I0608886

Honor of Assassins

Book 2 of the Graves of Good and Evil

A.B.B. Olson

Honor of Assassins

A.B.B.OLSON

ISBN: Soft Cover 978-0997257212

This edition dedicated to:
Foxy, Overdose, Cinders, Mel, Kali, Dante, & Lew.
You know who you are and what you've done.

Melallieyayekalilewdantoxydos forever

R·kunad Sea
High Reef
Andik
Purteae Harbor
Belgarath
Blackhaven Harbor
Blackhaven City
Elnya Highlands
Obsidian Way
Argyn River
Bari
Schelum
Purteae
Purteae Forest
Corridor of Asthius
The Highlands
Sethyn Lake
Blackhahen Forest
The Bridge
Jaquisa River
Orlan
Kismath
Strait of Arwen
Onyx Forest
Flousen Dua
Duan
Bijoz
Zeynuun
Tomasi Forest
Kyiji
Nafālyn Bay
Fārthyn Ocean

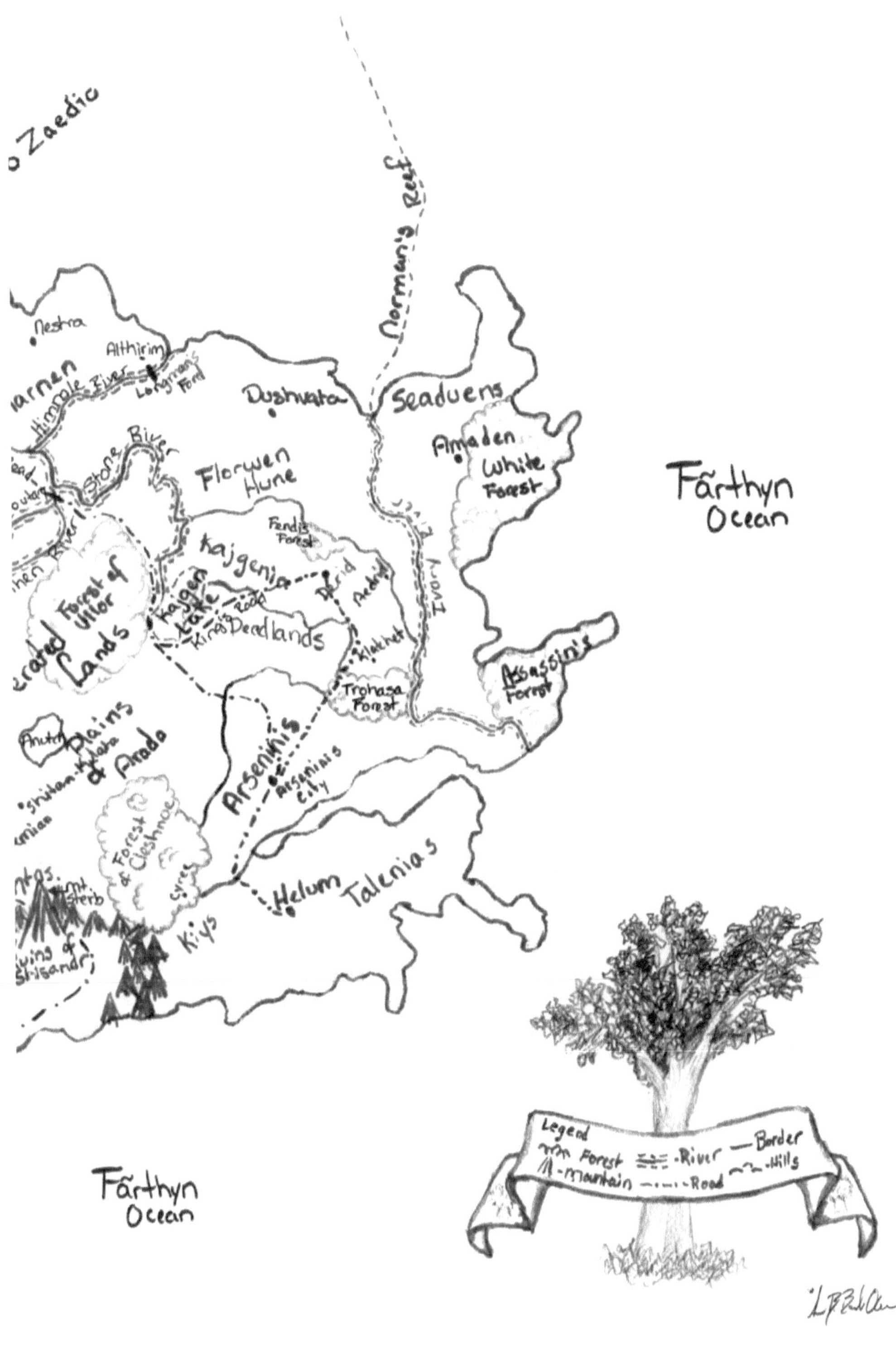
Norman's Reef
Nestra
Althirim
Himrale River
Longman's Ford
Dushvata
Seaduens
Amaden
White Forest
Fārthyn Ocean
Stone River
Florwen Hune
Fendis Forest
Kajgenia
Forest of Ullor
Kajgen Lake
Deadlands
Trohasa Forest
Assassin's Forest
Anutch
Plains of Arado
Arsenians
Forest of Cleshnoe
Helum
Talenias
Kiys
Fārthyn Ocean
Legend
Forest
River
Border
Mountain
Road
Hills

CONTENTS:

Prologue

When the child was born, he was mutated, not in any physical defection, but in the color of his skin and eyes. He was a dark elf, with tawny skin and emerald eyes, even his wispy hair was sable black, strange and different. He was one of three sons born to the Sestuns family, and all of them were tainted.

"Bailan, why? What have we done to deserve this?" Alena Sestuns cried, holding out her newborn child to her husband.

"I do not know, my love, but it is no punishment, I am sure. Our sons are healthy and strong, and we can ask for nothing more," the male replied, taking the boy.

"What are we going to do? Three sons, all genetic mutants? We are already cursed at, people are frightened of us. And poor Aladorn, he disappeared the other day when the others were teasing him, and it only made it worse, and little Aolan, chased by a mob just yesterday. Now this?"

Bailan shook his head again. "I know, but what can we do? We cannot change him, just as we cannot change Aladorn or Aolan. Give him a name, and we shall raise him as we have his brothers."

Alena looked down at her child, whose emerald eyes stared up at her, wisps of raven hair swaying gently with the wind of her breath. "Aidyn," she murmured, and the boy smiled slightly.

"Aidyn Sestuns, third son of House Sestuns. He will make us proud," Bailan said, grinning.

"If he survives."

"Now, Lena, do not make fear for yourself. Perhaps his skin will lighten. It has been known to happen."

"As it did with his brothers? No, Bailan, he too will be hunted and feared. My poor sons, dark elves and wiats. What have we done?"

Bailan clutched the newborn Aidyn and bounced him gently against his broad chest. "We have created another beautiful boy. Come, my son, meet your brothers."

The fair skinned male carried the infant to the next room, where two young elves sat nervously, waiting for the outcome. The eldest at ninety-three, Aladorn was tan-skinned and raven haired like his newborn brother, with verdant eyes and inky lashes. Half of his body was invisible, the worn and faded yellow of the chair he was sitting on perfectly visible from the waist down. When his father walked into the room, his lower half winked back into view as he focused, bringing his thoughts under control.

The middle boy, Aolan, was sixty-eight and just as fine featured as the rest of his family. He, however, was ash-toned. His eyes were a bright amber and his hair a stark white, but it was his skin that caused the most surprise. Dark gray, nearly black, it gave to him an alluring contrast, but it also inspired fear of the different.

"Aladorn, Aolan, meet your brother, Aidyn," Bailan said, smiling at his sons.

"Is he normal?" Aladorn asked softly, fearing to look at the new addition. His father's hesitation brought his green eyes up in a flash, unable not to look at the bundle.

"He is...a perfect child."

"He looks like you, Al," Aolan said, peering into the swaddling clothes. "At least he is not like me."

"Do not say that, Aolan," Bailan said sternly, nudging his son. "You too are a perfect child."

"I am a freak, a mutant."

"As am I," Aladorn muttered, standing to join his father and brother. "Ah, poor bastard. He will have to hide from the world like a craven human, if he lives. Why, father? What in your seed causes this?"

Bailan shrugged, handing Aidyn to Aolan. "I do not know, son. But it is no sin, and you are no craven human. You are a wiat, which people fear because they do not understand it. It is not your fault, nor mine, nor your mother's. You must not blame anyone for who you are, for it is no bad thing. You will see. Once we get to Blackhaven things will be better. Under the dictate of King Damian, all people are to be treated with equanimity. We just have to get there."

"Yes, travel across the entire breadth of Nymyños. Should not be a problem," Aolan muttered, studying his sibling. "He is rather attentive, is he not? Look at the way his eyes follow everything. Should he do that so young?"

Bailan frowned. "You are right. He is very attentive. As though he wants to know his surroundings by heart. Ah look, he follows sounds as well."

Aidyn's eyes were locked on his father, and then shifted to Aladorn when the wiat sighed loudly. "Perhaps he can be our sentry when he is older," he said softly.

"As you said, if he survives. How is Mother?" Aolan asked, handing Aidyn back to his father.

"Tired and worried, frightened for her children, and proud of them as well. She rests, so be quiet. Put Aidyn in his crib, and I will get dinner going."

Weeks later, Aladorn burst into the two-room house, becoming visible as he shut the door. "Father! Mother! Aolan!"

"What is it?" the middle boy demanded, turning from Aidyn's crib.

"A mob is headed our way. A decree has been set against all dark elves, wiats, and half-breeds. We need to go now or we will all be torn apart."

"Are you certain?" Alena asked, clutching Bailan's arm.

"Absolutely. Come on! We need to go!" Aladorn cried, grabbing a sack and shoving their meager belongings into it. "Aolan, get Aidyn ready to go. Hurry, they were only one street behind me."

The family leapt into a flurry of activity, grabbing foodstuffs and blankets, shoving things into the two packs they owned. Moments later, the sound of hundreds of angry people reached them, and they fled the shabby abode, Aolan clutching the silent Aidyn to his chest.

For a while they simply ran, slipping through the shadows and keeping to alleys and backstreets as much as possible. Arseninis City was ablaze with the fires of gangs and the screams of the dying. Once they were away from the activity, the family slowed and took their bearings. Their home had been near the center of the city, and they stood now on the edge of the markets, still a long way from the gate.

"Where do we go? I am sure we will not be allowed out if an edict has been issued," Alena queried nervously, taking Aidyn from her son and placing him in a pouch across her chest.

"We head south, hit the harbor, and try to slip off that way," Aladorn said, his sharp mind already working. "If nothing else, we can hide more easily there, what with all the foreigners from the docks."

The four elves began moving once more, the infant Aidyn watching intently from his pouch. It took them more than an hour to get across the city, avoiding the shrieking hordes and their revealing torches. When they were finally at the harbor, the family stared about in dismay. The ships were being searched, and all the sailors were lined up on the docks to be inspected. Alena stifled a sob in Bailan's chest, crouched down between crates.

"What now?" she whispered, looking to her eldest.

Aladorn was nearly invisible in the shadows, only the tell-tale glimmer of his dark eyes revealing his presence. "I will slip off and find a place to hide. Stay here unless the search gets close."

"What then?" Aolan demanded, fear etched in his face.

Aladorn cast about for an idea, and then he noticed a nail sticking out from one of the crates. Quickly, he pulled the nail out, along with all the others, and carefully removed one side of the crate. Thankfully it was large, but not large enough for the whole family. He shoved his mother and Aolan into it, careful to remain silent. Bailan tried to fit in as well, but he was too large. Aladorn swore softly, trying to think of another solution.

Suddenly the glow of fire appeared at the end of the crate stack, and the wiat disappeared in fear. "I will stay with Mother and Aolan. Father, you take Aidyn and head back. You are the least suspect of all of us. We will meet up again at the monolith in Cleshnoe Forest. Here, take my concealment cream."

Aladorn pressed a small jar of whitish cream into his father's hands as Alena reluctantly removed Aidyn from her body and secured him to her husband. "Please take care, Bailan. I love you. Please...tell me you will find us."

"I will find you, Lena. Aolan, Aladorn, my boys...I could never ask for better sons. You have made me proud. I will see you in Cleshnoe. Hurry now, they are coming."

Aladorn, still invisible, replaced the side of the crate, hiding his mother and brother, and then gouged an identifiable mark into the corner. He watched as his father slipped away, clutching his baby brother, the brother he would not see for another seven hundred and eighty-four years.

Aidyn sniffled, looking down in shame.

"Come on, Aidyn, you are getting it!" Bailan said, trying to bolster his son's attitude.

"I will never get it!" the child cried, throwing down the wooden practice sword.

"Yes you will. You have all the talent, and all the attributes... you just need the ambition, son. One more try, at least."

Aidyn sulked, but he picked up the waster and held it at ready, watching his father. When Bailan started to move, the six-year-old boy turned on his heel, sweeping the wooden blade in an arc to block the thrust he knew was coming. The wasters clacked, and then his father was moving again, poking and sweeping his blade in an attempt to get by Aidyn's defense. Bailan was awed by his son's skill, even at such a young age, though the child refused to accept that he was gifted, never happy with his work. Then the boy made the mistake he always made, letting the momentum of the sword carry his guard out too wide, allowing for a killing blow.

Bailan stepped in, lightly tapping Aidyn's chest with the tip of his waster, and awaited the outburst of self-criticism.

The child tossed his weapon away and plunked down in the dirt, crying.

"Aidyn...Aidyn now come on, son. There is no need for that," Bailan said, unsure of this new reaction.

"I bet Aladorn and Aolan were better than me!"

Bailan's heart leapt into his throat and he squeezed his eyes shut. Sitting down across from his child, the elf shook his head. "No, son, no."

"What?"

"You are six, my boy, and you will one day be the best blademaster in all of Nymyños. I swear it."

"I wish I could remember them. Tell me about them, please?"

The adult opened his mouth to oblige, and then he saw the desperate loss in his son's eyes. "No, Aidyn. I think...I think it best you forget that I ever told you about them. They are long gone, and they are never coming back. I should never have told you."

"But Dad!"

"No, Aidyn. You will forget their names. From now on, it is just you and me, all right? Just us two, as it has always been," Bailan said sternly, trying to keep from breaking down.

"What about Mother?"

"Her too. She is dead, Aidyn, six years dead."

"But I do not want her to be dead! I want to meet her! And Aladorn and Aolan! Please Dad! Please!" Aidyn cried, tears splashing down his face.

"I said forget them!" Bailan snapped, his heart breaking. "You have no brothers, you have no mother! You have me and that is it!"

Aidyn jumped to his feet and fled the small yard, sable locks flying. Bailan remained where he was, his legs numb with self-loathing and grief.

Aidyn turned inward then, becoming more and more distant from his father over the years. His skill with weapons continued to increase until one day he knocked Bailan to the ground in one single offensive move.

"You are defeated," the seventeen-year-old said coldly, standing over his father in the hazy mist that often accompanied the Andik evenings.

Andik was a small coastal village on the northern most peninsula of Blackhaven Kingdom, and the Sestuns residence was on the very edge of the seaward cliffs. The two dozen other residents of the village were nervous around the young dark elf and his stricken father, but they accepted them with the legendary Blackhaven tolerance. Only one other elf was as young as Aidyn, and he was reclusive at the best of times. So Aidyn, with only his crude weapons and his father's mournful determination to keep him company, had excelled.

Bailan sucked in a breath, trying to reclaim the wind that his son had knocked from him, and smiled. "Indeed I am. Even Aolan could not land me so fast," he replied, and then gasped when he realized what he had said. For eleven years, the names of their missing kin had not been spoken.

But his son did not even blink. Aidyn simply pulled back his waster and let his father stand. "You said the day I landed you, I could go to the capital to join the army."

"So I did, but Aidyn, are you sure that is what you want?" Bailan asked, furious at himself for ever making such a claim, but he kept his face calm.

"I am. If not for that, why have we trained every day of my life? What use are my skills if I am to be a hunter, or a fisherman? What, Father, am I to do with the talents you were so determined I attain?"

"I do not know, Aidyn, but I did not think you were so eager to leave me. I thought you liked it here in Andik. We have a home, a place in society. I taught you warfare because that is all I know. I was a sergeant in the Arseninisian Royal Guard until...until your mother and brothers were killed in the fire that took our home as well. What else could I teach you? I do not know how to sell things, or make things, or even how to write! I gave you the only thing I could, and you have taken it and made it an art, a fusing of power and grace and control. You are the warrior I always dreamed of being, and you are still a child. You have made me so proud, my boy, so proud, and I do not want you going off to join an army where you will be swallowed by a hundred other soldiers, never to make a name for yourself."

"How do you know I will not make a name for myself?" Aidyn demanded, picking up the training weapons and placing them inside the door of their house.

"I do not, but being a soldier, even a remarkable soldier, does not lead to success. You become a soldier, and you stay a soldier. Only a very small, select few ever go on to become captains or generals, especially in Blackhaven. The chain of command is incredibly small, as all soldiers are expected to know their duty to the last letter, obedient to the point of mindlessness."

"Then I will be one of those few."

"No, Aidyn, you will not. They are the city's elite, the sons of lords and other nobles. The sons of wealth and opportunity. You go to the city, and you will be cast aside for a lesser fighter with deeper pockets. You will be placed in a rank of a thousand others, and you will be forgotten by all but your regiment captain, your brothers-in-arms, and me. You are far too skilled for that, son. You must trust me on this."

"So what would you have me do?" Aidyn retorted, folding his arms. "Stay here and be a nameless citizen of a fly-speck village? Join a band of mercenaries and roam the countryside, irritating the thieves and murderers? Or perhaps I should set off on my own, become a rogue dark elf, chasing down and killing the less-savory?"

"Do not be crass, Aidyn. Go to Blackhaven City, but do not join the army. Find someone who can help you become something else."

"Like what?"

Bailan sighed, annoyed with his son's difficult moods. "I do not know! Perhaps a bodyguard for a baron, a trainer, or even a flaming assassin! Choose what you will, but do not join the army and be lost!"

Aidyn's emerald eyes narrowed as a single word from his father's tirade stuck. "An assassin?"

"What? No, I was just making a point. I do not want you to become a nameless face."

"I would make a good assassin, though, would I not? I bet it pays well, and I would not have to accept assignations I did not want. There must be someone who would hire me, and then I would make a name for myself!"

Bailan was horrified. "No, please think, Aidyn! You cannot do this! You are a good person, a kind elf. If you become an assassin, you will lose your soul. They are cold-blooded killers!"

But Aidyn wasn't listening anymore, his mind already set. "I leave tomorrow. There must be someone who needs me."

"Aidyn!" Bailan cried, reaching out for his only surviving son, but he was too late.

The next morning, Aidyn left the village of Andik without a single glance back. It took him five days to reach the magnificent capital of Blackhaven. The young elf, swathed in a coarse brown cloak, stood at the massive open gates concealed within the famous Blackhaven Forest. White-barked *kairhotuss* trees with leaves so dark they were nearly black glistened in the early morning, dripping with dew. The elf gazed upward in awe at the guards who curiously stared down at him.

Once he had stood there for a few minutes, one of them called down. "Are you lost?"

Aidyn was taken aback, but he lowered his hood and shook his head. "Not unless this is not Blackhaven City."

"A dark elf!" someone exclaimed, but it was simply surprise and not animosity. "Where are you from?"

"Andik."

"What are you here for?" the first guard asked.

"Uh...I want to become a warrior," Aidyn replied nervously.

"Really? Well, you have to come inside before you can do anything. There is a large wagon train coming in about five minutes, so unless you want to get run over, I suggest you move."

Aidyn hurried inside the gates and then stopped again, staring in amazement. The city, while still completely forested, spread out before him in gently curving rows, the streets wide and made of woven grass, somehow still green with life. They were the only things that appeared to have been cleared of trees, though all species of vegetation lined them, dominated by the *kairhotuss* trees. Aidyn was still gaping about when a hand gripped his shoulder. Spinning about, the dark elf ducked reflexively, bringing his hands up in a defensive position.

"Whoa! Steady on, boy!" the guard laughed, removing his helmet.

Aidyn stared, straightening in embarrassment. The adult elf was a sharp-featured male with hard blue eyes and light red hair. "I am Lieutenant Bindre, welcome to Blackhaven City, the greatest city in all Nymyños!"

"Thank you Lieutenant Bindre. I am called Aidyn Sestuns."

"A pleasure, young Aidyn. So, how are you planning to become a warrior?"

Aidyn shrugged. "I have no idea. I was trained by my father Bailan Sestuns every day since my fourth birthday. I am seventeen now, so I am not inexperienced."

"Why not join the army?"

Again the boy shrugged. "I do not want to be nameless."

Bindre frowned, but he said nothing on the matter. "Then go to Mafien Street, find the sign of the black beast, and tell the doorman you want a shadow."

Aidyn scowled in confusion, not understanding the vagary, but the soldier gave him a light push. "Mafien Street is north of here, and halfway back through the city. Go on. Luck to you, Aidyn of Andik."

The boy moved off, hesitant. He kept looking back at Bindre, but he was already climbing back atop the wall, plumed helm back on his head. Bewildered but determined, Aidyn followed the vague directions, and eventually found Mafien Street after asking around. From the disturbed looks he was getting, the dark elf realized the prejudices were not as distant from Blackhaven as his father had believed, and also that Mafien Street was not a pleasant place to be.

It was a seedy little avenue, lined with taverns and brothels, though still oddly covered in healthy trees and green grass-weave. Only one person occupied the street with Aidyn, a young human wearing a very inadequate dress. As the elf passed, she pressed herself against him, begging.

"No."

She slid her hand down his chiseled stomach and between his legs, squeezing. Revolted, Aidyn shoved her away and looked desperately for a black beast. Finally, he spotted a weathered sign painted with a crude panther, and rushed the shabby building, fearing the woman would touch him again.

He rapped his knuckles on the splintery door and waited, his fingers tingling with nerves. A thin section slid open and dark eyes glared out at him. "What?"

"I uh...I want a shadow."

"Do you, now? Who sent you?"

Unnerved, Aidyn shifted his feet. "Lieutenant Bindre."

The section slammed shut and the door opened slightly, allowing Aidyn to slip through. Once he was inside, the door was locked behind him and his skin prickled unpleasantly. The room was dim and the only light source was a small hearth filled with smoldering coals. Dark figures sat at tables, murmuring quietly over steaming mugs and plates of food. The doorman moved in front of Aidyn and took his time studying the uncomfortable elf.

"So... a dark elf."

The room became silent, and it echoed in Aidyn's pointed ears. He glanced about, his keen eyes picking out features where any other race would only see shapes. He said nothing.

"What is your name?"

"Aidyn."

"Why are you here?"

"I want to be a warrior."

"This is no place for warriors, boy. This is a place for fighters beyond that realm of duty and restriction. This is a place where you become your own master, your own ultimate self. Is that what you want, or do you want to be a sparkly little soldier?"

Aidyn leaned back as the man shoved his face close to his. At his age, he was not fully grown, so he was a few inches shorter, and much leaner than the bulky human. "I want to be the best weapons master Nymyños has ever seen. I want to be an assassin."

The man glared at him a moment longer and then stepped back. "Then you are in the right place. I am Master Driszn. Welcome to the College of Assassins."

For six months, Aidyn was pushed to the limit of his prowess, and then pushed over. He was put through brutal obstacle courses rife with danger, and every turn could have been the end of him. During a particularly difficult course, the dark elf leapt over a tripwire while ducking his head to avoid a spinning log, and landed in a roll, twisting his slender body away from several bladed mines. Gasping for breath, he bounded back to his feet and jumped again, barely clearing a rolling log. Seconds later he landed on the opposite side of a high fence, and he nearly fell. He had reached the end of the course, and had not received a single wound.

Driszn strode up to him, beaming in pride, and then swung a heavy club into his face. Aidyn barely evaded the attack, shoving his entire body backward only to be stopped by the fence. Several of the other assassins, all graduated and with several years of experience behind them, rushed him, wielding blunt weapons. Try as he might, Aidyn could not avoid all the hits, and he eventually went down, his broken nose pouring blood down his face.

"Wha-?" Aidyn groaned, rolling onto his side.

"You must be immune to pain!" Driszn roared, slamming the club into the elf's back.

The boy grunted in pain, but he rolled away, avoiding the next blow.

"You must accept it, and turn it into strength!" the Master bellowed, grabbing Aidyn's hair and yanking him backward, driving the club into his midriff.

The elf wrenched away, but the human clubbed him in the side of his head, and he went down.

"Welcome back."

Aidyn opened his eyes hours later and reflexively flinched when Driszn raised his hand. "Why did you punish me?"

"I did not punish you, Aidyn. Your Weapons Term has ended, and the next begins. This will be the tenure that makes or breaks you. It is the Torture Term."

"What?" the elf cried, certain he had heard wrong.

"For the next six months, you will be cruelly beaten in order to condition you in case you are ever caught and tortured. It will make you stronger, both physically and mentally, and it will make you an unbeatable force. Neither pain nor fear will ever affect you. Or you will die and that will be the end."

"You are going to *torture* me?" Aidyn gasped, still unable to accept the words.

"Viciously, yes. You will beg for us to end it, scream your lungs raw, cry until you have nothing left to give, and still we will continue, until you no longer feel it. Be ready for it."

"When?"

"Now."

"What?"

Driszn grabbed Aidyn and dragged him from his cot. Swiftly, he bound the elf's hands together so tight the ropes gouged his tawny skin. "For what it's worth, boy, I'm sorry."

Aidyn could not fathom the words, and so he stayed silent as his teacher shoved him through the halls that housed the College of Assassins. As he was the only student, the dark elf was alone in his dilemma, and the graduated assassins within the building watched him pass with eager eyes. They all were impressed by the young elf, and they held high hopes for him. His eighteenth birthday had been a rare experience within the Guild, and they had all joined in the celebration by hosting a day-long tournament. Aidyn had come in fifth of the eleven assassins in residence.

Suddenly, Driszn stopped and pushed his bound student into a small room with all the implements of torture arranged on the walls and a small firepit and a drain sunk into the floor. Aidyn spun around, but Driszn shut the door before the boy could get out, and walked away.

Aidyn hugged himself, staring at the door in front of him. Panic had seized him and he could not look at the tools hanging from the walls all around him. When the door suddenly opened again, the elf thought it had all been a trick, and began to walk forward. A fist slammed into his face, knocking him flat, sending waves of agony through his already shattered nose.

Gadrin, the Guild's Punisher, pushed the door shut and locked it. As Aidyn climbed to his feet, the human picked up a wicked looking knife and spun it expertly in the air. The dark elf's eyes went wide with terror and he spun around, looking for an escape. When he felt the cool blade touch the back of his neck, a keening noise burst from his lips, unheeded and unconscious. The blade slid down his spine, just brushing his skin. Aidyn's loose tunic slid from his shoulders, and his pants soon followed. Shivering, he stood naked before Gadrin, who glared at him.

"You will be reborn in this room. You will not be the same person as you are now, or you will be dead. Are you ready?"

"I will not be broken," Aidyn breathed, but the knife sliced into his shoulder anyway.

Again and again it skimmed across his skin, leaving thin, shallow cuts that stung and bled.

"I will not be broken!" the dark elf screamed in defiance, screamed until his voice was nothing more than a hoarse croak.

After nearly three hours of being slashed at, pressing himself against the cold stone wall in an effort to get away, the boy was nearly catatonic. When finally Gadrin stepped away from the bloody elf, Aidyn slid to the floor, thinking, praying, he was done for the day. Then the Punisher grabbed the large kettle from the tiny hearth, removed the lid, and tossed it on the boy.

Aidyn screamed as boiling water mixed with a hearty amount of salt burned into his tender flesh, angering the open wounds. His fingers and toes bent in agony, his toned muscles straining against his hazel skin. Bloody water cascaded down his body and ran to the middle of the floor where it disappeared down the drain. Gasping and crying, the dark elf crouched against the wall, trembling. For the rest of the day, Gadrin simply beat him. When he was finally allowed to sleep, curled up in the middle of the chamber, Aidyn fell into an exhausted slumber, fearing the next day.

For the next six months, Aidyn was beaten, cut, burned, scalded, pierced, stretched, hung for days from broken limbs, whipped, clubbed, and stabbed. The worst in his mind were the dunkings, however. As an elf, he could withstand much more pain than a human, and it took much longer to drown him. A bag was placed over his head and he was dunked in a freezing cold tub of water. For minutes at a time he was submerged, fighting futilely against Gadrin's merciless arms. His lungs and eyes burned, and he sometimes went blind for hours afterward, and he actually died twice, but was revived by the Guild's apothecary, and Gadrin had been brutally reprimanded each time.

It was two days before the term was up and Aidyn was glaring at the floor he so hated as Gadrin wailed on his back with a bamboo rod. So far, the Punisher had broken three of the rods, which was unprecedented, and it sounded as though this one was about done in as well. The pain lingered for the entirety of the blow, and then was gone before the next one struck. Aidyn did not even flinch as his flesh was torn open, his ribs broken, and his muscles bruised. He barely even registered the pain now. His hands were splayed on the floor beneath him, his body stretched out, balanced on his toes. He was doing push-ups, and every time he was at the apex of one, a blow was struck.

Gadrin swore with each blow as well, unable to comprehend the elf's strength. He had expected him to survive the ordeal physically, but not mentally. Every time he looked into Aidyn's emerald eyes, he saw neither hatred nor fear. The only things that smoldered there were determination and pride. The only other elf accepted to the guild had been a blubbering mess by the end of the Torture Term, unable to comprehend the cruelties enacted by the Guild. He had been utterly useless, and had been silenced.

Now there was the eighteen-year-old Aidyn, his face blank as he completed another push-up, and received another strike. The push-ups were not part of Gadrin's curriculum, but the elf said it was good exercise. The human could not believe it. Muscles rippled along Aidyn's body, perfectly toned and long allowing the elf to retain his naturally slim build, though he was incredibly strong.

With a loud crack, the rod snapped in half, and Aidyn turned his head to look at Gadrin from his peripheral. "That was the last one."

Gadrin glared down at the boy, disgusted with the knowledge. "I know...I guess it's the lash for you, then."

"Joy to you," Aidyn muttered sarcastically, resuming his exercise.

Gadrin shook his head in amazement as he took the scourge from the wall. Its nine knotted heads dug into the elf's already scoured back. The boy did not even react, though bits of flesh flew through the air, along with splatters of blood. Gadrin wailed at him until his own arm pained him too much. Panting, he set the scourge back and clapped his hands together once. Aidyn obediently got to his feet, rolling his shoulders and flexing his hands.

"One more day," the Punisher grunted, studying his victim.

"Does it make a difference?" Aidyn asked simply. "Tomorrow will be the same as today, and yesterday, and every day prior."

"True, except that tomorrow, rather than curl up on the floor, you go back to your cot."

The elf's lips turned up in a smile, but it was neither happy nor humorous. Gadrin knew that it would be a smile people one day feared. "What will you do then, oh Punisher of Assassins?"

"I will go back to my usual routine. I am the enforcer of laws among men who do not have any real laws. I scar those who fail, I beat those who break the Honor, and I execute those who endanger us."

"And what of me?"

Gadrin shrugged. "You will begin your third and final term. The Shadow Term."

"A bit dramatic, is it not?" Aidyn grunted.

"It is where you learn stealth and subtlety, and finally you will put all three of your skills into one mastery."

The elf grinned now, a flash of white in the chamber of torture. "I will be the master," he stated simply, and turned away from Gadrin.

After one final day of complete torture, where Gadrin threw everything he had at the young elf, Aidyn strode from the chamber he had been locked in for six months and found himself face to face with Driszn.

The Master's expression went from disbelief to awe when Aidyn stood before him.

"What?"

"No one has ever *walked* out of the chamber before. You are unbelievable, my boy."

"I will not be broken, ever."

"I believe it. Now begins your final test, the Shadow Term, where you learn all the fine arts of assassination. You will learn how to pick locks, disassemble various entrapments, you will learn how to sneak, how to disappear, how to move silently, and many other things. You will also be instructed in the ways of diplomacy and court behavior. And finally, you will put weapons mastery, pain desensitization, and subtlety into one cohesive way of life. At the end, you will graduate as an Assassin of the College."

Aidyn looked at Driszn, and realized suddenly that he was the same height as the big man. He had grown in the chamber. "How did you leave the room, Master Driszn?"

The human stared back at the elf, gauging his student's mental faculty after so long. "I crawled," he said finally, unashamedly.

"Gadrin said the only other elf to be accepted was killed after his term. Said he was a witless creature who was too unstable to be allowed to live. What do you think of my race, now?"

Driszn glanced at Gadrin who was standing behind Aidyn shaking his head in disbelief. "I think that you are an incredible boy to withstand the augmented beatings Gadrin bestowed upon you."

"That was not my question, Master Driszn," Aidyn said monotonously.

The Master once again studied the student. "I believe your race is capable of many great things, but they are too afraid of negative outcomes to do them."

Aidyn smiled his humorless smile, and walked back to the small cell that had previously been his room, the two men watching him.

Disappearing and silence came easy to Aidyn who never remembered his wiat brother who could vanish into thin air. Unbeknownst to him, he shared a small bit of that trait, and he mastered the art in just a handful of days. In fact, everything the third term had to offer came easily to the elf. He was tested again and again, pitted against several men at once, given ridiculously short amounts of time in which to pick a lock, get inside a room, "assassinate" his target, and slip out, all the while not setting off any of the alarms. He was ambushed and deceived, dragged from his bed and attacked during meals. Always he came out victorious, but rarely satisfied with his efforts.

His nineteenth birthday came and went and only he noticed. Sitting alone in his room, the assassin-in-training studied himself in a hand mirror. He had high cheek bones and fine features, his emerald eyes slightly tilted, rimmed with inky lashes. His sable hair hung just past his shoulders, pointed ears poking through. His shoulders were strong and his waist and hips slender. Long, muscled yet lean legs stretched out beneath him, ending in fine-boned feet. Looking down at his middle, Aidyn studied the hard rows of abdominal muscles that narrowed in a V toward his groin.

The dark elf ran his hand over his thigh, feeling the smooth, hairless skin beneath his palm, wondering. All the others in the Guild had hair on their chests, legs, arms, backs, necks, and everywhere else. He, however, had hair only on his head. He also did not sweat as they did, or itch or get blemishes. He wondered at these things, wondered if they were part of the reason he was so much faster, stronger, and better than they were.

Aidyn's eyes narrowed as he looked at his groin, thinking of the stories the men always told of the women they bedded. He had never even touched a woman, other than the whore that had assaulted him his first day in Blackhaven. He wondered about that, too. He wondered about females in general, as he had only seen a few flitting through the dark halls of the College as the other men brought them home. He thought of his mother, wondered what she had looked like, acted like, and even sounded like. Suddenly he thought of his father, and a terrible sense of guilt washed over him.

Was Bailan even alive? It had only been a year since Aidyn had seen his father, but to him it felt like an eternity. Shaking his head, the elf pulled on a loose pair of cotton pants and lay back on his bed. With his hands resting on his belly, he dozed off, all of his thoughts warring within his head.

Two weeks later, he graduated. The ceremony was quick and to the point. Master Driszn presented Aidyn with a set of black clothes made of a special material called *ärdyz.* They were so dark they appeared to elude light, playing tricks on the eyes. He was also given a dagger that strapped to his thigh. Driszn then took Aidyn's hand, now having to look up at his student, and placed in his palm a small leather ball stained brown with the blood of every assassin to complete the three Terms in the College.

"I, Master Assassin Driszn Noshbaren of the College of Assassins, do hereby grant you, Aidyn Sestuns, the title of Assassin, and place upon you all the honor and restrictions that accompany such responsibility. You came here a boy, and became a...male. There are but three creeds we, the College of Assassins, maintain.

"Do you swear by the Honor of Assassins to use your skill only when it is right and true to do so?"

"I do."

Aidyn took a deep breath as Driszn took his dagger and scored a line in the elf's palm.

"Do you swear by the Honor of Assassins to trust your brethren, and your kin, and always maintain your loyalties?"

"I do."

He scored another cut.

"Do you swear by the Honor of Assassins to step in the line of danger to protect the defenseless, and be brave in the face of evil?"

"I do."

The third slice reddened Aidyn's palm, staining the leather ball crimson.

"Then I bind you, Aidyn Sestuns, to the Honor of Assassins, and may the gods take mercy upon you if you break it," Driszn proclaimed, and then struck Aidyn across the face. Taking the stained ball, he held it aloft so that all the assembled assassins could see it.

"Behold! The Stain of Blood upon the Orb! Rejoice, and acknowledge your new brother!"

Months later, Aidyn returned to Andik, clothed in his Assassin's garb and riding a barrel-chested gelding. People stared at him, vaguely recognizing the boy that had left two years gone. With three assassinations behind him, each one executed perfectly, Aidyn had money to spend and a reputation that was fast becoming legend. Dismounting outside the shabby little cabin he had spent much of his life in, the assassin strode to the door and inside the house, not bothering to knock.

His father lurched to his feet, grabbed a fire poker, and jabbed it at the intruder. "Who are you?"

"Father, it is me! Calm down!" Aidyn yelled, expertly twisting the poker from Bailan's startled hands.

"Aidyn? My son! Oh I believed I would never see you again!" the older elf proclaimed, grabbing his son and hugging him close. "You have grown so much, nearly twenty and almost fully grown!"

Aidyn pried himself loose and sat down at the table, shaking his head. "You look well. How have you been?"

Bailan seated himself as well, still blown away by his child's appearance. "Bored, to tell the truth. You were my only occupation, son! But what of you? What are you wearing? My eyes skip around you."

"The garb of the assassin."

A sudden and tense silence filled the small house, the two males staring at each other, trying to fill a gap that was old and wide.

"So, you became one of them."

"Yes, but you do not understand, Father. The differences between the College of Assassins and the renegades you know of, oh, they are profound. Have you ever heard of the Honor of Assassins?"

"No, and I cannot believe such a farce exists."

Aidyn ignored the insult. "To be noble, loyal, and brave, to know right from wrong, to accept only the assignations that feel right to you, to honor your kin. Please know that I am not a monster, nor do I kill for the joy of murder."

"Yet you do it anyway?" Bailan asked, confused.

"I do it because I believe that there are evil people out there, people that need to be eliminated. And I am not reviled as you might think. They accept me as a dark elf, and as an assassin. The Honor of

Assassins decrees that no one should fear an assassination as long as they are upright citizens. I am an honored member of society, and people know my name! I even have an interview lined up with Prince Dietirin in a week."

"To do what?"

"A royal assassin! I would be given both title and land. A small lot, but land nonetheless."

Despite his protestations, Bailan was finding himself eager for his son. "Land? Nobility? This is guaranteed if you get the job?"

"Absolutely. And Master Driszn believes I have a one hundred percent chance of getting it. I am the best there is," Aidyn exclaimed, unable to contain his grin.

"That is fantastic, son! I am glad you came to tell me this! What say you we go out back and duel, one more time before you start your new life, hmm? Before you head back?"

Aidyn frowned. "What are you talking about?"

"If you do not want to, I understand," Bailan replied, his heart bruised. "Surely dueling with your old father would be of little challenge to you, now."

"No, I mean I came here to bring you to the city. You always said you wanted to live in the capital. Even if I do not get the position at the castle, I have a small house."

Bailan stared at his son in complete shock. The offer was so unexpected he didn't know what to say. Finally, he gathered his wits. "You want me to come with you? Live with you?"

Aidyn nodded, swallowing against his nervousness.

"What would I do?"

"Anything you wanted, Father! They are about to open up an academy, you could go and learn to read! You could open up a training facility! You could sit at home and do whatever you please!"

Bailan let out a disbelieving laugh. "You are serious?"

"I would never make the offer if I were not," Aidyn replied solemnly, briefly touching his father's hand.

The father studied the son for a long time, relearning the depth of the ever-watchful emerald eyes that had so astounded Aolan. He examined the agile muscle that glided beneath the tawny skin, the prominent cheek bones that reminded him so much of Alena.

"So young, and yet...so much older than you were. I will never ask what they did to you, but if you will let me, I will be there if you ever need to tell someone. I will come with you, Aidyn."

The assassin grinned again, standing. "Excellent. I have to be back in the city in five days at the latest. How long will it take you to be ready?"

Bailan shrugged. "A day, maybe two. There is not much here."

"Well then, let us begin," Aidyn said cheerfully.

A week later, Aidyn was sworn into the service of Prince Dietirin as Royal Assassin, and Bailan was set up in a small manor house on the edge of the Peerage District of the city. Years passed as tensions rose among religious factions and racial disputes were brought to the fore. Aidyn served faithfully and unerringly, becoming close friends with the young prince. After a very public assassination to force the hand of one dictator in the Liberated Lands, Aidyn and Dietirin were relaxing in the prince's lounge.

"Aidyn my friend, I have a feeling that you and I are going to see some serious changes in the future of Nymyños. Did you know they have just recently found a book of prophecies at the site of the Tower of Magins? Said to belong to the Seer Astinus."

The assassin chuckled. "Yes, well, when prophecy becomes a reliable source of information, I will listen. And even then, it will only have to do with blokes like you. It will never affect an underling like me."

"Well, as long as you are bound to me, you might just be affected," Dietirin joked, never knowing how true his words were.

"Alas, as long as I am bound to the Honor of Assassins, I do not have to accept anything I do not want to."

"Ah, the Honor of Assassins, forever a thorn in my side."

"And forever a blessing in mine," Aidyn retorted, laughing. "To the Honor of Assassins!"

Dietirin laughed as well and clinked his glass to the dark elf's. "To the Honor of Assassins!"

The Honor of Assassins is upheld still in all communities.
To be Noble, Loyal, and Brave is the creed, and to break it means death.

The Aftermath Continues.

Chapter 1

The Journey Goes On

Nebet'thu looked up from where he squatted next to the moldering corpse in the middle of the road, squinting thoughtfully at his giant deer, Leartia. She sniffed at him, obviously displeased by the smell of decaying human flesh.

"This screams Magin," Neb said to her as though she understood, and stood with a sigh of resignation.

He was a Plains Elf, one of the Hidden, and he stood shorter than the more populous High Elves, though populous is indeed a relative term. His dark blond hair fell straight to his shoulder blades, held back by a leather band at his temples.

The plains elves were a tribal culture, living in small, clustered villages camouflaged in the sweeping plains of eastern Blackhaven. They were known for their reclusive behavior and well-honed fighting skills, which was why the recruiters for the Blackhaven Militia were often seen scouting the plains in hope of coaxing them into service. Secretly, Neb harbored the dream of standing in the proud ranks under the iron command of the beautiful, albeit insane, Yayènia er'Tiena. But he was just a hunter, spending nearly nine months of the year on his own, returning to his village of Asheyl every so often to deposit his kills. Only during the dead winter months did he stay in the village, recouping and giving Leartia a chance to breed.

Leartia was harnessed to a cart that was nearly half full of meat and foraged items, and she was angry at the delay. Nebet'thu patted her on the nose and picked up the corpse. His mount danced away, but allowed her master to put the body in the cart, carefully separating the food from it, wondering if he should just throw it all away rather than risking it.

"Tèkar will know what to do with him, I suppose," Neb said absently.

The plains elf swung his leg over the deer and settled himself in the light saddle. He clicked to her and Leartia bound off toward Asheyl, home. The journey home took him another day, and the food began to spoil. Irritated at the waste, Nebet'thu tossed it on the ground and covered the body in the remaining sackcloth. Leartia eyed him over her shoulder every now and then, displeased. Neb pulled out a scarf and tied it around his mouth and nose.

"Just a little further, girl. Come on," he urged, patting her neck.

Asheyl was situated within a narrow gorge, the only way in or out was a sloping, winding pathway carefully tended by the villagers. It was a small village of deer-hide yurts clustered together, and the walls of the canyon rose up high above them, shielding them from both the elements and unwanted visitors. Located in the south-eastern part of Blackhaven Kingdom, the closest town was Hastert, near the Strait of Arwênlhias that separated Blackhaven from Kismath. Cook fires filled the evening as Nebet'thu rode down, smiling.

Young elves flitted around, laughing and dancing. Older elves, elves his age, waved at him, smiling and greeting him. The chieftain Tèkar, his wife Fellar, and their beautiful daughter Kepthari beamed at Nebet'thu as he dismounted before them. The hunter bowed and smiled back.

"It is good to be home," he said heartily.

"Neb, I missed you. You are the last to return home. Even Daegin came in two nights ago. What held you?" Kepthari asked, her brown eyes wide.

"I ran into some trouble. There is danger on the plains, just yesterday I found this..." Neb took the body out of the cart and presented it to his chieftain.

Tèkar glanced at the wrappings fleetingly. "You two," he pointed at two boys standing to the side, "take this cart and store it. Nebet'thu, follow me. Fellar, Kepthari, come."

The four walked to the mending hut, ignoring the startled glances from their familiars. Once inside they were assaulted by two menders, their hands immediately reaching for the dead body in Neb's hands.

"Nay, menders. Put aside your hands."

The two elves grudgingly let go of the body and backed away. Neb placed the body on a table in the center of the hut. He unwrapped the corpse and then looked away. The entire middle section was burned away, leaving the guts shredded and open. Maggots writhed in the blacked blood, making the innards move and wriggle. Fellar gasped and immediately left the hut. Kepthari placed her hands at her mouth and squeezed shut her eyes, though she stayed. Tèkar merely glanced at it, his legendary stoicism keeping his back straight. It was because of that he had held onto the chieftainship when devastation had churned the kingdom.

"Where did you find him?"

"About twenty leagues from here. There were no tracks around him, nothing to tell who did it or why. There was no evidence of a struggle, not even blood. He was just there, in the center of the road."

The menders fidgeted, blatantly eager to examine the body.

"The death was obviously caused by magic, Chief, Magins. No weapon could do this and leave no other wound," Nebet'thu said.

Tèkar nodded. "Yes, that is true. This must be brought before King Dietirin, he is not of our people," the elf pushed the head to one side, revealing a miniscule tattoo just behind the ear.

"Many tribes have tattoos that identify them, I do not see the significance of it," Neb said, his brow furrowed.

"Yes, but I know all the brands, and this one is unfamiliar to me, and he is human, obviously not of the tribes. And no tribe places a tattoo behind the left ear, anyhow. If it is a small one, it is placed on the skin between the thumb and finger, or on the wrist. He has the look of a Blackhavenite, but no more than that can I say. Perhaps a farmer, for his skin is darkened and rough. Someone must travel to Blackhaven City and tell of this, immediately."

"I will go. I have no farm to tend, nor trade to hold," Nebet'thu said.

"Good. I shall get your provisions ready. You will want to leave as soon as possible, after the celebration of course," Tèkar replied, flicking the cover over the corpse once more. He left the hut, his daughter following him.

Neb watched her hungrily, pondering slightly what the chieftain had said about a celebration, and then noticing the gazes of the menders, left hastily. Hands grabbed him from the right and yanked him into the shadows of the hut. The hunter was slammed against the wall and felt hands pulling at his shirt. When his shock subsided, he saw Eesa, the High Councilor's daughter. She was the vehement but sultry rival of Kepthari, and Nebet'thu's old interest.

Before the hunter could defend himself, Eesa shoved him into her yurt and against the wall. With her foot, she shut the door and kicked the lock into place. The vivacious elf had pulled open the laces on Neb's vest and was wrestling with his trousers. Finally, awareness slammed into the male's head and he pushed the female away from him. Her amber eyes stared at him passionately, her breathing haggard and quick. Her red hair was tousled and her clothing wrinkled. "Hello, Nebet'thu."

"Eesa. What are you doing?"

"Did you miss me? I missed you. I could not stop myself from thinking about you, and that night..."

Nebet'thu sighed, rubbing a hand through his ruffled hair. "Eesa, we are not together anymore. You know that."

"Tsh! I love you and you love me. We belong together. Everyone knows we are to be wed, and while you were gone, I arranged it all! We are to be wed today!"

"What? Eesa! I am not going to marry you! And I do not love you!"

Eesa laughed. "Oh Neb! You will have your jests! Come on! It is about to start, and you and I have to get ready!"

"What? No! Eesa!" Before Nebet'thu could do anything though, she had pulled loose the laces of her dress and pushed it down around her ankles.

He stared at her in shock, every sense within his head utterly stunned at the sight of her naked body. He'd never seen such a thing, and he could not tear his eyes away. Eesa smiled wickedly, her hips swaying slightly. "You have no choice, now," she murmured, advancing.

Finally, Nebet'thu's faculties returned to him and he squeezed shut his eyes, feeling doom descend. It was taboo to see a tribal female naked less you were married. Despair settled over him and he sighed.

"Why?" he whispered, his eyes still tightly closed.

Eesa snickered. "Because we belong together, Nebet'thu, everyone knows it. You are the only one who seems to be blind to our love. It *is* love."

"It was love," Neb countered, finally looking up, ignoring her body and staring straight into her eyes. "No longer."

Eesa's face fell, but then stiffened with determination. "It could be again. Besides, who else would have you now? Kepthari? She is to marry Daegin, and sees nothing in you other than a friend. Give in to me, Neb, and you will find your happiness."

Nebet'thu scowled at her, unable to come to terms with what fate had just handed him. Silent, he pushed out of her yurt and headed for his own. People danced around him in excitement, shouting their congratulations. He walked into his home and locked the door behind him. A pair of black trousers and a brown tunic was laid out on his bed, along with two bronze bands that would fit over his and Eesa's biceps, the symbol of marriage within the Plains Elf tribes. Cursing the whole while, Nebet'thu dressed in the ceremonial clothes and shoved the bands into his pocket. He found his pack next to his bed and looked in it. Provisions for his journey were stuffed into the leather bag, no doubt thanks to the chief.

Depressed, Neb left his small house and found the entire tribe gathered under the open village tent. Eesa stood ready, in a dress of white cotton, a wreath of flowers in her hair. The hunter progressed to the tent and walked up the aisle, his eyes downcast. The village elder stood at the front, beaming with joy. Just behind Eesa sat Kepthari and Daegin, and the leading families.

Nebet'thu stood silent while the elder said the words of matrimony, holding Eesa's hands. Finally, it came to the point where he had to say yeah or nay. The entire village watched him struggle, thinking him overcome. A single tear slid out of his eye, his despair at the situation crushing his free soul. The expectant watchers waited in romanticized silence. In the end, his honor and obeisance defeated his desires, that, and Eesa's squeezing grip on his hands, reminding him of what he had seen.

"Yes, I do."

The elder grinned. "It is done then. I present, Eesa and Nebet'thu, husband and wife forever," then in a whisper the older elf said, "now to the matrimonial bed, eh?"

Eesa all but pulled him down the aisle and into his yurt. There, she undressed almost as fast as she had just an hour before and stood before him in all her glory. Silently, slowly, Nebet'thu undressed and folded his clothes, piling them on the floor. Eesa leapt and shoved him onto the bed. There, she bound him to her forever.

Chapter 2

Breaking the Rules

Sithian waited outside the gate, his aural shield protecting him from the wind and rain. The soldiers atop the battlements stared down at him as though he were some god come to earth. The boy agreed with them, though as he gloated the rain began to pour harder, forcing him to strengthen his shield.

His journey to Blackhaven had made him stronger in power and body. The long days of riding horses into the ground had stripped the fat from his body, leaving hard, lean muscle. The constant change in weather had required him to use shields day in and day out, forcing him to work hard at maintaining a balance between power energy and body energy. People had watched him pass with wary eyes, their haggard faces turning slowly as he rode on, registering the shocking resemblance to Midian Rahlan, his father, and their only recently deposed subjugator.

He'd had no reason to kill any of them until that one man just inside the border of Blackhaven province. The idiot had demanded that he show proper respect to custom, and show his face. He had been irritated at the time, and the man had been arrogant. He had died slowly, and painfully. Sithian fingered the waterskin at his side, now filled with blood. It would come in handy when he got back to Zaedic. Sithian chuckled. Then there was the boy, a handsome messenger boy for the castle. Though he felt no attraction to the same sex, it was the fear, the fear in the boy's eyes that made Sithian hungry for more than just the feel of blood on his hands.

Suddenly the clarion call of elfish trumpets rang throughout the air, startling the reminiscing Sithian. The horns played out a short and obviously human fanfare though the players were undeniably elven, then the bells began ringing, the horns beginning again. This time Dwarfish copper and brass gave the tune a strength that unnerved *all* visitors to the city, and then finally the Human cadence rattled into the third repetition, completing the Changing of the Guard routine. Sithian's spine crawled as the song came to a sudden and ringing end, and he looked up to see the guards now switching positions with the ones that had just arrived. They moved smartly, their actions so perfectly precise that the Zaedican could only stare with awe and no little fear.

The new watch planted their bows against the wall and refused to give the arrogant young king the pleasure of acknowledging him. The guards consisted of all races, though mostly humans, elves, and dwarves, and they all had oiled cloaks pulled up over their heads to ward off the biting rain. One strange looking creature glanced down at Sithian with pure blue eyes. She brushed her cowl back to reveal shocking blue hair, and then resumed her conversation with a taller-than-average dwarf.

The Zaedican could hardly contain his disgust at women being in the guard, or in any sort of military branch, but he knew that anyone in the famed Blackhaven Guard was no one to trifle with. Sithian folded his arms. Annoyance was starting to gnaw at him. He had sent the boy away almost half an hour ago. The sun was cresting the horizon, and the rain still had not slackened, having actually doubled its fury. The wind howled in the trees behind him, creating an eerie atmosphere, the black leaves rattling like old bones as the rain assaulted them. The noise was almost a roar and his patience was wearing thin. He did not notice the subtle shifting in the watch, the fingers rubbing against oiled bowstrings, wrapping around gleaming ebony bow hafts, or the tensing of eyes trained on him, if only through peripheral vision. He noticed only the time that was slipping away.

Tlonna ignored the rain slicing through her clothes and battering her face. Her companions hurried after her, exchanging worried glances at this sudden turn of events, everyone except Yayènia and Ghealan. They strode purposefully, cloaks of office whipping in the storm, helmet plumes swaying back and forth. The city around them was coming to life, the people stopping their morning routines to watch the unusual procession with confused eyes.

The princess's mind was a whirlwind of questions and possible theories, each being dismissed as soon as it came to fruition. She could not understand what Sithian wanted, could not fathom any reason he would traverse hostile country in order to stand before the gates of the city that most hated his family. There was no mistaking whose son he was, for the boy looked identical to Midian, if a younger version with pointed ears. She shook her head in sudden denial of the events around her, trying to forget the terrible incident of the night previous, and the terror of the messenger boy's face this morning.

Losolin too was caught up in thought, though his eyes were fixed on the slumping shoulders of his beloved. Tlonna seemed broken, her eyes dull and hooded, her steps, while direct, where slow and hesitant. He glanced at Yayènia who shrugged, her hands crossed over her belly to grip her longblade hilt and dagger. Her bared abdomen was slick with rain and the part of her pants that was visible beneath her greaves and belts was dark with moisture. She moved with the surety of a warrior, the ridged muscles of her abdomen and arms gliding with each stride, her beautiful face stone-cold and deceptively calm.

On her other side walked Aidyn, his skin-tight black leather pants warding off the rain, but his black *ärdyz* tunic stuck to his skin, soaked all the way through, though his cloak, made of the same inky black silk-like material billowed out behind him, undisturbed by the rain. The assassin moved with a style all of his own, making Losolin slightly queasy. He moved at the same pace as the others, but with a fluidity and grace that seemed to blur his form as though he were walking through another plain of existence, one that defied logic to earth-dwellers.

Losolin wondered why he had never noticed it before. Perhaps he had been too engrossed in the trials around him to actually watch the deadly killer, to see his incredibly fast, precise movements, the strength in which he moved through life, nothing getting by his ever-attentive gaze.

Indeed, Aidyn felt the other elf's eyes on him, but he refrained from meeting the gaze, instead focusing on the odd pain in his heart, as though something were tugging at him, trying to feed him emotions that were not his own. The assassin caught his billowing cloak in one hand and snapped it tight to his body, his hand tensing as he slipped a wicked spike out from under his wrist, and then released it back into its muscle-tensioned sheath. His nerves were on end from the constant barrage of foreign emotion, and he could not help himself from triggering and releasing the deadly weapon.

As the Changing of the Guard herald rang out, Tlonna and her entourage reached the gate and they stood calmly amidst the smartly moving soldiers. The routine was strictly Suneelo's work, and he looked on with pride. When the change was complete, one of the ranking soldiers from the previous watch strode up to the group and executed the militant bow, a fierce display of strength and balance. His knees bent halfway to the ground, but did not connect, his head bowed and his arms crossed to grab the two hilts at his back. When he snapped upright again, fire burned in his eyes as he looked Tlonna directly in the eye.

"He stands within a bubble, calm and arrogant. Who is he?" the guard demanded, unafraid of the deadly elves before him.

Tlonna eyed him, unable to come up with a name for the bold human. "Sithian, King of Zaedic, and son of Midian Rahlan."

The human's face contorted with hatred and his eyes flashed to Yayènia and Suneelo standing calm off to the side. "You will let him in?"

"He can do little harm," Tlonna assured him, though she did not believe her own words. "Move aside."

Aidyn shifted, once again releasing the spike, but this time he wrapped his fingers around it and kept it there. Aladorn watched his brother curiously, finally noticing the subtle movement of his right hand. Moving to the assassin's side, he briefly touched the tawny hand.

"You are worried," he stated, not bothering to look at his sibling.

Aidyn did not move, his eyes trained on the gate doors. "A chance to kill him before he gets any older, any more powerful."

"You cannot do it, Tlonna will rip you limb from limb. He is her son."

"Tlonna will not be fast enough to stop me, nor will anyone else," the trained weapon whispered, shifting slightly again.

"You forget your place," Aladorn accused, this time wrapping his fingers about his brother's slender wrist, feeling the steel implement cold against his skin.

"No, Aladorn, I remember it quite vividly," he replied, and with a lightning quick movement, released his arm and shoved his brother back.

It happened so fast even Aladorn did not know what had happened until he was standing a good two yards away from the killer, rubbing his torqued wrist. Ghealan and Miazie noticed the exchange, but they were confused as to why the wiat had suddenly jumped back from the other dark elf.

"What is it?" the Second Commander asked, eyeing Aidyn curiously, who was once again standing alone and perfectly still.

"Nothing," Aladorn snapped, still rubbing his wrist.

Ghealan was about to respond when everyone's attention was grabbed by the sudden release of the gate's wheel lock. Guards moved about, keeping their oiled cloaks close about their bodies, readying the enormous gate to be opened. Two guards grabbed large hammers and began pounding at the massive ironbound bar that augmented the gate locks.

Apprehension filled the air around the companions as they waited in the rain. The bar was removed and the guards took up eight chains and began pulling, struggling against the incredible weight. The gate groaned and a crack appeared between the doors. A lone figure gradually materialized on the other side, surrounded by a pulsing blue aura. The rain ran off the edges in tiny rivers to puddle around the shield, causing the boy to be surrounded by a small pool. Tlonna's hands clenched and unclenched, her jaw tightening as the young half-breed was revealed. Aladorn glanced at his brother, saw Aidyn's feet shift yet again on the rain-slicked grass-weave street. Nerves tingled up his spine as he saw the assassin's body tense ever-so-slightly. Tlonna slowly walked forward until she was abreast of the guards.

Sithian smiled. He moved so that he was less than a yard away and bowed, mocking her. "Hello, Mother."

"Sithian," Tlonna began, but felt a sudden rushing of wind and cried out in alarm as a black blur swept by her and slammed into the boy.

The young king howled in agony as Aidyn slammed the iron spike into his thigh, grinding it deep into the bone. The elf's teeth were bared as he viciously twisted his arm, and yanked out the weapon. Sithian screamed and fell, clutching at his devastated thigh, trying to stem the flow of femoral blood.

"Aidyn!" Tlonna screamed, yanking the enraged assassin back.

"Let him die like his father, before he too becomes the hand of evil," he roared, punching his right hand into the air, the bloody spike visible to all.

"*Aiya*, let him bleed to death in the mud," Yayènia agreed, her face just as fierce as Aidyn's.

"No. Losolin, heal him. Aidyn, Yayènia, back off," Tlonna snarled, shoving the male back hard, the palm of her hand connecting with his sternum.

The assassin barely felt the hit, his mind focused entirely on the groaning boy as Losolin knelt over him. Fury rolled through his body, and moments later he had his bow off his back, knocked an arrow, and let it loose. The arrow narrowly missed Sithian's head as Tlonna careened into Aidyn, smacking him hard up against the gate wall. The strength with which the princess slammed into the assassin knocked his bow from his hands and he found himself dangling a foot off the ground, one arm held up high by Tlonna's.

"I said back off!" she roared.

Everyone watched in amazement as Aidyn twisted weirdly, dropped to the ground, and stalked away, his blacker-than-black clothing shimmering in the lashing rain. Tlonna stepped backward, holding her hands out, unable to figure out how in the nine hells Aidyn had freed himself. Looking to her companions, she found little sympathy in their eyes, and even less agreement.

"He is my son," she said, her only defense.

"And Midian's," Yayènia snapped. "I made the mistake of letting one Rahlan live, believing myself honor bound, and now I agree with Aidyn. Kill him, and end the threat."

Tlonna shook her head and turned around to find Losolin supporting the limping Sithian. "You did not heal him fully," she accused.

"Why should I?" the Lord Consort demanded, roughly grabbing the boy and tossing him at Tlonna. "He is your flaming problem now."

Tlonna caught her injured son and held him up, despite his struggles against her. Feeling abandoned and betrayed, she turned about and steadied Sithian, letting him hold onto any sliver of dignity he had left.

"They'll pay for that," he muttered, jerking his shoulder away from his mother.

"Not any time soon," she returned, not at all happy with the way things had gone. "Just remember you owe your life to me, now. Not that you did not anyway."

"What are you talking about? You never saved me before," Sithian snapped, "nor cared to."

"I gave you your life, Sithian," Tlonna snarled back, shoving him toward a horse. "Get on."

The guardsman to whom the horse belonged was not at all pleased by having the boy touch his mount, but the look Tlonna gave him silenced any protestations. "Your horse will be at the castle stables. You will be compensated for your troubles," she said to appease him.

He bowed away and went back to his post, doing a valiant job at looking unperturbed. Tlonna hoisted herself up after her son and flicked the reins, heading off toward the castle, leaving behind her companions.

Together, they began the long trek back to the castle, and whatever disasters awaited them there.

Water dripped unnoticed onto the fine Zeynuwnian carpet while a healthy fire crackled in the hearth in a gallantly furnished room. The atmosphere would have been comfortable on a normal rainy day, but today it was tense and angry, and very hostile. Tlonna sat in a high backed chair watching her son drink a large glass of imported brandy. His wounded leg had been tended to by a healer, and the looks he had given the woman unnerved Tlonna. Now she watched him with curiosity and worry, which caused her quite a headache.

"Sithian, why have you come here?"

"Apparently to be murdered by a sociopathic dark elf."

Tlonna took a deep breath to calm herself and leaned back, trying to appear languid and sure. "You should not have come."

"I see that. But now I am here, and what to do about it? Why, Mother, do you think I came to your elf-infested kingdom?"

Tlonna sniffed derisively. "Your sister."

Sithian leaned forward and set his glass on the table next to him. "Indeed."

"Rhiannan is not leaving my presence," Tlonna told him coldly.

"So you say. As far as I am concerned, you don't have the power to stop me," Sithian replied, raising his eyebrows.

Tlonna laughed. "You are far outnumbered and out-powered, make no mistake about that. More Magins reside in this castle than live anywhere outside these walls. No threat from you will scare me into giving Anna to you. Did not the lesson at the gate get through to you? You would be pinned to the ground through your eye socket right now if I had not stopped Aidyn."

Sithian's jaw clenched, but he said nothing in response, knowing full well that his parent spoke the truth. He had indeed felt the air of the arrow as it whisked by his head, and his leg throbbed in agonizing waves. Though Losolin had healed the femoral puncture and his smashed femur, the elf had done little other healing, leaving the torn and bruised flesh. The woman had only applied a salve and stopped the bleeding, wrapping his thigh in a tight cravat.

Tlonna watched his expression, watched his hand gingerly touch the swollen skin of his leg. "Why do you want Rhiannan?"

"Because she is my sister."

"What about your brother?"

"He is no brother of mine."

"You both came from my womb and your father's seed."

"We share blood, but I would rather spill his than look at him."

"He is stronger than you. He is almost more powerful than Midian was," Tlonna murmured, steepling her fingers.

Sithian stood suddenly. "Let me see Rhiannan. Now."

"Sit. We have not finished our discussion," Tlonna snarled, snapping her fingers and pointing to the chair. When the boy had followed her demand, the Magin Queen eyed him suspiciously. "You have left your inherited kingdom with no ruler, traveled across half of Nymyños, by yourself, and with meager supplies. You are a king, despite your ineptitude. I would expect you to have an entire entourage."

Sithian glared, but said nothing as he finished off his brandy.

"What are you doing here?" Tlonna asked again, her voice even sharper.

This time the boy's sapphire eyes seemed to flash with anger, and something darker lurked behind the flames. "Can I not move about of my own free will?

"No, you cannot! You are King of Zaedic, last I heard, and no ruler has the freedom to roam about the countryside for no reason!" Tlonna snapped, pushed beyond all bearing with her child. "When you were an infant I taught you reason and justice, honor and loyalty. Where did those lessons go?"

"I honored my father, but your friends took him away! I was loyal to him, and remain loyal to Zaedic to this day! I know reason, and we have our system of justice that suits the lifestyle of Zaedicans just fine. And if you call what happened out there justice, then you are just as wicked as I am!"

"Aidyn is an assassin, and held by codes of his own, do not equate my morals with his. And the state your people are in is not a lifestyle, nor is it fine. It is more than poverty and worse than slavery.

Your people are miserable, lifeless, ignorant of law and order, and unused to fair treatment. They deserve better from you, their leader!"

"Why? They choose to live there, I did not choose it for them. They sit at home doing nothing, moaning about their lot in life when all they have to do is go out and *do* something. No one does a bleeding thing, and they all want me to fix it for them. I tell them to fix their own stupid well and they curse me like a devil. Father never did anything for them, why should I?"

Tlonna shook her head. "Your father was a cruel, sadistic narcissist who murdered people for his own pleasure. You were not far behind him when I was his captive."

Sithian sat rigid, his slender fingers gripping the arms of his chair so tightly his knuckles were white. "You knew nothing of Father. He was an amazing person, powerful beyond measure and true to his quest."

"I knew too much of him, Sithian. He and I, we were mirror images of each other, light and dark, though any turn in our lives could have changed our positions. Midian was vile and cruel, and his only love was the love of power. He had many weaknesses, and in the end they were his demise. You must see that. Now, tell me, why did you honestly come here?"

The young king stood once more. "I wish to see Rhiannan. That is why I came. She belongs with me, in our home."

Tlonna stood as well, conceding to his desire. "Then you shall have your wish, though do not think you will ever have a moment alone," she turned and followed him out of the room into the hall where everyone else stood impatiently waiting, having returned to the castle to find that Tlonna was already sequestered in the room with her vile son. Aidyn was nowhere to be found.

With Tlonna's beckoning gesture, the companions proceeded down the corridor and up the second floor stairs, Yayènia glowering at Sithian the whole time, fingering the longblade at her hip, a quiet growl escaping every now and then. Suneelo, in formal capacity as Tlonna's guard, glanced sidelong at his wife and shook his head to warn her. Finally, they came to the noble housing wing and went to the far end. Tlonna produced a key, but knocked before inserting it. "Rhiannan?"

"What?"

"You have a visitor, and we are coming in," the princess said, unlocking the door and swinging it wide.

Rhiannan glared out at them, her eyes searching their faces, tightening with fear at Yayènia, until finally landing on Sithian. A bright grin spread across her comely features and she flew through the door. Brother and sister embraced warmly, laughing like children. When they separated, Sithian held his sister at arms' length.

"They haven't been treating you badly have they, Anna?"

"Undeniably so, disgusting creatures that they are," the young woman glared at Tlonna. "But come, let us talk about things with less of an audience, shall we?" she started to close the door but Tlonna held it open.

"You two may have some time together, but you will not talk in privacy lest you think to plot some plan," she said, pulling Rhiannan out of her room.

The two were escorted down the hall and back to the second floor. Once they were securely locked into the room they had recently vacated, Tlonna turned to one of the guards. "Go find Prince Haydyn. Tell him that Sithian has arrived and I need him to hold the seal on Anna. Hurry."

The guard sped off down the hall and disappeared around the corner. Losolin took the guard's place. "I will keep a watch on them. If I feel anything, I will contact you immediately, until Haydyn arrives."

"Good. I have to go sit in court, and it will be all day. Find Aidyn and tell him I want to see him in his room at dusk. I do not want *any* of you interfering with them," she pointed at the door, "unless they make a move. Keep the guard strong, and let me know if anything does happen," Tlonna said, and turned down the corridor.

She walked to the throne room and sat in her chair next to her father. Dietirin glanced at her, his bright blue eyes curious. "Where have you been?"

"I have a visitor," was all she said.

The herald pounded his staff on the floor three times and called out in a loud voice, "Petitioners of the royal family may progress into the throne room." He moved out of the way and allowed the guards to open the double doors.

A seemingly endless line of petitioners poured through to kneel in homage before their rulers. The first man came forward and squashed his worn hat nervously in his hands. He was an elderly human, from Andik, his weathered face brown from the sun.

"My Lieges, my name is Andreas Boyther. I have a signed petition of ninety percent of my fellows. We ask for a stronger military guard because lions, bears, and the occasional rampant boar have caused us much grief. The small guard we have is not sufficient enough to protect our land and people. Please your Highnesses, we beg of your protection."

Tlonna sighed and settled back for the rest of the day, her mind utterly blank. At some point Miazie appeared to take her place behind Tlonna, and she whispered that Haydyn was holding the seal on Rhiannan and that Losolin had gone to find Aidyn. Erdwyf stood behind Dietirin's throne, a look of impatience on her normally diplomatic face. About halfway through day Tlonna was startled out of her dull attention when two figures appeared in the door.

They stood a few inches above the humans, and a few inches shorter than the other elves, but moved with the gracefulness of elf kind. Their apparel was earthy, made of hide and slightly crude. The male's hair was dark blond, nearly brown, and held in place by a leather band about his forehead. His companion was slightly shorter than him, her bushy red hair rather dull. They were both slight and fit, and moved with dangerous ease.

When there was a small break for lunch and the petitioners opened their sack lunches, Tlonna twisted in her seat so she could face Miazie. "What are those people at the doors, the short ones?"

"I don't know. I've never seen them before. They look like elves," Miazie replied, genuine surprise in her voice, for there was few things she did not know.

"They are Plains Elves, and it is on rare occasion that they come to the city. Something big must have happened, the only reason they come to court is a faulty marriage, murder, or land disputes. Even so, those are usually taken care of by village councils," Erdwyf supplied, leaning on Tlonna's chair. "They swear allegiance to the Throne of Blackhaven, but only twice have I ever seen them within the city. But, following events of this morning, I am not all that surprised something has happened."

Tlonna eyed her friend for a moment, thinking. "True...Sithian would not be one to," she glanced cautiously at her parents, "go about quietly."

Both Erdwyf and Miazie shook their heads, glancing up at the strangers. The lunch break ended and the villagers pressed forward once more. It was a couple of hours before the elves reached the dais where the royals sat. They both stood calmly, neither bowing nor showing any sort of submission whatsoever.

"Your Highnesses, I am Nebet'thu of Tribe Asheyl, and this is my wife Eesa, daughter of Alden," Neb said, tucking his thumbs into his braided leather belt and slumping his shoulders comfortably.

"Welcome to the city, Nebet'thu and Eesa. What is your plea?" Dietirin asked, looking slightly surprised.

"It is no plea, but a message. On my route home, I found a body on the road. It was a man who appeared to be from one of the border towns, a farmer perhaps. There were no tracks, blood, or other evidence of a struggle."

"How had the man been killed then?" Constancias asked.

"His stomach was blown open. My belief is that this man was murdered by magic, Your Highness."

"Where is the body now?" Dietirin asked.

"I took it home and we buried it."

Tlonna watched the couple in interest, noting the way Nebet'thu seemed to ignore his wife's very presence, while she stood with the rigidity of one unsure of their status. Eesa had a peculiar look to her, a longer face than either high or dark elves, and wide set amber eyes. The female noticed Tlonna's' interest and boldly stared back, her face tightening.

The princess forced her gaze away and resumed listening to Nebet'thu and her father, for they were now discussing the involvement of his people.

"...plains elf has been seen in Blackhaven City since my own inauguration. This bothers me, my friend."

"It should not, King Dietirin. The Tribe of Asheyl remains loyal to the Throne of Blackhaven, and the Ewôsdírn family. We enjoy our solitude, and our lifestyle remains unchanged since the time of our founding."

"Be that as it may, Master Nebet'thu, it would comfort me if you would stay a while in the city. I have many questions for you," the king said, not unkindly.

"As do I," Tlonna added suddenly, her curiosity getting the best of her.

Dietirin gave his daughter a small, knowing smile, and he lightly slapped the arm of his chair. "It is settled then. Nebet'thu, Eesa, you will remain here for the time being. Do you have quarters within the city?"

Nebet'thu shook his head, obviously displeased by the arrangements, but wise enough to stay silent.

"Then you shall stay here. Nikta will show you to your room. Dismissed," the elf king said, turning his attention to the next people in line.

The two plains elves again did not bow, but they turned uncertainly to follow the maid out of the throne room. Tlonna squeezed her eyes shut as the day wore on, trying to keep her mind focused. Nothing had come to her of how Rhiannan and Sithian were. She had not seen Haydyn once, and she worried for him. Finally, the herald announced the end of the day and the petitioners that remained groaned and grumpily left the room. Tlonna and her friends began to leave when Dietirin called them back.

"Who is this visitor you have, Tlonna?"

"Ah...a friend from Narnen."

"Will I get to meet this friend?"

"No, no I do not think so. He is not exactly the most courteous person. He would offend you greatly, Father," Tlonna replied quickly.

"Dwarf," Erdwyf supplied.

"Ah...right," the king said, his eyes narrowing, knowing his daughter too well to be convinced. "See you at dinner."

Tlonna turned on her heel and fled the room, closely followed by Miazie and Erdwyf. They did not slow until they reached the door where Haydyn sat, his head against the door, his hands linked under his knees. The young half-breed looked exhausted. Dark circles ringed his closed eyes and his shoulders sagged. His delicate face was pulled tight as though he was in great agony. Tlonna knelt by him, concerned, ignoring the absolutely bored faces of Ghealan, Suneelo, and Aladorn across the hall.

"Haydyn?"

The half-elf's head jerked up and his eyes opened. "Mother, you startled me."

"Are you all right?"

"Uhnh, yeah. Jus' tired. Sithian keeps attempting to unseal Rhiannan. I have been able to stop him so far, but if he tries much more..." he stopped to allow his company to come to their own conclusions.

"Come on then, get up. I am going in there. Do you think it possible to seal Sithian?" Tlonna asked, helping her son to stand.

"It would prove extremely difficult. He would have to be bound and shielded while I did it. Even Father had a hard time shielding him during our lessons. He has a strong defense against such Weaves. I am not sure I have the strength to do it tonight, anyway."

Tlonna nodded and opened the door. Sithian sat slumped in his chair, an empty snifter abandoned on the floor beside his chair. Rhiannan was curled into a ball by the fire, her hair slick with sweat, as was her brother's. Haydyn followed her in, unconcerned at being in the same room as two people who genuinely hated him. Sithian's eyes glanced in his brother's direction, but went back to the floor with nothing more than a weary glare.

Tlonna had never seen her three children looking so dejected and tired before. It shocked her. Their likenesses came to her suddenly, their fine boned faces, lean bodies, slightly pointed ears, shaggy, curly hair, and larger eyes than is typical of humans. The door clicked closed behind her and she turned to see Losolin.

The awkwardness of the situation hit Tlonna like a physical blow. Her three children, and her Lord Consort, the male who should have been the father, but was not.

Haydyn put his hand on her shoulder and shook his head. "Sithian has nearly drained himself of all his power trying to fight me. Rhiannan is weakened terribly because she has been on the brink of power all day, but unable to touch it. It is a tactic Father used on you. It is meant as a torture device for magic users to drive them mad. I did not know our struggle would do this to her," his voice was rough and quiet.

A low grating moan issued from Sithian's mouth. It took a moment for Tlonna to realize he was laughing. "So, little brother, you proved yourself stronger than me. I didn't believe it. I can't believe it." Sithian's eyes bulged as though they themselves could not believe it.

Rhiannan whimpered, twitching in her misery. Losolin knelt lifted her chin so he could look at her. Her dark eyes were dilated with pain and her skin was white and clammy. "I can do nothing for her. Any more alien magic in her body would most likely kill her. She must fight this battle alone." He gently released her chin and picked her up. "I will have Aladorn take her back to her room."

Sithian made as if to stand, but managed only to kick his leg out. He did not even lift his head to glare at Losolin as the elf carried his sister away. Haydyn watched his older brother, his face expressionless. Tlonna sat in the chair across from her corrupt and tainted son. Silence filled the room until Losolin returned a moment later. The Magin took a deep breath and steadied herself.

"Did you kill a man, near the border?"

"Yes."

"Why?"

Sithian grunted. "Because that is what I do."

"Why did you not take one of your father's birds, instead of coming by ship and foot?"

"They all left when Father died. He had a hold over them, and it died with him."

"What are you really doing here?" she asked for the third time that day, still unwilling to believe her son's simple explanation.

Sithian summoned the will to look his mother in the eye, annoyed by her shifting topics. "To see my sister. I want her with me. She is Princess of Zaedic, and she will die here, with all you filthy little elves. Especially the one who killed Father. I want her blood. She left him in the hall with his throat slit ear to ear. Left him there, as though he were a mere human," his face contorted as his words and thoughts ran together in near incoherence, and the princess knew her son's mind was as twisted as Midian's had been, if not worse.

"Midian *was* a mere human, Sithian. A man of power and evil, but flesh and blood as we are, and you yourself are half-elf, as is Rhiannan, and Haydyn." Tlonna replied quietly.

Her son lifted his head to glare at her. "You and he had *nothing* in common."

"No, we did not, at least not in the way you think. But there were things that bound us together. Power, strength, you, and your brother and sister, things that we cannot change now. What do you have to gain by following in Midian's footsteps? Why can you not rule as a good and kind king? Bring your people to prosperity instead of leaving them in the squalor your father forced on them."

"The road to the nine hells is much easier and faster than the mountain you must climb to reach the heavens. I want to live my life as free and wildly as I choose. I don't want to be ruled by law or limitation. It is my life and I will live it as such."

"What about an heir? You must find one, and therefore you must lie with a woman, and not kill her."

Sithian's lips turned up into a sickly half smile. "I can always do what Father did."

Tlonna's breath rushed out of her as revulsion and horror stuck in her throat, but she quickly contained her emotion and stared blankly at her son. "That is what caused Midian's death, in the end. The wisest choice would be to take a wife. Your grandfather was married to the same woman his entire life."

"Aderiaen was also murdered for his choice. Us Rahlans have a habit of being killed by family members."

"Midian was not killed by family members, Sithian, he was killed by Yayènia," Tlonna countered quickly, trying to poke a hole, any hole, through his skewed logic.

The boy glared at her with such hate she felt the room cool. "You were his mate...and Haydyn may as well have held the sword that slit his throat. He is a coward and a traitor."

"I was *not* his mate!" the elf nearly screamed in wild fury at the thought. "I was his captive slave, a body he held for his own uses. He held me more securely than any cell ever could by the simple strength of his magic and his cruelty. If you ever think for one moment that I lay with your father willingly I will tear out your tongue myself! And Haydyn chose the path of righteousness rather than become another useless tyrant like yourself. Never call what he did cowardice, for it was more brave than what you did."

Sithian cowered in his chair, terrified of the growling rage that roiled in his mother's voice. His sapphire eyes were wide as he stared at her menacingly towering over his chair. Tlonna did not remember standing up or walking the short distance, but when she calmed she backed off immediately, afraid that she might lose control and hurt him.

Once the elf had regained her chair, they stared at each other for a long, awkward moment, neither sure what to say in case the other might say something and tip off another explosion. They had both also forgotten that Haydyn was in the room with them and he chose now to speak.

"Sithian, you saw what it was for you when I held you bound. Can you not see that my strength is so because of my choices? My magic is not tainted, it is not weakened by corruption. You once showed me kindness when Midian beat me for not killing a man, and I know that kindness is not lost. You still have a chance to redeem yourself before you do something irreparably cruel and rip your soul into shreds."

Sithian sneered at his young brother, disgusted. "You think you have all the answers because you ran away and were able to shield me without breaking. Let me tell you something, *brother*, when I am strong enough, I will guide the knife that slits your throat."

"If killing me will make you see remorse, or even sate your thirst for murder, than I give my life gladly."

The Zaedican king's menace disappeared as Haydyn stole all the fun out of his threat. Finally, Tlonna sighed.

"You will regret your life, Sithian, and I am sorry it is so," she said quietly, feeling miserable.

"Why, because I am not like you?" the young Magin demanded. "I am content in my life, other than the fact that you murdered my father and kidnapped my sister. Let me take her home and I swear I shall never come here again."

"You are a bad liar, Sithian. You will come as your father did, and your grandfather, and like them you will be utterly destroyed. And when you do come, I will not hold back my friends to save your life. If you put the lives of my people in danger, your life will indeed be forfeit."

"You think you can really win this war of good and evil, don't you?" Sithian asked, amusement lacing his every word. "You think your ideals and your morals have a chance at victory."

"I do not. I know it and I demand it, and it is more than you will ever have if you stay on the path you are on. Whether at the end of your life or tomorrow, you will come to see the idiocy of your choice, and I feel sorry for you."

"Do not waste your pity on me, Mother. Don't forget I have tasted both good and what you call evil, and I find the freedom of the latter far more attractive. What I do, what I plan to do, is purge the world of those who belittle and humiliate the rest of the population. I will wipe out the dissent and let the strongest race take over their rightful place as rulers."

"Once again you forget to look in the mirror. You have elfin blood running through your veins. If you choose to do this, you will be demanded to kill yourself and Rhiannan. Can you do that? Do you have the conviction to make the ultimate sacrifice for your ideals?"

Sithian smiled his half smile, the parody, and Tlonna shivered. "No one knows I'm half-elf. They think the Rahlans are simply higher humans...gods."

"You are not a god, Sithian, you are a selfish two year old in the body of a seventeen year old. You need to recognize your failures and your weaknesses before you inflate your already enlarged ego and do something that will cost lives on both sides. You know your folly, it is the same as your ancestors. You do not use your mind. Use it now and see your madness."

Sithian's cold blue eyes glared at her for a moment before shifting to his brother. "What of you, Haydyn? Why choose this life? Why choose naivety and weakness when you could have so much more?"

"The way I see it, *brother*, I am the one who is free, and without injury. I have true friends and will live a life full of love and honesty. What do you have? A lonesome castle on a windswept, barren island with a kingdom full of dejected, miserly people? I choose my route, though it comes with greater responsibility."

"You are a fool," Sithian sneered, looking away. For a moment the room was silent, and then he looked up at Losolin, standing silently behind Tlonna. "And you? You have risen in status, you have gained wealth and fame, but at what cost? You must cater to a lover who is tainted and weak, one who leans on others who are stronger but in less of a position of power. You hold her up, never fully becoming what you could be were you set free of these self-applied chains. Of all the people in this benighted kingdom, you are the only one who has earned my respect, and you squander it by pandering to her."

Losolin's face remained impeccable, not a lash moving in spite of the roaring rage building within him. "Your words prove your ignorance, Sithian. If only you could see the massive fault in your logic. You are only fooling yourself. I am not weakened by love, nay, I am strengthened by it. I have a reason to fight, a reason to come home at night, a reason to better myself in every way possible. I pity you, for I fear you will never know love, and will live a lonely existence because of it."

"Though you will not accept your lover's children into your heart?" Sithian whispered, sending a vicious glance at Haydyn. "Not even the one who turned his back on a life you deem evil?"

Both Losolin and Haydyn stiffened at the words, the former refusing to look at the latter. Haydyn stared at the elf, not in challenge or even frustration, but simply because he wanted to see his reaction. Finally, the older male sighed and looked at the younger.

"Haydyn is my consort's son, not mine, though I will love him for the man he is becoming, and as long as he stays on the path he now walks, I will love him as I love all my friends."

The blond half-breed's heart swelled slightly at the words, but Sithian's mocking laughter stole the joy from him. "What does that amount to? Certainly not the affection of a true family member. Our father loved him more than you do."

"Midian did not have the capacity to love," Tlonna snapped, seeing the look of hopeless desperation on both Haydyn's and Losolin's face. "He knew only ambition and want. He did not even love you, Sithian, though you continue to be blind to your father's cruelty. He would not have wept were you killed."

The oldest Rahlan sneered again then turned his face away to look into the fire. Tlonna sighed and stood, shaking her head. "I hope you will do as I say, and use your head, Sithian, for otherwise you will find yourself on a path too dark and too solitary, one that will turn you about so that you will never find your way back."

The brooding young man did not reply, so Tlonna quickly ushered Haydyn and Losolin from the room. She had not forgotten the previous day's troubles, the dire explanation of prophecy, and Yayènia's violent reactions, and they awaited her now like an ever-present plague. Haydyn turned to her as soon as the door closed, looking as dejected as she felt. Her constant attendants, dubbed both the Council and the Family, but usually called simply the companions: Yayènia, Ghealan, Suneelo, Erdwyf, Miazie, and Aladorn, were leaning against the opposite wall, every one of them tensed like a coil, ready to spring in a second, Aidyn once again conspicuously absent. Tlonna and Yayènia locked gazes, the fight from the night before, and this morning, tightening both their faces.

"Well that was joyous," Haydyn said acidly. "How I do love verbal slaps in the face."

"Do not let his barbs get to you, my son. Remember who you are and why you are that way," the Magin replied tiredly, her voice thick with sorrow.

"I wonder if it would've been better for me to stay behind on Zaedic. I could've overthrown Sithian and taken the throne myself. I could have had him executed and brought to justice," the half-breed snarled to himself.

"It is not a goal beyond our reach," Losolin said calmly, studying the boy. "In fact, it is a very good idea."

"No, it is not," Tlonna snapped, her hand slashing the air before her. "Maybe in a few years, but Haydyn is not ready for that kind of responsibility yet, and even if he were, the state of Zaedic is too unstable after Midian's death to handle such an upheaval."

"And you think having Sithian as a king is going to help it? Tlonna, the boy is a menace and a philanderer. He will never provide stability!"

"It is not our place to decide such things!" the Magin Queen shouted back, going up on her toes in her ire.

"Such behavior does not suit you," a seething voice said behind the group and they all spun to face Constancias, and Dietirin, who had been standing there, unnoticed for many moments.

Tlonna swallowed and slowly moved up to face her parents. Constancias's eyes pinned her daughter with a disgusted glare before searching the companions' faces and landing on Haydyn, who was being shielded by a vigilant Erdwyf.

"Step aside, High Advisor," the queen demanded coldly, her gaze never leaving the nervous boy's face.

"I will not, my lady," Erdwyf calmly responded, pushing Haydyn further behind her.

"Tlonna," Dietirin said in a weary voice. "Who is this young man?"

"Haydyn," Tlonna immediately replied, refusing to back down, "as I told you when we arrived."

"What is his last name?"

Tlonna's voice stuck in her throat and she looked frantically back at Losolin, who offered no help, instead staring at the king.

"You called him your son!" Constancias shrieked, finally turning to her daughter. "And he spoke of the throne of Zaedic! Who is he?"

The princess let out a defeated breath, her shoulders slumping. "He is my son, and his name is Haydyn Rahlan-Ewôsdírn."

Constancias's eye twitched. Dietirin stared at Haydyn. The group stood in tense, defensive hush, their arguments momentarily forgotten.

After a long, awkward silence, Dietirin recovered slightly. "Rahlan-Ewôsdírn?"

"Midian was his father, and I am his mother. The girl we have with us is Rhiannan, Haydyn's twin sister, and the boy in the room is Sithian, my...our...eldest."

The king's sharp intake of breath sounded almost painful as his gaze flickered between Tlonna, Haydyn, and Losolin. The latter looked away, ashamed for some inexplicable reason. Finally the oldest elf present closed his eyes and seemed to gather himself.

"You were gone for nine years, though this child is much older than that. How in the nine hells is this possible?" he asked softly.

"Midian used his power to change all three children while they were still within me. They aged sixteen years in sixteen weeks, and were altered to Midian's desires. Haydyn and Rhiannan caused him some confusion for he did not realize they were both there at the time. Haydyn escaped most of his tampering, and therefore his soul is his own, and he chose willingly to flee with us when we left Zaedic," Tlonna explained quietly, exposing secrets she had kept to herself for nearly a year.

Everyone present gasped when they realized the extent of what she had been through on the island, and then silence fell once more.

After a moment Constancias strode forward, shoving Erdwyf and a growling Ghealan out of the way, her hands latching onto Haydyn's shoulders. Purple magic pulsed out of her hands and the half-breed fell to his knees, crying out in pain. Tlonna angrily grabbed her mother and yanked her away from her son, fury writhing in her every movement.

Constancias shook her daughter off and pointed an accusing finger at Haydyn, who was being helped to his feet by Ghealan. "You will rue the day you ever stepped foot in my kingdom, Rahlan filth! Consider your life forfeit!"

Tlonna slapped the queen so hard the elf's head and shoulder smacked into the wall behind her, momentarily blinding her. "Haydyn may be half Rahlan, but he is also half Ewôsdírn. It is to him you owe thanks for my life, for he kept me sane, and alive, for the months I endured captivity. He is the one who found Losolin and the others and released me from my prison. He stood face to face with Midian and denied him, and his siblings. I will not let you reject him on the mere basis of parentage. He is a good, kind soul, and he is my son."

Constancias swallowed, her jeweled eye-patch catching the light as she quivered with emotion. Dietirin studied his grandson with calculating eyes, ignoring his voracious wife.

"I cannot say it pleases me to hear that my daughter birthed children to that monster, but I am glad to know that at least one of them carries her heart. Young Haydyn, I am honored to meet you, and gladly accept you into my family as Prince of Blackhaven. I hope to get to know you more in the next few months," the king said after a moment.

Tlonna looked at her parent with tear-filled eyes, relieved by his words. Haydyn simply nodded, still recovering from his grandmother's attack. Constancias was still glaring at him with her one eye, and it conveyed enough emotion for two.

"I shall be sure he is given the proper adornments, apartment, and privileges," Dietirin added, smiling fully.

The Magin Queen let out a sigh of relief. "He will go to the academy, and receive lessons in how to rule a country from select personnel among the family," Tlonna said, gesturing to the group behind her. "Now, we have other things to do, so I bid you good evening. Mother."

"Good night, Tlonna," Dietirin replied, embracing his daughter, holding her tight to his broad chest. "I love you so much, my child, and I weep for what you went through."

"*A'da*," was all Tlonna said, burying her face in her father's shoulder.

Dietirin pulled away from his child and roughly grabbed Constancias, who was angrily leaning against the wall. He dragged her away, shaking his head as she ranted at him.

Tlonna turned to face the dear friends and family behind her. "That is the second time today I have had to defend my children against attempts on their life," she said sadly. "Yayènia, take Haydyn back to his room. Ghealan, Aladorn, Suneelo, keep watch on Sithian. You two," she pointed at Erdwyf and Miazie, "Make sure he is entered into the records, and given the proper attire and titles."

As everyone turned to do their respective duties, she turned to Losolin who looked at her with shame-filled eyes. "Losolin, why do you look so pained?"

"I should be their father," he stated simply, shrugging. "I should be able to bring Haydyn into my heart, but I cannot find the strength. The little bastard was right," he said, nodding at the door the three other males had just entered. "I cannot love even the one who is kindhearted and righteous."

"It is not your fault, it is Midian's. And though I dearly wish that you and I could have a child, it is not so, and I fear that it may never be so. I love you, and that is all that matters, is it not?"

Losolin caught her hand and kissed it, closing his eyes against the pain that seemed always to afflict him. "It is."

Tlonna smiled sadly and brushed her free hand against his cheek. "Go on, now, I have to meet with Aidyn."

"I am sorry you have been through so much today," he said suddenly, seeing the agony in his lover's eyes.

Tlonna shrugged helplessly. "It shall pass."

"Remember that Aidyn is our friend, dear and devoted, perhaps to a fault but a friend nonetheless," Losolin said as he turned to go. "Do not revile him for his actions this morning, for it was on all our minds. He just had the courage to act upon it."

Tlonna took a deep breath and walked across the fourth floor of the castle, going the long route toward the front of the building and circling back toward Aidyn's apartment. When she knocked, she heard the click of a lock being released, but the door did not open nor did any voice grant her entrance. Taking the unlocking as such, Tlonna opened the carved door and stepped inside.

She had never before been within the assassin's room, at least not in her memory, and she was not surprised. Red and black drapes hung from the ceiling, sporting an insignia that Tlonna vaguely recognized, but couldn't recall where from. It was a slightly oblong circle, mostly black but with a red crescent on the right side. On opposite sides, one pointing up and one down, were two claw-like appendages. The one connected to the greater black side was red, and the one on the red side was black. Tlonna stared at it for a moment before recalling her purpose. Looking about the darkly furnished foyer, she found Aidyn standing off to the side, his arms folded across his chest. She eyed him carefully, and then started when she saw the symbol on his belt buckle, and then noticed it again on the hilts of his scimitars.

"I thought your insignia was a white dot on a field of black," Tlonna said quietly, confused.

"That is the emblem of House Sestuns, yes, but like you, I have my own," the assassin replied in the same manner, unfolding his arms and walking toward her. "Tlonna, you are my dearest friend and I love you, but you made an impossibly foolish decision this morning. Sithian may be your son, but he is not of you. He will carry on worse than Midian or Aderiaen, even Hadian. I know, I have lived through four generations of Rahlan ego. More, in fact, but none before

Hadian had the gall to do anything more than sit on their pitiful little island and beat their poor people into submission."

"You knew they were there?" Tlonna demanded, suddenly suspicious.

Aidyn's lip curled as he caught the tone of her voice. "Of course not, but there were always reports of some wicked human power up north. They knew we were here, though we did not know they were. The Rahlans have always been present in Nymyños, always been a source of discomfort for elves and dwarves alike. And now you have preserved the line because you falsely think that your vile son has some hope of becoming a good person? What of Rhiannan? You have watched for a year now, and she has not become anything different. She is still the sadistic little brat you brought from Zaedic. How can you think Sithian, who has been on his own for that same year, will be any better?"

"I have to hope!" Tlonna shouted, throwing her arms in the air.

"Hope is a foolish thing when reality is knocking at the door. You will condemn hundreds, perhaps thousands, yourself among them, to death if you do not rid the world of Sithian and Rhiannan," the assassin's voice was uncharacteristically harsh and loud as anger and bitterness welled within him.

"And of Haydyn? Would you have me take his life as well, just in case?"

"Haydyn has proven himself to be an ally, and you know it. The boy has nothing in common with his siblings, or his father, other than a need to finish his battles quickly and decisively. He even favors your appearance, not Midian's, and do not think my heart so cold I would kill him just because of heritage."

"You would kill Sithian and Anna because of heritage," Tlonna accused furiously.

"No," Aidyn snapped, "I would kill them because of their actions, their cruelty and disregard for anyone's life other than their own."

Tlonna bit back her retort, knowing she was wrong. Spotting a black velvet chair, she slid into it and buried her face in her hands, letting all the worries she carried come to the fore. Aidyn watched her succumb, and then moved silently to kneel before her. Drawing the female into his arms, he held her for a long time. Kneeling as he was, the assassin was between her legs, his arms wrapped about her waist as she clung to his shoulders, her face buried in the crook of his neck.

Long after he had lost track of the time, he felt her body soften against his, the sobs subside, and her arms slip down to rest against his. For one incredulous moment, Aidyn thought she was making a move on him, and then he realized she was asleep. Carefully extracting one arm, he slid his hand under her thigh and gently stood, bringing her up with him. Cradling Tlonna like a child, he carried her into his bedroom and laid her on his bed.

Extricating himself from the sleeping princess, Aidyn looked down at her, so pale against his black duvet, and let himself believe, for one small moment, that she was his to hold forever. Then he shook himself and wisely left his apartment, searching for Losolin. It was the Lord Consort that found him, instead.

"Aidyn!"

The assassin spun on his heel, completely reversing direction in order to face Losolin. The high elf eyed him curiously as he came to stand before the dark one.

"I was just looking for you," he said, his emerald eyes filled with some strange emotion Losolin could not quite interpret.

"Where is Tlonna?"

"Asleep. She finally let herself feel, and she fell asleep. She is in my room. I would let her rest, if I were you," Aidyn replied, putting a staying hand on the suddenly tense elf.

"She is on your bed?"

"Where else would she sleep, Losolin? As I said, leave her be...unless of course you do not trust me with your lover."

The words sounded odd in the half-Magin's ear, a resonance of truth to them that bothered him, but he did not believe Aidyn would ever betray him in such a way. "I trust you with my life," he replied after a moment. "Where will you sleep?"

The assassin shrugged. "Somewhere. Goodnight, Losolin."

"Aye, goodnight," the Lord Consort said, turning to watch as Aidyn moved away, noticing once again the strange, blurry movements that spoke of great control and speed, and yet something more deadly, something beyond powerful. Shaking his head, the male trod back to his room, the small suite that he stayed in when not with Tlonna.

Tlonna woke with a start, noticing immediately the unfamiliar scent and feel of the bed she lay in. The aroma was definitely intoxicating, somewhere between the smell of fresh cloves and ginger, and beneath it all the musky scent of maleness. Rubbing her cheek against the softness of the black silk pillow, she cracked her eyes open and took in the strange surroundings. Carved bedposts rose about her, supporting a black and gray curtain tied back to let in the moonlights. It was early morning, predawn, she thought, rolling about trying to figure out where she was.

The room was medium sized, but taken up mostly by the large bed and the wardrobe off to the right. A small painting adorned the wall above the closet, a portrait of a silver-haired female, beautiful and smiling. Tlonna frowned, not recognizing the girl. Sitting up, she realized she was still wearing the clothes from the day previous, including her belt, and one boot. The other she had apparently kicked off in her sleep, for it still lay on the bed. She was twisted up in the ebony duvet, one leg curled atop while the other was under.

Her foggy brain finally started working when she spotted one long, sable hair on the pillow, barely visible against the black material.

"Aidyn," she whispered, the night before coming back to her.

Gingerly picking up the hair, she studied it in the moonlights, feeling odd and not a little out of place. It seemed so strange a thing, to hold something so fragile, so personal, of the indomitable assassin. It seemed more precious to her than letting her sleep in his bed, holding that single strand of Aidyn's raven locks. He was her closest friend, Tlonna realized with shock. Closer than Miazie, Erdwyf, even Yayènia, Aidyn held a special place in her heart. His long life had filled his verdant eyes with a thousand thousand memories, had carved his mind into a cunning, brilliant engine of tactics, worldly knowledge, and an ever-present readiness. Her eyes strayed to the small portrait above the wardrobe, and she wondered.

"*Yndrysl,*" Aidyn said quietly from the door to his room, the elfish word for "good morning."

Tlonna turned about in the bed to look at him, warmed by his presence, though she felt foolish holding up a strand of his hair. She dropped it. "Who is she?"

The assassin walked into his bedroom and leaned against a bedpost, gazing at the picture. "Her name was Rahna."

"Was?"

Aidyn nodded, swallowing. “I would have married her, had she not been driven away by my darkness. She came back to me, but only because she thought we were going to die.” He went silent for a moment, reliving the painful memory. “She was half right. She was running toward me, reaching out, and I toward her, when an arrow went right through her head. She stumbled into me, bleeding, already dead...I would have married her.”

Tlonna patted the bed beside her and he looked at her, confused. When she held out her hand, he took it out of pure instinct, and when she drew him close, the assassin’s breath caught. The Magin Queen wrapped her arms about him and lay back, pulling him down with her. Aidyn swallowed again, closing his eyes as her lips brushed his.

“You did not sleep, did you?” she asked quietly.

Aidyn breathed his answer, his eyes now half open. “No.”

“Then sleep,” Tlonna murmured, gently brushing the stubborn strands of sable hair out of his face, though they fell back into place moments later.

The assassin’s shoulders slumped as he fell asleep, curling inward as his muscles, always tense and ready when awake, relaxed. This sleep was much deeper than what he usually experienced, for a warrior never truly rests, except for when he feels completely safe, and even then, it is a lighter slumber than all others. Tlonna watched him for a moment before rolling away to remove her belt and her other boot, placing them on the floor. Still drained, she tucked herself against the somnolent assassin, and slept once more.

Aidyn woke with a start, and, when he realized his limbs were wrapped about Tlonna, rolled away so fast he landed on the floor, taking the blankets with him. The princess shrieked in surprise as she was yanked halfway across the mattress, rudely awakened. Aidyn was up in a flash, straightening his shirt, which had twisted up to his armpits in his frantic move. Tlonna took one look at him and burst into laughter, unable to contain herself. She had never seen the assassin so flustered, so disoriented. There was a red blotch on his shoulder where her head had been, visible only because the collar of the usually perfect tunic was gaping open, and lopsided as well.

The male stared at her, breathing hard, quite unsure of what to do. He thanked the gods he had locked the door, as was his custom, when coming in to wake Tlonna, otherwise Losolin might have had the same idea, and walked in on them, asleep, together. The thought brought a myriad thoughts and feelings flooding through him, but he tamped them down, hard. Tlonna was still giggling, sitting on the half stripped bed with her hair all mussed and her clothing wrinkled.

Aidyn continued to stare at her, his hands making their slow way up his own body, unconsciously and purposelessly. Tearing his gaze from the female, he glanced out the window and was relieved to see that only an hour or so had passed, and the sky was just beginning to lighten.

"No one will have missed you, yet," he said suddenly, feeling horribly guilty.

Tlonna snorted. "Of course not. And if they did so what?"

"Losolin will kill me."

"Oh, I am sure you could beat him," she replied cheerfully, sliding off the bed to stand before her disconcerted friend. "Besides, why would he?"

"We slept together."

"Aye, *slept.* We did nothing else, all of which consists of very little to no sleep. And, he, nor anyone else, has to know," Tlonna countered, kissing the already stressed assassin on the cheek. When she saw his face, the princess eased away from him, her expression suddenly somber. "Go back to sleep, Aidyn. You need to rest."

The male shook his head in pure befuddlement as she gathered her boots and belt, and left his room. As soon as she was gone, he followed her path, locked his door once again, and wearily climbed into bed, dragging the blankets back onto the mattress and piling them about himself, trying hard to ignore the feminine scent of Tlonna. Soon enough, sleep claimed him once more.

As Tlonna walked back to her tower after leaving Aidyn, she found herself facing the elf Eesa. Slightly embarrassed by her obviously mussed appearance, and the fact that she was barefoot, the Magin stopped before the plains elf.

"Eesa, what are you doing here?"

"Princess Tlonna! I had hoped to find you," the elf said, looking unnerved.

"Well, I hope I am worth the effort. What can I do for you?" Tlonna gestured to a bench and sat, dropping her effects on the ground.

As Eesa sat, a circular disc on a leather band fell out of her woolen tunic. It was rather dull looking but for four runes that were embossed on its bronze face.

"What is that?" Tlonna asked.

"Oh, this? It is just an old family heirloom. My father is High Councilor, and it has been handed down for thousands of years, because, in the Tribes, all stations are inherited. The four runes are for strength, courage, wisdom, and virtue," Eesa replied, looking at the disc.

"May I see it?"

The plains elf lifted the heirloom off her neck and handed it to Tlonna. The Magin took it and rubbed her thumb across the surface. The runes glowed faintly and then faded. Eesa gasped weakly, her eyes wide.

Tlonna gave the disc back and smiled. "It is very old, and made with power. I am not sure *it* is powerful, but whoever made it was."

"There are stories, legends of the founding elves that created havoc or peace within the Tribes, depending. It is said that these elves established the Tribes of the Plains Elves and forged twelve discs of power that were used to hold important vows and alliances so that they could never be broken. There were once twelve tribes, but only three remain, the others lost, along with the discs. I never thought mine could be one of them..." Eesa's voice trailed off into a whisper.

"What was it you needed?" Tlonna asked finally.

Eesa jerked as though awakening. "Is it possible for a couple to get divorced if only one partner wants it?"

"I do not know...why?"

"Well, you see...I tricked Nebet'thu into marrying me. He loves Kepthari, our chieftain's daughter, but she is betrothed to my brother, Daegin. I really love Neb, but I think he hates me now. We used to be a couple, and he said he wanted to marry me, but then he fell for Kepthari, and did not want anything to do with me."

"How did you force him to marry you?"

"I tricked him into seeing me naked. In the *Leh shä Eben Läläinwabirn*, "Creed of the Plains Elves," our law, it is taboo for a male to see a female naked unless they are married. Neb is a very lawful elf, and I knew he would rather die than commit such a heinous act. So he married me that night and then left for here. He told me to stay, but I came anyway. Neb barely spoke to me, and it is nearly a four day ride. I really do love him, and I thought that being with me would make him fall back into love, but his bitterness only grows."

Tlonna took a few moments to collect her thoughts before replying. She had innumerable reasons to despise anything and anyone to do with forced marriages. "So now you are afraid he will leave you?"

Eesa nodded, plainly grateful she did not have to explain her plight anymore to the princess.

"Maybe you should talk to him. Tell him everything you just told me. Then, if he wants to forsake his vows, let him. If you love him, truly, then you will want him to be happy."

"But he will not listen to me!"

"Get him alone and start talking. He will hear you no matter what," Tlonna paused and picked at a wrinkle in her pants. "I think I am off to change. Remember what I said and tell me tomorrow what happens. Only half the day tomorrow is for court. Good day, Eesa."

"Good day Princess, and thank you."

Tlonna raised a hand to acknowledge her, and walked into her tower stairs. Feeling the stark absence of Losolin like a blow, she locked the door and strolled to the west balcony doors that overlooked the harbor. Settling in one of the chairs, she let the rain touch her and felt the cooling wetness partially cleanse her mood, and it concealed the fact she was crying, no matter that no one was there to witness it.

"What is happening?" Tlonna asked quietly after a while, trying to address the spirits that so often whispered to her in inarticulate murmurs. With beseeching eyes, she looked up at the small blue moon that hung peacefully over the lightening skies, shedding its light along with the others, the moon that was the remnant soul of Tonora, her ancestor. Vaguely, she wondered if any other elf had become a moon.

No answer was forthcoming and the elf dropped her gaze to the swaying ocean beyond the castle wall. Ships of all types wallowed at the docks, schooners and dhows, sloops and fishing boats, while dockhands and sailors ran amok, even at this early hour. Tlonna watched them a good while, her far-seeing eyes catching individuals where human eyes would catch only movement. Her sadness abated somewhat as she watched them, wondering what her corsair friends were doing.

Finally realizing that she had other things to attend to, Tlonna walked to the washtub and began pumping the water. As it filled, she removed her clothing, but hesitated in placing them in the hamper to be washed. Aidyn's scent filled them, and she pressed her face into the soft folds, breathing deep. Though she loved Losolin, and could love no other, Tlonna knew there was something more than friendship between her and the assassin, and she refused to push it away. Feeling slightly foolish, a little guilty, and all-around ridiculous, the elf took one more deep breath, and then carefully folded the clothes and stored them away in her bedside table. Stepping into the now full tub, Tlonna sank into the steaming water and regretfully washed away the memory of the dark elf's touch and fragrance from her skin.

Losolin entered her room later, soundlessly jogging up the three steps that rose from the platform the door rested on and walked over to Tlonna. She was sitting at her desk, her head bent over a piece of parchment as she wrote a letter to Demetrius, King of Kajgenia and their good friend. The Lord Consort leaned over her and smiled, idly pulling back the section of her hair that was always contained by a silver cuff hanging by her temple. Her delicate, pointed ear poked through the part, just below a braid that held the rest of her pale hair in place. He kissed her cheek and grinned when her lip twitched up in a preoccupied smile.

"Tell him I said 'hello'," Losolin murmured, rubbing his thumbs into her shoulders.

"I already did," Tlonna replied distractedly as she signed her name at the bottom of the letter.

"Dietirin sent for all the craftsmen in the city, and they are all assembled in Haydyn's rooms, waiting for a decision to be made about whose furniture will be used," Losolin stated. "Your father moves very quickly."

"A thousand years will do that, I suppose," Tlonna chuckled, finally turning her attention to the male. "Move quickly or do not move at all."

The Lord Consort laughed, pulling her up and out of the chair. "I think I prefer to move slowly," he breathed, kissing her cheek again.

Tlonna giggled and wrapped her hands in his hair. It started slowly, then he gripped her waist and pulled her tight against him, deepening the kiss until their breath came short and their bodies roared with passion. Losolin's hands skillfully undid her clothes, leaving burning desire in their wake. He deftly picked her up and carried her to the bed, and as they joined, Tlonna's fingers pressed into his biceps hard enough to bruise, her teeth scraping along his lower lip. Soon, Losolin's body was slick with sweat as he moved within her, Tlonna's breath came shorter and shorter as the hour passed, her eyes changing with alacrity.

"Marry me," Losolin gasped, tensing as he spent himself.

"What?" Tlonna breathed, her body roaring, making her tremble and lose sight for a moment.

"Marry me."

"No!"

"WHAT?"

"Do it right, Losolin. Ask me properly."

"Are you flaming serious?"

"Yes."

"Fine," Losolin said as he kissed her on the forehead and rolled out of the bed. "I love you anyway."

"Mm...I love you too," Tlonna said, forcing herself not to laugh at the bemused expression on her lover's face.

He pulled on his pants and then he knelt and riffled through his belongings for a moment. She watched him curiously until he stood and turned back to her. In his hand he held up a blue hyacinth, her favorite flower. Tlonna felt her heart expand with love as she stared at the silver ring decorating the delicate plant.

Losolin motioned for her to stand as he went to his knees. Despite the fact that she knew what was coming, Tlonna felt her heart start to thud and her throat constrict as she stood, clutching the bed sheet to her body.

"Tlonna, I love you more than life itself. I love every inch of you, every aspect of your heart and mind, and I cannot stand to be apart from you. We have been through so much and still we are together, and I could never ask for anything else. I love you. Will you marry me?"

Tlonna had to swallow twice before she could speak. "Yes. I will, Losolin, I love you so much."

Losolin leapt to his feet and swept her up in a swinging embrace. "You just had to make it difficult, did you not?" he laughed, setting her back down.

"It is what I do. Oh, Losolin, you have made my life so much brighter," she replied, giggling through tears.

"It happens," he returned blandly, and kissed her again.

Sithian brooded, a half empty glass of brandy hanging from his limp fingers. The fire had died down to glowing embers, the warmth lingering in the walls. He fancied he could just see through the opaque obsidian stone. The young Magin jerked the glass further into his hand and drank the last of the alcohol. The glass shattered to the floor, beads of liquid spraying across the expensive carpet. Across the room Ghealan glanced at him, his head resting in his palm as he read. Suneelo and Aladorn were both asleep in their chairs, having already taken their watch shifts.

Sithian glared at them, envious of their perfection and their ease. He hated Suneelo most of all, the husband of that cursed Yayènia. He considered blasting the pale elf with his magic, but quickly reconsidered when he looked to Ghealan. He was easily the largest elf Sithian had ever seen with muscles that, though long and shapely, bulged against his fair skin every time he moved. He stood closer to eight feet than seven, and though most humans averaged between six and seven feet, Ghealan still towered over everyone, elves included. Sithian shook his head once, glowering.

Midnight eyes sparkled wetly in the lamp light, lit by a long-departed servant. Sithian stared at his big hand, fingers splayed across the chair arm. They were fine boned, the knuckles protruding against milky white skin. He stretched his long legs and hooked his right boot over his left. He sighed. He could still hear Anna's screams in his mind, echoing off the walls of memory. Blood dripped out of the corner of her mouth, staining the pale skin, the black hair glistening damply with sweat and tears. She writhed on the floor, her fingers bent at sharp angles, the corners of her lips ripping as she opened her mouth further.

Once again, as it had been all day, Sithian had run into that damned solid wall. He probed it, searching for weakness. He could feel it becoming less and less impermeable as the day wore on, but still he could not penetrate it. It was a wall of black power, but unlike his father's, it was pure, untainted by madness. The strength of it was awesome, something Sithian had not even considered possible. Haydyn's power almost surpassed his father's. The mere fact that he had been able to hold the seal up all day without really weakening was proof enough.

If only he could harness that power, make it *his*...

Ah...the possibilities...

Sithian let his breath out with a hiss. Haydyn's power entranced him. Why was it that his younger brother's capability was so much more than his or his sister's? What was it that Haydyn had that they didn't? It couldn't be how he was raised, his decision to follow their mother, could it?

Of course not. The path of evil was so much *freer.* He could do as he wanted, with whomever he wanted, no strings attached. No laws, limitations, or regrets. Nothing could stop him and his sister from moving up in the world. Already they were the ruling family of Zaedic. Nothing, that is, except his mother and brother. They could destroy everything. They had already killed Midian, who's to say that they couldn't kill him and Anna?

Or was that it? His father's death...?

Ghealan turned the page of his book, a collection of stories Erdwyf wanted him to be familiar with by the time their child was born. He breathed in deeply, glancing at the nearly comatose Sithian, checking his body language for signs of assertiveness. Seeing none, the Second Commander went back to his story, trying to stay alert against the boredom.

Tlonna smiled faintly as the last manservant left the elegant room, and then looked questioningly at a young woman who slipped through the door, holding two packages, one long and slender, the other quite bulky and squarish.

"Your Majesty, I am here on behalf of Lady Yayènia. She asked me to drop these off for Prince Haydyn this morning. Where should I put them?"

The princess wondered what the warrior had gotten her son, but she pointed toward Haydyn's new bedroom without asking the maid. "In there should be fine."

Chapter 3

The Escape

Rhiannan shivered in her blankets, sweat pouring from her body like a sieve. A little blood stained the perspiration pink, leaving streaks on the bed. Her dark eyes stared forward, unseeing, drawn into the depths of her mind. Whimpers escaped her lips every now and then, accompanied by violent seizures. Her usually radiant hair was dull and limp, soaked in blood and sweat. Tears dripped out of the corners of her eyes, unfelt.

Awash in memories of her incredibly short childhood, the young woman remembered Tlonna leaning over her crib, talking to the demon Kelus about letting her die. She saw her mother holding her and Haydyn while reading from a book of history, smiling faintly. She watched her father show her where the most vulnerable parts of the body were, and how to apply just enough magic to cause the muscles to spasm out of control. She watched the bitch Yayènia slide her cursed katan across Midian's throat, a sick wicked grin on her poppet face.

With a jolt, Rhiannan awoke and began screaming, the corners of her cracked lips ripping apart where scabs had begun to form. She writhed on her bed for what seemed hours before the door burst open and elves poured in. She felt hands on her, warm and soft, more gentle than anything she had ever experienced. People talking, arguing, then a muted green light filled her eyes and she saw Losolin dimly through the haze, angelic and beautiful. Even as the pain began to recede, she tried to fight him, push him away.

He did not stop, casually swatting away her protesting hands as he continued to heal her. The corners of her lips netted together, the scabs disappearing. Giving in, Rhiannan lay back and felt her body responding to the magic now coursing through her.

Nebet'thu swung his legs over the edge of the bed and scrubbed at his face with his hands. Eesa whimpered in her sleep next to him. Her hair was thrown across her face as though she too had had a bad night. The storm that had started the morning before still raged, doubling its fury during the night after a short respite. The castle seemed stuffy and cold in its steel gray surroundings. Lightning flashed in the sky off to the north, illuminating the harbor. Ships wallowed in the roiling sea, their masts like bony fingers reaching to the heavens for help.

Silently thanking the gods that he was not at home waiting out the storm in his light yurt, or worse, in his hunting tent, Neb stood and stretched. He poked at the dying embers in the hearth and quickly rekindled a fire. After his morning ritual, the elf left his room and wandered the massive castle, searching for the kitchens. A stocky human maid was busy dusting a vase when he turned a corner.

"Excuse me, where are the kitchens?"

The woman yelped and nearly dropped the vase. "Oh...oh I'm sorry. The kitchen is just at the end of this hall on the right. It's a mite bit early so there might not be many cooks in there, sir, but I'm sure they can fix something up for..." the maid trailed off, her eyes going wide.

Nebet'thu whirled around and found himself face to face with the most dangerous looking...elf? he had ever seen. Thick black hair partially hid the most stunning blue eyes he had ever seen, but the aura pulsating around the male was astonishing. A spider web of blood dripped down both hands onto the fine carpet.

"Uh...h-hello. I am Nebet'thu of Asheyl"

"Joy to you. I was looking for a little messenger boy, ran a message to Princess Tlonna yesterday morning."

The maid curtsied deeply. "The messenger hall is on the second floor, my Lord, just below this one. I can take you there if it please you."

"Yes, it does please me."

The two walked off down the hall and disappeared by the stairwell. Nebet'thu watched them uneasily, having an awkward feeling about the youth. Forgetting his hunger, the plains elf headed in the direction of the stairs. He found the royal floor easily enough, what with all the priceless carpets, tapestries, and other décor. At a word from a passing servant, Neb found the entrance to Tlonna's tower. He ran the winding length of the stairs until he found himself on the topmost stair in the center of the vast tower, a single door before him, sticking out of the ceiling, a small walled block behind it. Out of the gloomy, storm-darkened shadows loomed two guardsmen, walking casually on narrow bridges that arched around and down to meet another door that, unbeknownst to Neb, led to Tlonna's guardroom.

"What is your business in the Princess's private tower?"

"I...I have a message for her. It is very urgent."

"Yeah? Why don't ye give me the message and I'll make sure she gets it."

Nebet'thu almost conceded, but a sinking feeling in the pit of his stomach warned him not to. "No, please get her. I have to tell her this myself. Please!"

The guard was about to reply when the door was opened and Tlonna stood staring at them. "What is going on, Alij? Ah...Master Nebet'thu, what can I do for you?"

The guard, Alij, grudgingly stepped back out of the way and allowed Neb to step through to talk with the princess.

"My lady, a young...elf...just asked to see the boy who delivered a message to you yesterday morn. I would not bother you about this, but he did not seem quite right. He pulsed with an aura that felt, well, evil to me. I thought I should inform you."

As he spoke, Nebet'thu felt dumber and dumber, but then he saw the Magin's face lose its hue and her eyes alight with fear. She pushed by him and ran down the winding steps. After a moment's hesitation, the two guardsmen ran after her. Neb found himself alone in the princess's private quarters, and was soon wandering around in amazement. The door was in the center, rising from the floor, and a few feet away, steps that led to the room itself, glorious in its soft colors.

Tapestries and maps decorated the walls in a pleasing way, gigantic glass-filled openings filled the rest. A set of doors stood open to a balcony that overlooked the city and the sea beyond, filmy curtains flapping in the torrent of rain and wind. The other doors opposite were closed, and he was amazed to see that it looked over the courtyard. He was just about to close the open doors when a thoroughly entertained voice called out.

"You are that plains elf from the petitions, are you not? What do you think you are doing in here?"

Nebet'thu whipped around to stare at the curious elf leaning against the door jamb. "I...uh...well, the princess she...she left without telling me what to do," he said lamely.

"Ah, so you come in and check out her room?"

"I just wanted to shut the doors so rain did not come in."

"Indeed. I am Losolin, the Lord Consort. You are Nebet'thu, right? Have a seat."

Neb stood rooted to the spot, not sure what to do. Finally, he took the chair offered him by the prince. The Lord Consort. A deadly elf, if the stories were true. There seemed to be a large amount of dangerous legends within the castle. He had even glimpsed his idol, the High Commander Yayènia er'Tiena chatting unconcernedly with the fey-looking elf he had seen at the petitions, armed to the teeth.

Losolin passed him a plate of sandwiches and watched him select one. "What is your home like? I was reading up on Plains Tribes, but I think a firsthand account would be so much better."

"You mean Asheyl? Well, it's on the south eastern plains of Blackhaven and takes up about ten acres in all directions. Not too big, nothing in comparison to the city. We all live in yurts and have specific trades."

Losolin frowned. "What is a yurt?"

"Round permanent tents," Neb said shortly. "Most of the tribe farms or does community jobs like cobbling or tanning. Only a few are hunters. My brother, and Eesa's brother are hunters along with myself, and I think there are maybe half a dozen or so more. I am not quite sure."

"Uh huh," the other elf replied, staring at Neb. "What is your government system? You do not really follow this oligarchy, do you?"

"In a way. We abide by the laws, but we have our own way of getting things done. Highest up is the Chieftain and Chieftess, Chieftain Tèkar and Chieftess Fellar. Then it is the House of Councilors, of which Eesa's father is High Councilor. Then the village elder, Marther and finally the rest of the village. It is kind of a democracy, but chief status is gained only through blood. Daegin and Kepthari will become the next when Fellar and Tèkar perform *Haithen.*"

Losolin blinked, his thoughts evidently somewhere else. "What did you tell Tlonna?"

Neb frowned at the change of subject. "Just that some elf was looking for the messenger who gave her a message yesterday morning. It was nothing, really."

Losolin leapt to his feet, fury clouding his features. "What did the elf look like? Black hair, sapphire eyes?"

"Yes, that would be him. Why?"

"He is the son of Midian Rahlan, and Tlonna," the prince replied, pulling a bow off the back of the chair he had vacated.

The elf followed Tlonna's footsteps, disappearing almost before Nebet'thu could react.

"Spirits!" the plains elf cried, running after him.

The two males arrived at the messenger's hall just as a shriek echoed off the walls. It was impossible to tell whether it was male or female, only that it was a howl of pain. Cursing, Losolin burst into the room, bow drawn, and body as tense as the string.

Sithian was holding a young boy against the wall, blue light shivering out of his hands into the boy's chest. Tlonna held her own hands out, cords of white magic roaring out of her fingers and into her son. Sithian and the boy were yelping in pain as magic slowly consumed their bodies. Losolin loosed an arrow and the shaft thudded into the young Magin's thigh, directly into the wound Aidyn had given him. Instantly, Sithian dropped the messenger boy and clutched at his leg, screaming in agony. Tlonna grounded her Weave and ran to the boy. She sent him over to Losolin who knelt to inspect him.

"Are you all right? Let me see you," the elf gently pulled off the boy's smock and placed his hand on the shredded chest. Flesh knit itself back into place and his tears subsided. Losolin pulled his shirt back on and patted him on the head. "Go on to the kitchens and tell the Head Chef that Lord Losolin sent you there for some sweets, all right? Give him this."

The boy took the token Losolin handed him and after a shaky bow, fled the room. Tlonna was busy directing her guards in chaining Sithian and taking him to the dungeons.

"No steel and stone will hold him, but we might be able to put a ward on the cell at least. Hurry, before he wakes. Send a Healer down as well," she turned to Losolin and gave him a weary smile.

"Losolin...if Father had not been giving me lessons, I would not have been able to hold him. He is almost as strong as I am. I am glad you showed up when you did."

"That is not what worries me. Where are Ghealan, Suneelo, and Aladorn? They were supposed to be guarding him."

Shock and fear replaced the resignation on Tlonna's face and she stared up at Losolin in horror. The male felt the worry as well, thinking of his brother. Together, they pushed past the confused Nebet'thu and sprinted from the room, narrowly avoiding several collisions with the morning staff. The door to the room Sithian had been in was hanging slightly ajar, the area around the lock and handle blackened and still smoking. Losolin cursed and carefully opened the door, letting it fall away when the hinges broke. Inside, the room was covered with a thick smoke that swirled menacingly, electric charges shocking through the clouds every so often.

"Suneelo?" Losolin said loudly, stepping fearlessly into the room.

Tlonna followed more slowly, not out of trepidation but so that she could discern the Weave. It took her a moment, but she located the key thread of power, a thick bar of Water that ran the perimeter of the room, parallel to the floor. Touching her forefinger to the thread, the Magin sent a flash of Earth into it. The bar sparked enough so that even Losolin could see it, and then it dissipated, allowing the smoke to filter out into the hallway.

As soon as the air cleared enough to see, Tlonna's hands went to her mouth. Ghealan lay slumped in his chair, one hand limp on a book he'd been reading, the other nearly brushing the floor, his lips stained crimson. Suneelo sat across from him, his head tilted to one side, thin lines of blood running from the corners of his mouth to his chin. Aladorn was on the floor, with blood dripping from his mouth and nose as he lay heaped against the wall.

Losolin rushed to his brother's side and pressed his fingers to Suneelo's throat, checking for a pulse. Tlonna did the same with Ghealan. The male let out a relieved sigh and bent over Aladorn, his face calming.

"They are alive. Badly stunned, but alive," he said, straightening the wiat. "Al? Aladorn can you hear me?"

The dark elf's eyes flickered but he did not respond any more. Losolin let his head drop gently to his chest and stood, looking at his lover. Tlonna stood in the middle of the room, her fingers raised and tapping the air, eyes focused in on something he could not see.

"What is it?"

"I am trying to undo Sithian's work, so that I may know what he did. The smoke was a simple illusion, which is why it did not make us cough, and it had no scent. A Weave of Water and Fire, with a single thread of Spirit."

"What are you talking about?" Losolin asked, having never heard her talk about the magic in any sort of specific formula.

Tlonna dropped her hands and looked at him, smiling slightly. "Maginic magic is called Weaving for a reason, Losolin. Every 'spell' is a combination of five elements, Earth, Air, Fire, Water, and Spirit.

When we Weave, we are in essence weaving together a pattern of elements to create a certain outcome. Usually we do it so fast we are not cognizant of the fact that we are using separate entities to do so, but Father has been showing me a lot of simple Weaves and then freezing them so that I may study them. It truly is fascinating."

"And you can learn new Weaves through this technique?" Losolin asked, intrigued. He was kneeling beside his brother now, his hands on the warrior's face.

Suneelo's eyes opened wide and he wheezed in a breath, choking on the blood in his mouth. He coughed, spraying the table, and Ghealan's book, with crimson dots. Losolin patted his brother on the shoulder and moved to the Second Commander. Tlonna walked over to Suneelo and handed him a cloth to wipe his lips.

"Yes. You can remove the threads individually and therefore learn the Weave, as long as you remember to reverse the order when you go to do it. Sometimes, forgetting to reverse them can result in new Weaves, or devastation. Father spent much of his youth experimenting with creating new Weaves. He has several scars to prove it," Tlonna continued.

By this time Aladorn was awake, wiping his bloody nose on the back of his sleeve. Suneelo had nearly fully recovered and was watching his brother move about the room, glancing back at Tlonna every now and then.

"What happened?" Ghealan demanded as soon as he was able to speak, glaring at Suneelo when he noticed the ruby drops on his book.

"Sithian used a concussive Weave to stun all three of you, and then filled the room with a fog too thick to see through," Tlonna explained in a preoccupied voice.

"How could he have gotten the chance to do so?" Aladorn muttered from where he still sat against the wall. "We were all watching him, and would have been able to stop him from doing anything."

"You did try to stop him," Losolin stated from the other side of the room, holding up a throwing knife.

The edge was stained red. He handed it to a confused Aladorn, who wiped it clean and replaced it in his belt. The other two warriors looked grossly bewildered and offended until Tlonna began to speak again.

"The Weave he used was completed in less than a second, sort of a flash of power that takes little thought, but a lot of energy. It is used mainly as a defense mechanism, and is meant for an area much larger than this room, which is why it was so potent."

"If he could do this, why wait until this morning? Why not do it as soon as everyone went to bed?" Suneelo asked, rubbing his chest against the dull ache that was beginning to form.

Tlonna frowned for a moment and then chuckled softly. "He needed to regain enough of his strength to be able to release the concussion while holding a protective aura about himself. Such magic takes a large strain on your energy force, and he had wasted most of his reserves throughout the day working on Anna."

"Little bastard," Aladorn muttered, getting to his feet. "I am going to my room now. Good day," he snarled, stalking out of the room.

Ghealan sighed and got up as well, shutting his book and dragging it to his side. "I will be in my office, probably learning just how Daniel the Bird Boy became king through sheer honesty," he said, holding up the book of children's stories. "If I do not, Erdwyf will read them to me instead."

Suneelo and Losolin smirked at their friend as he walked away, the hefty book looking small in his large hands. When the two brothers looked back at each other, their eyes inadvertently shifted to Tlonna.

"There are things that need to be solved, Tlonna," Suneelo said quietly. "Come home with me and sort them out."

"Would I be welcomed?" the princess asked bitterly, turning to face the warrior.

"If you come with good intentions, of course. If you come just to start up another fight, then you will probably be insulted and offended," the male answered honestly, shrugging. "Nia is desperate, she just got you back. We all did, to lose you now would be like slowly cutting out our own hearts. When you both disappeared, none of us could feel our limbs because our hearts went numb. When we saw you skinned alive it was as though our bodies were on fire from within, so great was the agony. To know that you are willing to die for a prophecy, for a purpose we do not understand, you cannot know what that feels like."

Tlonna was taken aback by the sheer emotion in Suneelo's voice and words. She had never before heard him speak so eloquently and so freely. Losolin clutched his brother's shoulder, both the males looking at her with eyes full of emotion, pleading for her to understand. Taking a deep breath, she nodded.

"Let us go, then."

A while later, they left the castle and, pulling their waxed hoods over their heads, walked to the stables. Neñyos and Takîreaes, and Suneelo's Smithy, all whickered loudly when their masters entered. A sleepy stable hand readied the horses and bowed as the nobles rode out.

The Peerage District sat on the far right side of the city, the properties each separated by a thick, sight and sound stopping wall of vegetation. Yayènia and Suneelo lived in the largest and most luxurious manor on the left side of the district. Beneath an arching canopy of cedar trees was a grass-weave path that led up to the sandstone manor, curving and flowing with the trees around it. The yard was seventeen acres of perfectly wild gardens and fields. Two stable boys came running around the side of the mansion when they heard the clop of the horses coming up the way. Their livery was waxed leather, for the weather, dyed silver and dark blue. The two young elves smiled and bowed gracefully, their hair hidden beneath cowls.

Tlonna and Losolin dismounted and handed over the reins as Suneelo led the way to the door. An exotic, grinning maid met them with a wide smile and a graceful curtsy.

"Lord Suneelo, good morning. Princess Tlonna, Lord Losolin, good morning," she said in a careful accent, as though trying very hard to sound native to Blackhaven.

"Morning Sayoir. Where is Yayènia?" Suneelo asked, handing the young human a small pouch, which she took with a toothy grin.

"In the library. Is this it?"

The elf chuckled. "Yes, now do not waste it, young lady. It is not easy to get!"

The maid shrieked in joy and danced away, startling the couple standing behind Suneelo.

"What was that?" Losolin asked as Suneelo began to head up the staircase to the second floor.

The captain shook his head, his shoulders shaking with mirth. "A jar of Aidyn's soap."

"What?" both Tlonna and Losolin gasped, sure they had heard wrong.

"A jar of Aidyn's soap," Suneelo repeated, laughing fully now. "Every time he visits Sayoir just about faints. She is so head over heels for him, and she kept badgering me about getting some of his cologne for her. I had to explain to her that elves do not wear cologne, and she nearly burst into tears. So I asked him for some of his soap, and he gave me that little vial."

"Aidyn gave it to you?" Tlonna asked, incredulous. "Does he know why you asked for it?"

"Of course. That is probably why he did not throw a huge fit over it. He knows about Sayoir's lust, and he would rather give her something small to allow her to get over him than have her do something embarrassing and potentially disastrous."

"Does he visit often?" Losolin queried, never suspecting that his brother, Yayènia, and the assassin were so close.

Suneelo shrugged as they reached the door at the end of the wide hallway. "We have dinner twice a month at least, and sometimes Aladorn joins us. We always have done so, at least with Aidyn. Yayènia and he have known each other since the day *she* was born. Well," he frowned slightly, "he knew of her, and she of him. Aidyn knows something but has, as of yet, refused to tell us."

"Aidyn knows a lot of things, and is very adept at keeping his mouth shut," Losolin muttered.

Suneelo was about to reply but the door swung open and Yayènia glared out at them. "Some people consider a library a quiet place to read and work," she said, glowering mostly at her husband. "Why do you have blood stains on your chin?"

Losolin quickly filled in what had happened with Sithian while his brother wiped self-consciously at his face. Yayènia sighed and motioned them inside, flopping back down into the chair she had obviously vacated. Suneelo grinned at his half-brother, unwilling to be dragged into the female's anger.

"We have been doing homework. After our little escapade across the continent, Nia and I decided we are too ignorant about the goings-on in other provinces. We just started on Zeynuwn. Fascinating land. That is where Sayoir is from. We hired her when we finished the house," Suneelo said, pushing aside a few books so that he could lean on the table.

Yayènia handed Tlonna a cup of spiced wine and a tray of little cakes, shoving it forward with little decorum. "Their army is extraordinary. Each soldier is selected from birth, males only, and trained from the time they can walk to the time they die. They have an odd kind of fighting too, it is called...*Uyai*...*Uyai-shin.* Deals a lot with fighting in close range using only your body and maybe a curved sword called a katan, like my twin swords. They also have things that are similar to dagger blades connected to the end of a chain and you use them like whips, *Na'sha.* Erdwyf wanted me to order a pair for her. I did not get one myself, but I can order another for you."

"No, that is all right. I have enough weapons for now. I cannot even carry them all," Tlonna replied, realizing her commander was making an attempt to forget their argument. "They sound like too much trouble anyway. Hard to control. I cannot use whips, I hit myself too often."

"That is not all, they have a patriarchy. Women are not allowed to be anything but wives, mothers, entertainers, or servants. They cannot own land, speak to a man unless spoken too, look a man directly in the eye without explicit permission, or even marry whom they want to. Men control everything!" Suneelo said, his eyes wide with wonder. "They even have women called Azawie, which are like...noble whores. A whole bunch of them live together in a house and they are at the disposal of any man who has enough money to pay for them. The emperor even has his own little army of Azawie. It is amazing. Sayoir used to be one, but she fled her village and we eventually found her living in the streets. She said it is the highest ranking a woman can get in Zeynuwn, except for being one of the emperor's wives. He has seven or eight I guess."

"Spirits! How can anyone live in a place like that? I am so glad we live in a free kingdom," Tlonna exclaimed.

"Not like it would really apply to you, being the princess and all," said Suneelo, flipping open a silk covered book. "This is one of the text books they have in the schools in Zeynuwn. Sayoir brought it with her when she fled."

Losolin, always interested in any book, took the material and flipped through it. "What is this language? It makes no sense whatsoever. It is just a bunch of lines."

"It is called Kien. Each set of lines is a different word. There are hundreds of thousands of different symbols, just like we have as many different spellings, they have symbols. Nia and I have been studying this language for years, and we only have a basic understanding of it. Of course it is better to have an actual teacher from Zeynuwn, but we have done decently," Suneelo explained, smiling at his wife.

"I thought all humans spoke Hindarün," Tlonna muttered, glancing at the strange language.

"They do, but Zeynuwnians have been isolated for so long they just seemed to have adapted their own culture. Kien is actually a derivative of Parlêthian, as Zeynuwn is where the Serenyi elves lived when they first landed. According to Sayoir, Shisandr, the first Elven dwelling, is considered a holy place," Suneelo said.

"It is still standing? Shisandr was abandoned nearly two thousand years ago," Losolin asked, amazed.

The captain shook his head. "It is a ruin, all that remains is the foundation and a few partial walls. Pilgrimages are made every year by scholars and holy men, when the ice melts enough to allow passage through the mountains."

Yayènia shook her head at her husband and his brother, always amazed by their interest in all things ancient. Briefly touching Tlonna's hand, she nodded toward the door, and the two females left without the notice of their mates. The Magin Queen followed the High Commander down the stairs to the bottom floor and into an open-air room, gauzy curtains swaying in the wind. The air smelled of rain, the vegetation all around glistening with moisture. Tlonna took a deep breath and closed her eyes, savoring the smell of renewed earth.

"What are we going to do?" Yayènia asked behind her, leaning against a beam.

The younger elf turned to study the weapons master. "There is not much we can do, Nia. What happens to me does not matter as long as it is for the benefit of all goodly folk, yes? It is something you have said yourself. Honor above all, duty above all, justice above all."

"You speak not of justice, but of suicide. And as far as the benefit of all goodly folk, what do you think will happen if you die? You are a hero, *the* hero of this city. You cannot do this thing you are so determined to do!" Yayènia cried, pushing away from the beam.

"I am no hero," Tlonna said quietly, refusing to give in to the warrior's adamancy.

"Yes you are! You cannot deny what every person in this city believes, you cannot deny what more than half of the continent of Nymyños believes! You are the hero of the people!"

"No, I am not!" Tlonna shouted, turning on Yayènia.

"Why not?"

"Because I cannot be a hero and do the things I must do! I cannot be a hero and destroy my own son! If I am bound by the weights of heroism, I cannot make the decisions I have to make. I have killed innocent people, I have killed elves and humans, and I have made the decision to stand by when others were killed…heroes do not do such things."

"I have killed a child, what does that make me?" Yayènia demanded, shoving her face into Tlonna's. "You have made the decisions no one else could because you are the savior of the people, the destroyer of evil, and the hope of nations. Those people died because you cannot save everyone! No matter what the cause, people will always die! You cannot prevent that, but if you give up your life because someone two thousand years ago said you must, then you doom *everyone*."

"And what of the Slaves of Death? Do I just let them go?"

"Who, the Darkwights? Cursed blighters deserve nothing less than a hot poker to the ear," Yayènia snarled viciously.

"They are our kin, Nia! The surviving remnants of the Elven Race twisted and maimed by Midian and Aderiaen Rahlan. You tell me to abandon them to a life of evil and reckless carnage?"

"They have a choice, just as we all do. They could choose to desert, to walk a different path, but they stay on Zaedic to do the Rahlan's bidding. Why should they be treated any different than any other murderer, rapist, or thief?"

"They do not have a choice, though," Tlonna countered quietly, remembering the tortured screams of the Darkwights in Zaedic, Kelus's broken gaze. "They still have their souls, their conscience, but they have no control of their violent urges. They were slaves to Midian's rule, knowing that they did wrong, but unable to stop. Kelus said the pain inflicted by giving in to their natural morals was a hundred times worse than anything Midian could ever physically do. I have to free them, release them from their enslavement, or all that we have fought for will mean nothing. I will have failed in the ultimate end."

Yayènia sniffed in disagreement. "Our way of life is no longer necessary, Tlonna. Humans will soon be all that is left in this world, and perhaps that is the way it should be." Tlonna spun about in horror at such a statement, but the warrior was not looking at her. "Our kind is too big to fit into this world anymore. We are too tall, our lives too long, our minds too sharp. The Seadueni interbreed to keep the bloodlines pure, and look what it cost them. They are a brutal culture, bitter and arrogant, defiant of any change. What have we to offer this growing world? Our people hardly age, hardly change, hardly even step outside our own boundaries. There are few of us left who know of the other provinces because we have locked ourselves behind our gates, refusing to have anything to do with the humans or the dwarves or any other race that inhabits Nymyños. We are selfish and proud to a fault, and unless we change, what use is it to renew our race? If you free the Darkwights, do you think they will revert after living so long under the mind of a tyrant? You will unleash an evil with the face of elf-kind."

Though she badly wanted to, Tlonna could not argue the truth of Yayènia's words. A ruckus from inside the house proper stopped her from coming to any sort of statement however, and she and the High Commander walked back inside. Losolin and Suneelo were rushing down the stairs, led by Sayoir.

"A messenger from the castle," Suneelo explained to the two females.

A skinny boy with shoulder length mousy hair stood by the entrance to the manor house, fists crossed at his chest. Tlonna turned to him, confused and worried by his troubled countenance. The boy bowed, and with eyes averted, related his message.

Sithian woke groggily, his head pounding and side throbbing. A crimson bandage was stuck to his thigh, in desperate need of changing. His hands were shackled to his feet, making it nearly impossible to stand, which remained painful because of Aidyn's stabbing, and the arrow wound from Losolin. Cursing, the half-breed shifted his head to look out into the dimly lit corridor and saw numerous glints of steel, betraying the presence of a strong guard. Letting his head lie back on the straw that sparsely covered the cold stone floor, the young Magin began to Weave.

The chains shattered, startling the guards and freeing Sithian. When he stood, a haze of nausea took hold of him, making him grope for the bars. The guards scuttled backward, fear etched on every face. When the nausea lifted, Sithian looked up and grinned, feeling the ward someone had put on his cell. He searched the invisible wall and found a slightly weaker spot, where the magic fused into the brick on either side of the door. After a few minutes of probing and pushing, the wall exploded, creating a gaping hole in which Sithian easily stepped through. The guards died seconds later, just a simple matter of increasing the heat within their armor to extreme temperatures in a matter of seconds, boiling them to death almost instantly.

Limping, Sithian traversed the labyrinthine elfin prison, getting lost several times. Once free, he pulled together a Weave that made him a little insubstantial. He had never been good at completely cloaking himself, but the boy now looked like a misty reflection, and those who noticed him simply shook their heads in confusion. He found his sister's room, opened the door quietly and entered, his eyes falling on her sleeping form. Revealing himself, Sithian moved to the bedside and bent down.

"Anna, wake up, Anna."

Rhiannan opened her eyes and grinned. "Sithian. Finally...a friendly face."

"It's time we got out of this place and went home. Come."

Sithian shielded both him and his sister, and they left the room. It was simple to get down to the stable and steal horses. The stable hands were asleep in the loft and woke only when they heard the pounding of hooves.

Chapter 9

Live and Die in Every Breath

The four elves shoved the messenger and Sayoir out of the way and ran down the hall, out of the manor, and into the stable. Not bothering to get tack, they mounted and flew down the lane. By the time they reached the city proper, the horses were lathered in sweat and prancing with adrenaline. A few people had seen two horses running through the city with insubstantial cloaked figures atop them headed for the gate.

Tlonna took the lead, guiding Takîreaes through the packed streets, cursing at people who got in their way. When they reached the outer gate, Tlonna dismounted and grabbed the nearest guardsmen by the lapels.

"Did you let two horses through here? Two horses together, with cloaked riders?"

"N-no ma'am, we tied 'em up over there, and there weren't no riders either. They looked like royal stock so we figured them to be escapees."

Yayènia and Suneelo went over to where the two horses were tethered and began poking around in the air above and below the horses, receiving strange looks from the guards.

"There is nothing here, Tlonna. They must have slipped by when the horses were detained," Yayènia said and then turned to one of her husband's guardsmen. "You, when did this happen?"

"About an hour ago, High Commander Yayènia. We haven't had our turn of the guard yet, so we haven't brought the horses up. I'm sorry, High Commander."

"I do not give a damn about the horses, I want to know about the riders!" Yayènia shouted, glaring at her man.

"High Commander, there were no riders."

"They were...they were invisible," the female explained, looking defeated. "Has the gate been opened at all? Or the door?"

The guard shook his head. "Not once, High Commander. No one has entered or left the city yet this morning."

Yayènia looked to Tlonna, who was staring at the ground by the horses. "Tracks, and blood," she said, kneeling. "Sithian is grievously injured, and neither he nor Rhiannan have healing powers."

She moved along the ground, her back arched as she bent low to keep the faint tracks in sight. Her three companions followed, scanning the area around them, frowning at the guards who scowled or gaped at the sight of their Crown Princess crouching over a trail of blood. Tlonna sighed when the tracks stopped at the stairs to the wall, but the blood trail continued.

"They went over the wall," she said dully, running up the steps to lean out between the crenellations. "Look, that is where they landed."

Losolin, Yayènia, Suneelo and a few of the closer guards leaned out as well and stared down at the muddy, blood splattered spot a few feet away from the base of the wall.

"The trail will be easy to follow. I will send out trackers with a quad of soldiers and a Magin. We will have them back by noon," Suneelo said, looking to Tlonna.

"No, it will be of no use. We will catch them, and they will escape once more. It is obvious we do not have the ability to contain Sithian," the Magin Queen countered, shaking her head. "Let them run, and continue to look behind them. Most likely their deaths will come from the front."

The High Commander nodded her agreement. "Still, I am going to prepare for their return."

"Their return?"

"Those two will come back with an army and no few demons behind them, I guarantee it. The harbor needs to be informed, and all outlying villages warned. Not to say that a war is imminent, but Sithian has certain aspects of his father that are...troubling."

Tlonna's narrowed gaze did nothing for Yayènia other than amuse her. "Make sure we are ready, then," the princess said after a moment, admitting the fact. "I shall go to the harbor and inform Jamìn, tell him to keep an eye out for white ships."

The four elves left the gate and rode back to the castle. There, Tlonna rode on by herself, albeit trailed by a guard of eight. The harbor was busy with its noon duties, and everywhere sailors sat on barrels eating their light lunches and taking swigs of mysterious drink. They all bowed low when Tlonna passed.

When she reached the harbor master's office, she bid her guard stay outside in case of offending her friend. "Master Jamìn! It has been too long since I have been down to see you and your harbor. How fare things?"

"Ah, yer too kind, Milady. Things be great. Trade and traffic has increased twofold since ye allowed corsairs to trade here. We be no longer under the threat of attack from 'em. A great move, that," the dwarf said, standing head to waist with the elf.

"I am glad. Speaking of corsairs, have you heard from Alexander and Troaz?"

"Aye, they be scheduled to come in three nights hence. I heard they plunder the ports at Zaedic all the time now. Good idea, that," Jamìn said, slapping his girth for emphasis. His balding head turned toward the map that hung above his large desk. "I have one of the few maps that has that evil island on it, thanks to ye and yer corsair friends. The most charted land ever, and I have the map of it. It be me pride and joy, miss."

"I am glad to hear it, Master Jamìn. Listen, I need you to do something for me," Tlonna said, sitting on a low stool so that the dwarf would not have to stare up at her. "I want ships posted along the route to Zaedic starting at the edge of High Reef. There may be an attack coming, and I do not want it to be a surprise. As soon as Alexander and Troaz come in, send them to the castle."

The harbor master listened attentively, his eyes narrowing more and more with each word. "Ach, miss. This be grave tidings. I'll be sure to pass on the word for ye. I'll get the notes readied, and find ships to take up the posts."

"Thank you Master Jamìn, it eases my mind to know you will take care of it for me. I will be sure to stop in soon," Tlonna left the office and rounded up her idle guard.

They toured the dock until afternoon, Tlonna having been negligent in her appearances there, and then headed back to the castle. When they arrived at the stables, the two horses Sithian and Rhiannan had stolen were back in their stalls and the boys were red faced and timid. The stable master had gotten hold of them.

Haydyn was furious with his mother and Losolin when Tlonna found him. He glared at her and then exploded, his face twisted with a rage that was disturbingly reminiscent of Midian.

"How could you not let me know what was going on? I know how to ward Sithian and Rhiannan so that they cannot break it! I was trained to it! What were you thinking, Mother? And you, Losolin! Spirits! They are my brother and *twin* sister! I know how to handle them in ways neither of you do! They will do just as Father did, maybe worse! They are two to his one! How could you be so naïve? HOW?"

"Haydyn! Calm down, we are not naïve, and we are prepared to deal with whatever comes at us. What Sithian and Rhiannan do with their power will be nothing good, I know, but we can only wait for them to make the first move," Tlonna said quietly, grabbing her son. "It has been almost a year since Midian died, and I just got word from the docks that Zaedic is still going downhill. Sithian has spent all of his money on his personal wants, the Keylodes have abandoned him, and there is no army. The Darkwights are the only ones who have stayed, though several hundred have fled all across the island and the new general of the army is someone named Orlando, all the others deserted."

Haydyn turned and gripped his mother's shoulders. "Look, you do not know what the city folk are like. You were always kept in the castle. Those people were *loyal* to Father, they did not know anything else. What Father gave them was the best they ever knew. When Sithian, Anna, and I went into the city, we were seen as gods. With Sithian and Anna home, they will recoup and things will go back to the way things were, if not worse."

Losolin tensed and drew the younger Magin away. "Tlonna, maybe we should send a ship there and check things out, just to ease Haydyn's mind, and to see for ourselves. We do have a shorter route charted out."

"No. I will not become a paranoid leader. I will trust in the posted ships to give us fair warning if and when they come. You two need to take a deep breath and trust in my judgment," Tlonna replied, her voice cool.

"I do, I do not trust in theirs," Losolin said, turning away.

"Losolin, just go. Haydyn, your rooms are ready. I will show them to you."

The two turned down the corridor that led to the massive center staircase and up into the fourth floor. Haydyn's apartment consisted of a large bedroom, a personal bathing room, a study, a small dining area, and common room. It was covered in dark teal and lavender tapestries that hung from the ceiling, long enough to just brush the obsidian floor. The large center rug was a lustrous crimson, embellished with silver and lavender spirals and Maginic symbols.

Haydyn stared in amazement at his new apartment. "This is incredible! My room in Zaedic was so sparse, bare, almost bleak. This is...are you sure it's mine? When did you have time to do this?"

"Yes, of course. You are the heir to the throne, Haydyn, not just my personal visitor. The room has always been kept ready, it is, along with two others, the apartment of the royal child. We just decided on the furniture and had it delivered this morning. Enjoy your time off, my son, remember that you are to go to the Academy in three days to start your term. Because of your father's rush, you are relatively unlearned, so you will be behind the rest of the students."

"I have learned a lot since then, Mum. Maybe I will be ahead of them?"

Tlonna tried to smile. "Haydyn, they all had seventeen years to learn. You have had little more than a year. You are intelligent for your experience, but...I am afraid your scholarly mind is about eight years old."

The young half-blood flushed with embarrassment. "Midian ruined everything, didn't he? He held nothing sacred, nothing was of importance but his own ambitions. Why couldn't he have let you alone? Why'd he do this to us?"

The princess gave up the pretense of being in a good mood and her eyes welled with tears. "Oh, my son," she whispered, stroking his hair. "I do not know. But we will make it through this life together, and everything will be fine in the end. It has to be. Now, go wash up, enjoy your rooms, and ready yourself for school." She started to turn away, and then, remembering, turned back. "Yayènia had something delivered for you this morning as well. I believe it is on your bed."

Frowning slightly, Haydyn led his mother through the apartment to the sleeping chamber and saw the High Commander's gift. There was a long, thin box and a book sitting on the edge of bed. Picking up the book, Tlonna felt a great rush of affection for her reputedly emotionless friend.

"You will find this rather interesting, Haydyn. And useful. She does not give this to you lightly," she said, handing the book to her son.

Haydyn tore his eyes from the box and took the book. "*Fealos eann klamen Kantle*... Sleep by the Sword?"

"Yes. It is the warrior's creed, sort of a 'how to live your life' book. If I am not mistaken, this is Yayènia's, the one she read during her training in the army. I believe Ghealan gave it to her shortly after they met."

Haydyn nearly dropped the tome. "It must be almost three hundred years old!"

"Yes, it is."

"Why would she give me this?"

Tlonna smiled a genuine smile for once. "She considers you not only her prince, but her own protégé as well. Now that, I am sure, is what you are most excited about," she said, pointing at the box.

Haydyn grinned and gently set the book on the bed. Then he ripped open the ties and revealed the sword inside the box. It was a single-edged bastard sword, four feet long, and slightly curved upward. The hilt was bound in black leather and adorned with the Tree of Blackhaven. It also had an engraving near the base of the blade. Haydyn put the cross guard near his eyes and read the etchings. "*Zuskadi Naht Xellt.* Duty Above All. Isn't that...that is House Tiena's motto...isn't it?"

Tlonna blinked away the tears that had formed and smiled again. "Yes it is."

Stunned, and overwhelmed by the High Commander's generosity, Haydyn felt a little guilty he was afraid of her. He voiced his issue to Tlonna.

She chuckled. "We are all a little scared of Yayènia, Haydyn. It is what makes her so good. But she is also a steadfast friend and an unbeatable protector. Know you have nothing to fear from her."

The young male nodded. "What should I do?"

Tlonna frowned slightly. "Well, Nia is not an expressive person, nor does she like others to be so. I would catch her eye the next time you see her, and nod your thanks. She will know what you mean."

"Really? I feel as though I should send her something. Does she like flowers?"

"No. Haydyn, listen to me. Do as I said, and know it is enough. She snuck these in here, which means she did not want it to be a huge deal. Let her have her privacy."

Haydyn nodded his acquiescence. "I will."

"Good, now, I have things to do, so enjoy all this, and I will see you at dinner," Tlonna replied and left her son.

She rounded up her personal staff and called an impromptu meeting. Her head advisors, Erdwyf and Miazie, arrived just as the meeting started, looking hassled and irritated. Yayènia showed up a few minutes later, having returned to her manor just to receive the summons Tlonna had sent out.

"What is this about, Tlonna?"

"Sithian and Rhiannan have escaped and will eventually make it back to their home. The two are ambitious enough to do what Midian did, or worse, it will just take them longer. They will not stop at anything. They think that because of their escape from here under the eyes of some of the most powerful Magins in the world, they are invincible. And they pretty much are, together. Apart, they are not, but they are powerful."

"But, Princess, they aren't as strong as you, are they?" asked the newly hired Public Liaison.

Tlonna smiled lightly. "They are my children, Arganor, and Midian's; they are not as powerful as me, no, but with practice Sithian will one day be so. Anna probably not, but she has a viciousness to her that will more than make up for it. They were also trained by Midian, a Magin, as I have not been."

"But...my lady, you have been trained, now, by the king!" the Keeper of Treasury exclaimed.

"Yes, Daphne, but that is not why we are here. A year ago, my friends and I returned and reclaimed the city. The domestic and market districts were rebuilt, as was the castle, but the outskirts of the city have yet to be looked at. If Sithian and Rhiannan were to come back and wage war against us, our outer defenses would crumble like sand. Edwin, I need you to look over the walls and reinforce them wherever it is needed. Daphne, I need you to get your records of the treasury and have them ready for the next meeting," Tlonna turned to three identical men sitting next to each other, the Masters of Trade. "Brothers, I need you to find the least expensive, good quality armorers and hire them as soon as possible."

"But, my lady, my brothers and I-

"Only work with materials-

"Never labor."

"We know little-

"Very little about-

"Finding cheap, quality labor."

"Masters, you are the best in the land at getting cheap, quality anything. Just think of these armorers as wood and you will be fine.

Now, go. You three are dismissed. You three as well, Daphne, Arganor, Edwin," Tlonna said, turning to the last guest.

"Mr. Crotes."

A tall, well defined human lifted his eyebrows at her. "Yes?"

"I need your help. I understand you run a rather...illicit...business?"

"Now, ma'am, if I were, why would I tell you, the highest of authorities?" the human shot back, his expression slightly cocky.

"Do not play that game with me, Mr. Crotes; I know perfectly well what you do. I need you to run some of your eyes and ears into the other lands. See how their economy is doing, what their leaders are up to. Alliances must be made before another war breaks out. This land barely skimmed the slime on the top of the barrel earlier. Whatever happens next will be many times worse. *I need to know who I can count on.*"

Marten Crotes sneered. He was gentry of Blackhaven, an entrepreneur of livestock and carriages. He also ran a widely feared network of spies and thieves, but had remained at large because of his wealth and influence. It was rumored that he also owned some very high class brothels in the city center.

"Why should I help you, *Princess*? What gain is there for me?"

"I am your superior. If I command it, you will do it whether you will it or no."

Crotes did a double take. Rarely did Tlonna pull rank on anyone.

She continued. "I will pay you double what it costs you and pardon you from any future petty crimes within reason."

The noble's eyebrows rose in honest astonishment. He tamed them quickly, however. "It sounds decent. How many of my...people...are we talking about?"

"Well, there are twelve different provinces, including the Liberated Lands, and this all needs to be done rather quickly. Anna and Sithian are not going to sit around waiting for us to get our act together."

"So about a six men for each province...that is quite a bit of money, Princess. Are you quite sure about this?"

"Of course. You get your men together and have them ready for departure by dawn, and I will have half the money and horses for them. Is that agreeable?" Tlonna replied, leaning forward and staring into the human's eyes.

"Very much so. I shall get them now. Good day sirs and madams."

After he left, all of Tlonna's friends jumped forward.

"Are you crazy, Loni? Trusting these people with explicit information, especially that last man? How can you be comfortable with this?" asked Miazie, her temper shorter than usual.

"I do not trust them, they are who I need. If I play the game right, they will do anything and everything I tell them to. Marten Crotes is as slimy and conniving as they come, but even he can be persuaded to do someone else's bidding, for a price."

"Yes, but he is a creep! And those triplets? That is just weird," Yayènia put in, slapping the table for emphasis, her gauntlet creating an imprint in the hard wood.

"Well done, Nia. You are a six foot four female elf who is the High Commander of the most fabled militia in the whole land, and you think triplets are weird?" Tlonna said, chuckling.

"Okay, fine. So I am a freak too, what else is on the table today? You did not call us out again in this bleeding weather so we could watch you manipulate rich humans, did you?" Yayènia shot back.

"Surprisingly, no. I actually wanted to talk about Losolin's and my wedding."

"WHAT?" came the instant reply from all present.

"Loni! Why did you not tell us?" Miazie cried, laughing.

"When did he propose?" Erdwyf asked, also laughing, patting her swollen belly.

Tlonna held her hand up for silence. "This morning. I thought of not saying anything, because of recent circumstances, but it is not something I could hold in." She looked at Yayènia.

"Pressure weighs on us all, Loni, not just you, and we understand. I hold no grudge. But today! First war, then marriage, it is a dream come true for me," Yayènia sighed, a wistful expression on her beautiful face.

"Spirits, Nia. You are so flaming cracked!" joked Erdwyf, but when she turned to Tlonna her composure became very serious. "So...who is Matron of Honor?"

The room became deadly quiet. Tlonna swallowed. "Well, I was hoping you would all decide amongst yourselves, and tell me later."

Her three friends immediately broke out in argument amongst themselves, allowing for Tlonna to slip out unnoticed. She soon found herself wandering the paths in the inner courtyard, a famed thirty-two acres containing three massive Kairhotuss trees that reached far above the castle. Their great canopies sheltered the fragile elfin flowers beneath from the relentless rain. The delicate petals swayed gently in the breeze, wafting their scent across the courtyard. Her mind went with them, lost amid a thousand thoughts.

She thought of Losolin, the seemingly only bright spot in her life at times, the very air she needed to breathe. He was her everything, the reason she was able to get up each morning and trudge through the difficult day. He frustrated her, amazed her, and all around irritated her, but she loved him with every ounce of her heart. The huskiness of his voice seemed created only to make her legs weak, the harvest scent of him made only to make her lose her mind. But Tlonna knew Losolin loved her the same way, desperately, helplessly, passionately.

At the same time, it seemed as though there was a darker presence in her life, something new and foreign, and at the same time incredibly familiar. Aidyn. The assassin was the complete opposite of Losolin, dark and violent, his voice low and smooth, his sexuality exceptionally honed and perfected. Somehow she knew that. She knew that Aidyn could make *any* female lose her mind in an eye-rolling, toe-numbing, breath-stealing night, without fail. Tlonna blushed, thankful that no one was around, as she thought of the dark elf.

He was older than her by far, though, and probably thought of her as a daughter. She knew that her father and Aidyn were close friends, had been for seven hundred years. Tlonna sighed, wondering.

Dietirin was sitting at his desk when the door to his office opened and Aidyn slipped in, looking unusually perturbed. The king gestured silently at the chair, though the assassin was already halfway into it. He finished signing the few documents he had left and looked up at his oldest friend. Aidyn's tawny hands fidgeted, an unusual thing for him.

"What is it?" the high elf asked, leaning back in his chair and studying the assassin.

"I need your help, Dietirin. I need your advice about something."

Dietirin waited for his friend to continue, but when Aidyn remained silent, the king sat forward, leaning on his desk. "Does this have to do with my daughter? Perhaps...your long held feelings for her?"

The dark elf scoffed for a moment, and then slumped dejectedly, nodding. "She is mad at me because I stabbed her thrice-damned son in the thigh, and would have finished him off if she had not pushed me away."

"You tried to kill Haydyn?" Dietirin asked, surprised.

"No, Sithian. Did she not tell you of him?" Aidyn replied, his eyes widening.

"No, she did, I just forgot. So, you tried to kill Sithian and Tlonna stopped you. I just heard that Sithian and the other one, Rhiannan, escaped. Are we about to have a war on our hands?"

The assassin shrugged, looking at the carpet between his boots. "I do not know. But, Dietirin, what do I do? For so long I have held my love at bay, knowing that it could never be, and there was Rahna, and...I just thought I would never have to deal with this. I am seven hundred and eighty-five years old, for spirit's sake! Why am I even dealing with this?"

"You are not dealing with it, Aidyn. You are avoiding it, as you always have. I told you once that she and you could never be, but that was because I thought Constancias would succeed in marrying her off to a Lostug. Now, again, I reiterate that point because of Losolin. He is your friend, and you cannot deny that he and Tlonna will spend eternity together."

"No, I cannot," Aidyn agreed, broken-hearted. "But how do I get beyond this? It could have been me, Dietirin, she could love me right now!"

"True, but you never took the chance. You had an opportunity when Herrich Lostug died, before she met Losolin, but you remained silent, fleeing to your manor house in the forest for months, and when you returned, she had met Losolin and her heart was taken. You have no one to blame but yourself. It was the only time I ever called you a coward."

Aidyn's emerald eyes flashed to the king, anger simmering deep within. "You told me it could never happen! Her father, and my closest friend! What did you expect me to do? Break all confidences and sweep her off her feet, carry her away and make her mine? Your own daughter?"

"Yes!" Dietirin shouted, fed up with the assassin's gloomy attitude. "That is what I wanted, for the great gods' sake, Aidyn; I wanted you to be my son-in-law! You held her only once, and for days after you were the happiest I had ever seen you! As was she! She loved you, and probably does to this day! But you lost your chance, and Losolin will be her husband, I know it. I like the boy, I will gladly hand my daughter off to him, but I always dreamed I would pass her to you. You can look death straight in the eye and deny it, but Aidyn, when it comes to love you are the greatest coward I have ever known!"

"What would you have me do now?" the assassin cried, slamming his head onto the desk and covering it with his hands.

"Find someone else. Let her go, find someone else to love," Dietirin said gently, patting the assassin's exposed forearm.

"I cannot," came the muffled reply.

The king allowed himself a small, sad smile, knowing the dark elf would not see it. "I know, my friend."

Tlonna was still in the courtyard when Losolin found her. He slid onto the bench next to her and wrapped his arm about her shoulders, pulling her head close so he could kiss her forehead. "I never asked how you slept last night."

She chuckled, figuring Aidyn had told him. "Very well. Aidyn has quite the comfortable bed."

The Lord Consort snorted, pressing his cheek to the side of her head. "I thought it was Aidyn that made it so comfortable," he teased, a little voice in his head warning him that there may be a little truth to his words.

Tlonna snickered, closing her eyes and leaning against him. "Perhaps. I am sure you have heard the stories of his skill."

He snorted again, though he had indeed heard the rumors. "Should I be worried, then? Are you going to step up from peasant to assassin?"

The Magin twisted in his embrace to give him a wicked smile, though it was tinged with sadness. He saw the look, and immediate pushed away so that she could face him fully.

"Talk to me, Loni," Losolin said quietly, brushing the hair out of her face.

Tlonna looked up at the sky, the hazy sunlight drifting through the early spring atmosphere. The rain storms had left the world refreshed, the shielding canopy of trees sparkling above the hidden city.

"I worry," she began, unable to look him in the eye. "I worry about Sithian following in Midian's path. Should I have let Aidyn kill him? Has my decision cost innocent people their lives and freedom? Am I the true evil here, for letting him live?"

"He is your son," Losolin reminded her, though he heartily agreed with Aidyn's actions.

The Magin swallowed, "Perhaps this is it, what the prophecy speaks about. Perhaps this is me bending to evil. Sithian is undeniably tainted, Anna as well, but I still hold a hope in my heart for them."

"It is not evil to hope for lost souls, Tlonna. It is the hope of all free people, the dream of rulers, to see those that fall to darkness climb out and walk a path of light. You are not alone in your wish to see Sithian and Rhiannan turn around, but the reality is that they will not."

"Aidyn said much the same thing," she muttered, "and it is indeed sound reasoning, but something within me cannot accept it. I need to believe that my children, no matter how ill-begotten, have a kindness to them."

Losolin sighed, his heart breaking at the sight of her tormented expression. "That is no evil thing, my heart."

"Losolin, I feel so lost," she replied, pulling him closer.

"I do not doubt it, Tlonna, but I will always be here to help you find your way back. Always," the male said emphatically, kissing her gently.

The next few days passed uneventfully until Erdwyf had her baby. Jaryikin was a beautiful baby girl with astonishing gray eyes, strawberry blonde curls, and a perfect round face. The infant was blessed by the high priest and received many wonderful gifts from all over. Erdwyf's parents brought a beautiful basinet made from the trunk of a single birch willow and hung with dark green curtains. Tlonna and Losolin gave the baby girl the rarest stone in all of Nymyños, moonstone, mounted in a delicate leaf pendant. Yayènia and Suneelo gave her a sword engraved with the family crest, Aidyn a cloak of the purest black, made from the *ärdyz* material that his assassin's garb was made out of, rare, and incredibly expensive, and Miazie a set of books on history and several other subjects.

After the initial thrill of the birth, things went back to normal. Marten Crotes' spies were long departed and the reports had come back from the wall and the treasury. Dietirin and Constancias approved of the plans and construction started within the week. Later on, Tlonna and Losolin announced their engagement and the news was met with joy and celebration all around–almost.

Erdwyf and Miazie, dragging along a protesting Yayènia, cornered Tlonna in the library, where she often fled for moments alone. The princess spun around as the three clattered into the room, the warrior between them looking frenzied.

"What is it?" she asked, fearing an attack on the city.

Erdwyf latched her arm around Yayènia's neck, stilling the shorter elf, and openly glared at Tlonna. "You are engaged now, and some decisions need to be made."

Tlonna frowned, wondering why the High Commander looked so frightened. Miazie and Erdwyf looked nearly giddy, though they were trying to mask it with sternness. "Such as?"

"Who is Matron of Honor?"

"You were supposed to solve that amongst yourselves," Tlonna muttered, blanching.

Yayènia wriggled slightly, plainly not wanting to be involved in such a lady-like affair, though a gleam in her eyes betrayed her true feelings to Tlonna.

Miazie scowled at her. "We could never make a decision like that."

The princess chuckled nervously, not knowing what to say to her three friends. When Miazie growled and Erdwyf's eyes narrowed, Tlonna edged toward the door behind her. As she made a dash for it, a dagger sliced by her and stood quivering in the wood, inches from her outstretched hand. Turning slowly about, the Magin stared in disbelief at Erdwyf, who still had her hand outstretched, and Yayènia, who was staring at her empty sheath.

"You want an answer now?" Tlonna inquired shakily, secretly impressed by the normally diplomatic High Advisor.

"Yes," Miazie said, also shocked by the fey-faced elf's display. "Know that whomever you choose will sit well with any of us, we just want to know."

"Sure," Tlonna replied skeptically, yanking the dagger out of the door. "Well, you all mean so much to me, and I count you all equal. There really is no way for me to decide between you."

"You cannot have three Matrons of Honor, Tlonna. We cannot all stand in the same place or carry Losolin's ring," Erdwyf stated.

"And what do you have to say?" the princess asked of the sulking warrior standing between the two councilors.

Yayènia shrugged one shoulder. "I have to wear a dress no matter what, I suppose. It does not matter to me where the bloody nine hells I stand, so long as I am in attendance."

"You did not throw a dagger at me, so I suppose it means more to Erdwyf than it does to you, Miazie," Tlonna decided, hoping her friend would not be upset.

By the smile that bloomed on all three faces, she knew she had made the right decision. Miazie squealed in sudden joy, startling the three elves so much that Yayènia actually drew one of her katans and looked about for the threat. The human, unabashed by her outburst, knocked the blade away from the still off-balance warrior and hugged her. Yayènia stood up so straight and rigid that she brought Miazie off the ground by a few inches. The High Commander was short in comparison to all other elves, but she still stood several inches taller than Miazie, who was short by human standards.

The baffled expression on Yayènia's face caused Tlonna and Erdwyf to fall over laughing. Miazie released the flustered fighter, dropping the seven inches to the ground, and joined in the laughter until even Yayènia was chuckling at herself. It was a rare moment of pure joy that the four females would cling to in the dark times to come.

"Tlonna! I refuse to let this wedding proceed! I will not have my daughter wed a beggar! Stab me thrice and drown me, how did I get such a worthless and unthankful daughter!" Constancias raged, her one eye red-rimmed with tears. It was after dinner and Tlonna had just mentioned the wedding, hoping that her mother would, for once, be happy for her.

Tlonna tossed her head in fury, trying to get her rage under control. "You are powerless to stop us, Mother, as you always have been," she said coldly, after a moment of tense silence.

"I will stop you and this abomination! I will not have *that* kind of blood tainting my line! I will not have filthy mongrel descendents!" the queen snarled, pointing at Losolin, who crossed his arms and glared back.

Tlonna stopped moving, her face went emotionless and the room began to chill. When she spoke, her voice was like ice. "You are the taint, Mother. *You* are the stain on this family. If you try to stop this wedding, I will take more than your eye. I will take your life. Do you understand me? I have killed people who deserved to die less than you. No one will mourn your death. It will be celebrated."

Every single being in the room stopped moving, too astonished even to flee. Constancias did not blink, did not breath, did not move a single inch.

Finally, she spoke in a harsh whisper. "How dare you? I gave you life, and you have the gall to say this to me, your own mother? I will have you and all your cohorts removed from any sort of standing within the kingdom, and Feorien will be the new heir. He at least will listen to his betters."

The queen's advisor knelt before her, shock plain on his angled face. "My lady, I am honored with this opportunity, I will do my best to please you."

Tlonna shoved him out of the way with her boot. "Shut up, weasel. Mother, you do not have the power for any such action. Even if you did, the people would never accept it. They despise you, as they should."

"You lying little beast! I shall take every one of your nasty little friends and burn them at the stake to show you and the rest of your treasonous followers that *I am the queen!*"

"You will do no such thing, Constancias," Dietirin said stiffly, coming into the conversation.

Disbelief briefly covered the rage on the queen's face. "Dietirin! I am your wife! You have no right to tell me what I can and cannot do. Besides, this is an oligarchy. I have as much power as you do."

"True, but I am king through blood, and you are just through marriage. If I were to divorce you, you would lose all power. Tlonna would remain heiress as she too is royal through blood."

"B-but you would not do that, would you? You do *love* me, right?" Constancias stammered, looking stricken.

"I love my daughter."

The only sound in the room was the opening and closing of Constancias' mouth. "Y-you do?"

"Yes."

"Why?"

For those who had never seen a livid Magin elf king, it was a terror. Those who had ran for cover. Lightning exploded within the hall, ricocheting off the walls and floor. Lamps and vases shattered and flew in all directions. Dietirin grabbed his wife by the neck and slammed her against the wall.

"She is *my daughter*! I raised her from an infant, you did not. You refused to touch her; afraid you might have to do some work. I was betrothed to you when I was twelve years old, and I hated you then, as I hate you now. I had no say in what my parents did to me. You forget that I tried to flee the night before our wedding so as not to marry you. Pretty though you may be, you were more fit to be the wife of Hadian Rahlan, not me. You will not do the same to my daughter. She will marry whomever she pleases."

Constancias shrieked in grief and rage, writhing in her husband's wrath. A pale purple beam of light erupted from her fingertips and sank into Dietirin. He let go and clutched his chest, his fingers digging into his shirt. Blood suddenly blossomed on the gray silk, spreading slowly outward. He pulled at his robes of office and bared his chest, the muscles still well tamed, quivering beneath the pale hairless skin. A hole, nearly two inches wide, was burnt into his chest, blood pouring out in gleaming bubbles. Losolin ran to his aid, laying the king down and putting his hand against the wound. Dietirin gritted his teeth, never crying out.

Too distracted by the danger their beloved king was in, the nobles in the hall never saw Tlonna draw her blade. Seeing her daughter approach, Constancias tried to flee, knocking tables and chairs over to block Tlonna. She never made it to the end of the hall. The queen screamed as the crimson tip of Tlonna's sword exploded from between her breasts. The younger elf shoved the sword through, all the way to the hilt, her teeth bared in a savage snarl, red-hot tears splashing down her face.

The queen clutched at the blade, slicing her fingers on the razor sharp edge. She died screaming, the blood in her throat making it more of a gurgle. Tlonna rolled the body over and, putting her foot on the corpse, yanked her blade free, and wiped it clean on the dead elf. The Magin's ice blue eyes were clouded over, pupils dilating and elongating with speed. Light pulsed out of her, angry and sizzling.

Tlonna turned and walked slowly back to her father, blade dragging on the floor. Losolin had closed the wound and stopped the bleeding, but Dietirin had lost too much blood. His skin was yellow and his face taut with pain. He opened his eyes at his daughter's approach.

"Little Loni..."

"*A'da,*" Tlonna cried softly.

"You avenged me, my beloved child. I am sorry, my daughter, that you have to suffer through this. I should have had her taken years ago, then none of this would have happened. I am sorry, Tlonna, that I failed you. You and Losolin will be wed, and you will rule this land with a strong and fair hand, I know. I wish I could be there to give you away."

Tlonna began to weep, shaking her head, clutching her father's hands.

"Before I go, there is something I must tell you. I named you Tlonna Arune for a reason. There is a story that says when the elf Tonora died, it was an act of love and hatred, a violent tragedy brought on by one who loved her as much as he hated her. When she died, her spirit forgave him, for she knew he had loved her and would weep for his deed. And so he did. When his tears fell upon her body, it began to rise and change. It changed into a beautiful blue orb that lit up the entire forest. The man saw at once that it was her in ethereal form and he was afraid that anyone who saw her would try to hurt her, so he threw her into the sky where she stayed to watch over all. That is why Tonora is visible longest, because she is watching over all, keeping them safe, providing light even in the darkest of times. You, Tlonna, are Tonora's descendent, her last name was Arune. She is the one who gave birth to Jair, which you know. You, Tlonna, are descended from the moons. Tomorrow night, look to the sky, for there will be a new moon. It will be red, and it will be me, looking down on you. It is our bloodline's legacy, though it happens only when we are killed by another's hands. Tlonna, I love you. Losolin, I give you my daughter," Dietirin weakly grabbed both his daughter's and Losolin's right hand.

"I, Dietirin, Father of Tlonna, and King of Blackhaven Forest, formally betroth Tlonna Arune Ewôsdírn and Losolin Ullor Grisholm, so they may be together forever beneath their ancestors and the moons, which are one. *Senniaeann säära klyshet, Inkan yayena valõn.* Goodbye my daughter, I love you." A single tear slid down the king's face, and he closed his eyes forever.

The hall was silent but for Tlonna's grief-stricken weeping. She knelt hunched over her father's body, arms wrapped around him, shoulders trembling. Losolin too wept, though he allowed Tlonna all the space around her father. Aidyn stood ramrod still, pain and disbelief lancing through his body as he stared at the body of his oldest friend. Unable to take the sight any longer, the assassin spun on his heel and fled the room.

The funeral was two days later. Dietirin's body was wrapped in a sapphire and pure white robe with the Tree of Blackhaven and the family crest, a left-facing crescent moon with an eight-point star between them. His hair was tied back with strands of grass and on his brow was his favorite circlet of silver and onyx.

His litter was carried by Suneelo, Ghealan, Losolin, and Aidyn, each robed in black, hoods up, and wreathed with the rare sky blue flowers from the *kairhotuss* tree. The four males marched slowly with their precious burden down the main thoroughfare of the city. All the inhabitants came out and tossed bunches of flowers tied with black, white, and blue ribbons. The street was covered in them. The procession consisted of the pallbearers in front, Tlonna riding Takîreaes, shrouded in black from head to toe, and then the royal staff, Erdwyf and Yayènia foremost, the former in her ceremonial dress, the latter in full war regalia, polished to a gleam. The procession continued through the streets where all the people joined, adding their sorrows. When the procession reached the royal graveyard, only friends and family were allowed in the gates.

Tlonna dismounted and stood before her father's mausoleum. Her face was stained with tears but she no longer wept, her beautiful face frozen in grief.

"My brethren, we come here today to mourn the passing of my father, King Dietirin Ewôsdírn, first of his name. He was a kind and true leader, one who would talk with the maids of things no more important than the weather, or protect an entire city from the rule of evil. He protected everything he loved and loved everything about his people. He was a great father and friend, someone you could talk to or laugh with, you could sit in a garden for hours listening to his stories or scream at just because you had to scream. We all have our private thoughts of him, and I wish for us all to take a moment to remember them."

A long moment of silence ensued, broken by much weeping and whispered prayers. After a time, Tlonna began to sing. Everyone stopped to listen to her voice. It was low and smooth, never wavering, though sometimes cracking in sorrow. Those who had not been sobbing began now, just for the beauty and sadness of her voice.

Shadows of thunder
Breaking asunder
Against the light
Goodness' might

Striving for peace
Vowing ne'er to cease
Good king's promise
Honor shall ne'er miss

Full of glory
Dietirin's story
Brought to bear
Evil's glare

His legacy
No less a memory
Shall linger through
Of kindness true

When she finished, the echo of her voice trailed softly in the wind. The four pallbearers picked up the casket and slowly walked into the mausoleum. When they exited the tomb, the door grated shut on its own, sealing itself with blinding red light. Above the door, the light flashed again and the epitaph appeared.

King Dietirin Ewôsdírn
First of His Name
Son of King Damian
Father of Tlonna Arune
Loved by all
Blessed by the Moons

1,032 Years of Age
Year 544 of the 9th Age, Muan

Queen Constancias was given a burial in the lesser nobility graveyard, marked with a simple tombstone that read her name and age. There was no funeral in her honor, and Tlonna refused to go to the gravesite when the priest went to bless it.

"Tlonna, she was your mother! At least go and say goodbye," Losolin pleaded once more.

"No! She killed my father! She is no mother of mine. I will not go to that grave no matter what. She can rot in the nine hells for all I care," Tlonna replied, angrily swiping at the male's extended arm.

He sighed, glancing at his brother for aid, but Suneelo simply lounged against the wall, present only because his job demanded it. The Captain of the Guard stared back, unwilling to be dragged into an argument yet again. Only an hour ago Tlonna had nearly taken his head off for suggesting she eat. Losolin gave the older male a look that promised revenge and went back to pestering his fiancée, trying to reason with the distraught female.

Finally Tlonna slammed down the books she was unnecessarily rearranging and spun around, her eyes full of grief and frustration. "I do not care what you think! Constancias murdered my father! Because of her I feel as though I live and die in every breath. She took from me my father, who I had just gotten to know once more. Her name shall be stricken from the royal lineage, all memory of her burned away. She was a murderer and a fiend, and I will be damned if I ever go to stand before her grave for any reason other than to dance upon it."

"Tlonna..." Losolin began but she silenced him with a look.

"Get out, both of you," she snarled, pointed toward the door sunk in the middle of her room.

"No, I will not leave you alone when you are like this," the Lord Consort replied softly, "please do not ask me to leave."

Tlonna looked up at him with fire in her eyes. "I am not. I am telling you to leave. Now." She looked pointedly at Suneelo.

"I am sorry, Princess Tlonna," the warrior said unexpectedly, snapping into a formal military bow. "I cannot leave your presence unguarded for a moment. To do so will be to foreswear myself and to break the code of honor by which the Blackhaven Militia operates."

Both elves stared at him, their faces slack with surprise. Losolin recovered first, eyeing his brother suspiciously, but when he opened his mouth to reply, Tlonna roughly shoved him forward. "You have no such bindings. Leave," she snapped, effectively pushing him through the door with power.

Losolin stood outside the door, stunned by the sudden disappearance of Tlonna's room. Irritated and stubborn, he turned and grasped the handle to walk back inside, but electricity shot up his arm, causing him to jump back a step and nearly fall off the ledge of the narrow stairway. Cursing in frustration, the male stalked away toward his own room.

Tlonna tried to ignore Suneelo, but the male watched her every move, though he was seemingly interested in the maps that decorated her walls.

"What are you waiting for?" she snapped finally, annoyed by his presence.

The male looked at her, his eyes dark, almost violet. "For you to do something stupid," he replied casually.

"Such as?"

"I do not know. It is my job to be here when you try to harm yourself, my job to stop you, as I am bound by oath to-"

"Oh do shut it," Tlonna cried, throwing her hands in the air. "All I want is to be alone so that I may mourn my father on my own!"

Suneelo dropped his act immediately and rushed over to the suddenly tearful female. "I am not just your guard, Tlonna, not just your fiancé's brother. I am your friend," he said, holding her as she sobbed into his shoulder.

"Ah, spirits, Suneelo! I miss him so much!" she blubbered, burying her face in his neck. The Magin was unaware of him gently picking her up and carrying her to the bed. When he began to release her, Tlonna tightened her arms around his neck, keeping him close.

Obliging, Suneelo straightened on the bed and let her cling to him. After a long while she fell asleep, tears soaking half his shoulder and the pillow beneath him. Carefully, he extracted himself and moved silently to the door. Stepping out, he instructed the guards to find Losolin, and took up the post himself. When the Lord Consort arrived looking confused and worried, Suneelo explained.

"It would be best if you were there when she wakes up," he finished quietly, watching his brother's reaction.

Losolin nodded, gripping the other's shoulder. "I realize that this must be hard for you. I know you and Ghealan were close to Dietirin."

Suneelo looked away, unwilling to show his true pain. "I would check Aidyn before myself or Lan. He knew him much longer, and was probably closer to Dietirin than anyone alive. They knew each other for nearly all of Aidyn's life."

The Lord Consort nodded in acquiescence before stepping into Tlonna's room, careful not to wake the sleeping princess. He found a chair and eased into it, letting his mind wander as he watched her. He had not known about Aidyn and Dietirin's relationship, though he had suspected something when the king seemed to brighten whenever the assassin was around. Indeed, Losolin mused, most people seemed to cheer up in Aidyn's presence, which seemed odd and quite opposite the point of being an assassin. Perhaps it was the mere fact that there was no safer place than beside him, especially because he and Yayènia were always in the same vicinity. Having those two about lent a sense of security to even the most paranoid of people.

Tlonna moaned in her sleep, drawing Losolin out of his reverie, but she simply turned on her side and fell quiet once more. His heart was broken for her, and he knew not what to do. His own parents had died while he was away, and he had not really regained a memory of them yet, anyway. He felt useless. Shifting, the elf stretched his long legs out and leaned back, resting his head against the chair. He was so exhausted, but could not sleep for fear Tlonna would wake. Watching her, he eventually let his mind wander back into the misty places of theory and wonder, mulling over the plainly blanketed words of his brother.

Suneelo and Ghealan had been famously close to Dietirin, even earning the nickname "my sons" from the enigmatic king. The captain however, much like his wife, was known for secreting his true feelings away and hiding them from everyone in his life. Losolin worried that his brother might one day explode from the sheer volume of bottled emotions. It was not normal for elves to be so stoic, for when one lives so long, one learns to simply feel.

Perhaps they had seen too much, been through too much, to be able to allow themselves to loosen up, the elf mused silently. It could be that, he supposed. He had noticed that Ghealan had not taken his usual walk through the throne room as he had nearly every day for the last two hundred years, instead relegating the duty to an under officer. Erdwyf no longer beat Tlonna to the throne room on petition days as she always had in order to spend some time with Dietirin, debating and deliberating over every possible topic. Things had changed, and Losolin wondered if the close family would ever truly heal.

Tlonna had taken the hardest blow, having watched her father die by her mother's hand, and then driving a sword through her mother's chest. Though she claimed to have no regrets about the kill, Losolin saw the darkness in her eyes that spoke of more than simple grief. There was repentance and shame lurking there, and it seemed to drain her of ambition.

Tlonna stirred again, her eyes sliding open and she looked at Losolin through a haze of sleepiness. Without a word, she held out her hand, waiting for him to take it. He kicked off his boots and laced his fingers with hers, sliding between the covers to hold his beloved. Tlonna's eyes closed once more and she drifted away, her head nestled against Losolin's shoulder. He smiled faintly, and remained awake, watching her.

When next she woke, Tlonna turned and met Losolin's gaze. "I am sorry," she murmured, kissing him lightly on the cheek.

The male huffed, brushing her hair from her face. "Do not be. It was what you needed at the time."

"No, I needed you, but could not see it."

"You do not need to see it, for I will always be here beside you. That is one thing you can count on for the rest of your life. I swear it."

Tlonna smiled faintly, staying quiet in order to enjoy the mere presence of him.

Several days later Tlonna stood amidst a whirlwind of blabbering people, completely overwhelmed and more than a little disturbed. Each one was talking about the things she must do to take over the throne as Queen of Blackhaven. Losolin was also being pestered, but as they were not married yet he was bothered less. Yayènia, standing beside Tlonna, shoved a blustering man back hard enough that he stumbled and fell, taking two others with him.

"Get back!" she growled, quieting all their protestations. "This is not appropriate behavior, and it is unsafe. Now, before I lose my temper, you will all make room for the Everwood Princess and reconvene in the council room in thirty minutes. Is that in anyway unclear?"

The gathered people shook their heads, terrified of the imposing High Commander, and split apart to allow her and Tlonna through.

"Excellent work," the Magin said, smiling faintly. "Will you stay with me?"

"As I am bound," Yayènia replied, linking her arm with Tlonna's as they started up the winding stairs to the third floor.

The two females sat in the council room, slightly refreshed by the cool teas brought by one of the ever-present servants. It did not seem all that long before the council rushed into the room, and the badgering began again. By the end of the day, a new crown had been commissioned, the ceremony decided upon, and the living arrangements switched about.

Tlonna sighed as a small army of servants made a continuous train from her room, out of the tower and across the hall to the royal tower, formally called the Tower of Winds. More personnel worked furiously in the tower to change it to Tlonna and Losolin's tastes. The massive bed Constancias and Dietirin had slept in was taken out and burned by Tlonna's order. All of the former queen's belongings were handed out to the people of the city, including towels, jewels, and shoes. Everything Tlonna had was being transferred. The canopy bed took a dozen guards to move into the royal suite. The entire move took a week, including renovations and redecorating.

The pale yellow and red walls Constancias had painted were covered with the blues and greens Tlonna favored, the tapestries and paintings of flowers were replaced with the landscapes and maps that had graced the princess's walls. One of the walk-in closets was transformed into a weapon hold. The many swords, bows, staffs, and knives Losolin and Tlonna had acquired over the years were carefully stored away, each in their respective cases.

The Tower of Winds was identical in shape and form as Tlonna's, though much larger. The balconies still looked out over the harbor and courtyard, but from opposite directions of her previous views.

Haydyn had his new furnishings moved into the Moon Tower. He was delighted with his new surroundings.

"Mother! This is amazing! I thought my other quarters were nice, but these are...whew! I can't believe this!"

Tlonna smiled faintly. "Yes, and you are speaking like a human, love, and you are no longer just the heir. You *are* the prince now, I hope you are glad. You have to sit parliament and petitions with me now, too."

Haydyn grinned back, blue eyes alight. "I am more than glad. I cannot wait to learn everything. The lessons that Lady Yayènia and Lady Erdwyf give me are more intimidating than anything else. The High Commander likes to scare me as much as possible."

Laughing softly, the queen hugged her son. "She scares us all. That is why she is High Commander and not something else. Most enemies see her on the battlefield and run away screaming before she even draws her blade."

"You would not happen to be talking about me, would you, Loni?" Yayènia said, smirking and walking toward them.

Haydyn blushed and ducked his head. Tlonna shook her head, grinning now. "Of course we are. No one else is quite as fascinating as you, friend."

Yayènia reached the twosome and put her hands on her hips. "Those weapons came in from Zeynuwn and I gave Erd her Na'sha. She is so excited. Has not put the damnable things down since she got them. She is out in the training yard with Guard Master Ulwin. Poor old dwarf cannot keep up with her, even with the baby just being born."

"I am surprised Ghealan has not put a stop to that."

"Oh, he is about ready to have a fit. He is so restless he keeps asking me to fight with him. He is even starting to wear *me* out, it almost feels like when we first met."

"Good. I want you to start training Haydyn soon, and I do not want you to kill him, so if Ghealan can keep you worn out, that is excellent."

"Ha! Very funny Tlonna," Yayènia replied, crossing her arms. "You boy," she turned to Haydyn, "will start next week. Be at the training yard at daybreak next Monday. I want you to wear light, loose clothes that allow you to move freely, and nothing fancy. You will get a little bloody."

Haydyn gulped. "Bloody?"

"I said muddy. Good day to you both," Yayènia said, fleeing the hallway packed with servants.

Chapter 5

Tournament to Forget

"Two of the world's greatest warriors, quarreling like children. What a kingdom we live in," Erdwyf remarked, climbing up to her chair beside the throne.

It was midday and the throne room had been cleared for lunch, a new rule Tlonna had set. Losolin nodded, watching his fiancée and Yayènia argue. Though Tlonna was nearly a foot taller than her friend, the commander was her equal in severity. "I would hate to see those two go at it with a purpose."

"I wonder who would win? Using magic anyway, Tlonna most certainly, but if they were on an equal plane...?" Suneelo added, leaning across the two thrones to join in the conversation.

Losolin looked at his brother, a smile playing about his lips. "They would never go for it."

"Ah...are you so sure? We all need a little entertainment, and the arena is always looking for new ways to make money. It would be a good way for *us* to make money. And both of them have been so tense since Dietirin...passed."

Erdwyf's grin slid off her face, but she continued idly playing with her arm band. "Do you think they would?"

Losolin stretched out his legs and lounged in his throne. "As High Advisor, it is your place to ask the question."

Erdwyf glared half-heartedly at him for a moment and then turned to Yayènia and Tlonna, who were now laughing as they tried to push each other over. "Tlonna, Nia, I have a question."

Tlonna and Yayènia stopped grappling with each other to stare at their friend, suspicion lurking in their eyes.

"There is somewhat of a debate roaming around about who would win in a fair fight. No magic, that is. It seems to me the only way to solve such a question is to have a tournament, a public tournament."

Tlonna straightened to her full height. Yayènia crossed her arms and raised a brow at Erdwyf. The High Advisor cocked her head slightly, "We would, of course, be charging the public for seats at the arena, resulting in what I am sure would be the largest turnout ever, and a large profit for the throne."

"I am for it, then. What about you Tlonna?" Yayènia replied, grinning.

"Ah...no. First of all, it would not be proper, second of all, we have better things to do, and third of all, you would lose horribly," Tlonna said, walking away.

"I do not think so! There is no way you would beat me, no one can," Yayènia retorted, grabbing her queen's shoulder.

"You believe so? Then fine, set it up!" Tlonna laughed, hoping she could exhaust herself sufficiently to forget, even for a moment, recent events.

The entire kingdom, it seemed, turned out for the event. The tournament arena was packed full to the brim and people were still pouring in. Tlonna and Yayènia were standing by the entrance to the grounds, calmly checking their gear. All their friends were jittery and anxious, despite the fact that they had been the ones to push the idea ahead. The two bristled with weapons, their clothes tight and unrestrictive. Vambraces were the only armor they wore and their hair was pulled back and coiled around their heads so it would stay out of their faces. As soon as the arena was full, Erdwyf and Losolin jogged onto the field and stood back to back. Together, they spoke the rules. As they finished, Tlonna and Yayènia sprinted to the center, eyeing the excited crowd with amazement.

Turning, Yayènia made the first move. She darted to the left and pulled her two swords out in a flash. Tlonna responded in kind, yanking her sword and crouching to avoid the deadly edges. Their swords met and rang off each other. No one breathed. They whirled away and braced once more. Tlonna moved in, spinning her weapon in her hands and catching it on the rim of Yayènia's vambrace, but the commander shoved the blade off with a heave and spun around. Tlonna regained her footing and kicked out. Sheathing one of the swords, Yayènia caught her ankle and twisted. The queen-to-be flipped in mid air and landed on her back, rolling to avoid the stronger female's downward hack. A moment later she was back on her feet, her sword crossed before her in a defensive block as Yayènia came at her in a blur, twin katans spinning too fast. For several moments the ring of steel seemed an endless song as the blades parried one another so fast no one could see the individual weapons.

Then, with a deft twist, Yayènia's left katan hit Tlonna's shortsword on the cross guard and knocked it from the Magin's hands. With a subtle flick, the High Commander did the same to the other shortsword, disarming her opponent. The crowd erupted into cheers, but then silenced as Tlonna yanked out her quarterstaff.

Yayènia reeled back as the wood smacked into her chin, dazing her for a moment. With a wild howl, she jumped into the air and spun, her blades spinning at arm's length. Tlonna shoved the staff up in defense, but against the razor edges of the swords, it held no chance.

Instead of discarding the wood, the Magin repositioned her hands on the severed ends and went after her soon to be sister-in-law with fervor. The wood and steel met in uncountable movements, the splintering sound of sword against staff the only sound. Curls of wood littered the arena floor in a strange spiral pattern, outlining the movements of the elves. The audience was silent and staring, most of them standing. Losolin and the others stood rigid, their mouths agape and their eyes wide. Dust floated up from the arena floor as the two contenders battled back and forth. Finally, Tlonna sent one of Yayènia's blades spinning across the dirt with a strong jab to the warrior's hip, accepting the glancing blow on her temple in order to do so. Tossing away her shaven sticks, the Magin pulled out two blunted daggers and sent both flying toward her opponent. With an almost lazy motion, Yayènia flicked them out of the air. Dusty and bleeding, both elves put their heads down and leaned on their knees for a second. Yayènia was the first to recover and yanked out her bow.

The crowd gasped as she tossed away her blunt arrows. As Tlonna lifted her face, she saw only Yayènia, for the warrior was already in mid air. Yayènia tapped the end of her bow on Tlonna's head and then landed. Spinning around, she swung her bow around and clipped the Magin across the jaw. Tlonna pulled out her longblade and jabbed it at Yayènia. The commander feinted right and then darted left. Her bow whistled in front of Tlonna's nose, and then the string caught around her neck. With an expert spin, Yayènia reversed her bow so that the wood was against her friend's neck. Choking, Tlonna attempted to free herself from the weapon, sliding her blade between her shoulder and the string, and slashing downward. The filament whipped around, lashed Yayènia across the face, and wrapped around her shoulders. Growling, the fighter untangled herself and launched herself at Tlonna.

The taller female was ready though, and brought up her sword. Somehow, Yayènia was able to slap her hands on the flats of the blade and flip around. Tlonna gasped, but didn't hesitate to turn and jerk the sword forward. A line of blood appeared on Yayènia's side where the blade razored across, slicing open leather and skin alike. Tlonna ducked a vicious swing from the fighter's fist and rolled, grabbing up the longer portion of her decimated quarterstaff. Aiming, the Magin attempted to launch it at the other, but the commander whipped around and wrapped her leg around the shaft. Yanking her leg down, the wood broke in half. Left with only their bodies, the two elves went at each other.

Tlonna was pummeled back a few steps before she responded and grabbed Yayènia's wrist as it came at her. The commander was thrown to the ground and the queen placed her boot on her chest. Yayènia pulled Tlonna down and rolled away, kicking her legs out and hitting Tlonna full in the face and chest. Standing, Yayènia picked up one of the discarded swords and waited for Tlonna to rise. When she did, the Magin easily pushed the blade out of Yayènia's weary hands. Both elves were beginning to slow, having gone on for a very long time. With a final burst of adrenaline, Yayènia punched Tlonna in the nose and then cracked her elbow across her chin. Blood shot out the Magin's mouth and she fell to her knees. Breathing harshly, Yayènia pulled out her daggers and crossed them at Tlonna's neck.

"You are dead."

For a second, nothing happened. Then, the crowd erupted in howls and cheers. Flowers and other things rained down upon the two. Sweat poured down their faces and they both collapsed wearily in the middle of the arena.

After a short visit to the infirmary for a few stitches, Tlonna and Yayènia walked arm in arm down the corridor of the great castle, laughing and discussing various tactics the other had used. Losolin spotted them and jogged over. Neither female had allowed him to heal her, convinced the wounds were too superficial for such a thing.

"I just got a letter from Demetri. He says that he will 'welcome the spies with unknowingly open arms'. Here," the king-to-be handed his betrothed a roll of parchment and waited for her to read it.

When she finished, Tlonna chuckled lightly. "If only all the rulers were so kind and intelligent. I really do miss him, and Tyular. It does not seem fair that our only true and honest allies are all the way across the continent. I suppose that could be an advantage, but it is not very nice of the spirits to play this joke."

"I know, I miss them too. Are you both feeling well?"

Yayènia cast her brother-in-law a sidelong glare. "Of course. Why would we not be? We have much more stamina than you males," she finished coyly.

"Aha," Losolin grunted, "anyway, Tlonna, your son would like a word with you. He is in the library, the archival library."

"What does he want?"

"I do not know. He just asked me if I had seen you," the Lord Consort replied, scratching at the spot where his circlet rested on his temple.

Tlonna straightened the crown and smiled. "All right. Nia, I will be seeing you?"

The High Commander nodded. "Oh, the Trade Masters got me their list of armorers, and I commissioned them to supply the new armor. I told them to copy the design made by Demetrius's armorers. Do you want the militia treasury to fund it, or will the throne?"

The queen bit her lip, a light pounding beginning in her head. "I do not know, let us talk later. I have to speak with Daphne tomorrow anyway, so meet me in the treasury after lunch. Bring the military records if you can."

Yayènia nodded, saluted casually, and strode away, her weapons clinking. Losolin put his hand on the newel post. "There have been reports from the wall that the trees are starting to grow dangerously close to the wall. I need to go see what needs to be done."

"I do not like cutting the trees away, even if it is reasonable," Tlonna replied sadly, shaking her head. "Let me know what you find."

Losolin nodded and descended the stairs. Tlonna hurried through the corridors until she reached the archives and her son. Haydyn was bent over a massive tome bound in tatty leather, running a finger down what appeared to be a never ending list on the cracking pages. He looked up only when Tlonna propped her feet up on the table, leaning back in her chair.

"Mum, do you know any tutors?"

Caught off guard, Tlonna let the chair thump back onto all four legs. "Yes, why?"

"Is there one here?"

"In the castle? Yes. Why?"

Haydyn again ignored the question. "What about Maginic teachers?"

"Haydyn, do you not like the Academy? Are you not doing well there? I have not heard anything from them to suggest so," Tlonna said in concern.

Haydyn marked his spot in the book and shook his head. "It's not that. The Academy teaches me about history, mathematics, languages...*academia.* I need other training, and, to be honest, I do not feel as though I am up to par with the rest of the students. I am not as far behind as we feared I would be, but far enough to warrant some issues. I want to learn all that I can before I have to face Sithian again. I want to be able to control my powers and know what it is that I am doing. Yayènia is teaching me the skills I will need for physical combat, but I am a *Magin* and I need to know how to be useful."

"So, you are telling me that you want to go to the Institute of Magic and learn tricks from a bunch of crotchety old wizards?"

The young half-breed grinned. "Precisely. Can you sign me up?"

"I will send out the letter today. And what about this tutor. What are you looking for?"

Haydyn shrugged. "Someone who knows the stuff the academy is teaching me, but can augment it. It is just embarrassing when I cannot answer the questions that my fellow students have known since their kinder years."

"I will talk to Miazie. Of anyone, a Belau will make the best of teachers, and you like her, do you not?"

"Yeah, but...I don't think she likes me."

Tlonna frowned. "Why do you think that?"

"She rarely speaks to me, and is haughty when she does," Haydyn said, blushing faintly.

The female snorted quietly. "Miazie is that way with everyone, believe me. She was once a princess, and has never forgotten that lifestyle. I will speak with her and let you know, all right? Anything else? I need to go meet with Feorien."

"No, that is all."

Tlonna left the archives and meandered down the halls until she found Feorien standing outside her office, his hands dry-washing each other almost frantically.

"Feor, what are you doing?"

The displaced advisor jumped, looked around, and bowed to his knees when he spotted the queen. "Queen Tlonna, I have wanted to speak to you for many days now. Ever since your mother...well...you killed...well..."

"What do you want, Feorien?" Tlonna said coldly.

The elf took a deep breath and closed his eyes. "Your mother gave me a life. Before her, I was just another page boy, running errands for the cooks in the servant kitchen. She gave me advancement and every opportunity I needed to make a better life. Since her...absence...I have found myself and my family falling into disgrace. I fear that soon we shall lose any affluence we have gained. I would ask you, my queen, to allow me to continue my services for you, as I did your mother. I will deliver messages throughout the castle and kingdom, take the lesser audiences, help with petitions, and basically be your advisor in such matters."

Tlonna squinted at him. "Feorien, you are aware that I already have two advisors that I trust completely, correct?"

"Yes, ma'am, but I would gladly be their assistant, or fill in if they are incapacitated. I have no job in this castle, and therefore have no means of income or support. My wife is very high class, and I cannot afford to keep her in comfort at this rate."

"And who is your wife?"

"Lady Sharntun, milady."

"Sharntun? The palace minstrel?"

"Yes, my Queen," Feorien replied, his voice nervous.

"I am still the princess," Tlonna sighed wearily. "Your wife has a fair hand with the harp. You may help Miazie and Erdwyf, but if I hear of one incident, you are out, understand? I do not want any trouble from you. I will not easily forget that you were, or are, loyal to my mother. You will do what Miazie and Erdwyf tell you to without hesitation. You will receive the pay you earned previously, as well. Go on then, I have things to do," Tlonna said, turning away. "Ah, Feor, I will have your new livery sent to you by tomorrow. There is a petition session tomorrow as well, after lunch. See you then," the princess strode away, turning down the corridor that branched off to the right.

She spent the rest of the day listening to various complaints from the city council members, being measured by the seamstress for her wedding dress, and approving lists of food, music, and guests for the wedding.

Chapter 6

Fear for the Humans

Exhausted and weakened, Sithian and Rhiannan rode out of the barn on two stolen horses. They rode until the morning, spotting the city of Orlan, the port of Kismath. After Tlonna had closed all harbors, the duo had fled east into Schelum but had found only resistance and hatred. Orlan had been the first city in Kismath to have a harbor, and was now in fact the only populated settlement in Kismath. The kingdom had been nearly obliterated by Aderiaen and Midian decades ago, and only a few wayward pioneers had returned to the cold province. The few merchants traded only with Zeynuwn, shying away from any Elven community for fear that it might incite the rage of the Rahlans again. Finding the harbormaster, Sithian bought two tickets aboard a merchant vessel sailing for Zeynuwn that evening.

Once the caravel docked in the exotic Zeynuwnian port, Sithian and Rhiannan bought a room at an inn for the night, wallowing in silks and expensive cotton, tasting of the rare seafood cuisine. Rhiannan smoothed her hand down the red silk robe she wore, plucking at a heron embroidered into the side. "We must get some of this for the palace, Sithian. Such finery is not to be wasted on peasantry."

The king nodded absently as he carefully pulled off the newest bandage on his thigh and winced as the skin reopened.

"Bastards did quite the job on you, didn't they?" his sister asked, kneeling before him to examine the wound. "You should call for a healer, or whatever they have here. It could take septic if you're not careful."

"No, our mother's blood will prevent that," Sithian replied, handing Anna a clean wrap. "The only thing she ever gave us that was worth anything."

"She did not mistreat me," Rhiannan said suddenly, softly, as she cleaned her brother's wound and tied the cravat. "It was more that bitch Yayènia, the looks she gave me, the snobbish attitude suggesting she was better than me. I want to take her life as she took Father's. I want to hear her scream for hours."

The king watched her work, noticing the clear difference between the Blackhaven healers and his sister. Their fingers had been firm and steady, gentle but effective. Rhiannan tugged and pressed, heedless of the pain it caused, more in tune with her own ravings than his suffering.

"You will get your chance, I promise you that," he said when she had finished. "When we march against them, you will have your chance to take her life."

"We are marching against them?" Anna asked, a wicked gleam to her eyes.

Sithian sighed and leaned back, lacing his fingers behind his head. "Not for a while, but yes, eventually. We are going to need an army, and commanders. Several of the Darkwights have fled, though more than half remain. I have made a new commander of a man named Orlando. He is from the Scattered Isles far to the east of Zaedic. And I have a network of spies running within Nymyños, even Blackhaven. But we need more. We need soldiers, and lots of them. We are going to need ships and engineers, and Magins."

"Did your spy contact you? Why did he never contact me?" Rhiannan asked, suspicious.

"You do not know our code. And yes he did contact me once, but he was only able to leave a single marking telling me he had made contact with a special group of agents living in Talenias under Athelias's protection," the young half-breed said to mollify his sister.

Anna made a face and lay down on her bed, staring up at the ceiling. "It will be good to be home."

Sithian snorted. "You have lived longer in Blackhaven than Zaedic, and you say you were not mistreated."

"What are you saying?" the young woman demanded, looking over at her brother. "And anyway, you're the one who came to get *me*. And now I wonder why."

"For my own personal greed," the king replied lightly. "I need you."

Rhiannan smirked at the last statement, never thinking that the way she was needed was not one she would enjoy at all.

The next morning they bought passage on another merchant vessel, this one a large ship headed for Narnen. The voyage took nearly a month in the heavy ship, but when it finished unloading its cargo and restocking for the trip back, Sithian strode into the captain's cabin, surprising the man.

"What are you doing in here? Our business is finished, boy," the captain said, stepping away from the unsettling young half-breed.

"You are going to take my sister and me to Zaedic," Sithian crooned, cornering the poor man.

"Zaedic? That cursed island up north? Why in the nine hells would you want to go there?"

"Because I am its king!" the young Rahlan roared, backhanding the captain, blue power crackling between his fingers. "You will do as I say!"

An hour later, the ship set sail north, Sithian and Rhiannan comfortably situated in the roomier captain's quarters. Three weeks later the ship pulled into port with half of its crew left, the captain swinging from the crow's nest. Sithian and his sister left the ship without ceremony, knowing it would never get back to Nymyños.

When they reached the castle, servants fell over each other in their haste to do their errant king's bidding. An hour later, when they were appropriately washed and dressed, Sithian guided Rhiannan into his office, commanding a servant to find Kelus, the Darkwight leader.

A few minutes later he entered the study, looking very much the same. His black velvet robes swirled about his body like a cloud, the hood up to hide the distorted face and neck. Silver eyes shone out from the shadows like lamps.

"You sent for me?" he asked casually, as though they had not been gone for months.

"Yes, I did. It would behoove you to give me and my sister the respect that you gave our father. I will not put up with boorish and disobedient servants, especially demons. You are to begin training a new army for me, one that will sweep over Blackhaven like a plague, unstoppable. Do you understand?"

The demon hissed, laughing, folding his arms before him. Sithian noticed with confusion that one hand was covered in a black glove. "I am surprised to see you. I had hoped you perished in your mother's land, a fitting end. Why did you come back?"

Sithian seethed at the demon's words, but he did well to hide his anger. "I am Zaedic's king. That is all you need to know, and you will accept me as your ruler or perish. You ran my father's army, you will do so with mine."

Kelus shook his head. "Things have changed, half-breed, and the winds do not favor you. I will not work for an upstart brat of Midian Rahlan. You and your whorish little sister can rule this rock, but you will never rule me."

With that, Kelus swept out of the room and away. The next morning, he bought passage on a small trader's ship sailing to Schelum. Sithian and Rhiannan watched him go from the castle gate, their eyes lit with fury.

"It is no matter, Anna. I have something far better than a demon. During my stay at Blackhaven, I read up a bit on archaic rituals. With enough power and the right incantations and talisman, it is possible to do the impossible. Come, we have much to do."

The brother and sister walked back to their castle and disappeared for many days.

Tlonna was sitting in her throne on the left of Dietirin's when a messenger came running in. He fell to one knee, bowed his head, and placed his right fist on the floor. "My lady, there is a...well...a man-thing waiting at the castle gates. He says he has come very far to see you and requests an immediate audience."

Sitting up ramrod straight, Tlonna clenched her fists. "What do you mean a man-thing?"

The young boy looked at her chin and bit his lip. "I think, milady, that he is a demon. He wears black robes, almost like an assassin, and the only thing I could see was the silver of his eyes. He said his name is Kelus."

"Kelus? Bring him to me immediately," the elf said, sending for Haydyn, Losolin, and Aidyn.

Yayènia, who was leaning against the throne, shook her head. "Do you think it wise bringing Aidyn here, with what happened at the gate with Sithian?"

Tlonna sighed. "Kelus has a kindness within him that he cannot shake. He must be here for a reason, and he would not come alone if he were on Zaedican business."

The High Commander loosened her sword in its sheath anyway and stood up as the three males walked into the room. It was an ominous procession, the dark assassin striding behind the two fairer males like a blurry shadow. Losolin slid into his throne with a look of discomfort as Haydyn thunked into his, and Aidyn stood on the Lord Consort's right. It was not long before the messenger and the Darkwight entered the throne room.

"Kelus, Leader of the Darkwights. What brings you to me?" Tlonna asked coolly, attempting to see the shadowed visage of the demon.

"You do, elf. The skin that you freed, and then Midian ruined again, is growing back. My whole arm is as it once was. I feel myself growing lighter and healthier by the day. I feared that if I stayed in Zaedic much longer, I would have been killed," he said, the silver irises of his eyes flickering to the others in the room, pausing on Haydyn and Yayènia, who had shot him in the hand not two years ago.

Tlonna descended the dais steps and reached out. "Show me your arm, Kelus."

The Darkwight pushed up his sleeve and removed the elbow-length glove beneath, revealing a muscled arm covered in healthy pale skin. "I am becoming an elf once more."

"Is this a bad thing?"

The demon hesitated. "I...I do not know. It has been so long since I was taken by Midian. I do not think I will be able to live as I once did."

"Kelus, you said that you have been changing by the day. If you left Zaedic when your arm was whole, how far have you changed now?" Tlonna asked, stepping closer.

The male before her lowered his hood with one clawed hand and one perfect hand. The face that stared at her was taught with apprehension. Kelus's eyes had remained much the same, black with silver irises, but the rest had changed back. His face was fine-boned with high cheekbones, a slightly pointed nose, and thin pinkish lips. The hair that had once been ragged and clumpy now hung in a shining auburn braid that cascaded down into the depths of the robes. His neck, however, remained black and oozing blood as it always had.

"Oh, Kelus! You are beautiful! I cannot believe this!" Tlonna laughed, grinning. She grabbed the transformed demon and hugged him until he groaned.

"Elf, get off before someone sees. I did not come here to be hugged by over-dramatic queens. I came here for safe haven. Do I have it?"

"Yes, of course, let me get you a room until we figure something out."

Haydyn stood, walking from his throne to stand before Kelus. "What of Sithian and Rhiannan?"

"What of them?" the demon asked, eyeing the young prince warily. "When I left they were glowering down at me from the gate."

"Then they made it back to Zaedic," the half-breed murmured, giving his mother a significant look. "Perhaps they had need of a spy."

"I am no spy, Haydyn Rahlan," Kelus hissed, sounding like his old self. "Dare to accuse me of such a thing once more and we shall find out if your father's training had any impact on your thick skull!"

"Hold," Tlonna said firmly as the two braced. "Kelus, his name is Haydyn Ewôsdírn, Prince of Blackhaven. I believe that you came here for the reason you gave, not subterfuge. This is a peaceful kingdom, and I will not have such things brought into the light."

"I understand," the demon said softly, relaxing. "I thank you for your generosity."

Tlonna smiled. "Good." She bade a servant to take Kelus to a room and then turned to Aidyn. "Follow him, but be discreet. I trust him, but his arrival has odd timing."

The assassin nodded, moving after the demon and his escort, his body seeming to melt into the few shadows that lay about the room. Tlonna watched him go with admiration, never noticing her son slipping off in another direction. Turning back to Yayènia and Losolin, she sighed, rubbing her fingers through her hair.

Aidyn leaned against a corridor wall, peering over the corner as the maid handed Kelus a key to one of the guestrooms and then walked away. The demon opened his door and stepped inside, not bothering to shut it all the way. That simple motion relaxed the assassin somewhat, but then he tensed again as Haydyn appeared around another corner, skulking.

Curious and slightly alarmed, Aidyn watched the young half-breed sidle up to the door and peek inside. Suddenly he disappeared and the dark elf swore, moving swiftly down the hall.

Kelus turned around, completely unsurprised by the boy's appearance. "Still do not trust me?" When Haydyn continued to glare at him, the demon bowed in Zaedican fashion. Halfway to the floor, he realized his mistake. Haydyn hoisted him up by the armpits and slammed him against the wall.

"What are you doing here? Answer me before I break your filthy neck!"

"You have gotten quite a bit stronger, Haydyn. Put me down, will you?"

"I will not! Tell me what you are doing here? Did Sithian or Rhiannan send you?"

"Haydyn!" Aidyn yelled from the door. "Put him down."

The prince cast a glare at the assassin. "Do not tell me you trust him, too. He was my father's lapdog, Aidyn!"

"He is your mother's friend," Aidyn countered, easily jerking the boy away, causing him to drop the demon.

Kelus landed lightly, surprised by the assassin's words.

The dark elf held Haydyn out at arm's length, his steel grip keeping him in place. "You will not attack Kelus again, is that clear?"

Haydyn opened his mouth in protest, a petulant look on his face, but the assassin shook him roughly, emerald eyes narrowed in a glare. "Yes, Aidyn."

"Good, now go."

The prince shuffled from the room, his shoulders slumping. When they were alone, the two adults turned to face each other, sizing the other up. Kelus dropped his cowl again and tossed the key on the small dresser.

"Aidyn Sestuns, I know of you. I have always wondered which of us has killed more," he said after a moment.

The assassin lifted an eyebrow, wondering the same thing. "Should I be concerned?"

Kelus chuckled. "Not if half of what I heard was even partially true. You have nothing to fear from me. Did Tlonna set you on my shadow?"

"She meant no offense."

"I know. I lived for a hundred years under the rule of a man so cruel he could not even think the word kindness. I would be more concerned if she simply let me go on my own. I am honored she sends one as powerful as you."'

Aidyn placed his hands on his hips, looking about the small apartment. It was a bedroom and another little room with a desk and chair. "You brought no pack," he said after a moment, noticing the lack of personal items.

"Aye. I fled Zaedic, there is no other way to put it. My room was in the castle, and I left the day Sithian and Rhiannan returned."

"Why did you not come sooner?"

"What would have happened had I run into Sithian while I was here? I knew where he went, figured he would not come back. In fact...he had distinctive limp when he returned. Know anything about that?" the demon asked, eyeing the assassin.

For an answer, Aidyn lifted his right hand and flexed his fingers, releasing the hidden blade from its special sheath. Kelus's eyes went wide as the weapon appeared from apparently nowhere, and he grinned. The assassin flexed again and the weapon returned to its hiding spot.

"I think you and I will get along just fine," Kelus murmured, appreciating the dark elf's wicked look.

"Sithian would not have returned to Zaedic had Tlonna not stopped me. Even so, he will carry scars for the rest of his life."

"No less than he deserves, the little prick," the demon replied.

Aidyn laughed, running his fingers into his hair and swiftly moving his hands back and forth, ratting up his sable hair. "Ah, at last, someone who understands the necessity of murder," he chuckled. Automatically his fingers began smoothing out the tangles, Kelus watching in confusion.

"Why do you do that?" he finally asked as the assassin ran his fingers backward over his scalp.

Aidyn suddenly realized his own actions and dropped his hands. "A way to stop my hands from finding a blade to drive through your skull."

"What?" Kelus yelped, stepping away from the dark elf.

"I can sense the taint within you, the evil Midian raked your body with, and the urge to kill rides through my blood like a living thing," Aidyn replied honestly.

The demon forced himself to stay where he was, rather than flee the little room. "Well then..."

"You should not fear me, Kelus. I will not harm you," the assassin said as his hands clutched at his waist, digging into the flesh just below his ribcage.

"You may not, but your hands might," the Zaedican chuckled uneasily.

Aidyn smiled, turning to go. "You will want to keep a low profile for a while. Zaedicans, even reformed Zaedicans, are not easily accepted here, I am sure you understand. I would guess you know your way around well enough."

Kelus nodded shortly, accepting the jab as fitting. He did indeed know his way around Blackhaven, the castle and its grounds specifically, from the time he had been here with Midian. Indeed, on the way to this room he had passed the one in which he had occupied two years ago. As the assassin left, his hands still clenched to his sides, Kelus felt a sudden shift in his world.

After court the next day, Tlonna, Losolin, and Erdwyf met Ghealan at the stables and they mounted up. Takîreaes and Neñyos frisked, having grown restless in the pasture.

"There are renovations still needed at the guard towers," the Second Commander said as they rode out into the city proper.

"What kind of renovations?" Tlonna asked, fearing the answer would drain the treasury even more.

Ghealan smiled knowingly. "The mortar needs to be replaced, there are still some holes from the siege, and the oil ramps need to be smoothed."

"And how much is this going to cost me?"

"Oh, a good thousand geld, if you get cheap stuff. For the best, you should probably terminate some positions in the castle. I have always said it uses too many servants."

"Oh, you are foul," Tlonna joked, shaking her head at Erdwyf, who merely grinned at her husband's sad joke.

They rode the length of the wall, Ghealan pointing out places that still needed work, and where the guards were thinnest. Losolin then took them to where the trees were encroaching on the wall, and the three dismounted, mounting the steps as the sun began its slow descent.

"Ah, my lords and ladies," an officer said, striding over to them, plumed helm hanging around his neck. "I'm glad you're here. As I explained to Lord Consort Losolin yesterday, several trees have grown within less than five yards of the wall. One nearly touches it. They're going to have to be cleared away."

"Taken out completely, or cut back?" Tlonna asked, walking over to lean out between the crenellations.

"Taken out completely, your Highness," the man replied, moving to her side. He stuck his arm out and pointed to one tree that seemed to be reaching toward the wall. "That one especially. It presents a danger to the city, and if we don't get rid of them now, it will be too late once a battle has begun."

"We do not yet know if a battle is going to happen," Tlonna stated blandly, though she knew the probability of one.

The human stared at her back until she straightened and turned to look at him. "I will have gardeners over tomorrow to begin the removal."

"But my lady, we can do it just as well."

"The trees will be transplanted within the city, somewhere they are needed. There are many bare places where the land was decimated by the siege and has not yet had the time to grow back. I will not slaughter trees for no reason if I can help it."

"But...they're just trees!" the soldier protested, confused.

Tlonna raised an eyebrow at him. "They are living beings with a wisdom and life all their own. I do not want to have to transport them around the wall, so set up a pulley system to bring the trees over the wall. I will send out a team of dwarves as soon as I can if you need them."

The man scowled, but he wiped it away quickly when he remembered whom he was talking to. "No, Lady Tlonna, we can construct one easily enough. Though one or two dwarves might be nice to have around just to help us with the ballast. Any other orders?"

The Magin caught the acid tone, but decided to let the man slide. "That is all. Make sure your patrolmen do not harm the trees in any way, Officer."

The man bowed and then marched off, muttering under his breath, never realizing that the elves' sharp ears caught every word. Tlonna looked at Ghealan, who sighed, shrugging.

"They are soldiers, Tlonna, and human. They do not have our love for the flora and fauna," the Second Commander said, leading them back down the stairs. "One day they will realize their mistake and try to rectify it."

Erdwyf grunted. "Let us just hope it will not be too late for them."

The other three elves all exchanged knowing glances, and feared for the future of the humans.

Chapter 7

Ceremonies

The week of the wedding arrived, and people swarmed through the gates: elves, humans, dwarves, sprytes, and dryads, all of different status. A large horse-drawn carriage of forest green and teal announced the arrival of King Demetrius.

"Demetri!" Tlonna cried when the king rode through the castle gates, looking proud and strong atop a leggy piebald mare.

"Tlonna, Losolin! Aidyn!" the king laughed, startling many of the surrounding people with the last name.

The normally calm and unexpressive assassin jogged forward, grinning, and embraced the king warmly, nearly engulfing the smaller male in his black cloak. Tlonna and Losolin exchanged bewildered looks when the killer stepped away from the beaming king to eagerly shake the hand of a younger version of Demetrius.

When the man stepped forward to greet the engaged couple, he chuckled at their expressions. "Aidyn and I go way back, my friends. That is Tristan, my son."

"It is so good to see you, Demetrius," Losolin said, bending slightly to welcome the king. "We worried you might not make it in time."

"Oh, I would never miss such a thing. Long have I waited for such an invitation!"

"I have missed you greatly Demetri," Tlonna said, wrapping her arms around him and hugging him tightly. "Come, you must be weary from the journey."

"Very. Tristan! Stop blabbering and come!" Demetrius yelled back to his son, who was talking non-stop to a suddenly bemused Aidyn.

The handsome prince gripped the assassin's elbow and pulled him along as he followed his father, Tlonna, and the entourage that had greeted them.

"Aidyn taught my Tristan nearly everything he knows about battle, and nearly as much about women. Your assassin has been a friend of my family for a very long time," the King of Kajgenia explained to his hosts. "He was my great grandfather's mentor."

Losolin looked back at Tristan, who was still talking at great speed, and Aidyn, who had his head bent in order to look at the young man. The assassin moved normally, as though he were purposefully keeping himself in check around the already nervous staff from Kajgenia, who were following behind with the bags. The Lord Consort shook his head and wondered what other surprises the assassin had left to spring upon them.

On the day of wedding, people woke early to wreathe their homes and yards in leis of flowers and cover the streets with bouquets of lavender, frankincense, and patchouli, the ancient herbs of happiness, blessing, and fertility. Tlonna stared into her mirror, her handmaiden running a brush through her damp hair, the scent of jasmine clinging to the golden strands. The royal seamstress rushed into the room carrying a pile of shiny white satin. When she let it fall, it became a stunning imperial dress with a glittering silver belt and organza sleeves. Tiny blue and silver flowers dotted the veil overlay on the skirt, and the train was nearly four feet long.

The Magin gasped, her mouth hanging open in awe. "It...it is so beautiful, Mattie! You are a genius! I cannot believe it!"

The head maid and the seamstress beamed at their adored princess. "It took me quite a while to decide how it was to look. It gave me quite the amount of dilly dallies."

The three females grinned while the maid did Tlonna's hair. After a few hours of primping, Tlonna stood and let her dressers slide a silk slip over her head and arrange it around her hips. Carefully, they helped the elf step into the wedding gown and lace up the back. When the silver belt was fastened, Tlonna began to weep. Her attendants looked at each other, alarmed.

"Lady Tlonna, what ever is the matter?" asked the maid, Carlotta.

"I just cannot believe I am finally getting married to the elf I love, after everything. It is so unbelievable, I cannot get it through my head! So many times I believed us done for, that the next breath we took would be our last. And now, it all seems so petty, so..." Tlonna waved her hand in the air, at a loss for words. "Unimportant," she finally managed, wiping away her tears.

"Aye, and Lord Losolin is getting quite the deal. A beautiful, loving wife, and a throne. And he's gorgeous too!" Mattie squealed.

"There is that," Tlonna replied, laughing as the seamstress placed the veil on her hair.

It was a delicate tiara of silver attached to waves of sheer lace that fell from just above the ears. Finally, Tlonna placed her feet into the white slippers and took a deep breath. "How long do I have?"

Carlotta looked out of the window to where the city clock tower stood. "About twenty minutes. We should go down to the ballroom so we can be ready."

After a nervous nod from the princess, the trio traversed the castle, carefully directing Tlonna away from traffic.

Losolin cleared his throat for the hundredth time and studied himself in the mirror before him. He was dressed in white cotton trousers, gray knee-length boots, a white belted tunic of satin, and a magnificent gray velvet cape lined with white silk. On his head was a silver circlet, and at his waist, the blade from Demetrius. Ghealan, Suneelo, Haydyn, and Aidyn grinned at him in the mirror, resplendent in their own white and gray suits, minus the cape and circlet.

"Are we ready, boys?" Ghealan asked, tugging on his lapels.

"Yes, I think we are," replied Losolin, copying his friend.

The males left the room and made their way down to the ballroom.

When Tlonna, Carlotta, and Mattie opened the door to the temporary room, they found Yayènia, Erdwyf, and Miazie fussing with their own dresses. Erdwyf, as the Maid of Honor, wore a silver and white dress of satin. It was elegantly simple and the skirt seemed to move on its own, so light was the fabric. Her slippers were silver, as were the ribbons in her hair. Yayènia and Miazie wore dresses of the same cut, but of white and blue.

Yayènia blushed crimson at being caught worrying at the white ribbons in her knee-length hair. Her hair fell down in spirals and looked oddly feminine, as she usually had it tied up so that it reached to only her thighs in a thick braid. Miazie grinned and shook back her own mane of raven hair accented with blue ribbons.

Tlonna beamed back at them, tears sparkling in her eyes. "You are all so beautiful!"

Erdwyf laughed and hugged her friend. "I am so happy for you. Ghealan and I could not sleep last night because we were both so excited."

"Yes, I am sure that is why you could not sleep last night," teased Yayènia, pointing to the other elf's arms, in which lay baby Jaryikin.

The females burst out laughing, too giddy to stop. It wasn't until the bells rang that they quieted. Narda the Seneschal, hastened into the room and stopped short when she saw them all in their dresses. "My word! Excuse me, I'm sorry, it is about to start. High Advisor Erdwyf, High Commander Yayènia, Advisor Miazie, you are to go out in that order. Erdwyf, with Commander Ghealan, Commander Yayènia with Captain Suneelo, Miazie with Lord Aidyn. Prince Haydyn will go first, carrying the rings. All clear? Come come, follow me. Princess Tlonna, I will come get you when it is time," the dryad said, pulling the bridesmaids out.

"All right Narda. Thanks," Tlonna replied.

Across the room, the males came out and joined the females. The couples linked arms and they proceeded out of the ballroom into the inner courtyard. When Aidyn's arm slipped through hers, Miazie felt a shiver of desire run up her spine. The assassin felt the motion and he grinned down at her, a knowing gleam in his verdant eyes. Hundreds of people sat in chairs and watched in excitement as the couples walked down the long aisle to take their places on the dais at the end. The musicians switched songs when Losolin entered, flanked by Aladorn and Demetrius. The chorus and the band faded into silence when he reached the dais and climbed the steps to stand in front of the priest. Once more, the doors opened from the ballroom, and the music began again. Tlonna stepped out and was greeted with stunned gasps and sighs from the gathered. Losolin clenched his hands in staggered awe.

Tlonna walked the aisle alone, holding a bouquet of flowers and herbs. When she finally reached Losolin, she handed the bouquet to Erdwyf and turned to face her betrothed.

The priest began. "Today we are gathered for a Hand-fasting Ceremony between Tlonna Arune Ewôsdírn and Losolin Ullor Grisholm before the Lady and the Lord of the Wild Wood."

Losolin took a deep breath. "Before the Lady and the Lord, do I pledge to love and honor this female, that we be in the image of the Heavens, two who are one."

Tlonna repeated him.

The priest spoke once again. "The flowers of the field beyond the Life River give testament to the joy of love and unity. Give now your vow to your beloved, so that she may know who it is she weds."

Taking a deep but shaky breath, Losolin began. "Tlonna, we have been through many things together that would have torn most apart. Because of these crucibles, I know that our love will survive the ages that we will live. I have never known another being that has had such an impact on my life, and I am glad that it was you. I want you to know that I will always be your strength when you are weak, your light when you are lost in darkness, your hands when yours are tied, your legs when you can no longer walk, and your laughter when you are sad. Your beauty is outshone only by your heart, which is honest and pure, loving and honorable. I love you. I love you more each day, and the sun itself pales in envy of your beauty and brilliance," Losolin said quietly, a half smile on his perfect face.

"Give now your vow to your cherished, so that he may know who it is he weds."

Choking back tears, Tlonna began her own vows. "Losolin, I have never known a male so stubbornly perfect that he can make my knees weak and my heart stop beating. You have guided me out of so many mazes wherein I was lost. I fear the nights when I do not know if I am touching you, and I fear the days when we are apart. When you are around, I know I am safe and loved. When I thought I was strong enough to handle something that I could not, you always put yourself in death's way and brought me back. There is no one I would rather spend my everlasting life with than you. There is no one I would rather face the battles and celebrations of life with than you. I believe in my heart and soul that you were made for me, and that our hearts are a single entity, beating as one. You are the very air I breathe, Losolin, I love you so much."

The priest waited a moment before saying, "Do you have a token of fidelity to give one another?"

Haydyn stepped forward and handed the rings to the bride and groom. They placed the rings on each other's fingers and said in unison, "This ring is the symbol of the love and the honor I give unto you. With this Band do I bind myself to the one I love."

"Before the Lady and the Lord; before the Elements; before this assemblage of friends and family; with the power and authority vested in me, I pronounce you husband and wife. Now you are wed; two made one. May the Lady and the Lord bless and keep you both in Their love. May They shower you with Their bounty and may you bring forth the fruit allotted you from the Life River. As I will it, so mote it be!"

The couple turned to face the crowd and the priest raised his arms. "I present Queen Tlonna Arune Ewôsdírn-er'Grisholm, and King Losolin Ullor Grisholm-en'Ewôsdírn. You may seal your vows now."

Losolin yanked Tlonna against him and crushed his lips to hers, nearly bending her backward as the crowd roared in appreciation. When the male finally released the breathless and star-struck Tlonna, the priest, smiling all the while, spoke once more.

"The rite is ended. Depart in peace Elemental Kin, Lady and Lord, our blessings take with thee, and thine upon us. With blessings given and blessings received, the River is renewed. Go now, and be one together."

Tlonna and Losolin stepped down from the dais and walked down the aisle, laughing as rose petals were thrown in glittering arches above them. They reached the ballroom, which was now empty but for decorations, and took up their places at the head table. When the ballroom was full with people, Erdwyf stood and held up her hands for silence.

"Let us rejoice this day in the way of our ancestors," she said formally and the musicians once again struck up a song. In accordance with tradition, the national anthem was sung and the first cask of wine was broken by Tlonna and Losolin's joined hands.

People cheered and clapped as the anthem ended, until the music lured them back to dancing. The night was wiled away with the free flow of alcohol, food, and dance. The ball did not end until dawn the next morning. Slowly, the people of Blackhaven wandered back to their own beds and the visitors back to the inns. Tlonna and Losolin grinned at each other as they danced. They were the last to leave, Losolin carrying Tlonna all the way back their tower. They did not emerge until midday.

Tlonna and Losolin's official coronation ceremony took place a few days later. The entire kingdom came out to see the rite, including sailors from distant lands and corsairs that had been welcomed into the harbor. The common folk danced in the streets, children twined themselves on the maypoles and cast boughs of hyacinth in the streets. As the two elves prepared for their coronation in one of the state rooms, the doors burst open and an explosion of sound erupted into the room.

Turning around, the couple was ambushed from all sides by roaring, laughing men and one woman, all in baggy, salt-stained clothes. Tlonna shrieked, grinning all the while

"Commodore Alexander! Captain Troaz! I have missed you greatly. I did not see you at the wedding ball, though I am surprised Kayra was able to get dressed up nicely for me. I hear she wears men's clothes, yes?"

"Even a lady of great comfort can get acclimated to a life, as long as there is plenty of enticement, eh, my queen?" a young, tousle-haired man asked, swinging his arms around Kayra.

"Aye, that I am, Jack. I am glad to see you once more," Tlonna replied, kissing the young man on the forehead.

The commodore, a tall human with his hair in plaits and beads inclined his head. "We were there, Tlonna, don't ye fret. We were there. Saw ye and yers all dressed up all pretty and such. Though, it seems I have much to thank ye for. There has ne'er been a time when we corsairs were so...welcomed and wealthy. If ye remember, a few years back me crew's ambitions to open a few taverns in some ports? Well, due to yer allowances, we own a few here in the 'haven, and a few in the eastern provinces. Without ye, we would never ha' made the funds to open up such fine places."

Tlonna beamed. "Ah, well, Commodore Alexander, it is all a pleasure just to know you and your men, and lady. How fares the fleet?"

"Very well, actually. We have two new additions, one that you might be very interested in, Lady Tlonna. Crewed by only elves, won't allow any humans on, other than the rest of the bastards in the bunch. An amazing sight to see, a bunch of bloody elves hauling at lines and doing an honest sailor's work, I'll tell you that," Troaz interjected, flicking his eyes to the left where a tall corsair stood. "This is Adii, captain of the *Sidyov*, and a damn fine captain, if I may say so."

The tall corsair lifted his head and gave a silver-toothed grin. He was an elf, painted around the eyes and nose with henna, earrings flashing, amber eyes glowing. "Good day to ye, my liege. I be Adiiran Liwian, and it is an honor to meet such an elf as yerself."

"Fortune to you, Adiiran, you follow in the command of a great man, few have I met that even come close to his grandeur. I hope you find the hospitality of *Kairhotuss* to your liking?" Tlonna replied, smiling still.

Alexander chuckled. "Of course, of course, we be staying in one of our taverns. Nice and peaceful after a long trek on the waves, though I wouldn't give it up fer nothin'."

"I would hope not. Well..." bells in the city began to toll, cutting off the female. "There is the beginning of the ceremony, I hope to see you all afterward at the feast. Losolin and I must go. Goodbye for now!" Tlonna said, running out of the room.

Soon after, they were kneeling on the colossal steps, named the Steps of the Wind, which led to the main floor of the castle. The steps numbered four hundred and rose to the third floor entrance to the castle, titled the Door of Winds. One hundred feet across at the base, the stairs tapered until the very last step, which was a mere three feet. Beneath the steps was open so one could walk beneath and look up to see the angles of each step inversed, slender yet strong pillars of white marble holding up the black marble stairs. The pillars and the stairs were the only main structure of the castle that was not made out of obsidian, and they were famed across the land as one of the greatest architectural feats in all of history, the castle close behind.

The castle was made from blocks of obsidian nearly a foot thick, ten inches high, and twenty long, carved along the entire façade with veins of pearl, silver, and gold. Though some magic had been used to make the obsidian stronger and to keep it from flaking, most of the work had been done by hand. Dwarves were acknowledged for building the palace, but a few elven designers and human masons were credited as well.

Rolling meadow-like gardens circled the castle with the ever-present forest hedging it and a few trees growing wildly in the middle of the plots. Usually the place was serene and quite, the soft musical sound of wooden chimes the only noise, but now it was filled with the roar that always accompanies great crowds.

People were spread out at the base of the stairs, craning their necks and ears, and still more were inching up the steps, pressing against the guards that Suneelo had set. Complete silence fell when Erdwyf, the Officiate of the Crowns, raised her hands. Suneelo and

Yayènia stood on the step below Tlonna and Losolin, holding black and silver pillows with the bejeweled, intricate crowns that were purely ceremonial.

When Erdwyf finished binding the two elves in their many oaths and giving the blessings of the Divine Spirits and the people of Nymyños, Yayènia and Suneelo carefully took up the crowns, handing the pillows to Aidyn and Aladorn who stood behind them. In unison, they lowered the crowns onto the bowed heads of Losolin and Tlonna, and then stepped back. When the newly crowned elves stood, the crowd below roared their pleasure, shaking the foundation of the stairs. The couple raised their joined hands and waved at their people. All manner of races stomped and hollered, tossing hyacinth and other flowers and herbs upon the great stair. Erdwyf stepped forward once again and raised her hands until the congregation quieted.

"I give you, Queen Tlonna Arune Ewôsdírn-er'Grisholm, and King Losolin Ullor Grisholm-en'Ewôsdírn, Monarchs of Blackhaven!"

Again, the crowd cheered and waved their hands. Two stable boys brought Takîreaes and Neñyos out of the castle, in which they had been temporarily housed. The monarchs mounted their horses and carefully ran them down the Steps of the Wind and into the streets for the traditional ride through the city. People followed them, waving and cheering, until finally they were forced back by the necessity of work. Tlonna and Losolin returned to the castle and were welcomed whole-heartedly into the feast hall, where all the nobility, guests of the throne, and friends of the couple were seated, waiting. They cheered and clapped when they entered and took their places at the head of the table on the dais.

Their corsair friends, and other non-noble companions were seated at the table just below the dais, and the four other tables were filled with nobles and dignitaries. A mass of servants appeared, each carrying two plates, which they set down in front of the guests, one servant to every two people. An appetizer of salted and fried bread, oiled salad, and stewed pears came first. After the dishes had been taken away, the six course entrée arrived, filling the feast hall with wafting aromas. Laughter, chatter, and the clink of silver on glass deafened the room. Tlonna and Losolin talked endlessly with their closest friends. Miazie and her ill-begotten husband Damon spoke of the condition of the Liberated Lands in the center of Nymyños to

Demetrius while Erdwyf and Yayènia argued their decades-old argument of which fighting tactics were better. Suneelo and Ghealan swapped stories with Losolin about their long-lost past occupations, and Tlonna chatted with Demetrius's son, whom she had not had the chance to speak with, along with Aidyn, whom the human would not let out of his sight.

He was a young man of twenty-five, tall and broad shouldered like his father. Gray eyes grinned from behind straight dusty brown hair that just brushed his collar. His face was a mirror of the king's, strong-jawed, wide cheekbones, and a hawk's nose.

Tlonna leaned back to let the servant take her plate and then took her goblet in her hands. "Now, Tristan, I understand that you roam the lands looking for a wife?"

"Yes, I do. Or something to kill, I'll take either," the human grinned.

Tlonna laughed and then took a drink of cooled cider. "Mayhap you will find a wife here. There are many women in this city. But, are you not supposed to marry a princess?"

"Now, my queen! I hear the new king is a peasant or do I hear incorrectly?"

Laughing hard, Tlonna wiped tears from her eyes. "No, no you hear correctly. So, what is it exactly you are looking for?"

"I want a woman who isn't afraid to go hunting on horseback, camp on the ground beneath the stars, eat roasted meat off the bone. I want a woman who is beautiful and humorous, good-natured and kind, strong, and not afraid to try new things, in and out of the view of public, if you catch my meaning," the prince confessed, nudging the queen in the arm.

"Oh, I think I caught it. Although I must admit, it will be difficult to find a woman of such perfect proportions..."

"Yeah, the only one around is sitting next to you, and she is just recently taken, my boy!" Demetrius howled, entering the conversation. "You missed your chance, son!"

Tristan grinned and took the goblet from his father's hand. "Father, I'm afraid to tell you this, but I think you've had enough to drink this eve."

"Nonsense!" the king guffawed and snatched his cup back. "I can hold my liquor as well as any!"

The dais table laughed and then oohed when the desserts came, sugared fruits, frozen creams, cakes, and pies.

Aidyn chuckled and subtly flicked Tristan's elbow, shaking his head. "I remember once when your father became so sloshed he kept running into the walls of the dining room, looking for the exit. The next morning, I found him face down on the kitchen table, sound asleep."

"I name you liar!" Demetrius slurred, a sloppy smile on his kindly face. "'Twas *I* you found on the tabled kitchen. And...and you were very shifty, I 'member. Very... shifty."

The assassin was laughing so hard he had tears running out his eyes, eliciting shocked and amused looks from his friends. They had rarely, if ever, seen him this animated.

"Shifty? I think you mean blurry my friend, you were seeing double, or triple perhaps. And you were what, thirty at the time? Weak blood I say," the dark elf finally retorted, his voice bubbling with mirth.

Demetrius eyed him with bloodshot orbs and smacked his lips. "Dribsle lerrt," he muttered, and everyone burst into laughter.

Tlonna leaned back and ran a finger along the stem of her goblet, grinning. The crystal vessel shone in the lamplight, the red liquor within becoming translucent as it sloshed against the cup. She sighed contentedly, smiling at her friends. The night wore on as people slowly started to drift off to bed; the servants came in and began clearing the tables.

Several minutes after everyone but the main table had departed, Demetrius began snoring, his head tilted to one side of his chair. Aidyn gently picked up his old friend and carried him off, Tristan following, shaking his head. Tlonna and Losolin crawled into bed much later, yawning and laughing.

Many leagues away, Sithian and Rhiannan were staring out of their throne room window as their experiment ran slow laps about the courtyard, limping slightly, but getting faster.

Chapter 8

Many Meetings

That week, thousands of nobility came to offer their congratulations to the newly crowned and wedded couple. Demetrius sat next to them, whispering rumors and juicy tidbits about each dignitary, making the two elves and their advisors snigger. The biggest surprise was when an olive-skinned man in a short turban and a pompous demeanor stood before them, bowing slightly.

"'Ello, King Losolin and Queen Tlonna. I am Emperor Tahi-tat of Zeynuwn, and I vish you zee best of luck een your marreege."

"It is said that Tahi-tat has seven wives, each one prettier than the next. He brought them all, I hear." Demetri whispered.

Tlonna leaned forward and looked down at the small man. "Emperor Tahi-tat, an honor it is to receive you in my home. I had feared you would not be able to make it in time."

"I am ruler of Zeynuwn, and I can command zee gods to make zee vheels of my careege fly vith great speed. I vould not miss such an eevent."

"I am glad," Tlonna replied as she dismounted the dais and bowed to the emperor. He looked taken aback, but relaxed when Losolin joined his wife and repeated her action.

"It is has been a long time since there was a Zeynuwnian emperor within the walls of Blackhaven," the king stated. "We must not let such a great opportunity pass us by."

"Zeynuwn has alvays been a friend to zee eelfs," Tahi-tat replied defensively, folding his hands before him as though in prayer.

"Aye, that I know. Please, join us for dinner before you depart, and bring your wives," Losolin returned. "I would like to learn about your...empire."

The small man nodded his assent and strode away, his bright robes fluttering behind him. The next leader to arrive was greeted with smiles and hugs all around. Tyular Ambrose, King of Arseninis, heartily embraced his neighbor, Demetrius, and then swung Tlonna around in a great hug. The female giggled in pure joy, and no little surprise, as the human was nearly six inches shorter than her.

"Tyular!" Losolin said, embracing his friend. "I have been waiting to see you!"

"I passed old Tahi-tat on my way in. Didn't give you any advice on your second wife, did he?" the king laughed, slapping the elf on the shoulder. "He's still mad at me for not marrying his daughter."

The four rulers laughed and returned to the dais, someone fetching a high-back chair for Tyular. The youngest king pulled out two sealed letters and handed them to Tlonna. "Barukh gave me one, and Athelias the other. Bar had a sudden crisis with collapsing tunnels and had to turn back. We had planned to travel together once we reached the Forest of Ullor, but there was only a messenger waiting when I arrived there. This is from him."

Tlonna took the scroll sealed with gray wax embossed with a pickaxe, the emblem of Florwen Hune. Opening it, she squinted at the blocky, dark letters crammed onto the rather small piece of vellum.

Tlonna Ewôsdírn and Losolin Grisholm,

It saddens me greatly that our meeting is delayed, for I fear I cannot make your wedding or coronation due to a tragic accident within one of our mining shafts. Several of my people have lost their lives, and I must put my efforts to the repairs and the honors of these poor souls. Please know that I do hope to meet you both soon, and to seal once again the treaty I had with Dietirin. May the stone around you be solid.

Barukh Odrinsson of Florwen Hune

"He sounds like a good dwarf," Losolin remarked once he had read the letter. "I hope to meet him soon."

Tlonna nodded. "He knew Father, it seems. Thank you for bringing it, Tyular."

The handsome king shrugged. "I'm afraid this one will not be as kind. It is from Athelias, who also could not, or would not, come."

Wary, the Magin Queen took the letter pressed with the wavy-rayed sun and snapped it open, rolling her eyes at the one-liner.

Magin,

It is too far for me to travel at this time, forgive my absence.

King Athelias Embina of Talenias

"How very contrite," Erdwyf growled sarcastically, reading over the back of Tlonna's chair. "I always hated the man."

"You know him?" Miazie asked, looking to her friend.

Erdwyf nodded. "*Aiya,* unfortunately. I had to stay in Talenias for nearly two weeks once on a mission to arrange a treaty. It failed, utterly, and I had to deal with the bastard and his repulsive son."

"I have never heard a good thing about Athelan," Tlonna put in, looking to Demetrius and Tyular, who shook their heads.

"That one is a gnarly brat," the older king said, shaking his head. "Tristan cannot stand him at all, which is not good if they are going to rule at the same time."

"I think we should dispose of the whole flaming family," Tyular muttered, folding his arms and slumping against his chair. "It would certainly ease a lot of minds to know they were no longer in control."

"We cannot justify wiping out the entire Embina line, Ty," Demetrius said, his tone letting everyone know that this was an old argument.

"But think of the end results of such a thing! We could set someone new, someone worthy, on the Sun Throne and not have to worry about it so much. Demetri, how many hours of communication do we spend on Talenias?"

"I agree with Demetrius," Tlonna said unexpectedly. "How could we claim to uphold justice and honor if we did such a thing? We need to do it legally, and with witnesses, and Athelias must admit to wrong doing. Otherwise we are no better than he."

"Well spoken," the Kajgenian leader said, beaming at the elf. "Relax, Ty, and enjoy the day. For once, *we* have no duties."

The younger king sighed, but he nodded, secretly relieved his claim had been turned down. Several more dignitaries strode into the throne room that day and the next in order to congratulate the young couple. The rulers of the three kingdoms sat side by side, laughing and reaffirming their friendship and treaties. To Tlonna's and Demetrius's joy, Haydyn and Tristan took to one another quickly, sparring and testing each other on the various things men their age should know. It did the half-breed good to have someone near his physical age, and his faculties and self-confidence seemed to grow.

Chapter 9

The New War

"Send out messengers to all the villages calling for all the able men. I don't care who they are or what they do, they will be here in three days or face the consequences of my wrath. They must bring enough food for a month, and any weapons they have. Otherwise, they go to war with only their bare hands to protect them. Do you understand?" Sithian asked, pacing, several months later.

The scribe finished the sentence and turned the paper. "It needs only your signature, King Sithian."

The young man signed the order and shoved it back at the scribe, who stood and bowed deeply. "I will have the message on its way, Sir. Your command shall be heeded."

Sithian waved the scribe out of his study and turned to Rhiannan, who stood with her arms crossed, staring out the window. Walking over, he put his hand on her shoulder.

"Do you think he will be ready? Do you think he will be strong enough?" she asked, turning away from the glass.

"Of course he will, he was the best, and he shall be again. Anna, look at what he's been through, no one has survived more."

Rhiannan bit her lip and then nodded, "Of course. I should not doubt him, or our work. Come, we have to check on our armor."

The siblings walked down to the armory and were greeted by the burly blacksmiths and armorers that worked in the castle.

The Master Smith bowed and grinned. "My lieges, your armor, and my masterpiece, is finished. Both suits are far greater than the one I made your father, may the spirits bless his soul, wherever it may be. Shall I show them to you?"

Sithian impatiently waved his hand and then followed the smith into the armory. The armorer pulled out bag after bag, showing them his handiwork. The armor was nearly identical, but had modifications for Rhiannan's female body. The breastplates, coifs, gauntlets, and hauberks were all blackened metal with the sword and flames of Zaedic emblazoned on the breastplate while the greaves and chain mail were colored red. The helmets sported long red and black plumes of horse hair. Both panoplies were impressive and daunting, and the brother and sister grinned at each other until the armorer carefully extracted two long wooden boxes from the bottom of the cart.

"These, you did not commission, but as Late King Midian had his own sword, I thought you should both have your own arms as well. Princess Rhiannan, I present to you Fâth, it means victory in archaic Hindarün."

Rhiannan opened the box and cackled wickedly. Inside was a scabbard of black leather and red thread. Next to it was a rapier with red gold filigree, black leather, and a hilt threaded with red satin rope. The young woman pulled both out and placed the scabbard on her belt. She sheathed her sword and grinned, adjusting the weight.

"To you, my king, I give you Magra, the magic word of death."

Sithian took his box and opened it almost reverently. It was a single edged longsword, the steel tempered so dark it was nearly black, with a fitted hilt and the word Magra etched into the fuller. The hilt was bound in red leather and the pommel engraved with the sword and flame emblem. The young Magin sheathed it in its red scabbard and strapped it on.

"Excellent, your work is truly magnificent. Will you have the armor brought to our rooms immediately?"

"Yes, Lord Sithian, of course. Right away."

The duo left the armory and strolled to their war room. All of their recently recruited captains and commanders were already seated, talking amongst themselves when the king and princess walked in. The seven men stood and bowed, and then took their seats once more.

Sithian leaned forward and addressed his men, loving the fear and nervousness etched on their faces. "In a few days, we sail across the R'Kunad to wage war upon the vile Nymyñosians, most especially the elfin kingdom of Blackhaven, and its leaders. As we speak, messengers are on the way to recruit all the able men from the villages. Ships are being readied, weapons are being polished in the armories and horses are being brought in from all over. Your men have all been training and my sister and I have been readying our weapon. The city of Blackhaven is not prepared for combat. The walls are weak, the city still recovering. The provinces are in havoc from the war my father wreaked on them years ago. The king and queen of Blackhaven are in dissent with my mother, and they are weak. There is no way we can lose this war."

One of the older men cleared his throat and sighed. “My king, have you ever experienced war against elves? They have the stamina of ten Men, the ability of twenty, and the strength of many more. Pardon my boldness, but that army will have many more Magins and other magic users than we do. We have only yourself and the princess.”

“You’re wrong, Mordrin. Rhiannan and I have our weapon, and that is more powerful than my mother. Several Magins have joined our cause, and we have the Darkwights.”

“How many of the demons are still here? Their leader fled the island, and rumor has it he is residing in Blackhaven,” said another captain.

“Kelus abandoned his nation. He is a traitor to the throne, and the memory of my father. If he was foolish enough to seek the hospitality of the elves, he will die as one of them,” Rhiannan interjected, glaring at the man.

Sithian was about to concede when the door burst open and a worn man stumbled in and fell to his knees. “My lieges, my lords. I have returned from the mainland.”

All present rose to their feet and stared at the man, unsure of who he was. Finally, Sithian recognized him as one of several spies sent out to wander the free kingdoms. “Sebastion, how good to see you back among the civilized. Come sit, tell all that you have seen.”

Sebastion stood and took the offered chair. “Blackhaven is in an uproar. The king and queen are dead, the king was killed by the queen, and the daughter killed her. The princess and her consort have been wed and crowned. Queen Tlonna has begun restorations on the outer walls and the elf bitch Yayènia er’Tiena has been training her army like never before. My king, the city is preparing for war.”

Rhiannan cursed. “How large is the army?”

“There are thousands flocking to the city from the countryside. Still more are coming in from the other towns within Blackhaven, and corsairs from the sea have started docking. As I left it, the army was near ten thousand strong. When I first arrived, there was a rumor in the city that two plains elves were in the castle. If this is true, it may mean that the tribes have joined the war and if that is so, we have very little chance of success.”

“Why should a few barbaric elves make any difference?” Sithian growled, fiddling with a knife, unaware that he had cut himself.

"My king, a Plains Elf trains from age fifteen until their dying day in warfare. Every day they spend at least three hours working with weapons and their body. They are vicious fighters and incredibly strong. You and the princess may have your special weapon, but the elves may have over a hundred. Even if just one elf from each village joins the army, we would be far overpowered. Despite the righteousness of your quest, the army would be torn apart even if it were four times the size of the elves'," said Orlando, General of the Army.

Thick silence followed Orlando's words. No one was willing to speak for fear that Sithian's wrath would explode. Finally, the young king took a deep breath.

"You've done well, Sebastion. General Orlando, send an embassy to the north. Find any mercenaries you can, if what Sebastion says is correct, we will have to wait a few more days to sail, and we need about seven thousand more men. Get slaves, mercenaries, thieves, bandits, rogues, whoever, and get them here by next week. I want that bitch who killed my father's head on a plate, and I can't have that with three thousand men. The rest of you, I suggest you take your troops and put them through the most extraneous training you can until we leave. Go on."

"Yes, my king, right away."

The men left and Rhiannan and Sithian turned back to the window. Finally, Sithian spoke, his voice heavy.

"Anna, you know that between the two of us, I am *the* king."

"Yes, why?"

"I have to find a bride and produce an heir. What if we don't survive this war? Father didn't survive the last war, how can we expect to do better than him? I need your help finding the suitable woman."

"Why? Father never married, he just captured Mother and got her pregnant. Why can't you do the same?"

"Because look at the trouble that has caused. I need a woman I can count on to be mine and only mine. I need her to be fertile and healthy as well."

"I am your heir."

"And if you die? There needs to be more than you as security for our line. You are to get with child as well," Sithian replied, turning away from his sister to examine the map of Blackhaven on the wall. "It is what you were created to do, anyway."

Rhiannan grimaced. "I would prefer to make that decision on my own, Sithian."

The young man pivoted, his eyes sapphire fires pinning her to the spot. "You will do as I say. I was created to follow in Midian's steps, Haydyn to lead the army, and you to ensure the continuation of the line. Haydyn has betrayed us, but you will do your duty!"

"Am I to be a brood mare, then?" Rhiannan frowned. "Who would you have me mate with, hmm? The villagers? Or perhaps your hideous war councilors?"

The king sneered at her, irritated. "Orlando. You will carry Orlando's child."

"Your general? Sithian, how can you not even give me a choice in this?" Anna cried, horrified that her brother meant her to do this thing.

"It is your duty, your purpose in life. He has agreed to this, and so will you. You are to go to him tonight, lie with him as often as possible until you quicken with his seed. Do not disobey me, Rhiannan, do not make me regret bringing you back here at the risk of my own life. During the day, you will find me a suitable wife, and during the night you will be one. Is that clear?"

"You mean for me to marry him?"

"Of course, otherwise the child would not be truly legitimate."

"Father and Tlonna were not married," Rhiannan snarled, frantically trying to weasel out of her predicament.

"That was different. Father needed her power and her bloodline. We need heirs," Sithian growled back, "now go. You will need to be ready for Orlando when he returns. He will be expecting you."

Rhiannan reclined on Orlando's bed, wearing nothing but a light robe, which lay open. The man had not returned, but the young half-breed was not about to go against her nefarious brother's command. For a while, she hoped that the warrior would not return at all, but her hopes were dashed when the door opened and he strode in. He was not ugly, and was in fact quite young, but Anna favored wiry, fair men, and Orlando was bulky with muscles and dark haired.

"Sithian kept his promise," the soldier said as he locked the door behind him.

"King Sithian," Rhiannan corrected automatically, not bothering to shut her robe. "He is your liege, as am I."

"Not any more. You are to be my wife, not my princess, and I will be Prince of Zaedic, as will our sons," Orlando grunted, swiftly removing his clothing.

Anna swallowed and looked away as he crawled onto the bed and spread her robe out all the way. "I have always coveted your body, Rhiannan. There have been nights when I have lain awake, sweating and restless at the mere memory of your curves. I shall enjoy our union."

"Joy to you," she said acidly as his strong hands unceremoniously gripped her legs and pulled them apart.

"Very much so," Orlando replied, and drove himself inside, his hands hard against her breasts.

Rhiannan moaned and writhed, and she did not fight him, but her night passed slowly.

Over the next week, people poured into the city until every house, inn, and field was packed with armed men. Sithian ordered the preparation of ships and had his commanders separate the men into companies. Rhiannan found a pretty young woman named Learia and took her from her family with little ceremony. The girl was the daughter of a high ranking soldier and ignorant. Her soft features and chocolaty doe eyes gave her an innocent look that escaped most of the haggard Zaedicans. Sithian strode into his sister's parlor, irritated that she dared to summon him, but curious as to the reason. When he saw the young woman sitting nervously on a chair, he allowed himself a small smile.

"Her name is Learia, and comes from a family with a healthy history. Her mother has four other children, and her grandmother had six. She is an unwed virgin, the daughter of Sergeant Michael Sing, and educated up to fourth year," Rhiannan recited dully from her position on a lounge chair.

Learia gave Sithian a terrified glance and hugged herself, trembling. The cold young man walked over to her and brushed his knuckles against her cheek. "What year were you born?" he asked, slightly bothered by her youthful appearance.

"Five hundred and thirty-first, King Sithian," she managed in a small voice.

"Sixteen years old then, tell me, Learia, what do you see when you look at me?" Sithian crooned, moving closer and running his fingers into her fine auburn hair.

The girl shivered in both ecstasy and terror as the mad king gazed down at her. "Power," she finally breathed, "and beauty."

Sithian grinned and released her. Turning to Rhiannan he folded his arms and waited until she looked up at him. "You have done well in choosing her. And from what Orlando tells me, you are doing as I bid you. Have you quickened, yet?"

Anna sneered at him. "It is too early to tell, but by Orlando's lack of talent in bed, I doubt it."

"Then you will do more. He says you satisfy him, but that his need is not completely sated. You will do everything in your power to do so."

"As my lord commands," Rhiannan snarled, sliding off the lounge and letting her robe fall open. It was all she ever wore now, as her newly acquired husband popped in at all hours of the day.

The look of disgust that crossed her brother's face at the sight of her naked body made her chuckle. "Poor Sithian," she murmured, moving closer, ignoring the look of revulsion on both his and Learia's faces. "So quick to give my body away in service to the throne, so quick to demand a girl for your own needs. But can you make the sacrifice? What if Orlando is sterile? Will you take the risk and breed with me?"

Sithian shoved her away, gagging. "You would even think of such a thing?"

Anna growled in anger. "Of course not, but you do not think of what you ask of me! You demand and demand, never giving thought to the consequence or the price. You are foolish in your greed, and someday you will lament your decisions!"

The Magin's backhanded slap sent his sister flying over the lounge chair to land in a heap, raven hair tossed about wildly. Learia shrieked but when Sithian turned to her, she went to her knees.

"I will do as you need, My Lord! I swear it! Please, do not strike me!"

"Come. We must be wed," he replied monotonously, pulling her out of Rhiannan's parlor.

The priest was called and with half of the court in attendance, an impromptu wedding was held in the feast hall of Zaedic Castle. Learia was shoved into a slim-fitting white dress at the last minute, and Sithian changed into his ceremonial clothes that consisted of black pants, black shirt, and a red cape lined with black flames. The wedding was quick and to the point, less than five minutes long, and as soon as it was finished, Sithian pulled his terrified young bride into his room and tore away her virginity, ignoring her cries of pain and discomfort.

The city was in a frenzy as blacksmiths handed out hastily made swords, armorers fitted all that they could, and tanners armored the rest. Fletchers and pole turners made small fortunes as the men bought bows, arrows, spears, and axes. Two weeks later, the armada was pulling out of the harbor, the men waving to those left behind.

Tlonna, Losolin, and Aidyn stood shoulder to shoulder watching as Demetrius's carriage and entourage left the city. They were atop the city gate, looking east as the sun rose before them, feeling abandoned. When the procession was no longer visible, Tlonna turned to her assassin.

"Why did you never tell me of your relation with Demetrius and his family?"

Aidyn shrugged. "It never came up, and I never thought it would matter. It was something I did for your father because I loved him. The Plauklers have been my friends for six hundred years or so, and I would not see it changed."

"Did you think I would change it?" the queen asked, hurt.

"No, but as I said, it never came up. Do not be offended by the omission, for it was not done on purpose. I have known a lot of people in my life. It is hard to remember who all I have told you about," Aidyn returned, his tone a little short.

"I only wondered," Tlonna muttered as Tyular's group appeared and disappeared into the gate.

A moment later it reappeared, the king riding at the head of his troupe, golden flame crown winking in the early sunlight. He twisted in the saddle and raised his arm at the three elves on the gate, and then waved again as Aladorn appeared suddenly, startling several of the guards on duty.

"I hate to admit that I miss him," the wiat said quietly, standing next to Losolin.

"We all do, all of them" the king replied, clapping the older elf on the shoulder. "They are good men, and it hurts to see them go."

Once Tyular had disappeared into the wild forest, the four dismounted the gate and rode back to the castle, passing the newly transplanted trees from the wall. Tlonna smiled at the sight of people wandering amongst the trunks, glad to have foliage in the once-barren area. The city was nearly fully healed after its devastation, and the people were rejoicing. The four elves rode slowly, enjoying the warm morning, glad to be among the happy citizens. The day passed uneventfully as the mundane life of running a kingdom moved back into priority.

Once back in his rooms, Aidyn packed a small bag and tracked Tlonna down in her office, ready to travel. "I am going to visit my property for a few days. I will be back by the end of the week."

The queen stared up at him, surprised. "Is there a problem?"

The assassin shook his head. "It is my estate, and I make it point to visit when I can. As I said, I should not be gone long."

"I know who you house in your manor, Aidyn. You do not need to hide it from me," Tlonna said as the dark elf turned toward her door.

"They are my people, and it is my responsibility to see to their security."

"As you wish," she sighed, but he was already gone.

He rode fast through the forest, keeping to the narrow trail that wound through the ancient trees, and he reached his estate by the end of the day. It was set on a ten acre plot, nestled amongst the forest with virtually no visible boundary. The trees edged right up to the wide covered walkway that ringed the two story building, and only a two acre yard behind it was cleared. Aidyn dismounted and led Whäd to the stable that housed one other horse.

When he strode into the foyer of his mansion, he was greeted by the startled and awe-stricken gaze of a young man. "Master Aidyn!"

"Hello, is Moiran here?"

"Yes, Master Aidyn, in his office, Sir. I will get him," the apprentice assassin stammered, pale in the presence of his idol.

"No, go back to whatever it was you were doing. I will find him," Aidyn replied coolly and set off, jogging up the wide stairs and into a long corridor.

Three more students gaped at him, their mouths open and eyes wide as he strode by, moving with that impeccable blend of grace and stealth. When he walked right into a room that once was an observatory, a strongly built man spun around and flicked a knife at him, realizing his mistake too late. Aidyn knocked the blade away with ease, however, and chuckled.

"Ever wary, Moiran, ever wary," he said, sliding into a chair as the Master of the Assassin's College blew out a heavy breath.

"Aidyn, I could have killed you!"

"Hardly. How are things?"

The man sat in his chair across from his mentor and shrugged. "The same as ever. The recruiters bring me kids, and about a fourth of them make it to be full-fledged assassins, and about half of those survive beyond their second year. Right now I have six students, three instructors, and five field assassins. One just returned from a rather nasty contract in the Liberated Lands, chased halfway across the damn place by the bloody Shitan-Kulata. I tell you, ever since they lost their general, the bastards have been running around murdering more than ever. Innocents, mind you, not people who deserve to die. But at least he managed to eliminate his target, some slave driver in the Highlands."

Aidyn smiled faintly, always forgetful of how talkative his friend was. As he continued to ramble about the daily goings on of the College, the elf studied the room, remembering. His father had loved this room, loved looking out at the stars and dreaming. Bailan had in fact loved the entire house, filling rooms with the books he had finally learned to read and the various weapons he came across on his trips to Blackhaven City. The dark elf realized that Moiran was staring at him.

"What are you doing here, Aidyn? You get our correspondence, and we always receive your funds. You have not been to visit us in several years, not since just after the siege was lifted.

The assassin shifted, uncomfortable. "Perhaps I thought I would like to see you and my house again. Am I not welcome in my own college, on my own property?"

"Of course you are! But you have the look of an assassin hunted. I know no contract was failed, not by you, so something is amiss," the perceptive human stated.

"I needed to get away for a while," Aidyn finally confided. "I just need some peace."

"Well, you'll find it here, my friend. Your room is, as always, just as you left it. One of the students' duties is to air it out once a week and to do general cleaning. You will find it quite comfortable."

"My thanks Moiran. I think I will retire for the night, and I will see you in the morning," Aidyn said and walked to his room, memories flooding through him.

When he stepped inside the large bedroom, the dark elf paused, always thrown off-balance by the room. It was sparse, as most of his belongings were in Blackhaven, but the bed was large and antique, nearly four hundred years old, held together by Dietirin's Weave of preservation. The painting on the wall had been a gift of the deceased king as well, a depiction of a beautiful elf maiden and a shadowy figure clasping hands across a break of light. It was entitled *Love of the Assassin,* and it had originally been a joke between the two males.

Aidyn had always proclaimed himself needless of females and pesky love, but Dietirin had seen the bleakness in his friend's emerald eyes. The king had commissioned the painting and given it to Aidyn on his birthday, claiming that he could pretend he was the shadowy figure, and they had laughed. But the assassin had been deeply moved by the painting, and that is why it hung still in his house, in his room. Shaking his head, he dropped his pack on the floor and flopped onto the bed, grimacing at the groan of the wood. Four hundred years was long indeed, even with magic to keep it together.

The next day he gave the assassins-in-training a lesson that none of them would ever forget. Most of them were too awed by his mere presence that they could only stare at him, forgetting that they were supposed to be trying to defeat him. Within seconds he had the six students on the ground, moaning in pain. Two of them had already completed their Torture Term and were halfway through the Shadow term, but the strength and speed with which the elf moved simply destroyed them. Moiran winced when Aidyn sent him a baleful look as the six youngsters got back to their feet, grimacing.

"Not everyone can be as good as you, Aidyn," he said when the elf walked over to him.

"No, but I would think they could handle one against their six. What have they been doing? Cleaning my house is not that important. The College is here for a reason, Moiran, why are they so...inept?"

"They are not inept, Aidyn, they are in awe. Give them a little time to get used to you, and you will see that they do have skill."

"Assassins cannot afford the pleasure of being awed," Aidyn replied stiffly, loudly, and walked back to the group.

"You must live within your mind, aware of everything yet focused on a single thing, your target. If you have no target you must be available to one. We live in very dangerous times, you never know when someone is going to attack you, or if there is someone else that you can protect. Assassins are not just blades in the darkness, we are protectors of the innocent and the righteous, defenders of liberty and goodliness. You know our Creed, to be noble, loyal, and brave, to hold honor deep within the very marrow of our bones," the dark elf said, pacing before the six.

"Every move you make must be made with strength and agility, and you must always be improving your skill. Every day I work myself through a set, varying it slightly each time, else it becomes a day here and there that you ignore it, and soon enough you will have lost your skill through sheer laziness. You must never lose sight of the reason you came here."

"To become an assassin," one of the students blurted, a boy with a too-proud set to his shoulders. "To kill people."

Aidyn's hand itched to strike the impertinent youth, but he settled for a deadly glare. The human folded inward, going pale and trembling with fear. The elf shook his head, sweeping his scowl across the other five.

"If that is the only reason you are here, then you should pack your bags and head east until you reach the Shitan-Kulata. They are the vile murderers who give assassins a bad reputation. They slaughter people for the sheer joy of it, the taste of power, and the touch of geld. We are the College of Assassins, honor bound by the three oaths to retain our morals and allow the freedom of others. We are the professional descendants of Furntil Eldrout, the elven assassin who murdered Brandon Stynbek, freeing the enslaved people of Nymyños. It is because of him that we are here, because of him that the Honor of Assassins even exists. We kill those who would destroy all that we and our fellow citizens hold dear. We kill slave traders and rapists, murderers and corrupt leaders. We protect those we love with our very lives, and if that is not enough for you, get off my estate."

"But you haven't assassinated anyone in a long time, Master Aidyn. You stand by the queen and king as protector, but you don't kill anymore," another of the trainees asked, the only girl in the group.

"I do as I need to, child. As I have said, our purpose is not only to assassinate tainted people, but to protect those who need it. Else we are simply what the ignorant claim us to be, murderers."

The six shared looks of deep wonder, and settled back to listen to the greatest assassin alive.

A few days later Aidyn left the estate, feeling slightly better about the students and his life in general. He took a roundabout course, riding east out of the forest and then turning west once more when he reached Obsidian Way near Sha Bridge. He was halfway back to Blackhaven City when a rider thundered by him and his mount Whäd, who was plodding along slowly as her master delayed returning to his busy life. The assassin watched the fast-fading rider with narrowed eyes for a moment and then shook his head, murmuring to his mare. She snorted back at him, tossing her multi-colored mane and side stepping to show her opinion of the galloping stranger. Aidyn chuckled at his horse, always amused and impressed by her show of emotions. The dark elf let his mare plod onward, and his thoughts turned away from the rider.

Tlonna, Losolin, Haydyn, and Erdwyf were meeting with Daphne, the Keeper of Treasury, to see the expenses of the wall restorations. Tlonna was signing the contract when Yayènia burst in, her eyes wild, her long hair windswept and in tangles all the way to her knees.

"Tlonna, Losolin, a rider from Narnen! The kingdom is under attack. Sithian and Rhiannan have rekindled the war! The other provinces are calling for help."

The four sat in stunned silence until Yayènia growled with impatience. Tlonna stood, her back ramrod straight and her chin proud. "Prepare your troops, High Commander. Daphne, bring me some messengers. Hurry."

Yayènia bowed and then ran from the room, disappearing down the stairs. Daphne curtsied, gathered her papers, and left as well. Within minutes, messengers were running into the room, looking frenzied.

Tlonna addressed each one. "I want you to ring the bell in the Tower of the Moons. Let the city know we are at war. You, I want you to go to the docks, find Harbor Master Jamìn and tell him I need my corsairs. I need you to go to the city armory and get me a full list of what we have, and what we need. You will go to the granary and tell them I need an army's worth of food for a long time, no, bring back the manager, I want to speak with him myself. Go on, hurry!"

The last messenger bowed his head and took off, his blue and silver livery flashing in the torchlight. Tlonna turned to Erdwyf and Losolin.

"I guess we had better get ourselves ready for war. Goodnight Erd."

"Goodnight."

The three elves went off to bed to catch a few hours of sleep, dodging frightened servants and nobles. Just as they reached their tower, the king and queen heard the peal of a massive bell that would be heard throughout the countryside for miles.

The next morning dawned bright and sunny, mocking the fear of the day. After her wash and breakfast, Tlonna met with the manager of the granary and set up the food that would need to be prepared for the army. The messenger came back with the list from the armory, and Tlonna was relieved to see it was full and missing only a few extra pieces. Yayènia showed up looking exhausted, and in the same clothes she had been wearing the day before.

"My troops all store their own weapons and armor at their home. The armory is for beginners and those too poor to buy their own until they earn enough. That is something I command of them. Everyone has been issued the new armor and all the trimmings, we are just waiting for it all to be done. I was up all night with my captains discussing the conditions the troops are in, and the order in which we should march. Tlonna, I do not want you to worry about the army. I will take full responsibility for my soldiers."

"Yayènia, that is a massive burden."

"Yes, but it is my burden. Leave it to me."

"As you wish. Get some rest, Nia, you are going to need it," Tlonna replied, gently pushing the warrior out of her office.

It was three days later when the army lined up on the main thoroughfare, Obsidian Way, and marched out of the gates. Yayènia and Ghealan rode at the head with Tlonna and Losolin. Erdwyf, Miazie, Suneelo, Aladorn, and the humans Tyre, Damon, and Ryun rode behind them along with the standard bearers. Forty-six corsairs rode behind them, laughing and singing bawdy songs. Behind came the army, the foot soldiers first, and then the cavalry, and finally the wagon trains, cooks, blacksmiths, and servants. Nearly ten thousand strong, the army stretched all the way into the forest. Drummers beat out a constant cadence that could be heard miles away.

The head of the line turned as the light pounding of a deer reached their ears. Nebet'thu caught up with them, his pack bursting. The tall elf bowed hastily to Tlonna and Losolin from the saddle.

"My lieges, I will ride to the tribes to rally them. I will find you as soon as I have enough. Do I have such permission?"

Tlonna smiled grimly. "Ride hard, Nebet'thu. Do you need anything?"

The male hesitated and then passed her a piece of bark with a small parchment pinned to it. "They may not listen to me, but if you command it, they will come."

Tlonna took the quill he held out to her and wrote a hasty note, asking the tribes to spare what they could for the army. She handed it back to the hunter and clapped hands with him.

"Take care my friend," Tlonna said, smiling faintly. The plains elf wheeled his giant deer around and rode away from the column at a gallop.

Days passed by slowly as the military snaked across Schelum and the southern corner of Purheae, keeping close to the Jaquisa River and the Kismath Mountains to the south. Halfway through the third full day of moving, Aidyn rode up, looking irritated.

"I returned to the city just as you all marched out. I stayed long enough to supplement my pack and moved out. A message would have been appreciated," the assassin grouched, pinning his friends with an emerald glare, giving his brother a particularly nasty one.

"We thought you were still at your estate," Tlonna said defensively, not liking the look on her dearest friend's exquisite face.

"I said I would be back by the end of the week, and I was," Aidyn snapped in reply, needlessly adjusting his right vambrace. "March off on the bloody war path and leave me behind. Your son was in a flaming fit, too, trying to keep me there. He thinks Feorien is going to try and kill him."

Losolin snorted. "Haydyn can take care of himself. He is just bitter because we made him stay behind."

The assassin shrugged angrily. "Which is fine, but I do not like being told by a frantic prince that half the bleeding city has left for war!"

"Aidyn, you are here now, drop the issue," Yayènia said, punching the dark elf in the shoulder.

He reacted on pure instinct by grabbing her slender wrist and shoving it backward in such a way that it forced her entire body to follow the movement. Everyone gasped as Yayènia jerked involuntarily when Aidyn released her, tossing her arm away from him. With a final lethal glower the assassin stormed away, leaving a rather stunned group of friends behind.

The next evening, as the company set up camp just on the border of the Liberated Lands and the Purheae Forest, a rider galloped into their midst. The man sped through the camp until he reached the large tent where Tlonna, Losolin, and their companions slept.

Dismounting before the horse even stopped, the messenger slid to a halt and gasped out his message to Yayènia and Tlonna. "The Zaedican Army has moved out of the provinces and has begun spreading devastation in the free lands. It has taken hostage the kingdom of Anutch and is headed south, toward the circuit of Alchemian. It is said that the army has a great weapon, a cloaked beast that wields death and ruin with its black hands."

Yayènia cursed. "If they reach Alchemian, they will have access to a great many weapons, things that could destroy entire companies in one blow. We have to beat them there, Tlonna. We will have to surround the city and defend it as best we can." Turning to the messenger she asked, "How many are in the army?"

"Around thirteen thousand, High Commander. But half of it is made up of mercenaries and farm boys."

"Mercenaries can be the most dangerous of enemy, because they have nothing to lose. Go get something to eat and some rest. I need you to leave tomorrow morning and keep track of the enemy. Hopefully, we can reach Alchemian before they do."

The messenger bowed and strode off, his shoulders slumped with weariness. Yayènia turned to Tlonna and grinned. "I need a map, and my captains."

The two walked inside the tent and found all their friends engaged in deep conversation. Erdwyf sat with her head on Ghealan's shoulder, fidgeting with a baby toy. Jaryikin had been left in the city with her nurse. Yayènia leaned on Suneelo's head and cleared her throat.

"My friends, we have some dire news. Our enemy has moved into the Liberated Lands and is headed toward Alchemian. Anutch has been taken, I am sorry Miazie."

Miazie let out a gasp and covered her face in her hands, Damon patted her back though she flinched at his touch. Tyre swallowed, his eyes pained, as were Ryun's. Yayènia continued. "We need to chart out the fastest course to Alchemian, which should be near the Bijoz mountain range. Straight, we will find ourselves in the realm of both marshes, and goblins. I believe there is a pass through the Kismath Mountains, but it is hard to find, and very narrow. It would slow us down. Anyone have any suggestions?" she said, pinning down a map so that everyone could see.

Miazie leaned forward, her face white with grief. "We should take the Corridor of Astinus. It's so old now that most of it is grown over and it has narrowed to a small trail between Sethryn Lake and the mountains, but it would cut our travel in half. Most humans do not even know of its existence so it should be safe."

"The Corridor of Astinus was built when my father was born," Yayènia said in wonderment. "It may be hard marching for the foot soldiers."

"A little exercise never hurt anyone," Aladorn put in, scrutinizing his brother's silence.

Aidyn sat in the corner of the tent, halfway in shadow which, for him, was like sitting in pure blackness so perfectly did he blend. The only sign of him was the glimmer of his eyes as he watched the council.

"But we need to arrive fresh and ready to fight as soon as we reach Alchemian, perhaps sooner. We cannot exhaust the humans in the militia," Yayènia added, not really arguing but simply pointing out any snags in the idea.

Miazie shook her head. "If they're at Anutch, then they have some serious traveling ahead of them. First they must get beyond the canyon lands, and then through the Plains of Arada, which at this time of year are incredibly hot and dry. The Corridor skirts both of those and runs fairly straight through the lowlands. There will be plenty of fresh water and cooler temperatures which should negate a lot of the rough terrain."

Yayènia thought for a moment and then nodded, looking to her council to see if there were any more objections. When there was none, she slapped her knee. "Then it is agreed. We shall take the Corridor. Miazie, where is the closest entrance?" Yayènia asked, pointing to the map and handing the woman a quill.

"About two or three hours from here, I believe, through a pass in the Kismath foothills," the Belau explained, drawing a dot on the map. "It extends all the way to the Bijozs, goes through Mount Sterb, and splits at ancient Shisandr and continues on to Zeynuwn's capital, Kyiji, on Nafâlen Bay. Alchemian sits right on the Corridor of Astinus, at the foot of Mount Sterb," she drew a curving line across the map and ended it on the far tip of Zeynuwn's eastern peninsula. Then she drew a small arrow indicating the foothills of Mount Sterb, where Alchemian was supposed to be.

"Good. We march at dawn. Ghealan, we need to work out our defense plans for when we get to Alchemian," Yayènia said, dismissing everyone else.

The Second Commander stood and stretched, hugging his wife who followed the rest of the leaders out of the tent. It was only a few hours until dawn when they folded the map, stamped out the candles, and bid each other goodnight.

The next morning was misty and cool. The camp disassembled and moved into line, yawning and stamping their feet to warm up. Yayènia stood atop her mount, Verity, and raised her arms for attention; Tlonna used a Weave of the natural wind to carry her voice to the rear of the camp.

"Today, we march toward war and death. Let it not be on this side! We travel on the ancient Corridor of Astinus to Alchemian to attempt to save many innocent lives. We must move swiftly and efficiently. You are the great Blackhaven Militia! You are something to be feared! Drummers! Beat us out a rapid pace!" the elf yelled to the cheers of her soldiers.

The drummers began a steady cadence, a quick march that moved the army. By midmorning, they had reached the entrance to the Corridor, a narrow passage between the vast Sethryn Lake and the mass of rugged mountains that spiraled into the clouds. The soldiers became silent as they approached the foundation of the Kismath Mountains, stepping onto an ancient path, bits of cobblestone peeking out of the mossy ground.

The only sound was the sloshing of the Sethryn against the Corridor's base, and the jingle of armor and horses. There was no wind in the Corridor of Astinus, and the air smelled greatly of moss and decaying wood. Four days passed before the army marched out of the shadow of the Kismath Mountains, and their accompanying shallow canyons, and onto the edge of the Plains of Arada. Breathing a sigh of relief, the company spread out and drank in the fresh air. On the far horizon behind them, they could see the plateau on which the kingdom of Anutch had once stood. Now all that could be seen was a plume of smoke rising against the sky.

The march continued for another week as the Bijoz Mountains came into view. The army was tired and dirty and Yayènia called a halt a day's march away from the base of Mount Sterb. They stopped next to a small lake that sparkled in the sunlight, lapping quietly in the soft breeze. All the soldiers stripped off their armor and dove into the cool water, elf, man, dwarf, and faery laughed and splashed about, the lines of race ever blurred by the Blackhavenites. After a few hours' rest, the army pressed on, feeling lighter and more rested than they had in days. It was nearing midnight when shimmering black walls loomed against the inky sky, wafting softly. No sound came from within the walls of Alchemian, so the fore riders dismounted before the door. Miazie and Damon knocked on the soft door and then leaned in when a patch was pulled back and a face peered out.

"Who goes there?"

"Miazie and Damon, we come with an army and grave tidings. Please let us pass through."

"Miazie? Is it really you?" the door was yanked open and a tall elf grabbed the human up.

"Ardenay! Oh, how I have missed you!" Miazie cried, hugging her friend back.

The elf put the Belau down and squinted at the group behind her. "And who are your friends?"

Miazie beckoned them all forward and introduced them formally to the alchemist, hardly breathing while she did. "This is Magin Queen Tlonna Arune Ewôsdírn-er'Grisholm, King Magin Losolin Ullor Grisholm-en'Ewôsdírn, High Commander Yayènia er'Tiena, Second Commander Ghealan Tomyvon, Captain of the Guard Suneelo Tiena, High Advisor Erdwyf er'Tomyvon, Lord Aladorn of the Wiats, Master Assassin Aidyn Sestuns, Captain Ryun, Captain Tyre, and Commodore Alexander Willis and his First Mate Captain Troaz Griffin."

Her companions all exchanged amused glances, for they were rarely introduced so formally, and all together.

"Ah, you are in high company these days, eh? Come on in then. Lady Elwyn will be asleep, but I will wake her. Follow me," Ardenay said, motioning for them to follow.

The others stared at the immaculate rows of gray, white, and black tents with trepidation and distrust. The nomadic city of Alchemian was a favored bedtime story, half-believed by some, scoffed at by most others. Portable gardens, statues, markets, and everything else were spaced equally between sections of the city. When they reached a large striped tent, Ardenay stopped them and disappeared inside. A few minutes later, they were beckoned inside and were greeted by a firm, albeit pretty woman.

High Alchemist Elwyn Arkayn was a human with cinnamon curls and dark green eyes. She was a bit stout, but moved with grace. She smiled at them and motioned for them to sit on the stools arranged around her desk. She leveled a stare at Miazie, and then sat herself.

"So, Ardenay tells me you are people of great importance, and come with ill news?"

Tlonna stood and inclined her head toward the alchemist. "Yes, I am Tlonna, Queen of Blackhaven, and I bring with me ten thousand warriors, commanded by the greatest elves and men in all the land. They are here to defend your city against an evil force headed this way. They have carved a path of destruction from Narnen all the way to Anutch, and were last seen headed toward your circuit."

The two alchemists present cast each other wary glances and then looked back at Tlonna. Elwyn cleared her throat. "And who, exactly, commands these armies?"

"I command the one that is here to protect you, and Commander Ghealan is my second," Yayènia said, standing. "I am High Commander Yayènia er'Tiena. My army is the finest in the world, and will not shy away from their duties to protect the innocent, no matter how annoying."

"Yes, Yayènia," Tlonna growled, slashing at her friend. "Sithian Midian Rahlan and Rhiannan Leona Rahlan sit at the head of the army that is marching toward us now."

"Rahlan? As in Midian Rahlan? Aderiaen Rahlan's lineage?"

"The very same. They are his children."

"And what abomination bore these monsters?"

"I did," Tlonna whispered, her eyes cold.

The air began to freeze and the alchemists stared at the elf with terror. Elwyn stood and wrapped her shawl tighter against her shoulders. "Ah. So the rumors were true, for once. I am sorry. When is this army supposed to be here?"

"I would not count on sleeping late, human, they were right on our tails, though they did not see us. We took the Corridor of Astinus," Ghealan said, angry.

"All right. Where is your army?"

"They are waiting just outside the walls, Lady Elwyn," Ardenay interjected.

"Then do with them as you will. I will get my people prepared. Ardenay, will you sound the horn?"

"Of course," the elf said, and bowed her way out of the tent.

The others left Tlonna, Losolin, and Miazie in the tent with the woman and went to ready the army. Outside, a low-pitched horn sounded, vibrating through the air. Immediately, lights sprang to life and within minutes, a group of variously dressed beings were rushing into the high alchemist's tent. Miazie was greeted warmheartedly by all, save two, while the others were given a wide berth. Finally, Elwyn snapped her fingers and waited for silence.

"My friends, as you are now aware, we are under attack. Our visitors here have brought us a great army to defend the city," she then introduced them. "There are about a dozen more that were in here earlier. Many of them are quite famous actually. My Lord and Lady, these are Alchemists Sodo, Ardenay, whom you've met, Kryll, Darmian, and Caydy. They are the alchemists who deciphered your prophecy. They are also the most powerful and highest ranking in all of Alchemian."

"Merry meet, all of you. Miazie has told me about all of you. I thank you deeply for your aid," Tlonna said, smiling at them, noticing that it was the elf Sodo and the spryte Kryll that had not greeted Miazie with any enthusiasm, had not greeted her at all.

Her eyes focused on Sodo, remembering the whispered story Miazie had told her, tears in her eyes. He was handsome and elegant, but the change that had been started by the Darkwights had left him looking feral and quite evil.

The elf came forward slightly and looked at Miazie, his mismatched eyes tight. "Miazie...spoke of us?"

"Yes."

"And I bet she told you all of our little secrets, did she? I warned Elwyn of the implications of letting the bitch go," growled Kryll.

"Kryll, hold your tongue," barked Darmian, grabbing her arm.

Losolin frowned slightly at Darmian, and then started when Kryll snapped her teeth at him, which were all razor sharp.

The tense moment was broken by the eleven others returning. They too were all introduced, with startled glances at Yayènia and Ghealan, who were renowned throughout Nymyños for their prowess in battle. They were given a spot to pitch the command tent and fell immediately asleep.

Morning came fast. The sound of drums and horns woke the camp near dawn. Yayènia, Ghealan, and their captains jumped atop their mounts in full armor and rode out of the city before anyone else had dressed. Tlonna and Losolin were the next out, followed by Aidyn and Aladorn. Soon, the entire group had joined the army, as had the high alchemist and her skilled comrades.

On a distant rise, three figures appeared. All wore dark cloaks that hid their faces, though Tlonna knew instinctively who two of them were. The trio directed their horses into a trot and pulled up just a few yards from the group. Rhiannan and Sithian lowered their cowls and leered at their mother. The other rider did not move, but the two siblings dismounted and walked the rest of the distance. The armor they wore was impressive and daunting, covering their entire bodies.

"I see you beat us to the prize, Mother," Sithian stated, waving his arms at the army behind his enemies.

"So we did. What do you want with Alchemian?"

"Their power and the alchemists. With them under my control, we would be truly unstoppable. I'm surprised you haven't thought of it yourself," the young king said, smiling.

"Truth be told, I make a point to not enslave innocent people. Also, they live in the free lands, they answer to no one," Tlonna countered, folding her arms.

"They will answer to me!" her son growled, jabbing at his own chest.

"My people will never answer to you, nor any of your kind, boy," Elwyn snarled, forcing her way next to Tlonna.

"Then it is war. Any last words?" Rhiannan sneered.

When no one said anything, the two walked back to their mounts, and with the third rider, rode back to their hidden army.

Yayènia unhooked her longbow from its place among her many weapons and strung it. Turning around, she and Ghealan mounted their horses and waved their bows at the militia. The warriors roared with apprehension and adrenaline. The leaders mounted as well and rode to join the commanders.

The companions looked at each other and nodded their best of lucks. Silence reigned for a few tense minutes before Yayènia bellowed at the top of her lungs, "SHIELDS!"

Just as the soldiers raised their shields above their heads, a great volley of arrows came screaming through the air.

Ghealan wheeled his horse around and rode through the ranks. "Archers to the front! Archers to the front! Three lines, front line firing and staggered! Move!"

The archers ran to the front and those who were first hit their knees to the ground and drew back their bows. As the advancing army appeared over the rise, the front line let loose and knocked out the enemy front line. The elfin longbows had a much farther range than human or dwarf-made bows, so the defenders had a better chance. The Zaedican Army poured over the rise and crashed into the great Blackhaven Militia. Blood sprayed as the two lines met, men screamed, horses screamed, steel screamed.

Yayènia strapped her bow back on and drew her beloved twin blades. The elf was knocked off Verity and slammed hard into the ground. Leaping to her feet, the High Commander laid about her with her swords. A clearing grew about her as she moved through the mass of people. Different colored flashes of light sparked everywhere as Magins met and battled. Tlonna fought with her sword in one hand and magic with her other, fireballs lancing away from her.

She skipped backward, avoiding two snarling humans and then twisted, her left hand encased in fire, the sword in her right dancing circles about the Zaedican's thrusts. The other man screamed as fire latched onto his clothes and began to incinerate him. Tlonna exhaled and leaned to the right as a spear came thrusting at her from over the flaming man's shoulder. She brought her elbow down hard against her side, trapping the long weapon and jerked forward. The pommel of her sword shattered the man's nose, and took him out of the fight for good. Shaking herself, the queen blew out a breath, and let herself be drawn into the fight.

Losolin flowed through stance after stance, ducking and leaping to avoid whipping blades, sliding his longblade into foe after foe. He went to his knees as a club came sailing end over end for his head, and took the man out by the legs. The elf rolled back to his feet, snatching a Darkwight by the collar and tossing him over his head so that he landed on another of his kinsmen's spears. The demon who owned the spear shrieked in surprise and confusion, staring up at the impaled creature with his mouth open, until a curving longsword grew from that same open mouth. Losolin yanked his sword free and brought it up just in time to deflect a whistling mace aimed for his shoulder. As he shook the most recent unfortunate human off his blade, the king stalked into the fray.

Ghealan stood a few paces from Erdwyf, the former dancing a deadly waltz with his bladed quarterstaff while the latter lashed out with her new bladed whips. Suneelo slid through his foes with his longblade, moving too fast to catch. The corsairs fought with sword and knife, reveling in the battle. The alchemists defended their home with whatever weapon they had, which resulted in a lot of contained explosions.

Aladorn and Aidyn kept their eyes on their king and queen while they brawled away, two dark figures flickering through the milling masses, silver flashes of steel the only sign that they were fighting rather than dancing. Damon stood by Miazie, his red magic keeping most enemies away, but the few that got by Miazie skewered with her katan. The melee moved slowly back toward the canvas wall. As the thousands pressed upon it, the beams tumbled downward, and the combat poured into Alchemian itself. Apprentices and children fled farther into the city. Tents crumpled under the onslaught as the day wore on. After a few hours, the fight was still going strong, against all odds. Both armies, numbers against skill, battled back and forth, neither gaining the advantage for long. As night fell, so did a light rain, turning the ground to slush as both rain and blood soaked it. People fell, stumbled, tripped, or slipped, only to be trampled as they attempted to stand.

Days passed.

The Blackhaven Militia surged back and forth under Yayènia and Ghealan's iron command. Pike men in the front line rushed the sneering mercenaries who aimed crossbow bolts at their hearts.

Tlonna blocked the armor piercing bolts with an undulating shield of magic as her army forced themselves further, chanting. Tlonna spotted Sithian roaring commands at a group of men who charged forward with their arms in the air. Multicolored magic sizzled through the air and slammed into Tlonna's shield. With a grunt, she enforced it so that it kept the other Magin's power away too. She spotted Yayènia opening her mouth in a command that was lost amid the return howls of her soldiers. Ghealan rode down the lines waving his battle axe in the air, having snapped his quarterstaff in the first brawl. His horse, Selwyn, snorted at the tangy smell of blood, rolling his eyes. The large elf finally reached her, his breath whistling from between his teeth.

"My queen, how are you holding up?"

"I am fine, Commander. You?"

"Never better. Listen, the enemy lines have advanced in a few places where we do not have Magins holding a shield. They have reached the city and begun slaughtering the alchemists. We outnumber them, but the alchemists are too panicked to allow us to help them. We cannot get through."

Tlonna cursed and then motioned to three Magins that had volunteered their services back in Blackhaven. They bowed.

"Can you hold this shield while I am gone, or someone comes to relieve you?"

The men studied the shield for a moment and then looked out across the advancing enemy. "Aye, we can."

Tlonna wordlessly passed them the pulsating magic, which immediately turned orange, brown, and blue when it touched the other Magins' hands. Tlonna reined Takîreaes around and followed Ghealan away from the lines. They emerged into the city proper and stopped to study the havoc being wreaked within. Alchemists ran from laughing soldiers, tossing glass vials behind them that exploded in different ways. The Magin spotted the elf Sodo snapping his fingers in the air seconds before flames burst into an enemy. When Tlonna and Ghealan reached him, he smiled grimly.

"Nytrynhimmel, means flaming water. It is a new chemical Ardenay discovered when Miazie was here. Dangerous and deadly to any who are touched by it and the heat caused by friction."

Ghealan grinned and watched in fascination as a soldier who lunged at Tlonna was consumed by liquid fire. "Good work," the commander said and led Tlonna away.

The two rode through the city, cutting off any foe that had made it into the encampment. A howling man missing a leg grabbed Tlonna's ankle as she rode by and nearly wrenched her out of the saddle. Hissing in fury, the elf brought her sword down and sliced his hand off, and then his head. She hacked away at men who were terrorizing screaming alchemists, dismembered bodies filling the trail behind her and the commander.

Another night passed, and the attacking army withdrew, not in retreat, but in exhaustion. Yayènia had her army set up camp where they had when they reached Alchemian, and begin to set up defenses. The wounded were tended to, the dead burned upon pyres of war. Elwyn and Jacinth had been killed, among a thousand others. Ryun wept bitterly, as he had bidden his wife to stay behind with the maids so that she would be safe, but Jacinth had greatly feared for him, and the idea of living in a world without him, and had followed him into battle, where she had been slaughtered.

Wearily, Tlonna and her companions went into the command tent and sat around the table. Yayènia pulled out a map Elwyn had provided her with earlier.

"Here, we let down our defenses and therefore we endangered the very people we are trying to protect," she marked the parchment with a charcoal pencil. "Here, we held strong, but a few people were worried that we held too strong and let our inner defenses fall. Around the edges, we fell to their pressure. We do not know this land any more than the enemy does, but we have allied ourselves with those who do. Sadly, they just lost their beloved leader and are not very willing to help us anymore. I rode down to the edge of the city, and there is a ravine to our backs. If we get forced to retreat farther into the city, we will be endangered. We must swing the armies around, reverse positions." Yayènia swept her charcoal around the map and then crossed where she had marked the positions of the armies.

Ryun leaned forward, his eyes red from grief. "High Commander..."

"Yes, Captain?"

"If we reverse the enemy, then won't we be forcing them into the city, into the innocent populous?"

"Yes Captain, but we will not allow them a chance to even think about the city. We will be hot on their flanks until we force them into the ravine, where they will fall to their deaths."

Suneelo cleared his throat and adjusted his chair. "How...exactly do you intend to...reverse...the enemy?"

Yayènia smirked at her husband. "Well, Captain of the Guard, we push them around."

"What she is trying to say," Ghealan interjected, "is that if we push at one of their flanks, and only one of their flanks, it will eventually force the soldiers to rotate. Like this," he put his hands together so that his right fingertips pushed on his left wrist. He rotated them.

Those who had not caught the concept let out an understanding 'aahh'. Yayènia snorted. Commodore Alexander glared.

"That is a nautical tactic, High Commander, clubhauling actually. Land lubbers aren't often heard to use such ways."

"Why not use them when they fit so well, Commodore?" the elf shot back.

The man rolled his eyes.

Tlonna sighed and rubbed her eyes. "Look I am tired, so I know the rest of you must be tired. Go to bed, I am afraid we have a long day ahead of us, several, in fact."

The officers nodded, mumbled their assent and staggered to their own tents.

The Zaedican Army did not attack them the next day. Yayènia and Ghealan had each squadron switch off throughout the day building defenses and resting. A barricade of sharpened poles was positioned facing toward the enemy, the wood having been salvaged from the destroyed wall. The children and elderly were moved to the, thus far, untouched eastern side of the city. As evening encroached, Yayènia looked up in amusement when something soft and cold landed on her face. Snow was drifting from the indigo sky, wafting gently on the currents of cold air. Winter had descended upon them. The soldiers were let off duty so that the next few patrols could take their place.

They arrived in full armor, as had the others, but they also wore their thick mantles and fur-lined gauntlets. Losolin rode up and dismounted before the warrior. He watched her momentarily as she ran a thick cable across the top of the spikes. Standing atop a ladder, she was able to look down on him.

"Tlonna wishes me to ask you what more needs to be done to the western side."

Yayènia hopped down and had a tall fire nymph take her place. The warrior smiled at the creature in encouragement and genuine affection. The nymph had risen swiftly through the ranks of the army and was now a squadron leader, and a wicked fighter.

Out of earshot, the warrior grinned. "Losolin, even if we left half the wall open and unguarded, there would be no way we would lose this war. You see," she held out her hand, "winter has come to spread her cloak over us, and the snow is white, not black. A good omen. The people of Zaedic live in a warm climate, they will suffer. We may not live here in this area, but we know this land. My soldiers are prepared for winter, the others are not. Miazie told me that Alchemian never let offending weather into their city, but were often out on the land looking for materials and elements and such. They will know how to handle such conditions.

"When we were on Zaedic, do you recall ever seeing a cold day, even though we were there during winter? It never rained there. The bitter winter of central and western Nymyños will destroy them."

Losolin shifted. "Yayènia, do you really think we will be here that long?"

The female snorted. "Wars cannot be won in a few days, Losolin. That is the mistake so many generals and commanders make. They do not take into consideration that their army might be destroyed. They do not bring enough supplies to support their army for more than a few weeks. We have brought enough to supply us for a few months, and I will periodically send out an issue for more if and when we need them."

"But, you do not think we will be here for very long, do you?"

Yayènia stopped. "Look, wars can drag on for years. My campaign against Aderiaen lasted almost five years, and never really ended. It just ground to a stalemate. It only came out in our favor when Aderiaen was killed by Midian. Then their forces withdrew to Zaedic, although we did not know that at the time. A few years later, Midian started it up once more. Now the battle has been flared up again by Sithian and Rhiannan. I am not leaving this position until either I am dead, or they are. We may be here for three more days, or three more years, it does not matter. War does not stop just because we all have better things to do."

"But, what about my city? Our city?" Losolin demanded.

"What about it? Haydyn is ruling in your stead. He has been instructed by all of us in how to be an efficient, benevolent, strong leader. He has Tlonna's blood in his veins. Besides, Narda is there, Feorien, Kelus, people Tlonna trusts to run her kingdom. Your mind cannot be there while you are here. Otherwise, you will find yourself digesting steel before you know it."

Losolin mulled that over as they walked through the streets of soldiers and alchemists to the western side. Neñyos followed obediently behind, snorting his displeasure at not being ridden.

After a few paces of silence, Losolin addressed her again, his brow slightly furrowed. "Aderiaen was Midian's father, was he not?"

"Yes."

"But you said a second ago that Aderiaen was killed by Midian. Aderiaen was killed seventy-seven years ago. Midian was only, what, thirty?"

Yayènia made a derisive noise in her throat. "Midian was one hundred and sixty years old, give or take a year, when I slit his throat. He had slowed time's touch on himself. Midian thought his parents were too lenient on the people, too weak in war, and most of all, not good enough for him. A few days after his eighty-sixth birthday, he raped and murdered his mother and then drove a magically enhanced sword through his father's skull."

"He killed his own parents?"

"Losolin, do not sound so disbelieving. After all, Tlonna killed her mother."

"I am not surprised, I just thought Midian was proud of being Aderiaen's son. He was a deeply disturbed man, was he not?"

Yayènia laughed, a long, belly laugh that caused her soldiers to stare at her in concern. "Understatement is your specialty tonight, my friend. Midian lost himself in his ambitions and his false belief that he was better than everyone around him. He destroyed lives in order to justify his own. I remember when Aderiaen's death was announced. There was no celebrating in the streets by the people he had tormented because they knew his son was so much worse. People stayed inside for days, afraid to come out lest they be slain. The sad part was that they were not far off the mark. When Midian first came to power the death toll rose indelibly. Hundreds were slaughtered by him and his minions."

The High Commander's mirth was long gone, turned now to serious recollection. Her icy eyes were clouded with painful reminiscence. "I remember riding out every night with the Silvers, when we were down in Kismath and Schelum. Each time we returned with at least half a dozen bodies, massacred in their own homes. Then suddenly it stopped, all of the Rahlan forces disappeared into thin air. Now we know they went back to Zaedic, but for nearly three decades there was not a whisper of trouble other than the fact that elves were disappearing with rapidity. And again, now we know that it was Midian's Darkwights enhancing their numbers."

She sighed, removing one gauntlet to brush stray hairs out of her face. "Midian Rahlan was his father's equal in ruthlessness and racism, but he was a thousand times more insane. Aderiaen let me walk out of his camp, Midian would never have done that. In fact he frequently used it to try and bait me into fighting him. Called me a coward and a traitor to my own cause. A child killer," she gave Losolin a small smile. "He knew how to goad me."

"But you never fought him, face to face, until Zaedic?" Losolin asked, not about to let the rare moments where Yayènia was talkative pass him by.

For an answer she pulled off her other gauntlet and pushed up her vambrace, revealing the inside of her wrist. A scar, puckered and white, ran the length of her forearm, cutting at a slight angle toward her thumb. It wasn't big but the wound had obviously been grievous.

"Eleven years ago we fought inside the gate of Blackhaven just before the city fell. Someone shot me in the back of the knee, making me stumble, and Midian stepped inside my guard. This is from his blade as I went down. I was able to scramble away and stabbed him in the side, but that was the only time other than Zaedic we ever personally fought. There were several occasions where we tried to get at each other but our officers always stepped in the way."

"Twice I fought him, and twice he beat me so severely I was in the infirmary for a very long time," Losolin said, shaking his head. "He was so fast and strong."

"You fought him twice in the same day, and survived. Not many can claim such a thing. Only Aidyn, I believe, and he was with you," Yayènia reminded her brother-in-law.

The king nodded his acquiescence but remained silent.

"You are right, though," she said after a moment. "He was incredibly fast."

"Who was?" Aidyn interjected, coming upon them as they walked.

"Midian," both the elves said in unison, staring at the assassin, wondering where he had come from.

"Ah, where is Miazie's husband?"

Losolin frowned at his dark friend. "Damon? Last I saw him he was headed back toward his and Miazie's tent. Why?"

Aidyn merely shrugged an answer and moved off, blurring away from his startled friends.

"Did he always move like that?" the king asked, incredulous.

Yayènia scowled after the assassin. "No. Only within the last year or so, though he has always moved with a style all his own. I remember when we first met. He was...somewhere in his four hundreds. I was in my sixties. Florwen Hune had just collapsed into civil war and I was in the company of Governor Arakis, taken to the castle to be paraded about like the whore that I was forced to be. Dietirin was disgusted and left the room, but Aidyn stayed, always vigilant." Yayènia chuckled faintly, shaking her head again. "He broke Arakis's wrist when the bastard slapped me for not acting happy."

"That was your first meeting?" Losolin asked, always surprised by Yayènia's brutal past.

"After that I was indeed smitten. He has always been beautiful, but only recently has he affected that strange, blurred way of moving. Actually," she frowned, thinking. "It has been since we found you and Tlonna."

"Do you think that has anything to do with it?"

"I cannot know, but it may be. I fear it is a mystery that will not be solved any time soon," the warrior replied, stopping as they reached Tlonna.

The queen turned when she heard Yayènia's voice and smiled at her husband.

Yayènia pulled on her gauntlets again and cocked a hip. "Your dearly besotted told me you wanted to know what else needs to be done over here."

Tlonna nodded, sighing. "We have the barricade up and the cable is in place. The trench is dug, and the pitch has been spread."

The High Commander nodded her head and then clapped her queen on the shoulder. "Sounds like you are done here. Let the soldiers get some rest."

The men and women within earshot thanked their leader profusely and staggered to their campsites. A dwarf in full armor stomped up to Yayènia and gave her a quick salute.

"High Commander, scouts report movement in the enemy force."

"What kind of movement, Captain?"

"It looks like half the cavalry is riding back northward. A few of their horse archers went with them too, probably as guards."

Losolin turned to his sister-in-law. "What do you think they are doing?"

Yayènia rubbed the hilt of her hip sword with a gauntleted hand. After a minute, she cursed. "They are going back for reinforcements. Captain, find Commander Ghealan and give him the report. Tell him to meet me at the gate and bring the Silvers. Dismissed."

The dwarf bowed and jogged off in what could be considered a sprint for his people. Yayènia strode off, her silver and black cloak of office fluttering behind her. Losolin and Tlonna ran after her.

She walked into her tent and began pulling her long hair into a tight braid. She coiled it around the back of her head and pinned it down. The king and queen watched her adjust all of her armor starting with the greaves of braided and burnished steel over her leather trousers. She stripped off her airy tunic and replaced it with one of thick wool, though it only reached to her lower ribs, leaving her muscled midriff bare. A breastplate of the same style as her greaves went on next, reaching to just above the end of her shirt. Yayènia strapped matching vambraces onto her forearms and then picked up her thick cloak. They all bore the bloody-clawed badger of House Tiena and the Tree of Blackhaven.

"I wish your armor covered more of you," Tlonna said as the warrior draped the cloak about her shoulders.

"This allows me to ride easier, it is more comfortable, and I like the way it looks on me," the warrior replied, picking up her helmet.

"Indeed," Losolin said, his eyebrows raised.

"Indeed?" Tlonna drawled.

The elf rammed a skull cap over her braid and then followed it with her plumed helmet. She looked positively alarming. Yayènia began to strap weapons to her body, her twin katans first.

"Besides, when you are as good as I am, you do not need full body armor. I have to head off this party. I am going to leave Ghealan in charge in my stead. Next will be Suneelo and then Sargotarh. I am going to take with me my personal elite. Ghealan knows what to do in case the enemy attacks, as do the soldiers. I do not know how long we will be gone, but you will all be fine. I promise," she started to leave her tent and then turned back. "Whatever you do, do not let them win."

Tlonna opened her mouth to reply, but the elf was already through the flap. They caught up with her as she mounted Verity. The long-legged mare snorted as her owner pulled her head around. With a half-smile, Yayènia nodded to her friends and rode off. They watched in apprehension as the light caught her and shot in all directions off her numerous weapons. She had taken them all.

Riders appeared out of all sorts of places, falling into line, all cloaked in silver and blue. They were Yayènia's personal elite, rumored across the lands to be the fiercest fighters anywhere. Most people called them the Silvers because of their special cloaks, which almost matched the High Commander's. Their true name was *Zephyr Leifen*, Silver Damnation.

They numbered only forty-six, both male and female, of all races. In fighting, Yayènia only discriminated in skill.

Tlonna and Losolin ran to the gate to find Yayènia and Ghealan in an intense argument. Both elves were screaming in Parlêthian. The *Zephyr Leifen* sat atop their mounts in armor matching Yayènia's, though the males wore no upper armor at all, just close-fitting leather tunics, their helmets, and cloaks, which they had wrapped around them to ward off the cold.

Finally, Ghealan threw his hands up in the air and took his orders from Yayènia. When she finished, her second in command grabbed her into a fierce embrace and then let go just as quickly. The elf rode off, brown hair flying.

Yayènia remounted and saluted the king and queen. Her fist clapped over her heart and then shot into the air. Without another word, she swung Verity around and galloped out, followed by her Silvers.

Aidyn grabbed Damon's elbow as the man began to turn into his tent. Miazie stopped as well, studying the dangerous elf with a suspicious eye.

"Get your filthy hands off me, college assassin," Damon spat, twisting his arm out of Aidyn's grasp and stepping back, one hand on his sword hilt.

The elf shoved him violently, a disgusted sneer on his face. "You are a disgrace to both the name assassin and Magin. You live without honor and you are married to a woman who does not love you. How does that make you feel?"

Damon lunged forward, his hands punching out toward the dark assassin's face. The two grappled for a short moment, but though the human was a skilled fighter, the elf had centuries on him. Aidyn deftly turned aside one of the Magin's jabs and slammed his own fist into the man's sternum, knocking the wind from him and sending him to the ground.

"You would do well not to do that again," the elf said calmly, placing his boot on the back of Damon's neck.

"Stop it," Miazie snapped, her eyes filled with frustration and guilt. "Let him up, Aidyn."

"I simply want to talk to him," the assassin coldly. "But I do not take insults from a murderer very lightly."

"I am no more a murderer than you are," Damon snarled into the ground, wheezing as Aidyn's boot pressed harder into his neck.

"I do not kill innocent people. I do not raid campsites and rape women. I do not force women to marry me, I do not head a contingent of killers bent on the decapitation of leaders within Nymyños. I do not slaughter tribes of nomadic people just because they have better feeding ground than I do. Do not *ever* compare myself with you."

"Sweet spirits, Aidyn you're killing him!" Miazie cried as the elf's foot pressed harder into her husband's neck, cutting off all air.

With a snarl of fury, the assassin released the other and allowed him to get to his feet. "Why do you care, Miazie? What is he to you other than your captor?"

"He is my friend, Aidyn. I will not let you kill him," the woman replied after a moment's hesitation. "He may have been misguided when he took me into his bed, but he is a good man with a good heart. If what you say is true, you cannot kill him without becoming a murderer yourself. Damon, listen to what he has to say."

Both males stared hard at her, but in the end she simply stepped to the side, holding open the tent so that they could walk inside. Aidyn went first, ducking low inside the human's tent and searching for a place to sit. He situated himself on Miazie's cot and waited impatiently for Damon to follow.

The man glared at his wife. "You do not know what you ask of me, Mia."

The Belau lifted her chin. "I know exactly what I ask of you. The Shitan-Kulata *are* a bunch of murdering thieves, and you know it. Aidyn is held by the Honor of Assassins. Can you say such a thing?"

The Magin sneered at her, but he snapped aside the tent flap and stalked into the room, standing upright before the dark elf. "Say your piece."

Aidyn sniffed at him, for once having to look up at someone. "Sit."

Damon huffed a great sigh but he obliged, sitting on his own cot across the little aisle. "What?"

"This battle, this war is not going to be won by our army alone, not with the alchemists, and not with whatever plains elves Nebet'thu brings in. We need warriors used to severe odds. Bring your people some honor, Damon, General of the Shitan-Kulata, bring them here and set them loose on prey that deserve to die."

"You want me to return to my camp and lead the assassins into battle against the Zaedicans? Are you nuts? They would kill me on sight, first of all, and never would they agree to put themselves in danger for a cause not their own."

"Again you prove the vileness of the guild assassins," Aidyn scoffed, disgusted. "You once led them, why should you be afraid of them?"

"It is our way to kill anyone who has been away from the camp for more than a month. And they believe I deserted."

"Not far from the truth, the way I hear it. But go your own way, Damon, just know that the addition of the assassins would prove invaluable to our cause. It could save thousands of lives."

"You think to convince me with notions of nobility and loyalty? That is your creed, not ours, not mine."

The elf sniffed again, shaking his head. "All right, let me put it another way. Either you go to your people and bring them here, or I will go to them, along with some associates of mine, and there will no longer be a guild to bother the college. Your choice."

"You think you and a few of your friends could take out the entire Shitan-Kulata? You are crazy!" Damon exclaimed, though Aidyn heard the tremor of uncertainty in his voice.

He simply smiled slowly, his emerald eyes never blinking. "Your choice," he whispered finally and stood to leave. "I would make up my mind soon, were I you. There are several...graduates...in this camp."

As Aidyn strode from the tent, Damon gulped in spite of himself, a sliver of fear stabbing his chest. Miazie entered a few moments later, concern writ on her face.

"I saw Aidyn leave, what did you talk about?" she asked, noticing the slight depression in her bedroll where the assassin had been sitting. She inhaled briefly, catching the alluring scent of the elf and then sat down in the same spot.

Her husband looked at her with empty eyes, the brown dulled by the choice before him. "I must either go to my people and bring them here, or condemn them to death."

"If you go to them you will probably die," Miazie said, catching on to his fear.

Damon nodded his head. "I do not understand why you like that...college assassin. He is vile and cocky. What gives him the right to demand the things he does?"

The Belau chuckled. "Aidyn is cocky indeed, but he has lived many lives in the line of fire, protecting those who feared him even as they hid behind him. He has lost a great many people in his life, the most recent of whom is Dietirin, who could probably say he knew Aidyn better than anyone. They had been friends for several hundred years. I suppose when you get to his age, with his experiences behind him, you are allowed to be demanding. He has a kind heart, and he is an unwavering friend. You would do well to follow his advice."

"And get myself killed?"

Again Miazie chuckled. "Either way, it is your choice, Damon. Piss Aidyn off, or don't. Many would choose the latter even if it was suicidal, because the former most certainly is more so."

Chapter 10

The Counter

Yayènia and her elite soldiers passed the encampment of the Zaedic army a few hours after nightfall. Hundreds of fires burned, veritably screaming their position. A few of the Silvers begged her to let them take a few shots, but in order to catch the cavalry, Yayènia forbid them. In their fierce loyalty, they did not question her judgment or even frown, but swiftly put away their bows and reached for their reins once more. After almost two days of nonstop riding, even Yayènia was drained. She called a halt just before the mountain entrance to the Corridor of Astinus.

They did not use tents, but slept beneath the stars, rolled in their cloaks. Yayènia was taking first watch when she felt, rather than heard, one of her warriors approach. A woman of incredible agility, dressed in gray pants and the cuirass that did not quite reach her navel, stood waiting for permission to join her commander.

Yayènia patted the ground next to her, "Sit, Abbey."

The woman obliged and sat next to her commander. "They will not wait for the reinforcements."

Yayènia shook her head. "I do not think so. The Rahlans have always been ambitious, and these two more so."

"When, do you think, will they attack?"

"I do not know. Tomorrow or next week. I just do not know. I only wish I could be there when it happens."

Abigail wrapped her arms around her knees and pulled them in. "High Commander, I...I think I am with child."

Yayènia sat still for a moment and then finally sighed. "Why is that?"

"I am late, and I have been getting ill in the mornings. High Commander, I am sorry if I have upset you in any way. A woman at the city gave me a mixture of herbs that would kill the infant before it is born."

"Abbey! I would never ask you to do a thing like that! And I am not upset by any means. It is a wonderful thing, having a child. I just wish you had told me earlier. I would have had you stay home so that you and the baby would be safe."

Abbey looked hurt. “High Commander, I would never do such a thing. It is my fault, and my burden that I am with child, not yours, or the peoples’.”

“It is no burden,” Yayènia replied.

“Yes, it is. I am weakened and vulnerable, I will grow large and cumbersome, and when it is born, I will be unable to do anything but take care of it,” the woman argued, her voice acidic.

“No, that is not true. Lady Erdwyf has an infant and look where she is now. Here, along with Commander Ghealan, and when we were home, she and he both came to their work. Their lives are just merely enhanced.”

The human punched the ground. “Damn it! I don’t even know who the father is, Yayènia! I don’t have the strength of an elf, and I don’t have the money of the personal friend and advisor to the queen. I don’t want this child!”

Shocked, Yayènia stared at her companion. After a few tense seconds, she asked, “How do you not know who the father is?”

Abbey gave a sick laugh. “I was at a ceremony a while ago, and drank too much. I slept with many men that night, and cannot even remember who they all were.”

“Were any of them Silvers?”

She laughed again. “Almost all of them, maybe even all of them.”

Yayènia had to laugh. “I admit, Abbey, that most of the males are pretty attractive, but to sleep with them?” she said.

“I know, I know. But, if you want to know, I have a feeling who it is...”

“Yes?”

“William.”

Yayènia guffawed. “William? Why do you think it is him?”

The human blushed crimson so that even in the dark Yayènia could see it. “He was the only one who...who pleased me,” she whispered the last words.

“Then tell him you are pregnant with his kid and forget about it. Will is a good man, and very pleasing to the eye. He will be proud of himself.”

At that moment, someone else approached. Both females turned to see who it was, and then stared. William was standing behind them, curious.

“I heard my name.”

Yayènia looked at her warrior in a new light. He was tall and slim, muscular as they all were; with round, hazel eyes and chin length brown hair. His long lips were smiling, slim hips cocked as he stared down at the females. His leather tunic did little to hide the rippling muscles down his stomach or the shapely pectorals. She stood and brushed off the seat of her pants.

"Well," Yayènia said, "I will leave you two kids alone. Goodnight," she drifted off into the dark and took up her watch on the other side of the camp.

Morning dawned with a light dusting of snow and a quiet wind that ruffled their hair. The Silvers broke camp in a matter of minutes and were riding before the sun was halfway up the horizon. By midmorning, Laren, an extremely short elf, coming up a few inches shorter than most humans, scanned the ground and pointed. A line of depressions in the soft ground showed where the riders they were chasing had camped.

Yayènia reined Verity around and looked off into the distance where the tracks led. "Well, at least we know where they are headed."

Far away, a miniscule dot rose on the background. The plateau city of Anutch.

The land passed swiftly, as did the days, while the Silvers rode. It was midday when they caught up with their prey. Over a hundred archers and cavalry rode toward the city at a casual pace, arrogant in their superior force. Yayènia signaled a halt and let her warriors adjust themselves for battle. Their quarry was still within eyesight when they remounted and rode off once more. The Silvers silently surround the party and took aim. Forty-seven riders fell to the ground, arrows piercing their flesh. The Zaedicans burst into confusion. They swiveled around, looking for their attackers, but found none. Another volley of arrows whistled through the air and took down another forty-seven.

Finally, one of the archers spotted one the Silvers and shouted to his companions. The warrior, Yaedin, burst from his cover, his warhorse bellowing. The elf strapped his bow to the saddle and drew his sword. The other *Zephyr Leifen* exploded out of camouflage and joined him. The party stared in shock as nearly two and a quarter score scantily armored warriors rode in full charge toward them. The archers let loose volley after volley, but their attackers' skill kept them from being skewered.

Regaining their senses, the Zaedicans arranged themselves into position. The Silvers burst through their front line, slaughtering those in the front. Soldiers stabbed at horses, but the animals were trained in battle and kicked out with all four hooves. Their teeth ripped away cloth and flesh, hooves crushing skulls. A dwarf bellowed in battle fury as he swung his hammer, destroying a horse and rider, who, as they fell, took out two others with their weight and momentum.

The men felt impossible terror as they recognized the legendary silver cloaks their assailants wore, and saw the plumed helmet of their leader. The captain, however, gritted his teeth and howled a war cry, brandishing his halberd in the air. His men reformed and began going after single warriors. A crowd of nearly twenty men grabbed the legs of a spryte's horse and heaved. The horse fell, snapping its neck on the ground while the spryte was thrown off.

She landed on her back, the wind knocked out of her lungs. Gasping, she struggled to her feet only to have a lance run through her breastplate and into her heart. When she was dead, the score of men turned to another warrior.

Yayènia dismounted, baring her teeth in a soundless growl as the men turned to her. Recognizing her, some tried to flee. She yanked a spear out of a dying soldier's belly and pointed it at the group of struggling men. The elf lunged forward, turning. The head of the spear whipped across the faces of the front men, ripping out eyes and shattering noses. They screamed, clutching at gaping wounds. Using her momentum, Yayènia aimed as she spun, she sent the spear thudding into a Zaedican's back as he tried to overpower Yaedin. Screaming guttural nonsense, the warrior turned back to the pack of men, drawing her twin katans. Yayènia twisted through the milling soldiers, ducking and spinning, her blades constantly slashing, reversing, and parrying.

Two men came at her wielding cumbersome halberds, trying to poke at her bare midriff. The elf brought one blade down on top of the weapon coming in at her left, severing the head from the haft with one powerful blow. The stick still jabbed her slightly, but it simply scraped her side, not even breaking the skin. Then, with her right sword keeping the other at bay, Yayènia leaned to the side and brought her foot up into the broken end of the haft and kicked outward. The pole slammed backward into its wielder, driving hard into his groin. As soon as he hit the ground, the warrior spun, bringing her sword up under the other halberd and stepped inside the man's guard.

His eyes went wide as the snarling elf slashed her right katan down, splitting him open from shoulder to hip, and slammed her elbow into his face. He stumbled backward, letting go of his halberd and falling to the ground, where he was then trampled by his own soldiers. Good thing he was already dead. Yayènia spun, shaking the cumbersome weapon off her left katan, and brought it up just in time to deflect a cleaving broadsword aimed at her head. She kept her parrying blade up high, sliding it along the Zaedican's until they locked hilts, and then she rammed her other sword into his unguarded belly.

With a hiss, she yanked it out and let him fall.

"Haooh!" someone yelled and it was repeated by all the standing Zephyr Leifen, which numbered forty-five.

Yayènia turned and surveyed the scene, her eye twitching when they landed on her two dead warriors. Laren strode up to her and shook his head, the top of which came to her chin.

"They butchered Ceephen, twenty against one, and they killed her horse as well," the elf reported. "And Moarn was caught by three in the back while he was battling another. He managed to take them all down, but they had pierced his lung."

"Then they died with honor," Yayènia said solemnly, always heartbroken yet proud when one of her elite was slain.

"The leader is with William," Laren continued, pointing at the blood covered human who was holding a stiff-looking man by his hair.

"My name is Yayènia er'Tiena, High Commander of the Blackhaven Militia and the *Zephyr Leifen.* What is your name?" she said as she strode up to the furious man.

His lip curled and he spat a sticky glob at Yayènia's feet. "Elfin slut. I shall die before revealing anything to you."

"Why is it always that? Death can be easily arranged, but everyone always tells me what I want to know long before they even start begging for death. Begging, you see, like hapless dogs," the warrior returned tritely, removing her gauntlets.

Again the human hocked at Yayènia, but before the spit landed Yaedin slammed the butt of a lance into his cheek, nearly driving it all the way through. The man let out a surprised howl of pain and then spat once more, this time to remove the several shattered teeth. He cursed avidly, shaking his head, blood and spittle flying from his lips.

"What is your name?" Yayènia demanded.

"Captain Seamus," he moaned, leaning to one side.

"Well, Captain Seamus, I did say you would cooperate, did I not? Will, tie the good captain up. The rest of you, see if the survivors have anything useful to say. If not..." she shrugged, making a face that was full of mock regret.

Her warriors all chuckled and moved off, checking the few living Zaedicans. Minutes later there were none left, and a very wide-eyed Seamus was being strapped to Yayènia's mare. He glared at her with baleful eyes, his lips snarling at her though he could no longer utter an intelligent sound for the gag shoved in his mouth. When the Silvers had once again mounted, carrying with them their two slain comrades, Yayènia gave the signal to move. When Seamus began to writhe in the saddle in a last attempt to free himself, she simply slugged him across the face and urged her mare onward.

The return journey took almost a week. When they passed the Zaedican Army, Yayènia was pleased to see that their numbers were fewer than before, by a substantial margin. The Silvers rode into Alchemian to the sound of cheers and clapping. The High Commander was even more pleased to see that her own army's numbers hadn't been damaged too much. Losolin, Tlonna, and the officers met the warriors at the command tent. When Yayènia dismounted, she shoved Seamus down before Tlonna. Her warriors gently lifted Ceephen and Moarn from their saddles and took them to the prep tent for the fallen.

"We caught them just a few leagues short of Anutch. It appears they have turned the plateau into a base of operation, with another full garrison standing watch."

Tlonna gestured at the man on the ground. "And this is?"

"This here is Captain Seamus, leader of the cavalry sent back for recruits," Yayènia replied, patting him on the head.

Ghealan grinned. "Nia, I am proud of you. Usually, you do not show enough mercy to keep prisoners alive."

Yayènia grinned back, pulling off her helmet and tucking it under her arm. "I know, I must be growing soft-hearted, eh?"

"What can he tell us?"

The warrior pursed her lips. "Not much, he was not very trusted. But, he knows numbers, and I figured you would want to speak with him yourself."

Tlonna nodded, staring down at the trembling man, Losolin looking off in the direction of the departed *Zephyr Leifen.* "How many did you lose?"

Yayènia's face twitched in a slight wince. "Two, Ceephen and Moarn. They died bravely, fighting off several of these wretches."

"Then they shall be remembered with honor," the king said solemnly and sighed. "Damon is missing."

The warrior blinked at him. "Miazie's husband? The Magin assassin?"

Tlonna nodded. "Both Miazie and Aidyn know something, but neither one is talking."

Yayènia snorted. "They probably killed him, which is no less than the blighter deserves. Forcing anyone into marriage is a crime against...life."

"As much as your concern for my freedom touches me, Nia, I feel obliged to inform you all that Damon is alive, as far as I know," Miazie said, coming up from behind the elves.

The warrior narrowed her eyes at the human, staring down at her. "As far as you know?"

The Belau gave the taller female a sly grin. "Aye, as far as I know. Aidyn may know more, but I doubt you'll get any information from him."

"Are you bedding him?" Yayènia asked bluntly, voicing everyone's secret thoughts.

The look of surprised amusement that passed over Miazie's face was genuine. She let out a barking laugh and ended up wheezing. "*Bedding...Aidyn*? Are you insane?"

"What, I would if I were not married," the warrior said honestly, winking at her husband who was glaring at her from behind Losolin. "As would Tlonna, I am positive."

Both Losolin and Suneelo turned to regard the queen with inquiring eyes, but she simply laughed, waving her hand in the air. "My physical relationship with Aidyn is of no one's business but mine, and his. Do not worry my love," she said, patting Losolin's cheek, "We have only ever slept in the same bed once, that I can remember."

That silenced everyone but Yayènia, who was howling with laughter even as the still kneeling Seamus fell over when her knee *accidentally* connected with the back of his head.

Chapter 11

College versus Guild

Two days later, the Zaedicans attacked. The shrouded third rider headed the charge, black robes billowing behind. The army careened into the defending ranks. Soldiers screamed, howled, and roared at each other. The snow fell in thick sheets, slowing the progress of the mêlée.

Yayènia, who had been polishing her armor, leapt atop Verity. The mare had no tack on her; the elf wore only her gray riding clothes. Tlonna and Losolin met up with Aidyn as he was adjusting his scimitars on his hips.

The assassin grinned wickedly. "Let us go kill some humans, eh?"

Tlonna shook his hand and replied, "Good luck my friend. I hope to see you at the end of the day."

The elves bid each other farewell and rode into the fray, catching sight of Erdwyf and Suneelo as they crashed into the battle, blood spraying with their every attack. The male threw himself backward when a black-eyed demon came at him with an attack faster and more furious than the Darkwights under Midian's control. Swearing, Suneelo ducked low and drove his shoulder into the demon's belly, launching it up into the air and flipping it over his back.

The creature bellowed in anger as the elf dropped it hard, and screamed when he buried his sword deep into its chest. Yanking the blade out, Suneelo ducked again as a broadsword came whistling toward his head, and he lifted his own weapon and let the adrenal-rushed human impale himself. Shaking his head at the ridiculousness of it all, the Captain of the Guard was finally allowed into the milling masses of the battle.

Erdwyf hissed in surprise as three demons came sprinting toward her, scarred and bleeding faces twisted into howls of loathing and fury. With a loud command, she cleared the area of Blackhaven soldiers and drew two lengths of chain from her belt. Whirling her arms in the air, the chains unfurled and at the end of each sat two small but wickedly curved blades that screamed through air as they snapped at full-length. The three Darkwights fell away, clutching at various dismemberments, screeching in agony. Erdwyf swirled her arms again, spinning her entire body, then tucked her arms to her chest. All around her lay moaning and writhing adversaries and her chains went still, coiling about her feet as they lost their velocity.

Gasping, Erdwyf looked about her in astonishment, and then looked up as the Zaedicans that had been approaching fled in absolute terror.

Aidyn had both of his scimitars out and winking in the sun as they twisted through the attackers. He bent low and stuck his arms out, slashing two humans across the belly, disemboweling them. As he came up, his foot connected hard with a Darkwight's nose, driving the bone deep into the brain, and his elbow cracked across the surprised face of another Zaedican. He felt the wind of a spear pass close by his head and he turned in time to catch the missile by the very end. The momentum jerked his arm back, but he used it to keep it moving as he swung his arm out, reversing the direction of the spear. The thrower stared at him in terror as the dark elf launched himself into a spinning leap, the spear screaming out before him.

When Aidyn landed, he dropped the spear and looked down at the back of the man's head. Then he realized it should have been the front of the man's head. He grinned down at the grotesque sight of the man's torqued neck, and had to dive out of the way of a brawling mass of soldiers.

Ghealan swept his hips out of the way of a jabbing sword and brought his elbow down on the soldier's hand, numbing it so that he dropped his weapon. The elf brought his knee into the man's sternum, cracking the process and driving the wind from his lungs. With a well-aimed kick, the Second Commander launched the man backward, where he landed on top of two of his fellows. Roaring in battle lust, Ghealan drew his battleaxe and spun it out to the side, splitting another man in half as he came in at him with a sword raised to strike. He shook the gruesome decoration from his axe and had to quick-step backward to avoid a Darkwight's slashing cutlass.

"Big elfie, lots of muscleses!" the demon shrieked, its red eyes staring off in different directions.

Despite his obvious mental impediment, the demon knew how to work a blade. The elf dropped his axe into its loop on his belt and drew his sword, a wickedly curving, double-edged shortsword. Ghealan found himself on the defensive until finally he blocked the cutlass with a parry hard enough to send it out wide and he ended the wight's suffering with a strong thrust to its heart. With a disgusted shiver, the warrior stepped away from the dying demon and turned back into the brawling fight.

Losolin leapt over two soldiers rolling in the muck and skewered a Zaedican in the back of the neck. Extracting his blade proved to be a challenge, and so when the next foe ran up to the seemingly defenseless elf, the king simply lifted the sword, human and all, and battered at the horrified soldier until the corpse flew free. With a short chop, Losolin cleaved the man's shoulder from his neck and sighed as his blade became lodged yet again. When a Zaedican came at him from behind, Losolin kicked out, slamming his boot heel into the unfortunate man's knee, snapping it backward so that for a second the soldier was standing on legs facing opposite directions. Then he toppled and lay writhing in agony. When the king finally got his sword free, again, he extracted a bottle of oil and splashed it over the steel. When next he hewed a man in twain, the blade slid free and Losolin heaved a sigh of relief.

Tlonna lifted her blade to block an incoming attack and pushed it off, sending the man over backward. She turned to parry a thrusting javelin and grunted when someone rammed into her from behind. She grabbed at the hand that was trying to get a hold on her armor and jerked it forward, slamming the unfortunate soldier's head into her back, knocking him unconscious. The javelin wielder stared at her uncertainly, his eyes wide behind the visor of his simple iron helmet.

He jabbered at her in some unknown language and poked at her again, blinking wildly. Tlonna's face contorted in repulsed confusion and she grabbed the javelin and hacked off the end with her sword, twisting the haft from the foreigner's fingers. He dropped it and drew a shortsword, once again jabbering.

"Quiet," the Magin Queen snarled and flicked her fingers outward, launching white magic into the man.

He screamed as the magic crawled up his body and then he became very silent indeed as the magic dove inside his chest and blew up his heart. Tlonna shook her head and stepped over the body, her sword diving into the back of one man while her free hand loosed devastating magic into another.

As the soldiers milled around her, Tlonna sliced away at them, creating a swathe in the battling armies. Suddenly she realized a whole contingent of soldiers was trying to get to her, heedless of how many of their kinsmen were dying around them. From the corner of her eye, the elf caught the sign of a burning M pounded carelessly onto their breastplates.

Remembering Deric Wellenton, Tlonna's lip curled in disgust.

Cleicks.

With renewed vehemence, she lifted her hand, fingers perpendicular to the ground, palm facing outward as her sword continued to keep the regular soldiers at bay. A pulsing ball of white light formed against her palm, and when it grew large enough, the queen shoved it forward. It careened into the advancing Cleicks, incinerating a dozen of them before burning out. Then she was surrounded, fingers digging into her arm, trying to pry off the defending steel. Furiously, she swept her sword out and down, cleaving two Cleicks in half and freeing a space for her to escape. She successfully removed herself from the surrounding ring, but was still sorely outnumbered. Her sword and power worked frantically to keep them away, but there were just so many. Panting, Tlonna felt the bite of a sword as it slipped past her defenses and sliced across her forearm. Worry started to edge its way into her mind, that is until an obscure black form whirled into the attackers, laying three out in the first two seconds of its arrival.

"Aidyn!" Tlonna gasped as the assassin bounded to her side, scimitars working so fast she could not determine the individual blades.

"Glad to see me?" the dark elf laughed, sliding his right blade across the throat of an encroaching Cleick.

"I always am," she returned, now standing back to back with him as they fended off the humans.

Several minutes later, they stood panting in a ring of dead or dying bodies, all alone in their struggle. Tlonna turned and wrapped her arms about Aidyn's slender waist.

"I thought I was done for. You arrived just in time, as always," she mumbled, hugging him tightly.

Disconcerted, the assassin patted her on the back, careful not to hit her with his sword. "It is my job, after all," he replied when she let go.

Tlonna looked up as a great shout went up, and she watched in amazement as the Zaedicans and their cohorts fled, sprinting across the battleground as fast as their weary legs could carry them. Behind them was a field full of the dead and dying, their cries filling the air. Aidyn took a deep breath and put his hand on the Magin's shoulder.

"Come, we need to meet back at Alchemian," he said, drawing her away from the terrible sight.

The battle was in full fury the next day when a horn sounded from the eastern border of Alchemian. Tlonna and Suneelo, who were fighting shoulder to shoulder, looked up in disbelief as the herald announced reinforcements, though whether they were friendly or not, the two elves could not know. A great cry went up from the back of the Zaedican force, but the cry quickly became screams as their rear was shredded by the whirling katans of midnight-robed assassins. Tlonna and Suneelo, who stood at least a head taller than a good portion of the seething fighters gaped in astonishment as, at the head of the unexpected group, rode Damon. He only had one eye, but he rode in with a snarling scream of vengeance.

"And you thought I was bedding his wife," Aidyn muttered as he came to stand beside them. "I do good things every now and then."

Tlonna sent him a nefarious smirk and nudged him in the elbow. "Miazie is a good thing, Aidyn."

Suneelo burst into laughter when the assassin grinned, flashing his pearly teeth. When the high elf's mirth faded, the dark one sighed, shaking his head.

"I simply thought to bring Damon and his lost souls some honor. It seems my shaky faith was rightfully placed."

"It looks as though Damon paid a price, however," the queen remarked, pointing out the bloody bandage over his eye. "But he has honor, thanks to you."

Aidyn shrugged. "We shall see how well my collegiate assassins handle having guild rats in their ranks."

"You think there will be dissention?" Suneelo asked, stabbing a fleeing Darkwight in the shoulder as it flew by.

"I know there will be, but I have informed my boys to remain focused, and to not let prejudice or pride goad them into tarnishing their creed."

Tlonna turned a speculative eye on the assassin. "How many of your 'boys' are here, Aidyn?"

One side of the dark elf's mouth curled up into a wicked smile. "Seven. Though four of them are not actually from *my* college. Two are from the Narnenian house, and two from Seaduens."

"There are Seadueni elves fighting for Blackhaven?" Suneelo gasped in astonishment.

Aidyn shook his head. "The College of Assassins is a network of brothers, brought together by a creed, by the three Oaths, to uphold nobility, loyalty, bravery, and most of all honor. The Seadueni assassins were raised the same way I was, under the same edicts. We are of a similar mind, and they will fight for a cause they believe in until their dying day. Do not fear any subterfuge from them."

"If they are your friends, then I will not," Tlonna stated calmly, though she too was shocked by the revelation. "I did not know you had brought friends."

"I did not bring them," the assassin admitted. "They came of their own free will. The Seadueni were in Schelum, hunting a warlord, when I rode through and they saw my campfire. The Narnenians were in the Kismath Mountains chasing a goblin shaman and much the same happened. My three met up with me at Sha Bridge when I was hastening after you, after hearing the same news I had."

"Then, pass on my love and deepest thanks," Tlonna replied, bowing her head to Aidyn who nodded.

The three elves turned when the Shitan-Kulata rode up to them, their general dismounting before them. "Queen Tlonna, I bring you the entire encampment of the Shitan-Kulata. They will follow none but my command, but I am yours to command, as always."

"I am in your debt, Damon," the Magin Queen murmured quietly, noticing the murmurs of dissent coming from the assassins before her as they spotted Aidyn, who was quite recognizable.

The Magin assassin turned to face the elven one and bowed his head ever so slightly, allowing him a good look at his missing eye. "I wish no trouble from your associates, dark elf. Keep them away from my men, and mine will stay away from yours."

"And if they meet in battle?"

"How are mine to know yours?" Damon said, shrugging. "As I said, keep yours from mine, and mine will stay away."

Aidyn merely smiled and stepped out of the way of the general, sweeping his arm out. The human remounted his horse and signaled him men forward. They followed him slowly, each one passing the elf and glaring down at him in utter revulsion.

"They hate you, yet they come when you send their general off to get them, for that is what happened, is it not?" Tlonna asked when the last assassin had ridden away.

"It is. And yet they came," the dark elf replied, shaking his head. "I did not believe they would."

"And so you are proven wrong?" the queen assumed, frowning as she, the assassin, and Suneelo began to make their own way back to Alchemian.

"We shall see," was all Aidyn said.

Chapter 12

Sheer Frustrations

Officers of the Blackhaven force rode back and forth shouting commands at their troops. Yayènia and Ghealan had put a strong defense in the front. Legions were advancing, their long weapons diminishing any threat of outbreak. Archers ducked behind the Legion shields, rotating for a continuous assault of arrows.

The soldiers were chanting, their voices rising into the snow-flecked sky. Their words were incomprehensible, but the effect was daunting.

With each word, the soldiers advanced a step, shoving their foes backward. Those who fell were trampled. Three figures sat atop a slight rise watching. Tlonna felt a chill run down her spine at the trio. Her fear was not long lived, for the cheers of her people reached her ears. Looking back at the battle, Tlonna saw the Zaedicans fleeing. Arrows rained down upon them, dropping the stragglers. She glanced back at the rise to see that the trio had disappeared.

Losolin and Damon hailed her and the Magin rode to them. Her husband sported a new gash on his shoulder where the armor had gaped. Damon had many wounds, though none of great concern. Both males smiled at her as she dismounted.

"Another victory today," Losolin said, hugging her.

"Yes, but how many more will we have? They caught us off guard today. Though it did not do them any good, next time we might not be so lucky."

The males squinted at her. Tlonna frowned. "What?"

"A bit bitter, are we?" Damon replied, irritated.

"I tire of watching people die while most of the time I am shielded behind the lines, forced to watch when I could, and should, be aiding them."

Losolin gave her an agreeing look, but Damon shook his head. "You are the queen, my lady, we cannot risk your life as we have been. Yayènia's decision is one I will agree with."

"A queen, and king, should be at the head of their people, taking the first hit and killing the first foe. We led them here, why should we not lead them to the battlefield itself?" Tlonna replied, folding her arms as she glowered at the human.

"Perhaps they do not even know of you," he pressed, shrugging. "Perhaps they believe you are just another queen, which, to the regular soldier you are."

She snorted. "I am queen, Magin, and I brought about the death of their damned king! And have you not forgotten that just a few years ago, you and I were running for our lives because mine was constantly in danger? What is wrong with you?" Fuming, Tlonna jumped atop Takîreaes and rode away.

Losolin followed her, telling Damon to find Miazie.

"Loni, Damon is doing his best to reconcile what he has done in the past. He is trying to make you feel better, and you know he has it right. A good portion of those soldiers out there do not know of you or me. I do not like standing on the sidelines any more than you do, but what happens if we do die? Haydyn is not ready to be king, no matter how great his improvement."

Tlonna ignored him until she reached their tent and stepped inside. He handed Neñyos's reins over to their servant and followed his wife inside.

"Tlonna, will you listen to me?"

She turned around and glared at him.

"With every day that passes I feel more and more of a showpiece, a mantle upon which a crown rests, and nothing more. The soldiers bend to Yayena just as deeply, if not more so, than me, and most do not know my face. They see the crown and bow. I know why Nia asked that we stay behind and not fight, but then why did we come? Why march at all?"

Losolin sat down on their big cot and put his fingertips together. "Perhaps just being here is bolstering the army, giving them strength of hope and determination. Your story is legend after all, the greatest Magin ever to live, spoken of in prophesies. You rode at the head of the army and commanded them when we were recruiting. Even if you sat here, in this tent, for the duration of the war, they would fight for you because they believe in what you can and have accomplished. Yayènia is the face of the army, their mother of sorts, of course they are going to know her face. She is the one who gave them glory and honor and tells them what to do. Do not feel useless just because she gives the commands."

Tlonna nodded slowly, still frustrated but willing to accept her husband's words.

At that moment, Yayènia herself walked into the tent. "Tlonna, Losolin, I need to speak with you."

The two elves made room on the bed and turned so that they could see the warrior.

Without preamble, she said, "I am getting old."

" *What?*"

"I am getting old! I have never been caught off guard like that, and I fear it will only get worse. I was slower today, too. I missed a block too, and got sliced for my incompetence. I am losing my touch."

Losolin had to swallow a bark of laughter. "Yayènia, my friend, you are not losing your touch, or getting old. You are only four hundred and ninety-eight! Everyone else is older than you are except the humans, me, Tlonna, and Erdwyf, and her only by seven years! No one can fight or move like you, except Ghealan, and he is five hundred and fifty!"

Yayènia held up a finger to silence her king. "I got worried today. I thought I might get hurt. I am growing old and cowardly."

Tlonna fought the urge to slap her sister-in-law. "Nia, getting nervous does not mean that you are either old or cowardly! Nine hells! You were at the front line in the center of a full out battle, without armor, and you got *nervous*. Few people can claim that they get just nervous. Besides, courage is not the lack of fear, but rather knowing that something greater than fear is in danger and must be protected.

"Yayènia, you are one of the greatest warriors and protectors in the entire land. Probably the entire world! You are unpredictable, and that makes you dangerous. You do not stick to one strategy just because it worked before. You change your style, you think things out before you go into battle. You have a quick mind and even quicker reflexes. Your heart and mind is not bent on merely slaughtering as many foes as you can, but rather preserving as many innocent people as possible.

"People know who you are because you have done such great things for them before. Those who do not know you are quick to learn because they admire the stories people tell them. Heroes who 'get old' before their time, or 'lose their touch' are never great heroes, but rather the side stories to those others, others like you.

"You fight for the greater good because you know what it is like to be at the command of evil. You have been there, and so you help as best you can to save others from the fate you have suffered. I would be more worried about you if you did not feel anything at all during a fight. I am relieved to know that you can be nervous. Honestly, it is a weight off my shoulders to know you have that spectrum of emotions," Tlonna said, watching Yayènia carefully.

The warrior was staring at the ground. After a long pause, she said, "No one has ever put it that way. I always tried to explain it to myself, but failed. Tlonna, do you actually believe that?"

"Yes, I do."

"All of it?"

"Yes, every word."

Yayènia stood, brushed off her knees, and sighed. With a salute, she walked out of the tent.

The battle stalled for many days. The winter came in full force, shielding the armies from one another. The Zaedicans floundered in the snow, many dying within a few days of the storms. The alchemists managed to reinstall their weather shield so that the city and its defenders were warm and dry.

When nearly a week passed and no attack came, Tlonna had Yayènia send out a scout. The man came back with dire news.

"Their reinforcements have arrived. Apparently, they were informed of the disappearance of the messengers that High Commander Yayènia dispatched. They have doubled the numbers of the Zaedican military."

Tlonna dismissed him and turned to her commander. "So, what do we do?"

The officers all looked around at Yayènia who was staring at her hands. "We have no reinforcements. We brought with us all that was available. With their numbers doubled, we have little chance of success in a pitched battle."

Ghealan shifted. "Send emissaries to the other provinces. I know some of them have supplied us with a number of men, but this is a war for the freedom of all lands, not just Blackhaven. My queen, you said once that King Demetrius of Kajgenia would be friend and ally to any of our causes. Would he be willing to meet us?"

Tlonna sucked on her bottom lip. "Demetrius has already provided us with thousands of men. He is afraid to leave his kingdom unprotected. Send an embassy to him, but do not hope for much. He has spared all he can."

Yayènia pulled a piece of parchment from a container behind her seat. With a quill, she wrote down Kajgenia.

"What about the others? Seaduens?"

"Would we be willing to risk civil war within the ranks to have the numbers of the Seaduens Militant?" the one and only dwarf captain asked.

"Their numbers are great, Captain," Ghealan replied, shrugging.

"Orthak is correct though," Yayènia commented. "Our two forces, and rulers, have never gotten along." With a smirk, she glanced at Tlonna.

"Send to them anyway. If they come, we will know they are more concerned about the war than a blood feud," Losolin said.

Yayènia began to write it down, but then paused. "Wait...do you forget that Losolin murdered Iyaner? And several of his other family members have found death at the end of a Blackhavenite sword."

Erdwyf sighed, "Losolin is right, if they come, we will know they are more concerned with their livelihood than a stupid feud."

When everyone started arguing with each other, Tlonna raised her fist and the tent fell silent. "Yayènia, send word anyway. It will do no harm."

"Fine," Yayènia grunted, "Schelum?"

The elf captain Sargotarh snorted. "And who would come, High Commander? That kingdom, and Kismath and Purheae have been trounced to within an inch of extinction. We could only hope for maybe a hundred from all three, combined."

"Yes, but a hundred nonetheless. Remember, Sargotarh, in war, a single soldier can tip the scale of victory," Yayènia replied.

Erdwyf shook her head. "Yayènia, what soldiers they have left are too terrified to do more than stand atop a wall and shoot arrows. It would not be worth the risk of the messenger sending to them for aid."

"All right, Narnen, then."

"Yes, definitely," Erdwyf said. "They were the first to be attacked, and they will come, if any survived. Besides, I do have diplomatic pull there. If anything, I can command some forces to come."

"Florwen Hune?"

"They are an army of Dwarves. Their soldiers would be a great addition to our force. They command brute strength," Suneelo said. "Orthak, you originate from Florwen Hune, what say you? Would they come?"

The dwarf grunted uncomfortably. "King Barukh is a good dwarf with a strong set of morals. He would send aid if he can afford it, but we must not forget that Florwen Hune is the neighbor of Narnen. They may be under attack already."

Yayènia wrote it down and then sighed. "Flousen Dua."

When no one said anything, she groaned. "Should we at least send to the damned reclusive land? It cannot hurt, can it?"

"Begging your pardon, High Commander, but no one has heard anything out of Flousen Dua for years and years," Sargotarh said. "Not since the fall of Aderiaen have they done anything. After Duan was razed by his hordes, all the people fled into the deep forest and have not been heard from since."

"I am aware of that, Captain. But it would not do any harm to send a request to them."

Tlonna rubbed her eyes. "How many more are left?"

"Only three. Talenias, Arseninis, and Zeynuwn."

"Not Talenias. Athelias is crazy, and was allied with Midian. We do not know where he stands, but Demetrius said the economy has been suffering greatly. He is just as likely to spear his own men as the enemy," Tlonna said. "I would not trust him with a letter opener."

Orthak bowed his head. "Excuse me, my Queen, but don't you think that even sending an emissary would be at least a decent gesture? I mean, you were there about four years ago. Maybe with the death of Midian Rahlan, Athelias has calmed?"

"No, Athelias did not come to the coronation, a sign of his allegiance, and there is no way his insanity could ever be taken away. The man's mind is lost," Tlonna replied.

"Then I would rather not risk it. Arseninis?" Yayènia asked.

"Tyular may not let go of any more troops, but it would be worth a try. He is a good man," Aladorn put in, toying with his sleeve cuff.

"Last one, Zeynuwn."

Suneelo patted his wife on the shoulder. "Nia, from what we have read up on them, they are not a country to be trifled with. They are near to where we are and will be a very valuable asset. Send to them. Emperor Tahi-tat would be glad to help in our little war; he likes to align himself with power."

All the officers and leaders laughed dryly at the elf's dark humor. It was any excuse to laugh.

Erdwyf drummed her fingers on the table. "Might there be a little problem with calling to Zeynuwn?"

Yayènia looked at her, eyebrows raised. "What?"

"A messenger would have to cross the Bijoz Range during winter. Only highly trained elves would be able to stand that kind of crucible," she turned to the humans and dwarves who were now glaring at her. "No offence, officers, but it is true that only an elf's body can withstand such severe conditions. Our anatomy can adapt to extreme environments better than other races."

Grudging agreements were murmured and the elves relaxed.

Yayènia sighed. "You are right, Erdwyf. I did not think of that. We cannot really afford to send out any of our elven soldiers. Our forces are already too small."

At that moment, Trey, a *Zephyr Leifen* warrior bowed himself into the command tent. The human bowed to Tlonna and Losolin and then dropped into the formal bow to Yayènia.

"High Commander, Abbey is very sick...she cannot stop vomiting."

Without preamble, Yayènia jumped to her feet and shoved her soldier out of the tent.

"Take me to her."

The council in the tent hastened after her, wondering. When they reached the Silvers campsite, they saw Abbey clutching her stomach and retching into the latrine.

Yayènia rushed forward and knelt beside the woman.

"Abbey...is it...*the baby*?"

Abbey nodded, gulping. "I can't stop. I think I lost it."

"No. Where is William?"

Trey responded as Abbey began vomiting again. "He's in his tent. Won't come out, High Commander."

"Stay with her. Losolin, do you think you can help her?"

Losolin nodded and put a comforting hand on her heaving back. His magic sank into her and immediately she stopped retching. Exhausted, Abbey collapsed in his lap, gasping for air. Yayènia found William in his tent pacing, his flesh white and his hands clammy.

"William!"

The human turned and immediately went to his knees. "High Commander. Abbey, is she…?"

"She is fine. Why are you not out there with her?"

"I-I tried, but suddenly I couldn't go past the tent yard. I was so scared something would happen to her or the baby. I just…I freaked. I knew that if she or the infant died I would be responsible, as the father and lover. What if she threw the baby up or-or…"

Yayènia shook her warrior until he stopped babbling. "She is not going to die or lose the baby, and she certainly is not going to *throw the child up*. I do not think that is even possible. Now get out there and help her!"

The elf shoved the human out of his tent and dragged him to where Abbey was still laying in Losolin's lap. The crowd that had gathered drew apart to let the warriors through. William knelt next to Losolin and took Abbey from him. The elf stood and brushed off his pants.

Tlonna nodded at him, watching the human couple in concern. When Yayènia came within reach, the queen snatched her. "Do you mind explaining this?"

"It is the business of the warriors to confide that to any who do not already know, Tlonna."

"Nine hells, Nia. I am your queen and you will do what I command you to do. Now, I *command* you to tell me what is going on."

"Yes, my *queen*," Yayènia sneered, wrenching away. "Abbey told me when we left to stop the recruit team that she is pregnant. And that William is the father. They are not married, and they were both intoxicated. I do not know what they plan on doing, and I do not know why being pregnant would cause such an illness in Abbey. It concerns me greatly. I was hoping Losolin would be able to tell me more than what I know."

Taking the hint, Losolin spoke. "The infant within her is healthy and as it should be, but I am not sure she is. Obviously, her body is fit and healthy on the outside, but I do not think her insides are all that wonderful. When I was cooling her stomach, I felt something…tainted. It was like…something was fluctuating faster than normal in her womb. I do not know."

"Her hormones are going crazy. It happens in all human women during their gestation period. It induces vomiting because the muscles around the womb are tightening and loosening rapidly. Elves don't experience it because you are too immune to illness and your bodies adapt to such changes faster," a breathless Miazie said, catching up.

"It's common in human women, really. It's typically called morning sickness but can sometimes happen at any time in the day. It also has to do with blood level and whatnot. Depending on what Abbey has eaten recently, it could be what is affecting her."

The elves stared at her.

Finally, Tlonna put an arm around her friend and grinned. "Are we not lucky to have a Belau with us?"

The foursome smiled and walked back to the command tent.

Chapter 13

Back in the Battle

The war exploded the next day with unforeseen fervor. The Zaedican Army crashed into Alchemian before the sun fully rose before the horizon. The camp burst into a frenzy. Horses screamed and whinnied as soldiers leapt upon their bare backs. Men and women shouted to each other across the yards and the sound of weapons being hastily drawn rang through the air.

The three blacked-cloaked riders pulled off to the side of the havoc. Sithian and Rhiannan watched coolly as their third companion danced in his saddle, eager for battle. Tlonna watched them warily. She felt the sickening tingling in her spine and stomach that meant someone extremely powerful and evil was nearby. Snarling, the elf egged Takîreaes onward toward the trio. Sithian spotted her when she was still a few hundred yards away and patted his fellows on the arms to alert them.

They all stared at her until she was but a few yards away. Her son grinned and bowed his head mockingly. "Ah, Mother. So nice to see that you're still alive."

"Would you really care, Sithian? Would you mourn for my life if I was dead?"

Rhiannan snorted. "Like you would were it us? I don't think so. We're in the middle of war, Mother. You have unwisely put yourself in grave danger by coming up here. I do not think this is what we should be talking about. We should be talking about what should be said at your funeral."

The younger Magin lunged forward on her horse and swung at Tlonna. Bending backward, the queen slammed her fist into her daughter's abdomen, knocking her out of the saddle.

"Never come at me, Anna. I will always win," Tlonna snarled and then turned her glare on the third rider. "And do not think I do not know who you are. There is no one as tainted as you. No one, other than those that are already dead, that make me feel such hatred. My people will be warned of your presence."

She spun around and rode away from the threesome, her heart pounding. So caught up in her worry, the elf did not notice the lance flying toward her. The steel tip crashed into her shoulder plate with such force that it knocked her off Takîreaes.

Tlonna rolled to her feet and wrapped her hands around the wooden pole protruding from her pauldron. Blood was rolling down from the wound, staining the inside of her arm. Breathing rapidly, she pulled the weapon out of her shoulder. Blood stopped rolling and started oozing out of the hole. She pressed her hand to the wound and beckoned to Takîreaes.

The stallion trotted up to her and she mounted painfully. She rearranged her grip on the lance and sought out its owner. He was easy to find.

The soldier was staring at her with a mix of pure terror and disbelief. He was standing on a small rise that had allowed him his aim. Seeing her find him, the man attempted to turn and flee, but the pressing mass around him disallowed that. Takîreaes forced himself through the crowd until Tlonna halted him. The soldier stood trembling in his sabatons.

Tlonna bounced the lance in her palm and smiled at him, her eyes cold. Fear glazed over his face and she shoved the point through his chest. Takîreaes screamed as a stray sword nicked his flanks and sheared away a piece of flesh. Tlonna beheaded the man with a swing of her sword. His body fell and was trampled by his comrades.

The Magin looked up and watched in horror as the walls of Alchemian crumpled once more. The lines had broken. She saw Yayènia and Ghealan practically standing atop their horses screaming at the soldiers. Tlonna urged her stallion forward, but his progress was slowed by the milling fighters surrounding them. The horse kicked out, killing any who were unfortunate to be in range, but more filled the gaps.

They were almost half a league away from the city, stranded in the midst of both enemy and friendly soldiers. The screams and chants of men erupted twofold into the air. Yayènia's voice rose above the din in a wordless howl that sent her warriors into frenzy.

The silver, black, and blue clad soldiers plowed through their crimson foes. Tlonna forced Takîreaes into a swarm of Blackhaven soldiers who immediately recognized her as their queen and formed a strong wall against enemies. That way, she was carried back to the city and left her temporary guards when they reached Yayènia.

"We need to talk, now."

"Tlonna, you are not supposed to be here!" the weapons master shrieked, her eyes going wide when she spotted her sister-in-law.

"Gods damn it Yayènia! Now!" Tlonna grabbed Verity's reins and pulled her away from the ranks.

As soon as they were far enough away to be heard without shouting, Tlonna told her who the third rider was.

Yayènia did not allow Tlonna to finish her last sentence before shoving past the Magin and leaping upon Verity. Tlonna followed, loosening her swords in their scabbards. She grabbed the warrior's reins.

"What about the rest of them? We cannot win without you."

"There is plenty enemy to go around, my queen. Help yourself to some."

"What do you think you are going to do?" Tlonna shouted, yanking on Verity's reins hard enough to earn a snort from the horse. "You cannot win this battle, Yayènia, *I* cannot win this battle."

"Well someone has to do it!" the warrior growled jerking on the reins, a flicker of surprise on her face when Tlonna's arm merely tensed.

"You will die!"

Yayènia dropped the reins and bent down in the saddle, her deceptively pretty face looking as though it were carved from stone. "And what else am I supposed to do? I was born for this, Tlonna. I, alone. I will die in battle, which I know, as you should. If it be this one, it be this one. Who else will take this charge? Who else is strong enough, or skilled enough? Besides, prophecy dictates it be so, sound familiar?"

The queen cursed fluidly, making her companion's brow rise in shock. The two females glared at one another for a moment, the screams and poundings of battle seemed far away. Finally Tlonna reached up and gripped Yayènia's armored collar. The Magin yanked the High Commander out of her saddle and pulled her close, so that the older elf had to stand on her toes or else hang there.

"And what of your husband, or your friends, or your army? What of them? Answer me that, High Commander Yayènia er'Tiena, and tell me that it is your duty to go to needless slaughter. I forbid you, as your queen, to go before this enemy and sacrifice yourself. I will not have it. There are thousands of warriors fighting for you, *right now*, not for me, or Losolin, or even Nymyños. They fight for you, and were you to go do this thing, you will die, and they will die as well. They would follow you into the heart of the ninth hell, unblinking, Yayènia, and I will not let you abandon them," Tlonna hissed.

Yayènia stared at her, blue eyes narrowed slightly. Tlonna let her back down and the warrior yanked on her short cuirass to straighten it.

"As you command, my Queen, but remember your own words the next time you are so determined to throw yourself to your death because of that flaming prophecy," she said shortly, remounted, and rode away, silver cloak swelling behind her.

Tlonna watched her go, and then slammed her plumed helmet back onto her head. Catching Takîreaes's reins, the Magin Queen swung into her saddle and rejoined the battle.

The battle slowed down in the evening as the night grew colder and the attacking soldiers began to retreat. The officers reassembled in the command tent to have dinner and to discuss the day. Erdwyf held open the tent flap for the others who ducked by. Yayènia shoved in after Tlonna, bypassing the queen and plopping down in her chair. The others, sensing her mood, quieted. Suneelo and Losolin stared at each other, then at their wives. The two females glared at one another across the table.

Erdwyf took her seat, wary of her friends' moods, while Miazie sighed resignedly, taking the seat opposite the High Advisor. Finally, when the awkward silence had stretched long enough to become uncomfortable, Erdwyf ordered dinner to be brought in.

Her actions seemed to loosen the others. Aidyn leaned back in his chair, propping his feet on the table, and started cleaning one of his knives. Ghealan rubbed his wife's back and pulled the assassin and Sargotarh into a discussion about the archers. Aidyn did not move from his languid position, but he eagerly joined the conversation. The others delved into talks, all but Tlonna, Yayènia, and their spouses, who continued to exchange worried glances.

While the steaming dinner of salted pork and snow-chilled ale was served, Erdwyf finished writing the letters that were being sent out to the provinces for aid. With a conclusive action, she placed the last period on the last letter.

"They are all ready for signatures," the High Advisor said, passing the parchment, ink, and quill to Tlonna.

Tlonna signed them and handed the stack to Losolin. When he had finished, he signed them and passed it to Yayènia. The warrior added her scrawling signature and tossed them back at Tlonna, making the papers fly out of order.

Everyone jumped. Erdwyf glared at her and began picking up the parchments that had fallen on the floor. Silence ensued again, until the High Advisor had stacked them neatly back into place and handed them to Tlonna with deliberate care. She cast another scathing look at Yayènia. The High Commander sneered back.

Even Ghealan rubbed his temples.

Tlonna traced the edge of the letters with a finger. "I think it would be best if everyone signed them for purposes of persuasion."

"How so, my queen?" Sargotarh asked, his brow furrowed, obviously attempting to ignore the flaring tempers.

"Well, for instance, the letter going to Florwen Hune, if King Barukh sees Orthak's signature, he will see this is more than just an elf and human war, understand?"

"Yes, I do, Queen Tlonna," the elf captain said, grinning.

When everyone had signed the letters, the selected messengers were called in. To Kajgenia, a human archer named Ellion was sent. An elf called Astar rode to Seaduens, and an elf named Cora rode to Narnen. To Florwen Hune, a dwarf lancer Dorik and to Flousen Dua the human Lara. Riding to Arseninis was another human named Tyron. Two elves selected from the Silvers were going into the Bijozs to brave the pass toward Zeynuwn.

When they had all received their orders and were being prepared on the fastest horses, Erdwyf and Tlonna drew aside the two elves traveling together, Tarounen and Liena.

"My friends, I know you have been trained for this sort of task, but be warned, this is very important and dangerous," Erdwyf said, holding them by the shoulder.

Tlonna nodded, "Yes, and though you both have proven yourself warriors that will brave most anything, few have ever survived this pass in winter. You have been supplied with plenty of furs, flint, and steel, but warmth will still be difficult to find."

Tarounen smiled carelessly. "Queen Tlonna, High Advisor, we will not let you down. Liena and I are well equipped for this journey, and we do not worry. You should not either. We will return with an army at our back."

Erdwyf sighed. "All right, I trust you both. Go, be safe, and return to us."

The elves turned and mounted their horses. With a smart salute, they rode out of the camp behind the others. Yayènia watched them go from the depth of the tent, arms folded stubbornly.

It was earlier the next morning when a horn woke the camp, a clear sound that echoed of its own accord. Yayènia and Tlonna were at the gates before anyone else joined them. They both started at seeing the other.

"Yayènia..." Tlonna said, spreading her hands.

Yayènia sighed, unfolded her arms, and then folded them again. "Do not think on it. You were right. Look, the Plains Elves come."

Tlonna nearly laughed at the sight of the long-legged giant deer carrying nearly a thousand tall, fiercely armed elves. Nebet'thu dismounted and bowed formally to both Tlonna and Yayènia. He turned to indicate the mass behind him.

"My Queen, High Commander, I bring you all the hunter warriors from every clan in Blackhaven Forest. They came willingly, prepared to fight to their dying breath. It took us a while to find you, otherwise we would have been here much sooner. I hope I have done well."

Yayènia took a deep breath and then grasped the shorter elf's shoulders.

"Nebet'thu, we are deeply gratified by your effort. You have done...extremely well. Tell your men to make camp where they will. Afterward, come to the command tent."

Nebet'thu bowed again and turned to his men. The orders were given and the fighters dismounted and led their deer into the main camp. After taking Leartia to the picket lines, he found the command tent and entered it. A few of the captains, Orthak, Sargotarh, and Ryun, and the companions, hailed him with cheers and a mug of ale. The plains elf ducked his head in appreciation and took the offered seat.

Yayènia grinned at him and passed him a plate of food. "You have done well for our people, Nebet'thu. You will be given a spot here in the city with the rest of the ranking officers."

"But, High Commander, I am not an officer. I am not even a recruit," Neb said, setting down the bread he had been about to eat.

"Nonsense, Lieutenant. While we fight, you are an officer of the Blackhaven Militia. You will command your men, answer only to officers above you: sergeants, majors, captains, Second Commander Ghealan, then me, in that order. If Captain Orthak here gives you an order that defies a major or colonel, you will still obey Orthak, but above all, you will obey myself, Commander Ghealan, or either of your monarchs. Understand?"

Nebet'thu looked stunned. "Y-yes High Commander."

Yayènia snapped her fingers and leaned in, "Another thing, Commodore Alexander and Captain Troaz are considered military captains in this war. You will obey them as you would any other. Now, what does the rest of the land look like?"

The new lieutenant gave his report between hurried bites of food. According to him, the Zaedican force had merely plowed through the center of Narnen, not bothering to destroy it completely. At hearing this, Erdwyf nearly melted with relief for her parents, who lived on the eastern edge. Any villages in the army's path were simply obliterated. It had carved a path of destruction through the center of Nymyños in order to reach Alchemian. By the end of his report, the mood in the tent had been sufficiently doused.

The plains elf was dismissed for bed and the others in the tent followed him. Though the arrival of the elves had been a booster, the knowledge that so many innocent lives had been wiped out of existence threatened to lead them to despair.

Chapter 14

Walking Legends

The war raged on for two weeks before any of the messengers returned. The first was from Tyron leading a few hundred cavalry from Arseninis. The reinforcements were cheered with fervor as they rode into the camp. Yayènia, Tlonna, and all the others greeted the soldiers and had their camp set up within an hour. Tyron was given a hot meal and a black plume added to his helmet for his services.

The Zaedican Army began using barbaric tactics to throw the defenders off their rigid strategy. They began tossing heads they had hewn off the bodies of their enemies into the camp. The bodies were heaped in piles around their own camp in plain view of Alchemian. However, the wind coming of the Bijoz range usually swept the stench of rot back into the Zaedic camp.

They used their Magins to create horrid howling sounds that were directed into the camp by streams of power. The howling caused the soldiers unrest and irritation. The alchemists did their best to apply barriers that the Magins could not supply. They also dealt out tonics that helped deal with the headaches and stress caused by the incessant noise. Most of the people dealt with it by stuffing bits of cotton in their ears beneath their helmets.

Almost on the heels of the Arseninisians, Ellion rode in with over a thousand soldiers from Kajgenia, along with King Demetrius's son, Tristan. The young man greeted his acquaintances with a grim smile.

"My father sends his apologies that he could not supply more men, but he fears leaving his borders unprotected. He also apologizes that he himself could not come, but a pressing matter has come to his attention. It seems that a guild of the Magin-haters, the Cleicks have made our city a base of theirs. They have started rioting in the streets every so often. Rather irritating after a while. Speaking of irritating, what in the nine hells is that noise?"

Tlonna scowled. "The enemy. Tristan, I am glad to see you alive and well, and with as many men as you have. Your father has once again proven himself a valuable and dear friend, and you as well."

"Thank you, Queen Tlonna. I am proud to serve beneath you and your honorable High Commander. Lady Yayènia, where would you like the men?"

Yayènia inclined her head and clapped wrists with the young human. "Anywhere. We have no predetermined lines of camp. I believe an intermingled army is better committed on the field."

"Words from my own mouth, Lady," Tristan bowed to her and then turned to the soldiers behind him. "All right, find a place where you can. Report to your captain when you are ready and get your orders. Understood?"

"Hii-gyn!" they yelled in unison, the battle cry of Kajgenia.

The men dispersed into the camp and were soon lost amid the other soldiers. Losolin gripped the young man by the shoulder and steered him in the direction of the command tent. Ellion received his plume and was off to bed.

Tlonna sat across the table from Tristan in her usual chair and folded her hands on the table. "How go things in the east?"

"They are as well as can be hoped. Like I said, the Cleicks are running rampant all over and people are starting to panic as word of the war reaches them. My father is trying to keep word of distress low, but it is difficult. Riots are breaking out all over the land."

"The Cleicks are going to be more of a problem than I ever thought they would be," Tlonna said, picking at a sliver in the table. "I never thought they would be much more than a nuisance."

"Well, with the rise of Midian, they were bound to get a larger support group, Tlonna," Losolin said. "Magic is not a very common ability, especially among humans and dwarves, and so it is feared as the unknown."

"True, but that is not the main worry. I got us off track. Tristan, has there been any news of Zaedicans in the east?" Tlonna interjected.

"No, at least, not enough for me to hear about. It seems their main goal was to cut right through Nymyños to Alchemian so they could get a hold of whatever secrets they have. I don't have any idea about what their goal was after that. I'm just glad you got here in time."

"Barely," Yayènia snorted. "We did not have time to wipe our noses before the horns started blowing. I am just glad this winter is holding out so strong. I just hope it is a long winter."

The prince frowned at her. "Why? Doesn't it make the threat of disease and weakness stronger?"

"Yes, for those not acclimated to this sort of weather. Those of us who *are* used to it, however, can take advantage of those weaker than us."

"My men aren't used to this environment. Our winters are rather mild in comparison," Tristan said, a bit put off.

"Yes, but you are among those who are, and we will be able to take care of that little problem," Erdwyf said, before Yayènia could offend him again.

The talk went on for hours into the night. The officers pondered about Sithian and Rhiannan's eventual plans, the length of the winter, fortifications, and whether or not the other provinces would reply.

The battle reignited the next morning.

After a few dozen soldiers came to the command post and complained about the noise, Yayènia and Ghealan decided to attack for once. The soldiers lined up outside of Alchemian, just out of sight of the Zaedic camp. From the lack of noise, the invaders were still asleep.

The commanders rode in front shouting their directions.

"Target the Magins and kill or capture them. If they attempt to attack you, do not worry about capturing them, cut out their innards. I would rather have soldiers than captives. We will advance at a full charge and smash into their front like fire on a parched field of wheat. Make this day a victorious one!"

The soldiers raised their weapons and roared. When they were within bow range of the sleeping camp, they burst into a full charge. The guards attempted to raise the alarm but were silence by a few well aimed shots. The cries of the men woke the rest of the camp.

The Blackhaven Militia and its additions pounded into their foe without mercy. Tents were set ablaze, horses let loose from their tethers, wagons tipped over and put to flame. The officers headed straight into the heart of camp where the largest tents were. Sithian stood in front of his in only a pair of breeches, staring at the advancing warriors. Tlonna, Losolin, and another Magin, Conan, unleashed their magic on him.

The young half-breed flew backward into his tent, which crumpled with the impact. He did not stir. Rhiannan and the other leader were nowhere to be found. As the sun rose further into the sky, the Zaedicans finally began to gather their wits.

Tlonna yanked her sword out of a screaming Magin and turned to find another. Losolin snarled at a soldier who was trying to pull him out of the saddle. The elf king hacked his hand off, and then his head. He looked up and grinned viciously at his wife.

Tlonna nodded back at him and then turned away. A few yards away she saw Yayènia ram her fist through a Darkwight's throat, the barbs on her gauntlet tearing through flesh and bone, propelled by enormous strength. Takîreaes screamed in alarm as a dozen soldiers charged him. Their fingers wrapped in his chest harness in an attempt to pull him down. The stallion bit and kicked at his assailants as Tlonna jabbed at them with a spear she yanked from a downed Darkwight. Three died instantly, but the others continued to pull on the horse. Tlonna's efforts kept them from doing any real harm, but Takîreaes was struggling to stay on all fours.

The Magin leapt from his back and drew her sword at the same time. She hacked at the men in fury. Finally Takîreaes got his hooves beneath him and reared. Elf and horse laid about them, blood spraying in a mist. When she remounted, Tlonna saw Ghealan raise his sword for the retreat, as did Yayènia. The Blackhaven Militia poured out of the enemy camp, shields on their backs to protect them from a following rain of arrows.

When they reached Alchemian, the soldiers raised a cheer, knowing they had caused the enemy much pain, and taken few losses in return. Yayènia and Ghealan found Tlonna and Losolin and dismounted. Ghealan raised his sword above his head and bellowed in good humor. Yayènia grinned and wiped blood off her cheek with the back of her arm.

"A good start to the day, eh? The enemy's blood will soak the ground for many days. I do like the sound of a man screaming to wake me up," the High Commander said, pulling out her sword and running a cloth down its gory length.

"Absolutely," Losolin replied, taking off his helmet.

Only a few hours had passed when horns were heard off to the west. Tlonna and Ghealan walked out to greet the newcomers alone, as everyone else was busy with some task.

Tlonna squinted. "What in the name...?"

Ghealan grabbed her arm and in the same movement put his other hand to his mouth.

"Dear Gods...Tlonna...Elves. They are Duani Elves! Flousen Dua answered!"

Just as he finished exclaiming, two robed elves halted the army at their backs and stepped forward to meet the pair. Both were male, blond, and extremely fair. Their faces betrayed no emotion as their eyes took in Tlonna and Ghealan. The taller of the two bowed his head ever so slightly.

"I am Prince Erandur, High Captain of the Onyx Forest Army, and this is Lelfwin my Second Lieutenant. We are here to help the Queen of the Everwood," he spoke in a slow drawl.

Ghealan smiled before Tlonna could respond. "High Captain Erandur, our gratitude is in order. I am Second Commander of the Blackhaven Militia. This is Magin Tlonna Arune Ewôsdírn er'Grisholm, Queen of the Everwood City."

Erandur smiled a pale smile, his dark green eyes lightening a bit. "Where do you want my warriors?"

Finally Tlonna spoke, holding back her questions with a tight leash, "How many do you have?"

"What remains of the Onyx Forest Army followed me, eight hundred all told, a small number, but fierce and well trained every one of them."

"They may go where they wish. High Commander Yayènia believes in an intermingled army. We would appreciate it if you would follow us to the command tent to meet the others."

Erandur bowed and then turned to the eight hundred behind him. "*Yolom lãn oyer lault valõn jerwlyn. Nyn flounen fineal jemptson!*" he commanded, giving them their orders to spread out and remain passive.

The elves lifted their bows high in the air and shouted "*Ayna!*" a loud and short proclamation of power and strength.

Tlonna eyed Erandur and Lelfwin as they handed their packs to soldiers and then turned to wait for Tlonna and Ghealan to move. They pivoted and headed back into Alchemian as Lara, the messenger sent to Flousen Dua, emerged from the mass of elves.

"Second Commander Ghealan, Queen Tlonna, do you have any orders for me before I retire?"

"Yes, come with us to the command tent please," Tlonna replied, smiling at her. "How was your trip?"

"Cold, and boring. I ran into a few outposts, but they let me through as soon as they saw my cloak. My queen, you should see the Onyx City...it is...stunning. A city hidden within the depths of such a forest as I have never known, deep green with trunks of ebony. Few of their buildings were on the ground, most were on platforms between the trees, which admittedly were low to the ground, but I could walk beneath them and have feet above my head. It truly was magnificent.

"It was ever dark, but it was a pure darkness, as though nothing evil had ever touched it. In places there were clearings where the elves would dance in the sunlight like the faerys of Purheae must. At home, the city is beautiful and everything wondrous, of course, but Flousen Dua was like a forgotten paradise of ancient culture and pure enjoyment of life," the human said, coloring faintly when she saw how rapt her listeners were.

Lelfwin smiled softly at Lara. "You do us such honor, Human Lara, to compare us so to the Everwood City."

Tlonna smiled at the elf and said, "It must be beautiful, Lelfwin. I hope one day to travel there and see it."

"It would be a great honor, Queen Tlonna."

When finally they reached the command tent, it seemed everyone had convened. Losolin, Tristan, and Erdwyf were playing the impossible game Three-Fold Dice, Aidyn and Aladorn watching amusedly. Miazie and Damon were sitting in the corner, talking quietly. The rest of the captains were staring at maps and arguing quietly over a particular spot of their defenses. Yayènia was lounging against Suneelo's chair, toying with his braid, watching them. As soon as they entered, all idle motion was abandoned and the tent was full of intensity.

Yayènia straightened and smiled at Lara. "My congratulations, Lara. You have done a great service for this campaign, your helmet, please."

The human surrendered her cap and watched eagerly as Yayènia attached the black plume of duty. She was grinning by the time the elf handed it back to her.

"You are dismissed, go now, and get some rest."

When she was gone, the High Commander turned to the newcomers. "I am High Commander Yayènia er'Tiena, whom do I have the pleasure of meeting?"

"Erandur Eldrout, High Captain of the Onyx Forest Army. It is an honor to meet you; High Commander, your deeds and courage are well known among my people. May this acquaintance lead to friendship at the end of this war."

No one noticed Aidyn's jaw drop or his feet slide from the table to the floor with an uncharacteristic thump.

Yayènia returned his formal bow with her own and smiled. "May it, indeed. Your story is no less known to me as mine is to you. An honor for me, as well," she turned to Lelfwin. "What is your name?"

"Lelfwin Greenlan, Second Lieutenant to Prince High Captain Erandur. An honor, my lady, to meet you."

Before Yayènia could reply, Miazie stood and squinted at Erandur. "You said your last name was Eldrout? As in...Furntil Eldrout?"

"The very same, Lady. He is my father," the elf said, studying her with bafflement.

Miazie looked as though she was going to have apoplexy. "*Is*? He is still alive?"

"Of course. Why would he not be?" Erandur asked, frowning at the human.

"He...he assassinated Brandon Stynbek! Over two thousand years ago!"

Erandur looked truly confused at Miazie's shock. "Yes, he did. He has been ruling Flousen Dua since then. I do not seek the throne, so he continues to rule until he grows tired of it and wishes to perform *Haithen*. Neither of us is in a big hurry, so we do not worry. Father rules well, I fight well. It works out."

Yayènia put her hand out to stop another outburst from Miazie. "You are my kind of leader, High Captain. Come, join us, and we will discuss our position."

Only then did the two Duani elves noticed the open-mouthed stare Aidyn was giving them, and the prince smiled.

"Aidyn Sestuns, a great, great honor it is to meet you. My father has watched your progress for many centuries. He desires to meet you," Erandur said, beaming at the dark elf.

The assassin was stunned, staring up at the other elf in complete shock. "He...wants to meet me?"

"Very much so. He sees in you a kindred spirit."

Everyone stared at the two males as they stared at each other. Aidyn finally nodded, settling back in his chair. "And I him," was all he said, but his friends heard the utter astonishment and disbelief in his voice.

Yayènia clapped her hands together after a moment and looked to her companions. "Shall we talk, then?" she asked.

The leaders of the armies and militias present squeezed themselves around the table and delved into a lengthy discussion about the next move.

The next day, neither army attacked. Yayènia and Ghealan summoned the council, as they had taken to calling the leaders. When everyone was assembled, the High Commander slapped a large, detailed map on the table.

"Our defenses must change. The enemy is too used to our tactics for them to be effective anymore. I have a few ideas, but I would like to hear yours, first."

After a few seconds of silence, Erandur leaned forward and laced his fingers together on the edge of the table. "If you do not mind my asking, High Commander, what about the attacks you led on Aderiaen Rahlan's army during the last years of the war? Especially your last attack?"

When Yayènia did not say anything, Ghealan cleared his throat. "We very nearly lost on that last attack, the High Commander almost lost her life. Had desperation not called for such a raid, it would never have taken place. The enemy lost thousands, but our soldiers suffered great loss as well. I would not pull such a move again."

When uneasy silence fell again, it was Captain Sargotarh who next broke it. "Commanders, what if we surrounded them in the dead of night, harrying them on all sides, never letting them know which direction to form defenses?"

Yayènia folded her arms and began pacing back and forth. "It may work, but I fear spreading our fighters so thin. We do not yet have their numbers, and with reinforcements flowing into their camp all the time from distant lands unknown to us, I would not risk putting soldiers so far out of reach of Alchemian. Their camp is massive, and only the superior fighting skills of our soldiers have kept them at bay. Anyone else?"

The dwarf captain Orthak fingered his heavy axe while he spoke. "Split our numbers, make a full on attack with a third of the soldiers, make them think we have suffered more casualties than we really have. Then, when they start to get cocky, send in the rest from the flanks. Most of their men are soldiers of fortune, or blacksmiths strong enough to wield a sword, using strength rather than skill. Cleave through their defenses as though they had none."

Yayènia stopped pacing. "Precisely what I was thinking, Captain. Make their numbers useless. With full elven strength driving the charge, they will not be able to hold their lines. We will send in my Silvers, the Plains Elves, and the Onyx Forest together. A third of the cavalry next with a third of the foot soldiers behind them. We will stage a retreat then, pulling on their victory to make them chase after us. Set archers up here," she pointed at a spot a mile from Alchemian's walls. "As soon as the third volley goes, the rest of the army will come in and flank them, driving two wedges in from the side, splitting them. As soon as the retreat is sounded, those between the bait soldiers and the flankers will be crushed."

"An ancient tactic, to be sure, but it is a classic for a reason," Ghealan said, smirking.

"How many elves are in this camp altogether?" Erandur asked, eyes wide.

Tlonna shifted, settling her gaze on the warrior. "Just over two thousand, High Captain. Why?"

Lelfwin let out a whoosh of air. Erandur closed his eyes and opened them again slowly. "We had thought that perhaps our race had dwindled beyond hope, but if two thousand elves are in this army alone, how many more are in the other provinces, or in the Everwood city alone?"

Miazie answered him, as everyone else had fallen silent. "Maybe another thousand are left in Blackhaven, less in Narnen. Arseninis and Kajgenia have together perhaps five hundred. Seaduens has retained their numbers, around seventeen thousand, and Flousen Dua, you say, around sixteen hundred. A mere twenty or so are left on Zaedic. At my estimation, hardly more than twenty thousand elves left in all of Nymyños, of which we know of, at least."

Erandur and Lelfwin's excitement was depleted by the time Miazie finished speaking. The High Captain shook his head. "We were once the greatest race of all, powerful and large. What has happened?"

When no one answered, the Duani elves left the tent in despair. With the mood efficiently doused, no one so much as whispered.

Yayènia roused the soldiers and had them lined up to move by the time the sky had scarcely begun to lighten. The soldiers breathed into cupped hands, as the air was foggy and blisteringly cold. Wearing fur-lined trousers and shirts beneath their armor staved off most of the cold, but the moisture seeped in anyway. Only the elves succeeded in making sure the temperature did not affect them. The others merely shook their heads at the steam rising from the elves' armor as their bodies adapted to the cold and warmed itself. Dwarves wrapped their hands in their thick beards and hunched their shoulders. Every now and then a fire would erupt, but it was only from the fire nymphs, who used it to keep themselves warm. Humans stuck their hands in their armpits, annoyed at the other races' abilities. Tlonna and Losolin rode to the head of the lines where Yayènia, Erdwyf, Ghealan, and Suneelo were.

The companions merely nodded at their king and queen, too anxious to talk. It was a few more minutes before Erandur, Lelfwin, Tristan, and Nebet'thu rode to join them. The rest of the captains were leading the flanks into the surrounding hills. The three non-Blackhavenites stared in awe at the solid line of silver-clad warriors sitting a few yards from them at the front of the line. Abbey and William had been ordered to stay behind to protect their unborn child, but the forty-two others were grim and perfectly still, though their trained war-horses snorted and stamped around.

When the last stragglers found their place in the ranks, Yayènia raised her hand to command silence, which fell immediately.

"You all know what you are supposed to do. We ride slowly at first, as quietly as possible until we are within sight of enemy lines. Then into a full charge. We drive in fast, wedge formation. Myself, Commander Ghealan, High Captain Erandur, Second Lieutenant Lelfwin, General Tristan, and Lieutenant Nebet'thu, King and Queen Ewôsdírn, Captain Suneelo, and Advisor Erdwyf are leading the charge. *Zephyr Leifen* forming the wedge to drive in, Plains Elves next, and Onyx Forest coming in behind. All clear?"

In one thunderous roar, the near two thousand elves replied with a "HAOOH!"

Yayènia grinned at her companions who grinned back. She raised her twin blades high in the air.

"Then let us go kill some filth!"

She spun Verity around and she and the council rode off in a straight line with the wedge behind.

"High Captain," the warrior waited for him to look at her. "Are you sure your men can keep up on foot once we start the charge?"

Erandur grinned slowly. "High Commander, you could advance the whole way at a gallop and my men could still keep up, have no fear."

"Good. I shall have none," she replied, returning the grin, though hers was accompanied by a chuckle that would have frightened any but those who rode with her.

By the time they crested the small ridge that hid the Zaedican camp from sight, the entire regiment was silent as shadow. The sun was a sliver on the far horizon, just coming up. Yayènia called a halt as she surveyed the best place to drive the charge. Finding it, she yanked her fist up and forward to signal the move. They accelerated slowly, mist coming from all nostrils as they advanced. The Zaedican guards tried to raise an alarm but were silenced by arrows. Nonetheless, a few soldiers heard the death cries and attempted to rouse their fellows. Too late. The council slammed into the camp like an unstoppable force, the wedge coming in seconds later. Men screamed as they were trampled beneath their tents. By the time they were a quarter way through the camp, the Zaedicans had formed their defenses. As they started to push back on the elves, Yayènia started counting. When they finally had a good defense up and the elves started to take casualties, she called the retreat.

Mad with the scent of blood and tang of victory, the Zaedican soldiers raced after the retreating regiment, just as they had hoped. When they reached the line of archers, the elves reined in and trotted to wait behind them. The enemy force, unable to stop for their momentum, were hewn down by near three thousand arrows. As they realized their mistake and tried to retreat, the flanks poured down the hills and into the sides. The Zaedicans were split in two. The back half abandoned their fellows and fled back to their camp. Those trapped between the three regiments attempted a defense. They were slaughtered despite their effort.

Nearly ten thousand foul soldiers died that day.

Chapter 15

Blood Traitors

The next day, as the camp rejoiced at their victory, Erdwyf rode in from her watch. Finding Tlonna, Ghealan, and Yayènia, the elf dove into the fray. Revelers attempted to pull her from Odilia's saddle but Erdwyf cursed at them, shoving their arms away. When she finally reached the trio, those that had been in her path were silent and waiting, wondering at the graveness of the High Advisor's face.

She sketched a hasty bow to Tlonna for the sake of the soldiers and then turned to the commanders.

"High Commander, Second Commander, reinforcements have arrived from beyond the horizon. Sithian's numbers have tripled. He has near forty thousand soldiers. We are outnumbered beyond hope."

Yayènia cursed. "Where are they coming from? WHERE? What massive land lay beyond the sight of our ships? Has Serenyi resurfaced? I do not understand!"

Tlonna wrapped a strong hand around Yayènia's arm and held her back.

"Erdwyf, let us go inside and speak of this matter. We do not want to destroy hope when it is all we have."

"Of course, my queen."

They adjourned to the command tent with summons to the captains, Losolin, and Suneelo, who were making rounds behind Alchemian. When finally everyone had arrived, Erdwyf stood and recited what she had seen. Many of the captains shared Yayènia's wrath and frustration; others merely stared at the chipped camp table.

Losolin rubbed his temples. "What messengers have yet to arrive from the provinces?"

"Astar from Seaduens."

"Cora from Narnen."

"Dorik from Florwen Hune.

"Tarounen and Liena from Zeynuwn."

"I would not expect Tarounen and Liena back for a few more weeks at least. The Bijoz Pass is difficult, even in summer," Suneelo said, looking at his wife.

Tlonna sighed. "And the others? Zaedicans are coming from across the sea and through Narnen and arrived here many times over, now. What is taking so long?"

"Maybe they are dead," Troaz said bluntly. "You sent the best warriors possible, but even they would not be able to survive running into the Zaedic army."

"It is possible. Narnen has become a conduit of evil. We may have sent Cora to her death," Yayènia added, finally taking a seat.

The camp table was full. Twenty warriors crowded around, each of them a leader in their own right. Tlonna, Losolin, Yayènia, Erdwyf, Ghealan, Suneelo, Aidyn, Aladorn, Nebet'thu, Sargotarh, Orthak, Ryun, Alexander, Troaz, Damon, and Miazie from Blackhaven. Erandur and Lelfwin from Flousen Dua. Tristan from Kajgenia and Jordan, the captain from Arseninis.

They were all grim. They were all tired. They were all angry.

Ghealan pulled out the much-used map and tacked it to the table. At the sight of the Zaedic encampment, he added seven more upside-down Vs, one for every five thousand.

"If my wife is right, we are outnumbered by more than thirty-thousand. We have, what Nia, eight and half thousand in camp right now? They will have *over* forty thousand," Ghealan said after he had finished.

Tristan pulled out his dagger and started toying with the tip. "Do we have a chance? Does Nymyños?"

"Yes." Tlonna said quietly yet passionately, catching and holding the gaze of every man, elf, and dwarf. "Gods and spirits, we have a chance. We have to! How many more Magins do we have? They have craftsmen and mercenaries. We have warriors. They are driven by evil and greed, we are driven by love. Love of our people, our lands, and our families. We are fighting for our freedom and our lives. What are they fighting for? They seek only to take, we seek to protect and preserve. Our blood, our sweat, *our* flesh, is what made this land what it is. Not theirs. They came here, trying to take what is ours, and they thought we would roll over and beg for mercy at the sight of their banners and red armor.

"We are warriors of Nymyños. Our fighters can kill five to their one. Pain means nothing to us, for we have all suffered at the hands of evil before. Despair, horror, fear, and weakness may come upon us, but if we let the hate of our enemies and love of our people fill our hearts, we will prevail. Blood will be spilt, but by the gods' will, let it be our enemy's blood that runs like a river!"

The leaders roared in unison, pumping fists in the air. Human, dwarf, and elf clasped hands together and bellowed their allegiance. Tlonna looked on with fire in her eyes, fierce pride swelling in her bosom like an elixir. Once everyone had quieted, Tlonna spoke again.

"I have an idea, but we need the alchemists and their potions. Miazie, can you get them here?"

The Belau nodded and left. She returned trailing Sodo and the others that were still alive. The tainted elf had taken Elwyn's place when she died, assuming her duties during the length of the war.

"What can we do for you, Queen Tlonna?"

"High Alchemist Sodo, a few weeks back, you were using a viscous material that explodes when friction is applied to it. Do you have lots of it?"

Sodo shifted. "It is called Nytrynhimmel, and we have some. Why?"

Tlonna twitched nervously. "Can...can we have it?"

"Why?"

"I...what would it do if thrown at enemy lines while encased in jars?"

"It explodes. That is what it does."

Ghealan mumbled under his breath and then grabbed the alchemist by his robes. "My queen is obviously asking you if she can have your potion so that we can have an element of surprise on the enemy that is trying to destroy your people. Now, go *get it before I break you in half*."

The High Alchemist stumbled back a few steps when the warrior shoved him away. His exquisite face tightened with anger and stubbornness, his one black eye twitching. "Threatening me will not get you any closer to your goal, Ghealan Tomyvon. Do not seek to outlet your anger and your frustration on me, for I am one more enemy you really do not need, or want," he said, then turned and strode out of the tent. The other alchemists hastily followed him.

Tlonna caught Miazie staring after him, a small smile on her face. The elf gripped her shoulder and gently squeezed, giving her friend a little shake. "I can see why you love him so," she whispered, careful not to let her words carry to anyone else.

"Aye, though it seems he no longer loves me. It was folly anyway," the human replied just as quietly, sadness lacing her voice. "I am so much less than he, than all of you."

"He still loves you," Tlonna countered, glancing at the tent opening. "I can see it when he risks looking at you. And it is no folly, Miazie, to love another, no matter how great the difference in race or status. And I love you, though it is indeed against my better judgment," she said, laughing softly.

Across the tent, Ghealan was rolling his eyes as Erdwyf scolded him for threatening Sodo, while Yayènia grinned at him. A few minutes later, the alchemists reappeared, carrying large clay jars full of the glutinous, clear liquid.

They placed them carefully on the table and backed away. Tlonna looked at Sodo expectantly.

"Well? How do we use it?"

"You throw it."

Yayènia growled and picked up one of the jars. She aimed it at Sodo and smiled, though it was more of a sneer. The alchemists about him gasped in fear and backed further away, but the elf merely shrugged. "Do it, and you will find out just how fast it spreads."

"Don't," Miazie interjected quickly, pulling up her wide pant leg, exposing her calf. "It burns quickly."

Everyone stared at the white splotch on the human's leg, looking about for an explanation.

"When last I was here, some of it exploded and I would have been burnt to a crisp had not Sodo covered me with his body. It eats through flesh like acid and neither water nor air will douse it. The only way to put it out is to smother it completely, and that usually takes quite a long time, often too long. We must be very careful with it, for if we drop a jar," she looked pointed at Yayènia, "then many of us will be dead within seconds," the Belau lectured.

Sodo was staring at the ground a few inches away from Suneelo's boots, his jaw clenched, his arms folded tightly across his chest. Ardenay stepped forward, putting a friendly hand on Miazie's back.

"If you want to use it as a weapon, then you should put it in smaller jars that are able to be thrown. The stuff is viscous, and easily agitated. Heat caused by friction, such as snapping it between your fingers, will cause elements within to move faster, and if it happens to hit anything with a force of velocity behind it, those elements will explode. It happens in less than a heartbeat, but I have studied it long and hard. My assistants are busy making several batches for use when these are depleted, and I will get some glassblowers to begin making jars."

"Thank you," Tlonna said, taking the jar from Yayènia. "How long until they are ready?"

"We will have enough to store this batch by morning, but the others will not be ready for a few more days, as we must let the Nytrynhimmel cure," Ardenay replied, grabbing Sodo's elbow and tugging on him. "We will leave you now, but please be careful with the Nytrynhimmel. A spill would be disastrous."

The Alchemists departed once more and Erdwyf opened the jar closest to her. She stuck a finger in it and drew out a tiny droplet. Walking outside, she snapped her fingers and the droplet exploded into the ground a few feet away. She giggled.

Ghealan wiped a hand across his chest, nervous. "Gods have mercy."

As soon as they were out of sight of the command tent, Sodo jerked his arm out of Ardenay's grasp. "Why are you being so cooperative?" he demanded.

The female resisted the urge to slap him. "Because they are trying to protect us, and they have lost some thousands in doing so already, a large number of their force. Are you so blinded by your rage that you cannot see past your own misery?"

"She is there, Ardenay, mere steps away, and yet she does not look at me. She watches *him*, the bastard who raped her and took her freedom. I want to rip his throat out with my bare hands, I want to-"

"Shh," the female soothed, placing one slender finger against his lips. "Remember who you are, Sodo. Do not let the evil touch your heart, *säära dü*."

"I am no longer your friend, Ardenay, I am something corrupt and foul, something less than I was. Certainly not worthy of your companionship. I wonder how many times she has lain with him and uttered his name, bathing in that human's touch," the elf snarled, unable to keep his mind away from the woman he loves.

"Miazie is human as well, Sodo. Never forget that. And she does look at you, but you are always looking away. Her eyes plead for you, her face softening with a pain I cannot even begin to imagine.

She loves you yet, but cannot come to you. If you want her, you must go to her."

"While that Man sleeps beside her, I will not touch her," Sodo snapped and strode away, fuming and desperate.

Ardenay stood alone in the deepening light, staring after her friend, her heart torn for both him and Miazie. Finally, she took a deep breath and went back to her own tent.

The council spent the morning pouring the Nytrynhimmel into small glass jars plugged with cork. When they finished, nearly fifty jars were sitting in a crate, padded with clothing.

It was approaching midnight when an alarm was sounded and a lone rider was admitted into camp. Astar, the elf dispatched to Seaduens dismounted slowly and fell to her knees before the leaders.

"High Commander, my lieges, I am sorry but I failed. King Stoffnias of Seaduens refused to come, but he gave me a message. He said Seaduens is too proud and pure to come to the aid of traitors and murderers. And...and this," she pulled off her gauntlets and showed them the inside of her right arm.

A blade had been dug into her flesh from shoulder to wrist. Astar had attempted to wrap it, but the ride back had made her lose any strength in the arm.

"I am sorry. I have failed."

Yayènia watched her for a moment before turning to Losolin. "Well?"

The half-Magin took Astar's hand in his and ran his other hand over the wound. The flesh knitted back together and the elf's face loosened as most of the pain receded.

"I cannot heal it all the way. It is too late for that, but you might regain some use of it. However...a sword may be too heavy, I am sorry."

Astar took a deep breath and looked to her commanders. "What would you have me do?"

"How well is your aim?" Yayènia replied.

"All right. I usually hit what I am aiming at."

"Good. You can be in charge of these," she pointed to the crate of jars, "They blow up."

Astar's brows climbed her forehead. "Really?"

"Really," Ghealan said, smiling.

"I can do that."

"Good," Yayènia said and handed her a black plume. "For your service. Go get some rest."

Astar shook her head. "But...I failed to bring reinforcements."

Tlonna sighed. "None of us really thought Stoffnias would come to our aid. You did your duty, and suffered besides. You have earned it. Take it."

The female glanced at Yayènia who shoved the plume into her hands. "Take it and go to bed."

Astar bowed and departed.

Aidyn sighed, "Well, what did we expect?"

Erandur looked about to explode. "Murderers and traitors? What madness does Stoffnias suffer from? We are defending Nymyños! Not Blackhaven! Long have I hated that king, and now he abandons us to doom? He is the traitor! Blood traitor! When this is over, Seaduens will pay with blood."

Tlonna laid a hand on the older elf. "Erandur, calm yourself. Our enemy is Zaedic. We will deal with Seaduens when the time comes."

The Duani prince took a deep breath and nodded. "I believe, my lady, they are one in the same, now."

The next afternoon, while the camp was resting, the Zaedicans attacked. They came over the rise like a swarm of ants, the army's red armor clashing with the hodgepodge armor the mercenaries and craftsmen. Thousands slammed into the lines of the Alchemian defenders, slicing through the lesser numbers like a knife through butter. Yayènia screamed at the soldiers chosen as Nytrynhimmel flingers.

They rode up in a line as the defenders retreated, pulling back the wounded. Using the slings Miazie and some of the other civilians had hastily woven together, the flingers loosed the jars of flaming glycerin. Soldiers screamed as the jars shattered, glass and Nytrynhimmel spraying everywhere. The liquid burst into blue and green flames, consuming anything in their path whether metal, flesh, or bone. Glass sank deep into limbs and unprotected necks, severing arteries, digging into eyes and lungs, blinding and choking. The advance was stopped as the Nytrynhimmel spread through the ranks, decimating the lines.

The flingers loosed a second round of the jars, tossing them higher to reach farther back into the ranks. Again soldiers screamed as they were consumed by the unnatural fire. Magins attempted to stop the flames with magic, but the viscous material simply spread faster, bolstered by the magic's heat. As the front lines tried to fall back, Ghealan roared to the archers who loosed three thousand arrows into the smoking air.

A wall of corpses began to form as the arrows picked off what the Nytrynhimmel left behind. Erdwyf waved a small flag at a waiting soldier by the wall of Alchemian and he sent the signal into the city. Alchemists and camp followers punched down on levers that sent a thousand flaming balls of hardened oil and grass into the already smoking air. The newly arrived enemies screamed in terror as the small projectile weapons descended upon them. Harrowed by fire, the soldiers retreated.

The small balls and their launchers had been Tristan's idea. He had seen something similar in a book and brought it up to Yayènia and Ghealan. They were small catapults, pulled tight, and launched with little effort. The missiles were balls of grass soaked in oil and rolled in the pebbles from the bottom of the ravine. Used as such, they became invaluable weapons, inexpensive and deadly.

Tlonna watched as massive numbers were hewn down, but still more replaced them. Seething with fury and wretchedness, she bowled Takîreaes through the lines until she reached the front. Ghealan saw her and his eyes widened when she dismounted.

"Tlonna! No!" he roared, understanding her intention.

The Magin Queen ignored him.

She handed Takîreaes's reins to a surprised soldier, a grizzly human with worry-wide eyes. Forming an aural shield around herself, Tlonna walked out between the armies. Hundreds of arrows tried to reach her, but they bounced harmlessly off her shield, white magic crackling with each hit. Steeling herself, Tlonna took a deep breath and emptied her mind. The earth spirits whispered to her, crooning and weeping. Their sibilant voices were hollow, their words she understood, but the meaning was lost.

The ground beneath her began to tremble and the front lines of both armies cried out in shock and fear. Behind her, Tlonna vaguely heard Ghealan ordering the troops back, heard Losolin calling to her, his voice an addition to the spirits'. She held up her arms, palms flat to the sky, head thrown back as the earth spirits joined her body. The ground was lurching, breaking open in places, the sky above a roiling mass of angry thunderheads, bruised and rumbling. The first strikes of lightning were aimless, barely reaching the ground around her. But they came faster, and more defined, striking with Tlonna's thoughts. Distantly, she heard the screams of dying men. The smell of charred flesh barely touched her. She opened her eyes, unseeing. Her pupils were contracting and elongating, the irises changing from blue, to gray, to white, faster as the lightning grew in strength. The Staff of Cyree, which was attached to her back at all times, glowed bright, an invisible anchor of power to the Magin Queen.

Tlonna took a step forward, and another, blindly hacking down the Zaedicans. Power whirled around her. As other Magins tried to curb her attack, her shield merely absorbed their Weaves, casting their strength back in the form of striking death. With a final gargantuan effort, Tlonna opened her mouth in a primal scream as the sky tore itself open at her command and fell upon the Zaedican Army.

The Zaedicans, though greatly outnumbering their opponent, fled.

Losolin launched himself out of Suneelo's arms as Tlonna screamed. Wind tore at his armor, keening around him, ripping the breath from his lungs. The enemy was a fleeing mass of confusion as fist sized hail and body-seeking lightning pounded on them. Behind him, the sky was an angry purple and blue, but nothing fell, and the combined army of Nymyños watched in awe as their greatest champion stood alone in the midst of it all.

As he broke free of the lines, Tlonna fell to her knees, the shield disappearing like a guttering flame, and his wife toppled over. The Magin Storm still raged on the Zaedicans, but now a soft snow was falling everywhere else.

"Tlonna!" Losolin screamed as he reached her.

She was unconscious, blood trickling from her mouth. He scooped her up with little ceremony and sprinted back to the lines. They parted without command, and then fell in as he passed until they reached Alchemian. Yayènia was irate, held down by Ghealan, Aidyn, and Erandur, and still managing to make a job of it.

"I will kill her! I swear to Maln I will kill her!" she screamed as Losolin came into view, the listless Tlonna in his arms.

Ignoring his sister-in-law, Losolin strode to their tent and laid her down on their cot. Miazie walked in behind him, and for a moment he felt like they were back where they had started, wandering aimlessly through the Liberated Lands.

"She used all her energy for that. I have read of Magin Storms, but I never thought I'd witness one. It was terrifying," the Belau said, coming to stand next to the king.

"She saved this army today, but what about tomorrow? How many did she take down?" Losolin asked quietly.

"Enough to make it count, I think," Miazie replied.

"I hope so."

"Do you remember when we were attacked by Athelias's men? She called down lightning, and killed every single man but for the one you jumped on. No Magin has ever had the power to do that, not even Midian. What she did today, a Magin Storm, is a theory. No one has ever successfully created one, not on such a large scale. Usually they last a few seconds and devastate a dozen people. She...Losolin she could destroy the world."

The male turned to Miazie. "But she never would."

"No, she never would," the Belau agreed quietly, gazing down on Tlonna's calm face.

"Did you know she could do that?"

Yayènia looked up at Erandur from across the table. He, Ghealan, and Aidyn had released her a few moments ago. "No."

"I saw her do something like that once. On a much smaller scale, but it was still frightening. It was outside Arseninis," Aladorn said softly, half-faded out.

"Really?" Ghealan asked.

"Midian could do it too...sort of," Aidyn supplied. "He nearly killed me in the middle of one."

"But nothing that big, right?" Erandur asked.

"No, nothing that big," the assassin confirmed, his soft voice barely a whisper.

"She really is the Magin Queen, then?"

"Yes," Yayènia snapped as Tristan ducked into the tent.

The young man was pale, but he smiled at the five elves nonetheless. "Seems like we just had a rather large and unexpected victory. No wonder my father is so fond of Queen Tlonna."

"Aren't we all?" Damon said as he followed the prince in, looking more and more haggard as wounds took their toll.

After that, everyone was ducking into the tent until it was full of the council, minus Ryun, Jordan, Suneelo, Losolin, and Tlonna. Miazie was the last in and she stood before them all, hands on her hips.

"Tlonna used every reserve of energy she had, plus she drew on the earth for even more. What she did is called a Magin Storm. It has never been successfully performed before tonight. Not even Roluf Gwemheoad was able to maintain one larger than a room. Tlonna will not regain consciousness for a few hours, if that. She gave you another day. What do you plan to do with it?"

"Our numbers are not enough. High Commander, if they attack again, we will not be able to stop them," Sargotarh said, unable to tear his eyes from Miazie's worried visage.

"Captain Sargotarh, I am aware of the direness of our situation, but we cannot flee. If we do, they will raid Alchemian, gain what knowledge they can, and then come after us. We will either stop them here, or die here, and Tlonna's...gift...will have been for nothing. We have no other choice...unless you want me to abandon Nymyños to doom just to save ourselves?" Yayènia snapped, never glancing away from the map spread before her.

The elf bowed slightly, his armor creaking, a sign of much use for elfin armor. "Of course not, High Commander."

Ghealan sighed as he sat down next to his oldest friend. "Nia, what tricks do we have left?"

"The Nytrynhimmel is depleted for now. Until the next batch is ready, we are done. Tristan's pebble things we have plenty of, but they are not enough. Tlonna is out. The only thing left is...well, it does not matter. It is the only string we have left to pull."

The few people in the command tent looked at Yayènia. It was Tristan who finally asked, "What string?"

Yayènia huffed, folded her arms beneath her bosom, and glared at the table.

Ghealan bit his lip and looked at Erdwyf who stood a few feet away. She looked away.

"A suicide raid," Orthak grunted coldly.

Aidyn shook his head and sighed. "It is not worth it. We can hold out a bit longer. Maybe long enough for the rest of the messengers to return. We do not yet know how much damage Tlonna caused the bastards."

Erandur nodded his head. "I concur. You were right, High Commander, to put me down when I suggested it. We have more options than that. We have a superior fighting force, and we can win, if we put our entire collective minds together."

Yayènia slapped her hand on the table, startling everyone. "No! I have never seen an army this large in my entire career, not in one place. If we stay here, we will die. If we flee, we will die. The only way to give our land a fighting chance is to go in fast and hard, and if every soldier kills three of the enemy, we will reduce their numbers almost by half. The remaining armies in the provinces can deal with what is left, if they stand together."

"That is the problem, Nia," Erdwyf said plaintively. "*If* they stand together. Blackhaven, Flousen Dua, and Kajgenia would for sure, but what of the others? And there are no armies left in those three kingdoms anyway. Who would answer the call? Seaduens? They have already shown their deceit."

"I do not know! Erdwyf, I wish I did but I do not! I am no queen, or advisor! I am a fighter and I am doing my best to decide the fate of Nymyños. What more do you want?" Yayènia shouted, her face scrunched up in despair.

It was then that Suneelo strode in. He sniffed once and said, "Ryun and Jordan are dead."

Erdwyf burst into tears and Yayènia flopped back down into her chair, hiding her face in her hands. After a few moments of quiet, Yayènia raised her head.

"They will be given pyres of honor tonight?"

Suneelo nodded, "I will get them prepared." He left.

Yayènia looked at the people around her. "Well? What do you want me to do? My second? My advisor? Prince of Legends?"

Erandur scowled at the title. Tristan looked confused.

The Duani elf's jaw tightened. "My legend is no more known than yours, Yayènia. Less so, actually. Do not mock me."

"I mock no one, Prince Erandur. Your battle history is no child's tale. What would you suggest I do?" Yayènia replied angrily.

"As I said, we must all work to find a solution."

Losolin walked in and silence fell. He had passed his brother and received the news of the two men's deaths. "She will be up in the morning," he said to the unvoiced question.

"Good. Maybe she can pull another miracle out of the sky and save us all," Yayènia snapped.

Losolin's weary face turned furious. "Yayènia, your barbed words are helping no one. Leave."

"Losolin, do not push me."

"I am not. I am ordering you. Leave."

The warrior and the king glared at each other for a full ten seconds before Yayènia stormed out of the tent. Losolin took a deep breath and turned to Ghealan.

"For tonight, you are High Commander."

Tristan turned to the half-Magin. "King Losolin, was it a good idea to dismiss the High Commander like that?"

Losolin shrugged. "I do not know, Tristan, but she is very much on edge right now and not fit to be making decisions, and, I am King of Blackhaven."

"Of course. I did not mean to doubt you."

"Yes you did, and that is why you are a good leader, Tristan. Do not ever take anything for granted just because the person who said it is of some influence. That is one of the last lessons Tlonna's father taught me. Often times, such people are corrupt, or unwise. I know little of war, I know little of ruling, I am a novice in the company of masters," Losolin countered.

"King Dietirin was very wise," Erandur said before Tristan could argue. "I would like to visit his tomb one day."

Losolin nodded. "I would like to show it to you, Prince Erandur."

When silence fell again, Ghealan started placing wooden chips on the map, indicating where companies would harry the enemy camp, keeping them from getting rest. Archers were to be set up at all times with the far-reaching elfin long bows.

In the small hours of the morning, fifty squads of archers left Alchemian on foot, moving swiftly and silently, having abandoned their heavy armor for leather jerkins and greaves. They spread out in the trees surrounding the Zaedican Army, hidden and up high. Each of them had four quivers full of arrows, and fletchers were busy making more to be sent periodically to replenish them.

Tlonna woke with a start, her eyes feeling lead-heavy and her body trembling with exhaustion. Her throat was parched and she couldn't breathe without wincing. Rolling onto her side, the elf saw Miazie dozing next to her bed.

"Miazie..." Tlonna murmured, painfully extracting her arm to wake her friend.

"Tlonna! Oh, you're awake," the Belau said sleepily.

"Yes. This feels familiar."

Miazie grinned half-heartedly. "What? You unconscious and me keeping vigil? No. I think it was usually the other way around. But I suppose this happened often enough too. How are you feeling?"

Tlonna struggled to sit up. "Tired beyond reasoning. I do not know what I did. Was it worth it?"

The woman hesitated, taking the time to adjust her shirt before responding. "What you did...it's never been accomplished before. Not in such magnitude. It's called a Magin Storm, and you basically used all your bodily energy, plus the energy of the earth around you, to tear open the skies in a determined area. You were able to keep all the damage before you. Not a single Nymyñosian was hurt other than bruises from falling."

Visibly relieved, Tlonna swung her legs out from under the blankets. "How many did I take out?"

"Hard to say. Yayènia estimates around four thousand, others say more, others less. They sent scouts out to make a count, so we will know by midnight."

The elf nodded and reached for a clean pair of breeches. Her body seemed to be moving through mud, taking twice as much energy as it should. Miazie stood hastily, habitually straightening her hair and clothes.

"You really should rest some more, Tlonna. Losolin commanded Yayènia to take a break, and put Ghealan in charge for a while. There's no reason for you to strain yourself."

"No, other than the fact that every soldier in this camp is here because of me, they get no rest, they fight at my word. Why should I be pampered when they are not?"

Miazie shook her head. "You're never going to be a noble, are you? You will always be stubborn and unwilling to admit the fact that you don't have to put yourself in the line of fire every time. You have done enough."

The Magin glared up at the human, and then purposefully stood. "And you will never learn that I always do what I believe to be right and fair. You have been in this fight longer than most of them out there. You have met Sithian and Rhiannan. You have seen Midian's work first hand. How can you say that I have done enough, when there sits an army of ruthless murderers in the middle of Nymyños, threatening all I love?"

"By seeing what you have gone through already. Tlonna, you can only handle so much. Your mind or your body will give up one day, and you will be less than you could be. Do not believe that because you are an elf you can go beyond the limits of everyone else. Even Yayènia has to rest, and she is a hero right out of the stories. Don't kill yourself before you have a chance to live. You are barely wed, barely crowned. Let others take some of the responsibility."

Tlonna sighed when she realized the wisdom of her friend's words. Her legs were trembling with the effort of standing. Flopping back onto the cot, the Magin nodded wearily. "You are right, as usual."

Miazie smiled. "I know. Let me get you something to eat."

Resigned, the Magin Queen of Blackhaven lay back on her cot while the exiled princess of Anutch fetched her cooling soup from the camp kitchen.

Suneelo found his wife stretched out on their camp bed, sound asleep. Smiling, the Captain of the Guard removed his helmet and carefully placed it on the armor stand. Yayènia had removed her cuirass, but she still wore her greaves, vambraces, boots, and gauntlets. Relieved that she was finally resting, Suneelo carefully lay down next to her after removing most of his armor.

"'Neelo?" Yayènia murmured quietly, turning her head to smile sleepily at him.

Cursing at himself for waking her, the male smiled back. "Yes?"

"Can we win?"

Sighing, Suneelo closed his eyes momentarily. "I do not know, love. That is your department. We have won against incredible odds before, and we have lost against incredible odds. It is up to the gods now, and the soldiers. We have a lot of things on our side."

"But do we have enough? You saw what Tlonna did, and that wiped out a fraction of their numbers."

"Tlonna is one person, Nia, albeit a very powerful person. They have no one like her. Sithian and Rhiannan are nowhere near her level, and they do not even fight. They sit on the hill while men die for them. We have all the advantages but for the numbers."

Breathing deeply, Yayènia curled up next to her husband and rested her head against his shoulder. "I hope so, for I feel deep in my bones that this war is only the first of many, and I fear that we may not be standing at the end."

"We are Warriors of Blackhaven, of the Greatest House Tiena, and very much in love. Nothing can defeat us, yes?" Suneelo said, referencing an old elfin proverb.

"Yes. Yes, indeed," Yayènia murmured, and fell asleep.

Erdwyf groaned quietly as she pulled off her right vambrace. Ghealan sent her a concerned look over Tyre's shoulder. Ignoring her husband, the High Advisor flexed her stiff fingers, studying the blackened area on her forearm where an enemy mace had slammed into it. Her muscles slid beneath the bruised skin as she twisted her wrist back and forth to make sure it wasn't broken. Satisfied, she began rubbing ointment on the area.

"All right, send them out, but make sure none of them venture beyond the hill. We have few enough mounts as it is," Ghealan said to the human, dismissing him. "How did you manage to get that?" he said to his wife when they were finally alone in the large command tent.

"I was at the end of the front line when Tlonna Wove that Storm. A couple Zaedicans were tossed against us, and a few of them decided to try and win the war by themselves. One got a little lucky," Erdwyf replied quietly, resting her gaze on Ghealan's creased forehead. "Do not do that," she said, smoothing the frown away. "It makes you look like a human."

Ghealan smiled wickedly. "Well, how would you like to try sleeping with a human tonight? I hear they are rather rough."

Laughing, Erdwyf flicked some ointment at the warrior. "You have a job to do, sir, and you will do it well. I am going to get some sleep. Love you," she said, kissing him goodnight.

"That is not fair, Erdwyf," Ghealan groaned as she strutted toward the exit.

"Well, High Commander Ghealan, you will have to make up for it later, then."

Losolin walked a few steps behind Miazie, who had a bowl of soup and a waterskin. "Is that for Tlonna or have you commandeered my place in the tent?"

Grinning Miazie ducked into the shelter. "Well, it could be like old times and we could fight over it."

"We never fought over—Tlonna! You are awake!"

Tlonna looked up wearily, and managed a weak smile. "Fought over what?"

"Who got to sleep with you," Miazie butted in with a toothy grin at Losolin.

"Oh," the queen chuckled, taking the bowl of soup from the human.

"How are you feeling?" Losolin asked, sitting next to Tlonna's feet.

"Horrible. But nothing I cannot handle. How are things progressing?"

The king sighed. "I booted Yayènia from position for tonight. I just checked in on her, and both she and Suneelo are asleep. Half-ready to walk outside and do battle, but asleep nonetheless. I ran into Sodo on the way over here, looking like he was fit to take on the whole enemy by himself. The pyres for Ryun and Jordan are built, but they will be lit tomorrow night. I am sorry Miazie," Losolin said, putting a consoling hand on his friend's shoulder.

Miazie shook her head. "I have become numb to it, I think," she said in a nasally voice. "At first, it was such a shock, but... he was ready to die. After Jacinth died, he kept telling me he wanted to follow her. I hope they found peace together."

"I really liked Ryun," Tlonna stated quietly. "I wish I had known Jordan better. Tyular will not be pleased his captain is dead."

"Tyular would be here if he could, as would Demetri," Losolin reminded her. "They know war as well as us. Better. They know the risk, especially for officers."

"I know, but it does not make it any easier," the queen replied.

A few hours later, Dorik marched in with five hundred dwarves from Florwen Hune. Tlonna and Ghealan greeted them and sent them into the camp and handed Dorik his black plume. It was then that a hulking figure sauntered over and gave Ghealan a hard smack on the back. When the elf regained his balance, he gave Anadin the Dwarf-Elf an unsure smile.

"Welcome to the tenth hell, Anadin. May I present you to Magin Queen Tlonna Arune Ewôsdírn er'Grisholm?"

The half-breed grinned and bowed his head to Tlonna, who continued to stare at him, still weary from her ordeal the previous day. "An honor to meet you, my lady, after hearing so much about you."

"Y-you have heard of me?"

"Oh, aye. I led your lover and his companions, including this one," he clapped Ghealan on the back again, "through Florwen Hune almost two years ago. They did their best to kill me, but...I am still walking today."

Tlonna turned her stare onto Ghealan. "You tried to kill him?"

"Yayènia."

"Ah."

"Aye, where is the little elfling? I would like to show her that Anadin still lives."

Tlonna turned back to the half-breed. "High Commander Yayènia is...resting."

Anadin guffawed, "Why in the nine bleeding hells is she resting at a time like this? This is war, not elfie nap time!"

"The High Commander has been running this defense for months now, and exhaustion took its toll on her. She will be back in a few hours," Ghealan replied quietly.

"Oh, aye. I will leave you to whatever it is you were doing. See you on the field."

Tlonna and Ghealan watched the massive male stroll away in disbelief.

"That...he is very odd, is he not?" Tlonna said as they turned to go back to camp.

"Aye," Ghealan replied, rubbing his fingers over his lips to hide a grin. "Yayènia is not going to like this."

"Did she really try to kill him?"

Ghealan sighed. "Nia does not like unnatural things, and when there is a dwarf in mix, she likes them even less."

Tlonna held the door open for him. "But, she has dwarves in her militia. There is even a dwarf in the Silvers, and there is Orthak."

"Nia does not dislike dwarves, she respects them, but she views their culture to be coarse and unrefined. Yayènia takes great pride in being clean, in her soldiers being clean, and her ranks being clean. Dwarves, well...the dirtier they are, the happier, it seems. When it comes to fighting, she does not discriminate if they are up to her standard. Her *Zephyr Leifen* warriors are all trained personally by her and are therefore the greatest fighters around, whether they are an elf or not. Anadin clashed with her immediately, despite his abilities. They do not get along, and I worry about her reaction."

They reached the command tent and found Yayènia and Suneelo in a tight embrace. The High Commander drew away from her husband and looked at Tlonna, her eyes dark with reserve.

"Scouts have reported that reinforcements have stopped coming into Sithian's camp. It looks like we finally have a solid group to work with. You took out about seven thousand by yourself. What Ghealan did is going to work to fray the edges, make them nervous. Keep this tactic up for a few days and then we will see what I need to order. Dorik came in here to receive his plume, but I did not question him. How many dwarves do we have?"

"Five hundred, Yayènia-" Ghealan began.

"Who is leading them?"

The Second Commander took a deep breath, "Anadin."

There was a second of tense silence as both Ghealan and Suneelo waited for Yayènia to move.

"What?" the elf asked sharply.

"Anadin, the...the Dwarf-Elf from Florwen Hune," Ghealan repeated.

Yayènia closed her eyes and rubbed her temples. "Why, of all people, would King Barukh send that abomination to lead his soldiers? What madness is this?"

Suneelo wrapped his hand around her arm. "Love, he is a good warrior. Our dislike of him does not hinder his ability to wield that massive blade of his."

"I do not care! I do not want him here, with me, in *my* defense. Oh, we are doomed," she said plaintively, throwing her hands in the air.

"Wouldn't happen to be talkin' about me, would ye?" Anadin boomed as he ducked inside the tent.

Yayènia looked about to explode. Suneelo stepped forward and extended his hand. "Anadin, how nice to see you again."

As the dwarf-elf took the hand offered, he grinned and looked to Yayènia. "I am told it is ye who are in charge of this here camp?"

Yayènia glared. "*Aiya.* What do you want?"

Anadin released Suneelo's hand and turned to face the warrior. "I was told by a..." he tapped his fingers together, "Captain

Orthak that I should come here, introduce meself to ye, and become a part of this so-called council ye all have here."

Yayènia snorted, "You want to be on my war council?"

"Oh, aye. I want to know how the legendary Yayènia er'Tiena runs her wars. Ye aren't gonna deny me such a right, are ye?"

Tlonna raised her brow at her friend and gave a slight shake of her head. Yayènia cursed. "No. We always meet here, whenever you hear one lingering horn blast. Two short blasts mean a change of the guard. Three mean attack and two long blasts mean to ready the troops. Got it?"

"Oh, aye. I will be back then, good day," the massive male ducked out of the tent and sauntered away.

Suneelo patted his wife's shoulder. "You did well, my love. Better than I expected."

"Oh, aye," Yayènia replied, mocking Anadin.

Chapter 16

And the Guardian Falls

A week went by as the archers in the trees harrowed the Zaedicans. The days turned bitter cold and snow fell incessantly, making tents look like little mounds. The attacking army did not move from their camp. At night, fires could be seen a few miles away from Alchemian, where the soldiers crowded to get a respite from the cold and damp. The camp city was bustling. Where soldiers weren't huddling, alchemists worked with their chemicals. Tubs of Nytrynhimmel were readied for battle, iron was melted down and forged into weapons, and trees were hewn down to supply wood for bows and arrows. Idle children were put to work cleaning armor and running messages. Some children, those fifteen and older, were recruited and trained with squadrons. Worried parents watched their children spar, their knuckles and faces white with worry.

Sodo started attending the council meetings, his mismatched eyes steady on Yayènia's face. He had stopped wearing his white robes and now wore his day clothes. Aidyn and he had formed an unlikely friendship. The assassin and the tainted elf were prone to closeting themselves in Sodo's tent and tampering with dangerous chemicals and weapons while Miazie looked on in baffled wonderment.

The Belau was distraught over the loss of Ryun, her lifelong friend, but continued to attend the meetings. Damon, Tlonna, and Losolin worked together, honing their raw Weaving skills. Erandur and Lelfwin often were found with Tristan and Aladorn, sparring or trading secrets of battle. Sargotarh, Nebet'thu, and Orthak had taken the corsairs, Alexander and Troaz, under their wing and were teaching them the finer arts of battle fighting.

As the council grew tighter in friendships, the war camp watched their enemy whither under the harsh hand of winter. Though they lost hundreds to disease, their numbers still dwarfed Yayènia's. Younglings from the camp sat on watch for Tarounen and Liena, the Silvers sent to Zeynuwn, and Cora sent to Narnen.

It was the late month of Lamat, six months after the start of the battle, that Cora finally returned, looking the worse for wear.

Erdwyf met her at the gate, as it was the dead of night and most of the council was abed.

The elf nearly toppled off her horse as she dismounted. Erdwyf steadied her and then told a passing soldier to take the beast.

"Cora, come on," Erdwyf said, leading the female to the command tent.

Yayènia and her council were summoned and they arrived shortly after Cora had taken a few sips of watered ale. When they assembled, the elf wearily told them of what had befallen her.

"The trip to Narnen was not so bad, I was able to bypass the army easily by going back through the Corridor of Astinus and then over along the edge of Purheae. But when I got there, it was hard going. The enemy had taken over all the major cities and was on watch for any travelers. I had to abandon my horse at a farmstead just on the western border of Narnen. I traveled on foot to Nestra, and then had to hide for a week there, as soldiers were being taken for 'questioning'." The elf put a sarcastic edge on the last word. "The king and queen were still ruling, but it was obvious that they held no actual power. Some representative from Zaedic was running the city. I want to say his name was...Marcel?"

Everyone looked to Tlonna, who shook her head. "I do not know this name. He probably took over the role held by Kelus before he fled."

Cora nodded. "Well, when I realized I was not going to get any help from the king, I retrieved my horse and rode to Althirim. There I talked to Count and Countess Rhaeetigan, Lady Erdwyf's parents."

Erdwyf nodded, "They are well, then?"

"As well as can be hoped. I spent a few days with them, listening to their account of the siege. They said a farmer and his wife had first seen the ships coming from the north. They fled to Nestra and warned the monarchs, but they believed them to be trade ships. It was not until the soldiers disembarked and slew every urchin, seaman, and citizen at the docks that a warning was sent out. Houses were barred from the outside and set aflame. People were slaughtered in the streets, farms burned, nobles and citizens herded like animals into the city square and hewn down. Women and girls raped, men and boys forced to watch, their limbs hacked off to prevent them from interfering. It was a massacre, my lords and ladies. Complete carnage.

I have never seen anything so gruesome, except for the siege of Blackhaven. It happened the same way.

"Ships continued to dock, and the border was being watched. I could not get out. Finally, about two weeks ago, the watch disappeared and the ships stopped coming in. Soldiers poured out of Narnen, headed here. I bid the Rhaeetigans farewell, with a promise to give their love to Erdwyf and Ghealan, and returned to Nestra. I found King Emar and Queen Atlan hiding in the dungeons of the castle. They were afraid their own people would assassinate them, and for good reason.

"Narnenians were furious and homeless. They painted a large red Z on the door of the castle, for Zaedic, and I have a feeling they did not use paint. There was enough blood in the gutters to paint every door in the city red," Cora took a long swallow of her ale. "I found them in the dungeon and I told them of the state of their kingdom. They were too scared to talk. I asked them for soldiers, and they refused, saying they needed fighters to defend their city. I told them it was too late. They did not care. I think they may have lost their minds, or had it tortured out of them. So, I left. I had to swing wide of Anutch from the east, traveling along the southern edge of the Plains of Arada. I am sorry, but I tried."

Tlonna leaned forward and patted the elf's hand. "It is not your fault, Cora."

"Indeed," Yayènia added as she attached the black plume of special services to her helmet. "You have provided us with much needed information, and for that I thank you. It must have been a hard journey. Please, retire and catch some rest."

The elf thanked her superiors and limped out of the tent. Ghealan yawned and turned to Yayènia. "Well, now we know we were right in suspecting that they have no more reinforcements."

"Aye, and that Narnen is severely wounded, but still alive," Tristan added, glancing at Erdwyf, who was slightly paler than normal.

The advisor bit her lip and excused herself from the tent. With a nod from Tlonna, Ghealan followed his wife.

Yayènia watched them go with concern. Suneelo nudged her and she turned back to the council. Reluctantly, she regarded Anadin. "Nothing like this has reached Florwen Hune, that you know of, has it?"

"Nay, High Commander, otherwise I'd've told ye," the half-breed replied, "I knew a lot of people were fleeing Narnen, but I figured it to be because of the war itself."

Tristan nodded in agreement. "I, as well, noticed that refugees were coming in swarms, but I thought nothing of it. People relocate all the time during war. I never thought something like Blackhaven would happen all over again."

Sargotarh swallowed audibly. "That was the most horrible thing I have ever seen, the siege. To think it happened elsewhere..." he shook his head.

"Did Dietirin and Constancias do anything to stop the siege?" Losolin asked.

Aidyn nodded. "They did. Stores were brought in, the underground tunnels reinforced, which eventually became the underground city, but we did not realize that would happen at the time. The gates were barred, no one entered, and no one left. The harbor was emptied, the militia ready at a moment's notice. The only problem was that we were too late. We did not get the warning until the army was already at the border. Runners had been dispatched from the other kingdoms, but they had been cut down. They did their best; it was just...too late."

"And yet, the same slaughter happened," Tlonna mused.

Suneelo sniffed, "We put up a good defense. We had larger numbers, and much more city than Nestra. Thousands died before their numbers defeated us. I only wonder what would have happened had we not put up a defense."

The council fell silent for a few brooding minutes. It was finally broken by three short blasts of a horn. The council leapt to its feet and everyone took off in a different direction to prepare. They reconvened a few minutes later in full armament, arms and armor gleaming in the moonlights.

Yayènia pointed to the Dwarf-Elf. "Captain Anadin, take charge of your dwarves. Captain Orthak, Captain Sargotarh, get your companies on the flanks, Orthak take the right. Tristan, High Captain Erandur, take your troops to the front lines, full shields, legions front. Neb, get your men surrounding Orthak and Sargotarh and defend with archers only until useless. Understand?"

"*Aiya Zo Konyia,*" the plains elf, said, slipping into Parlêthian as he addressed the female, then galloped off on his deer.

"Captain Troaz, Commodore Alexander, I want your men behind the front lines, crouching so the bastards do not see you until you are on top of them. Lieutenant Lelfwin, you do the same. Captain Tyre, I want yours at the rear. Aladorn get your soldiers with them, shields held above to guard from arrows. Damon, take your men to the flanks and defend Nebet'thu's archers with swords. Everyone understand?"

The remaining council replied with a loud bellow and then sped off.

Yayènia, Ghealan, Tlonna, Losolin, Aidyn, and Suneelo galloped to the front lines where Tristan and Erandur were shouting their companies into lines. Tristan's legion soldiers were standing with their long shields held edge to edge, long spears held forward. They gave their war cry as they rode by.

"*Hïi-gynn*!"

Yayènia burst into laughter as they rode on. Tlonna glanced at her. "What does it mean?"

"It is ancient Hindarün. It means 'come and get us'."

Tlonna grinned. "I like it."

"I do too."

They reached the center of the line and then turned their mounts to face the oncoming army, which was a continuous boom just out of sight.

Yayènia turned around and raised her twin blades high as she stood in her saddle. The nine thousand, seven hundred and fifty-seven soldiers roared back at her, weapons glinting in the dawning sunlight. When she sat again, Tlonna grinned at her, slammed her helmet down onto her head, and looked back at the army of nations.

Banners fluttered in the wind. The bloody clawed badger on a slashed field of blue and white, Standard of House Tiena; the shadowed arrow on a quadrant of red and white, Standard of House Tomyvon. The silver tree on black, Standard of Blackhaven, eight point star and sun on a field of pale blue, House Ewôsdírn, and the white orb on black, House Sestuns, the broken sword on gold was House Ambrose of Arseninis, and the crossed spears on slashed teal and forest green was House Plaukler of Kajgenia. There was a giant deer on a field of brown for the Plains Elf tribes, a pickaxe on brown from Florwen Hune, a black dart on a field of dark green, House Eldrout of Flousen Dua. The corsair flag was there as well, casting its own shadow beside the ancient and famous emblems. Snow billowed around the flags, obscuring them for seconds at a time. For a moment, time seemed frozen.

Ghealan looked at Yayènia and said, "This is it."

Yayènia nodded.

Tlonna breathed deeply. "How many will die today, at the end?"

"Only Maln knows," the High Commander replied.

The queen rode a little farther down the ranks and clasped hands with two Magins. Blue and yellow light surrounded the other two and then faded. Blindingly bright white expanded from Tlonna's body as she took in the other Magins' power and transformed it into hers. Losolin and Damon did the same with four other Magins, though all together they could not match the magic pulsing out of the Magin Queen, especially with the Staff of Cyree glowing at her back.

As the enemy crested the small rise and came pouring down toward the defenders, the Magins unleashed their power. Thick bars of light sliced deep holes in the ranks, only to be filled in by more soldiers. Enemy Magins attempted to counter Tlonna, Losolin, and Damon, but were cut down before their magic became tangible. Thousands of arrows whistled overhead as the archers let loose volley after volley.

The advancing lines faltered as they stumbled over their own dead. Yayènia and her council roared the order to brace. The Legions in the phalanx formation at the apex of the army shifted as one, shouting their war cry. Behind them, the rest of the army shifted as well with a massive boom. Each soldier pressed hard against the back in front of him with his shield to lend stability. Not a word was uttered, complete silence falling over the combined armies. The advancing soldiers bellowed, running in wavering lines to avoid the devastating power of magic.

Damon's strength faltered first, and then Losolin's as their anchors' energy fizzled. Mounting, the six Magins pulled their material weapons and waited for the lines to reach them.

Finally, Tlonna, now standing by herself having completely drained her anchors, pulled herself atop Takîreaes, and let her Weave fade. The enemy lines slammed into the Kajgenian phalanx.

Yayènia, Suneelo, and Ghealan were swept up in the tide, their horses screaming and kicking out. Tlonna watched Ghealan disappear beneath the mass and reared Takîreaes up. Soldiers swarmed around her like a maelstrom, their weapons glancing off her armor. The queen kicked a man in the face and stabbed another through the neck. Snarling, she put Takîreaes down and charged as best she could. The stallion bellowed, gnashed the bit, and plunged head long into the fray. Bodies pressed against each other so tight some were merely squeezed to death.

Tlonna yanked her sword free from another soldier and looked up. Yayènia was missing, but Suneelo was still atop Smithy, lying about with his sword.

The enemy advanced further into the defense and met up with the crouching corsairs and two hundred and sixty-eight Onyx Forest swords. They leapt to their feet and stopped the attack for a moment. The elves and corsairs roared as they shoved the massive force of the enemy back a few steps. Then they splintered and the Zaedicans advanced further. The five hundred and thirty-two Onyx Forest archers put away their bows and drew blades. They slaughtered the first ranks. Their superior strength and skill easily overpowered the original rush of foes, but then the sheer force of numbers pushed a wedge between the elves and the Zaedicans ran on only to be met by five hundred angry dwarves and four hundred desperate Arseninisians. Behind them, five thousand vengeful Blackhaven soldiers pushed against the backs of their comrades.

The Zaedicans were forced back into the clutches of the fighters they had bypassed. Now surrounded on three sides, the mercenaries and workmen panicked as they looked at the fierce elf, dwarf, and human warriors on each side. Erandur and Lelfwin shouted to their troops as Yayènia climbed back atop Verity, snarling as she yanked out an arrow that had found her shoulder.

At their officers' call, the Onyx Forest elves advanced, spinning their spears and swords until they became blurs. Zaedicans died in droves. The ground became slippery with offal, the snow a red slush. The head of the Zaedican force, those soldiers caught between the three sides of the defense, was squashed. The rest of the soldiers shoved against the defense and, with their massive numbers, pushed them back.

Tlonna was attempting to free Takîreaes's reins and saddle from grasping soldiers when Erdwyf rode up and dispatched the front most ones. Takîreaes and Tlonna finished off the remainders and then swung around to confront the female.

"Erdwyf, what in the nine hells are you doing out here? I thought you had been ordered to stay inside today!"

The advisor snarled. "And how much safer would that be? This is war, Tlonna, and I will not stand idly by!"

"What about your child?"

Erdwyf paled a bit, but her face hardened. "I will not stand idly by while others die. I came to tell you, there is a column approaching from the southeast, from the Bijozs."

"Zeynuwnians?" Tlonna gasped as she kicked a soldier in the face hard enough to shove his nose bone into his brain.

"I think so. Where is Yayènia?"

The queen looked for the long plumed helmet of the High Commander, but couldn't find it. "I do not know. Find Ghealan, tell him. I will find Yayènia."

Erdwyf nodded and galloped off.

Tlonna swung Takîreaes around and cursed as he reared back on his hind legs yet again. The stallion screamed as a lancer charged, and then slammed to all fours. The soldier died as massive hooves smashed into his face. The Magin scanned the tops of the fighting melee and finally saw the bouncing blue, silver, and black plume of Yayènia's helmet...in the center of the battle.

She sighed and charged into the thick of the fight. Takîreaes lashed out with tooth and hoof, his rider with sword and magic. The stallion bellowed again as a thick mass of soldiers slammed against his side, and he toppled. Tlonna rolled free of the saddle and winced as a sharp pain lanced up her leg. Forcing the pain to the back of her mind, the queen backed against her struggling horse and swiped out with her sword. Soldiers fell back, ruby smiles carved into their throats. She ducked under a swinging mace and stabbed the man in the belly, jerking him around to throw the balance off another Zaedican.

Finally, Takîreaes was able to get back to his feet and she remounted. Though having exhausted most of her reserve with the beam of Magin flame, Tlonna was able to Weave little blasts of fire. It took almost ten more minutes for her to carve a path to the High Commander. When she reached her, Yayènia spat out a glob of blood. An arrow was sticking out of her thigh, broken off so that only an inch stuck out. One of her vambraces had been lost and her forearm was covered in sticky blood. Something was lodged in her shoulder, by the awkward way she moved her arm, as well.

"Yayènia!"

The warrior looked around and her battle-fevered gaze alighted on her queen.

"A column is marching toward us from the Bijozs!"

"Zeynuwnians?"

"I believe so!" Tlonna had to scream in order to be heard over the clamor.

Without responding, Yayènia pulled Verity around and gestured for Tlonna to lead. The two females cut a path back the way Tlonna had come. They finally made it out and raced headlong to where Erdwyf and Ghealan were waiting. When Yayènia saw Erdwyf, she nearly vaulted out of her saddle to throttle her friend.

"I told you to stay away from here!"

Erdwyf glared at her. "You are losing too much blood, Nia. Perhaps you should lie down."

"I will not stand on the edge of battle while others die."

The advisor gave the warrior a meaningful glance.

Yayènia snarled. "Fine."

The four rode off in the direction of the column headed toward the rear of Alchemian. It was Tarounen who hailed them. The elf gazed at his leaders in pride. Liena, beside him, looked antsy.

Yayènia gave them a crooked smile which looked all the more frightening for her wounds. "Tarounen, Liena..." she pulled two black plumes out of her satchel and handed them to the elves.

As the *Zephyr Leifens* attached their adornments, a warrior in green leather armor rode forward. Through the terrifying visage of his masked helmet, slanted brown eyes took in the foursome.

He pushed his long-legged mare between Liena's and Tarounen's and bowed his head.

"I am Shin Hatsu, General of the Zeynuwnian Green Army. I presume the High Commander Yay-ena? Queen Tionna?"

"Correct, and Second Commander Ghealan, High Advisor Erdwyf. An honor to meet you, General Hatsu, how many have you brought?" Tlonna replied, extending her hand.

The general looked over her shoulder to the battle beyond. "Five thousand. Shall we fight?"

Ghealan appraised the ranks of men behind Shin. "Are they ready to fight? You have marched a long way."

"Why do we not ask them?" Shin replied and turned.

Speaking in rapid Zeynuwnian, the general addressed his army.

As one, they raised crossed katan swords and shouted, "*Hei!*"

"They are ready," Shin said, his eyes crinkling in a smile, though his mouth was hidden by his mask.

"Good," Yayènia and Ghealan said in unison.

"Good," Shin repeated, nodding shortly.

The five leaders and the Green Army poured over the distance to the battlefield and slammed into the flanks of the Zaedicans. They screamed as they died beneath the charge. By the time they reached the center, the Green Army had been filtered throughout the battle. Tlonna and Shin were both knocked from their mounts and leapt up back to back. The Zeynuwnian moved through formations with a speed and ease unknown to most humans. A ring formed around the two as soldiers tried to flee from their flickering blades. Shin received a hard blow to his thigh and fell back against Tlonna. The elf shouldered him back onto his feet and he bounced back into the fray.

It was approaching midday when the snow stopped falling. The battle had been going on for hours, and things had slowed. The fighting had reached Alchemian and poured within the city. People slipped and slid in the sludge. Bodies clogged the streets like driftwood, those still alive crawling desperately out of the way to avoid being trampled.

Horses bellowed and snorted, their breath frosting in the cold. Tlonna watched in exhausted triumph as Zaedicans were mown down by the combined armies of Nymyños. Large skirmishes were still going on in the city however, and dozens were still dying. Tents burst into flame as soldiers dropped torches in their hurry to get away. Alchemian was becoming a sea of blood, smoke, and bodies.

Caydy the spryte hitched up her robes to her knees and tried to flee through the ankle deep sludge now filling the streets. The mud sucked at her shoes until she finally kicked them off and ran barefoot, the sounds of running feet behind her. Gasping in terror and desperation, the alchemist dodged bodies littering the ground, screaming at the faces she knew and honored. Reaching one of the ruined gardens, Caydy tripped, slamming to her knees painfully, scrabbling at the bloody grass. A cold hand gripped her throat from behind and she froze. Sobbing, the female flailed, scratching at the arm holding her.

A man's voice hissed by her ear, "Where's the elf queen?"

Caydy sobbed harder, clenching her teeth.

"I said, where's the elf queen?"

"I-I do not know, please..."

"Don't lie to me. I can sense fear, I can feel lies, I can *smell* treachery," the man said, whispering.

From the corner of her eye, Caydy caught a glimpse of shaggy black hair and pale skin. "M-M-Midian?"

"Yes, that's right. Now, I will ask you one more time. Where's the elf?"

"But, you're supposed to be dead!"

Midian shoved the alchemist forward. Her forehead slammed into the rail of the garden, gouging out a chunk of skin. She felt a foot press hard on the small of her back, grinding her pelvis into the gory muck. She screamed, knowing as she did that it was lost amidst the screams of her people, that it was useless. She was going to die. The hand pushed down between her shoulder blades. Caydy opened her eyes, vowing to herself she would not die with her eyes closed, trembling in fear. She glimpsed the hem of a black cloak, blood soaked, lying inches away from her face in the garden.

"Obviously, there are those in the world who are *much* more powerful than yourself, bitch. Time to die. *Magra.*"

Caydy felt fire and ice flare up her body and reach her brain. In that instant, she died.

Yayènia stalked forward, arms going up to unsheathe the twin blades at her back. Warriors paced along behind her, faces grim. The crowd of running people shifted to allow them through. A single figure stood in the elf's line of vision, black cloaked, light seeming to gather against him, making him blacker than night. Tlonna's order skittered across the warrior's mind.

You will die...

With blood on her hands and sweet revenge in her eyes, insanity was creeping in. It was always there. She transformed it into skill, but now it was growing. A smile cracked her lips. She was not aware of the warriors behind her moving off to fight their own battles. She was alone. Wind caught her black-lined silver cloak and sent it billowing into the wind.

The snow around Midian whirled black. The ground he stood upon lay bare as the tainted snow whipped around him, the incarnation of evil itself. A curved longblade of black steel glinted in the flickering light. Darkness gathered around him. He stared at Yayènia as she approached. He could feel her blade ripping though his back. The very same blade sliding across his throat. He flexed his wrists where puckered scars had risen to mark where she had pressed cold steel into them. The elf reached him.

"I watched you die."

"You cannot kill a god, High Commander," Midian hissed, his voice deep and gravelly where once it had been smooth and crooning.

"You are no god. You are a man, brought back to life by a pendant made by those more powerful than you," Yayènia shot back, leaning on her swords.

"I have defeated death; there is no one more powerful than me."

"Your father once said something like that to me. What was it? Oh yes... *I am a walking god, and I shall taste neither fear nor death.* Seems to me he is seventy-seven years dead."

"He was a fool," Midian snapped.

"Seems to be a family trait, boy," Yayènia laughed, and yanked her swords out of the ground. "Come, let us settle this for once and all."

Midian grinned, and raised his blade.

Ghealan and Suneelo rode through the milling soldiers, roaring at the top of their lungs. The soldiers rallied around their officers, training taking over the fear. Their ranks reformed, shoving the Zaedicans back. The enemy army was bundled in heavy furs and thick materials that greatly inhibited their movement. Their slower movements enabled the defending militia to push them over.

Tlonna, Losolin, Miazie, Damon, and Aidyn ran through the streets looking for more of their companions, dispatching the fleeing Zaedicans. With a scream, Miazie stopped short and pointed. At the end of the street, Yayènia went to her knees before the third rider, one of her swords falling to the ground. The cloaked figure moved with lethal grace, black snow whipping around him, then turning white again as it passed.

"Midian," Losolin whispered, disbelieving.

Yayènia felt the ring of her sword all through her body, stunning her into paralysis. It seemed he had no weakness. She had been fighting all day, and she was injured. The strength of Midian's next blow shocked her into movement. Their blades kissed again and again, weariness hampering Yayènia. Midian slammed his sword hard onto hers, and her wounded shoulder and forearm gave out and she dropped her blade. With her other hand, she groped blindly for another weapon. He grabbed her elbow and shoved her roughly down to the ground. Afraid for her life for the first time ever, Yayènia closed her eyes. Midian pounded his free hand into her face over and over again until it bled freely. Her jaw shattered and her nose broke. The Magin's super strength overpowered even her elven might. She cried out as Midian wrenched her arm around, shoved it behind her back, and yanked it upward. Her shoulder shattered.

"Did you think you could beat me? I, who am born again, I who have been resurrected? Did you honestly think you could win? Now, finally, you get to pay. You escaped me once, you won't do so again. I will watch the light leave your eyes when you die. I will taste your blood and it will be sweet."

He turned her around so that she faced him. His fist smashed into her face once more. With her suspended on her knees, the human tore at her flesh until every inch of her was covered in blood. He peeled skin from her muscle, yanked hair out by the fistful, and pummeled her gut until she vomited blood. Yayènia opened her mouth to scream, but could only manage a hoarse moan. She tried to hit her assailant, but he caught her wrist and snapped it.

Midian groped around behind him until he grabbed one of Yayènia's blades and held it tight to her throat. Blood gurgled in her gullet; as the blade sliced through her flesh and severed her throat. He grinned as her eyes glazed over and her body relaxed in his arms. He bent down and ran his tongue along her neck, eyes rolling back in ecstasy. Standing, Midian dragged her body across the ground to the edge of the city, dropped her sword down the ravine that stood next to it, and then tossed the elf after it.

Yayènia's body slid down the soft, damp earth until it reached the bottom, lying next to her bloody sword. Midian grunted contentedly and strode away.

The others fought to get through the pressing masses. As Midian turned away in triumph, Tlonna slammed into him with full force, taking him down. The others struggled behind her, heedless of friend or foe.

In severe agony, Yayènia clutched at her bleeding throat with twisted fingers. Tears leaked down her face as she pulled herself painstakingly toward a trickle of water. Not moving her head, she dipped her hand in the water and attempted to wipe away the blood. Whimpering, the elf continued to wipe her bloody neck. Her hand shook violently, spraying crimson water everywhere. Opening her eyes, she gazed up at the edge from where she had fallen, her vision clouding at the edges. Gurgling pitifully, the warrior saw a dark figure above, saw golden hair appear, heard a cry of desperation.

"Someone help! Losolin! Tlonna! Spirits help! Please! Tlonna! Oh Gods! Suneelo! Please!" Erdwyf screamed.

There was a moment of silence, then a cry. Erdwyf launched over the ledge. Yayènia blinked slowly as booted feet crunched toward her in a run. Erdwyf hit her knees, sobbing in fear. Unable to move, Yayènia laid still, breath gurgling through her ruined throat.

"Spirits! Nia? Please do not be dead. Oh plea-"

A scream echoed across the ravine as people scattered away from the edge. Black figures swarmed over as people shied and leapt away from them. A soldier's hand wrapped around Erdwyf's waist and she was yanked away.

Her eyes widened and her hands grasped toward Yayènia's tensely quivering body. The man behind her shoved Erdwyf up and over his shoulder as she screamed. Another man rode up to Yayènia and turned his visor up to study her. Another stopped next to it and studied her as well. The first man grunted.

"This one is done for. Leave her, she is doomed to the depths of the nine hells," the man growled and rode away.

Erdwyf wrestled with the man, tears of rage and terror swimming in her eyes. A fist of determination settled in her stomach like a burning coal. Fury welled inside the elf, and she screamed, this time in wrath instead of dread. Grinding her teeth, Erdwyf wrenched around and struck her captor in the back of the neck. His head snapped back and his elbow slammed into her gut. Nauseated, the elf clamped down her teeth harder and aimed another successful blow at the man's skull. The human went rigid and slid off his horse, which did not stop. The other riders galloped by, not noticing their fallen comrade. Wrenching away from the man, Erdwyf put one booted foot on his chest, reached down, and ripped the lower half of his jaw off. Tossing away the bone and flesh, the female broke into a frantic sprint to where Yayènia still lay.

A knot of people surrounded her, though nobody moved. Above, another group of people still battled, spurts of magic blowing holes in whatever it touched. Erdwyf shoved people out of her way and stumbled to her knees beside Yayènia. With a single glance, the advisor felt her worst fear come to life. Split from ear to ear, her best friend's throat was bare. No more blood gurgled out, no more gulping sobs. Yayènia was dead. The guardian had fallen.

Howling in rage, Tlonna clambered off Midian. He got to his feet, vaguely surprised. Pure white magic exploded into his chest as the elf bore down on him again. A slight tingle made him lift his hand to scratch where the power pumped into him. She skidded to a halt a few feet from him, her eyes wide.

"Hello, Tlonna."

"How, in all the hells are you alive?" she screamed, her voice rough with fury.

"It seems to me that our son and daughter have the combined ability to resurrect the dead. An amazing trick, really. Too bad the failure offspring cannot do that. I know watching your sister die must have been hard for you."

A tempestuous desire to kill raged in Tlonna as she stared at her enemy. Refusing to play his game, she said, "She was not my sister."

"Oh? Don't you think it a bit odd that two elves, two *female* elves, would both possess extraordinary weaponry talent, unheard of natural beauty, *and* have magical abilities?"

"You lie. Yayènia is not a Magin!"

"Oh no, no she was not a Magin. She *was* a Maig; she could not use her power outwardly, but inwardly. She could heal herself from the inside, unless of course, she died too quickly or lost too much blood or energy. Few knew it of course. How do think it is that she survived so many fatal wounds and still managed to walk away with barely even any scars? Think about it, Tlonna. Ask anyone, no one knows where exactly she came from, or how she managed to rise so high in the political chain, when her parents *sold her.* Yayènia was born to Constancias and Dietirin Ewôsdírn in the year nine thousand forty-six, month of Kayab. Ashamed of her small size, Constancias secretly sold the two-day-old infant to a couple, gave them the title of baron, and told her saddened husband that the babe had died. Yayènia was sold over and over again throughout Blackhaven until rescued by Ghealan Tomyvon. I gather that you know the rest of the story."

Tlonna stared at the man. Disbelief and horror were waging a war inside of her as she stood, dumbstruck. When her inner battle reached its climax, her vision hazed and she lost control of her body.

Midian barely had enough time to block the blade that came swinging at him. Tlonna mounted a full-fledged attack on him, her eyes changing rapidly in both color and pupil shape. It wasn't until Midian finally got in a strong thrust that tore through her upper arm that she slowed. The queen dropped her sword from her useless fingers and clutched at her wound. The undead Magin was preparing himself for the killing blow when green and red magic slammed into him. Twisting in pain, Midian focused on his new assailants, stepping over to straddle Tlonna's body.

Losolin and Damon stood with their feet spread, hands outstretched. With a single blow, Midian tore Damon in half. Miazie screamed and leapt for her mutilated husband. Losolin's power had nearly doubled in strength and he held Midian at bay long enough for Tlonna to recover from the shock of her injury. Yanking a dagger out of her boot, the elf plunged the blade into the man's spine and wrenched it downward. Midian froze, paralyzed. The black magic coming from his hands snapped back into his body and sent him spinning. Not caring about what happened to him, Losolin lurched to where Tlonna knelt, cradling her shredded arm. In a few agonizing seconds, he healed it and helped her to her feet. She stumbled to where Midian lay, his eyes open, breathing raggedly. The elf gripped her dagger and with a sneer, plunged it into his neck, directly into the scar where Yayènia had sliced it two years before. She beheaded him, carved out his heart, and stabbed it over and over until it was just a bloody, gooey mess.

"Come back from that, you gods-damned bastard," Tlonna growled, wiping her blade clean even though she herself was already covered in slick blood.

Little bursts of fighting still existed, but most of the battle had died out. The Nymyñosian Militia had won, spurred on by the fury and desperation at seeing their commander fall. Abandoning the stunned Miazie, Tlonna, and Losolin scrambled down the ravine to where Erdwyf still genuflected over the unmoving form of Yayènia. People stared down at the elves, most of them silently crying at the loss of their beloved commander. They parted numbly for the king and queen who gently pushed Erdwyf out of the way.

The knowledge of whom and what Yayènia was still lay fresh on Tlonna's mind as she stared down at the bloody wreck. "Losolin...can...can you...?"

The elf put his hands over the dead warrior's neck and chest. The skin knitted together and a long, pink scar swelled up out of the flesh. Blood still covered nearly every inch of the elf, though she looked much better without the massive rip in her throat. Losolin sighed wearily and sat back. "I do not have the skill to bring back the dead. I am so sorry."

Erdwyf, who had been sitting with her body bowed over Yayènia's legs, let out a wrenching sob.

"I tried to get to her fast enough. I tried. I could not leave her lying here all by herself. Not that, never that. She is my best friend. She is...she is our salvation." The words came out garbled and in a throaty voice. "Oh gods, Suneelo and Ghealan. He still loves her. I know it. They love each other. But I do not care. They love us, too. They do not know, do they?"

When Tlonna shook her head, sniffing, Erdwyf collapsed, weeping helplessly over her fallen friend. Tlonna wearily stood and wiped her eyes with the back of her hand. Pointing to a few men, she ordered them to take Yayènia to the camp and prepare her body. Erdwyf was aided up by Losolin and together, the three went to find Miazie.

The human sat stroking the head and torso of Damon. The rest of him lay a few feet away. Tears poured silently down her dirty face and landed on the Magin's. More guards took both parts and followed all the others who were carrying the dead. Very few of the Zaedican Army had survived. The Nymyñosian defenders had suffered massive losses as well, and many were greatly mourned.

Tlonna, Losolin, and Erdwyf found Ghealan and Suneelo effectively executing a group of mercenaries. Their armor was splattered in blood and gore, just like everyone else's. Ghealan rushed to his wife's side, his face in shock.

"What happened?"

When neither Tlonna nor Erdwyf said anything, Losolin took his half-brother Suneelo, and Ghealan a few feet away. "Yayènia...she...she fell. Midian cut her throat."

Neither elf moved. It was Suneelo who spoke first, a scornful look on his face. "No, no. She is not dead. No human could kill her, Midian is dead. No."

Losolin gripped his brother's shoulder. "Suneelo."

"NO!"

"Suneelo..."

"Gods damn you, she is not dead! She cannot die!"

"Brother, listen-

"Shut your mouth! Yayènia! Yayènia!" the elf began to wander away, his voice cracking.

Losolin nodded to some soldiers, who followed him at a distance, making sure he didn't go too far. He turned to Ghealan. The commander still stared at Losolin, his eyes pained. Crinkles appeared at the edges of his eyes, betraying him. When the king started to reach for him, the elf broke down and fell to his knees, great sobs shaking his body. Unable to control himself any longer, Losolin too fell to his knees and wept.

An hour later, Aidyn, Sargotarh, and Aladorn, each of them grief-stricken and bleary eyed, brought Suneelo into the command tent. The Captain of the Guard was blood-streaked and riddled with ash and mud. His golden hair was mussed and frayed from his fingers as they tore at it in a frantic and unconscious rage. Dark eyes were reddened with tears, the pupils dilated with madness.

Losolin was sitting with his head pillowed on his arms when the four elves entered the tent. His brother was strung listlessly between the assassin and the wiat, his feet dragging. Sargotarh followed behind, carrying Suneelo's confiscated weapons. The king stood when Aidyn dropped the mourning elf into a chair, and wiped his own eyes.

"We had to restrain him from leaving."

"Leaving?" Losolin asked, looking up from his brother's dead eyes.

"The camp," Aladorn explained. "He wanted to kill them all by himself. Losolin, he has gone mad."

"Would you not?" the half-Magin said quietly, thinking of Tlonna, and what her death would mean.

"I did," Aladorn reminded him, thinking of his own wife, now dead for over a hundred years. "What do you want to do with him?"

Losolin shrugged, kneeling before his elder sibling. "Suneelo?"

The warrior did not respond but for a slight flicker of his eyes. Losolin pointed toward the entrance, looking at the three elves behind him, and they left.

"*Bruun*?"

"She is gone," Suneelo moaned, tears welling once more. "My wife, my love. Gone."

"Suneelo, you must not lose yourself. Yayènia would..." for a moment his voice broke. "She would want you to keep moving, to keep fighting. Please do not lose yourself."

The captain shook his head and began to weep in earnest, soul-wrenching sobs that broke Losolin's heart as his brother gripped his shoulders. "I cannot live without her!"

"I know," the king whispered, "I know."

Tlonna looked up as Miazie entered her tent, looking forlorn. The queen let out a shaky breath and wiped her eyes again. She wondered if there was a single smile in the entire camp, and doubted it. Her friend sat down beside her on the cot and sobbed once.

"A day of loss," she muttered, leaning on Tlonna's shoulder.

"I did not know you loved him," the elf replied in kind.

"I did not, not as a husband, but he was a friend. I passed the command tent on my way and heard Suneelo and Losolin. Suneelo's love for Yayènia is profound. I cannot imagine his pain," the Belau said.

"She was loved by many. Miazie, did you know she was my sister?" Tlonna asked, still unsure of whether she believed Midian.

The human started to shake her head, but suddenly her pupils contracted and her mind bent to a time long ago. She saw the sale of Yayènia by Constancias. Gasping, Miazie came back to the present and gripped Tlonna's hand.

"She was sold. Oh, Tlonna, how did you find out? Did Yayènia know?"

The Magin shook her head. "Midian told me, right before I tore out his heart."

Miazie made a small sound in the back of her throat, wrapping one arm around her best friend. “I am sorry,” she whispered.

“I am too,” Tlonna replied, hugging her back, great heaving sobs rolling up her body to burst forth in an uncontainable rush.

Chapter 17

Grief and Love

That night, pyres were built, and the dead were burned. However, when they went to build one for Yayènia, a nearly comatose Ghealan stopped them, shaking his head.

"She never wanted to be burned. She hated fire. Bring her home. Please, let us take her home."

Tlonna agreed, and they wrapped Yayènia up in her cloak after her body had been cleansed. When the mass funeral was over with, the council reconvened in the command tent, though it seemed a dreadfully empty place. Shin-Hatsu and Anadin sat side by side, their faces masks of disbelief and confusion. Erandur was silent, brooding. Tristan leaned against Aidyn's chest, his eyes closed, the assassin's slow tears dripping down his own face. Aladorn, Lelfwin, and Miazie sat in a row, their eyes downcast and sullen, the human's face pressed against the wiat's shoulder. Tlonna and Losolin clung to each other, desperate, while Suneelo lay hunched against his brother, unresponsive. Erdwyf lay curled against Ghealan, both of them crying silently. Troaz and Alexander sat in the back with Tyre, one of the few remaining human captains. Orthak and Sargotarh were despondent, looking lost without their commander.

The army stayed at the demolished city of Alchemian almost a week to help rebuild. The wall was repaired and put back in its place. Ardenay was christened High Alchemist when Sodo resigned, having lost all drive.

As the camps were struck and the armies began to prepare to leave, the demoralized war council convened one last time.

"I will take my people straight home, but do not think our relations over, Queen Tlonna. My people have lain in hiding for far too long. We will bring news of this war to my father, and then I shall most likely be on my way to your city," Erandur said, bowing slightly before the female elf. Then he turned to Aidyn, who blinked at him. "As I said before, my father very much wishes to speak to you. When this battle is over, I pray you will come to Flousen Dua and honor us with your presence."

"I shall," the assassin murmured, shaking the Duani elf's offered hand.

As Erandur moved off to say his farewells to the others, Shin-Hatsu marched up to Tlonna. "I marched a long way to get here, and I do not plan on returning immediately. I will move my army across the breadth of the Liberated Lands and finish off any surviving bands. We will turn home when the passes open enough to admit us safely through. I will report my findings to Emperor Tahi-tat as soon as I can. When you call, unless strictly forbidden, my men and I will march with you. Zeynuwn stands beside Blackhaven and her allies once more."

Tlonna smiled, genuinely touched. "You won this battle for us, General, I cannot thank you enough. Send my regards to your Emperor, and know that should Zeynuwn find itself in trouble, my people will come."

The exotic looking human bowed sharply and marched away, barking in his own foreign tongue at the various lieutenants standing outside the tent waiting for him. Anadin waved his gigantic hand at her and departed without saying much of anything, though he paused beside Ghealan and patted him on the shoulder.

"Barukh will know what happened here," he rumbled and moved off.

Then Tristan moved over to Tlonna, pulling along a disturbed looking Aidyn. "I need to get my people home as soon as I can, for all of Tyular's remaining men are marching with us until the border. I am sure Father will send word as soon as he can, once I'm back. Tlonna, I'm so sorry."

The queen pulled the young prince into a tight embrace, sending a curious glance at the assassin standing behind him. When Aidyn merely shrugged and walked off, she released Tristan.

"I do not know how deep your relationship with Aidyn goes, but he seems to care for you a great deal," she said to the dispirited man.

Tristan shrugged one shoulder. "He has many stories," he replied dully. "I will leave it to him to divulge them."

"You sound like your father," Tlonna retorted with a shake of her head. "Go home, Tristan, and take along our love."

The individual armies split at last and began their various marches home. The Blackhaven Militia, which had suffered the greatest loss and had poured their full strength into the war, prepared to go home as well, planning to stay one more night in order to rest for their long march home.

Miazie sat in the tent she had once lived in, stroking the katan Damon had given her. Tears splashed onto the lacquered sheath as she cried. She had grown to care for him in the year gone, and now he had been torn away from her, literally. She lay down and wrapped the baldric around her fist. Sleep took her at last.

It was a sudden burst of sunlight, and then shadow again that woke her from her dead slumber. Slowly opening her eyes, the Belau gazed around at her surroundings and then alighted on the figure standing in the entryway to her room. Sitting up, she rubbed at her swollen face and sniffed.

"Yes?"

"Miazie. I am sorry."

"Sodo? Dear spirits!"

The elf lowered his cowl and gazed at her through his mismatched eyes, one normal, the other black where it should have been white. His hair, which had once been summer gold, was now streaked with sable.

"Miazie, forgive me. I should not have come here," he turned and slapped the tent flaps out of his way as he left.

The woman jumped to her feet and ran after him. "Sodo! Wait, don't."

The elf pivoted. "Do not what?"

"Don't...leave."

Sodo faced her fully and walked back into the tent. "I came here only to say that I am sorry for your loss. I did not know you loved him, as you did."

"He was my friend. I have never stopped loving you. I...don't...shouldn't....uh..."

The elf rushed her, wrapped his arms around her, and pressed his mouth to hers, tears splashing down his face as he finally held the woman he loved. Miazie gasped, pushing away slightly to study the elven face, her lips trembling as she fought to keep her wits.

"I love you."

"*Klamen inkan yayena dü*," Sodo replied, unable to stop his tears.

Sodo left the next day with the army, waving goodbye to his friends and sharing a long embrace with Ardenay, who smiled sadly but acceptingly.

The army snaked back through the Corridor of Astinus, now much slower because of their wounded. Yayènia lay alone in her own wagon, guarded always by Erdwyf, Suneelo, or Ghealan. They reached Blackhaven nearly a month later, tired and footsore.

Chapter 18

A New King

Kelus and Haydyn met them at the castle gate. Both had been bidden to stay behind to keep the kingdom under control and they looked on with horrified gazes when they saw the shortened lines of soldiers. Tlonna hugged her son and gripped wrists with Kelus, barely able to look either in the eye.

Suneelo and Aidyn took Yayènia's body to the castle morgue, where she would be prepared for her funeral. Because elven bodies do not decay anywhere near as rapidly as humans or dwarves, the fallen warrior looked as though she were merely sleeping, though her skin was gray and cool to the touch. The two males stood in the room, looking down at her, silent and grieving.

Finally Suneelo took a deep breath. "I do not think I can go on, Aidyn. My heart feels like dust, my world has turned gray and empty."

The dark elf gently brushed Yayènia's stiff fingers. "The pain fades, after a while. The heart mends, but the scars remain. Color and sound returns, but slowly, until one day you find yourself smiling once more. And then you catch yourself and you stop, believing your happiness to be a dishonor to her, until again you find yourself smiling. Eventually, you realize that she would want you to continue living, to live for her and yourself."

Across the bed, Suneelo was weeping softly, gazing down at his wife, his forehead crinkled up as he tried to hold back the tears. Yayènia's head twitched to the side in a small movement and Aidyn backed away, not wanting to bump the bed again, though he had not felt any contact with the edge.

Suneelo looked up at him, his eyes watery and reddened. "Do you remember the day we got married? So many people said I was mad to marry her, that she was more likely to slit my throat in bed than anything else. But I loved her so much. She had a tenderness to her that could steal your breath away in the rare moments she let it come through. She was afraid of showing her true heart, afraid that once she did, her reputation would be shattered and her soldiers would believe her weak. Gods, Aidyn, I love her so much!"

The dark elf rushed to the other side of the bed and held the high elf up as he collapsed inward, his knees losing their strength. Suneelo's face was buried in Aidyn's chest and he wept for a long time. As the grieving elf struggled to get himself under control, the assassin looked down and frowned as Yayènia's face turned slightly, seeming to search for the sun. He stared downward, swearing to himself that he was imagining things, and then her eyelids flickered.

"Sweet spirits!" Aidyn shouted, leaping away, dragging a startled Suneelo with him. "She is alive!"

Suneelo gaped at him for a moment and then slugged him hard across the face, dazing the dark elf. Aidyn took the hit without complaint and pointed at Yayènia.

"Suneelo, she just moved. I swear to the gods she did!"

The elf turned slowly and walked over to his wife, staring down at her. Her eyelids twitched and this time his knees hit the floor before Aidyn could get to him.

"Nia," Suneelo wheezed, reaching out to brush his knuckles down her cheek, tears streaming anew. "How, my love?"

Aidyn rushed from the morgue, black hair and cloak flying behind him as he sprinted to the infirmary. He burst into the large hall and skidded to a stop, grabbing the closest healer.

"High Commander Yayènia is in the morgue, but she lives yet! Get down there and help her!" he shouted, shoving the frightened human out of the door.

Two others followed his steps while the assassin rushed about, searching for Tlonna. He found the queen sitting in her room with her head on her desk, weeping quietly.

"Tlonna, Yayènia is alive!"

"What?" the Magin asked, her voice nasally from tears.

"Yayènia, I just saw her move. She is alive."

Tlonna stared at him, her mouth slightly open, for a long long time. Finally she blinked and drew in a deep breath. "I will get Losolin."

Minutes later the three were sprinting back to the morgue, where Suneelo stood a few feet away, pacing behind the frantic and bemused healers.

"Move!" Losolin roared and shoved his way to Yayènia's side. His hands pulsed with green light as he moved them up and down her body, muttering under his breath.

Finally he dropped them and shook his head, turning to his brother. "I do not understand. She had no life force within her, not a single wisp of energy. But now, there is. Not a lot, mind you but enough to keep her alive."

"Can you heal her all the way?" Suneelo asked, his voice frantic.

Losolin shook his head. "The amount of energy I would need to take from her in order to do so would kill her, this time for sure. She must heal from within. But she will heal, my brother, she will."

Suneelo went back to pacing, his eyes closed and his face tight. Yayènia was carefully moved into the infirmary and her friends and family were with her day and night, switching shifts as they prepared for the imminent battle to come.

It took almost three months for Yayènia to heal well enough to walk without help. Even with Losolin's aid, her own innate magic, and the best healers, bringing a semi-immortal back from the brink of death was difficult. It was mid-spring when she finally walked out of the infirmary, wincing in pain. Her skin bore the signs of Midian's brutal beating, a new set of pink scars that slashed across her arms and chest. Her throat bore the most horrid of these, running from both sides of her jaw and rising about a quarter of an inch, and dark pink. Castle inhabitants bowed deeply when she passed, murmuring their condolences. She ignored them all.

Yayènia reached the wide double doors to the throne room, where she had been told everyone was congregated. Taking in a deep breath, the elf grabbed both handles of the doors and slowly pulled them open. The room, which had seconds ago been clamoring with noise, fell dead silent. Suneelo, Tlonna, Erdwyf, and all the rest rose to their feet in astonishment. The crowd of peasants, nobles, and visitors stared at her in consternation.

It took a few moments before Suneelo moved. He leapt down the dais stairs and gathered her up in his arms, as he had not been able to do for months. She yelped with pain, and her husband quickly, but gently, set her down. With the support of him, Yayènia scuffled to the front of the line and knelt in military fashion: right knee pressed to the floor across from the left fist, left knee at a ninety degree angle, right hand fisted over the heart.

She spoke for the first time since the attack. The voice that was once beautiful and melodious now had a strong tone of pain and harshness added to it. Everyone present blinked in sadness. “My king and queen, forgive me for my failures.”

Tlonna started to deny her but Yayènia shook her head slightly.

“Forgive me for my failures. I was the High Commander of the finest combined militia ever known, and I was taken down by one man, a man that I thought I had killed. There I have failed twice. I was not able to protect you, or anyone else from fates that they should have been spared. Dear friends lost loved ones, a civilization lost their leader. There, I have failed many times over. The two leaders of the enemy army were not counted among the dead, nor were they seen during the battle. They escaped with nothing more than a scratch, if that. Once more, I have failed. My king and queen, please, I beg of your mercy to grant me one of two choices. My first choice, is to be allowed a swift death at the end of the sword. My second choice, if you decide that cannot be granted, is to be allowed to join the ranks as a common foot soldier, stripped of all my ranks, titles, and properties. My husband, Suneelo, will continue on as he will, with everything he has now. I will not burden him with my name any more. What is your answer?”

Tlonna and Losolin stood stunned, unable to speak. Suneelo knelt beside his wife and put one hand on her shoulder. “Nia, please, do not do this. I love you and you have not failed at anything. Please, I beg of *you.* You are still the High Commander, my love. You were not stripped of your rank because you were hurt. Do you think so little of our friends or me that we would all forget who and what you are just because you were injured?”

When Yayènia did not say anything but knelt stonily before the dais, Suneelo moved away, his shoulders quivering in silent grief. Tlonna descended to stand before the abeyant elf.

“Yayènia er’Tiena, rise for your judgment. I will look you in the eye and see your true intentions when I lay before you your punishment.”

The crowd gasped and Losolin’s jaw dropped with horror.

When Yayènia stood, Tlonna continued. “Better, I do not like speaking with my chin in my chest. It is uncomfortable. Now, I will grant neither of your wishes. Your punishment, as you may see it, is to remain with all your titles, ranks, and properties intact, along with your marital vows to one Suneelo Tiena. You will report for duty, as always, at three past dawn, to work both yourself and your army. You will retire, as always, at four to dusk, to do whatever it is you please *except* take your life in any act of self-demeaning, selfish, uncouth, barbaric, *loathsome, groveling, self-pitying, weak, or any sort of unhappy woe-is-me heroics! Do you understand*?"

The hall was silent. Losolin was silent and Suneelo was standing ramrod straight, waiting for his wife's reply.

Yayènia gazed in bewilderment at Tlonna, searching her eyes for any sign of sarcasm. Finding none, the elf bowed her head and crossed her fists in an awkward position, as there were no hilts to grip as there should have been. "Yes, of course, my queen."

Tlonna smiled, and was the only one who saw the grateful and semi-happy smile the warrior flashed. She took a single step backward, pivoted, and marched painfully out of the throne room. After a few seconds, Suneelo ran after her, ignoring his duties as Captain of the Guard.

The hall slowly grew louder as the petitioners began gossiping about what had just happened. Tlonna and Losolin looked at each other and their fingers found one another, lacing tightly. The queen took a deep breath and sat back in her throne, closing her eyes and shaking her head.

"It will take a long time to heal," she murmured, looking at Losolin.

He simply nodded and kissed her knuckles.

The next week, Yayènia arrived at the military barracks almost an hour early and wiped down all her weapons. When she drew the one that Midian had used to slice her neck, the elf studied it fervently. Sighing, she took it to the royal blacksmith who was just starting his fires.

The dwarf turned and inclined his hairy head to her. "High Commander Yayènia. Glad I am to see you walking once more. What service can I be to you?"

"Master Ulrow, this sword, as you know, is my favorite, one of two. It is also the one that cut my throat. Would you be so kind as to melt it down and forge it into a new blade?"

"And what, pray tell, would you like it to look like?" the dwarf asked, taking the weapon in his thick hands.

"I was hoping you could decide that for me. As it was your grandfather who made them, I thought it would be right to have you make this one. He was a master of his craft, as I know you are. He designed it from scratch for me when I made High Commander, along with its twin. Would you be willing to do the same for me now?"

Ulrow scratched at his beard for a moment, studying the sword. He looked up at the elf who was sitting on one of his anvils so she could be closer to his level of height. "High Commander... it would be my pride and my honor to forge this sword. However, it will take some time for me to come up with a proper design, melt it down, separate the materials, and make it again."

Yayènia waved her hand. "No matter, Ulrow. This is not a matter of time, but a matter of making something turned evil into something great, as it once was."

The dwarf gave her a sad smile. "High Commander, as you have been a friend of my family for many years, and of mine for all my life, I will do my absolute best. It shall be my masterpiece."

"Thank you Master Ulrow. I must get back to the barracks now, but I will come and see you soon. Blessed be, my friend."

"Blessed be," the dwarf returned as the elf walked out of his shop.

Yawning, Tlonna wrapped her fine cloak around her waist and tucked it under her folded arms. She descended from her tower suite onto the fourth floor of the castle, the top floor as well, and wandered through the office section, across one of the arcing, open-air bridges, and into the library, her mind drifting.

The second library in the castle was reserved for the royal family, upper staff, and friends. However, any civilian could apply for a temporary access permit that restricted them to a set amount of days in which they could peruse the extensive library.

A six foot wide column rose from the center of the floor, a massive tree trunk that had been built around, the crown sticking out of the top of the roof. Pitch had been used to seal the opening, keeping the books safe from the elements. The walls were covered in soft red and silver material that gave the library a warm feeling, especially with the giant obsidian fireplace glowing at the far end of the squarish room. The library was actually split in two by a hallway, the north side dedicated to the archives and records of the entire Blackhaven Kingdom, which stretched from the Fãrthyn Ocean to the R'Kunad Sea, separated from the rest of Nymyños by the Strait of Arwênlhias and the Argynd River.

The south was filled with story books and history, books on the various empires, geological studies, Maginic studies, and everything in between. Small tables and overstuffed chairs dotted the center floor and between the three aisles. The carpet was thick, a deep burgundy that reminded Tlonna of good wine. She smiled at a water nymph that was curled up in a chair reading, her blue-ish skin and hair shimmering in the light. The nymph gave a shy smile back and then turned the page of her book. Tlonna climbed one of the tall rolling ladders that allowed people to reach the highest books and swung herself over a few feet. She scanned a few titles until finding the one she sought. *The Bloodlines of Prominent Elves* by Lederin Hayber. Tucking the book beneath her arm, the elf climbed down the ladder and plopped down in a plush chair by the fire.

She opened the book and began reading.

The nymph had left long before Tlonna felt a gentle tap on her shoulder. She was so preoccupied by the material in her lap that she actually started, looking up sheepishly to smile at Nebet'thu.

The plains elf pulled a chair up next to hers and indicated if it was all right.

"Of course, sit."

"Queen Tlonna...I have a concern I would like to address to you, if it is right with you," the male said quietly, respecting the library.

Tlonna shut her book after marking the page and waited expectantly.

"My wife, Eesa, said she talked to you a while back, before the battle. She said she asked you about divorce?"

"Yes, I remember. What is your question?"

The elf shifted, obviously uncomfortable. "Over the past few months...I have...well, come to see Eesa as my wife. Before this whole ordeal, we were a match."

"You mean lovers?"

"Not quite. In the Creed of Asheyl, a male cannot see-"

"A female naked, yes, now I remember. Okay, so you two were friendly friends."

"And then I fell in love with Kepthari, our clan chief's daughter. But she is sorrowfully betrothed to Daegin, Eesa's brother."

Tlonna squinted. "Yes, Eesa told me all of this before."

"I am sorry, I did not know she went into detail. Well, when she forced me to marry her, I hated her. I did not want anything to do with her until a few months ago. For some reason, when she was coming back from a bath, she was wearing nothing but a sheer robe, and I saw her in a new light."

Tlonna chuckled. "So, you hate this lady who forces you into a loveless marriage, and then you see her wet and naked and all of sudden she is your fantasy?"

Nebet'thu blushed crimson as he realized what he had said. "It was like I had never seen her this way before, all sad, quiet...defeated."

"Ah..." the queen murmured, studying her company. " She is not the elf you married, is she?"

"No."

"And do you love her now?"

"I do not know. Perhaps it was the battle at Alchemian that changed me, perhaps not, I cannot be sure."

The Magin set her book on the ground and turned to face the hunter full on. "Master Nebet'thu, Eesa came to me as you said. She was very distraught over the fact that she had done this terrible thing to you. She asked me if it was possible to get a divorce if only one member of the party wished it. I told her I did not know, which was true. What I did tell her was to talk to you, make you listen; make you understand why she did this deed. She was very upset that she had hurt you, only thinking of what her heart desired. I take it from the look on your face that she did not talk to you."

The male bit his lip and ducked his head. "When Eesa said she wanted to talk to me, I hit her, walked out, and stayed in a brothel for a week. I had never fornicated with anyone other than Eesa and her only once. Now I have the sins of at least a dozen different females, both elf and not, on my flesh. When I came back, she was still bruised on the mouth from where I had hit her. She did nothing but cry and mumble to herself when I came back. I felt so despondent about my actions that I went to a tavern and actually drank enough liquor to get myself drunk, which I have never done. I did not know it was possible for us to get drunk. The next day, I took her out to feed our deer, something of which I had been doing up till then. I thought bringing her with me would make her a bit happier, but it did not. I killed her spirit, my lady. I am no better than a human."

Tlonna watched the male struggle with himself until he finally broke down and let out a single sob. She knelt down and wrapped her arms around his shoulders. He laid his head on her shoulder and wept. When he was finally able to pull himself together, Neb jerked back, realizing that the Queen of Blackhaven was kneeling in front of him as he cried into her sleeve. Blushing, the elf turned his face away.

The Magin frowned. "Nebet'thu, I am just as capable as comforting a friend as any other person. Do not be ashamed that it was me who saw you release your pains."

"I am-I am sorry, your majesty."

"Do not be," Tlonna reclaimed her seat. "I never really thanked you for your aid at the battle of Alchemian. You did a wonderful, selfless thing, Nebet'thu, and I am grateful for it."

"I did a duty many thousands did, I just survived. I do not know how, either."

Tlonna smiled gently. "I have been reading up on you Plains Elves. It is said you train every day in the arts of warfare. How can you not know how you survived? I saw your elves fighting, Nebet'thu, and I was greatly impressed."

The elf blushed under her praise once more. "Thank you, my queen."

"Tlonna. Is there something you need from me my friend?"

"Do you have any advice for me, with Eesa, I mean? I know you have many more important things to deal with, I just thought...perhaps...you might have an idea."

"What, dear Nebet'thu, could be more important than matters of love? Now, what I would suggest you do is talk to your wife. Tell her what you just told me, then ask her what she wants. If it is to split, then I will arrange it. If not, then I will do whatever it is you require of me. How is that?"

The short elf nodded. "I think I can do that. Thank you, your maje-Tlonna," he put his chair back and, after bowing, left the library.

Smiling to herself, Tlonna shifted further into her chair and resumed reading.

Losolin looked up as there was a knock on his office door. "Enter," he said, wondering. His surprise and curiosity was deepened when Haydyn stepped inside, gently closing the door.

"Are you busy?" the prince asked, standing rigidly.

"Yes, but I can spare some time. What is it you need, Haydyn?" Losolin replied, moving his papers over to free some space on his desk.

The prince sat, gripping his knees with his hands until his knuckles turned white. "We need to speak."

The king did not reply, but leaned back in his chair and waited for his stepson to explain his cryptic statement.

"You and Mother have been married now for a while, and crowned. And I have been recognized as the Heir Apparent, yet you still treat me as a stranger. Why is that?" the young half-blood asked in a rushed tone.

Losolin stared, caught off guard. He sat up slowly, laced his fingers together, and placed them carefully before him. "We have...spoken about this already, Haydyn."

"No. Not recently. You told me last year that you wouldn't because you and Mother were not yet married, and that it was too soon for you to accept me. I understand that, but it has been a year, and still you do not like me?"

"It is not that I dislike you, Haydyn, it is not that at all."

"Then what is it?" the prince demanded, irritated now.

Losolin's lips thinned as he pulled his temper into check. "You are not my blood. You are not my son. You are my heir, you are widely accepted and liked. You do well at the academy, Yayènia cannot say anything negative about you. Why is my affection so important to you?"

"Because you are my mother's husband! You are my predecessor! You are...my...you are my idol! All I do, I do to be accepted by you! I make every effort so that you would look at me and see someone you are proud of!" Haydyn shouted, losing control.

Losolin let the young man rage at him, keeping his eyes on his hands, silently hoping no one was in their office, overhearing the desperate words of the prince. When Haydyn finally silenced, he slumped in his chair and riveted his eyes on the rug beneath his feet.

"Haydyn..." Losolin began calmly. "I am proud of you, I believe you are an extraordinary person, capable of great emotion and great success. You have been through too much in your life. You have been alive for three years, yet you are eighteen. You did not have a childhood, you did not have a father, really. Do not think I underestimate the impact these things have had on you. You have grown exceedingly in the last year. You are very intelligent, and righteous. I respect you as a person, and as my heir. But...you are *not* my son. You are my wife's son, and I will love you as such. I do love you as such, but you are not mine. I wish with all my heart that Tlonna and I could have a child, but if we did, you would be shunted aside for it because it would be the legitimate heir. That would be accepted, maybe even demanded, but I do not think it would be wise. You are fit to rule, and have been trained by people far better than myself to do so."

Haydyn blinked in surprise. "I had not thought of that. So...because of me, you will not have a child of your own?"

"Yes," Losolin replied softly.

"But...I am only half-elf. I will not live as long as you, any of you. You will still be young when I die. Unless you abdicate, I will not ever rule. You need to have a child," Haydyn said, giving voice to his own fear for the first time.

Losolin looked up at his stepson. "What makes you think that?"

"It is the truth, isn't it?"

"No. Just because you have only half-elven blood, you will live a very long time. Look at your father. Midian lived twice as long as any human, and he was still young when he died. And humans are living longer every year. Now the average life-span is up to one hundred. Unless something unexpected happens, Haydyn, you will live to one day to take the throne."

The prince stared at the king, lips parted slightly in surprise. "But I thought...I never really believed I would rule."

Losolin smiled faintly. "Ah, ignorance is bliss, is it not?"

Haydyn snorted. "You have no idea."

"So, even though you are not mine, I love you as much as I can. Is that good enough?"

"For now. Thank you for listening, Losolin. I'm sure that was the last thing you needed today," the young man chuckled, standing.

"It is what I am here for," Losolin replied

Yayènia paced up and down the lines of her new recruits, Men, Elves, Dwarves, Nymphs, Sprytes, Faeries, female and male, young and old, they watched her like hungry dogs, soaking up any morsel of information she might hand out. The elf wore a silken sash around her neck, hiding her horrendous scar. It was the one wound she was ashamed of and attempted to hide.

Her voice echoed against the walls of the large training compound, low and smooth with its harsh undertone. "When you fight, you will experience a range of emotions. Fury, wrath, fear, helplessness, despair, elation, empowerment, numbness. These emotions are your weapons, use them as such. Bottle them up until battle, and then release them with full force. They will do for you what adrenaline cannot. They will take you far and beyond your average adrenaline rush. During a battle, you will also experience physical sensations that you would not believe possible. In day to day life, you reach a point when you just cannot go any further. That is not an option in war. The enemy will kill whether or not you fight him back. Exhaustion and fatigue are merely walls that you must climb over. Once you climb over them, you will find yourself numb to pain, immune to exhaustion, invincible against weakness. Your mind will enter oblivion."

The soldiers stared at her at her as she paced, hands resting lightly on the hilts of her longsword and dagger. "During battle you will find at least one of the enemy who looks you in the eye as they die, and you will feel compassion for them. Do not be fooled! When they were swinging their sword, they would not care one iota for your life. You were just another number to them. You must feel the same! Each one of their lives is another life you spared on our side. You must show no pain. You may lose extremities, an eye, get a spear through your ribcage, or any other numerous wounds, and live. If you cannot go on, you must get yourself out of the line of fire as quickly as possible, otherwise you *will* die. We have healers in our ranks and out. Find one of them and get back to rank as soon as possible.

"I will not have weakness in my army," Yayènia barked loudly. "Weakness creates an opening that will shatter formations. I will train you hard, I will make you bleed and cry, but you will get over it. I will kick you around and then hit you when you are down. I will force you to do things that you believe impossible. I will push you mercilessly until you meet my standards. Some of you will die in training. If you fear for your life, leave now."

Yayènia looked up, but no one moved. They watched her with glittering, excited eyes. Fear filled most of them, but they did not leave.

"When you march into battle behind my banner, and the banner of the king and queen of Blackhaven, you will be in full war regalia. Your uniform has been paid for and will be issued to you within the week. When we march, I will personally inspect the lines to make sure that every lapel is in order, every stitch is in line. If you do not comply, you will be stripped and made to dress properly before all the militia. Do you understand?"

All present replied heartily, "Yes High Commander!"

Nodding, Yayènia continued her speech. "You are members of the elite Blackhaven Militia, under the command of myself, Second Commander Ghealan Tomyvon, and most importantly, Queen Tlonna and King Losolin. You wear their colors and march under their, and my banner. However, you are all also members of the free kingdom of Blackhaven. You will get in drunken brawls, fornicate with people who are not your spouse, get arrested for improper public conduct. You will do as you please, as long as you do not wear the uniform when you do so, do you understand?"

"Yes High Commander!"

"You all have the right to a number of sick days, personal days, and so on, however, if I get word from one of your captains, or generals, or anyone else of rank higher than yourself that you are missing too many days, I will personally come see exactly what the problem is. Now, I want each of you to pair off, grab a practice sword, and begin sparring. Go!" Yayènia watched in satisfaction as the recruits hastened into pairs and within moments were spacing each other out for sparring room.

She noticed one young elf that seemed to shimmer every now and again, particularly when he was hit. Narrowing her eyes, the warrior walked over to him and watched the young elf and his partner spar. The grim set of the jaw and the lankiness of the body sparked her memory. The young man he was practicing with went into an awkward position that Yayènia recognized as an attempt to lunge and she darted between them. The practice sword slid through her hand until she gripped it and yanked it upward and out of the human's hands. The two males stared at her in awe and fear.

"You," she pointed at the elf, "why are you here?"

He stammered, his face reddening. "I-I want to be in your army, High Commander."

"But you are not new to this career. You were one of the original recruits Queen Tlonna brought from the east. You are Aladorn's son, Locton."

"Yes, High Commander."

"Why are you here? You rode with us to Alchemian."

"I did not fight very well, High Commander. I killed only twenty-seven soldiers," Locton replied, his blush deepening.

Yayènia took a deep breath. "You marched with us, you fought, and you survived. You were not carried back by your comrades. You fought better than most." She reached up unconsciously and rubbed at the scarf that hid her scar.

The two young males stared at her.

"I am going to remove you from this program and take you under my training, personally. You will train with Prince Haydyn, and the Silvers. You may finish out today's practice, but I want you to meet the prince and me tomorrow at noon here. Understand?"

"Yes, High Commander."

"Good, now, you. What is your name?"

The human swallowed and then blushed a deeper crimson than Locton. "Troy, High Commander."

"Very well, Troy. When you are lunging like you were, you need to use your legs more than your shoulders and arms. Like this," she sprang forward and then turned back to the man. "Get it?"

"Yes, High Commander."

"Show me."

Yayènia watched Troy work on his lunge until she was satisfied with his form. She left them and walked around the training yard. Partners everywhere were yelping and giggling as they dueled. The warrior spent her time instructing her recruits on their individual weaknesses. They left the training yard covered in welts, bruises, and grins.

Yayènia was checking the practice swords for flaws when Tlonna strode around the corner of the store room. The warrior cast her queen a scornful glance before returning back to her work.

"What?"

"Since when do you wear dresses in a training yard?"

Tlonna laughed and then sat down on the bench next to her friend. "It is Narda's idea. She thinks the people will not respect a queen who wears male clothes. So I wore this today to ease her mind."

"They did not seem to disrespect you when you wore armor and walked around covered in blood. What is the difference now?" Yayènia asked, sanding down the splintered edge of a waster.

"I do not know, Nia. How is training going?"

"All right. This batch seemed to be competent enough, although you will not believe who showed up."

"Who?"

"Locton. Aladorn's son."

"What? Why?"

"Said he did not feel as though he fought well enough in the war. I told him he was to show up tomorrow and join in Haydyn's training. I have hopes of him joining *Zephyr Leifen.* He has the potential to be a warrior like his father.

Tlonna nodded and then grabbed a practice sword from the pile and began sanding it. Yayènia laughed. "If Narda were to see you now."

"I know I know," the Magin sighed and then stared at the pile of shavings in her lap. "Sometimes I think this whole queen business is not for me."

"You are the best thing to happen to this city in many years, Loni. Sure, I would love it if you could be a Silver, but there is so much more you can do as queen than you ever could as a fighter. Without you, we would be under the command of an elf-bastard and his human slut."

"But, you should have been queen, Yayènia."

Yayènia snorted and wiped the shavings off her lap. "What would make you say a stupid thing like that?"

"Do you know who your parents are?" Tlonna asked quietly.

"Of course I do. Yinji Yedoc was my father, and Selinia Yedoc was my mother. She died when I was fourteen."

"Is your father still alive?"

"I do not know. He sold me a few days after Mother died to Governor Arakis. I have not seen or heard from him since. He is not worth my spit."

Tlonna shifted uneasily. "I am not so sure the Yedoc's were your parents, Nia."

"What?"

"When I fought Midian, he told me that your parents were...my parents."

Yayènia stared at Tlonna for a moment before letting out a disbelieving laugh. "That is insane, Tlonna, and you know it."

"Nia, listen to me. I was in the library and found a book that listed all the prominent Elven bloodlines. Four hundred and ninety-eight years ago, Constancias had a child that died two days after birth. I checked the registry that lists all the royal deaths, and there is not one for that infant. There is, however, another registry that lists all titles and lands given to people, and why. On the day that the infant died, Yinji and Selinia made a very large purchase from the throne, and acquired the status of baron and baroness.

"There is no record as to what this purchase was, other than that Constancias signed and recognized the whole thing, while Father did not. His signature is nowhere to be found. A few days later, Selinia gave birth to a daughter, but without showing signs of a gestation period. No nurse was called to the house either."

Yayènia's forehead scrunched up. "Now, it was almost five hundred years ago, but if I am remembering correctly, Mother was always extremely thin. Maybe her pregnancy did not show much. I am rather small."

"Yayènia, the coincidences are too perfect. You are my sister, and not through marriage. You belong on this throne, not me. You are the Wind Throne heir."

"Look," the warrior said, standing, "even if I am your sister by blood, I do not belong on a throne. I belong here, in the barracks. You know I would hate it, and I would be a bad leader. Everyone would be put to death just because I do not want to listen to them whine. You are the Queen of Blackhaven, not I. I am the commander of troops, not everyone else.

"It may be possible, because we have so many similarities, but I have long since destroyed any ties to my past. I do not even know who my own son is. I know only his name. I could not pick him out of a line. If I met him face to face, I would not know him. The people who forged my past are long dead to me. I live for the now and the future. I do not care about who my parents are or where I come from."

She stacked the practice swords in their barrel and held her hand out for the one Tlonna still had in her lap.

The queen handed her the sword and gazed out at the training yard. "What about your magic?"

Yayènia sighed and leaned against one of the supporting poles. "It is not magic, really. I can just manipulate my body to heal faster than most. It is something I have always been able to do. I used to think everyone could do it, until I discovered that everyone else would die from some of the wounds I get," she rubbed her throat again, swallowing.

"Were either of your parents a Maig?"

"No, otherwise Mother would still be alive. And my father hated anything that had to do with magic. Said they were oddities of nature."

Tlonna forced a chuckle. "Yinji was not very smart was he? All elves have a sort of magic. Extended life, our ability with nature and animals, all that is magic. Anyway, power is inherited, Nia. It is not something that just shows up randomly in children."

Yayènia turned around and folded her arms. "It does not matter, Tlonna. It will not change anything. I still would not take the throne, you would stay queen, I would stay High Commander, and nothing would change. Our names would stay the same, everything. I would just have another stupid title added to my name. It is already long enough. People have a hard enough time with High Commander Yayènia er'Tiena, Countess of Blackhaven, Commander of *Zephyr Leifen*. I do not need the title princess added to it or whatever it would be."

Tlonna stood and walked to where her friend and sister stood. "I know, it has just been a shock that has been sitting in the back of my mind. I guess it has been a few hundred years since it really mattered."

"I guess," Yayènia replied, chuckling.

"Come on," Tlonna said, taking her by the elbow, "dinner should be ready by now."

The two walked through the training yard, which was surrounded by a high wooden fence, and onto the path that led to the castle. On the fourth floor was the private dining room for the royal family.

Tlonna and Yayènia strode into the room and were greeted by all their friends. Losolin, Suneelo, Erdwyf, Ghealan, Haydyn, Kelus, Aidyn, Miazie, Aladorn, and the new addition, Sodo. Dinner was served while the companions laughed and chatted animatedly.

Once the main course had been served, Tlonna knocked on the table to gain everyone's attention. When she had their attention, the queen took Losolin's hand and began to speak.

"We have all come a long way these last two years. The bonds of friendship within this room could not be stronger, nor could the love and respect we all feel for each other. But we have suffered great losses, experienced great fear. There are questions we all have that cannot be answered simply, nor can they be answered here."

When the council continued to stare at her blankly, Tlonna smiled, glancing at Losolin, who was also looking confused. She had been thinking about this for a long time, never revealing her plan to anyone until she was sure of it.

"My friends, I propose a quest."

"What sort of quest?" Suneelo asked, sharing a look with his wife.

Again Tlonna smiled. "When Jair destroyed the Tower of Magins, there was a backlash of power that twisted Purheae Forest, and left the land uninhabitable except for those already twisted. Miazie, you once told me that the Tower was still there, in ruins, but still there."

The Magin nodded, waiting for her friend to reveal her point.

"I propose we go to Purheae, find the ruins, and see what answers can be found there," the Magin Queen stated simply.

"What?" Erdwyf replied in disbelief. "Tlonna, no one has ventured there in two thousand years! Nothing will be left other than rock and rubble."

"Not if I am correct. I believe the strength of the Backlash left a strong Maginic dusting, which will have preserved much of what was there at the time."

Everyone looked to Miazie, and the Belau stared blankly at the table. After a while, she shrugged. "I have no sight here."

"What answers do you think you will find there, Tlonna?" Ghealan inquired.

The queen studied her Second Commander, his handsome face surrounded by wavy auburn hair, green eyes tilted slightly upward. "I cannot be sure, Lan. I believe there will be something there. We are talking about the place where all of this," she gestured at everyone at the table, "was started. My family is descended directly from the Magins, as was Midian's. Sithian, Rhiannan, and Haydyn are of those two bloodlines, a joining of the past to the present. The Ruins have stood basically untouched for two millennia, there has to be something there."

"The *Chronicles of Astinus* was found there," Erdwyf put in, linking her fingers with Ghealan's. "Right after the destruction, after everyone had fled, Amram, Jair's son, returned and took the book from the rubble. Since then, no one has heard anything about the place. I agree with Tlonna, it would be worth it to go have a look around."

"As do I. It is there that all of prophecy, alchemy, magic, and religion was started. Perhaps more prophecy will be unveiled, or even a weapon, such as the Cyree once predicted, yes?" Sodo interjected.

"Yes," Tlonna confirmed, smiling at Miazie. "I would leave soon, within the week. Who is with me?"

"I am," Erdwyf and Miazie said in unison. Sodo nodded his agreement.

"I have to," Yayènia mumbled, leaning back in her chair and crossing her arms. "I am the protector of the throne, and if the throne decides to up and leave, I have to go with it, no matter how foolish the throne is being."

Tlonna looked at her sister, eyeing her. "Are you well enough for such a thing?"

The High Commander bit her bottom lip and looked at the friends gathered around her. "I will be," she said finally, sitting back.

Losolin sighed. "I will not be separate from you, Tlonna. We go together."

"And I as well," Suneelo said. "Someone has to protect the protector."

Yayènia shoved her husband lightly, but she smiled.

"Ghealan, are you willing to stay and guard Blackhaven?" Tlonna asked, looking to Erdwyf.

The couple exchanged looks. "Our daughter is too young to go on such a journey, Erd. I will stay. Jaryikin and I will hold the place down."

Aidyn and Aladorn also elected to stay, the former hinting at another trip to his estate, this time bringing the latter along with him.

"I will stay, of course," Haydyn said, smiling at his mother. "I may be a joining of the two bloodlines, but I rather like my elf-blood better, and I would like to keep it that way."

"Smart boy," Yayènia said fondly, mussing the prince's shaggy hair.

The warrior had taken an unexpected liking to the half-breed, befriending him almost immediately. Tlonna smiled in genuine happiness at the odd pair. It was then that she realized Yayènia and Suneelo were Haydyn's aunt and uncle. The revelation shocked her so that she was not aware that she was staring at them for nearly a minute.

"Tlonna? Love?" Losolin asked, nudging her gently.

"Wha-What?" she said, coming to herself.

"Are you all right? You look pale, stunned."

Everyone was staring at her now, faces lined with worry and confusion.

"Yes, yes I am fine. Just thinking. So, what about you Kelus? Do you stay or go?"

The reformed Darkwight shook his head. "I will stay, Tlonna. I have no desire to see the roots of evil. Besides, I too like the solidity of my life now. I have no need to revisit the darkness."

"I understand my friend. Come, let us finish our meal and plan our trip," Tlonna said.

The week of planning passed quickly, and the seven journeyers departed Blackhaven City with little fanfare. They traveled quickly along the forested Obsidian Way, then turned north when the road forked. Three days later, they were at the foot of Lybera Bridge.

They drew rein at the base of the wide bridge, staring at the carven visage of Furntil Eldrout.

"I can't believe he is still alive," Miazie said.

"One day, we will travel to Flousen Dua and meet him, Miazie," Tlonna replied, urging Takîreaes onto the bridge.

"I wonder what he would think of this," Losolin mused aloud as Neñyos plodded over Furntil's face.

"Who can say. Erandur was pretty humble, and I would bet Furntil is as well," Yayènia said.

The small group began discussing the Duani elves, and then they were in Schelum. As usual, they drew up as they crossed into the human land, feeling the air thicken about them. Yayènia and Erdwyf exchanged glances, remembering the last time they had crossed this bridge. The Taint had been strong then, the land shadowed and dying, and the human lands had felt sickly to them. Now it felt less restive, less pure than Blackhaven, but it was not nauseating.

"I would prefer we head straight east, bypass Barl completely. We will reach Purheae in two days," Yayènia said, reining Udu, her new warhorse around to look at Tlonna and Losolin.

"Very well. Lead on, Nia," the king replied, gesturing at his sister-in-law.

As promised, they passed through the hilly landscape of Schelum and were standing at the border of Purheae at noon two days later. Miazie called everyone's attention and waited until the horses were quieted.

"Purheae, as with Narnen, is guarded with a border that prevents Weaving. It does not have the violent repercussions Narnen has, but it will be unpleasant for anyone trying to use magic. Also, your hypersensitivity will be dulled."

The six elves stared at the human until she squirmed. "Stop glaring at me. I did not make the border!"

"We know, Miazie, we know," Sodo laughed, kissing his lover on the forehead.

"Well, there is nothing for it," Tlonna said, and rode across the border into Purheae. She grimaced, but beckoned the others to follow her.

"Ugh," Erdwyf grunted as her hearing seemed to lessen and her sight to dull. "Is this how you usually see and hear, Miazie?"

The human snorted. "I do not feel any different, so probably. Your elven abilities are dampened until they are equal to that of a human. Now you know what you have."

"No wonder you squint so," Tlonna chuckled, blinking in discomfort.

"All right, all right, can we move on?" Miazie grumbled, urging Kaia into a trot.

Grinning and snickering, the six elves followed her into Purheae. The forest appeared less than an hour later, rising up against the horizon like a dark smudge. Yayènia squinted, caught herself, and forced herself to ignore the blurry trees. When they finally reached the tree line, they stared at it in revulsion.

"Can you feel it?" Losolin asked, leaning back in his saddle away from the forest. "It feels wrong, tainted."

At the word taint, his six companions shuddered, remembering Midian's Taint, the blackened snow, the choking rivers, the dying sun.

"Midian did claim to be a direct descendant of Roluf Gwemheoad," Tlonna murmured, almost to herself.

"Roluf was not evil, Tlonna. He was misguided, I think, ambitious and hasty, but...in his heart, I do not think he was cruel," Miazie said to her friend.

The queen nodded silently in acknowledgement, dismounted, and strode into the Purheae Forest. Her friends stared after her in alarm. Yayènia swore in Parlêthian, dismounted, and ran after her sister.

"Why do they do that?" Suneelo asked, joining Losolin at the edge of the forest. "Do they *like* making us worry for their sanity?"

Losolin grunted in amused agreement. "Probably trying to see if we will follow them."

The elder brother folded his arms across his chest and glowered at the trees where his wife and sister-in-law had gone. A minute later, they reappeared, strolling out of the shadows as though they had done nothing abnormal.

"What was that about?" Erdwyf asked, joining her friends.

Tlonna shrugged. "I wanted to see if I could sense anything."

Yayènia snorted, reached over her shoulders, and drew her two swords from their sheaths. One was the katan she still had, its twin yet in Blackhaven with Master Smith Ulrow. In its place, she had a slim-bladed shortsword. Tlonna studied it as her sister planted the two swords in the ground and leaned on them, glaring about. The shortsword was rather plain, the hilt wrapped in black and red leather strips, the ends dangling free. The blade itself, while well-maintained, was dull in color and a chunk was missing out of the edge near the cross guard.

The Magin continued to stare at the sword, perplexed. Yayènia's weapons were known for being the best quality, immaculate and ridiculously shiny.

"Sense what? Tlonna? What are you talking about?" Miazie pressed, frowning at her friend as she continued to stare at Yayènia's ugly blade.

"I...a power. Sentient. Dusting of magic," Tlonna said distractedly, "the forest is alive and I wanted to see. Yayènia, what is going on with that sword?"

The High Commander started, and then looked down at the shortsword. It didn't quite reach her ankle, but it felt odd for her to have one sword out without the other, even if it wasn't the twin. "What do you mean?"

"It is old, and chipped. Where is your other katan?"

Yayènia frowned, and then her eyes unwillingly strayed to Erdwyf. The High Advisor blinked at her, and then realization flared in her eyes. Her jaw tightened, but she stayed silent.

"It was my first sword. Ghealan gave it to me. It seemed appropriate. My left katan is being melted down and reforged."

Suneelo and Erdwyf shared a look behind Yayènia's back. Yayènia sighed and handed the blade to Tlonna. "It is nearly four hundred years old. It is not going to be in fabulous condition."

The Magin took the weapon and studied it. There was a small emblem embossed on the leather strips, distorted by time and use. It was heavier than the swords she was used to, definitely not elf or dwarf forged. "Man made?"

The warrior nodded shortly. "It was all he could afford at the time."

"And the emblem?" Tlonna inquired, deeply curious about the secretive past life of her sister.

Now Yayènia looked extremely uncomfortable, muttered something about nosy people, and grabbed the sword. She sheathed it along with the right katan and remounted. Her companions stared at her curiously until she snarled.

They mounted their horses and followed the irritated warrior deeper into Purheae. They traveled throughout the day without incident, Yayènia making sure to stay ahead of everyone else, avoiding eye-contact and keeping her face a frozen mask of annoyance. Tlonna and Losolin rode side by side, conversing little, taking in their surroundings. The rest of the group was spread out behind them, muttering every so often, then falling silent once more. Nightfall came with little change in scenery.

Purheae was covered three-quarters of the way by the forest that stretched from the R'Kunad Sea to the narrow southern tip flanked by the Jaquisa River, and the Kismath Mountains on the other side of the river. The western side of the province was bereft of any trees, instead covered with boulder-studded hills and cliffs that dropped down into shadowy gorges. It was through this landscape that the seven traveled, following the forest edge, curving away only when the way was barred by a crag. At each chasm, they found ancient stone bridges spanning the crevices, covered in slick moss and crumbling at the edges, or long-over grown pathways winding away into the rocky face.

Travel was slow, and they decided to continue on after dark, squinting against the unfamiliar nearsightedness. Only Miazie remained comfortable, having lost neither senses nor powers. Sometime after midnight, Yayènia held her fist up and they halted.

Tlonna looked around, shifting slightly in Takîreaes's saddle. They were atop a small hill, three sides gradually sloping away, the fourth steep and covered in rugged stone, only to flatten out a quarter-mile down to stretch away into darkness. The group dismounted and quickly set camp, not bothering with tents. Suneelo built a fire and ringed it with small boulders to keep it contained. The seven laid out their bedrolls around the fire and sat facing each other. Erdwyf passed around a basket of cold cuts and cheese. A bladder of wine was produced, and dinner commenced.

"It is an elephunt," Yayènia said suddenly.

Her six companions looked up in surprise, startled by her voice in the deep silence. Suneelo subtly gripped his wife's hand and then let go, leaning back to stare up at the sky.

"An elephunt's head, actually."

"Elephunts are mythical creatures, Yayènia," Miazie said quietly.

"How do you know? They could have lived somewhere else during some other age, and we would never know," the warrior shot back at the human. "Anyway, it was the insignia of the Warriors of the Shadow, a group of fighters that roamed Nymyños about two hundred and fifty years ago. Do you remember when Aladorn and Ghealan met on the road to Zaedic, Losolin?"

The king nodded, remembering the acid greeting Aladorn had used, speaking Parlêthian. '*Takireaeses shä klamen xetian lauk rakna, yumstan kinë lada*'.

"'Warriors of the shadow ride together, and never forget.' It was their motto, an oath never to abandon the crew. They were considered outlaws, rogues, but they rode around keeping the peace in their own terms. If I am not mistaken, they were the beginning of the Shitan-Kulata."

Miazie and Sodo jerked slightly, thinking of Damon. Yayènia awarded them with a guarded look, her eyes glittering in the firelight. "Yes, Miazie, you and I have much in common," she said quietly.

"Unfortunate circumstances they may be," the Belau returned.

The High Commander sniffed in amusement and continued her narration. "It was this band that Ghealan joined, leaving me. Before he went, he bought me the sword and had it stamped with the elephunt so that I would...remember him, I suppose."

"He is an idiot," Erdwyf muttered, shaking her head.

Yayènia laughed, slapping her friend on the knee. "Aye, well, that is not in contention. Lucky for you and Suneelo that he is."

Suneelo snorted, Erdwyf rolled her eyes. Yayènia gazed into the fire, slowly drawing the sword. She handed it to Losolin, who took it and studied the hazy imprint.

"Why a mythical creature?" he asked after a moment.

Yayènia shrugged. "The elephunt is considered to be the most powerful creature, intelligent and extremely loyal to their herd. It makes sense that a group such as the Warriors would choose it as their symbol."

Tlonna took the sword from her spouse and put the hilt close to her face. She could barely make out two large ears and an elongated nose. The rest was too faded to determine, but she had seen illustrations of the beast in fantasy books and paintings.

"So, he gave you a sword with the marking of the band he left you for. How very romantic," Losolin remarked dryly, leaning back in imitation of his brother to study the velvet sky.

"You have no idea," Erdwyf said sardonically, shaking her head again. "He is such a boor sometimes."

"Hey, he is not here to defend himself, now," Suneelo put in, sitting up. "And as much as I enjoy bashing my good friend, I would like to get some sleep tonight."

Yayènia smiled faintly, catching Tlonna's knowing eye. Silently, the warrior kicked out the fire and rolled into her blankets, scooting up to Suneelo to share his warmth. Soon, the three couples and Erdwyf were sleeping soundly.

Tlonna groaned as her mind clicked awake just before dawn. She shivered slightly, feeling Losolin tense as he woke as well. "I do not like being human," he murmured in her ear.

The queen stifled a laugh and wound up yawning instead. "It makes me pity Miazie," she replied, rolling around so she could face him.

The others were still sleeping, so Losolin quietly built up the fire and started breakfast. It was a mix of cheese, potato, bacon, and eggs that was a favorite of the king and queen. Yayènia woke minutes later, sitting up and rubbing her arms against the cold. She glared at Miazie as she did so, sniffling in the chill morning air.

"I do not like this," she muttered to her sister. "I want to be resilient again."

Tlonna shook her head, chuckling. Soon after, Suneelo and Sodo woke, followed by Erdwyf and Miazie.

The human noticed the shivering elves and burst out laughing, wrapping a fur-lined cloak about her body. "Oh, this is brilliant. After all this time, *I'm* the one dealing with the weather better. This is just fantastic."

Tlonna shoved her friend, sending her sprawling. "We still speak better, Miazie," she laughed.

The Belau picked herself up and brushed the dew and dirt off her clothes, glaring. "All right, fine. But I am glad you know how it is to be human, now."

"Aye, and I will be downright glad when we are back in civilized country where elves are elves and humans are humans," Erdwyf grumbled.

Breakfast was consumed quickly, and the seven resumed their tedious ride north. As the day warmed, the land flattened out slightly, and they urged their horses into an easy canter. It was midday when they reached yet another ravine, this one wider and much deeper than any of the others. They turned west and rode for almost an hour before finding the bridge.

Instead of a stone bridge, it was a rope and plank affair that swung in the howling wind of the canyon.

Tlonna rode to the very edge and gazed out across the expanse. "Oh, this ought to be fun," she said, dismounting.

Suneelo dismounted next to her and handed her his reins. Tlonna stepped back as he moved out onto the bridge. Yayènia watched him silently, but the others saw her knuckles whiten on her stallion Udu's reins. When he reached the center of the bridge, the elf stopped and stood looking toward the far end. Suddenly he was sprinting away from his companions, drawing his sword as he did so. Yayènia yelped in surprise, but Erdwyf held her friend back, squinting in the direction of Suneelo.

A wild howl drifted on the wind to them, nothing a person could make. Yayènia snarled, but Erdwyf held her fast. Losolin and Sodo moved onto the bridge, speeding over the planks before any of the females could object.

"Bloody flaming males!" Miazie shrieked as Sodo and the king disappeared, held back by Tlonna.

Tlonna and Erdwyf shared a look as they held back their struggling friends. "They are more than capable of taking care of themselves, Nia...Miazie," the Magin said calmly.

Inside, Tlonna's heart was thudding against her chest and her stomach was knotted with unease as she waited for her husband to reappear.

On the other side of the bridge, Sodo and Losolin slammed into the beast attacking Suneelo. The three males reeled backward, staring at the creature. It stood twice as tall as Sodo, who was the tallest at seven feet nine inches, covered in leathery skin and coarse hair. It snarled, showing sharp eyeteeth and a flickering black tongue.

"What the bleeding blazes is that?" Losolin gasped, crouching with the others as the creature roared.

"A demon!" Suneelo shouted, "Brought forth from the black maw of hell itself. A beast, twisted by power, given strength by lurking in the shadowy recesses of this blighted land. *Kalise*!" he swore as the creature bounded for them.

The three males moved, faster than the demon could expect, three blades slicing into its thick hide.

"A *brekthni*," Suneelo panted, giving the demon its elfin name. "Man wolf."

The *brekthni* screamed, the sound echoing off the hills for miles. It tore at the males, catching Sodo across the chest with one clawed limb, knocking him into Losolin. The king yanked a dagger out of his boot and threw it hard at the creature. The blade impaled itself to the hilt in the beast's neck, but the *brekthni* ignored it. Suneelo spun, tossing his sword as he did so.

The weapon whistled through the air faster than thought, sweeping toward the demon. Losolin dragged Sodo back, trying to staunch the blood now seeping down the elf's front. Suneelo stared at the approaching creature as his sword flew. With a howl, the *brekthni* lurched to the side, stumbling over its own feet. A spray of blood, caught by the wind, splattered into the three elves. Losolin stood next to his brother, both breathing hard, as the beast's head rolled away from its body, severed by Suneelo's sword.

The warrior strode up to the head and punted it across the ground so that it fell into the canyon beyond. He retrieved his sword, and Losolin's dagger, and returned to the two others. Sodo was sitting up, holding a torn bit of his cloak to his chest. He winced as Suneelo dropped to the ground beside him and took the cloth away. Losolin was digging through his belt pouch for an ointment, cursing his inability to Weave.

"How deep?" Suneelo asked the alchemist.

"Nearly a finger's width, far as I can tell," Sodo gasped, his lip curling. "I am no warrior, I am afraid."

Losolin snorted. "Better than most, friend. Now hold still."

The injured elf sucked in a breath as the king smoothed on a foul-smelling liquid over the two lacerations. "Miazie is going to kill me."

Suneelo shared a look with his brother. "Do you love her?"

Sodo looked at him oddly. "Of course I do. Why would I not?"

"She is human...she will age and die."

"She has elf blood in her lineage...she will age slowly," the alchemist replied quietly. "And even when she does, I will still love her. She...thrills me. There is something about her that turns aside doubt and reason and gives me only a sense of compassion and love. Do you understand that?"

The warrior laughed once, softly. "I do. It is much the same with Yayènia. She is harder than stone, colder than ice, and more lethal than a poisoned blade, but somehow, when I am with her, she is simply my wife, tender and quiet. I do not fear her any more than I would myself. Some call me mad, others suicidal but I love her more than life itself. So, when you say your love for Miazie blinds you to reason...I understand."

Losolin remained silent, though he smiled slightly in agreement. He thought back to the night he and Tlonna had found one another after so long, but still did not remember. She had torn into him with her power, and he had kissed her in the creek, feeling emotions he did not understand.

The three males fell silent, thinking about their loves, tending to Sodo's wound. After a moment, there was a cry and they looked up sharply, believing the *brekthni* come back to life. Instead, it was the females and the horses, no longer able to stand unknowing on the other side. Miazie, Yayènia, and Tlonna burst onto the scene like avenging angels, furious and terrified at the same time. Erdwyf followed behind with the horses, her face tight with anxiety.

For a blind moment, the three females could not tell who it was that was injured, as the males all had similar cloaks on, and their hair was all shades of blond. Tlonna stopped short when Losolin looked up at her, a fierce passion burning in his eyes. Relief and love washed through her as she realized it was not he who was injured.

Yayènia spotted Suneelo's sword on the ground, her heart skipping every other beat. Then she saw him bent over Sodo, and her stomach returned to its rightful place.

Miazie cried out as she recognized Sodo's figure between the other two males, dropping to her knees beside Suneelo. The alchemist's mismatched eyes found hers and there was a look of profound love in them that her throat tightened dangerously.

"What happened? Are you okay?" she whispered, eyeing the bloody patch of cloth on his chest.

"Just a few scratches, is all. It was a demon of some sort," Sodo replied, looking to Suneelo.

"A *brekthni,*" the warrior stated simply, gazing at his wife.

Yayènia frowned at him, arms crossed.

"A werewolf?" Miazie gasped. "I thought they were just stories. Like the elephunt."

"Werewolf? What is a werewolf?" Tlonna asked, casting around for the creature. She spotted the carcass yards away and turned toward it.

"A man wolf. A demon created in the Backlash, twisted and mindless, they feed off anything in their path. No one knows for sure if they used to be human, but they have a slight similarity," Erdwyf explained, following Tlonna's gaze. "Extremely dangerous, and strong. How did you kill it?"

"Suneelo threw his sword, cut off the head. Flaming good throw, by the way," Losolin said, grinning at his brother.

"I was lucky. The wind could have caught it and taken it into the gorge," the warrior replied blandly, standing.

Sodo stood as well, with the aid of Losolin. Together, the seven moved over to the beast's corpse and stood staring down at it.

"It seems smaller than it was," Sodo remarked.

"They are said to shrink in death," Erdwyf said, nudging a forelimb with her boot. "Myth says they return to their human form, but apparently that part is indeed myth."

"Well, shall we move on, or do you want to rest a bit, Sodo?" Losolin asked, taking Neñyos's reins from Erdwyf.

"I am fine," the alchemist replied, smiling at Miazie, who glared back at him.

They remounted and moved onward, heading back east toward the forest. At nightfall, Tlonna called the halt, and they set up camp. After a dinner of bread and stew, Losolin checked Sodo's injury, wrapped a clean cravat around his chest, and moved back to sit with Tlonna. Miazie rose and strode a few feet away, disappearing beyond the ring of light from the fire. Sodo began to rise, but Yayènia waved him back and stood herself. Her five companions stared at her.

"She has suffered a pain I know how to deal with," she said simply, and followed after the human.

Miazie turned around as she heard someone approach, ready to berate them for following her, but her words died when Yayènia materialized out of the shadows. Silently, the legendary warrior sat down next to her, drawing her knees to her chest and resting her chin on them. Miazie stared at her in surprise, unsure of what the elf wanted.

"It hurts, does it not?" Yayènia said suddenly.

"What?"

"Watching them suffer. Knowing they mask the pain so that you do not worry so much," the elf explained.

Miazie blinked. "It does. I remember when he was attacked by Darkwights outside Alchemian. I thought he was going to die, and I was so destroyed. It hurt to breathe."

Yayènia continued to gaze out at the darkness, her beautiful face outlined in vague shadows. The Maig turned away, looking up at the night sky, tracing the arch of the moons in the inky sky.

"It never gets easier, not that it should."

Once again Miazie was startled by the sudden words. "Then why do you do it? Fight, I mean. You and Suneelo, Erdwyf and Ghealan, even Tlonna and Losolin?"

Yayènia sighed and stretched out her legs, crossing them at the ankle. "Because someone has to, Miazie. There will always be people who are unhappy with the way of things, people who want to create disruption. People like me, and Suneelo, and the others, we are the balance. We place ourselves in the line of fire so that the majority of the world can live without fear and uncertainty."

"I could not do it," Miazie whispered.

"Nor could I, in the beginning. But sometimes things come to you whether you will them or not. I was very weak when I was young, in both heart and body. I allowed things to happen to me because I was not strong enough to deny them. I was thrown into a world of cruelty and lust that hardened me beyond thought. I was a ruin of a female, bereft of emotion, hollow and broken inside."

Miazie blinked a tear away as Yayènia's voice cracked slightly. "You have seen so much, Yayènia...been through so much. I cannot even begin to imagine your pain. But…I," she chuckled slightly in self deprecation, "I will listen."

The elf did not laugh as she looked at the human with glittering eyes. "I do not talk much about it."

"I know you don't."

"The world is a pit of hatred and despair, blanketed with falsities and veneers that lend hope to those strong enough to hold onto it. The mutilations of war, the wickedness of people, the…base immorality of rulers, it is slowly eating away at the fabric of civilization," Yayènia spat. "When you have things like love and friendship pitted against hatred and greed, ambition and lusts for things unholy, it is easy to understand why we fight. It is easy to take a life when you know they would just as easily take yours or another's. Why we fight, why we continuously put ourselves in the center of fire is because we know these things. We have seen the madness first hand, stared it down and walked into the blackness with our backs stiff and our minds set. It is why we come out alive each time, leaving behind us a legacy of death and power. It never gets easier to see your loved ones injured, but it indeed gets easier to take the life of someone else's loved one."

Miazie sat in stunned silence as the elf's voice faded away. The anger and hurt in Yayènia's words made the human want to gather her up and hold her. But as usual, the warrior was like iron, outwardly unaffected by her own narration.

"I never think about an enemy as being another person, I suppose," the Belau said finally. "I think it would make it much harder to fight them."

"Quite the opposite," Yayènia replied. "Makes it easier to realize they made the conscious decision to try and kill you. That is why I never promote war. It makes me the enemy, and negates my right to live."

"That is a rare sentiment, I think," Miazie stated.

The High Commander huffed softly. "That is what makes us different from our antagonists."

"Yayènia," Miazie started, then realized she rarely spoke to the warrior, much less said her name.

"I am not someone to be feared, Miazie," Yayènia said intuitively. "I am your friend."

"I know, but I feel so inferior," the human laughed.

Yayènia chuckled, finally looking at the woman. "Never inferior. Short, but not inferior. You are a valuable asset to our company, and a loyal comrade. Now, what would you ask me?"

Miazie inhaled deeply and let it out before answering. "Why did you follow me?"

The elf studied the human briefly before turning her face away. "I recognized your pain."

It was midmorning the next day when Yayènia sent Tlonna a hand signal and they halted. The others stopped with them, curious. The warrior rode a few steps ahead and then drew her longblade.

"I know you are there, come out now," she called.

After a while, there was a rustle and a man clad in rough hides stepped out of the trees. Everyone stared in shock as the man stared back. He was young and fit with broad shoulders and a piercing stare.

"Who are you?" he demanded in a strange accent, glaring at them suspiciously.

His accent was a little hard to understand, almost as if he were speaking through a mouthful of food.

Yayènia's back went ramrod straight. The others exchanged surprised glances. There had not been any reports of human habitation in Purheae for nearly two thousand years. Yayènia dismounted, sheathing her blade. The man was taller than average, his eyes level with Yayènia's neck.

"I am Yayènia er'Tiena of Blackhaven. Who are you?"

The human showed no recollection of the famous name. Instead he sucked on his teeth as if deciding whether or not to reply. Finally, he touched two of his fingers to his heart.

"I am Eyin Thorn, Clan Leader of the Stone Hunters. Your companions?"

Tlonna edged Takîreaes forward and dismounted next to Yayènia. "I am Tlonna Ewôsdírn, Magin Queen of Blackhaven. This is King Losolin of Blackhaven, Captain of the Guard Suneelo Tiena, and High Advisor Erdwyf er'Tomyvon, Belau Miazie Paron, and Alchemist Sodo of the White. We were not aware of Human inhabitants in Purheae. How do you come here?"

Eyin frowned at Tlonna. She gazed back at him coolly as the others dismounted as well. Behind him, Yayènia shifted in annoyance. The human turned to her, his head cocked.

"You are a great warrior, no?"

Yayènia's lip curled. "You can find out just how great if you continue to ignore my queen."

Surprisingly, Eyin chuckled. "You are hasty for an elf. I was born here, Queen of Elves and Magins. We, my people and I, are descended from those who fled so long ago. We have lived here for centuries now, moving from place to place so the magic would not settle on us. Now, why are you here?"

"We come seeking answers in the ruins of the Tower of Magins," Tlonna replied cautiously, unsure of his reaction.

He spat on the ground. "Cursed and wretched place. You will find few answers there, and if you do, you will not want them."

Tlonna shrugged. "Still, we must go."

"I cannot allow that," Eyin growled, stiffening.

Before anyone could react, Yayènia grabbed his arm, twisted it behind his back, and hauled him up on his toes. "Do you think you can stop us?" she hissed.

Eyin struggled, but stopped when his shoulder twisted alarmingly. Tlonna sighed in resignation. "Listen, friend, we go in search of answers so that we may be able to win a war against Roluf Gwemheoad's descendents, who rule an island kingdom to the north called Zaedic. There is reason to believe the Elves of Seaduens are allied with them, and we are outnumbered ten to one. What would you have us do?"

A look of pure loathing had crossed Eyin's face at the mention of the first Magin. "He has...descendents?" he asked in a livid whisper.

Tlonna nodded silently.

Eyin shuddered, looking all the more enraged by the fact that he was still forcibly on his toes, his wrist held by Yayènia at the nape of his neck.

Tlonna watched him, expressionless. Yayènia released him with a shove and he stumbled a few steps, rubbing his shoulder and muttering. After a moment, he turned to face Tlonna, his chin raised proudly.

"I...respect your adamancy," he said, glancing at Yayènia. "You are positive your enemies are descendents of the Sunderer?"

"Their leaders are, yes. It has been proven."

Eyin's cheek twitched. "I must speak with my people. Will you consent to wait three turns of the sun before continuing on?"

Tlonna turned to look at Miazie and Losolin. The Belau sighed resignedly, rolling her eyes. Losolin raised his brows, and remained silent. Tlonna snorted.

"Some help you lot are," she muttered. "Yes, Eyin, we will wait."

The man bowed his head slightly, turned and strode back into the forest.

"I cannot believe there are people fool enough to live in that twice blighted forest," Suneelo said, glaring at the offending trees.

"Well," Miazie mused, rubbing her chin, "it makes sense, doesn't it?"

"What do you mean?" Losolin asked.

The Magin shrugged. "The War of the Council ended two thousand years ago. When the people fled, it was a terrible shame to them. Purheae was the first Human settlement in Nymyños. Man was said to have been made from the Plant God Gagu's rib, weaker than both Elf and Dwarf, but resilient, weed-like. Purheae Forest was said to be Gagu's most beloved place."

The elves shifted. Miazie smirked. "Indeed, it was Purheae, *not* Blackhaven that held the Plant God's affections. It was darker, more wild, more tangled than restful Blackhaven and Gagu was mad, never comfortable in more civilized settings. So, Man was a flawed, raw, and angry version of Elf."

"What does that have to with this?" Suneelo asked, irritated.

Miazie smiled again. "Purheae is Man's ancestral home. When Roluf Gwemheoad waged war against the elves in the forest, he inadvertently drove the humans away as well. He forced them out of their homeland to seek refuge in the other kingdoms. The backlash of magic that stops Maginic Weaving, that mutes your elfin ability of hypersensitivity, has little or no effect on humans."

Miazie spread her arms wide and spun in a circle. "This is the perfect place for us, for humans! Elves and dwarves are uncomfortable here. This could be the first human empire!" she said, in awe of her own revelation. Suddenly, she realized she was the only human in a company of elves, two of them monarchs.

Blushing, she laughed nervously at their stony faces. "Not that that would be a good thing, though."

Yayènia snorted. "It is a bloody horrible idea. Now if we are going to stay in this god-forsaken place, I do not want to set camp in the dark."

With her words, the small company readied for their stay.

They were not a company that idled well. They sparred, debated, mused over their latest discovery, but still they found themselves impatient. When they began to lose faith in Eyin, he returned. It was late on the third day, and he did not return alone.

"What is this?" Yayènia demanded as the young man strode into their camp, followed by several others.

Eyin touched two fingers to his heart. "I apologize for making you wait. The news you brought, I related to my people, and they are not happy. It took some time to convince some of them to meet you."

"To what purpose?" Losolin snapped coldly.

"To make an agreement. My people are nervous, and though I do not detect any foulness in you, we must have assurance," Eyin replied.

The others behind him stared at the seven, dark eyes glittering suspiciously. The young man paid them no heed, obviously in charge and confident. Tlonna stepped forward, standing tall and proud.

"What is your...proposition?"

"You will tell no one of our presence here," he began.

Miazie opened her mouth, but the Purheaen shook his head. "We have lived a peaceful life here. We do not want to threaten that peace for the sake of riches and a more glamorous reputation. Second, you will send a border patrol to guard our borders from these vile descendants. And thirdly," Eyin hesitated here, his followers fidgety. "Thirdly, you will acknowledge me, Eyin Thorn, as the First King of Purheae."

Tlonna and her six companions stared at him. Losolin found his voice first. "These are ridiculous! Not only do they contradict one another, they are utterly insane! What makes you think we would agree to such absurd demands?"

Eyin and the others paled, but the young human squared his shoulders. "In return, I will allow you to pass unhindered to the Ruins. If, as planned, Purheae once again flourishes, you will have exclusive trade rights, and I will vow to obliterate any Seadueni or Zaedican that passes through Purheae, until time turns to dust."

Silence fell, thick and tense. Tlonna looked at Miazie for guidance. The Belau's eyes were cloudy with thought, but when they cleared, she shook her head. "There is no grave portent with either answer," she said quietly.

The queen made a face and then turned back to Eyin and his waiting followers. She sighed in annoyance. "Fine. I accept. I, Tlonna Arune Ewôsdírn, Magin Queen of Blackhaven, acknowledge you, Eyin Thorn, as First King of Purheae. I extend to you the invitation to join the Nymyñosian Racial Alliance," she ended with a bow, equal to equal.

Yayènia cursed under her breath, but she executed her military bow, fluid and assertive. Eyin bit his lip and leaned back, but he kept his footing. Losolin repeated Tlonna's words, his face stony, and his bow was a hair too short for it to be equal. Once everyone had acknowledged him, Eyin exhaled heartily.

"I accept the invitation, and will hold true to my promises. What will you do now?"

Tlonna stuck her hands on her hips. "What we initially came to do, search the Tower of Magins."

"You will not make it before dark."

Suneelo grunted. "Do we look like people who are afraid of the dark? We could be on our way back home by now if not for your interruption."

Eyin folded his arms and stared at the elf. "I did what had to be done. Other than the occasional scout, there has not been a traveler within Purheae for a very long time. I had to be sure of your intentions and to make sure you kept your word. You stayed for the full three days. My people had made their decisions by noon on the second day."

"You lying sack of-" Yayènia began but Tlonna cut her off.

"You have the markings of a very influential leader. Whether or not your influence will be good or bad remains to be seen. I will be watching you very careful, Eyin, King of Purheae."

One of the Purheaens finally spoke. "You are already threatening him? Your assertiveness bothers me, Elf Queen."

Tlonna turned her cold gaze on the old man. "I make no threats, Human. I am the Magin Queen. I can be as assertive as I wish to be."

"You have no powers here," one of the others said.

Tlonna raised her brows and her hand. White lightning crackled around the group behind Eyin. It was extremely weak, and Tlonna felt a sharp pain in her stomach, but the Purheaens knew of neither. Their astonished gazes turned to fear.

“I am the Magin Queen. My powers go beyond your imagination, beyond your country’s limits. Do not test me again.”

Chapter 19

The Tower of Magins

Tlonna stepped over a fallen tree and stopped short. The Purheae Forest had abruptly ended, as though a giant blade had simply sliced it off. The Magin Queen turned around to survey the line of trees and felt a stab of shock. The trees all bent backward, as though pushed by a heavy wind, though the day was calm as could be. The leaves did not rattle, but seemed frozen in petrifaction. Turning back, she surveyed the scene before her with awe.

A giant round foundation of worn granite rose into the sky nearly five times her height. Boulder-sized blocks lay strewn about, covering the mossy ground every few steps. Off to the left, half of a statue lay on its side. Tlonna stared at the weathered face, feeling slightly intrusive. Instinctively, she knew it to be the handsome, albeit chipped, visage of Roluf Gwemheoad, the First Magin.

Behind her, Miazie let out a stunned breath. "The Tower of Magins... I never thought I would stand here."

"A great bloody ruin. And look what those bastards did to the forest. Two thousand years later and the trees are still hurting," Yayènia grunted, glaring about the site.

"We are standing in history, right now, Yayènia, can you not feel it?" Erdwyf replied, smiling.

"What I feel is the rough aftershock of fools."

"Yes, but also the vibrancies of history, of legend. Tlonna, did you know that your *Chronicles of Astinus* was found right here, a thousand years ago?" Miazie said, wandering further into the ruins.

"What, exactly, are we hoping to find here?" Losolin asked, standing next to Yayènia and feeing the same reluctance to join the trio of females now excitedly poking around.

"This is where it all started, Losolin. Where Astinus made his prophecies, where Tonora died, where I was given a destiny. Where you three were entwined in my fate," Tlonna replied, pointing at Miazie, Yayènia, and her husband.

"All the more reason to not be here," the High Commander snapped, studying the bleak, broken tower. "Because of this place, my throat was slit."

Tlonna shook her head and started toward the tower. On the far side, she found the entrance. The door lay a few feet to the side, the carven remains of what must have once been a behemoth, twice her height and wide enough to accommodate three broad males standing shoulder to shoulder. Stepping into the shadowy, musty tower, she immediately felt the archaic presence of great power.

"Why do you insist on going into dangerous places?" Yayènia asked behind her.

"Because I am a dangerous person," Tlonna replied lightly, looking around.

It was a single room, most likely the main hall for all who lived in the tower. The granite floor was slick with moss, but contained no animal remains. Directly ahead of her was a moldering trestle table, half-sunk to the floor and scorched on one end. Sconces held used candles, thick with dust and mildew. There was a rotting tapestry clinging to the wall to the right.

Tlonna moved over to inspect it, shaking with excitement. What she could see of it was burgundy and gold. A female body clothed in billowing pants and nothing else knelt on one knee, its head obliterated by mold. Nothing else was discernible, but the queen could not stop staring. Veries Gurgen had looked at this tapestry. Astinus and Gwemheoad as well, and now she was.

"Nia, they were *here* two thousand years ago. Can you imagine? We are standing where the first Magins stood, where the last Seers ever stood."

"Yes, I know. But, two thousand years, Tlonna, all this stuff should have been dust by now. Why is it still here?"

"Magic," Tlonna replied automatically, turning around to grin at her sister. "The residues of the Weave that destroyed all of this rebounded, and settled over the tower. See, Miazie was telling me that Magins leave a trace wherever they go, sort of like a fine dust that falls from us from unused power. Hundreds of Magins lived here, powerful Magins, for a century. That left a lot of Maginic residue here in the tower, so when Jair destroyed everything, all the extra magic was simply left here."

"What happens when you Weave?" Yayènia asked, intrigued against her will.

"I leave a dusting, too, but not as much as the Backlash Jair caused. It goes into the earth to be reused some other time, by some other Magin." Tlonna explained, striding over to a set of stairs. "Come, let us see what this leads to."

The sisters climbed the stairs and found themselves in the exposed first floor. What looked like bedrooms curved to the right side, while the stairs continued upward, ending slightly above the rest of the walls. Tlonna rushed to a devastated room covered in pale green moss. A great canopy bed as ruined as the trestle table covered most of the room, but a rotted desk slanted off to one side, a decimated chair before it.

"I wonder whose room this was." Yayènia murmured, running a finger along the moldy yellow bed curtains.

Tlonna shook her head in wonder, and then stopped dead. A dull glint of silver had caught her eye from under the bed. Kneeling beside it, she reached under and gasped as her hand brushed something hard. Trembling, she pulled it out and nearly fell over in disbelief. The silver was a key, tarnished and slightly rusted, but still attached to a small bit of rotted leather. It rested atop a locked metal box.

The queen tried the key, but it would not turn. Confused, Tlonna turned to Yayènia, who was standing just behind her. "This key does not work."

"Then we will find some other way to open it. Not here, though."

Nodding, Tlonna handed the box to the warrior and tucked the key into her belt pouch. "I want to search the other rooms first, but I will hurry."

They searched the three other rooms but found nothing other than a few dry inkwells and a woman's hair pin stuck in a bedpost. Descending the stairs and exiting the ruined tower, the sisters found the rest of their group sitting a little ways away from the tower, apparently lounging.

"We found something," Tlonna said as they joined the others.

Miazie's eyes brightened and she leaned forward excitedly. Even Losolin, Sodo, and Suneelo looked anticipatory as Yayènia set the box down and Tlonna took the key from her pouch.

"This key does not go to the box, but I think it was the key Astinus wore around his neck, for his journal. The lock is broken, so whoever found the *Chronicles* obviously did not need the key. This box is locked, and we found no other key. A hairpin, but no key."

"Can I see the pin?" Miazie asked.

Tlonna handed the Belau the silver embellishment who studied it with fervor. It had once been elegant, decorated with a dogwood flower and studded lightly with diamonds. Miazie closed her eyes and gripped the pin tightly, swaying and muttering under her breath. She came out of her trance with a sharp breath.

"It was Cari Sumen's. She stuck it in the bedpost whenever she and Hylen made love. A gift from him to her, for her eighteenth birthday."

Sodo sucked in a breath and stared at his mate. "I cannot believe you can do that, love."

Miazie smiled weakly. "I can't believe I'm holding this. Now, open the flaming box before I explode."

Tlonna grinned and pressed her thumb to the lock, pushing upward until her muscles were straining. It snapped open, and she lifted the lid. Inside was a multitude of papers, a few sketches, and a single small painting. It was all preserved as though it were merely a century old, rather than two millennia. The painting was of a woman standing next to a young boy. The woman was short and thin with ginger hair tied in a tight bun atop her head. Her face was square, with full lips and a well shaped nose that created a pretty yet strong countenance. Her dress was tight at the bodice and then flared out sharply from the hips, and was covered in embroidery.

The boy looked to be nine or ten with the same square face but a squint to his eyes that made him look haughty. He was dressed all in black with falls of lace at his wrists and lapels.

Tlonna handed the painting to Miazie, and took a paper at random. She read it aloud.

"'*Veries, my precious, I hate to write this letter, but I find myself in a rather stern position. The Triads are fraying at the edges, and I know I must return to the Tower soon. I have missed you greatly, but when I return, we must end our dalliance. Roluf has commanded me to find out what Buftren is doing with his spare time. I fear that I will be set to following the snake, and I must not have any distractions. Please, we will talk when I return.*

Teral.'

"This was Veries Gurgen's..." Tlonna murmured, stroking the box.

Everyone was staring at the letter in her trembling hand, awe-struck.

"There are dozens of letters in here," Yayènia said, riffling gently through the box. "Read more."

Smiling, Tlonna obliged. "'*Veries, my precious, I rejoice at the news of our child! I will return to you soon, and we will speak of the future. Roluf has found a way to test strength without draining us, so we will be home in a few days, and we will be put into Triads. That is what Roluf wants to call them. Five Triads. I know that you and I will be in the same Triad, we must, for we belong together. I will see you soon, my heart, and we will be a family.*

Teral.'"

She read several others, all out of order. Most were from Teral, ranging from provocative love letters to harsh refusals of affection. Sadly, the latter seemed to be from later on. The birth of their son, Temas, seemed to be right in the middle. None of them were dated, but they seemed to be rather spread out over a few years. Other letters were from family members or friends in another long dead city of Purheae.

When she finished reading them, Tlonna set them aside and picked up the painting. It was Veries and Temas from the descriptions that were given in the letters. Going through the sketches, the elf felt a jolt go down her spine. One sketch was of a young man with a startlingly handsome face, but the eyes were drawn dark and lifeless, the mouth thin and the brows drawn down in anger. Beside it, Veries had scrawled the name Jair. Jair, the destroyer of the Tower of Magins. Jair, Tlonna's ancestor.

"So...what have we learned?" Yayènia asked that night, leaning against Suneelo, his long legs on either side of her hips.

Tlonna shook her head. "I am not sure, but I feel as though I have not yet found what I believe to be here. Veries' box is an amazing discovery, but it is not what I am after."

"What *are* you after?" Suneelo asked, resting his chin on Yayènia's head.

The Magin sighed, idly flipping a knife about, and shook her head again. "I do not know. Something... something that will explain to me why these terrible things are happening. What is my exact purpose here? How am I supposed to free the slaves of death? The Darkwights, if we are correct. What we have found so far only augments the fact that this is indeed the time, and I am indeed the

Moon Heiress, or whatever they want to call me. Nothing explains *how* I am supposed to do all these wondrous things."

"Tlonna, remember what the Cyree said?" Miazie inquired. "That I would discover something to help you? Maybe I am the one who is meant to find something here. There would be no place better, or more fitting. And the 'Guardian's Fall' was the first in the prophecy, and it has happened. The next is the "Lover's Rule," the human said, looking to Losolin.

The elf gazed at her friend, wrapped in Sodo's arms. "Mayhap. But I still feel the need to find something myself. I do not feel right about sacrificing myself without knowing exactly how and why."

"I do not feel right about you sacrificing yourself for anything," Losolin snapped, glaring about. "It is a bunch of dead men who said that, so I say forget about them, live for the sake of living. Who gives a bloody flaming blight what dead men want?"

Tlonna frowned at her husband. He resolutely insisted on denying the fact that she must die to free the Elven Race from their demonic prison. She had long since come to terms with it, but Losolin got furious every time it was mentioned. As did everyone else, but she found it easier to ignore their anger.

"Indeed," Yayènia muttered, shifting against Suneelo.

"Rather than argue, why do we not try and think of things to do tomorrow? The seven of us should each explore a place to see if we missed anything today," Erdwyf butted in before anyone else could start up.

Tlonna relaxed marginally as her friends began to debate about tomorrow. Silently, she gazed up at the dark sky, staring at the red moon of Dietirin, wishing he were with her. After a while, the conversation died as the six rolled into their blankets and fell asleep. Tlonna remained awake, staring into the dying fire, her mind crowded with a million thoughts. Sighing, she began to lay down when a flash of green light caught her eye. For a second, she thought Losolin was Weaving, then dismissed the notion when she remembered he could not do so within Purheae. Curious, she stood, careful not to disturb anyone.

Seconds later, another flash of green light sparked in the night. The next moment, hundreds of different colored flashes flickered into existence, only to disappear the next instant. Tlonna stood transfixed, awed by the spectacle, and terrified of what it could be. It was not until the lights had faded completely that she realized they had all been centered around the ruined foundation of the tower.

Silently, Tlonna moved away from her sleeping comrades and toward the ruin. She found nothing as she circled the base, and then finally she reached the gaping door. Inside it appeared as though all the lights had conjoined into one shimmering figure. The Magin drew up sharply, gaping at the twitching lights as they coalesced into something more or less solid. A thunderous cough shook the elf out of her trance, and she backed away a step.

-Child of my blood-

Tlonna's heart seized as the light-shade spoke, a grating, booming voice that filled her head until she thought it would burst.

-Come to me-

Against her will, Tlonna moved into the tower, rigid with foreboding. "Who are you?" she wheezed.

-Magin Jair-

"Jair? But...you are...two thousand years ago..."

-I am the Shade of Jair, child of my blood-

"How?"

-The power I left here when I destroyed the tower was done on purpose. I knew one day I would be needed. I have come now to tell you what you need to know-

Tlonna did not reply, fearful of the giant light-shade before her. He was more discernible now, a tall, powerful figure moving within the flickering lights, featureless, yet formidable. She could barely see the outline of a long robe swaying about his feet, and straight hair brushing his shoulders.

-You must die in order to save your race-

"I know that already," the elf muttered.

-You must take within yourself another, one less powerful than yourself, but more than any other. You must take the gift from the Cyree and shield yourself with it. You must remember who loved you first and longest for in the end it will be he who is your saving grace-

When the Shade of Jair stopped speaking, Tlonna gaped at him. "That is it? That is all you are going to tell me? You make no sense, but add to the riddles! Why can no one give me straight answers?"

-The answers you seek are not the answers you need-

Tlonna picked up a piece of loose rubble and hurled it at the shade. It simply passed through him, creating a swirling hole that closed immediately after. "Why?"

-Because you are the Moon Heiress-

"That is not an answer!" Tlonna shouted. "Why did you burn down the tower? Why did you kill all your comrades? Why did you destroy the Council of Magins?"

The shade seemed to grow and brighten, filling the large room until Tlonna shrank back from him in fear.

-They were killing our kind, slaughtering the forest, twisting the magic. They cared naught for the lives of all the innocent people under their rule. They experimented, tortured, and crippled thousands of elves, debilitating the entire race. I did what I had to-

The voice in Tlonna's head was so loud it made her weep as she cowered, her hands over her ears.

-They were careless, massacring entire villages, ravaging the forest in their stupidity. Some protested, but they were easily silenced. Witness what you would defend-

Jair's roaring voice faded, only to be replaced by a vision of horror. A robed Magin sliced open the throat of a squirming elf-child, his eyes glittering as the blood poured into a stone basin. Tlonna whimpered, and the vision changed. A dozen Magins rode into a small village, Weaving strands that blew individuals apart at first touch. A few they captured, dragging them bodily onto their horses and wheeling away, leaving the village behind.

The visions flashed through Tlonna's mind, each one more graphic and violent than the one before until she retched, tears streaming from her eyes. Finally, the visions faded, and the Shade of Jair was once more standing before her.

-Would you defend them now, child-

Tlonna did not answer, but she shook her head in denial.

-The Council of Magins began benignly, but it turned into a rabid beast, mindless in its infection. You are the child of my blood. Continue my quest, and rid the world of such evil. Soon, the tide will turn again, and you will be forced to make a decision-

"What decision?" Tlonna rasped.

-Save your family, or save your people-

The queen choked, rage and desperation rising into her throat. "You cannot demand that of me!" she screamed.

The shade remained silent.

"Damn you! I will not accept that! I will save them all!" Tlonna bellowed, getting to her feet and raising her fists at her dead ancestor.

-You cannot-

"Yes I can!"

-Then they will all die and the world will turn into a bottomless pit of anguish-

A sound erupted from Tlonna's throat that was so enraged it did not sound as though a person could create it. White magic burst out of her body like an aura, expanding until it filled the entire room, dimming the flashing lights that encompassed Jair's shade. The hair on Tlonna's head spread out, held up by the power radiating from her, her clothes billowed outward.

-STOP-

The command fell unheeded, and Tlonna stepped forward until she stood scant feet away from the ancient Magin. "You say things, but I will not allow them to happen. I am the Magin Queen, and I will win."

-You will die-

"But everyone else will live."

There was an echoing crack as Tlonna's power detonated, warring with the Boundary. The Shade of Jair was consumed, lancing into the elf's body, throwing her to the floor amid the rubble. Sudden darkness enveloped her, blinding after the light. Slowly, Tlonna climbed to her feet, staggering weakly. Utter silence greeted her as she groped her way to the door and fell to her knees on the dewy grass. Somewhere behind, her six companions still slept, unaware of the cataclysmic event that had just taken place.

"That was not supposed to happen," Tlonna panted to the night. She twisted around to fall on her back, groaning. "That was not supposed to happen," she said again. Holding up her hands, the elf studied them. They were steady, but at each of her fingertips, different colored lights flared briefly and died. Though she could not feel it, Tlonna knew her eyes were changing rapidly as they had done every time she Wove since the Cyree. Sudden terror filled her as she realized what had just happened. She had absorbed Jair's Shade. With clarity, she knew he was *not* the person she was supposed to take in. He had not been expecting that.

Tlonna let out a chuckle, disbelieving the experience. Seconds later she was laughing uncontrollably, burying her face in the ground

as tears slid from her eyes. She could not stop, even when she heard six pairs of feet running toward her in alarm.

Losolin skidded to a halt in astonishment when he saw Tlonna face down on the ground, laughing so hard she was shaking. He glanced uncertainly at Yayènia, who was staring at her sister with a look of utter fear on her face. Suddenly, he became aware that there were different colored lights glimmering around his wife's body, insubstantial little bursts of light that floated close to her body.

"Tlonna?" he finally ventured, anxious.

Tlonna's head snapped up and he gasped involuntarily. Her eyes were completely white, blood staining the corners of her nose and mouth.

"*Leif*!" Suneelo swore, taking a step back.

"Loni?" Losolin asked again, his voice cracking slightly.

Rather than answer him, the queen rose onto her knees and held her arms out straight. Her six companions took another step back in unison, terrified. A bar of light stretched between her hands, no longer white, as it should have been, but laced with dozens of different colors. Tlonna's arms were rigid, the muscles bulging against the skin as the bar pulsated slightly.

"I command it all, now," the Magin whispered finally, in a voice that was hers, yet somehow different.

"Tlonna, what is going on?" Miazie keened, clutching Sodo.

"All of it. It is all mine. All the Magins that came before are inside me now. Part of me," Tlonna said, giggling.

Losolin swallowed against the lump of revulsion in his throat and knelt by his wife. "Tlonna, what happened?"

"Jair came to me. Told me things. I absorbed him and all his power. All the lights, they were all that was left of the Magins who lived here. Now..." Tlonna let her hands drop and the bar of light disappeared. "Now I understand."

"Understand what?" Erdwyf insisted.

"Too much power...too much!" the queen laughed, getting to her feet. "Toooooo much. I will save you all. Yes..."

The six stared after their friend as she wandered away, weaving back and forth aimlessly, muttering to herself.

"She has gone mad," Yayènia whispered.

Losolin turned to her, numb. "No. No."

"If what she said is true, she just soaked up hundreds of Magin's dustings, more than what one...a *dozen* strong Magins could even comprehend containing. The effect will be...devastating," Miazie said softly, watching Tlonna wander about.

"Will she recover?" Suneelo demanded.

The human turned slowly to face the elf. "We'd better hope so."

Tense silence fell as the little company stared after their friend and queen, who was now laying on her back once more, tossing up multicolored flames and catching them before they fell, her power too great to be held back by the Boundary now.

Chapter 14

A New Form of Power

Sithian sat at his desk, his ankles crossed upon the pile of documents before him. Balancing his head on his thumb and forefinger, the half-blood stared blankly at the stone wall across from him. A fire crackled in the large hearth to his left, casting wavering shadows over the office, bringing the temperature of the room to an unpleasant degree of warmth. It was rarely cold on Zaedic, and this year had not been different. Now that it was well into Laynyan, the air itself seemed to perspire with the humidity. Sithian felt sweat run down his back, staining the silk inlay of his coat.

The door opened and the young king looked up disinterestedly as Rhiannan strode in, looking irritated as always.

"Why do you keep it so flaming hot in here?" she snapped, wiping at her brow.

He did not answer, just merely watched his sister watch him. After a long moment, she huffed her displeasure and folded her arms across her chest.

"Well? What do you suggest to do, Sithian? Your brilliant plan failed, miserably, and now...*now* those blighted Blackhaven bastards have been sighted in the harbor. Trade ships, brother. They are *trading* with us, as if we were not enemies!"

Finally, Sithian returned his feet to the floor and acknowledged his sister. "Let them trade, Anna. What harm does it do us?"

The young woman's face contorted in rage. "They are our enemies! If we trade with them, we support their economy! We support the economy, we are supporting the treasury, and by relation, the throne! Mother, Sithian! You are allowing this throne to support and accept Mother and that elf-bastard Losolin! Father would never-"

"Father is dead. He ran this kingdom into the ground, and he has joined it now," Sithian cut in angrily.

Rhiannan's slap caught him full in the face, jerking his head around. In a flash, the king was around his desk, pinning his sister against it, his fingers digging into her jaw. "Do not ever strike me."

The woman whimpered in pain, her back bent over the desk at a painfully sharp angle. Futilely she tried to free a hand, but her brother was too fast and ridiculously strong. He caught her wrist and pinned it to her shoulder.

"I am the king, and you will never strike me again," Sithian said coldly, his eyes dead, emotionless.

Fear crept into Rhiannan's throat, freezing her heart as she stared up at her brother. There was no love in his gaze; there was barely recognition. "Sithian?" she breathed.

"Get out."

When he released her, Rhiannan gingerly straightened, took a step toward her brother, and then fled when he turned his dead gaze away from her. Wearily, the Magin moved around to the fire and stood staring into it, mindlessly pouring himself a goblet full of brandy and downing it. The liquid burned down his throat, making his vision waver and his balance weaken. Stumbling, Sithian leaned against the mantle, sweat drenching his body.

They had buried Midian as soon as they had returned after the battle. His father was entombed in the ancestral graveyard, a rather small hilltop of massive mausoleums. There had been a total of thirty-two Kings of Zaedic, each one a direct descendant of Roluf Gwemheoad, a Rahlan since the marriage of Sithian Rahlan to Inabes Gwemheoad, the First Magin's granddaughter. It was not until the present-day Sithian's great-grandfather Hadian that Zaedic had become a true kingdom. Before, it had been a large island village, ruled over by the Rahlan family. The palace had been erected during Hadian's reign, replacing the thatch and timber hall that had stood since Sithian's time.

The Rahlans had always been Magins as well, powerful and ruthless, descended from leaders, sons of great men. Now, one of them was a traitor, living and training at the great kingdom of Blackhaven, Zaedic's sworn enemy for a thousand years. Sithian's lip curled as he thought of his fair brother, at his acceptance of the elfin culture, his betrayal of their father, and worst...Haydyn's determination in following their over-holy mother.

Tlonna's face swam into Sithian's imagination, staring at him with her frosty blue eyes, rimmed with inky lashes and framed with golden hair that fell to her waist. She was a fool, insipid and weak. With a snarl, the half-blood hurled his re-filled goblet of brandy into the fire, causing the flames to leap up as they consumed the fuel. The skin on his forearms reddened, the hair burning away. Sithian ignored the pain, Weaving almost unconsciously to heal himself.

Learia slipped inside the room, her curvaceous body shimmering in a gown of fine linen, so fine it was nearly transparent. The rosy color of her gown accentuated her pale flesh and dark hair, making her seem small and fragile within the dark palace.

"Sithian," she murmured, coming up behind him to wrap her arms around his waist.

"What do you want?" he demanded, irritated at yet another intrusion.

"Rhiannan says you are angry, and deeply hurt from the loss of King Midian. It is my duty as your wife to take care of your needs."

"Angry and hurt, am I?" Sithian chuckled humorlessly.

"I believe so, yes."

The Magin turned in the small woman's arms, his cold gaze coming to rest on her dainty face. "What do you think you can do, Learia?"

The Queen of Zaedic flowed to her knees and deftly untied his breeches. Within seconds, she had her mouth on him, stroking and caressing. Sithian rubbed his face with his hand, trying to keep back the violent urges sweeping through him. After a few futile minutes, Learia pulled away and stared up at him.

"You are so empty, Sithian," she said quietly.

"Is that an insult, wife?"

"No. It is an observation. Physically, you are whole and fit and healthy, but inside... oh my husband, you are more empty than a ring."

Sithian pulled half his lips into a grin, looking down at his wife. "You have failed to give me an heir, I have lost my father. My brother is a traitor, my mother a sworn enemy, and my sister a whining imbecile, who has also not quickened with a desperately needed heir. What do I have to be full about?"

"It has been less than a year, Sithian. You come to me rarely, not once since the battle. I cannot birth you a son if you do not give me your seed," Learia returned softly.

"Then I will come to you tonight, and we will make an heir. Now go. I have things to do and I do not need you to distract me."

Rising, Learia kissed him lightly on the lips and glided from the room. Sithian watched her go, wondering how it was that she loved him at all. He found her seductive, but he harbored no emotions toward the woman at all. She was a tool. Everyone was a tool. Slowly, he returned to his desk and picked up the first sheet of parchment. It was an account of how many Zaedicans had died in Nymyños.

Rolling his eyes, Sithian shoved the record away from him and returned to his torpid position. It was his kingdom, but he did not consider them his people. He did not care about them. They all deserved to die. Everyone, from the Fãrthyn Ocean south of Nymyños to the Scattered Isles hundreds of miles north and east of Zaedic. He sneered at his desk, fingernails digging into his temples.

Around his neck weighed the Resurrection Pendant, its infallible chain severed by the elf-bitch Yayènia's sword. How that had happened, Sithian could not fathom, but he had Woven the links back together. It was not the same as it had been, but it was good enough. Midian had failed to put it on again when he had ridden into the alchemist camp the last time. Not that it would have mattered. Tlonna had destroyed him completely, pounding his heart into a mushy glob that was completely irreparable.

He remembered seeing his father's body strewn about the ground, his spine laid open to the elements, his neck slit across the scar, eyes staring upward in silent agony. Sithian had slipped on what had been his heart, which had caused him to vomit. It was a vision that haunted him day and night.

He had thought his father invincible after the resurrection. Sithian remembered the day clearly, the way Midian had come to life with a gasp, writhing on the stone slab within his tomb. The midnight eyes had found his son, the pupils dilated, the rest bloodshot. The Magin had grabbed at his body, feeling himself alive once more, felt the blood coursing through his body. He had been dead for months, his body decaying slowly due to the magic he had used to extend his life.

He'd needed to replenish his blood every day for the first few weeks, sucking it from the people his son had brought him, puncturing their necks with his fingers and teeth. Sithian had watched in fascination, even taking part every now and then, just to feel the power of draining another's blood so...intimately. Midian had lavished it, often ordering the victims to be women so that he might be inside them while he fed. Then, slowly, the need for blood had diminished and then completely disappeared, and the undead king had come truly alive once more.

It was then that he had begun training, remaining hidden from everyone but his two offspring. His power was amazing, his strength and stamina above and beyond even the strongest elves. He had proved it, easily overtaking Yayènia, avenging himself.

That had been a wonderful day, Sithian mused, his eyes narrowing. A magnificent day, until his mother had appeared to rip everything away. And now he had just received news that the elf-bitch had survived, somehow, Yayènia was still alive. Blood began to drip from where his nails dug into his temples, slowly tracing down his fingers, over his knuckles, and onto his desk. The crimson drops landed on the letter that bore the news, spreading to mingle with the ink, distorting the words.

Without looking up, Sithian grabbed a large bell on his desk and rang it. Immediately, a servant bowed in, keeping his eyes averted. "Yes, Majesty?"

"Bring me a woman. Beautiful. Young."

"But the queen, Majesty, she is just outside."

Sithian glanced up. "I do not give a damn where the queen is. Bring me a woman as I command."

The man went pale and bowed out. A few minutes later he was pulling a young woman into the office, alternating between smiling and grimacing.

"Leave us," Sithian snapped, beckoning to the girl.

She was indeed beautiful, fair and slim, her large green eyes wide with terror. "How can I serve my king?"

"Please me."

"How, your Highness?"

Sithian glanced at her, his head still in his hands. "Figure it out yourself."

The young woman knelt between his legs, and took up the position his wife had half an hour ago. This time, he responded. As she ran her tongue and lips over him, Sithian wrapped his hands in her bounteous yellow hair, pushing her face against him. She gagged, but he held her tight.

"Finish it," he hissed, releasing her head a little.

She did as commanded, using her throat now, until he released his seed. When she started to pull away, Sithian grabbed a fistful of her hair and yanked her head to the side. "What is your name?"

"Merisel," she gasped, her lips flecked with his essence.

"Ah..." Sithian breathed, running his fingers down her pale neck.

With a sudden jerk, he threw her to the ground and climbed over her. She did not resist, but her body went rigid with fear. He yanked up her dress and sheathed himself, feeling her tense further with pain.

"Are you a virgin...Merisel?" he crooned.

"Yes," she whimpered.

"Not anymore," Sithian laughed, moving inside her. When he climaxed again, he grabbed her face and twisted it upward. She keened softly as he lowered his mouth to her pulsing vein. He licked her once, and then sank his teeth into her flesh. Merisel cried out, her fingers digging into his forearms as he drank, hot blood flowing into his mouth, dripping onto the rug beneath them. She lasted a while, longer than most. Then, her grip loosened, her struggling body moved less and less, until finally, she lay still.

Sithian drank until her heart stopped beating and then sat up, still straddling the dead girl, still inside her. He wiped his mouth the back of his sleeve, looking at his victim. He had not done this since his father had stopped, feeling it was unnecessary. But now...

He felt rejuvenated, alive more than ever before. He had never drained someone, only taken what his father had allowed. Even Midian had not completely emptied a person. Sithian leaned back, surveying the scene. There was a large splotch of blood on the rug that would need to be cleaned. Or not. He stood, staggering slightly, a little queasy but feeling immortal. Sithian retied his drawers, licked his lips, and called his servant again.

The man bowed in, then froze, seeing the young woman. "My lord...did she not p-please...you...?"

He stared up at Sithian, stared at the blood staining his lips and chin, stared at the girl's exposed lower half. "My king..."

"Get rid of her, Marco," Sithian hissed.

"Of course. Of course. Yes...I...yes."

As Marco dragged Merisel's body from his office, Sithian sat back down at his desk, and resumed reading reports.

Rhiannan watched Marco carry the dead girl's body out of her brother's office from around the corner. She was about to turn and leave for her own quarters when she saw the bloody wound on the corpse's neck. The princess fought down the urge to vomit and braced herself against the wall. She had known Sithian had taken part in the revolting act after bringing their father back from the dead, but until now she had thought him acquit of the habit. And now, he was allowing Blackhaven to continue trade with the people of Zaedic. He was losing his grip on the throne, and his sanity, and would take her with him when he fell.

"Are you well, Princess?" a voice said behind her.

Rhiannan turned and stared at the young woman who had spoken. She was a small thing in servant robes, terror writ on her pixie face. "Yes. I am well. What is your name, girl?"

"Marin, your highness, if it pleases you to know," she replied, curtseying low so that her umber hair spilled over her shoulders and brushed the floor.

"Ah," Rhiannan breathed, a plan forming in her mind. "Marin...come to my room with me."

"Your grace," Marin said, and obediently followed the princess through the palace to the upper floor where the royal suites were.

Once ensconced in her sitting room, Rhiannan turned to the girl and bade her sit. "So, Marin, how old are you?"

"Seventeen, my lady."

"Do you remember my twin, a fair boy, Haydyn?" the Magin asked, conjuring in her mind an image of her treacherous brother.

"Yes, my lady. He disappeared with the Magin Queen, the elf, two and a half years ago."

"Yes, he did. He turned his back on his people, on his family, and ran away to become the prince in our rival kingdom. Did you know that?"

Marin nodded. "Yes, highness."

"Do you...hate him...for that?" Rhiannan crooned.

The girl frowned slightly, squirming in her chair as the princess stared hard at her. "I... did not know him, my lady. But, he did betray our nation, he was our prince, and he left. I guess I hate him for doing such a thing."

"Good. Tell me, Marin, have you been with a man?"

"What?"

Rhiannan moved closer to the girl, cocking her head slightly. "Have you *been* with a man, Marin?"

"O-once, your grace."

"Good. I need you to do something for me. For Zaedic...for the king."

"The king?" Marin breathed, going flush.

Inwardly, the half-elf grinned. Outwardly, she smiled gently. "Yes, for King Sithian. Do you like him?"

"Oh...he's very beautiful your majesty. And very strong. We have never been so prosperous, Princess Rhiannan. I would do anything for the king."

"As you should. My brother has given much for his people, it is time the people gave back. He is a lonely man, the queen does not satisfy him. If you do this thing for me, he would be yours."

"Anything you ask, anything you need, I will give it to you," Marin panted, staring at Rhiannan.

"Excellent," Anna whispered, coming to kneel before her. "You are going to Blackhaven, and you are going to accuse Haydyn of raping you."

"What? But he never did," Marin gasped.

"Does not matter, girl," Rhiannan snapped. "Do you want Sithian?"

"Yes."

"Then you will do this. I will train you on how to act, on what to say. You will go to the kingdom of the elves and you will accuse my brother of rape. Haydyn betrayed Sithian. He brought about the death of King Midian, our father. They have laws there that demand a rapist be put to death."

"But it has been nearly three years, my lady. They will not believe me!"

"I will give you the means. You see, Haydyn has a birthmark...here," Anna rested her finger on the inside of Marin's left thigh. "It is small, easily missed, and shaped like a flame. Only someone who had been eyelevel with his thighs could know of it."

"How do you know?" Marin asked, disgust crossing her face.

Rhiannan sneered. "I grew up with him. He is my twin, girl, I know what he looks like. I do not practice incest."

"Oh, I never-" the girl began desperately but Anna cut her off with a slice of her hand.

"Forget it. You will do this, or you will be removed."

Marin swallowed audibly, her hazel eyes going wide with fear. Almost imperceptibly, she nodded. "What do I do?"

The half-blood grinned, and stood. "First, you will go to petitions, and lay your case before Tlonna and Losolin..."

As the princess coached the servant, Sithian was in his office, penning a letter to the king of Seaduens.

Losolin watched Tlonna as she sat next to him, her white eyes half closed, the colorful sparks flitting about her body like a fitful aura. The company was completely silent as the queen stared unblinking at the fire, a small smile on her lips. She was like a child, entranced and completely distracted by the light. Losolin looked to Miazie, trying to keep his panic at bay. The Belau shrugged and gave him an apologetic look, at a loss for an explanation. The queen looked over at her husband, no recognition on her face, and touched him lightly on the shoulder.

Sparks shot out everywhere. Losolin swore as pain lanced up and down his arm, green light sizzling about his limb where she had touched him. The half-Magin leapt to his feet, grounding his own power, the rest of his body tingling unpleasantly. His left hand clenched tight as his muscles tried to deal with being touched by Tlonna's immense power, his veins distending against his skin. Tlonna let out a bark of laughter, staring in rapture at the pulsing magic. Suneelo grabbed his brother's shoulder and shook it, trying to loosen the muscles.

"Tlonna?" Erdwyf asked cautiously, reaching out a hand toward her friend.

"Do not touch me," Tlonna growled in a voice that was not her own, all humor disappearing from her face.

"Loni?" Yayènia gasped, lightly touching her sister's arm.

Faster than thought, Tlonna wrapped her arm around the warrior's and yanked her close. Everyone froze as Yayènia grunted in surprise, trying to pull away. Just as with Losolin's, the muscles in the warrior's arm clenched alarmingly hard, shuddering with the tension. The Magin grinned maliciously and gripped her other hand on Yayènia's neck.

"No! Tlonna! Stop!" Losolin shouted, still trying to control his quivering arm.

Suneelo cursed and ran to help his wife who was now being forced backward, unable to free herself from Tlonna's grip. The captain tried to pry the queen's fingers off Yayènia's neck, but Tlonna back-handed him hard enough to knock him unconscious.

"*Kalise*!" Erdwyf swore, joining Losolin as he attempted to yank Tlonna away from her sister.

Yayènia was choking, her free hand digging into Tlonna's wrist, trying to free herself. Sodo and Miazie had their arms around her waist, pulling, but the queen's super-enhanced strength was too much. Erdwyf yelped in pain as a Weave caught her upside the head, shoving her away with enough force to knock the wind from her. Losolin felt another Weave slam into his side, but he gritted his teeth and kept his grip on his wife.

"Tlonna...this heart is where you belong," he gasped. "This life, this soul. We are your family, love, Nia is your sister and you only just found out! Loni, come back to us. Please, come back to me."

Tlonna snarled, white eyes narrowing as Yayènia started to turn blue.

"She is possessed!" Miazie cried, tugging unsuccessfully on Yayènia's shoulders.

"By what?" Losolin asked desperately.

"Evil. D-darkness. Whatever happened at the tower...it's inside her, a spirit of hatred and anger."

"The prophecy..." Erdwyf gasped, coming to her senses.

"Yes," Miazie breathed.

"She is strangling Yayènia!" Losolin shouted. "How do we get her back?"

"I don't know!" Miazie sobbed.

Tlonna could hear the voices battling back and forth in her mind, but all she could see was a red haze, and a dim figure that had tried to attack her. It was going to die. They were all going to die. She could feel Jair inside her, along with all the excess Maginic powers she had absorbed, their anger and bitterness filling her so completely she could not remember her own name. Her hand ached where her attacker was trying to wrench away, but she ignored the pain, focusing on the slowing pulse beneath her other hand.

Suddenly agony exploded in the side of her head, over and over again until darkness overcame her, and she slipped into oblivion.

Losolin dropped his sheathed sword and went to his knees, checking Tlonna's pulse. Yayènia was being revived by Sodo, while Erdwyf checked on Suneelo, who was slowly coming around. He'd had to hit Tlonna in the head four times before she collapsed, and now blood was leaking from her temple. Trying to blink away the tears that welled in his eyes, the king wiped the blood away and turned his wife onto her back. She was breathing regularly now, the strange flickering aura gone, and she looked as though she were merely sleeping.

His heart was tearing itself to pieces, and he shook as the knowledge that he had just beaten her into unconsciousness took hold of him. Yayènia had lost consciousness, and Tlonna had shown no sign of releasing her sister. Losolin gingerly picked up his wife and carried her to her sleeping roll.

"Bind her hands," Miazie said softly from behind.

"What?" Losolin asked, spinning around on his heels to stare in horror at the human.

"This evil will not pass with the night. You must bind her hands or she will kill us all in our sleep."

"No, she will not, I...cannot do that, Miazie. I cannot," Losolin breathed, turning back to study his listless love.

"You must, or have someone else do it. It is not her anymore, Losolin, it is something else, something tainted and bitter. She will come back, but for now, her soul is gone," Miazie insisted, looking around as Sodo, Yayènia, Erdwyf, and Suneelo walked up to the camp.

"What in the nine hells was that about?" Suneelo snapped, gesturing to the prostrate queen.

"Another branch of the prophecy has come true," Erdwyf cut in before Losolin broke out in anger. "Tlonna has been consumed by the vengeful spirit of Jair, whom she encountered at the tower, I assume. She has taken in his soul, and the magics that went with it, therefore finding the power she was meant to have, the power that is too much for her body and soul to endure all at once. Now, she is lost to us until she finds the strength to fight the foreign spirit within her."

"She must have known this would happen, why else would she have been so determined in coming?" Yayènia asked, gazing down at Tlonna, rubbing her throat, which hurt all the more because the area was still achy from being severed.

"I don't believe she knew *this* was going to happen, but she certainly knew something was going to happen. Tlonna has been through too much to go off chasing some hunch on a whim," Miazie replied.

"And look what it got her," Suneelo snarled, "she has gone completely mental."

"No she has not!" Losolin fumed, straightening from his crouch next to Tlonna. "She is strong and righteous, and she will come back to us!"

"She nearly killed Yayènia!"

"The evil being *within* her nearly killed Yayènia! Tlonna is fighting it!"

The brothers were nose to nose now, their breath ragged with fury as they faced each other. "Stop!" Yayènia commanded, and was ignored.

The warrior threw her hands in the air and looked to Erdwyf. The High Advisor shook her head in defeat. It was Sodo that stepped between the two males, shouldering them apart and putting his hands out to keep them at a distance.

"No one but the gods are at fault for this, my friends. Them, and those long dead who predicted and determined these events. Now, calm down."

Losolin and Suneelo glared at each other for another moment, and then both looked away in shame. Sodo put his hands down and stepped aside, ready to intervene should the two start fighting once more. The king turned away and looked down upon his wife, her face turned away from him, concealed in shadow.

"Bind her hands," he said softly to no one in particular, and walked away.

Tlonna woke with a start, her heart thudding in her chest and her head pounding. She could see very little, her vision fogged over but for a small amount, creating a tunnel effect. Rage and hostility infused her mind, and she began to shake with the need to get revenge. Revenge on what, she did not know, only that her desire for it was insatiable. The Magin Queen tried to sit up, but found herself struggling to do so. Her hands and elbows were bound behind her, not tightly, but firm enough to keep her from freeing herself.

Snarling, Tlonna rolled onto her stomach and crawled into a sitting position, baring her teeth. Figures lay about her, indiscernible people that ignored her presence. One was sitting up, a bright form that seemed to watch her with gleaming eyes, eyes that gave her an uneasy feeling of familiarity.

"Unbind me," she hissed, inching toward the figure.

"Lay back, Tlonna," it replied in a distant voice, one filled with pain and weariness.

"Free me!"

"Lay back, my love," said the bright form, firmer now.

The part of Tlonna that was still her, the part shielded from Jair's vengeful soul, recognized Losolin's voice and tried to obey him, struggling in vain against the furious being inhabiting her mind. Her body lurched awkwardly as the two individuals fought against each other, falling to the side.

Losolin started to his feet in one fluid motion, wanting to help the elf he loved, knowing he could not unbind her. For an instant, he saw her eyes clear and beseech him for aid, then they were white once more and she wheezed, writhing on the ground like a creature in torment.

"Free me!" she rasped in that voice that was not wholly her own.

"You must free yourself," Losolin cried, backing away once more, tears threatening.

Tlonna's mouth opened and a howl of such rage and hopelessness came out of her that the five others jerked awake in terror, even Yayènia, who had never known such fear. The Magin rose to her feet so gracefully it was as if she had been simply picked up and set down again. She bent backward until her head was level with her waist, muscles straining, her legs bent inward at the knee. The six companions stared in horror at the contorted elf, frozen by their own revulsion.

Suddenly Tlonna straightened, milky eyes half-closed, blood dripping from one nostril, her chest heaving with each breath. "This was not supposed to happen."

The voice that came out was no longer even close to Tlonna's. It was male, hollow and angry. Tlonna's body convulsed, the bonds breaking, her mouth slack as black blood oozed from her lips, her fingers contorted and stiff, tearing at her own body as though her skin pained her.

"She will destroy everything!" Jair shrieked, rolling Tlonna's head back and forth in furious denial. "Everything!"

The elf's body twitched violently and then flopped to the ground, where she twisted grotesquely, animalistic noises ripping from her throat as she did. Tlonna's shoulders rolled back and her legs tensed so that she was arched with the back of her head and the heel of her feet the only things touching the ground. She stayed liked that for several seconds, every muscle in her body tense and distended, and then she fell back, gasping and wheezing.

"Tlonna!" Losolin cried, rushing to her side, cradling her shuddering body in his arms.

Abruptly, she went limp, her head lolling to the side, blind eyes open and staring. Terror seized Losolin so completely he began to sob hopelessly, shaking Tlonna. No breath came from her lips, no pulse beat in her neck or at her wrists. He dropped her from numb arms, wrath and grief building within him until it burst in an explosion of green light.

"NO! NO!" he roared, his entire body rigid as he held his clawed hands above Tlonna's limp form.

The earth shifted beneath them, the night sky illuminated with green magic, silent thunder shaking the surrounding forest. Losolin's bellow echoed through the air, chased by his magic. A moment later, all the green light had gathered above the two elves, condensing into a writhing ball of power. It dropped into Tlonna's body and all went dark. There were no stars, no moons, no light of any kind. Yards away, the five from Blackhaven could hear their monarchs' harsh breathing. Miazie dropped to her knees, clutching at her head as her skull suddenly seemed to rip apart, images assaulting her mind, things she had never seen before. Sodo bent over her, alarmed.

Then, without warning Tlonna's chest heaved, her back arched, and her eyes opened wide, a clear and stunning blue, the pupils a reflective white. She let out a scream of such agony that everyone crouched, pressing their hands to their ears. Losolin was stooped over her, hands digging into the ground. The Magin Queen's hands reached up and wrapped around his shoulders, anchoring onto him. Slowly, he lifted his hands from the earth and held his wife close, shaking as sobs tore from him.

Tlonna bit into his shoulder, trying to stop screaming, feeling his hands warm on her back, his fresh woody scent filling her nostrils. She could taste blood, and wrenched away, horrified that she had punctured his skin, but Losolin did not pull away.

"Tlonna...Tlonna," he wept, holding her close.

"I lost you," she whispered, burying her face in his neck.

Chapter 21

So Many Tears

No one slept anymore that night, huddling close to the fire, not speaking, wrapped in their own thoughts. Every now and again one of them would glance over at Tlonna, catch a glimpse of her odd eyes, and look hastily away, fearful of what lay behind them. Tlonna herself was slumped against Losolin, exhausted and terrified, pain still singing through her body like acid in the veins. Every breath she took felt like breathing in ash, and she was acutely aware of her changed vision. She saw things now, auras and images that flickered about her companions and then faded, revealing bits of their secrets or their fate.

She was also aware that something had changed in the air, that her senses were as strong as any other time, rather than dulled as they had been. Tlonna sighed, and gave up trying to think. Slowly, she slipped into a light trance.

Losolin was shivering, his eyes riveted on the camp fire, thoughts racing through his mind. His shoulder ached slightly where Tlonna had bitten him, but he ignored it, focusing on the change within his body. His senses were sharp again, but it was more than that. His muscles tingled, and he felt as though he could run for days, or swim the distance between Nymyños and Zaedic and arrive fresh. The feeling worried him, and he sensed that he had broken something within him by summoning as much power as he had. He'd brought Tlonna back from the dead, used magic within the anti-magic border of Purheae. He knew what he had done, but the King of Blackhaven did not want to admit it to himself.

Miazie watched Tlonna and Losolin out of the corner of her eye, her head resting on Sodo's shoulder. Her skull still pounded, and she was assaulted by things she did not want to comprehend, so she ignored them. The two elves were silent and blank-faced, slumped against each other as though too tired to go on with their lives. She pitied them greatly. They had been through so much, experienced horrors beyond imagination, lived through torture and war, and still come out strong at the end. Now the Belau feared something had been broken. She had seen Tlonna clutch Losolin as though he were her only reality, watched them stumble to where they sat now, and cry silent tears, seemingly unaware that they were not alone. Miazie closed her eyes, remembering the time King Athelias of Talenias had sent a company to slaughter them, the way Losolin had gone mad, sweeping through the lines like a god, invincible, and then watching Tlonna snatch a spinning sword out of thin air and announce that she was the Magin Queen. It was such a vivid memory that Miazie shivered, thinking about how very powerful her two friends were, and now, they were something more. They were beyond powerful.

They were gods.

The next morning dawned a sullen gray, a heavy mist covering the ground like a shroud as though the earth was trying to hide under the covers like a frightened child. Frightened of the terrible things that had happened the night before. The seven companions woke unwillingly, yawning and stretching in the damp fog, forgetting momentarily the unfortunate events. Yayènia smiled at Tlonna, a sleepy smile born of sisterly affection and incoherent drowsiness. Then the memories returned and the warrior's face froze as she caught a glimpse of Tlonna's white pupils. The Magin frowned, and then her expression tightened as she realized what her sister was thinking.

"Tlonna..." Yayènia started, but the younger elf had turned away to greet Losolin, who was blinking up at the gray sky.

He shifted his face to Tlonna and gazed at her, unable to summon any sort of emotion. He sat up slowly, rubbing his arms to dispel the cold, and took a deep breath.

"What happens today?"

Tlonna shook her head. "I do not know. Perhaps we should go home."

"Did you find what you were looking for?" the male asked softly, ignoring the others as they watched with worried eyes.

"No, I found something more," she replied, standing. "You broke the border, Losolin."

"I know," Losolin said, following her. "What will it do?"

"It unleashed all the dormant power that was held at bay," Miazie broke in, folding her arms across her chest. "All the magic that was surrounding this area was funneled into a conduit."

"What conduit?" the king asked, fearing the answer.

"You, Losolin."

Everyone stopped moving, their eyes riveted on Losolin as he stared at Miazie, his eyes blank. When he did not move, Suneelo walked over and put an arm on his brother's shoulder.

"It does not change you, *bruun*. It just means you are stronger than you were, right?" the warrior said, glancing at Miazie, who jerked her head to the side.

Losolin eyed his sibling, smiling a little. "Right. We are the same people, just... amplified."

"Indeed," Suneelo said, shaking him lightly. "So, do we continue our search, or do we return home with what we have?"

"I think we need to return," Tlonna said softly, turning to face her small group of friends. "You must not fear me, I have died, and come back to you because of Losolin. He sacrificed his body for me, became something else, and you must not fear that. We are one step closer to our goal, we must not shirk away."

"No one fears you or Losolin, Tlonna, and no one is shirking away," Erdwyf said, smiling. "We know you, we love you, and we will not be turned away so easily. We will finish this thing, whatever it is, and we will all be there at the end, with you."

Tlonna gave her friend a faint smile and turned away to begin packing her things. Losolin moved away from Suneelo after patting his brother on the shoulder, and stared at the firepit until it burst into flame. Within minutes, he had breakfast cooking.

They retraced their steps back through Purheae, skirting along the decomposing *Brekthni* carcass and once more crossing the bridged and creviced face of the province. They were less than a day from the border when Eyin Thorn materialized before them, stepping from the forest as he had the day they had met.

"Did you find the answers you sought?" he asked abruptly in his thick accent.

Tlonna and Losolin stared down at him in silence, knowing it was not his true question.

When no one spoke, Eyin's face contorted with rage. "What did you do?" he screamed, startling the horses. "The forest is silent! The animals stay hidden! My people are terrified! We felt the world shift! You destroyed the barrier, the thing that kept us safe from Dwarf, Elf, and Magin alike! You have altered the physical and intangible structure of Purheae! What did you do?"

Tlonna shared a look with Yayènia, and then dismounted. She stepped up to the irate human and waited until he was looking her in the eye. Once his gaze landed on her white pupils, he shuddered, unable to look away.

"Times are changing, King Eyin Thorn of Purheae, and you had better be ready for it. You can no longer hide behind your boundary. It is time the alliance was struck again."

"What alliance?" Eyin breathed.

"The Alliance of the Four Kingdoms," Tlonna replied loudly. "Come to Blackhaven City with us, see how a kingdom is run, and strike the alliance anew with me. The next generation of rulers, a new generation of Nymyñosian peace."

Eyin shook his head, eyes still riveted on Tlonna's. "I cannot just leave, Queen of the Elves. I am responsible for a people, now...a kingdom."

"Then when you are ready, come to Blackhaven and you will be welcomed. Now, we return to our home. I hope to see you soon, Eyin Thorn," the Magin said, remounting. Just as they were about to ride away, she looked back at the human. "Remember your promise, King of Purheae."

They rode all through that day and the next, eager to be home, anxious to put this experience behind them. When they finally rested somewhere in the middle of Schelum, Erdwyf brought up the last encounter.

"Do you really plan to renew the Alliance of the Four Kingdoms, Tlonna? It was a desperate failure when King Dietirin called on it," the fey-faced elf said.

No. I plan to form the Great Nymyñosian Alliance, but it would overwhelm Eyin. I will not allow it to fail. Eyin is not ready to rule anything yet. He is young, untried, and uneducated. He will come to Blackhaven, just give it time. I must send to Furntil Eldrout of Flousen Dua and seek a meeting with him."

"Tlonna, Flousen Dua was not part of the alliance," Miazie interjected.

"Hence the Great Nymyñosian Alliance," Tlonna said simply. "Who rules Kismath and Schelum?"

"No one, so far as we know," Erdwyf said, frowning at the thought. "Barl was destroyed completely, and then rebuilt as a village about six years ago. There is a mayor, but King Richard was beheaded, along with his entire family. No one has risen up since to take the throne. Schelum is leaderless and wasted, its population less than a thousand."

Tlonna shook her head in disgust. "And Kismath?"

"I do not really know, for sure," the High Advisor replied bitterly. "No one has gone into Kismath since its razing. It had two main cities, Orlan, and the capital, Kismanelle. Orlan sits on the cliffs facing the Strait of Arwênlhias, a fortress of trade between Schelum, Flousen Dua, and Blackhaven. Aderiaen Rahlan burnt the entire city to the ground, Yayènia and Ghealan were there, if I remember correctly."

"*Aiya,* we arrived just hours too late," Yayènia agreed. "Lan and I attacked Aderiaen's force right after, but when we drove them off, there was no one left alive in the entire city. We searched for days for a single person, and those we did find died from injuries. Aderiaen had planned it well. The water supply had been laced with cooking oil the night before, and then lit on fire, destroying any attempt to put out the fires lit from outside the walls, arrows and trebuchets and whatnot. We finally had to give up and leave."

"Half the force had been sent to Kismanelle to head off any attack, but we just were not enough," the warrior continued. "No one came to our aid, and we were driven back time and again until there were none of us left. Kismanelle was torched as we fled, though we had been able to evacuate a small portion of the city. King Jaryn and Queen Sybilla were with us in the beginning, and then turned back. None of us saw them go, but the next morning, our scouts found their heads stuck to the city gates. They had no children."

"That is terrible," Tlonna sighed. "So, neither kingdom had a surviving member of the royal family after the war. Schelum has not evolved since, what of Kismath? No one has heard a thing?"

"Unfortunately not," Miazie said when Erdwyf merely shook her head. "There are only two routes into Kismath. A ford across the Jaquisa River, following Obsidian Way out of Blackhaven and Schelum, or a ten mile stretch between the Onyx Forest of Flousen Dua and the Kismath Mountains. It's only navigable during dead summer or winter, when the marsh land around it dries up or freezes. Now, it is home to goblins who like the marshes, which leaves only the ford, and no one is really up for a twenty-five mile hike through the Kismath tundra."

"That is true. Bringing the army through was a hell all on its own," Yayènia said, nodding.

Suneelo smiled at his wife. "I traveled through Kismath once, about three hundred years ago. It was an unpleasant experience. Once you reach Kismanelle, it is decent enough, but the rest of the kingdom is marsh or tundra. The entire place is on a constant up or down slope but for Kismanelle. Only the marshland and the banks of the Jaquisa are at a decent elevation. Then there is the mountain range, which you got a taste of on the way to Alchemian. Blasted mountains, home to goblins and beasts, frozen all the way, pocked with stunted trees and boulders. It is not a friendly place."

"I heard the Kismathians were sturdy people," Losolin interjected.

"Yeah, considered the strongest of the human breeds, short and stocky, thick skinned," Erdwyf replied. "Although, they were supposedly an attractive people, too. Fair."

"Indeed, usually had red or blonde hair, pale eyes, and pale skin, due to the elevation and lack of strong sunlight," Miazie supplied blandly. "Though most blame it on the fact that Kismath is sandwiched between two Elven kingdoms. Interbreeding with you pasty folk."

"Ah yes, us pale demons," Sodo snorted, fingering Miazie's raven-silk hair.

"Ignoring the pasty comment," Tlonna laughed softly, "Miazie might be on to something. What if the Kismathians fled into the neighboring kingdoms, Flousen Dua, Schelum, and Blackhaven?"

"I am telling you, there was no one left to flee, Tlonna. Those that came with us have long since been integrated into Blackhaven society. When you send to Furntil Eldrout, have the messenger go through Kismath rather than circle around like normal, if you want to know," Yayènia said, yawning.

"I will," Tlonna said, lacing her fingers with Losolin's. "Shall we say goodnight?"

Her tired company nodded in acquiescence and soon they were all asleep but for Suneelo, who had first watch.

They arrived back in Blackhaven three days later without fanfare, though they had run into Watch Guards just after entering the forest. Yayènia and Suneelo turned for home while the five others continued to the castle. Haydyn, Ghealan, and Aidyn greeted them at the castle gates where they dismounted. Ghealan held little Jaryikin in his massive arms, looking decidedly odd. Erdwyf took her daughter and rubbed her cheek against the infant's.

"Oh, Jaryikin... did you have fun with daddy?" she cooed in a soft voice, oblivious to the comical looks she got from her companions.

"Ah, Erd, she said my name!" Ghealan said gleefully.

"Really? She said Ghealan?" Tlonna teased.

"No, she said *dâd,* you know... daddy? She sort of gurgled it, but she is less than a year old," the warrior said defensively, frowning at his queen. Then he noticed her eyes. "Tlonna... what happened? Your eyes?"

"We will talk about it later, Lan," Erdwyf cut in, looking up from her daughter to catch Tlonna's tense expression. "Right now, I want to go home. Tlonna, is Ghealan needed for today?"

"No, go on home, Lan. Spend the day with your wife and daughter and I will talk to you tomorrow, okay? Thank you for holding things down here," the queen replied.

"*Aiya,* Tlonna. We will talk tomorrow. Losolin, Sodo, Miazie," he said, guiding his wife back toward the stables to get his horse.

Aidyn and Haydyn had stood silently during the entire exchange, and now they stared at Tlonna with identical expressions. When she gave them a suffering look, they shook themselves. Then the assassin rubbed his chest and glowered at her quite menacingly.

"Welcome home, mum," Haydyn said, hugging his mother. "Is everything all right? You are not hurt? None of you are? Where are Suneelo and Yayènia?"

"Home, and we are all fine, Haydyn. We will tell you all about it tomorrow, but for now, let us just enjoy being home and together. Aidyn, my friend, how are things?" Tlonna said.

"Dull and safe," the assassin replied, stiffly embracing her. "There was one little issue when one of the resident noble couples had a row in the middle of the third floor. She threw a vase at him, caught him upside the head. He is still in the infirmary."

"Who was it?" Miazie asked, curiosity getting the best of her.

"Lady Berik of Belgarath, the mayor's daughter, and her fiancé, Lord Josham of Althirim, from Narnen. He is the son of a very wealthy shipwright," Haydyn supplied, grinning.

Aidyn rolled his eyes, but allowed the young half-elf to continue the narrative as the five moved up the walkway toward the castle. "Apparently, Lord Josham got handsy with a maid, and Lady Berik walked in on them."

"Handsy?" Tlonna inquired, confused.

"Uh...you know..." Haydyn rubbed his hands all over his own chest. "Handsy."

The queen shared a baffled look with her adult companions, desperate for sympathy. They all returned the look.

"Anyway, Berik and Josham got into a huge argument that escalated into them having it out in the middle of the main hallway on the third floor. It took three guards to pry her off of him, and that's when she threw the vase. Knocked him out cold," the prince said merrily, flattening his hand out before him.

"And where is Lady Berik now?" Losolin asked tentatively.

"House arrest," Aidyn cut in before Haydyn could elaborate further. "I put a guard on her door until she calms down."

"When was this?" Tlonna inquired.

"Three days ago."

"And she still has not recovered?" the queen asked in disbelief.

"Think about it, Loni. She caught her fiancé in bed with a maid. She is not going to get over it in a few days," the assassin returned as they entered the castle proper.

Haydyn sniggered, and Tlonna sent him a narrow-eyed look. "What do you have to do with this, son?"

"Nothing!" the prince yelped hastily, turning crimson. "I did nothing!"

"He visited Lady Berik, Tlonna," Aidyn said meaningfully, shaking his head. "Not quite a week ago."

"Haydyn!" Tlonna gasped, turning on her son.

"What?"

"You cannot sleep with engaged people! You should not be sleeping with anyone! You are too young!"

"I'm eighteen!"

"Physically, yes, mentally, no!"

Haydyn went even more crimson, his mouth opening in embarrassment. His face began to crumple, and he turned and fled up the stairs to his suite.

"Haydyn!" Tlonna cried, starting after him, horrified at what she had said.

"Tlonna, let him go. He needs to be alone for a bit," Miazie said, putting a restraining hand on her friend.

"Oh, how could I say that to him?" the queen asked, shaking her head. "That was awful of me. I did not mean that he was stupid, but he really is only three years old!"

"Tlonna, love, it is something he needs to come to grips with. It is not your fault," Losolin soothed. "Now come on, let us go to our rooms and wash and rest, all right? You can talk to Haydyn later today."

"Yes, I suppose so," the queen agreed. "Aidyn, thank you for dealing with him. You seem to have become somewhat of a parent figure for him, just like Nia."

Aidyn flushed slightly at the comment, but said nothing on it. "Go get some rest, Tlonna, all of you. We have much to discuss from what I see. Welcome back."

"Thank you, Aidyn," Losolin said, smiling at his friend.

Together, the four climbed to the fourth level and split to their own rooms. Once there, Tlonna collapsed into the tub already full of steaming water and soaked. Losolin joined her after storing their gear, and within the hour they were napping on the bed.

That evening, they called a meeting with the council, feeling rested and at ease for once. Everyone was there, the city council and the close circle of friends that stood by Tlonna and Losolin no matter what. They all studied Tlonna's eerie eyes, silent and anxious to hear what had happened in Purheae.

"My friends, you can obviously see that I have changed, and I am sure you are curious to know what has happened," the queen began. "I will tell you, but first I would like to discuss something a little less personal. I have decided to form a new alliance, the Great Nymyñosian Alliance, with Purheae, Schelum, Kismath, Flousen Dua, and of course, Blackhaven. Also Zeynuwn, Kajgenia, Narnen, and Arseninis. We have a new friend in Purheae, a young human named Eyin Thorn, and I have acknowledged him as the first King of Purheae," and she told them of their encounter with the strange young man and the agreements made.

"So, in short, we need to send a company down to Purheae so that we may keep our end of the bargain. I expect a list of those ready to go by midday tomorrow," Tlonna finished, looking to her three military leaders.

Yayènia, Ghealan, and Suneelo all nodded their consent, jotting down notes as they did so.

"Secondly, I wish to send three on a mission to Flousen Dua, through Kismath."

"Why?" asked Arganor, the Public Liaison. He was in charge of dealing with the citizens of Blackhaven on a daily basis.

"Because I want to know what has become of the nation, Lord Arganor. I know of the siege, the razing, the massacre, but someone must be living there," Tlonna replied coolly.

"Goblins," someone spat.

"Other than goblins," the queen said. "I want to know, and I need to send a message to Furntil Eldrout, so both tasks will be done at the same time. I want a messenger, a scout, and a guard to go, preferably elves, other than the guard. I would like the *Zephyr Leifen* Lara to go, if she is willing."

"She will be," Yayènia said immediately.

"Good. Arganor, I will need you to find the other two."

"I will have them by tomorrow, my queen," the human said, making a note.

"I also need someone to go to Barl and seek out the mayor. If he is the only authority figure in Schelum left, I need to speak to him. If not, find out who is and send them to me. Jayce, can you arrange a meeting?"

The young Royal Diplomat nodded, flipping through a small book. "Last I heard, the mayor of Barl was one Nedd Ardyce. I have never spoken with him, but I will send a message out tomorrow."

"Thank you. Now, as to what happened at Purheae," Tlonna said, leaning forward and pinning each of her listeners with her white-pupil gaze. She told them what had transpired, from the finding of Veries Gurgen's lockbox to the absorptions of Jair and her possession. "Now, I see auras and images, I can tell when a person is a Magin just by looking at them. I can see in the dark as well as I can in daylight. I can sometimes see flows of energy, the wind, all sorts of invisible forces. It does not change me."

"To what purpose, may I ask?" inquired Daphne, Keeper of Treasury.

"I am not yet sure, but I know that in absorbing Jair and all the surrounding Maginic dustings, I augmented my power a hundredfold, and Losolin nearly tenfold by his use of the boundary to bring me back to life, becoming a full Magin through sheer force. We are strong enough now to deal with any magical being on earth."

"But what of your physical being, Tlonna? You know the prophecy as well as I. Does that not concern you?" Aidyn asked, green eyes glittering.

Tlonna sighed, slouching in her chair. "It is not worth being concerned over when I cannot control it. We all know what I am fated to, why deny it? Now we know that I will be strong enough when the time comes."

"Do you really believe your...sacrifice is necessary, my lady?" Narda asked, her large gray eyes round with sadness.

"We will only know when the time is here, Narda," Tlonna replied quietly. "But that is not what we are here to discuss."

"What else is there?" Aladorn snapped, finally speaking. "You want to send people all throughout Nymyños, fine. You want to create alliances with a thousand people, fine. But do not pretend to ignore the fact that in the end it all comes down to you. Do you really think we will ever forget that? Do you think we can just gloss over the tiny detail of your imminent sacrifice? Tlonna, we are not just your council of state, we are your friends and your companions. There are things that *must* be discussed before it is too late."

"I disagree," Losolin snarled, leaning forward to pin the wiat with a glare. "There will be no sacrifice, therefore there is nothing to discuss. Give over, Aladorn."

"No, Losolin, he is correct," Tlonna said after a moment's silence. "We cannot ignore the truth any longer. I am going to die, I am going to give my life for the sake of Nymyños and the Slaves of Death. It has been prophesied, I have made these prophecies true, I have determined that will be my fate. Yes. I understand your unwillingness to accept the fact. I do not want to give my life either, but if it ends this darkness, then I will give it willingly. What good is a life when it is not meant for something? What good is a life when it is lived and ended for no purpose? Tell me, should I turn my back on all the good people of Nymyños, of the world, just because of my selfish desire to live? Of your selfish desire for me to live?"

"Tlonna, it is not a selfish de-" Losolin began, but the queen cut him off.

"Yes it is. Why is my life more important than any other? Why should I turn away when I have a chance to free a people, *my* people, from slavery and torture? They are in constant agony, ask Kelus! He knows, he lived that life for many years until an accident freed him from it. He was forced to flee his home because of his emancipation. Tell me why should I allow that kind of...wrongness to persist?"

"It is not your responsibility to free everyone!" Losolin shouted, rising to his feet. "Nine hells, Tlonna! You were not born to die! You were not given a life just to throw it away! You do not *know* any of these supposed Slaves of Death! It is not your fault they are what they are! It is Midian's, and Aderiaen's before him! Why should you suffer when you have done nothing but live?"

"Because it is my destiny!" Tlonna yelled back.

"You make your own destiny!" Losolin bellowed.

"This is the destiny I choose!" the queen screamed, standing rigid, power flickering in the strange aura about her.

Everyone in the council room froze, staring at the elf in horror and despair. Then their gazes shifted as one to Losolin, their king. He stared at his wife, jaw clenched, fists pressed against the table, shaking.

"Then you choose it without me," he hissed, and stormed out of the room.

Taken

Hours later, Yayènia and Miazie stood outside the royal suite, avoiding each other's gaze, waiting anxiously for the door to open. Within, they could hear Tlonna sobbing, as she had been since Losolin's departure. They had been standing there for three hours now, knocking and calling to their friend, never receiving any answers.

"What do we do?" Yayènia asked after a while, feeling awkward and useless.

Miazie shrugged, "What can we do? Bloody Losolin has to fix this, not us. I can't believe he walked out, I just want to...to..."

Yayènia nodded, caressing the hilt of her longblade. "I know. At the worst flaming time, too. We should shank him."

Miazie snorted, and then looked at the warrior with a gleam in her eye.

"No, gods above, no, Miazie," Yayènia said, grabbing hold of the human's arm as she reached for the elf's blade.

"Come on! Just...catch him off guard, shave off some of his hair, something! He walked out on *Tlonna*! After all they've been through, after all this time! Nine bleeding hells Yayènia! He deserves to be bled for all he's worth!" the Belau hissed, rage bubbling inside her like boiling water.

"Since when do you thirst for blood? You have been strange since Purheae. Though I do not condemn your desires, we must think this through. There is an element we are not seeing. You are the Belau, you should know this. I will talk to Suneelo. They are brothers, perhaps he can talk some sense into Losolin," Yayènia said, rubbing her hands across her face wearily. "I am not good at this kind of thing!"

"Any change?" asked Erdwyf, approaching quietly.

The two females at the door shook their heads in unison. As the High Advisor reached them, she gripped their shoulders. "Ghealan and the boys all went to find Losolin. Aidyn was furious, I have never seen him so angry. And Suneelo! I had to take his blades away from him."

"And Lan's?" Yayènia asked guardedly, eyeing her friend.

"All of theirs, Aladorn's, Aidyn's, even Sodo's! They were all going to skin him, I would swear on it. It was not easy."

"He certainly deserves it," Miazie spat.

The three females crouched at the top of the stairs, quietly conversing, trying to block out the sound of Tlonna's heartbroken weeping.

Deep within Blackhaven Forest, north of the city, Losolin buried his face in the loam, his entire body wracked with sobs. His fingers dug into the earth, trying to become one. His own words haunted him, his actions a repeating vision in his head.

"Why?" he bellowed, his heart breaking. "Why do you demand this of her?"

The earth spirits around him whispered in their strange language, only audible to him since Purheae.

"Why are you taking her from me?" he demanded. "WHY?"

The forest around him shook with his rage, the leaves curling inward, creatures fleeing in terror. The air itself stilled, all sound seeming to disappear as the forest took a breath, waiting for the explosion. The elf kneeling in the center howled in dismay, unable to stop.

Aidyn, Ghealan, Suneelo, Aladorn, and Sodo burst onto the scene, reaching for weapons they didn't have. They crowded to a stop, shocked to the core by the scene before them. Losolin was huddled in the midst of the massive trees, green light pulsing around him, his clothing shredded from his own fingers, his hair tangled and mixed with leaves and debris. Blood stained the rips where his fingers had dug into his flesh.

Aidyn started forward but Suneelo stayed the assassin, shaking his head. Losolin convulsed, gasping.

"Losolin," his brother called quietly, "Losolin, can you hear me?"

"Go away."

"Only if you come with me," Suneelo replied.

"I can never go back. Ever."

"Of course you can, it is your home, your kingdom, your family."

Losolin did not reply, but covered his head in his hands and curled into a ball. The five males surrounded him, looking down upon their king and friend in dismay. Suneelo knelt at his brother's head, touching him lightly on the shoulder. The Magin twitched away, lost somewhere within himself.

"*Bruun*, you must not abandon hope."

"Hope has abandoned us all," Losolin hissed.

"No it has not," the captain argued softly, looking to Ghealan.

"We came here to lynch you, Losolin, but Erdwyf took our weapons," the warrior said bluntly.

"And yet you came anyway," the king whispered, his face still pressed against the earth.

"We do not need weapons to kill you."

The others gave Ghealan dark looks, disdaining his hard words, but they blinked in surprise as Losolin began to laugh. It was a harsh, throaty laugh that came from the depths of hysteria, a choking, rasping explosion of misery and resignation.

He turned onto his back, staring up at the forest canopy. "Then kill me, and be done with it. Then she can throw away her life without hesitation."

"Get up you worthless sack of wine," Ghealan spat, shoving the younger elf.

Suneelo snarled at the curly-haired elf, but the warrior gave him a look full of meaning. Realization dawned on the captain and he backed away. Aidyn, Aladorn, and Sodo followed his lead, still confused as to what was happening.

"Get up!"

Losolin swiped his hand at Ghealan, trying to push him away, but the warrior only grabbed his arm and yanked him to his feet.

"Fight me like the male you claim to be," Ghealan taunted, poking the other in the shoulder. "Fight me!"

"No."

"Damn you! Fight me!"

Losolin snarled, but shook his head. "No." He backed into Aidyn who shoved him away, now understanding what Ghealan was trying to do.

The others caught on and soon they were all jeering at the younger elf, surrounding him, taunting him, pushing him. Losolin finally lashed out, striking Ghealan across the face, jerking the other's head around.

Then they were fighting, a full knock down brawl, each of the five elves stepping in whenever Losolin got a good swing in, which was often. Aladorn went down from a strong right hook and Sodo stepped in. The alchemist smacked Losolin hard upside the head, enraging him further, and took a round of punches to the midriff that finally took him out.

The fight lasted a long time, until Losolin simply collapsed from the exertion. The five all staggered to their feet, sporting bruises, welts, cuts, and a few broken ribs. Suneelo ran his tongue along his lower lip, feeling a long split from where his brother had punched him straight on.

"Bastard put up a good fight," he muttered, bending over to grab Losolin's right arm.

"Yeah, I just hope it was worth it," Aidyn replied darkly, sporting a black eye and a laceration along his jaw, and took the king's left arm. It had taken every ounce of self-restraint to keep his life training in check, to stop himself from snapping the king into a thousand bloody pieces.

Together, limping and staggering through the forest, the five carried the comatose monarch back to the city and into the castle, using the evening shadows and back streets to avoid the public. Haydyn met them at the door, his young face troubled.

"Yayènia, Erdwyf, and Miazie are still with Mother, though she has not yet come out of her room. How is he?"

"Splendid," muttered Aladorn, hunched down to accommodate Sodo's shorter height, Losolin strung between them.

"You all look like you took a good beating. What happened?" asked the prince, studying his stepfather.

"What needed to happen," Ghealan snapped. "Losolin has a habit of keeping things bottled up until they explode, which, with him, is very damaging to everyone around him. He needed an outlet, and we provided him with one, though too late to stop a catastrophe from happening."

"Ah," the half-blood replied, rocking back on his heels. "Well, take him to the infirmary. I get to enjoy a meeting with Daphne."

"Get used to it, young prince," Aidyn said, and followed his friends up the stairs to the infirmary.

Tlonna sprawled in one of the balcony chairs, exhausted and spent. She felt numb, her eyes red rimmed and swollen. She felt lost and alone, broken and deceived, torn to pieces and ground into the dirt. Every breath seemed to be ripped from her lungs, her very life a horrible mockery. She could hear Losolin's voice like a litany, cold and distant, though they were the same words over and over again

Then you choose it without me.

There were no tears this time, she had none left. Everything seemed faded and cold, without meaning or purpose. Without Losolin she was only half a person.

"What do I do?" she whispered. "I cannot turn my back on innocent people, but I cannot live without him."

The spirits murmured to her, their voices unintelligible and sibilant. They teased her with their knowledge, keeping it just beyond her understanding.

"*Zuskadi naht xellt.*" She breathed. Duty above all.

"And stupidity above everything else," said an angry voice behind her.

Tlonna whipped around in her chair, magic pulsing about her hands, to find Yayènia, Erdwyf, and Miazie standing in the doorway.

"How did you get in here?" the queen demanded, rising.

Yayènia shoved her fist into her sister's face, showing off bloody fingers. "A doorknob cannot keep me out."

"Why did you not reply?" Erdwyf asked, her words clipped.

"Because I did not want to be disturbed, hence the locked door," Tlonna retorted, shoving her way through the others.

"You know, I once said that to Elwyn, the High Alchemist," Miazie said. "*Zuskadi naht xellt.* She did not understand it either."

"I understand it just fine," the Magin snapped. "This is why my husband is no longer here."

"Your husband is part of your duty."

"In what way? I already have an heir."

The slap from Yayènia caught Tlonna by surprise so much that she went to her knees. Glaring up at her sister, the queen rubbed her face petulantly. "What was that for?"

"For being an idiot. You know damn well that Losolin is much more than a stud for breeding. He is the reason you are alive, many times over. He is the reason you are sane. You truly think he would leave you? You honestly believe that he would walk out on you?"

"Did he not? Perhaps I mistook his absence as a trick!" Tlonna shouted, getting to her feet.

"Oh no, he left, but you know he could never leave! You...you drag him down! You drag us all down with your pessimistic ideals and your stubborn resistance to look at things another way. You decide you must die, there is no way around it. Well guess what! We are not going to put up with it anymore! And stop using my house motto as a reason to do so!" Yayènia yelled back, yanking her gauntlets off.

"We have stood by you for so long, and you think you can just throw your life away because some prophecy from two thousand years ago says you must? You are not doomed by that! You are doomed by your own decision!" Erdwyf cried, removing her band of office from her bicep.

Slowly advancing, the three females backed their queen against the wall, removing their accessories as they did so. Tlonna stared at them, uncertain of their motives. She scooted along the wall until she felt her bed hit the back of her legs. With a snarl, Yayènia leapt atop her, grabbing her by the midriff and hauling her backward. Tlonna kicked and writhed, trying to break free of her sister's frighteningly iron grip. Erdwyf and Miazie crawled onto the bed as well, revealing lengths of rope shimmering with some sort of Weave.

Uncertainty and irrational fear gripped Tlonna as Yayènia shoved her against the headboard and pulled a rope from her shirt. As soon as the rope touched her, the Magin felt the terribly familiar sense of blockage form around the core of her power.

"What are you doing?" she cried, wrenching about, trying to free herself, panic and frenzy welling inside her.

"Something that should have been done long ago," Miazie said, grunting as she tied Tlonna's legs together. "You have not listened to us since the beginning, and now you are going to do so. We have invested too much time and effort in you to allow you to recklessly throw yourself in front of everyone."

"Why are you binding me? Why the seal? I do not understand!" Tlonna replied, her voice keening with doubt and panic.

"Because you are stronger than we are, and you always run away," Erdwyf said, running a length of rope between Tlonna's feet to the footboard so that she could not move her legs at all.

Yayènia finished lashing her sister to the headboard and swiftly knotted her hands together as well, tying them at the elbow and wrists at the small of her back. When she finished, the three females moved away from the bed, staring at their securely trussed friend and queen.

Tlonna's breath was heaving from her chest, her changed eyes wide with alarm. She tried to wiggle, but found herself unable to do so. Her legs were bound together and then tightly strung to the footboard. Her shoulders and torso were strapped to the headboard, with her arms behind her. She glared at the three, unable to do anything further.

"You will all pay for this," she threatened angrily.

"Of course we will, but what we have to say is worth it," Yayènia retorted, folding her arms across her chest.

Tlonna watched the triceps and extensor muscles form rigid walls on the warrior's arms and swallowed nervously. "I do not understand why you are doing this to me, rather than to Losolin, who ran away. I am not the one you need to worry about panicking and fleeing. I am not afraid to face the truth. I accept my fate."

"You refuse to accept any other fate!" Miazie shrieked, losing her temper. "You refuse to allow that you might actually have to live! Is it so terrible, Tlonna, to live? Does all this mean absolutely nothing to you? Do we mean nothing to you? Do you think that if you die, we will just shrug it off and move on with our lives?"

"No, but I-" Tlonna began.

"You what? You do not care? You are not worried about what we will do once you are dead and rotting in the ground? Is that it? Is that why you are so flaming nonchalant about it all?" Erdwyf demanded, for once showing her volatile temper.

Tlonna once again opened her mouth to speak, but Yayĕnia ran over her words. "You are a fool and a child to think that we will just let you walk to your death. Or do you think us incapable of protecting you as we are sworn to do? Perhaps you believe us so ill-suited to the job that you have no chance of surviving your own god-forsaken life?"

This time the Magin remained silent, but no one added anything further. After a moment of them staring at her, Tlonna spoke. "I do not think you incapable or ill-suited, quite the opposite, and I fear for you. I do not willingly accept my death because I am tired of, or unhappy with, my life. I know that you all would mourn me, and that you would do your best to avenge me, no matter what the cost to your own lives. Do not think me selfish or determinedly blind, for I am not. I believe that I must die not because of any prophecy, but because it is what I feel must happen. I am a conduit of power, a living talisman against evil. I know this, I accept this, and I am honored by this, though I would wish it otherwise. I love my people, my kingdom, and my friends enough that I gladly give up my life so that they may have theirs. Is that so selfish? Is that so...weak?"

Miazie, Yayènia, and Erdwyf looked at each other, and then in unison sat on the bed with their bound friend. Yayènia took a deep breath, not looking at anyone. "I once thought I was born to die, but found reasons to live. If you promise not to interrupt, I will tell you my story... one I have never told anyone but Suneelo. Perhaps it will convince you that dying is never the only option, though it may seem so." She looked up to meet the three other gazes, and then quickly looked down again. "I was born the twenty-seventh of Kayab, four hundred and ninety-nine years ago in the middle of the night, and sold two days later..."

Ghealan leaned into the mirror, examining the black eye Losolin's first punch had caused. He heard the door behind him close and turned, expecting Erdwyf. Something heavy smashed into his face hard enough to send him reeling into the mirror, shattering the glass. Roaring, the large elf blinked to clear his vision, clambering to his feet. Before he could shape a thought, the blunt object slammed into his face again and again until he lost consciousness, and slid to the floor of his castle apartment.

Lost in thought, Suneelo bent over a chest full of medical ointments and bandages, searching for a salve to put on his numerous bruises. He heard something soft land on the rug beside him and started to turn in confusion. A boot clipped him hard on the chin, knocking him over. Swearing, the elf lurched to his feet just in time to catch a heavy statue about the middle, a marble badger someone had given Yayènia years ago for her birthday. He grunted with the impact and staggered backward. Before he could right himself, he caught a glimpse of a hairy and hideous face, and then his vision sparked, and Suneelo went down.

Losolin woke with start, his head and body pounding as it healed from the beating he had given himself. He blinked once, and then let out a shout that was cut short as a fist whacked him in the face. He turned painfully onto his side, but was forcibly dragged from the bed and received a beating far worse than the one he had given his friends earlier. It did not take long for him to slip into oblivion.

Sodo heard the door open, and turned, one hand pressed to his belly where Losolin had pummeled him. The alchemist frowned at the ugly creature that strode into his room, swathed completely in brown. "Who are you?" he demanded, reaching behind him for a weapon. As he moved, the stranger leapt forward, his foot connecting with Sodo's injured belly. The elf went down, taking with him the bedside table behind, where a dagger was sitting. He fought purely out of instinct, grappling with his assailant. But the alchemist was no warrior, and he felt himself tiring and before too long, he was overtaken.

Aidyn and Aladorn were walking to their separate suites when three strangers descended upon them from separate directions. The assassin and the wiat stopped short, surprised and on-guard. Weaponless, they crouched, ready for the attack. It did not come as expected, though. The three strangers stuck out their hands, and solid air pulsed against the two, knocking them senseless immediately.

No one in the castle took note of the seven brown-clad strangers that moved silently through the halls, carrying over their shoulders six limp forms covered in sackcloth. Somehow, their eyes merely skipped over them, forgetting their presence almost immediately, continuing on with their lives unconcernedly.

Yayènia finished her long, tragic story an hour later to the muffled sounds of her three friends sniffling. Tlonna, still trussed tightly to the bed, tried blinking her eyes clear, but could not wipe away the tears that fell despite her efforts.

"So," the warrior said quietly, dry-eyed. "Do you still think your life hopeless? Or can you try to push through, like I did, and survive to see another lifetime?"

Tlonna nodded, unable to speak. She was heartbroken for her sister, though she knew Yayènia was well over her past. Erdwyf rubbed at her face, her heart thudding painfully at finally hearing the full story of Yayènia and Ghealan's relationship. She'd never known they had been engaged, never even considered the thought. It hurt that her husband had never told her, though she was not surprised. Miazie cleared her throat softly, unable to imagine the horrors the High Commander had lived through, or the heartbreak.

They were all staring at each other bleakly, having been brought closer to each other during Yayènia's story, when the door burst open and several people rushed in. They stopped and stared at the odd sight of the three females surrounding the bound queen, but soon recovered and ran to the bed.

Feorien and Narda scrambled over each other's words in their haste to inform the queen of their news. Trying to ignore the humiliation and discomfort of being blabbered at by her subjects while completely helpless, Tlonna shook her head and bade they stop so she could hear the news outright. It was then that Haydyn strode in, looking thunderous, and shoving aside the people gathered about his mother.

"Untie her, Yayènia, we have a situation. Losolin, Ghealan, Suneelo, Aladorn, Aidyn, and Sodo have all been taken."

"What?" the four females gaped, unsure they had heard correctly.

"Losolin was apparently dragged from a bed in a spare room where he was resting, Suneelo taken from his suite, as were Ghealan and Sodo. They all left signs of a serious struggle. Aladorn and Aidyn simply disappeared, though there is an odd wrinkle in the obsidian of the fourth floor corridor near the western stairs. No one saw anything, or at least no one is talking," the prince related quickly, ignoring his mother's predicament. He was one who had Woven the block into the rope.

The four shared horrified looks, unable to believe the six males could be overtaken so easily. Hurriedly, they began untying Tlonna as Haydyn shooed the servants out of the royal suite.

"When did this happen?" the queen asked, flexing her arms and legs as they became free.

"We're not sure, but less than an hour ago, I would guess. I could feel a residue in the fourth floor corridor, so they were definitely Magins, though how no one saw them is beyond me. There was blood where Losolin, Ghealan, Sodo, and Suneelo were found, and lots of it. The rooms were all totally trashed, but not as though someone was looking for something. Simply the result of struggles."

Once she was free, Tlonna stood, looking at her three friends. "Any idea who would take them?" she asked, trying to keep back her despair. Then Haydyn's words struck her. "You said Losolin was resting? In the castle? Here?"

"Yeah, the others went and brought him back," Haydyn said, carefully avoiding the three other females' gazes.

Tlonna nodded, looking at Yayènia. The warrior shook her head, large blue eyes hard with suppressed fury.

"Why them and not us?" Miazie asked, trying to think clearly.

"They are bait," Erdwyf said quietly, hugging herself. "And we are the prey."

"For whom, and what purpose? I can see myself, and Tlonna, but you two? What is there to gain from capturing two advisors, even if one is a Belau?" Yayènia mused, squinting at nothing.

Erdwyf shook her head, unable to come up with an answer. Miazie just stared blankly at the fighter. Haydyn gazed helplessly at his mother, fearing for the six males he looked up to as role-models and friends. The queen was exchanging a long look with her sister. Finally she turned to her son.

"Find the best trackers in the city, immediately. I want them here within the hour. Erdwyf, Miazie, get your things. Yayènia..."

Without speaking, the High Commander nodded and set off for her room, the other two trailing her. Haydyn put a hand on Tlonna's arm as she turned toward her wardrobe. "Are you okay? What happened?"

"I needed to listen to a story, and it was difficult to accept that it was so," the queen replied quietly, turning back to her son. "Haydyn, you must stand strong in my absence."

"I will. But...what is happening? What are you going to do?" the young prince asked, swallowing against his trepidation.

"We are going to get them back, son."

"Be careful...and...I love you," Haydyn replied as he turned to go.

"I love you too, Haydyn," Tlonna said, embracing him impulsively.

The young half-blood hugged his mother back, and then left her to prepare for the hunt. He found two trackers easily enough and had them ready to go by the time the four females descended. Each wore dark clothes, fitted to their bodies to minimize cumbersomeness, and bristled with weapons, even Miazie. The human wore her katan, a brace of daggers around her thighs, and a long dagger on her hip. Yayènia and Tlonna, as usual, wore three swords apiece, dagger belts, boot knives, and a number of small throwing knives about their bodies. In addition, the High Commander carried a studded mace opposite her elfin longblade, which she used only when she wanted to inflict serious pain. Erdwyf also wore her elfin longblade, though hers was several inches longer than Yayènia's. The High Advisor also sported the bladed chain whips from

Zeynuwn, which swung with her step, the blades sheathed in separate leather scabbards.

Haydyn studied the four armed females with cautious eyes, and introduced the two trackers to them. Daniel and Ian bowed hastily, the two men apprehensive in the presence of the fierce females.

"Do you have mounts?" Tlonna asked the two men as they headed for the stables.

"Yes Queen Tlonna, both of us. A requirement of the job," Ian replied hastily, rubbing his hands together nervously.

"Excellent, excellent," the Magin replied absently, motioning the stableman to saddle Takîreaes.

Udu, Odilia, and Kaia were also saddled, whickering at their mistresses, snorting at the large and virile Takîreaes. For his part, the stallion ignored the mares and snapped at Udu, concentrating on Tlonna as she checked his girth and mounted him with ease. Soon, the six hunters were galloping down the dark streets of Blackhaven, following the only lead they had. A few late-working people had seen a wagon team passing through the city, though no one had noticed anyone other than the driver.

The six passed the city gates and burst into a full out gallop, giving the horses their heads, the wagon tracks clearly visible. Then it began to rain. Tlonna swore, but they pushed on until dawn as the horses began to tire, and the tracks to fade. They rested long enough to recover the horses, and then resumed their hunt. It was midday when they lost the trail completely. Daniel dismounted and crouched low the ground, moving in a widening spiral, trying to find the tracks.

"They just...end," he said, stupefied. "It's almost as though they grew wings and flew away. Like birds."

"Is that possible?" Ian asked, frowning.

"No... there is something else here," Tlonna said, closing her eyes and moving her hands through the air. "A Weave...if I could just...find it." Her hands seemed to catch on the air, and suddenly there were orange writhing lines visible to the rest of them flowing through air. The Magin's lips curled back to bare her teeth and she opened her eyes. The pupils were changing, though they remained white. The two trackers balked, the three females shook their heads, used to Tlonna's magic.

The queen yanked her hands downward, and the orange lines of the Weave disappeared, sparking blue as they did, and suddenly the trail was visible again, though extremely faint.

"Ah ha!" cried Ian, bending down to run his fingers over the tracks.

"This Weave is only a few hours old. They are not far ahead of us," Tlonna said, remounting Takîreaes. "We need to overtake them, and then head them off."

Yayènia nodded and they pressed on, ignoring their weary minds and bodies, focusing on the fading trail. Several times they had to stop so that the two trackers could find the marks again, or for Tlonna to remove a Weave. It was well into the evening when the small group came to a halt, having caught sight of the wagon at last. They were out of the forest now, and nearing the Hidden Plains, where the Plains Elves made their home.

The Plains were in a deep valley, that when viewed from either the west or east, seemed to disappear, giving them their name. The villages of Hastert and Asheyl were nestled within them, and a small town called Mardyn sat on the southeastern edge, near the Strait of Arwênlhias.

The six moved back and chose their route. They decided on a southern path, making a wide circle and advancing a mile up the wagon's path. They reached their position just before dawn, yawning and bleary eyed. They stood within a defile, barely wide enough for the six of them to stand shoulder to shoulder, with high walls that made the sky above a slim, navy blue ribbon. It was the only route through the Plains that did not mean traversing up and down the rocky landscape, rising out of the land like a wall, falling back into levelness a mile further east.

The two trackers took the horses deep into the defile and settled down to wait, their job done. Erdwyf, Miazie, and Tlonna dozed while Yayènia kept watch, used to sleeplessness. Nearly two hours later, as the sun sat halfway visible, the defile still dark as midnight, she heard the rumble and creak of the wagon approaching. The warrior shook her three friends awake and they prepared for battle. As planned, Tlonna was the only one visible, the other three behind her in the shadows until needed.

The wagon turned into the defile, its team of six horses snorting and huffing in the early morning chill. Tlonna stood with her feet spread, her elfin blade resting on one shoulder, her head down, in the middle of the path. The driver halted the wagon, a hooded figure in all brown, the eyes glimmering from within the shadows. The wagon covering twitched open and two more shaded faces peered out to see why they had stopped. Tlonna did not look up, but her thumb began to tap against the slim hilt of her blade.

"Move or I will kill you," the driver said in a cold voice, lifting the reins.

"You can try," Tlonna replied in a hard voice, finally looking up, white pupils dilated in the dark.

"What in Maln's name?" the driver cursed, yanking on the reins. "A demon!"

The team leapt forward, snorting and bellowing as they lunged toward the elf. Tlonna held out her free hand, her fingers bent at the last knuckle, and the horses veered to either side, the yoke splitting down the middle. Red magic pulsed around the Magin Queen as the wagon seat came up to meet her, the driver trying to jump from the wagon. With a loud crack, the wagon slammed into Tlonna, the back end lifting off the ground and then crashing down to the earth, the axles and wheels splitting and spinning away. The impacted space where Tlonna stood was bent concave, the mangled body of the driver impaled upon the boot.

The six other abductors spilled out of the wagon, drawing weapons and advancing upon the unharmed Magin Queen as she stepped from the wreckage. The six surrounded her, and then Miazie, Erdwyf, and Yayènia materialized into the faint light as the dawn finally reached the defile. The brown-robed figures pivoted about, alarmed by the sudden appearance of the others.

Then they began to laugh, dark hollow chuckles of malice and contempt. They retreated slightly so that they faced the four females, turned mostly toward Tlonna, their biggest threat.

"Who are you?" the Magin demanded, aiming her sword at the closest figure.

They stayed silent, brandishing their weapons slightly, keeping the four females at bay. Tlonna glared. "I can see which two of you are Magins, and you are of no threat to me, as you well know. Tell me who you are, who sent you."

Once again they did not respond, but Yayènia snarled angrily. "You know who we are, you know who you kidnapped, do not pretend ignorance! I grow weary of waiting."

"One more chance," Tlonna said quietly, and when the six ignored the warning, the four lunged forward in unison.

Orange and red Weaves flashed through the air, but Tlonna's hand swept up and, in a flash of white, voided them. By then, Yayènia had slit the throat of one and was dueling another. Miazie ducked under the swing of a mace, bloodied by Ghealan, though she did not know that, and stabbed the abductor in the belly. Erdwyf had a small portion of her bladed whips in one hand and her sword in the other, repeatedly slicing her target in the face and chest. Through the brown cloth, she could see hairy, pale skin, reddened with blood.

Tlonna had both the Magins locked in a Weave. Within minutes, five of the seven were dead, the last two were the Magins. In a surge of rage, Tlonna tightened the Weave, and the two were squashed like bugs, blood and gore exploding everywhere, splattering the four.

Not stopping to think of their disgust, they tore inside the ruined wagon and fell to the ground, unable to stand in the sloping wreck. Aidyn, Aladorn, Ghealan, Suneelo, Sodo, and Losolin were all slumped against the buckled walls, chained hand, foot, and neck. None of them was conscious, and all had wounds that still seeped blood. Using an elemental Weave of earth, Tlonna disintegrated the chains, and the males all collapsed listlessly to the ground.

Ghealan and Losolin were in the worst shape, Aidyn and Aladorn the best, though none were in decent condition. Erdwyf knelt by her husband, wiping the clotted blood from his face, examining the broken nose and split lip, the bruised eyes and forehead. His ribs were broken and he had lacerations all down his right side from the shattered mirror.

Yayènia lifted Suneelo up onto her shoulder and took him from the wreckage, laying him down in the shadow of the defile, and examined him head to toe. He too sported several broken ribs, but mostly bruises and bumps. Miazie had to drag Sodo out, unable to lift him, and she too gave him a full body inspection. Slowly, the four females retrieved the broken males from the rubble, checking them for serious injuries, treating what they could. Daniel and Ian appeared to help as well, staring at the wagon, and then settling to the task of washing cuts, wrapping injured torsos and heads.

Tlonna stood over the unconscious form of Losolin, staring at his battered face, hearing the last words he had spoken to her. *Then you choose it without me.* She studied his well-made frame, the strong limbs and beautiful face, seeing beyond the blood and bruises. Next to him lay Aidyn, blood staining the inside of his ear.

They were all alive, but deep within oblivion. Tlonna felt numb inside, looking down at her husband, the elf who had, not a day gone, walked out on her. She wondered what he had thought of when he walked away.

"My Queen?" Ian said, approaching with a wet rag. "Do you wish me to wash his face?"

"Yes, please, Ian. Thank you," the Magin replied hollowly, stepping back. She looked around and saw Aladorn stretched out next Aidyn.

Walking over to the wiat, Tlonna knelt by him, wiping a drop of blood from the corner of his mouth with her thumb. He stirred slightly, long lashes flickering as he moaned quietly. The queen stood, looking down the line of unconscious males. Yayènia, Erdwyf, and Miazie were all tenderly bathing their mates' face, gently wiping away the blood to reveal the stunning faces beneath. They were indeed all beautiful, finely wrought and sculpted to perfection. Tlonna turned once more to her own husband, now alone as Ian knelt by Aidyn. Daniel was bringing up the horses, and setting free five of the six from the wagon team. They had all survived, having been spared by Tlonna. Losolin's head moved slightly, and she felt her heart skip, and knew that her love was not dimmed, only aching.

It took them an hour to get the six males onto the horses, riding with someone. Daniel, accompanied by Aladorn, also led the sixth team horse, burdened with the five dead abductors still whole. They had searched the remains of the others for items, preferring to get back home before dealing with the situation. They arrived at the city that evening, riding through the streets to the curious stares and salutes of the citizens.

The small rescue group trotted into the stable yard and was immediately surrounded by servants, though there was no sign of Haydyn, or even Feorien. Frowning, Tlonna dismounted, pulling Losolin after her, and surrendered him to a healer. Yayènia was helping Aidyn walk, the assassin having regained consciousness a few hours earlier, though he had drifted in and out of sleep.

"Any ideas?" the High Commander asked, one strong arm under Aidyn's as he hobbled toward a healer.

Tlonna shook her head, "Not a single one. We will search the bodies, though I do not think we will find anything. How are you my friend?" this last was directed to the woozy assassin.

"I feel weird," he muttered, trying to focus his eyes on the queen.

Miazie snorted as she passed, half carrying Sodo, half dragging him. "It is called nausea, Aidyn."

The male glared after her, but he did not reply, instead concentrating on staying upright. It took several minutes for the six males to all be taken to the hospital wing, and still none of Tlonna's council appeared. When questioned, Erdwyf shook her head in puzzlement.

"Haydyn should be here, or Feor, even Kelus. He usually is informed when things like this happen and shows up to help Haydyn. I do not like it, Loni, not one bit. Someone should have been here, Narda...Daphne, anyone."

Tlonna studied her High Advisor a moment before turning into the castle, ignoring her weariness. The others trailed after, the two trackers as well, unsure what to do now. When the queen noticed them, she sent them to one of the many secretaries for payment. As the four females reached the fourth level of the castle, Narda headed off the quartet, her faery face pale with exhaustion and alarm.

"A woman from Zaedic, my Queen, is accusing Prince Haydyn of rape. Everyone is in a panic, we don't know what to do!"

Tlonna shared a startled look with Miazie. "How did she get here? Where is she now? Where is my son?"

"Everybody is in the map room, everyone. The girl says she came alone, on one of the trade ships."

"Haydyn left Zaedic over two years ago. Why, if he did rape her, is she coming forward now? This does not make any sense," Erdwyf said, scowling at the seneschal.

The dryad merely shook her head in defeat, dark eyes round with anxiety.

"How convenient..." Yayènia muttered, gripping her longblade in one hand, and her mace in the other.

Tlonna squinted at her, thinking. Without saying what she was thinking, the queen headed in the direction of the war room, also known as the map room, beckoning the others after her. When they entered the large room, pandemonium surrounded them. Along with the council members were Haydyn, Kelus, and a young woman Tlonna did not recognize.

The queen held up her hand, mindless of the fact that she and her three companions were still splattered with blood and grime. The room silenced immediately, and Narda slipped inside the room from behind Yayènia.

"Sit." Tlonna commanded, and everyone present immediately found a chair, except for herself and the three with her. "Good. Now, I am tired, hungry, and ill-tempered at the moment. Would someone please explain to me what is going on?"

Haydyn leaned forward, his expression thunderous. "This young woman, here," he gestured vaguely toward the stranger, not looking at her, "claims I forced myself upon her two years ago, in Zaedic. She has come here to press charges against me."

Tlonna stared at the Zaedican, blank-faced. "What is your name?" she asked finally, motioning to Erdwyf, who sat and began taking notes, using supplies from Daphne.

"Marin," she responded immediately, boldly.

"Who sent you?"

The young woman went sheet white, betraying herself. "No one, your majesty. I came because the prince accosted me."

Standing behind Tlonna, Yayènia snorted loudly. The queen felt like doing the same. "If that is true, then why wait two years to come forward? Did he get you with child? If so, where is it? Well?"

Marin's lip trembled as she gaped at the Magin. "I was afraid, your majesty. Afraid that he would see me and force himself upon me again. I did not get with child, thank the gods, but I am afraid that when the prince took his liberties, he broke something within me, for I am unable to have children now. See, I am wed, now, and my husband and I...we want children, but I am barren. I fear it was his brutality that did it."

By now the girl was sobbing, though she was the only one affected by her story other than Haydyn. The half-blood was scarlet with outrage and humiliation. "Mother, you cannot possible believe I-"

Tlonna shook her head once at her son, cutting him off. "Marin...do you have any proof of this?"

"Only one thing, my Lady."

Haydyn's head snapped up, as well as half the councils'. Tlonna swore inwardly, but she retained her blank expression. "Which is?"

Marin swallowed, obviously terrified. "He has...he has a birthmark...on the inside of his thigh. Sh-shaped like a flame."

The prince gaped open mouthed at the girl, unable to conceive how she knew that. Tlonna did not even blink. "Describe it."

Marin and Haydyn both whipped their heads around to stare at the elf, one with horror, the other with disbelief.

"It...it is the color of rose wine, about the size of...a cherry, and shaped like a flame. Round on the bottom and pointed in a curve at the top. The point faces his hip." The girl's words grew steady as she talked, her face even taking on a look of smugness.

Haydyn was quivering in his chair. Tlonna beckoned to him and he stood. "Haydyn, Erdwyf, Kelus, and I are going to step outside for a moment to check the validity of your description, Marin. Yayènia..."

The High Commander followed the four to the door and then turned, planting herself in front of the only exit, drawing both her katan and old shortsword, leaning against the longer sword. With a single look, she deterred everyone from moving or even talking.

Outside the room, Tlonna turned to her son.

"You cannot believe her, Mum! She would have been thirteen, perhaps fourteen when we left Zaedic, myself only sixteen. I'm not like Rhiannan and Sithian. You must know that!" the prince said immediately, anger and nerves lacing his words.

"I do not believe her, Haydyn, but we cannot dismiss the charge out of hand, however much we would like to. I am positive she was sent by either Sithian or your sister, and she admitted as much by her actions and her story. I need to see your birthmark."

Haydyn blanched, looking at Erdwyf and Kelus, who remained silent. Tlonna caught the look. "They are here for validation. Kelus was there during and after our escape from Zaedic. He will be our most valuable source of information, and Erdwyf must be present for such matters, as High Advisor. I am sorry, son. Show us your birthmark."

The half-blood made a face, but he unlaced his pants and pushed them down. He turned his left leg so that his inner thigh was visible to the three adults before him. The birthmark was there, as described by Marin, though with two distinct differences. It was upside down, and the size of an egg.

Tlonna nodded and the prince yanked his pants back up, lacing them, his face red with embarrassment. The queen turned to the witnesses. Her eyes found Kelus's.

"Rhiannan would have seen it when they were children. It would have grown with him since then," the ex-demon said softly. "It is something she would connive in order to get back at Haydyn. Though why the pettiness, I do not know."

"She knows the punishment for rape is death," Erdwyf put in, eyeing Kelus. "And she knows that you run a fair system, and will not, as you said, dismiss it out of hand. She hoped that supplying the girl with a description of Haydyn's mark would be sufficient evidence of rape. You would be forced to execute him, if you upheld the law, which you would."

"Would you?" Haydyn asked, his eyes wide.

Tlonna shook her head. "I do not know. I would be expected to, certainly I should, but...execute my own son? I do not know. Hopefully I will never have to answer it."

Haydyn shook his head. "I didn't do anything."

"I know."

"Please don't kill me."

"I am not going to," Tlonna said quietly, stroking his cheek with a finger.

"Kelus? Do you even recognize her?" Haydyn asked, blushing.

The auburn-haired elf shook his head. "Your father had so many whores around the palace it was impossible to tell one from the other. She looks like the ones he favored, though, but too young. Midian rarely touched a woman under sixteen. Claimed they did not move right."

"Sick bastard," Erdwyf snarled to herself, receiving agreeing looks from the others.

"Well? What now?" Tlonna asked.

"We prove her false, and go home," the High Advisor said, yawning. "I want a bath, and then bed."

"Mm," Tlonna concurred, stifling a yawn herself. "I do not think this will be as cut and dried as we wish it could be. Rhiannan, as I believe it is her behind this, is more cunning than that."

"True, but she is only three years old, Tlonna, and less intelligent than Haydyn. Just because she is in an adult's body does not mean she has an adult's mind. I highly doubt that she has received the same education as the prince," Kelus replied.

The queen nodded and knocked once on the door. Yayènia opened it and they strode back into the map room. Marin looked up expectantly, almost gleefully. Silently, everyone took their positions, sitting in their respective chairs and looking about those gathered. Finally, Tlonna spoke.

"I have seen the mark you described, Marin, and found it faulty. There were two very distinct differences, ones that you would have known had he actually raped you. What was described to you by Rhiannan was what she had seen when they were very young. It has since changed. I dismiss your charge and highly suggest you take the next ship out."

The council turned as one and gloated at the young woman, who turned vivid red, standing up so fast she knocked her chair over. Pointing a menacing finger at Tlonna, she seethed.

"You will rue the day you denied my charge, Queen of Elves and Fools. King Sithian is many times the leader you are, and ten-fold the Magin you are. Princess Rhiannan and he will lay your kingdom to waste and tear your family apart. Zaedic will become the capital of the world, and you will all bow before the might of the Rahlans. Mark my word, Tlonna Ewôsdírn, your reign is coming to a very sticky end."

"Enough!" Yayènia barked, grabbing the girl by her neck and wrenching her to the floor. "Your Highness?" she growled, looking to Tlonna for permission.

"No, Nia, do not kill her. Let her up."

Reluctantly, the warrior stepped away from the human, who scrambled to her feet, hubris vanished into thin air. Tlonna gave her a disgusted look.

"What were you going to do? Did you think you would just walk away after a speech like that? Are you daft?"

"I am a victim!" she wailed. "A victim!"

"Of what? Your own stupidity?" Miazie snapped, unable to keep quiet any longer.

"Of...of...monarchs and their machinations! Please! I just did what I was ordered to!" Marin cried, now becoming yet another person with another story.

"Get her out of here," Tlonna ordered, sick of listening. "Put her in the guard tower. I will speak to her later. For now, everyone go home. Go rest and be with your family. Do not, no matter what, disturb me for anything short of war."

The council members laughed wearily, and, with two guards taking hold of Marin, they dispersed to their separate homes. Some lived within the castle, others within the city. Haydyn hugged his mother and set off for the Tower of Moons, the heir's suite. Yayènia and Erdwyf went to their castle apartments, unwilling to leave when their husbands remained in the infirmary. Bidding each other goodnight, the four females tramped wearily to their quarters, washed the blood from their skin, and fell into bed, exhausted.

The next morning, Tlonna, Erdwyf, Miazie, and Yayènia met at the infirmary doors and strode inside, feeling apprehensive. Aidyn and Aladorn were sitting up in their beds, sharpening knives and talking quietly, Sodo was propped against his pillows, watching them from across the aisle. Losolin was awake as well and reading a long parchment, his face blank. Suneelo was still prostrate in his bed next to the king, but it appeared his eyes were open. Only Ghealan remained asleep, his head heavily bandaged.

When the females entered, the five males all looked up, a disturbing image of brutality as their bruises and cuts became visible. Erdwyf ran to her husband's side, stroking a visible patch of skin, staring down at him with wide eyes. Ghealan's head turned slightly, but he did not rise. Yayènia and Miazie each went to their males' bed, bending down, whispering and kissing as worried lovers do. Only Tlonna stood uncertain, glancing between her husband, Aidyn, and Aladorn. The assassin smiled at her, a brilliant expression that made her grin back, unable to resist her friend's charisma, and that cursed attraction that sizzled between them.

Aladorn, too, smiled at her, though the wiat was much more reserved than his comrade. The queen walked to them, passing Losolin's bed, and hunched down between them. "How are you my friends?"

"Sore, and embarrassed," Aidyn replied candidly, setting aside his gleaming knives. "Any idea what it was about?"

Tlonna shook her head, pursing her lips. "None. The seven men who captured you are all dead, though we were able to bring back a few. They are in the exam room below, but I have not gone to look at them. We wanted to make sure you all were okay. They said nothing to you?"

Aladorn frowned. "Aidyn and I were walking to our rooms when we were surrounded by three brown-cloaked people. Next thing we know, we are here. The healers filled us in when we woke this morning. That is all we know."

Aidyn nodded at his brother. "It is true. Only Sodo was conscious enough to hear anything, and he said they spoke in a language he had never heard."

The queen frowned, glancing at the alchemist, who was now patiently allowing Miazie to examine his wounds. "That is it? You know nothing else? You have never heard of happenings such as these?"

The dark elves both shook their heads negative, watching her with identical green gazes. Tlonna frowned at the resemblance, suspicions lurking in her mind. After a moment, Aidyn touched her hand. "Go talk to Losolin, Tlonna. This is not irreparable."

"I know," Tlonna breathed, squeezing his hand. Then she stood and walked to her husband's side.

Losolin glanced at her once and then back down at the paper he was reading. "Jonas told me Haydyn was accused of rape and found innocent."

"You heard correctly," Tlonna replied, standing stiffly by his knees. "It was a girl from Zaedic, probably sent by Rhiannan."

"Probably? Or positively? Did she say for certain?" the king asked, still reading.

Tlonna fought the urge to strike him, surprising herself with the violent power of the desire. "She said she was told by her monarchs, which means either Sithian or Rhiannan, and Sithian is not so petty."

Losolin nodded once and fell silent. Tlonna turned back to Aidyn and Aladorn, who were pretending to sharpen their blades. The assassin looked up, and then pointedly glanced at the curtain separating the beds. With a yank, the queen closed off her husband's bed, making him look up in surprise. Then she Wove a shield of silence around the curtain, sealing them off completely.

"What the bloody nine hells is your problem?" she shouted, throwing her hands up in the air.

Losolin stared at her, lips parted slightly in shock. "What?"

"How dare you run off like you did! How dare you leave me! Do you know what you did to me? Do you know?"

The male threw his paper the floor and hoisted himself into a straighter position. "Very well the same thing you did to me! Every time you talk so carelessly about giving up your life, it rips apart my heart! Every time, Tlonna. Because I love you more than life itself, more than anything in this world, it physically hurts me when you so blithely accept death! After all you have been through, after everything you and I have survived, why is this so easy for you to succumb to? I do not understand!"

Tlonna opened her mouth to reply, but her husband ran over her words. "And now... now you have other Magins' power within you, and Jair's soul, and you are distancing yourself from me! You may not think so, but I can feel it. I watch you, day by day, withdrawing a part of yourself so that when that time comes, you can let go and believe us safe from harm. I know what it is you do, and I know why. But you cannot do it! You cannot continue to become a different person, someone other than the elf I love, the female I married. Stab me thrice, Tlonna, why are you giving up already? Do you not understand that I, that all of us, will be with you until the very end? I love you, but I am losing you to yourself, to all those people who are trying to defeat you. You are defeating yourself by drawing away. Come back to me, Tlonna, please, before I go mad with the loss," Losolin finished, tears swimming in his eyes. When he blinked, they rushed onto his cheeks and he angrily wiped them away.

"Oh, Losolin," Tlonna sobbed, sitting on the edge of his bed. "I am so afraid! I do not want to die, I do not want to be away from you, but I just do not see another way to do what must be done. I am looking, I promise. I am just so weary of being challenged, and I want it all to end. I do not want to hurt you, and I can see it in your eyes, Losolin, please do not ever leave me again. Promise me you will not leave me alone."

Losolin drew her close as she cried, putting his arm around her shoulders and resting his chin on her head. Tears fell unbidden from his closed eyes, feeling a part of his heart begin to heal as his wife curled against him, mindful of his injuries.

"I promise, but you have to promise to that you will try to find a way, a different way. I need that much at least," he murmured into her hair.

"I promise. I am sorry...so sorry," Tlonna replied, her voice muffled by his chest and her tears.

Losolin did not respond, instead he squeezed her against him for a moment, ignoring the pain in his shoulder. They lay there for several minutes, and then Tlonna sat up, wiping her eyes.

"Did the healers tell you what happened?" she asked, running her finger gently along a bruise on his chin.

He nodded, thoughts darkening to the abduction. "I do not understand it, though. Why? To what point and purpose? Sure, they beat us all and were able to take us from the city, but in the end, what did they manage? Nothing! They never said anything to us when we were conscious. There were no insignias, tattoos, rings, nothing. It is very odd that someone would go the trouble of kidnapping all of us males, and then fail to do anything grand. Not that I am complaining that we were not mauled or anything, but do you not find it bizarre?"

Tlonna looked at him, thinking. "It is peculiar that the attempt was foiled so easily, and that there were no ransoms or demands. But...think about who they captured, Losolin. The king, the king's brother, the second in command of the militia, the personal assassin of the throne, the underground liaison, and the Second Advisor's lover. All of you have strong, personal ties to the throne, you particularly, being *the* king. Then, when we get back, Haydyn has been accused of rape. Seems a little convenient to me."

"And yet again, that accusation was easily proved false, and the girl put under arrest," Losolin pointed out, frowning slightly. "None of it makes sense."

The queen could not think of anything else to say on the matter, and after a while she dropped the Silence Weave, and pushed back the curtain. The others in the infirmary were all staring at her with uncertain gazes, worried and nervous. When they saw Losolin sitting up and looking calm, they relaxed back into their own conversations until Tlonna got their attention once more.

"Now," she said, sitting on the edge of Losolin's bed so that she could see all of them. "We all know what happened, we just do not know why. Any ideas?"

The room was silent a minute, and then Miazie spoke. "I have not been able to scry anything yet, but I would hazard a guess at a diversion."

"A diversion for what? That Zaedican's accusation of Haydyn? No, it is too simple," Sodo said, shaking his head.

"It was definitely a diversion, I just do not think we have seen the outcome yet," Aidyn muttered, plucking at his blanket. "Perhaps the two incidents were isolated, just a coincidence. Elsewise, they failed at both attempts, miserably."

"Now hold on a minute," Suneelo interjected, scowling. "Think of the way it was done. Obviously with Magins, that much has been decided, but who would have the means and the desire to abduct us? Why not the girls? That is the way most kidnappers operate, yes?"

Yayènia nodded at her husband. "And, we are the higher-ransom people, as well. Tlonna, me, Erdwyf, Miazie...we are the hierarchy leaders, whether or not we all act the part."

The males grumbled, but it was true. After a moment, Aladorn spoke up. "We are leaving out one important thing. Who was behind it? Who are our enemies. The Rahlans of course, Stoffnias of Seaduens...who else?"

"Athelias," Tlonna said suddenly. "We have forgotten about him. He is mad as can be, and was in thrall to Midian. It would make sense that his allegiance would pass to Sithian. And remember when he sent that file of men after us, knowing they would all die? The only person who survived was Erich, and that only because I would not let Losolin cut his throat."

"Erich? Who is Erich?" Aidyn asked, confused.

Suneelo explained. "A Talenian Tlonna recruited some years back when they were ranging across Nymyños. He is what...second rank captain in the infantry?" he asked of Yayènia.

She nodded, smiling in pride at her husband. "I received four excellent captains from that group, Erich, Bryce, Tyre, and Aselios. Each one has made me proud in their own way. I thought I would lose most of them when the officers from Kajgenia went back home, but they stayed on. Even Sargotarh and Orthak cannot find anything to berate them, despite the fact that they are all humans."

"We are good for something, then?" Miazie needled playfully, more comfortable with the warrior since the trip to Schelum.

"Aye, but nothing else," Yayènia shot back, grinning.

"So you say," Sodo laughed, affectionately running his hand along Miazie's spine.

The Belau blushed, but she grinned as well as the elves around her laughed congenially. They had become a tight knit group over the last few years, sharing experiences and events together that had allowed them to heal from their separation, and allowed the newcomers to find a place. The males of the group were like brothers, crude and jovial with each other, while the four females were more collected, yet just as able to supply wit and snide remarks as their boys.

They were composing themselves when Ghealan awakened, blinking his eyes and raising a hand to rub his face. He hissed in pain and let his hand drop, looking around he spotted his wife right next to him, and then studied the others.

"How are you feeling?" Erdwyf asked softly, bending over him and kissing his cheek.

"I have been better, Erd," the warrior laughed quietly, "but what a reception! Everyone is here!"

Tlonna grinned. "Ah, well, we could not let you wake alone, now could we? All you boys decided to take a little trip together, and we had to come save you."

"Like usual," Yayènia grunted, gently pushing Suneelo on the shoulder. The male glared at her, though his lips were twitching into a smile the whole time.

"We have been discussing the motive behind our abduction," Losolin said to Ghealan, scooting closer to Tlonna. "We were just moving onto Athelias."

"The King of Talenias?" Ghealan asked, his brow furrowing.

"The very same," Tlonna nodded. "He is utterly insane, and tied to Zaedic tighter than you can imagine."

"He would be a reasonable suspect in this matter," Aladorn added, tossing his dagger belt onto Aidyn's bed, who glared at him balefully. "He would want to prove his faithfulness to Sithian, and what better way than to capture the king and all the support of the throne?"

Tlonna chewed on her lip, looking at the wiat and thinking. "He has a knack for making plans and not thinking them through, like the attack on us four years ago. This has his touch. It was easily reversed, without too much damage, and little point."

"Write to Demetri and see if he has heard anything," Losolin suggested.

"Tyular too," Aladorn added. "Even Barukh might know something."

"We have not had much interaction with Barukh, though," Tlonna countered. "He might not look upon it favorably if we question him out of nowhere."

"He sent us five hundred dwarves," Yayènia reminded her.

Everyone looked at the High Commander, remembering the fierce battle-driven dwarves led by the exasperating Anadin. Tlonna nodded her assent. "I will write all three of them, then. Does Barukh speak Parlêthian? Or Hindarün?"

"He must speak Hindarün. It is a rare Dwarf that speaks elfish, though," Erdwyf supplied. "I would suggest writing it in Kierlak, but I doubt anyone here speaks it fluently?"

With negative remarks from everyone, Tlonna sighed. "I would not trust anyone else with the information I would have to include, so Hindarün it is. Any suggestions?"

As the council began to debate the content of the letters, the morning wore on, and the conspiracies flew through air.

Chapter 23

Fog

The next day, three messengers left the city, headed for Kajgenia, Arseninis, and Florwen Hune. Also departing was Lara the *Zephyr Leifen*, another messenger, a scout for Flousen Dua to chart Kismath and ask a meeting with Furntil Eldrout, King of the Duani Elves. Tlonna spoke with Haydyn about increasing his academic activities, trying to avoid another argument with her son, and then turned to the southern guard tower to speak with Marin. Suneelo met up with her at the entrance to the tower, still bandaged, but moving around just fine.

"There has been an issue, Tlonna," her brother-in-law said, looking annoyed.

"What kind of issue? I do not want to deal with anything else today, Suneelo," the queen warned.

"She committed suicide."

"What?" Tlonna gasped. "How?"

The Captain of the Guard shook his head. "I cannot tell. My guards found her just minutes ago when they went in to give her lunch."

Tlonna swore, stamping her foot in a huff. "Why is nothing ever easy?"

"What do you mean? She is dead, no more accusations, no more questions. Bury her and move on," the male said, shrugging his shoulders in a careless manner.

"I wish I had your conviction, but I do not think this is over. It is too easy, just like your abduction. Too easy, too clean. There is something deeper going on here, I feel it."

Suneelo eyed her, indigo gaze disturbed. "What are you thinking?"

Tlonna shook her head. "Too many thoughts to sort through. The messengers are sent, Lara and her entourage are off, now it is time to wait and see. I just hope we last long enough to get the replies."

"You are thinking rather pessimistically, are you not? We are pretty certain the attempt on me and the others was Athelias. Haydyn's verdict was innocent by proof, Marin killed herself because of it. I do not think she was even betrothed. I think it was all a lie to make you and Losolin want to feel bad for her, and indict Haydyn. She messed up, she lost control of her emotions, spilled her guts to you and the Council, and then, terrified of the repercussions awaiting her in Zaedic, she killed herself. You are seeing shadows where there are none, Tlonna," Suneelo said gently, squeezing her arm.

"The problem is... they are there, and only I can see them," she murmured back, looking up at him with her haunted eyes.

Suneelo did not look away, but he hugged her with one arm. "This is nothing compared to what we have all been through before, yes?"

"Yes, I suppose," the queen replied quietly, doubting. "Well, being as how there is no reason for me to talk to Marin now, I am going to a meeting with Edwin. He is worried about the eastern wall near the gate, and wants to go over budget issues with me and Daphne. I will be in my office if you need me."

"Where do you want me to put Marin?" Suneelo asked as his sister walked away.

"Bury her in the convict graveyard or burn her. Your choice, Suneelo."

"Great. I appreciate it," the elf replied sarcastically, but he moved into the tower to deal with the problem before the news spread too far that a Zaedican had died within their cells.

After her meeting with Steward of the Walls and the Keeper of Treasury, Tlonna hurried to the rear courtyard, and wound her way through the gardens to The Archer, who had stood guard above her nation for just over nine years. He was still standing guard over it, in fact. Tlonna had demanded that the underground be repaired and ready for occupation at a moment's notice, just in case. The city knew nothing of it, and she preferred to keep it that way, using only the most discreet of craftsmen to handle the job.

She descended into the dark tunnel and strode through the dirt corridors, now reinforced with barriers of her magic, inch thick Weaves that shimmered slightly in light. Ahead, she could see a small group of dwarves and one wood nymph working on re-hinging the doors to the tiny rooms. When they caught sight of her, they bowed as one.

"Your Majesty," they murmured, and she smiled back, moving beyond them toward the throne room.

She believed the throne room of utmost importance, not because it was her hub of authority, but because it lent a sense of normality to the people of Blackhaven City. Here, they could lay their claims and petitions at her feet just as they did now at the castle. Here, they could speak directly with her, face to face, and get a reply back immediately. Although Tlonna did not believe they would need the underground again, she did not want to leave her people stranded if they were overrun again.

On either side of the barren throne room were two massive caverns that had not existed a year ago, but she had hollowed the earth out and had the carpenters set up large cross weave anchors to hold up the ceiling. They were to be fruit and vegetable gardens. Above, the ground had been cut open to allow sunlight to filter through, and then she had the anchors put up so that the ceiling would not collapse, even if people walked above them. Directly above the caverns were flowers and shrubs, no trees, for their roots would go too deep. The air vents were not visible from above, even if a person was to stand next to one, as they were hidden by long grasses.

The underground was her secret project that only the craftsmen and her council knew about. Tlonna wanted to be prepared for anything, and she would not let her army stand their ground until they were all but obliterated. She would not be defeated. She would not.

Tlonna returned to the castle an hour later, having fully toured the underground. She walked alone, which was rare. Usually, one of her friends or family members would be with her, or a resident noble who believed themselves useful, and she was nearly always shadowed by two or three guards, though she was far more equipped to handle her enemies than they were. But today, however, she was truly alone. Reveling in the solitary moment, Tlonna wandered slowly, gazing at the black obsidian stone blocks that made up the castle. They shimmered in the torchlight that illuminated the indoor halls where no windows could be placed.

Always there was a faint breeze wafting through the high corridors, pleasant and warm even in winter. Foliage would skitter across the floors, petals in the spring and summer, leaves in autumn, and every now and then in winter, puffs of snow. Tlonna breathed deep, catching the faint smell of the apple trees planted in the western corner of the rear courtyard. Fall was approaching fast now and the harvesting had already begun. The granaries and cold cellars of the city were bursting with food newly brought in from the fields. It was a time of merriment and hard work, and soon, preparations would begin for the celebration of Samhain.

Tlonna smiled to herself. It was the first time in twelve years the city would celebrate the ancient festival, and already she was getting letters from nobles and other wealthy people of the city, asking whether she would attend their fête, or perhaps she was planning one? In truth, the queen was planning on attending the city fête, free for everyone, and probably the most fun of all the parties.

Samhain was the one night when everyone was equal, their faces masked, their bodies clothed in obscure, and sometimes obscene, costumes. It was the celebration of the parting of the veil between the world of living and dead, a night for inebriation and carousing, though the meaning behind it was rather skewed by the actions of the population. Some said the ancient gods came down to fornicate with the people of the world, others that they rode the Great Wild Hunt, in search of mortal souls.

Tlonna believed none of this, yet she also believed all of it. She was not a religious person, she did not care what the gods did on whatever day. But she was excited for the fête anyway. Her couturier, Mattie, was after her every day on what she wanted to dress as, and the queen always told her to choose for her. She trusted the woman, especially after seeing her wedding gown. Losolin was also being hounded about the celebration, though he was showing a rare patience with his tailor.

The Magin smiled faintly as she thought of the exasperated expression on his face every time he was asked about his costume. He truly was a beautiful elf, strong and masculine, yet somehow gentle and lethal at the same time. She loved him more every day, and it hurt to know that she worried him. Tlonna sighed, gazing up at the huge black and silver tapestry that hung in the foyer of the castle, depicting the Tree of Blackhaven, bordered by her star and sun emblem, all in thread-of-silver.

So much weight to carry, she mused silently, staring at the massive textile. So much power, yet it all came with suffocating restrictions, rigorous edicts, and irrational fears. Tlonna sighed, closing her eyes and leaning against the cool obsidian wall, feeling the glossy smooth surface beneath her tunic. It all seemed so hopeless. She wished for a moment to be back in the wilderness, ignorant of herself and her responsibilities, as she had once been. She wished for a private, passionate night with Losolin within the tight confines of their old tent.

But wishes and dreams were not for rulers, or for people who must carry the burden of others. They were bound to the real world, alone and hungry in a world that could supply them with neither lasting companionship nor sustaining hope. Tlonna swallowed back her despair and fear and opened her eyes once more. Losolin was standing before her, his hands in his pockets, his oceanic eyes calm and reassuring. No one else was around, and she realized it was dinner time.

Her husband did not speak, but he came and pressed her against the wall, kissing her with a burning passion that bespoke of things to come. It was a promise and a plea all in one. When Losolin pulled away, Tlonna was breathless, her heart fluttering within her chest.

They stood close for another several minutes, not speaking, yet conveying all that needed to be said. Tlonna rested her head against his shoulder, listening to his pulse beat against his throat, strong and steady. Losolin's hands pressed her close against him, his head bowed over hers. Tears formed at the corners of the queen's eyes, and she blinked them away, restraining herself. Above them, the black and silver tapestry wafted slightly in the apple-scented breeze, casting them in flickering shadows.

After a while, Tlonna stepped away and searched her husband's face. "Do you believe we can succeed?" she asked softly.

Losolin looked down at her, his perfect face void of expression, his eyes the only troubled thing about him. "If we both believe it, then yes. Tlonna, the world will not stop for us, it will not stop for anyone. We must make our fates, not the other way around. Believe in yourself...believe in us...and yes, we will succeed."

"Always the philosopher," Tlonna said, smiling faintly. "Ah, love, how can I fail with you at my side? You always keep me upright."

"Not always," Losolin laughed, tugging on the section of hair held by a silver cuff. "I like you horizontal every so often."

Now she laughed, linking her fingers with his. "Come, let us eat, and then to the horizontal."

"A good plan," the king said, guiding her to the fourth floor where they took their private dinner, and later, to their bedroom where they did little sleeping.

The morning seemed only an extension of night, coming gray and foggy, blanketing the quiet streets of Blackhaven with a mist that dampened sound and made one think of the Winter Solstice Celebration. It was not a bleak fog, but it was chill and the inhabitants of the city dressed themselves in long, thick layers and hurried to their destinations. Once there, they drank warm cider and gazed out into the grayness, their thoughts meandering along content trails.

The satisfied lethargy was not absent at the castle either. Tlonna wore a dress of white brocade and velvet, feeling the need to preen a little, and simply let her hair fall as it would. Losolin was the opposite, wearing a black cotton belted tunic, which he did not belt, and black suede pants. His boots were soft gray leather, the only color he seemed to approve of other than black.

"Well, aren't we night and day this morning?" Miazie asked them upon entering the dining room for breakfast.

The royal couple grinned, but said nothing, and breakfast passed uneventfully. Delaying the inevitable paperwork and council meetings, Tlonna and Losolin saddled Neñyos and Takîreaes, and rode through the foggy streets. Along every avenue there were groups of singers, their clarion voices rising through the morning to bring smiles and fantasies to all who passed. Usually they were small groups of elves, but every now and again it was humans or dwarves, caroling in their distinct languages and accents.

Dry leaves skittered along the verdant grass-weave streets, a mix of *kairhotuss* leaves, oak, birch, aspen, maple, and dogwood. Tlonna smiled, hoisting her white velvet hood further onto her head, enjoying the warmth it gave off.

"It was not like this last year, or the years before, was it?" Losolin asked suddenly, softly.

Tlonna looked at her husband from inside her hood. "No. This is the first year of true peace, I believe. Everything is done, all the repairs are finished, trade is flourishing...we are all truly home."

"It is nice, is it not?" the king murmured, catching her hand and holding it as they plodded along the misty streets.

"Very. This is a time for family and celebration, for love and hope and peace and all those things we fight for, Losolin. All those things that were struggling to survive just a year ago. And, it is beautiful to look at. Everything is hazy, the flaws and chinks faded away so that appearances are softened, old becomes new, worn becomes beautiful. Just like the Winter Queen giving birth to the Green Man, yes?"

Losolin smiled back and nodded. "I can definitely see why people tend to become more religious during this time," he mused, watching a young couple depart from a small shrine to the Earth God Ullor, of whom Losolin was named after.

"Do you?"

"What? See why?"

Tlonna chuckled. "Become more religious. We are not much into that, but we have never really discussed it."

Losolin frowned slightly, and then shook his head. "I cannot say I do. I am not one for worship."

"Nor am I. I do not like anything that puts me on my knees," Tlonna replied quietly, watching the couple as they wound their way through the fog and light traffic.

Losolin grunted, but said nothing more on the matter, and she let it pass. They wandered through the city for an hour more, attended now by two guards who had caught up with them as they passed the shrine. They were gray shadows on white and gray horses, soundless and easily missed if one were not looking for them. Even so, they were difficult to pinpoint. Suneelo had trained them well. Tlonna felt them immediately, some extra sense picking up their aura field as they came within yards of them.

She had noticed her senses becoming extremely heightened since Purheae, feelings and prickliness along her body that notified her of other Magins, people with weapons, people with different attributes, people with secrets. She also saw things, aural images and others that disoriented her and made her dizzy. Tlonna had remained silent about them, however, knowing that the mere physical appearance of her eyes bothered her friends. They bothered her, too, but she accepted it as she did most other things, with a great deal of resignation.

The Magin Queen snapped herself out of the self-induced funk and looked about her city. It was beautiful. The people were beautiful as well, sprytes, elves, dwarves, humans, dryads, nymphs, and the myriad half-breeds. Tlonna smiled at an odd looking creature as it drifted by her, and then she realized it was a mix of stone nymph and spryte, thin as her arm and the color of slate. It looked at her with large, flat gray eyes, and then bowed slightly.

"Your Majesty," he said, shocking her.

Tlonna had always held the impression that all sprytes were female, if only because of their lithe appearance, the offspring of dryads and elves.

"Merry meet," she replied tardily, masking her hesitation with a quick adjustment of her skirt.

Gray lips curled into a small smile and then he was beyond her, already a part of the mists. Tlonna turned to Losolin, who was grinning like a fool.

"You could not have been more obvious, love," he chuckled, moving the long-legged Neñyos into a faster walk.

Takîreaes snorted and moved alongside the gelding, not about to be left behind. Tlonna huffed, her breath frosting in the air before her. "I cannot be prepared for *every* person who says something to me!" she said, trying to defend herself, but Losolin was laughing and did not hear her.

They meandered back onto Obsidian Way from the side streets they had been using, and found the traffic a bit heavier, if no more hurried. No one seemed to want to move quickly, and the monarchs simply let the horses pick their way through the pedestrians. Now, every other person called out to them, and they could no longer talk. Losolin bent down to accept a sadly wilted handful of wildflowers from a young dwarf-girl, her small hands clinging to his.

She was a tiny thing, barely two feet tall, the top of her coarse red hair coming just above Losolin's knee, brown eyes wide with wonder. Losolin beamed as she released the flowers into his hand, and suddenly they flourished, their petals becoming vivid, the green of the stems brightening and stiffening with health. The child laughed in delight, and the king tucked one of the small daisies into her hair. Passersby were watching in awe, their own faces alight with smiles and watery eyes. It was one thing to see a king accept flowers from a child, it was another to see an adult elf accept flowers from a dwarf of any age.

Losolin climbed back onto Neñyos as the child scampered away, the blue daisy still bright against her hair. Tlonna gazed at him with love, her heart swelling. Slowly, they made it back to the castle, where they dismounted and walked the rest of the way through the front lawns and gardens. They were met by Erdwyf and Daphne, and their day started.

Later in the evening, Tlonna spotted the ragtag flowers in a small vase next to the bed on Losolin's side. She couldn't help but smile.

The fog stayed over Blackhaven for nearly two weeks, a persistent cloud that chilled the city and outlying forestland. People began to mutter to themselves, worried that it would never leave, but their fears were unfounded. One morning the sun rose, and the mists burned away, leaving the city dripping with dew, but clear and refreshed. Yayènia and Tlonna were inspecting the new armory when they looked up in surprise as the air about them cleared and the barracks became visible across the military training fields.

"Well, would you look at that," the warrior murmured, blinking in the sunshine.

Tlonna looked about the glistening fields with pride. Pairs and small groups of soldiers were grappling or sparring in one area, others ran the dirt track that wound around the entire military compound. Directly across from them, Ghealan was instructing a group of recruits in hand-to-hand combat. All the buildings were constructed of birch wood, each piece of soft white timber snug against its neighbor, and the foundations were of blue-veined marble. The military compound was a glorious thing to behold, pristine and lovingly tended. Trees lined the various pathways to the separate buildings: the barracks, armories, workshops, the forge, offices, and a small shed at the back of the forge that hid a new addition: a concealed trapdoor that led to the underground.

The queen and her sister were standing in the newest armory, examining the armor that was stored there, as yet unassigned to soldiers. Tlonna signed the last inspection list and passed it to Yayènia, who also signed it.

"When do you think they will be assigned?" the ruler asked, heading out of the armory.

Yayènia shrugged. "Within the next few weeks, I am sure. I have Rone and Bailan working on that right now," she said, referring to the Third Rank Infantry and Cavalry Captains.

Tlonna nodded and then stood watching Ghealan instruct a particularly large human. He grabbed the human's wrist, and then slowly went through the motions of disarming and flipping. The man nodded, and then they switched positions, moving slowly, sketchily. At one point, Ghealan shook his head and reviewed the whole thing once more. A few minutes later, they were moving much faster, the human blocking Ghealan's hands in an attempt to disarm the elf.

Yayènia came to stand next to her, arms folded, light glinting off her vambraces. "He is a good teacher," she said suddenly.

"Did he do this with you?" Tlonna asked impulsively.

The High Commander was silent for a moment, watching her second and the human spar. "He was not as gentle with me," she said finally. "I learned everything in about a month. I was a brawler, a melee fighter and a monster."

"I have seen you fight. *I* have fought you, Nia, and I have never seen such controlled grace. Every move you do seems calculated and yet natural. It is as though you can see not just moments, but *steps* ahead of your opponent. How did you learn that?"

Yayènia smiled slightly, shaking her head. "I was a common soldier for a year, Tlonna. I simply honed everything Ghealan had taught me into my weapon. It was all I cared about, all I had. Every night I read *Sleep by the Sword,* and every day I gave myself entirely to my training. At the time, I was only the fifth female in the entire militia. Ghealan fell behind during our last training exercise, he fell and jarred his knee. I then broke his leg, and received the High Commander promotion a month later. It was my revenge."

Tlonna watched Ghealan move onto the next recruit as the large human was assigned to spar with another. "You are the greatest warrior ever to live, Lan the second, and Suneelo the third. How is it we ever lose?"

Yayènia shook her head again at the comment. "We fight with honor and the belief that we are protecting, rather than destroying. It means we will not pull nasty tricks just to win. It is what separates us from our enemies."

"We must always fight back, never fight," Tlonna murmured, still watching Ghealan.

"Always and never," Yayènia replied just as quietly, and walked away.

Chapter 24

King Eyin

Days passed slowly as the celebration of Samhain approached and the city became more and more festive. Harvest plants appeared on every corner, pumpkins and gourds, bundles of wheat and barley. The trees finally succumbed to autumn's demand, and the leaves turned to crimson, gold, bronze and, on the *kairhotuss* trees, true black. They scuttled across the ever-green streets to pile against homes and stores in heaps.

Losolin was lounging in his chair, feet upon his office desk, when Erdwyf walked in. The king sat up, tossing the report he'd been reading onto his desk, and looked at the female. She had Jaryikin with her, the infant cradled in her arm. Losolin smiled, and took the girl into his own arms. Smiling down at her, he asked what Erdwyf needed.

The High Advisor shook her head in sheer disbelief. "You will not believe who is approaching the city."

"I am not worried unless it is Stoffnias or Sithian," he replied, his finger trapped in the little girl's fist.

"Oh no, it is Eyin Thorn of Purheae. He comes with three others, and will be here by midday."

"That little upstart Tlonna acknowledged as king?" Losolin asked, his eyebrows climbing his forehead in surprise.

"The very same. What do you want to do?" Erdwyf asked.

The king sighed, staring down at the child in his arms. She blinked up at him with large gray eyes, newly flecked with emerald reminiscent of Ghealan, and yawned. "I suppose we will have to meet him, but not at the city gates. He can get through the city just fine. We will have an entourage for him at the castle gates. Me, Tlonna, you, Nia, Suneelo, Ghealan...the rest. Have twenty guards in full regalia, ten on each side of the gate, to greet the little blighter. I suppose we will have to host him here."

Erdwyf laughed at her friend's obvious distress. "Try to be civil. I will take care of everything, if you take care of Jaryikin."

"Deal," Losolin said, and pushed the female out of his office.

Erdwyf giggled again, but she continued down the hallway until she disappeared. Her daughter watched her go, and then the emerald flecked gray gaze shifted to the king.

"Well little one, I really was not expecting her to leave you here. What now?"

The one year old child grinned at him, toothless yet, as elven children develop at half the rate of humans. Panicking a little, Losolin looked around for someone, finding himself utterly abandoned in the fourth floor office corridor of the castle. The only person present was Suneelo. Losolin burst into his brother's office, Jaryikin grasping at his hair, and stared at him.

Suneelo gaped back, indigo eyes flicking between the girl and the king. "What is with you and little girls recently? First the dwarf in the street, now this? Why do you have a baby?"

"It is Jaryikin, Suneelo. Erdwyf handed her to me and left. Just left! Eyin Thorn is on the way, and I have a baby! What do I do?"

The Captain of the Guard laughed at his brother's terror. "How am I supposed to know? Erdwyf left me not ten minutes ago, telling me about the human, and said she was on the way to your office. I told her to find Selick and do what she needed to do."

Losolin frowned, momentarily forgetting his problem. "Who is Selick?"

Suneelo rolled his eyes. "My Lieutenant, *bruun.* I do not run the entire Guard by myself."

"Right...so, help me?"

"You are the king. One little girl should not be a problem for you, Losolin."

"Then you take her if it is so easy! I have things to do!" Losolin replied, holding Jaryikin out to his older brother.

Suneelo's eyes widened, and he shook his head. "Oh no, I think not. You are the one responsible for her."

The Magin beseeched his brother, tucking the child into his arm once more, where she fell asleep. Suneelo pointed at her.

"Look, problem solved," he said, smiling. "Now go away."

Losolin glared at him. "You are going to pay for this, I tell you."

Suneelo was grinning now. "I am sure. I wait in fear of your retribution. Now, take your baby and leave me alone."

The king did just that, walking back to his office and sitting in his chair, Jaryikin slumbering on his chest. He tried reading more reports, but the sound of the baby breathing lulled him to sleep.

Tlonna and Yayènia walked into Losolin's office and stopped short, their mouths open in shock. He was dead to the world, splayed in his chair, with Jaryikin clinging to his shoulder, also sleeping.

"Did I miss something?" Yayènia whispered to her sister.

Tlonna shook her head. "I never thought I would see the day. Where is Ghealan, or Erdwyf?"

The High Commander shrugged, and then looked into the hallway as her husband approached. He was grinning like a fool, a mischievous glint in his eyes.

"Do you have something to do with this?" Yayènia asked as Suneelo joined them, looking in at Losolin.

"Of course not," he lied, still grinning. "Should we wake him?"

Tlonna was still shocked at the sight of her grumpy husband asleep with a baby girl. "Losolin?" she called.

The king jerked awake, and then looked down at his adornment. Muttering, he picked Jaryikin up and held the sleeping infant out to the two females with an imploring look. Yayènia snorted and backed into her husband.

"I think not, little brother," she said.

Tlonna sighed and took the child. "I am sure I will hear the story later. I take it you know Eyin is on his way?"

Losolin nodded, still fazed. "Erdwyf said he and his companions would be here by midday. I told her to take care of things, and she gave me her daughter."

"Yes. It is nearing midday now, and he is at the city gates. We need to get ready," Tlonna replied, balancing Jaryikin on her hip. "Yayènia, Suneelo, you are required to attend. I want you in full regalia and at the castle gates in twenty minutes. Losolin?"

He hoisted himself out of his chair and the four departed his office. They split for their separate preparations. Once ensconced in their suite, Tlonna laid Jaryikin on their bed and donned the black velvet dress she had once worn to attend King Tyular of Arseninis. It was embroidered in thread-of-silver with a tree that spread from the bodice to the hem. She watched Losolin dress in his usual garb, black pants, gray tunic, and gray boots.

Adorning their crowns and their cloaks, the couple headed out of their room once Tlonna had picked up a blinking Jaryikin. They reached the castle gates just steps ahead of Yayènia and Suneelo, resplendent in full armor, their cloaks of office billowing out behind them. Reluctantly, Yayènia took Jaryikin from Tlonna as her sister and husband went to speak with Selick, an elf of average height, but with glossy red hair and hazel eyes.

It was then that Erdwyf and Ghealan arrived, the former in her ceremonial garb, the latter in his armor, plumed helmet tucked under his arm. The couple grinned at Yayènia, who was having an even harder time than Losolin with their daughter. The warrior held Jaryikin out in front of her, gauntleted hands grasping the squirming child's middle.

Laughing, Erdwyf took her daughter, beamed at Losolin, who glowered back, and then took her place. Ahead, the sound of horses approaching the gate echoed through the quiet air. Suneelo and Tlonna hurried to their places, the guards snapping to full attention, banners of Blackhaven and House Ewôsdírn unfurling in the mild autumn breeze. From the closed gate were two lines of ten guards, each at attention. At the end of the militant aisle stood Tlonna and Losolin. Next to the queen were Yayènia and Ghealan, next to the king stood Erdwyf and Suneelo. Miazie and Sodo rushed to their spots on either side of Ghealan and Suneelo.

Slowly, the gates opened, and through the wall rode Eyin Thorn, three of his people, and a retinue of Blackhaven guards. The young human gaped at the presentation, his horse slowing. Then, shaking himself, the king urged his horse onward until his guides through the city stepped forward to grab his reins. Staring at Tlonna, Eyin dismounted rather ungracefully, and she noticed that the horses wore blankets with the Blackhaven insignia.

"Merry meet, Eyin Thorn, King of Purheae, and welcome to Blackhaven City," Tlonna said once the horses had been taken.

The young man seemed unsure of what to do, so he stood back a few feet from her, his three followers staring about in wonder. "Ah...yes...thanks. I mean...merry meet to you too, Queen Tlonna, King Losolin. I come under your invitation, not in any sort of aggression."

"Plainly," muttered Yayènia, but she said it so only Tlonna and Ghealan could hear. They had to hide smirks.

"Well, do you find my city to your liking?" the queen asked, gazing down at the human with grinning eyes.

"Yes. It's very beautiful, and well kept. I find it very welcoming," Eyin replied nervously, his eyes darting about the elves, and Miazie.

"Then I am pleased. Come, you and your companions must be weary after your journey. Let us reconvene at the castle, and we shall discuss what needs to be," Tlonna said, smiling.

Eyin nodded wordlessly, his gaze falling on the massive obsidian castle, gleaming in the sunlight. The entourage dispersed, Yayènia and Tlonna flanking Eyin as they moved up the walkway between *kairhotuss* trees and quaking aspen. The young king's eyes landed on the Stairway of the Winds and his mouth dropped open. They began to climb, rather than go under the passageway carved from the steps that led to the first floor. Midway, Eyin and his three followers were gasping for breath, sweat glistening on their skin despite the cool temperature and wind. Tlonna, Yayènia, Losolin, and Erdwyf slowed to a stop, allowing the humans to catch their breath.

After a moment's rest, Eyin nodded, and they resumed the climb. Once they reached the third floor, Tlonna ordered wine, water, and hors d'eouvres brought to a private audience room, and then sat. Yayènia took up her customary stance behind her chair, Losolin sat next to her, and Erdwyf next to him. Eyin and his sweaty companions stood awkwardly until Tlonna told them to sit as well.

"So, Eyin, what brings you to Blackhaven?"

The young man shifted. "It has been brought to my attention that I know little of ruling a people, and even less of the world. My people have not left Purheae in many generations, and so our knowledge is limited. I thought that perhaps, being a large and prosperous city, Blackhaven might have the education I need."

"You wish to go the Academy?" Losolin asked in surprise, not at all what he had expected.

"Yes, if I can. And any other place you might think I should. I want to be a successful king, one that is remembered not for his follies, but for his triumphs. I cannot do this if I am an ignorant," Eyin replied, dark eyes shifting to the king's.

"It is a wise decision, Eyin, but there are many more things involved in kingship than just basic education. There are diplomacies, edicts, treaties and petitions, law and order, economics and the welfare of your people. All these things take years to learn, if not a lifetime. How long do you plan to be here?" Tlonna said, frowning.

The human looked sickly. "I...would like to learn all that I can, but I must not be gone from my people too long."

"The average semester at the Academy is six months. Can you do that?" Erdwyf inquired.

"Yes, but I would have to take time to go back to Purheae. What must I do?"

"I will enroll you tomorrow," the High Advisor stated. "I will leave the rest up to Queen Tlonna and King Losolin."

"Would you prefer to stay here, or somewhere in the city?" Tlonna asked. "Either way, it is no trouble. And what of your companions?" She finally noticed that they were all of an age with Eyin, somewhere in their mid-twenties.

Eyin now looked nervous. "I brought them to see if they might also receive the education. I would like them to one day be my advisors, and military commanders."

At this, Yayènia started. "What sort of military are you planning?"

The human blanched, staring at the warrior with wide eyes. "One that would protect my people, and perhaps be of aid to you and others of similar means. I have no desires of conquest."

"Good, because you would lose," Yayènia snapped, easing back a little.

Tlonna hid a smile. "If you would sacrifice one of your men to Yayènia, she will teach him everything he needs to know about being a good commander."

Behind her, the warrior choked, but Eyin's face lit up in wonder. "Really? That would be very good! Meradyn, you are the best among us."

A handsome young man stepped forward, tall and slim with russet hair and hazel eyes. He bowed uncertainly, feathery hair gleaming in the light from the windows.

Eyin gestured at him vaguely. "Meradyn Obren, Your Majesties. He is the best hunter in all of Purheae. He once a killed a stag with only his hands. He will be my commander one day."

Meradyn did not speak, but he glanced once at Yayènia, and Tlonna saw his knees tremble. She sighed inwardly. "And what of the other two?"

"Jorunson and Marc, Queen Tlonna. Jorunson can read and write, Marc can make things out of anything. He has made a made it possible for our village to have warm water all year round by lighting a fire underground, where the water pooled, and keeping it lit. Quite amazing, Your Majesty."

"Indeed. Well, have it your way, Eyin, King of Purheae. The three of you will be enrolled in the Academy of Blackhaven tomorrow, while Meradyn is placed under the care of High Commander Yayènia. Anything else?" Tlonna stated.

"No, Queen Tlonna. That's all, I believe," the young man said, looking pleased.

"Good. You will be shown to your rooms, where you can bathe and rest before dinner. It is at seven. You may take it anywhere you please, or join us on the fourth floor. Just inform your assistants."

"Yes, my lady," Eyin said, standing with the rest of the elves. "Thank you for your generosity. I will not forget it."

"Good," Losolin said shortly, and they all exited the room.

Four servants were waiting to take the visitors to their quarters, and the four elves watched them go. As soon as they were out of sight, Yayènia swore.

"Why? What did I do to deserve this? Have I offended you somehow?" she cried, looking at Tlonna with wide eyes.

"What?"

"I do not *want* to baby-sit some inept human for the next six months! I do not have the time for it, anyway!"

Tlonna sighed. "Look, if you train Meradyn well, then we will never have anything to fear from Eyin and his ambitions, if there are any. And, we will have a strong ally. You train him, he trains others, and somewhere down the line, there will be an entire kingdom of people who live and practice our way. Think of it, Nia. Think of the opportunity here."

The warrior sighed, and threw her hands in the air. "Then you might as well send the other three to me as well, so I can influence all of them!"

"Good idea," Tlonna said, smiling. "They will be yours after school each day."

"No!" Yayènia howled, "I was kidding!"

"Yes, well, apparently today that means you are serious," Losolin interjected, glaring at Erdwyf, who gave him an innocent smile.

"No! No! No!" Nia cried, despairing.

"Yes, High Commander Yayènia er'Tiena. Yes," Tlonna said stiffly, and then grinned as her sister gave her the most pitiful look she had ever seen. "You can hand them off to Ghealan or Sargotarh some days, you know."

"Bloody well good," she snorted and stormed off.

The next day, Eyin Thorn, King of Purheae, along with his two companions, arrived at the steps of the large Academy of Blackhaven. It was a block marble building the color of snow, three stories high with a courtyard in the middle. The double front doors were red oak, carved with the Tree of Blackhaven, and bound with silver hinges in the shape of leaves.

Eyin tugged at his rustic clothing self-consciously. He wore leather pants, sewn down the sides, and a matching leather tunic, neither of which were dyed, and soft leather moccasins. Jorunson and Marc looked much the same.

"We do not belong here," Jorunson muttered as a group of students passed. They were of the same age, but many different races, and all clothed in silk, cotton, velvet, and a variety of others. They ignored the three humans standing at the base of the steps.

"We will soon," Eyin replied. "I am King..."

"Of a village, and two others," Marc replied acidly. "This city is bigger than all of them put together, Eyin. Purheae will never be this strong."

"You don't know that. Maybe we will learn what we need to!" Eyin replied, still gazing at the beautiful building.

"You heard the elf queen!" Jorunson shot back. "We can never learn all that we need in just six months! We know nothing of anything!"

"We will," the young king returned determinedly, and strode into the academy.

Once inside, the three men stare in awe. Large portraits in gilded frames lined the walls, potted plants and stone benches took up the edges of the foyer, and a young woman behind a large desk was at the end. She stared at them, brown eyes unblinking. "Who are you?"

"I am King Eyin Thorn of Purheae, this is Jorunson, and Marc. The High Advisor Erd...win, signed us up this morning."

"High Advisor Erdwyf, you mean?" the woman asked, scorn in her voice. "I believe she was in here this morning, indeed. You say you are a king? Of Purheae? No one lives there."

"We do," Marc said.

"Whatever," the woman returned airily. "Look, the High Advisor enrolled you in Linguistics, History, Alchemy, Diplomacy, Landcraft, and Basics. Your professors are... Morin, Tarsin, Sodo, Hered, Alisimon, and Olosyn."

Eyin stared at her, baffled.

She sighed. "Your first class is already in session. It is Landcraft, with Professor Alisimon. She is in the courtyard today. Wait!"

The three men had turned away, but stopped when she called. "You need your badges, and supplies. High Advisor Erdwyf said you had none."

"What supplies?" Eyin said as he took the silver badge from the woman. It was an odd symbol, a slanted line with a hook on the back.

The woman saw his confusion and sighed. "It is a 'B' in Parlêthian, for Blackhaven. Here," she handed the trio wax tablets and writing utensils. "You write down notes on the tablet, and then scribe them onto parchment later. I am sure that at the castle you can get the parchment and things you need. If you do not know how to write," she made a face, "then do whatever you need to do in order to remember what you are told."

When she said nothing more, the three Purheaens hustled out into the courtyard and found a small gathering of students, and one tall female elf. She glanced at them once, and continued her lecture, which, to the vast relief of the three, was in Hindarün.

By the end of the day, they had attended all six classes, done what they could with their tablets, and returned to the castle completely mystified. Erdwyf and Miazie met them at the entrance.

The Belau smiled kindly while the elf simply nodded at them. "How did you find the Academy?" Miazie asked.

Eyin shook his head. "Too much information in one go. Did I do okay?" he asked, handing her his tablet.

The Belau examined the sketches on the tablet and smiled faintly. "As long as you understand it, that is all that matters. What did you think of Alchemy?"

"Fascinating!" Marc interrupted, beaming. "I never dreamed of such things!"

"I am glad. Your professor is my...lover."

"Professor Sodo?" Eyin asked, surprised. "But he is an elf!"

"Yes, that he is," Miazie replied, smiling. "High Advisor Erdwyf and I are to be your tutors during your stay. It has also been decided that, when possible, you will join your friend Meradyn in military training with High Commander Yayènia."

The three humans paled, but they nodded their acquiescence. Erdwyf, who had remained silent, folded her arms. "In your quarters you will find parchment, ink, and quills, as well as books and other implements of learning. On the fourth floor there is a private library. You will all meet us there in half an hour with your writing tools."

"For what?" asked Eyin.

"You are going to learn how to write and read."

"But we are learning that in Basics. And Jorunson already knows how," Marc complained.

"Be that as it may, you will all three attend, and Advisor Miazie and I will determine what you need to learn while not at the Academy," Erdwyf said coolly.

So it was that Miazie and Erdwyf ensconced themselves in the fourth floor library with the three reluctant humans, and began their teaching.

Yayènia sighed, shook her hands to loosen them up, and went back into a crouch. Across from her, Meradyn's white face was streaked with sweat, dust, and a little blood. One nostril was crusted unpleasantly, and there was a long shallow split along the corner of his mouth. The human crouched down with her, teeth gleaming in the failing light. He had determination, she had to give him that. He had yet to lay hands on her and had spent most of the day on the ground, but when she had offered him any kind of break, he had refused until he simply fainted.

Now, Yayènia was beginning to feel the strain a little, her back pulling slightly when she bent over, an unusual sensation. She had not trained anyone from scratch in many years, and Meradyn was as close to scratch as possible. The only thing he had to offer was stealth, at which he was passable.

"Remember," she said, catching his gaze. "Make your decisions before you act. Do not rush at me without a plan."

He nodded, swallowed, and they continued to stare at each other. Finally, Yayènia watched his muscles tense, and prepared for the attack. That was something she would have to teach him to conceal. The human's left hand snatched her wrist as she threw it up to block, and yanked it down, making her bend over a little. His free hand latched onto her shoulder with an iron grip, his elbow out to prevent her from reaching around.

Yayènia was forced back a step, and was surprised. Then she gathered her thoughts, brought her hand under his, and slammed her palm into his sternum. Meradyn gasped as the wind was knocked from his lungs, but he did not release her. They grappled for a moment, each trying to get a stronger grip on the other. With her superior height and strength, Yayènia bore down on her student, simply leaning over, her hands still trapped by his. Then suddenly she ducked low, caught him in the middle with her shoulder, and laid him out yet again.

Meradyn coughed, his hands coming up to cover his face. "I'm never going to get this!" he moaned into them.

Yayènia sat down next to him, crossing her legs. "It is only your first day, Meradyn," she soothed, a small bit of affection simmering deep inside in spite of her conviction not to like him.

"But I will never reach your status! Not in six months, not in six years!"

Yayènia smiled at his thick accent, and the comment. "Probably not, but you will not live as long as I have, either. Do you think I learned everything in a couple months? It took years, Meradyn, just as it does everyone. I had even less training than you when I began."

"But you are elf-kind, and I am human," the young man said, finally removing his hands to look at her. "There will always be an element of separation."

"Tlonna says not."

"Who?"

"Queen Tlonna, my sister. She believes the only thing that separates us from each other is ourselves. She often says we all bleed the same."

"It is true, but you can regenerate your blood, and dwarves have super thick skin. Humans are-"

"The favorite children of Gagu, God of Plants, the improved version of Elf," Yayènia cut him short, surprising herself with the words.

Apparently they surprised Meradyn as well, for he stared at her with his mouth open. She glared suddenly, her reaction to uncertain moments, and he blanched.

"Come," Yayènia said, standing fluidly, holding out her hand to him. "It is past time we returned."

The human took the proffered hand and they wandered back to the castle, speaking of various legendary warriors, mostly human, and their tactics.

"Eyin did not know me, or any of us, when we rode through Purheae. How is it you know these things?" Yayènia asked as they rounded the last bend of pathway before entering the rear courtyard.

Meradyn shrugged. "Jorunson has his writing, Marc has his inventions, Eyin his ambition and dreams, and I have my legends. My father's father was not native to Purheae, he came from Talenias, fleeing Aderiaen Rahlan's oppression. He was not welcomed at first, but then the Stone Hunters, Eyin's clan, accepted him. He brought with him all the stories of his childhood, stories no one in Purheae had ever heard, things long past. I listened until I knew them all by heart. I wanted to be a bard, once, but there is no use for such a superfluous profession in a community where everyone must work together in order survive."

Yayènia listened silently, opening the door for him as they entered the castle. He told her of his family, his life as a hunter, and everything in between. He had three sisters, the eldest at seventeen. She felt for the young man, the same affection she did for Haydyn. It was odd for her, having loved only Suneelo for so long, to have two young men in her life that she looked at as nephews, young people she needed to educate and protect.

They reached the dining room after everyone else. Eyin looked up sharply as his friend entered the room, battered and bruised, but grinning. Tlonna and her friends stared in astonishment as Yayènia chuckled at something he said, ruffled Haydyn's hair as she passed him, and then sat down next to Suneelo. Meradyn took his seat between Eyin and Marc, staring at the fare on his plate.

"How did it go?" Losolin asked, studying the young human's worn appearance.

"He has promise," Yayènia said unexpectedly, making everyone stare at her, including Meradyn.

Suneelo shook his head at the vicissitudes of his wife and resumed eating dinner, his hand finding hers beneath the table. Eyin turned to Tlonna. "Are all of our days to be like this, long and arduous?"

The queen smiled faintly. "What do you think being a monarch is, Eyin? It is never easy, and rarely fun. If you are to learn as much as possible in six months, then yes, every day will be like this. Perhaps longer, as your day started later than normal, being the first. Tomorrow, your first class is at daybreak, and your training session at the Compound will end at dusk."

Jorunson muttered something and Marc looked condemned, but Eyin and Meradyn exchanged excited glances, their dreams beginning to take shape.

Five days later, Meradyn punched Yayènia in the face hard enough to bruise, and Eyin spoke his first sentence of Parlêthian. There was a small celebratory feast in their honor, and Tlonna felt one section of her tension slide away. The two young men would go far as long as they stayed on track. Jorunson and Marc looked on, feeling slightly embarrassed by their own failure to produce a coherent elfin phrase. The three students had been down at the training yard twice now, joining Meradyn and Yayènia for five-hour sessions.

The High Commander rolled her shoulders, easing the stiff muscles and tendons, watching Eyin and Meradyn mock-spar. They both had immense potential, the former more brawlish and strong, the latter more tactical and swift. Together they would make a good team. Meradyn had spoken with her about titles just yesterday, worried that the one he and Eyin chose would not fit him or his one-day army. The king had asked her about what she thought the army should be called, what sort of armor would be best, how to get that armor, and how to fund such a thing.

She had told her protégé any title he and his king felt comfortable with was the right one. She was the High Commander of the Blackhaven Militia. She knew High Captains, Generals, Commandants, and Chiefs. Each province had their own way of doing things, and Purheae should be no exception. Meradyn liked hers.

Yayènia told Eyin to speak with Daphne, Keeper of the Treasury, about how to fund things. She told him light armor was best, whether cavalry or infantry, though it should be tough. Finding it was only a matter of finding armorers, blacksmiths, tanners, and clothiers. Yes, clothiers. As for what the army should be called, that was his and Meradyn's decision.

“Well, you are full of vagaries, aren’t you?” Eyin remarked at one point, still unable to feel comfortable around the female who had suspended him on his toes by his wrist not so long ago.

Yayènia shrugged. “I know how to plan and win battles, Eyin of Purheae. Tlonna and her councilors take care of the geld issues. When my army needs private funding, I use geld from my own coffers. I am really not the person to speak with on these things. The treasury of your kingdom will always be an issue, as it is with every group in the world. There is not an endless supply of it, no matter how much of it you may seem to have. My husband takes care of that part of our lives, not I. You may also speak with him.”

“It seems you just want me to go talk to anyone so long as it isn’t you!” Eyin accused the elf, a little irritated.

“Perhaps!” Yayènia snapped and walked away.

A week later, Samhain arrived.

Chapter 15

Samhain and Murder

Mattie, Tlonna's couturier, arrived that afternoon to personally oversee the queen's fitting of the costume she had designed. It was more risqué than Tlonna had ever thought, but she trusted the woman, so she agreed to it.

"You will be Elph, first of your kind, beloved of the Nameless God. She had silver hair and moon-white skin. She wore nothing but her own skin, though I would not do that to you. Here," Mattie said, handing Tlonna a small ring with cascades of silver beads, the same length as her hair. "Place it on your head and we shall pin it in place so that it will give you silver hair. But after we dress you. After."

Tlonna smiled good-naturedly, laughing inwardly at the seamstress's whimsy. By the end of the fitting, the queen could only stare in admiration of the woman's genius. She wore a gown comprised only of sheer white chiffon, which was opaque only because of the six layers. It flowed with every movement, weightless and shimmering with tiny diamonds sewn on the outer level. It fit snugly across the bosom and flowed outward from there. On her head was the silver veil that really did make her hair look silver. Her slippers where white silk, and that was all there was to her costume.

The back fell open all the way to the small of her back, and there were no sleeves, only a silver elastic band that ran around the tops of her breasts and under her armpits to support the light fabric.

"You are sure this will not fall off?" Tlonna inquired yet again, plucking at the band.

Mattie smiled. "I swear it, my lady. On my life."

"Good," the queen said, also smiling. "What is Losolin wearing?"

Now the couturier grinned. "Oh, you will like it. He will probably fight it, but you will love it."

Tlonna laughed. "I bet." She picked up her mask, a white thing that covered the top part of her face, the eyeholes ringed with diamonds.

Together, they moved to where Losolin was getting ready in a separate room, and stared in awe. The king wore exceedingly tight black leather trousers that rode low, exposing his hipbones. Across his abdomen were several straps of black leather, each adorned with silver studs, that swept over his broad shoulders to gather in a row of knots down his spine. The same bands were on his biceps and wrists. He looked like a warrior out of legend, vengeful and devastatingly beautiful.

He was also scowling, his oceanic eyes resigned as Coran yanked on the leather stays down his spine. "I really hope that this night is worth all this, Tlonna."

"If you make it so, it will be, Losolin," she replied, laughing. He really was by far too beautiful for his own good.

"Do you like it?" Mattie asked, fidgeting nervously, clutching at Tlonna's fingers.

"I do. You were right, Mattie, as always. You are genius with cloth, and no one can gainsay that. Thank you, once more," the elf replied, staring at her leather-clad husband.

"Yes, once more you have found a way to put me into things that I should not be able to fit into. It is a wonderful day," Losolin snarled, yanking on the leather about his biceps.

"It is the legendary outfit of Ullor, the God you are named after, my king. I thought it appropriate, especially as the queen is Elph, the first of your race."

"Yes, well, does it have to be so bloody tight?" he complained, breathing deep.

"Else wise it would simply fall off, and you would not want that, would you my lord?" Coran replied, used to his master's irritation.

Losolin did not reply, but he sent Tlonna a look full of meaning. She grinned. "Ready?"

"I suppose. Anything else, Man?" the king sighed, turning around as Coran stepped away.

"This is all, my lord. Have a good celebration," he replied, handing the king his mask. It would cover his eyes and forehead, and had leather straps that dangled from the sides and down the back of his head.

"You know all house staff is free to join as well," Tlonna said, turning to Mattie. The woman gave her a smile.

"Yes, my lady, but we find it in our best interest to ignore such festivities. Too much wine, and we cannot work tomorrow," Coran replied coolly, his eyes flicking over to Mattie, and then back to Tlonna.

The queen eyed her couturier and Losolin's tailor through narrowed lids, suspicious. "Ah ha..." she breathed, looking to Losolin and finding him trying not to smile.

Mattie clapped her hands suddenly, diverting their attention. "You must go now, my lieges, else you will be late for the fête."

"Oh fine," Losolin grumbled, and guided Tlonna from the room.

They emerged from the castle surrounded by revelers and drunk nobles, all dancing about like fools. Tlonna and Losolin quickly saddled their mounts and rode into the city, shortly joined by Yayènia and Suneelo who materialized from the shady lane that led to the Peerage District. Erdwyf and Ghealan were not joining them, instead staying at home for some much needed family time.

The siblings blinked at each other, startled by their garb. Yayènia was in a dress, which was cause for comment in and of itself, but it was also made entirely of pale blue braids, and it clung to her body like a second skin. Dangling from her wrist was a mask of the same dusky blue, a simple thing that would cover her eyes and forehead, white feathers attached to the top. Suneelo wore black cotton pants and a shirt of the same braided material as his wife's dress. His mask was black and just as simple as Yayènia's, though without the feathers. On his wrists were black and blue cuff bracelets of leather, each studded with silver.

The two brothers stared resignedly at each other as their wives oohed and awed over the clothing.

"I never thought I would see you in a dress, Nia!" Tlonna exclaimed finally, having finished examining the braided garment.

"Yes, well, that is why we wear masks on this night," the warrior said, slipping hers on.

"Thank the gods for that," Losolin muttered, copying her. Suneelo nodded and did the same.

Tlonna shook her head and donned her mask as well, and the four rode to the inner city where the fête was being held. When they arrived, the party was already in full swing. Hundreds of people, all masked and costumed milled about, dancing, laughing, drinking, and cavorting. Guards took their horses, sending knowing glances to the two couples, identifying them by the animals. Revelers parted for them, picking up a vibe that ran through the crowd as the city's most influential couples headed for the center.

By the time they reached it, the crowd had grown as silent as possible with such a large gathering. Tlonna turned around, still masked, and pointed at the band upon a dais twenty yards away. It was a large band comprised mostly of elves, mixed with a few humans, and one dwarf, and consisted of violins, drums, flutes, trumpets, cellos, a piano, a few singers, and a new instrument called the guitar. Behind the dais was a curved wall made of lightweight wood that amplified the music across the city square. As the conductor caught sight of Tlonna's gesture, he raised his baton, and the music was struck up once more. Immediately, the people began to dance.

Suneelo grabbed Yayènia and spun her about, catching his wife off guard. She twisted away from him, and then came back, executing an elegant twirl that left Tlonna and Losolin staring. Suneelo caught her hand, stepped behind her, and they began to dance in earnest, a graceful waltz that took up half the dance floor. Tlonna and Losolin followed, more subdued as they did not know much dancing. Once, Yayènia whipped by her sister, the edges of her skirt running across Tlonna's back.

Losolin grinned, having fun in spite of himself. His hand tangled in Tlonna's hair and dragged her close and they twisted across the floor, oblivious to the awed stares directed at them. Their increased stamina allowed the elves to last much longer than the humans, who eventually cleared the dance floor to watch the fairer race. Tlonna, Losolin, Yayènia, and Suneelo were in the very middle, absorbed in their respective spouses.

Suneelo dragged his hand down Yayènia's back, grabbed her rear and spun her around. Yayènia lifted her leg and he caught her ankle, yanked her against him, and they danced off into the crowd. Tlonna pranced backward, pulling Losolin after her, until he threw her up in a toss that spun her into his arms.

It was nearing dawn when the band played their last song, a weeping slow song that brought even the most exhausted of couples back into the crowd. Tlonna caught sight of Miazie clutching Sodo close, her eyes closed as she laid her head against his chest. The tall alchemist had his arms around the little human's back, smiling serenely. The queen was surprised to see her friend there, knowing Miazie had little patience with large groups of people.

When the ballad ended, Losolin pulled back from Tlonna and kissed her with a passion that he rarely displayed in public. She dug her fingers into his leather-clad shoulders and kissed him back with all her fervor. When they parted, Yayènia and Suneelo were standing before them, radiant and relaxed, ice blue and indigo eyes heavy-lidded.

"Now it is the time of reflection and abeyance to the gods," the High Commander said calmly, the mask doing nothing to hide her identity. No one in the world could stand as Yayènia stood, a position of elegance and lethality all in one.

"What happens?" Losolin asked, blinking.

"We light these and make our respects to the dead," Suneelo replied, handing them white candles.

"Everyone will go to the graveyards where their loved ones are buried, and lay the candles at the base of the tombs. Then, at dawn, the spirits go back to Summerland, and we go to bed," Yayènia added.

Tlonna took her candle silently. She was thinking of her father, dead now a year. Her heart ached, but she smiled up at her husband. "Well, Ullor? Shall we go?"

"Mmm..." he murmured into her hair, and they found the guards and retrieved their horses.

"Who do you go to visit?" Tlonna asked of Yayènia and Suneelo, who looked startled at the question.

"We go to my...our father's grave," Suneelo replied, looking at Losolin. "And Selinia's."

"Where is his grave?" Losolin asked, realizing he had never gone to visit his dead parents.

"It is next to Mylea's, in the Fian Cemetery, down on Fian Street near the Harbor District. Would you like to come with me?"

Losolin looked at Tlonna, who smiled gently. "Yes," he replied to his brother.

So the four went first to Selinia's grave, Yayènia's foster-mother. The High Commander laid the white candle at the base of the tombstone, stood silently for a minute, her thoughts and pains private. Then they moved back onto Obsidian Way and traveled across the solemn city to Fian Street, a small side street edged up against the harbor markets.

Tlonna and Yayènia stood back by the horses as Suneelo and Losolin moved together to stand before their father's grave. Losolin knelt and tucked the candle between the two graves, Suneelo at the base of Loseen's. They stood shoulder to shoulder for a long while, two similar figures of identical height, looking down at the grave of their father and the king's mother.

Yayènia nudged Tlonna slightly, and they shared a smile of understanding. A wind was beginning to pick up, and it tugged at the females' skirts. The warrior muttered irritably, but Tlonna merely grabbed a fistful of hers and pulled it tight against her legs. Slowly, Losolin and Suneelo moved back to their wives, striking faces somber.

No one spoke as they rode to the royal cemetery to visit Dietirin's mausoleum. Tlonna felt the pain in her chest tighten as it came into view, and she lit her candle with a small Weave. Yet again, everyone stood back as she approached her father's tomb and knelt at the base.

"I miss you so much," she whispered, feeling a tear slide down her cheek. Hastily, the queen wiped it away and planted her candle in the ground.

The flame flickered in the wind, but stayed alive. Tlonna stayed there for several long minutes, thinking private thoughts of her father, wishing she had been given more time with him. After a while, she stood and moved back to her family. They all leaned against one another the way families do, taking and giving warmth and strength.

Yayènia and Suneelo broke away first, uncomfortable with the affection after so long of not having any. Without saying a word, they remounted and rode off, waving back to Tlonna and Losolin.

Slowly, the king and queen followed their example, and were back at the castle just as the sun was beginning its ascent. As soon as they hit the steps leading to their suite, they were tired. Once sequestered in their room, Losolin undressed Tlonna and she him, and they made love as the sun rose.

Eyin Thorn woke with a pounding headache, and he groaned loudly as he rolled out of his bed. Meradyn was asleep in an overstuffed chair outside his room, hair mussed, mouth open and snoring.

"Hey, get up," Eyin said, pushing his friend, squinting against the faint light leaking through the heavy curtains.

Meradyn swore, and then clutched his head in pain. He peeked up at his king and moaned. "What did we do?"

"We drank too much, stayed out too late, and slept too little," the young man replied, slowly shaking his head. "We may be in trouble with Queen Tlonna."

"Oh gods!" Meradyn gasped, and then squeezed his eyes shut against the pounding in his head. "Yayènia will kill me!"

At that moment, Marc and Jorunson stumbled into the suite, just as ill-looking as their friends. Jorunson held a note in his hand, and thrust it at Meradyn. "You lucky bastard," he muttered.

Meradyn took the piece of vellum and stared at the markings on it. All he understood was a symbol he knew stood for 'y'. "What does it say?" he asked.

"Your training is cancelled for today. Be ready tomorrow to make up for it. High Commander Yayènia er'Tiena," Jorunson replied sullenly. "We don't get a day off, though. *We* have to report to the Academy as usual."

Meradyn looked gleeful, slouching back down in the chair with his eyes closed. "Ahh... I like her more and more each day. Well, I am going to my room to get some real sleep. Have fun today!" he laughed softly and lurched out the door to his room next door.

"Some days I hate him," Marc complained, and then winced with the other three as the usual guard knocked on the door to notify them it was time to get up.

"He works just as hard as us, probably harder," Eyin reminded his friend, and then turned. "I'm going to wash and get ready. You two do what you want, but remember your own desires to learn."

Marc and Jorunson looked dolefully at each other, and then moved sluggishly to the room that they shared. Twenty minutes later, the three young Purheaens were moving down the front courtyard where a carriage awaited them. They rode through the misty morning, clutching their supplies and thinking of the miserable day ahead. Only Eyin was excited about what he might learn.

The four of them had joined in the Samhain celebration last night, and though they had retired much earlier than most, it was still an extremely late night for them. They had gotten drunk and caroused, and Meradyn had even disappeared with a girl at some point, retuning half an hour later with a sated look about him. Eyin had danced with Jalel, a Zeynuwnian girl from his Diplomacy class that he found intoxicating and exotic.

Jorunson swore he had seen the king and queen dancing some sensuous elf dance, but no one believed him. Marc had spent much of the time standing at the foot of the band dais, staring at the various instruments in wonder.

Eyin rested his head against the carriage wall and dreamed of the things he would do once he was back in Purheae, a bona fide king.

He had never expected such a thing could ever happen, though he had always been told that he was a born leader, the first in many generations. His parents had taught him as best as they could, giving him lessons on self-worth, honesty, fairness, and such. But now he had been given an opportunity to really learn, to be around those who led with greatness and he did not intend to waste it.

He was proud of Meradyn as well. His friend had proven to be a good choice for a military commander, even the mad warrior thought so. Jorunson and Marc...well, he would have to wait and see if they turned out to be good choices. So far, they had been a little disappointing, but Jorunson's literacy had improved, and Marc had learned a few of the written words.

The carriage pulled up in front of the Academy of Blackhaven and the three hung-over humans climbed out and walked up the steps, a few minutes early. They were always early, Eyin had commanded it, and if he was nothing else, he was the leader. Their first class of the day was Basics, where they learned mathematics, reading, writing, and a number of other random subjects that most children grew up learning.

Eyin sat down on the gray cushion he always occupied and readied his things. Professor Reetuh Olosyn walked in as he pulled out his tablet.

"Good morning Eyin, Marc, Jorunson. How are you this day?" she asked, looking more than a little tired.

"We are well, Professor. Did you go to the party last night?" Eyin asked, smiling up at her. He liked Professor Olosyn a lot. She was from Arseninis, and seemed to know everything. The woman was gray haired and short, but she was kind enough to the inept Purheaens.

"Unfortunately. How did you find Samhain in Blackhaven City?"

"It was more than I ever expected. In Purheae, we don't have any celebrations except for the winter and summer solstices. What are we going to study today?" Eyin replied, excited.

Olosyn blinked at him, always baffled by his eagerness. "We are continuing with subtraction, Hindarün grammar, and the story of Ishtar and the Giant."

Eyin grinned, looked at Jorunson, who smiled back, and then the other students began trickling into the class. It was a small group, mostly newcomers to the city and education, like them, and a few younglings getting a head start on their education.

The day passed slowly for the hung-over young men, and when lunch arrived, they gratefully ordered a heavy lunch from a street vendor. Tlonna had given them each an allowance for such things, and they took it happily, having no geld of their own.

"What do you think we will learn in Alchemy?" Marc ventured, chewing on a steaming meat pie.

Eyin shrugged. "Sodo never gives anything up. I did see him last night, dancing with Lady Miazie. Do you think it's weird that they are elf and human?"

Jorunson frowned. "I think they must be insane to even think of making such a thing work. No one seems to care much, though. They're all the best of friends."

"You sound bitter," Eyin replied, squinting at his companion. Marc nodded.

"It is just frustrating!" the man said, sniffing. "I don't see us ever reaching their level, Eyin, no matter what you say."

The young king studied his friend for a moment. "You underestimate me, Meradyn, Marc, and yourself, Jor. Look at what we have already learned, and we have only been here two weeks. Look at Meradyn, hitting the commander in the face like that! How can you still be so doubting?"

"I'm a realist, Eyin. I know we are not up to the same level as these elves. They have centuries of living on us!"

"Humans have fared just as well in other kingdoms," the king replied, finishing his sandwich. "Remember what Professor Tarsin said about King Demetrius of Kajgenia? That he is the most successful and liked king of the human race ever? How about King Tyular of Arseninis? He rose to the throne too young, and unprepared, when his father died, but now he is doing very well."

Jorunson made a face. "And what of Emperor Tahi-tat of Zeynuwn? King Athelias of Talenias, King Richard of Schelum? King Jaryn and Queen Sybilla of Kismath? Eyin, they're all dead or corrupt!"

"Tahi-tat is neither, he is merely a ruler of a different system than anywhere else in Nymyños," Eyin corrected. "Besides, being dead doesn't make you a terrible leader, it makes you dead."

"Roluf Gwemheoad?" Jorunson said quietly, looking at his friend out the corner of his eye.

Eyin's face contorted with rage, but he controlled it quickly. "Gwemheoad and his offspring are not human. They are blights of nature, cruel and sadistic demons from the pit of the ninth hell itself."

"He was human, Eyin, and you know it. What of these Rahlan's we have heard about? I even heard one of the nobles at the castle say that Prince Haydyn is Midian Rahlan's son, which would mean Queen Tlonna fucked him."

Eyin struck his friend across the face hard enough to knock him to the ground. The king was breathing hard, the air hissing through his teeth. "Don't you ever say that again!"

Marc, who had been standing silently during the whole exchange, grabbed Eyin's arms and held him back as Jorunson got to his feet, glaring. "Why don't you ask her, then? Find out the truth!"

The young king swore, yanked away from Marc, and strode off, furious. Jorunson and Marc exchanged glances, but they returned to the Academy for Alchemy. Eyin did not turn up.

"Tlonna, Eyin is here to see you, and he looks upset," Miazie said, coming into the queen's office.

The elf rubbed her face. She and Losolin, along with everyone else in the city, had gotten only a few hours of sleep. "Do you know why?"

The Belau shook her head. "No, but it is time for his class with Sodo, and I know Eyin would not skip for anything superfluous."

Tlonna sighed. "Send him in, then."

Miazie left the office, and soon after Eyin walked in, looking irritated indeed.

"Eyin, what can I do for you? Should you not be in class with Professor Sodo?"

The human dropped into a chair and looked at her sullenly. She noticed that the knuckles on one hand were raw. "Did you lie with Midian Rahlan?" he asked suddenly.

Tlonna blinked, caught off guard and shocked. "No, I never lay with him."

"Then Prince Haydyn is not his son?"

The Magin Queen narrowed her eyes, wondering. "He is, but I never lay with Midian Rahlan. He captured me, held me prisoner for months, and raped me repeatedly. Am I to be accused for this?"

Eyin looked ashen, but he held her gaze. "No. It was something that Jorunson said, and I could not think about anything else. Queen Tlonna..."

"You may call me Tlonna, Eyin."

"...do you think that I will ever be a good king? Do you think Purheae, and my people, will ever be more than an uncivilized group of tribes and frightened elders?"

"I believe that if you have the heart, the determination, and the fortitude, you can make Purheae whatever you want it to be. You have, as I once said, the makings of a great leader. It is up to you what form that greatness comes in."

"Can you be sure?"

Tlonna smiled. "I can be sure of nothing, my young friend, but I do know that you are the one who will lead Purheae to triumph, or destruction. You, and those three companions of yours. You must not judge yourself by the victories and downfalls of others, but rather by your own. Make your own decisions, and act upon them. You will fail, and you will succeed, but it is in the manner that you do both that will mark you as a great king... or a terrible one."

"But...what do *you* think?"

"Of you?"

"Yes."

Tlonna smiled. "I think you should go back to the Academy."

Eyin stared at her. "That is not what I meant."

"I know. Give me more time to make a decision on that. Go on. Oh, and Eyin?" she said as he got up and moved toward the door. "Do not hit your friends for my sake. I can take what judgments and accusations they can make, and I will deal with them. All right?"

"Yes my lady," Eyin replied, and left the room.

Tlonna watched the empty doorway for a long moment, thinking of the question he had asked her. The truth of the matter was that she did not know what to think of the ambitious human. Shaking her head, she went back to the contracts on her desk.

Sithian too sat at his desk, the only place he truly felt any power, and also where he felt the chains of responsibility. Despite his disdain for the lives of everyone around him, the matters of kinghood were still his to deal with. Angry and petulant, the Magin leaned back in his chair, studying the ancient parchment in his hands. It was something he had been mulling over for many days now, a power that could possibly destroy the hierarchy of his enemies. Finally succumbing to the need of action, he summoned his sister.

When Rhiannan strode into the office, she glared down at him. "What do you want?"

"I hear your petty little attempt to disrupt the Ewôsdírns went badly. Poor Marin, she was a pretty little thing," Sithian crooned, eyeing his sister.

"Well, at least I tried something rather than sit in my room all day brooding about things I can't have," Rhiannan spat, still glaring.

Sithian chuckled quietly, glancing back down at the parchment, his mind made up. "How true your words are, Anna. I have been a child, sulking and pathetic, but the time has come for a change. I have a plan that will truly behead the powers of Blackhaven."

Anna's interest sparked and she sat down unbidden, not noticing as she did the triumphant and cruel fire in her brother's sapphire eyes. "What is it?"

"Oh, the details would bore you, but let's say that when in action, it will force one of our mother's closest friends to betray her. See, one thing I have discounted and ignored all this time is her need for companionship and trust. My plan will see to it that both are betrayed, irreversibly."

Rhiannan saw the nefarious glimmer in Sithian's eyes, but she paid it little heed. "How? Simple infiltration will not do it. Tlonna and her group are tightly bound, no new friend will be able to get their confidences quickly. Your plan will take months, perhaps even years."

"That is why I am going to use an old friend, a trusted friend...a beloved friend," the young king said, his voice crackling with menace.

"Who?"

"Oh, you need not know the details, as I said. Besides, you will be there every step of the way."

Anna jerked her back straight, staring at her brother, suspicious. "What do you mean?"

"The Weave calls for a host body, one without any magical abilities, and one of the same gender as the target. You are going to provide me with such a body."

The princess's heart began to race, fear creeping in on her. "I can find someone sure enough."

"No, no," Sithian whispered, unable to contain his grin. "You *are* the body."

"What?" Anna cried, confused and worried.

Sithian stood and moved over behind his sister, covertly drawing forth a wicked dagger, pulsating with dark blue magic. Before Rhiannan could completely turn to keep an eye on him, he rammed the weapon deep into her side, piercing her kidney. She went taut, cold eyes snapping wide in agony. Her long black tresses jerked wildly as she tried to fight off her insane sibling.

"Anna, you've become a bit of a problem, and right now I don't need any more problems. Did you know Learia is pregnant? You are no longer needed as an heir if I die, and your failure to produce a child with Orlando proves your worthlessness. And now, I have come upon this ancient Weave set down by our ancestor Sithian, and I need a female body, bereft of life and power. This dagger within you right now is taking all of your magic, and storing it within the blade. I will then use it on myself, and transfer your power to mine. How do you like that?"

Sithian stared down at Rhiannan's head, but she didn't answer. He realized then she had stopped moving seconds ago, and now lay slumped against the chair, dead. The dagger burned in his hand, and he withdrew it, drawing a breath between his teeth in ecstasy as the blade now writhed in brown flames.

Muttering the archaic words to complete the Weave, Sithian dragged the dagger down his belly and watched in fascination as the magic was sucked into his body. For a minute he felt the two powers within him fighting until his greater magic triumphed, and converted Rhiannan's. His limbs, which had gone rigid with the strain, loosened and he threw his head back, laughing softly.

Then the reason he had killed his sister came back to him, and he knelt by her side, carefully summoning up the image of his intended target. He pulled several strands of hair from a pouch on his belt, along with a few dry pieces of flesh, and held them in his hand, a writhing ball of blue flames slowly melting them into nothingness. The room fairly glowed with the magic he called upon, and Rhiannan's corpse twitched violently, her hair lengthening and paling. After nearly an hour, Sithian sat back, winded, and examined his work. The female before him stared back, mindless and yet very much alive.

The Magin smiled faintly, and began the next set of Weaves, invading the empty mind with his desires and instructions.

Chapter 26

To Take a Punch

Once the city had been restored to its usual pace, Tlonna found herself bombarded by petitioners and the like. Haydyn remarked every now and again on seeing Eyin and his companions at the academy, or Meradyn at the Military Compound. The young prince seemed unsure of the four men, always wary of their intentions, though he, similar to Yayènia, grudgingly liked Meradyn.

Tlonna was in the private library when her son walked in. The queen was looking for a book on the Stynbek reign, hoping to find some clue about the kidnappers, for it had been discovered that they were not of any known race, though definitely humanoid.

"What do you think of the Purheaens?" Haydyn asked without preamble.

Tlonna turned, blinking at her son in surprise, her hands still on a section of books. "I am not yet sure. Why?"

The prince frowned and flopped into a chair, lacing his fingers behind his head. "I saw them at the celebration."

"And?"

"They were roaring drunk and loud, like a bunch of mindless bums," Haydyn snorted, shaking his curly head.

"So were a lot of people, Haydyn. That does not make them bad or stupid, it makes them humans. Why are you so concerned about them?"

Her son shrugged. "I don't know. Perhaps the fact that they are from Purheae, and have ambitions that could endanger Blackhaven in the future."

"Those ambitions have not been ignored, love," Tlonna said, taking a seat across from Haydyn. "There is a reason Yayènia is training Meradyn the way that she is, and that I am so willing to have them educated here. You see, if they learn the way that we did, that you are, then they will have loyalties to Blackhaven, and to this throne, thereby removing most of the issues. Do not think I am blinded because they are young. I know the threat Eyin and his people can pose to us later on."

"And what about now?"

"Now? I see no issue with them now," Tlonna replied, frowning slightly. "You are not normally this paranoid, Haydyn. Is there something specific that is bothering you?"

The half-blood leaned on the table, not looking at his mother. "Meradyn bedded a girl on Samhain."

"Was it consensual?" the queen asked softly.

"I can't be sure, but I believe so. It just bothers me that they have been here less than a month, and already have gotten that close to our citizens," Haydyn replied.

"They are young men, just as you are, Hayd. You bedded Lady Berik, and I know that you have been with a few of the other nobles as well. Do not give me that look."

Haydyn hastily wiped the scowl from his face. "Do you really think me too mentally young to do such a thing?"

Tlonna sucked in a breath. "I believe that you do not yet fully comprehend the consequences of your actions. What if one of them got with child? You would have an heir, Haydyn, and her family would probably demand that you marry her. What if she were already married, as Lady Berik was about to be? What if the child were sickly, or wrong? What if you attain the true affections of one, and you do not return the feeling? Do you see what I am saying? You have aged years since being brought here, but you are still a child, and it is not a bad thing. It is something we can rectify, and you should not be ashamed of it, but you must accept it."

"I do, but I think that I am older than you do. I have learned many things, and I know that I am mature for my age."

"You are, but my love, you are only three years old, still," Tlonna insisted quietly, grabbing his hand. "I know we have not had the chance to deal with this, and I swear to you, I am your mother, and I will always be here for you. Please do not be upset with me. I love you, Haydyn, you are the flesh of my flesh, and even though you were forced to age insanely fast, you retained your goodness, and your conscience, something that cannot be said of your siblings."

Haydyn made a face. "And yet they rule a kingdom, where the people bow and scrape for them, they have the influence to make war on an entire race, an entire continent. I sit on a throne, but I am just a title. I have no real authority, people barely recognize me in the streets. I have done nothing of note, nothing to put my name on the people's lips."

Tlonna leaned back, releasing his hand. "Sithian and Rhiannan are cruel and sadistic, they feed on the terror of others. Everything they do will be noted down in the histories as wrong. What is it you wish for? Do you have any ideas as to what you would like to do in order to be known?"

The prince stared at her. "You needn't be so harsh! I'm serious!"

"I am too, Haydyn. Did you have something you wanted to do? If so, tell me, and we will work on getting it done."

The two stared at each other for a long moment, judging the other's sincerity. Finally, Haydyn took a deep breath. "I want to open a library."

Tlonna blinked again. "There are already libraries around the city, lots, in fact. And this one, and the second floor library as well."

"I know, but those are all restricted areas, where you have to have a membership, or nobility to use, or be a resident of the castle. I want to open a library to the public, where they can learn to read without paying, without being looked down on for their ignorance."

"It is a noble idea, son, but how do you propose we pay for this library of yours? Where are we going to get the books, and the tutors? What about the building itself? These kinds of things take lots of geld, and we do not have it at the moment. Everything has gone toward the army, and the defenses, and the rebuilding of the city itself."

Haydyn rubbed his face. "I know, but isn't there something we could do? I have a trust, don't I? I have geld of my own."

"Not enough to do this, Haydyn. This will have to be taken from the people's taxes, if it is something you truly want to do."

"It is, but I will not make them pay for it, however indirectly. I will find a way. If I do, will you sign what needs to be signed, and whatnot?"

Tlonna studied her son a moment longer, then nodded. "Yes, I will. Now, is that all you have against Eyin and his companions?"

Haydyn thought a moment, and then stood. "For now, I suppose. But I will be watching them."

"Do what you have to, Haydyn."

He smiled faintly, and left the library, his thoughts turning. Tlonna watched him go, also thinking. Slowly, she reminded herself of her purpose in the library, and resumed looking for books on the Stynbeks.

The next day, Yayènia resumed her training with Meradyn, and Eyin refused to speak to Jorunson or Marc. It made for awkward classes, but they got through without incident. Haydyn and Eyin were two of the seven in Professor Hered's Diplomacy class, and they eyed each other uneasily. The two young men sat across the room from each other, with Marc and Jorunson in the middle, along with an ambassador's son between Marc and Eyin.

Hered, a rotund human with a bald head and shiny face noticed the rift between the prince and the king, and laughed inwardly. How apt it was for this class that two future rulers were at odds right now. He decided to work on it.

"Prince Haydyn, King Eyin, would you please come and stand up front?" he asked, making the two stare at him incredulously. "Now."

Reluctantly, they obeyed. "Good, now, I want you to debate something. How about...a hunter has crossed the boundary, and killed a deer in Purheae, when he is from Blackhaven. What do you do?"

The two glared at each other, unable to help themselves. Haydyn was the first to respond. "Find out why he crossed the border in the first place, and if the reason is understandable, give the animal back to ..." he glanced at Eyin, his mouth thinning, "to the people of the area."

"And if it isn't?" Hered asked, looking at the king as well.

Eyin stared at Haydyn, glanced at the others in the room, and then back to the prince. The half-blood folded his arms. "Give the deer back, and place the offender under arrest for three days."

"Very good, Prince Haydyn. King Eyin? What would be your judgment on the hunter?"

The tall human looked again at Hered. "I would kill him."

The class gasped, shocked. Even Haydyn looked disturbed. Hered cleared his throat and shifted his feet. "Would that not be a bit hasty?"

Eyin shrugged. "Such an act would be considered theft, in my country. A theft as large as an animal is punishable by death. Otherwise, I would chop off one of his hands and send him back here."

"You're barbaric!" the ambassador's son gasped, now leaning away from Marc as though the other might reach out and strike him.

"We're clan people, and without harsh rules, what society we have would fall apart," Jorunson countered, blushing.

Eyin was glaring so hard at Haydyn now, Hered feared the two would soon come to blows. "Gentlemen, gentlemen, sit down. I believe a lecture is in order, now!" he said, stepping between them.

"Professor, might I intervene?" someone said from the back, and the eight occupants of the room turned to look.

Miazie was leaning against the door, her arms crossed beneath her chest, raven hair done up in an intricate bun. She wore a simple dress of dark green silk, but over her shoulders was a long, narrow stole of black and silver, the stole of Royal Adviser. The students gaped at her, exempting Haydyn, who blinked at his mother's friend in confusion.

Hered bowed as much as his bulk would allow. "Lady Miazie, of course. We are honored by your presence."

Miazie smiled as she walked to the fore of the classroom. It was a small room, filled with books of edict, history, and law. On the floor were several cushions and lap desks, and on the slightly raised platform, a lectern from which Hered taught his students. The Belau came level with the professor, and inclined her head slightly.

"I am here by the Queen's wishes. The education of Prince Haydyn and King Eyin, and his fellow learners, indeed, all of the students, is of utmost importance to her. I do not mean to usurp your position, Professor, only to give a lecture today, and others every Thursday for the next few weeks, but those will be held at the castle. All are invited to come."

"We will all attend," Hered announced, eyeing his students, who stared back at him.

Miazie smiled again, and took a position at the podium, studying the young people before her. Though she herself was rather young, her experiences had made her elderly in wisdom, at least. She met Haydyn's gaze, and had to stop herself from frowning. The prince was furious at Eyin, still, and Tlonna had told Miazie of the conversation they had had. Eyin and the prince could easily become a serious issue.

"You are all here because you are each in a position of attaining power and titles, or at least some authority over others. You may not be aware of the fact that your Professor Hered was once, years back, part of the Blackhaven City Council, holding the title now held by Lord Jayce Blackwell, Royal Diplomat. He gave up his position in order to teach, and he has done a remarkable job thus far." She smiled at Hered, who was blushing furiously at the compliment. "Now, I tell you this because Queen Tlonna wishes you all to pay attention to him, as this is one of the most important subjects a young politician learns.

"There are different laws in each province, some more adamant than others, as illustrated by the vast differences brought to the fore by Prince Haydyn and King Eyin. Blackhaven law is strict, but fair, when such a thing is possible. Purheae is indeed peopled by clans, but it is soon to become a solid kingdom once again, as it was two thousand years ago. But look to Kismath or Schelum, once great kingdoms, now nothing more than struggling villages, if that. The times are changing, as they must, and you need to be ready to deal with many different ways of life.

"Queen Tlonna has sent envoys to many of the provinces in the hopes of forming the Great Nymyñosian Alliance, the strongest ever, if it succeeds." Miazie continued, highlighting the importance of maintaining a strong bond between the kingdoms, and indeed the races, of Nymyños. There was a common enemy, the sadistic and cruel Zaedicans to the north, the brutal and racist Seadueni elves, and the corrupt and ignorant Talenians to the east. What was left were the scattered remnants of the Elven people, the reclusive Dwarven communities, and the persecuted Men all across Nymyños.

The Twelve Lands were at war, she intoned, receiving startled and terrified looks from her small audience. Yes, they were at odds, even though most of the rulers did not accept it. Queen Tlonna and King Losolin, along with King Demetrius of Kajgenia, and King Tyular of Arseninis were working toward aligning the much weaker kingdoms, so that the good and innocent people of Nymyños stood a chance of the looming wars.

An hour later, the seven students and their teacher were shell-shocked by the Belau's revelations, horrified by the cruelties extended because of ignorance and racism, saddened by the injustice of war, and bolstered by the strength and determination of their rulers. Eyin and Haydyn eyed each other now with a small amount of consideration in their hard gazes.

As Hered and Miazie conversed, and the others in the class prepared to leave, Eyin moved over to where Haydyn knelt, gathering his things.

"I know of your parentage, and your siblings. I know that you were born of the bloodline that destroyed my people, on both sides. Can you blame me for mistrusting you?" he said quietly to the prince.

Haydyn stood slowly. "Yes. Just because my blood is of Roluf Gwemheoad and Jair, it does not make me one of them. Just because my father was the master of genocide and a conduit of evil you choose to hate me, even though I chose to leave with my mother, to lead a better life than that of my father or siblings, you find me abhorrent and unfit. What of you, Eyin Thorn, King of Purheae?"

"What of me?" the human asked, slightly humbled by the other's words.

"You come from an unknown heritage, a people of tribal law and order, you know nothing of the ways of others. How are you any more worthy than I?"

"I am not, but I am trying to be at least equal. You have the benefit of growing up, no matter how quickly, under the tutelage of rulers. You live in a castle with all your needs catered to. I may be king, but I am king of less than a hundred people, mostly old and ignorant. I have never been with a woman, I have never earned and spent my own geld, and I have never worn fine clothing. I can barely read, I know few letters, but I can track a rabbit. I do not speak the languages of the three main races with intelligence, but I can lure a deer out of hiding by speaking to it in its own tongue. I can do these things because my lifestyle demands it of me. Everything I have, I have either made, caught, or found. Everything you have, you have been given."

Haydyn scowled, standing with his back rigid. They were of a like height, but they were mirror opposites. The prince was fair and blessed with elfin beauty, thin and wiry. The king was dark and broad-jawed, muscled and solid. Blue eyes clashed with green, each laced with inky lashes that made women envious or lustful.

"I have had to fight for a lot of things, including my life, Eyin. Do not think me weak or untried," Haydyn finally said, folding his arms.

"I don't, merely spoiled," Eyin replied.

The prince shook his head. "It is true I have been given most of what I own, but I am not spoiled. Do you think having Tlonna as a mother, and Losolin as a stepfather is easy?"

Eyin frowned, thinking about the king and queen. They were tough, inside and out, and did not seem to put up with much. "No."

Haydyn laughed shortly, quietly, and then noticed Jorunson and Marc staring at him and their friend. "And what of them?" he asked, nodding toward the two.

Eyin turned his head and caught sight of his companions. "They are here because they have skills no one else in Purheae has. They are good men, but this is not something they ever envisioned. It is for that reason that I am king, and they are not. I have the ambition, the mind, and the heart to lead my people from their seclusion and ignorance. They will be my foundation, along with Meradyn."

"Meradyn will be a good warrior," Haydyn replied, thinking of the other Purheaen. "Yayènia likes him, which is unusual in and of itself."

"She is...an interesting creature," Eyin said, forgetting that he was supposed to hate the man he was talking to.

Haydyn smiled, catching Miazie's approving look. "That she is, but a powerful and righteous one too. How about a truce, Eyin?"

Caught off guard, the Purheaen stared at the prince, blinking. "What?"

"A truce, you and I, for now."

"Oh, yeah, sure. A truce," Eyin agreed, sounding a bit confused, but he smiled, a quick twisting of the lips that made Haydyn think he wasn't used to it.

The half-elf stuck out his hand and they shook, ignoring the baffled looks from Marc and Jorunson. Miazie and Hered shared a look as well, but it was one of profound hope and relief.

When the prince left the small room for his next class, Eyin turned to his two companions. "We have enough to worry about right now without making enemies of ourselves and the only allies we have. Agreed?"

Jorunson's lips twisted, the left side of his face bruised and swollen from Eyin's fist. Marc hesitated, and then nodded. "I agree," he said, looking his king directly in the eye, unaware that it was improper to do so. Eyin smiled slightly, also unaware.

"Jor?"

The literate one of the group looked away, his jaw tightening. He sucked in a deep breath and let it out, and then looked back at Eyin. "Fine. But I get to hit you back."

The young monarch did not even blink at the demand. It was the way of his people to do such things. He merely lifted his chin and looked at Jorunson, waiting. The man clenched his fists, and Eyin clasped his hands behind his back.

Miazie looked over Hered's shoulder and saw Eyin gripping his hands behind his back, chin raised, and staring at Jorunson, who was preparing himself for something. The Belau frowned, and Hered turned to seek out what held her attention. Realization dawned on her when she saw Jorunson draw his right arm back, and a cry was on her lips before she could stop herself.

"No!"

But it was too late. Jorunson's fist clipped Eyin hard on the side of his face, the sound of bone and flesh contacting with steeled force. The king's face jerked upward and to the side, but he stood his ground, bending back only a little, his arms clenching tight. Blood spurted from his mouth as his lips were cut open on his teeth, but his eyes never even flickered and he uttered no sound.

Miazie stared in open-mouthed shock, unable to think of a reason as to why the young man would punch his king. But more so, she was stunned by Eyin's reaction. He had taken the blow as though it meant little to him. He was now wiping the blood from his face with the back of his hand as Jorunson massaged his knuckles, which must ache like the nine hells. Then Eyin cricked his neck, rolled his shoulders, and bent down to pick up his things. The three young men walked out of the room as though nothing had just occurred, leaving the two adults absolutely mystified.

Later that evening, Miazie and Tlonna stood in the larger of the two lecture halls within the castle as students, residents, and teachers filed inside, finding seats and glancing at the two females at the podium. Yayènia strolled out from behind a pillar where she had been instructing a few guards on the security. Muted gasps of recognition and amazement filled the hall as the warrior stepped up to converse with the queen and advisor. When Erdwyf and Losolin appeared, there were cries of delight.

Tlonna shook her head and stifled a laugh at the reactions, wondering what the people were thinking. Yayènia was not even in her armor, but rather a pair of snug gray pants, a blue tunic, belted at the waist, and her vambraces and swords. She had yet to get her twin katan back, so she still wore the old sword with the elephunt on the hilt. Erdwyf was also in normal clothes, instead of her usual elegant dresses. While she still wore the band of office on her bicep, the High Advisor wore only a simple white dress, belted with a black foulard. Tonight was casual, even Tlonna was in a pair of black pants and a light pink belted tunic.

So, she wondered at their pleasure.

"Bunch of nuts," Yayènia growled, though her sister heard the laughter in her voice. When the lecture hall had filled, Miazie turned to her gathered friends. "Should we start now?"

"Yes," Tlonna nodded, and subtly shooed everyone away. Losolin, Erdwyf, and Yayènia disappeared like smoke, fading from the small stage to take up inconspicuous positions. The audiences murmured slightly, and then went silent as their queen stepped up to the lectern.

"Good evening, you have been invited to this place tonight for a singular purpose. Royal Advisor Miazie Paron will soon take my place to tell you about progressions in this kingdom, and others all across Nymyños. I have asked her to do this because I believe you have the right to know what goes on behind closed doors. You have a right, and a responsibility, to be informed about the goings on of rulers like myself, and others throughout the land. There are changes and trepidations coming to our beautiful land, and I wish for you all to be prepared and educated on such things. What you hear tonight is not secret, and I want each of you to spread this about the city. Feel free to question anything, and also to comment. I now give you over to Advisor Miazie, and hope that you take something away from this night."

Tlonna stepped away to silence, as hundreds of pairs of eyes were trained on her, and she moved next to Losolin. He stood in the shadows of the stage, leaning against the wall, a few guards around him, scanning the now muttering crowd. Miazie stood before the podium, arranging her sheet of notes on the lectern before her.

As Miazie began to speak, elaborating on the things she had spoken of in Eyin and Haydyn's class earlier, Tlonna watched her people. They were, for the most part, silent. A few leaned over to discuss a comment to their neighbors, and then were quiet again. When her friend brought up the impending war, the murmuring began anew, this time more worried and animated, until the Belau stopped talking, waiting for silence.

In the crowd sat Eyin and his companions, including Meradyn, still sweaty and dirty from his day of training. Tlonna watched them the most, having been told of the altercation between Haydyn and Eyin, as well as Jorunson. They were all four silent, their dark eyes riveted on the slender woman at the pulpit. Once, Eyin bent his head to listen to Meradyn, nodded once, and returned his attention returned to Miazie.

The queen was pleased, and as the lecture wore on, no one left, but a few more people trickled in, standing in the back. Mostly, they were people Tlonna had seen about the castle on a daily basis, resident nobles or servants on their break. At one point, Feorien and his wife, Sharntun, slipped in, and then, a while later, they slipped back out.

Miazie's words faded from her mind as the queen began to ponder recent events. The two odd attacks against the throne, both easily thwarted. Now, Marin was dead by her own hand, and the bodies of the kidnappers had revealed nothing. Nothing, that is, Tlonna remembered suddenly, but a single medallion, small and easily missed.

One of the guards who had been responsible for stripping and searching the bodies had found it embedded into one of the men's hip, apparently the skin had been burned and the medallion pressed into the ruined skin so that it would heal over it. It had been grotesque. Tlonna slipped her hand inside her pocket and found the medallion with her fingers. Bringing it out, she studied it. It was pewter, and the size of her thumb pad. Grimacing, she rubbed off a piece of dried flesh, trying not to think about it.

The symbol was of nothing she recognized, not really any tangible form at all, but rather a series of lines and squiggles that made no sense to her whatsoever. Tlonna had yet to show anyone else, having been preoccupied with Eyin, Samhain, and the other minor things going on about the city.

Then, suddenly, for just a second, the emblem flashed. It was not a flash of light or reflection, but a flash *from* the medallion. Tlonna brought it close to her face, trying to see what had happened. She rubbed her thumb over it again, then pressed it between her fingers, trying to get it to repeat the action. But the medallion stayed cold and silver. Had she imagined it?

Her instincts told her no, she had really seen the flash. Looking up at Miazie, then glancing at the crowd riveted on the Belau, Tlonna moved furtively into the shadows, slipping from

Losolin's side, and out of the hall. Stepping into the corridor, two guards turned and saluted her.

"Queen Tlonna. Is there something wrong?" one of them asked, frowning slightly.

"No. Take me to where the kidnappers are," she said quietly, once again pocketing the medallion.

"The dead ones, your Highness?"

"What other kidnappers do you know of?" Tlonna snapped, and immediately regretted it.

The guard blanched, and then turned on his heel. "Right this way, Queen Tlonna," he said, and strode away.

The other guard watched his companion go, and then started after. Tlonna held up her hand. "No, stay and keep your post."

The guard went back, and Tlonna hastened after the other. They descended the two flights of stairs, crossed the foyer, and entered the south Guard Tower. They climbed up the obsidian steps that wound around the walls of the tower. At each level, they passed an opening in the floor, catching either the startled looks of guards or the sullen looks of prisoners. There were not many of the latter, but those that were watched Tlonna with hateful eyes. She followed the guard all the way to the sixth level, only two from the top, and they stepped onto the floor.

The queen swallowed against the sight, closing her eyes for a small respite. The bodies of the five were laid out on tables, naked and shaved. They were not elves, obvious by the need to shave them, but they were not quite human either. Tlonna figured them to be some sort of hybrid.

"Where are those responsible for these bodies?" she asked the guard.

He shrugged. "Probably down in the common room. Shall I retrieve them?"

"Please." Tlonna said, turning away. She heard him leave, and went immediately to the side of the man with the open wound on his hip. "Who are you?" she whispered to the corpse, pulling out the emblem.

He had been a strange looking fellow. Neither young or old, rather androgynous, and heavily muscled. Tlonna stared down at him for a long time before she heard the approach of others. Stepping away from the table, the queen looked up, waiting. Three guards came into the room, followed by her escort. She dismissed him, and then turned to the others.

"What have you ascertained from these fellows?" she asked without preamble.

The oldest of the guards sighed. "Not much, I'm afraid. We would have told someone had we found anything."

"You still have no clue on their race, or history? No...tattoos, no more embedded items?" Tlonna pushed, showing them the medallion.

"No. Well, actually, we have an idea on the race. They have elfin blood in them, we've decided, because of their faces. Elfin and human, but, my Lady, we're only guards, not Healers or people of knowledge. I would suggest having someone like that look at them. We know where to search for things, and how to extract them, but that's about it."

"I understand," Tlonna said, her shoulders slumping. "What about this? You said when you gave it to me that you had never seen such a symbol. How about now? Does *anything* look familiar? Is it similar to any sign you have ever seen?"

The three stepped forward and took the emblem from the Magin's outstretched hand. They murmured over it, turned it over in their hands, held it up to their faces. The middling guard, a tall man of around thirty suddenly sucked in a breath, making Tlonna's heart race.

"What is it?" she asked, moving closer.

"I recognize this part, but that's it. See, this horizontal squiggle, intercepted by these three slanted lines?"

Everyone nodded. The man continued. "I was in Talenias a few years back, just before the siege of Blackhaven began, and I saw it. It is a rudimentary form of their religious symbol, sunrays coming over hills. I'd swear my life on it."

Tlonna frowned. "I had a feeling Athelias had something to do with it. Anything else?"

They studied it for a while longer, and then gave up. "No, nothing."

Cursing quietly, the queen walked back to the bodies and stared at them for a long time. "Where did they come from? What are they? Why did they make such a pathetic attempt at hijacking the kingdom?"

The guards looked at each other, wondering whether she expected answers. Then the older guard started as a thought came to him. "My Lady, remember during the Alchemian battle, there were all those mercenaries from neither Zaedic nor Nymyños?"

Tlonna nodded, looking up at him.

"What if these fellows came from the same place? What if they are not native to our world at all?"

"What, you mean like spirits?" one of the guards asked.

"No, as in from another land, Gerard! Three years ago, no one believed that Zaedic existed. Now look, we have trade vessels going there. There must be more out there. The Dwarves came from another continent, the Elves came from another island."

Tlonna studied the excited guard with narrowed eyes, thinking. It was very possible. They were certainly not from any explored area in Nymyños, which was nearly everywhere, so the fact that they were not Nymyñosians in the first place would make sense.

"But what about the Talenian symbol? Why would it be there if they are not from Nymyños?" she asked suddenly, looking to him.

He shrugged. "Perhaps King Athelias bought them, mercenaries, perhaps. My Lady, if I may, I would suggest finding every book on symbols and emblems and see if any other parts jump out at you."

"I will. Thank you gentlemen, you can go back to whatever you were doing before," Tlonna replied, moving toward the door, her mind already turning.

By the time she reached the lecture hall again, Miazie was finishing her speech, and people were beginning to stand, clapping. Tlonna slipped inside and moved to Losolin's side. He eyed her through narrowed lids.

"Where have you been?"

"Elsewhere," she evaded, clapping along with everyone else.

Losolin snorted, but he refrained from asking her more questions as the audience filtered out of the room, dozens of different conversations creating a loud buzz. Miazie stepped off the small stage and joined her friends by the wall.

"I think it went well. I think that they will spread the message fast, and soon everyone will be aware of the things going on. I'm really pleased," the Belau said, smiling at Erdwyf, who had come forward from the shadows.

"I agree. They seemed to be very open and accepting to what was said. Perhaps this time, we will have more warning," said the High Advisor.

"Warning for what, Erdwyf? Do you think we are going to be overrun again?" demanded Yayènia, gripping her longblade in an earnest attempt at controlling her temper.

Her fey-faced friend turned slightly, eyeing the weapon. "I only think of what might be, and what has been. Will you attack me for that, Nia?"

Yayènia yanked her hand away from the sword. "No, but do not think me ill-prepared, Erdwyf. I have a much larger network of scouts all within the forest, and without, than I did before. We will not be caught off guard again."

"As you say," the High Advisor replied blandly, and strode away.

The warrior's lip curled in irritation, but she stayed planted beside Tlonna. "Where did you go?"

Tlonna scowled at her. "To the Guard Tower. Have any of you seen this before? This symbol?" she said after a withering glance at Losolin, pulling out the medallion.

Miazie, Yayènia, and Losolin crowded around, trying to examine the small pewter emblem in her hand. The Belau finally took it from Tlonna, cupped it in her hand, and closed her eyes. Sweat beaded on the human's forehead, and she began to sway slightly, but she soon snapped out of her trance, and shoved it back into Tlonna's hand.

"It is imbued with darkness...evil, malignant desires that make my skin crawl. Three races are involved with it, two familiar, one not," Miazie hissed, wiping away the perspiration.

"Is it powerful? Does it endanger us?" Losolin asked, eyeing the medallion with disgust.

"No, it in itself is just a piece of metal. It is the meaning behind it that sickens me. The symbol, here," Miazie pointed at the wavy line dissected by three slanting ones, "is Talenian. Here..." she traced the center line, which, at its top, split into four branches, "is the Zaedican Burning Sword. But, both those factions are human. This is the River of the Seadueni."

"*Dûmvardyn*!" Yayènia spat furiously.

It was a word of such vulgarity that it caused her three companions to stare at her in alarm. The warrior glared viciously.

"Well, are they not?" she demanded, looking everyone in the eye.

No one denied her.

After a minute, Tlonna took a deep breath. "So...what we have here is a trio of enemies, obviously united against Blackhaven and her allies. What about the kidnappers? They are not from here, I am beginning to believe they are not even a race of Nymyños. Where do they fit in, and which faction brought them in?"

Miazie shook her head, frustrated. Losolin took the medallion and studied it, his forehead creased in thought. "I remember...something..." he said quietly, pulling up his memories and scrutinizing each of them in turn. "Loni, do you remember Wellenton?"

"The Cleick we killed in Kajgenia? The one with the black pendant?" Tlonna asked, frowning.

"Yes. Remember his accent?"

Realization dawned on Tlonna, and she looked at Miazie, who was also rather excited. "They had the same accent! And we know that Wellenton was a pawn of Midian's, so they must be from one of the outlying islands beyond Zaedic," the queen gasped, clutching her husband's arm.

Yayènia held up her hand. "Hold on, who is Wellenton, what is a Cleick, and what accent?" she demanded, confused.

Tlonna turned to her sister. "Deric Wellenton was a man we found in Kajgenia who had possession of this pendant," she drew the black pendant out of her shirt, where she always kept it. "It is called the Death Pendant, and it is the brother to the Resurrection Pendant, which still resides in Zaedic. Midian was wearing it when Losolin broke his neck, and you cut his throat."

Yayènia nodded. "And a Cleick?"

"Magin haters," Miazie informed her. "A sect of fanatics founded by the Rahlans years ago in order to wipe the land of all Magins other than themselves. They told the Cleicks that they were gods, rather than humans with magic. They are a lot more present than they were a few years ago. Their emblem is an emblazoned M. They were at Alchemian."

The High Commander scowled. "I remember seeing that. So, the abductors had the same accent as this Wellenton fellow, and he was from an island beyond Zaedic?"

"As far as we know. When we asked him, he said it was nowhere we knew," Losolin said, nodding.

"And, the kidnappers had the same accent as this man, who hated Magins, but they had two Magins with them?" Yayènia deduced flatly.

"Yes," said her three friends in unison.

"Sounds awfully complicated," she replied, taking the medallion from Losolin and glaring at it. "Are you sure about the accent?"

"Absolutely," Tlonna stated, looking to Miazie and Losolin for support.

When they nodded, Yayènia sighed. "I will send out patrols to look for anyone associated with any of these factions. Can you replicate the accent?"

Losolin frowned, and then snapped his fingers so that a tiny green flame flickered above his thumb. He shoved it at Miazie, who blinked, startled. "Say something in the accent, and this should record it."

The Belau eyed the green flame with trepidation, but she dutifully spoke a common phrase in the island accent, and then backed away. Losolin snapped again, and the flame turned to an orb, pulsing slightly. The king passed it to Yayènia, who held out her hand as the orb floated over to her, and then squinted at him.

"What do I do?" she asked, her hand still outstretched.

"Just touch it, and it will replay what Miazie said to it. When you are finished, squash it between your hands. Until then, it is going to follow you around, so get used to it."

Yayènia dropped her hand and the green ball of light moved over to float next to her head. She sighed. "This is going to be enjoyable," she muttered, moving her head to the side. The orb followed the motion.

Losolin smiled wickedly. Tlonna frowned, concentrating, and followed the exact same Weave she had seen her husband do. Malevolent blue sparks shot up from her fingers, scorched the vaulted ceiling, and then sparkled downward, winking out of existence.

The few people left in the hall screamed in fright and fled the room. Yayènia was laughing so hard she had tears in her eyes, Miazie was staring open-mouthed at Tlonna, and Losolin was grinning fit to split his face open. Tlonna was glaring at her husband, rubbing her hand in agitation.

"Why did it not work? I followed the same Weave you did!" she said finally.

Miazie shook her head at Losolin's shrug. "You are different Magins, Tlonna. Losolin is a Healer Magin, one who can create things, bring about healthy change, and gets his energy from his own body. You are a War Magin, one who destroys, alters physical traits, and draws your strength from everything. Everything you do will be different from him."

Tlonna huffed, folding her arms beneath her breasts. "So all I can do is kill and destroy? Is that what you mean?"

"Basically," Miazie replied shortly.

Tlonna stared at her, and then without a word, turned on her heel and strode from the hall. Her three companions watched her go, unsure of what to do. After a moment, Losolin followed after, swiping the pewter medallion from Yayènia's hand.

"Tlonna!" he shouted, jogging after his wife, who was sweeping down the corridor, headed in the direction of the library, which was fast becoming the room everyone fled to in times of duress.

She turned and waited for him, her jaw tight, eyes cold. "What?"

"Talk to me, love. You have grown more distant than ever, and it worries me. What is happening?" Losolin asked softly, coming to stand near her.

Tlonna sighed, looked everywhere but at her husband, and then faced him full on, blue eyes wide, the white pupils dilated. "There are too many unanswered questions, and the answers we do have, we have come across too easily. It is frustrating, knowing that we are missing something vital, something that could destroy us entirely. What would you have me do, Losolin? I am tired, yet I cannot sleep. I am hunted, yet I cannot see my hunter. I am surrounded by people, yet I am alone."

"You are not alone, Loni," he whispered, taking her hands in his. "I know sometimes it may seem that I waver, that I cannot handle the pressures, but I can. Tlonna, I love you more than I can stand, and it pains me to see you this distant. I ran away once, I will not do so again. We will find the answers, and we will find our hunters. We, not you alone. You will never be alone."

Tlonna sniffed lightly. "There are days I feel so empty, Losolin. All I want to do is crawl in bed and sleep until the end of days."

The king smiled sadly, and then wrapped his arms around her, hugging his wife tight. "Let me be your foundation, love. That is what I am here for. You cannot give up yet, I will not let you crumble."

The Magin buried her face in his neck, breathing in the familiar scent of him, the woody, slightly sweet smell that comforted her even in the worst of times. Her heart ached with love for him, and she clutched at his arms, desperate for his touch.

They stood in the center of the corridor for a long time, a few guards looking the other way, giving their rulers a little privacy. Yayènia and Miazie departed the lecture hall to find them still embracing each other, and strode off in the opposite direction, a little green bulb floating behind them.

Finally, Tlonna drew away and looked up at Losolin. "I was going to search for any clue as to where our mystery men came from."

"Good idea," he replied, and they continued to the library, where they spent the rest of the night combing through the many books of symbolism, archaic cults, races, and cultures.

It was nearing dawn when Losolin came across the answer. "Loni, come here," he called.

Tlonna moved around the table they had covered in books to lean over her husband's chair. He had an ancient tome open before him, and on the revealed page was a sketch of a male figure. He was the same hybrid race as the kidnappers, a mix between elf, human, and something else, androgynous yet hairy, muscled yet thin. The text of the book was in ancient Hindarün, handwritten, and faded.

The elves bent close to read.

This specially engineered species of warrior was created in the province of Arseninisia, from the races of Elf, Man, and Goblin. They were made for a singular purpose: to be the infallible guards of the human kings. Unfortunately, the psyche of three such different races caused the Eseirik only trouble. Unable to differentiate between their human needs, their elfin purpose, and their goblin war-mongering, the Eseirik went insane within the first year of their making. Having been born into adulthood, this soon became a serious issue. Three kings were murdered by their own guards before the Eseirik were destroyed. It is, however, the belief of many that several escaped to make a colony somewhere west.

They can be identified by their peculiar appearance, at once beautiful and grotesque. The leader of each septet, as their groups were called, was branded with a small medallion on the left hip. He was called the Eseir.

The author went on about the hierarchy of the Eseirik, and many other things that horrified Tlonna and Losolin. When they had come to the end of the passage, Tlonna slumped into a chair.

"How many more are out there, do you think? This book was written three-thousand years ago. They could have bred an entire city by now, if not more."

"But they were all male," Losolin pointed out, frowning. "So I do not understand how they survived even one generation, much less hundreds."

"It says nothing about how they were bred," Tlonna said, "perhaps they could mate with any female, and the child would inherit either race."

The king scratched at his chin thoughtfully, staring at the drawing. "Maybe," he conceded finally. "One thing is for sure, our friends were definitely Eseirik. They have the same appearance, and they were in a group of seven."

Tlonna nodded silently, and then picked up the medallion from where Losolin had set it. "The question is, what do Sithian, Athelias, and Stoffnias have in connection with them?"

"Well, we know what they have as far as motive: a hatred of us," Losolin stated, frowning slightly.

Again, Tlonna nodded. "None of it makes sense. Stoffnias hates humans, Athelias was Midian's pawn, and Sithian hates Stoffnias."

"He does?" the king asked, surprised.

"Yes. Midian hated Stoffnias, and passed it on to Sithian. They were allies of a sort, but always looking over their shoulders at each other. It is the racial thing yet again. But..." Tlonna sighed, looking into her past, "I would not put it beyond either of them to ally against me."

"Do you really believe so?" Losolin asked, honestly curious.

"I do. They have sufficient enough reason to want me dead, or worse. They both have reasons to harm you as well. You killed Iyaner, Stoffnias' son, and you are married to me," Tlonna shrugged, "to Sithian, that makes you a heretic."

Losolin shook his head. "People are stupid."

"People are greedy," Tlonna countered, resting her head on her folded arms. "Athelias would ally himself with them only because he is too weak and crazy to defy them. Stoffnias wants me dead, and he wants this throne. Sithian just wants me dead."

The door opened and Aidyn strolled in, a silent black shadow crossing the floor. "Already up?" he asked, taking a seat next to them.

"*Still* up," Losolin corrected, and yawned for emphasis.

The assassin made a face. "Any progress yet? Yayènia shoved a green ball in my face and made me listen to a strange accent. Said you were trying to find out about our abductors."

"Indeed," Tlonna said, and pushed the book toward her friend. "Take a look at that and tell us what you think."

Aidyn's green eyes took in the sketch, and then quickly read the passage about it. His expression tightened with each sentence, so that when he looked up at Tlonna, his face was a mask of stone. "I would say that these Eseirik are our guys."

Tlonna and Losolin nodded wearily. "Where do you think their base is?" the queen asked after a moment.

The assassin's eyes scanned the room as he pondered the question. "Talenias, near the Bijoz range. I would stake my life on it."

"Why?" his friends asked in unison, startled. "We believe they are not of Nymyños at all."

Aidyn shook his head. "Remember, Sodo heard them speak in a strange dialect, but definitely Hindarün, probably ancient Hindarün if anything. And, there is a large population of minority races in Talenias, some of superior standing within the community. And, no one goes to that area of the kingdom. Like Kismath and much of Zeynuwn, it is freezing cold, secluded, only one way in and out besides the ocean, and the shore is nothing but a range of rocky cliffs. There is no harbor, and no threat of ambush. A dozen men could defend against an army."

"What about one?" Tlonna asked softly.

Aidyn stared at her, comprehending. "One could slip inside without too much difficulty, if he were good enough."

Losolin and Tlonna exchanged glances, and then met their friend's steady gaze. He folded his hands before him on the table, and leaned slightly forward.

"I am the Royal Assassin because I am the best. I can do it, if you ask it of me, but you must release me from your oath, Tlonna."

The Magin blinked in surprise. "I do?"

"I cannot willingly leave your presence without dying, not over such a distance. Only by force, or your release, can we be separated," Aidyn replied quietly.

Losolin was scowling, previously unaware that his wife and the assassin had such a binding oath. Years ago he had burst into the room directly afterward, and never been told. Tlonna nodded, and stood. Aidyn followed her, and they were soon standing very close, the assassin and the queen. Losolin watched them uncertainly.

They linked hands, closed their eyes, and immediately a white glow appeared around their hands and forearms. Tlonna exhaled, and silent thunder shook the library, knocking a few books off the table. Losolin leapt to his feet as both Aidyn and Tlonna went to their knees, the white light dissipating in tendrils, sparkling different colors.

Shaking, they got back on their feet. Aidyn rubbed a hand across his chest, looking lost. Tlonna shuddered, shook her head, and stumbled to her chair.

"I do not remember it being that powerful," she said after a moment.

Aidyn snorted. "I do. You did not realize what you were doing, and because of that, you were not as affected. Though I did not appreciate the fact that I was somehow physically attached to you. There is an emptiness inside my chest."

Tlonna nodded. "Mine too."

Losolin frowned at them in turn. "Serves you both right for not telling me about it. Now what is happening?"

"I am going to send Aidyn to search for the Eseirik. If he finds them, he is going to kill them all."

The assassin nodded in agreement, a look of longing still evident in his expression. Losolin did not care for it. "When?"

"I will leave today. I just need to get my things, and I will be away," he returned. "Can I have that?" he pointed at the medallion.

"Whatever for?" Tlonna asked, handing it to him.

"There are hundreds of symbols all over Nymyños. It will be nice to have an image of the one I am looking for," Aidyn explained, pocketing it. "I ah...I guess I will start getting ready, then."

Tlonna nodded, and realized she had never sent Aidyn on a mission like this before, and never alone. Suddenly she was very worried for her dear friend. "Aidyn..."

"This is not my first assassination, Tlonna," he said, expecting her reluctance. "I will be fine. Losolin, take care of her."

The king nodded too, grasping his hand. "Be safe, Aidyn."

The assassin smiled, and slipped out of the library. He was out of the city two hours later, and no one saw him go but Aladorn, who watched from his apartment window, silently worried for his younger brother.

Chapter 27

Assassin

Aidyn traveled swiftly, his mare, Whäd, moving beneath him in long, smooth strides. They were beyond Blackhaven Forest in a day, and nearing the end of the Highlands when night fell, along with the first snow. The assassin pitched his small black tent within a stand of pine so that Whäd would have shelter as well. By dawn the next morning, they were moving again, the black and gray dappled horse pacing easily through the powder.

Aidyn's body steamed for the first few minutes, adjusting to the cold. He only passed a few people, and they watched him go by with wide, awed eyes. They made quite a sight, the assassin and the odd-colored horse. Aidyn was covered in the slithery black *ärdyz* material that appeared to absorb light. His heavy cloak billowed out behind him, the cowl swept back by the wind of his passage.

Whäd had black legs, but the rest of her body was spots of gray and black, even her mane and tail were dappled. She had all black tack, with only a silver medallion in the center of her chest. Aidyn had raised her from a foal, and they could communicate as easily as two people. By nightfall, they had passed into Schelum.

It took a week to travel across Schelum, the tip of Purheae, along the narrow Corridor of Astinus, into the Liberated Lands, around deserted Anutch, and into the Forest of Cleshnoe. Once within the dense wood, Aidyn slowed Whäd, letting her pick her way through the foliage. To his right, he could see the distant peaks of the Bijozs, the massive mountain range that separated Zeynuwn from the rest of the continent.

Unknowingly, Aidyn passed within less than a mile of the Cyree, almost tracing Tlonna and Losolin's steps from four years previous. He thought of that time, letting his mind wander the long and often bleak landscape of his past. He was seven hundred and eighty-six years old, though he did not look a day over twenty-five.

Snow was thick everywhere now, more than a foot thick in some places, even within the forest. Aidyn broke the path for Whäd every now and again, letting her rest. Together, they navigated the forest in three days, and came out on the western side of Talenias, just below the foothills of the Bijoz.

"Well?" Aidyn asked Whäd, who nuzzled him in answer.

He grinned and scratched her neck, feeling her warmth seep through his flesh. Even with his elven skin, he was chilled. Aidyn yanked the hood up to shield his face from the falling snow, pulled his cloak about his person, fastened the frogs, and mounted his mare. They traveled quickly, and soon the assassin was noticing small carvings or odd pilings of stones. Often, the carvings matched the medallion in his pouch, though he found others that did not. He walked now, letting Whäd follow at her leisure. He trekked through the frozen tundra, frost lacing his raven hair, the snow whipping around him in little spirals.

After nearly two days of tracking, Aidyn found a crevice in the ground that widened and finally sloped up to lead into a cavern. Knowing he had found his target, he made camp half a day's ride from the opening.

The next day, the assassin rode Whäd within a mile of the defile, and then dismounted. "Find a place to hide and stay until I call you," he said to her in Parlêthian.

The mare snorted and trotted off. Aidyn watched her go, a small smile on his lips, before turning to the last leg of his journey. He had pulled out his other cloak for today, but still wore his black under it. This cloak was pure white, the frogs, like his black, were cord rather than metal, which could reveal his presence. He hunched down when he reached the defile, becoming a mere hump in the snow, a drift against the rock.

Aidyn stayed there all day, waiting. One person emerged the entire time, a brown-cloaked shape that passed the assassin, heedless. He was obviously going on a journey by the size of his pack. Aidyn left his post to follow. He caught up once they were out of sight of the defile.

The Eseirik did not notice the drift of snow that followed him until it was far too late. Aidyn leapt out of the snow like a cat, his longsword unsheathed. His target turned as he was in midair, a look of surprise in his eyes, the only visible part of his face. Aidyn slammed the hilt into the Eseirik's temple, knocking him to the ground, and the elf landed on him.

The hybrid grunted in pain, trying to wriggle free of the assassin, but the elf held him firm. He wrapped his fingers around the brown-clad throat and pressed downward, shutting off his airway, and pulled the medallion from his pocket. The Eseirik stopped struggling as his eyes alighted on the pewter item.

"How many of you are running about Nymyños?" Aidyn hissed.

The man shook his head. Aidyn slid his knife into view. "Two septets!"

"Where are they dispatched?"

"One to Blackhaven and one to Kajgenia."

"How many are in camp?"

The Eseirik clammed up once more, his brown eyes tightening. The elf placed the medallion back in his pocket and picked up his knife. He jammed the blade into his victim's thigh, careful not to spill any blood, and shoved his forearm into his mouth to muffle the scream. Once the hybrid had regained his senses, he tried to bite the assassin, and received a broken nose for the attempt.

"How many?"

"Three septets!"

Aidyn sighed, and then broke the fellow's neck. He picked the body up and carried him away from the trail, retrieved his knife, and then backtracked, covering up his tracks. Once more, he took up his station.

When night fell, he was ready.

He moved into the defile, still wrapped in his white cloak. Ahead, there were sounds of laughter, conversation, and eating. Aidyn smiled to himself. Food was befuddling, it would give him a better chance of survival. Already the odds were severely against him, twenty-one to one, if the Eseirik had not lied.

A few minutes later, he was sitting at the entrance to a tiny cavern where two guards sat idly playing some sort of game involving a cup of beads and a dagger stuck in the table. Aidyn crouched on all fours, moving with the now thin wisps of snow that blew in from the defile. The guards did not notice him. He crawled all the way up to the table, laying flat on his stomach.

Like a ghost, he rose up, two long knives in his hands, and drove a blade into each guard's neck. They died with a gurgle, slumping onto the table, blood pooling in the center, staining the wooden beads, and dripping off the edge.

Aidyn sheathed his knives and propped the two men up, taking one of their hands and placing it on the hilt of the dagger in the table. Readjusting his cloak, the assassin moved into the corridor leading further into the foothills of the mountains. It was made of bedrock, carved by hand. The elf took a deep breath to ready himself for going underground. He hated it.

He encountered two more guards in the passageway, no doubt going to relieve the dead ones. Aidyn heard them coming, and hunkered down just beyond a bend. They were dead as soon as they came level with him, throwing daggers protruding from their throats. Shaking his head, Aidyn retrieved his daggers and took off his white cloak. It would only make him stick out at this point. He was encased in darkness now, underground at night as he was. As soon as his white cloak was neatly folded and placed uphill from the bloody trail of the dead Eseirik, the assassin simply faded from sight. He moved cautiously now, stopping at every turn to listen for movement. He heard none, and was soon standing at the opening of a larger cavern than the first. This one housed several Eseirik, though not all of them.

Aidyn stood silently at the opening, watching, invisible in the shadows. Nine were at a table, eating and drinking, three more sparring hand-to-hand. One was actually curled up in a chair, reading. The elf stared at him, dumbfounded, unsure of this rather abnormal sight.

Suddenly, the reader looked up, right at Aidyn. He narrowed his eyes to slits to avoid any gleam, and after a moment, the reader went back to his book.

He dies first, the assassin thought, *he is the most dangerous. The Eseir.* Carefully, he released two of his throwing knives into his hands, and held them ready. With quicksilver movements, he sent the two flying, one toward the reader, another toward one of the sparring Eseirik. They went down, and an alarm went up, the eleven others spinning around, searching for their attacker.

Aidyn shot two more knives out, taking out the other two sparring men. Then he sprinted into the cavern, drawing his longsword as he did. He leapt onto a table, vaulted over five of the Eseiriks, and landed behind the other four. Swiping his sword in a wide arc, Aidyn sliced all four open, splattering blood all over the floor and wall.

Two went down, but the other two stayed on their feet, lurching toward him. The elf backed up, swinging his blade constantly. They all appeared unarmed, but Aidyn knew better than to underestimate them. Indeed, as soon as he finished the thought, yellow magic lanced at him. He jerked aside in time, but found himself cornered by five of the hybrids. The sixth stood back, apparently the Magin of the group.

The elf went low and brawled into the midriffs of his foes. Surprised, they fell back, the two he had injured crying out in pain. Aidyn kicked out blindly, felt his foot connect with something, and heard bone break. He rolled and came up on the other side of the now four Eseirik, with the Magin still behind them. Again, yellow light shot toward him, blasting a hole in the granite wall behind the assassin.

Cursing, Aidyn tossed a long knife at the Magin, but, as it was not meant for throwing, it was easily avoided. The elf ducked again and sprinted to the other side of the cavern. He faded into the shadows, keeping his eyes riveted on the Magin. For a second, he had them fooled. And then one of them sighted him, and they rushed forward, but the assassin was ready. He had sheathed his longsword and now held his two scimitars.

Aidyn spun into their midst, arms flying through formations drilled into him for five centuries. The four went down in a heap of bleeding and screaming, and then all went very still. But now the eight others had arrived, and there was still the Magin. The Eseirik had told the truth. Aidyn crouched, waiting.

"Who are you?" the Magin asked suddenly.

Aidyn stayed crouched, but he was caught off-guard by the question. He did not answer.

The nine Eseirik came forward in a semi-circle, trying to surround him. "Who are you?" he was asked again.

"I prefer not to talk while I am working," he snapped, standing his ground. If they surrounded him, he could kill them easier.

"I would like to know who you are. You have incredible talent. You would be a great asset to our sect," the Magin said.

Aidyn shook his head slightly, but did not reply. He was watching the advancing line as it curved about him. Suddenly something stabbed him in the side, though no one was close enough to reach him. The elf grunted, and he felt blood trickle down his skin. Another stab, on the other side of his torso. Pain lanced upward, but he kept his feet. One of the brown-clad hybrids stepped within range, and Aidyn took his head off as another jab caught him in the small of his back.

His vision was clouding now, and two more invisible blades punctured his skin. He went to one knee, lashing out with his scimitars. The blades destroyed another Eseirik, cutting off his legs at the knee. Aidyn adjusted his grip on the left weapon and jabbed it into the belly of one of his attackers.

By now, he was fighting to stay upright as the stabbings increased in both speed and pain. His entire torso was slick with blood, his vision tinted red with agony. Aidyn shook his head, trying to clear his vision. One of the hybrids bravely stepped forward, and the elf felt something slice across his cheek. The Eseirik died seconds later.

"The poison will not kill you," the Magin said suddenly, grabbing his attention. "It will knock you out for a couple days though. The more you force me to inject you, the longer your recovery will be. You will join us, dark elf, whether you wish it or not."

Aidyn's focus snapped when he was named a dark elf, and he summoned the adrenaline to get back to his feet. Roaring like an animal, the assassin whirled in a ragged circle, arms outstretched, blades gleaming. Crimson sprayed as he severed limbs, heads, and tore open flesh to the bone.

The five remaining Eseirik went down howling, including the Magin. As he stumbled to his knees, Aidyn made sure to fully sever the Magin's neck, and the stabbing mercifully came to an end. Gasping, the elf crawled to each of his targets, and finished them off. With the last of his strength, he pulled himself up onto a ragged couch, and lost consciousness.

Dreams and nightmares plagued him. Visions of Tlonna, Yayènia, Miazie, and Erdwyf in situations he prayed he would never be in. He wondered, deep in his subconscious, if their bodies really looked that perfect. He watched his brother, Aladorn, die in several different ways, each more horrible than the last. He watched Losolin, Ghealan, and Suneelo slowly succumb to vicious torture, and give away all their secrets. He watched Nymyños burn. He watched Blackhaven descend into madness.

Three days later, Aidyn jerked awake. His body screamed in agony, but he sat up anyway. The stench of rotting bodies made him gag, and the elf turned to examine the carnage he had wrought.

Maggots and other beastly things writhed inside the corpses of the Eseirik, and Aidyn had to fight down a wave of nausea.

He stumbled about, picking up his weapons, cleaning them off the best he could in his condition. Finally, he groped his way back into the stone corridor, beyond the rotting bodies of the two guards, where he retrieved his white cloak, through the guard chamber, and into the defile. Screaming wind and snow buffeted him, blurring his vision, and knocking him into the rough defile wall. At the end stood Whäd. She was obviously hungry, but she whickered at him softly, lifting her head.

"Whäd," Aidyn whispered, unable to summon anything more. "I told you to wait," he chided gently, clinging to her.

The mare whuffled, and began to pull him along. The elf stumbled and tripped, but she moved slowly, patient and concerned. Finally, they reached a spot where the snow and razor wind was lessoned, within a sparse stand of pine. They were the only trees hardy enough to grow in the area. Exhausted and ill, Aidyn collapsed in a puff of snow. Barely clinging to consciousness, he tugged at his saddlebags until they came off his horse, and opened the feed bag. Then he started ripping at his clothes, pulling the expensive garb away from his torn body. He looked down at his torso once he had managed to get his shirt untucked and up around his armpits. Dried blood caked his entire abdomen, tiny puncture holes scabbed over in sets of three, whirling about his flesh. His cheek was swollen by the way his right eye seemed to be squinting of its own accord, but other than that one injury, none of the normal Eseirik had gotten to him, only the Magin.

Aidyn cleaned the dried blood off the best he could with the cold snow and then wriggled his shirt back down, not bothering to tuck it back in. Whäd descended to the ground, pressing her warm bulk against her master to shield him from the worst of the wind, and began to eat.

Aidyn woke again sometime around midnight. Whäd was watching him with one liquid eye, a rare blue. "Hello," he murmured.

She snorted and Aidyn managed a laugh. He still felt on the verge of death, but a little better than before. Slowly, he dug into the other saddlebag and fumbled around until he found something to eat. It was a piece of salted pork, nearly frozen. The assassin chewed on it, his eyes closed.

"This one nearly got me, Whäd. Twenty-one of them, and one a Magin. Poisoned me somehow, with magic darts. I dreamt too, of Tlonna and all the girls. You know them. They are beautiful females, supple," he mimicked their form in the air with his hands, "and perfect...but not for me. Oh no, they are all taken. See... no one can love an assassin. Except you," he dug his fingers into her mane, aware that he was seriously ill, for elves did not ramble.

He continued to talk to his horse until sleep claimed him once more, his hand still entangled in her mane. When it did, Whäd gripped the feedbag with her teeth and yanked it closer to her. Content, she ate.

Aidyn could hardly see or stand, but he forced himself onto Whäd's back and urged her into a trot. For the first time in his life, he felt frozen and ill, the pain in his sides and back was a pulsing constant, agonizing and never fading. But he knew he had to hurry. The first Eseirik he had slain had said two septets were out, one to Blackhaven, and one to Kajgenia. The one to Blackhaven was decimated, their bodies lying in the guard tower.

The only other target worth such effort was Demetrius, the king who posed the most threat other than Tlonna. So Aidyn ignored the pain and forced himself to ride. Snow billowed around him, splaying up from the ground and whipping down from the sky. Fire burned through him, his body fighting the poison.

Days slipped by in blurs, frost stiffening his hair and Whäd's mane and tail. He ate sparingly, eating only what his body needed to stay energized. As an elf, he could go days without food, special cells in his body releasing the necessary nourishment needed to stay alive, but lethargy would soon kick in. So he nibbled at his food, hunched over in the saddle, cloak pulled tight against him.

As pain buffeted him, Aidyn's mind went into hibernation, drifting through fog in order to avoid most of the pain. His right cheek throbbed as well, the swelling visible to his eye, but this too, he ignored.

It took Aidyn an entire week to reach Kajgenia. To his utter disgust, his strength had not yet fully returned. As he trotted Whäd into Derid, the assassin ignored the alarmed looks he caused. Bloodied and ragged, his elfin features were a stark contrast. Worried that his time was short, Aidyn went straight to the castle. Galloping into the courtyard, he threw himself off Whäd and stumbled to his knees. The guards rushed to his side, hands reaching.

"Are you okay there?" one of them asked, and then gasped when Aidyn looked up. "You're from Blackhaven, aren't you?" he asked, concern in his eyes.

"Yes, where is the king?"

"He's been in meetings all day. Sir, please let us help you!"

Aidyn shoved the guards away, grimacing. "No time," he gasped, and lurched up the stairs into the foyer, his two worn cloaks billowing out behind him, black and white flashing with each step.

As he staggered through the halls, people gaped and covered their mouths, eyes wide. He ignored them. Behind the elf rushed two of the guards, calling to him. When they reached the door to Demetrius's study, Aidyn grabbed the two men.

"My name is Aidyn Sestuns, Assassin for the Throne of Blackhaven. You must trust me."

The men gaped at him. Aidyn's jaw clenched, but he grasped the knob to the door. It was locked. Growling, the elf leaned back and kicked it open. Within was mayhem.

Three guards lay dead upon the floor, two more were locked in combat with the brown-cloaked Eseirik. King Demetrius was fighting for his life as well. Aidyn let out a roar of anger and pain as he whirled into the room, longsword flashing. Two Eseirik went down in seconds, the other five still turning. Behind him, Aidyn could hear the two guards burst into action. Another guard went down, and the Eseirik flung a blade at the elf.

Suffering from Maginic poison and wounds, Aidyn dodged enough to avoid a fatal hit, but the blade still ripped through his arm. Howling, he leapt over a chair and stabbed the hybrid in the face, yanked a scimitar out and caught the fourth assassin across the chest. Aidyn looked up in time to see Demetri stagger away from his two attackers, freeing himself. The elf launched his sword at one, and tackled the other.

The hybrid writhed beneath him, and he struck a powerful blow to the back of his skull. The Eseirik grunted, but rather than slump into unconsciousness he twisted suddenly, dragging Aidyn beneath him. Struggling, the elf grappled as the hybrid sought his neck.

Suddenly, the creature went stiff and toppled over. Aidyn looked up in shock to see Demetrius standing over him, a large candelabrum in his hands. The elf painfully rolled onto his side and got to his feet, emerald eyes searching out the last of the septet. The three remaining guards were removing their blades from the Eseirik's body, looking panicked.

"Aidyn..." Demetrius gasped, drawing his attention.

"My lord, please forgive me for not reaching you sooner. I was delay—my lord!" Aidyn caught the king as he lurched forward, clutching his stomach. "Demetrius, no!"

Blood pulsed down the man's front, staining his clothing and plopping onto the floor. "Aidyn...Tlonna must not give up."

"No!" Aidyn cried, holding the king in his arms.

The guards rushed over in shock and terror, calling for help. The elf gently laid him out on the floor and pressed his hands to the stab wound, the blood bubbling up and over his fingers. Demetrius gasped, his eyes closing. "Don't give up...tell Tristan...I could never ask...for a better...son. Tell him...to stay true...Promise me."

Aidyn let his tears come. "I promise, my friend."

The man sucked in an agonized breath, and tried to say something more, but it never came. Demetrius Plaukler, King of Kajgenia, died in Aidyn's arms.

Someone pulled him away from the body with firm but gentle hands, guided him down the hallway, and sequestered him in a room. Numb, Aidyn collapsed on the bed and slept the sleep of the dead. Hours later, he woke floundering in blankets, the sky outside the window moon-filled and dark. Sitting up, he rubbed his face and hissed in pain as his palm slid across his cheek.

The pain from his poisoning had faded to a dull throb, but his face felt on fire. Groaning, he crawled from the bed and walked to the gilded mirror hanging on the emerald wall. Leaning into it, Aidyn glared at his image. His eyes were shadowed with pain, his sable hair lank and dull, even his skin had a gray cast to it. But on his right cheek were two thin triangular gouges, pointing toward his nose. They were right on top of his cheek bone and curved slightly upward in sync. The two marks were blackened and scabbed, the flesh around red and swollen.

Vaguely, he remembered one of the Eseirik back at the defile swiping at him with an odd device, but he could not remember it making contact. He pushed his face closer to the mirror and stared at the wounds. They seemed to accentuate the tilt of his eye, and he sneered at his reflection. He lifted his fingers to the cuts, and realized his hands were covered in dried blood. Demetrius's blood. Sickened, Aidyn found the wash basin and scrubbed at his hands until the water turned translucent red. Then he stumbled into the actual wash room and stripped off his clothes.

Standing naked in the marble room, Aidyn stared at himself in the floor length mirror. He was lithe and muscled, his skin, on normal days, was a light tan, just this side of brown. Scars crisscrossed his body like a map of his life. Most were thin and white, but a few were puckered and red. He stepped up to the large tub and pumped steaming water into the basin. Submerging his body in the water, Aidyn felt the ache of strained muscles lessen and the sting of his numerous nicks and cuts flare and fade.

In his mind he watched the last week and a half play in his mind, realizing that for the first time he had been overmatched. The only reason he had survived was sheer determination and his body's ability to withstand most things. Aidyn ignored the memory of his hallucinations, stubbornly refusing to admit they exposed deeper feelings.

He was seven hundred and eighty-six and had lost the only person who had ever loved him. Once, long ago, he had harbored the thought of him and Tlonna, but that was before Losolin, and even then he knew it could never be. He replayed the conversation he'd had with Dietirin over in his mind.

"Tlonna can never be yours, Aidyn, you know that."

Aidyn nodded, not looking at his king. "I do."

"But...she needs to know what a true night of passion is. Constancias is determined to marry her off to a Seadueni heir, and if that happens, as I believe it will, Tlonna will never know love. Can you give her that?"

The King's Assassin's head jerked up in shock, eyes wide. "What are you talking about, Dietirin?"

"Go to Tlonna tonight. Give her something to remember."

"I cannot do such a thing! She is a princess, and I am no prince. I am a killer."

"You are my oldest friend, and my daughter loves you in the way only such young elves can. Got to her bedchamber tonight, and if she accepts you, then I will be thankful for the rest of my life. If not, then it is her choice."

Aidyn swallowed, and then nodded. "Are you sure?"

Dietirin smiled sadly. "If she were human, she would be old and married by now. I trust you, and she loves you. Perhaps not as much as you would like, but enough for now."

Aidyn had done as his king had wished, and gone to Tlonna's chamber that night. She had opened the door and smiled up at him, innocent eyes clouded with lust. They had embraced, and shared a night of passion. Never again had it happened and Aidyn barely remembered it. Tlonna, he knew, had no recollection of it whatsoever, and he fervently hoped that it stayed so.

Dietirin had been wrong, of course. Tlonna had met Losolin through the machinations of Yayènia and Suneelo, sparking a relationship so strong not even death could defy it. Aidyn could not be happier for them, knowing full well they belonged together. But...he still yearned for such companionship. Soaking in the tub, the elf stared at the opposite walls, the long years of his life dancing before him like a play. He'd been with hundreds of females, far more than he could remember, for he did not believe in chastity. And yet, he had never felt a true connection with any of them, save Rahna. Sighing, he stood, water dripping over his body.

Toweling off, Aidyn walked into his room and found his saddlebags slouched against a corner. Searching through them, he found a clean set of clothes and dressed, feeling much better. His face still throbbed, but it was manageable. Opening the door, the assassin glanced at the guard standing outside.

"Lord Aidyn."

Aidyn lifted on corner of his mouth in a half-hearted smile of greeting. "Am I a prisoner?"

The guard looked offended. "Of course not, Lord Aidyn. Prince Tristan worried for your safety only. With King Demetrius's..." the man's eyes turned sad, "with his death, the prince worried others might think you were responsible."

"Ah, how is he?"

"The prince?" the guard shrugged slightly. "He is strong, but he and his father were very close. He is in a meeting with the council right now to determine how to move on."

"Is it a closed meeting?"

The man smiled in understanding. "I was given orders to tell you that from this point on you are an honorary member of the Plaukler family, and that you should feel free to do as you wish, including attend the meetings."

Aidyn was overwhelmed, but he merely clapped the guard on the shoulder. "What room?"

"Council Hall, I will escort you there."

Together, the elf and the guard descended from the third floor, which housed the royal family and high ranking nobles, to the first, where the halls were placed. When they stood outside a set of heavily carved doors, the guard gestured to them.

"I am not allowed in, but you are. I will be here when you are ready to go back to your room."

"Thank you," Aidyn replied, and opened the left door. A dozen or so men looked up, including the young Tristan.

When they saw who he was, they rose as one and began clamoring for him to tell them what had happened. Only Tristan was subdued, looking grief-stricken and exhausted. "Aidyn..."

The assassin went to the prince's side and clasped his hand. "I am sorry, Tristan. I was too late. I tried so hard to get here in time, but I just could not go any faster. Please forgive me."

"Aidyn, the guards told me what happened. The one who killed my father is in the dungeon, awaiting my displeasure. Who are they?"

The elf took the seat offered him and told them of the Eseirik, and of his efforts the last week and a half. "That is why I was on my way here, I knew they were coming after Demetri," he concluded, feeling drained.

One of the council members shook his head in disbelief. "They nearly beheaded the two strongest nations in a few weeks. Who sent them?"

"Queen Tlonna believes they were bought by three leaders, an alliance against one enemy, us. Sithian Rahlan of Zaedic, Stoffnias Lostug of Seaduens, and Athelias Embina of Talenias."

"Why does the elf-queen believe this?"

Aidyn sighed, and pulled the medallion out of his pocket. "This was found embedded in the flesh of one assassin sent to capture and murder King Losolin, and others, including myself. It bears emblems linking the three nations."

He tossed the pewter disk onto the table, and everyone leaned in to see it. After a while, Tristan scooped up the medallion and handed it back to Aidyn. "Anything else we need to know?"

Aidyn filled them in on the Eseirik, and then returned to his room and penned a letter home. He felt sickened, depressed, and more than a little sore. Dawn was creeping in through the windows, and he yanked shut the thick green curtains. His cheek burned and his head pounded. Annoyed with his condition, Aidyn curled up on the bed and lay staring at his hand.

How many had he killed, and how many more were still in his future? He had few regrets, but the ones he had were large. He did not regret his profession, or his life, but he felt as though he had failed. King Demetrius was dead, and he had been in the room. If it had been Yayènia instead of him, Demetri would still be alive. Self-doubt and criticisms plagued him. If he hadn't hesitated at the door, if he hadn't stopped to rest once out of the defile, would it have made any difference? Or would Demetri still have died? The thoughts plagued him until, finally, sleep came.

Aidyn woke at midday and washed, tending to his wounds and pulling out the braids in his hair. He was combing out his sable locks when someone knocked on the door. Donning a robe, the elf opened the door and blinked in surprise.

"May I come in?" Tristan asked, looking exhausted.

"It is your castle," the elf replied, stepping out of the way.

The prince wearily sat on the bed and looked up at Aidyn. "I always forget how tall you are," he said, attempting a laugh.

Aidyn smiled and tightened the belt on his robe. "There are times it is a bit annoying. The doors are almost too short, the wash basins a little cramped. But," he shrugged, "after eight hundred years, you get used to it."

Tristan nodded distractedly and motioned for the assassin to sit. Once Aidyn was situated, the prince seemed unsure of what to say.

"I've...uh...never seen your hair like that," he blurted.

Aidyn frowned and ran his fingers through his wet hair, but said nothing. Finally, Tristan looked at him, gray eyes troubled.

"Do you think I'm next?"

The elf shook his head. "All the Eseirik are dead, Tristan. I will go down and talk to the last one to see what he knows, but you should not fear for your life."

The prince nodded, but still looked unsettled. "Aidyn... my father held together the entire Eastern Alliance. King Barukh, King Tyular... they're not going to respect me the way they did him... and why should they? I'm just a kid!"

Aidyn put his hand on the human's shoulder. "You are not alone, Tristan, remember that. You will make your father proud."

The human bit his lip and looked at the floor between his boots. "My father is dead, my mother died in childbirth, I have no siblings, no family. Aidyn, if I die, there will be no one left. All my councilors and advisors were loyal to my father, who's to say they will be loyal to me? Tlonna said there's a war coming. How am I to lead my people? What if I destroy what seven decades of Plauklers have worked toward? What if ruin my father's kingdom?"

Aidyn stared at the panicked young man. "You are twenty-five years old, young, even for a human. But, for ten years you have ridden the countryside, fighting enemies, mercenaries, and keeping the border safe from Seaduens. You rode with us at Alchemian and survived. You have been under your King Father's tutelage your entire life. And," the elf held up a hand, "you have strong ties to Blackhaven.

"Now, I cannot speak for Barukh, but what I know of Tyular Ambrose, you have a strong ally with him. Do you really think Tlonna, Losolin, or Tyular will let you fall?"

Tristan shook his head.

The elf patted him on the back. "I wrote to Tlonna and Losolin, so they should know by week's end. They will come as soon as possible I am sure, but I will stay here. Whatever you need me to do, I will" he said, standing.

The young man stood as well, and impulsively hugged the older male. Aidyn grunted in surprise. The prince's head came up to his collarbone, his arms wrapped around his middle. The elf patted his back again, and Tristan backed away with a cough, blushing.

"Sorry, Aidyn...I wasn't thinking."

The assassin shook his head dismissively. "You have not done that since you were very little."

"I know. I remember you coming with King Dietirin's messages when I was a boy. You used to give me wooden blades and practice with me. I always wondered why you never got older while everyone around me did. I was seven when Father told me you were a different race. Then you stopped coming, and I went into training, and didn't see you until Tlonna and Losolin's wedding."

Aidyn smiled faintly. "You have a good memory. I stopped coming because Yayènia needed me in battle, and then Tlonna disappeared, Blackhaven was razed, and my people fled. A different life, just like now."

Tristan nodded. "You are a good friend, Aidyn Sestuns."

"Let us see how good a friend I am when this is all done and over with, all right? Now, go get some rest before you fall over."

"What are you going to do?" the human asked as the elf bent down to riffle through his pack.

"I am going to pay our hybrid a visit. I will get the answers we all seek," Aidyn replied and stood, a set of clothing in his hands.

"Be careful Aidyn. Come get me as soon as you are finished," Tristan said, stepping out of the room. He looked back just as the elf took off his robe and the prince received a glimpse of rippling shoulder and back muscles, crisscrossed with scars, spinal extensors quivering with the movement. With a shake of his head, the young man left.

Chapter 28

Funeral

Erdwyf looked up as the message runner bowed into her office. The young water nymph handed her a tightly scrolled bit of vellum tied with a black string, Aidyn's signet pressed into the black wax. The nymph brushed his vibrant blue hair out of his silvery eyes.

"Message from Kajgenia, High Advisor. They said it was urgent."

"Thank you Nissus. I will take it to the king and queen."

The nymph smiled slightly and bowed his way out of her office. Erdwyf waited until he was completely out of her hearing range before opening the letter, her hands trembling. Aidyn's flowing script was tilted and uneven, a sure sign of exhaustion or pain, or both. As the High Advisor read, tears flowed down her face, plopping onto her desk. Finally, she dried her face and walked the hallway to Tlonna's office, where she found her and the king embracing, their hands linked and twisted behind Losolin's back.

Erdwyf knocked on the door, earning one-eyed glares from each monarch. As soon as they saw her face, Tlonna and Losolin pulled away from each other, looking concerned.

"What is it? What has happened?" Tlonna asked, then she saw the letter. "Aidyn...he is not... Please tell me he is not dead," the queen's voice cracked, her hand reaching for the parchment, knees buckling.

"No, Aidyn is fine...but, you need to read this, both of you," Erdwyf replied, handing the letter to Tlonna.

With Losolin reading over his wife's shoulder, the couple read the letter, their faces turning pale and grieved at the same moment. "Demetrius..." Tlonna breathed, forehead crinkling as she tried to hold in her tears. When they finished, she turned into Losolin's arms and cried, hiding her face in his shoulder. Erdwyf took the letter back from Losolin, and left them alone, going to find the others. Yayènia shook her head and looked solemn, Suneelo swore and angrily wiped at the tear forming in his eye. Ghealan sighed, his shoulders slumping and he pulled his wife into his arms. Miazie took it the worst, sobbing into Sodo's chest, clutching at his sleeves and shaking her head in denial. Even Aladorn had to swallow back his grief, dark verdant eyes sparkling with emotion, though his pain seemed more for Aidyn's trial than for the death.

After a while, Tlonna wiped her eyes and looked up at her husband. "We must go," she said, her voice shaking.

Losolin nodded, wiping away a stray tear from his wife's face. "We will have to ride fast in order to make it in time. Haydyn will have to stay, with Feorien and Kelus."

"It was all planned," Tlonna whispered. "Kidnap you and the others to draw us away from the city, enabling Marin to get in and accuse Haydyn, causing enough of a distraction to downplay the kidnapping. Sithian and his allies must have known the septet would never make it out of Blackhaven, so they expected us to find their hideout. Demetri had to die because he is our strongest ally, and they knew we would never miss his funeral. It will draw all of us out of the kingdom. Something is going to happen."

The king took a deep breath and looked over her head at empty space, mourning and angry. "It does not matter. Demetrius would have come for us."

Tlonna nodded and moved around to her desk. "Haydyn will again be given executive powers, with Feorien as Advisor. I will call Kelus in to help as well. I need Yayènia and the others—"

"Here," Yayènia said, stepping into the room. "Erdwyf just told us."

Losolin turned to find the whole family standing in the office. Yayènia and Suneelo, Erdwyf and Ghealan with Jaryikin, Miazie, Sodo, and Aladorn. Tlonna straightened, looking grave, white-pupil eyes rimmed with grief.

"We are all going to Demetri's funeral. He deserves nothing less. I am aware of the implications of beheading the entire kingdom for a while, but I do not care. We all have second and thirds that are capable of taking care of things for a while."

No one disputed her, and the queen turned to Erdwyf. "I want the Mourning Flag raised immediately with notices put out. Keep the details slim, but my people will be aware of Demetrius's death."

The High Advisor nodded. Turning to Yayènia and Ghealan, Tlonna eyed them. "Full garrison until we return. I do not know what is going to happen, if anything, but I have a feeling this is a very intricate and dangerous plan. Suneelo, guards at every entrance to the city, castle grounds, and the castle itself. I will put up Weaves that will set off alarms when cloaked people pass by. Aladorn, you will need to be out of the castle before I do that. Your magic will set them off."

The four elves nodded as well, and they all waited for Tlonna to continue. "We leave as soon as the orders are put out, and supplies are gathered. Miazie, Sodo, I need you to do that. Plan for eleven."

Miazie frowned. "Who are the other two?"

"Eyin and Meradyn. They need to come, they need to see what we are fighting for. They need to."

The Belau nodded, and with an unspoken agreement everyone rushed out of the office to do their queen's bidding. Losolin sighed and hugged his wife close. "I will send out a letter to warn them of our coming. How do you think Aidyn is handling this?"

Tlonna shook her head. "I have no idea, not well, I would imagine. He and Demetrius were close. Aidyn used to run messages for my father when they were of delicate contents. He told me he began Tristan's training. Did you know that?"

Losolin shook his head. "I only knew they knew each other because of their interaction when they came for our wedding. I still have not regained all my memories."

"Nor have I, and they seldom come, now," Tlonna replied, wiping away another tear as it ran down her cheek. "Oh, Losolin...how many more will we lose before this is all over?"

The king shook his head again, "Too many. Far too many."

Together, they wrote the proclamation for Haydyn, Feorien, and Kelus. Losolin left then to write the letter to Kajgenia, and handed it off to a message runner. He was on his way to find Haydyn when the prince ran into him.

"Oh! Losolin! Sorry, I didn't see you," Haydyn gasped, steadying himself as he gripped the corner of the hallway.

"I was looking for you Haydyn. King Demetrius of Kajgenia has been murdered, and your mother, the others, and I, are going to his funeral. You need to stay here again, with executive powers. Feor and Kelus will be here to aid you."

Haydyn frowned. "I liked King Demetrius. Uh...do you think something is going to happen while you are all away?"

"Most likely. The army will be on alert, and guards are being positioned at every possible entrance. Your mother is going to put up wards as well. Haydyn," Losolin put his hand on his stepson's shoulder. "You must be careful, and use your judgment and training wisely. Your mother believes that this is all an intricate plan to destroy us."

"Like a coup?"

"Perhaps, or another assassination, kidnapping, or even another siege. But whatever happens, you must listen to your heart, and choose what action is best."

The prince looked worried. "What about Eyin Thorn and his...friends?"

Losolin smiled. "We are taking Eyin and Meradyn with us. Jorunson and Marc are your problem until we get back. We are leaving today."

"But...if they can go, why can't I?" Haydyn pouted, folding his arms as Losolin turned to leave.

"Because you already know what we fight for, because you have a responsibility to your kingdom, and this is good for you. Besides, someone has to be here to sit on the flaming throne. Otherwise the city, the whole bloody kingdom, would be thrown into anarchy, and we would not want that," the king replied blandly, turning back.

Haydyn pouted more, glowering at his stepfather's back as the elf moved off. He always knew when Losolin was agitated because his language grew courser. The half-blood found it amusing. Shaking his head, he continued on to his apartment.

Losolin found Eyin and Meradyn in their room, poring over a book. They looked up when he entered, and then fumbled out of their chairs to bow. They had learned decorum since their arrival, at least theory if not true practice.

"Sit, boys. I have some news," Losolin said, wondering how he had received the job of talking to all the adolescents.

"Is everything okay, sire?" Meradyn asked, noticing the elf's sad eyes.

"King Demetrius of Kajgenia has been assassinated," Losolin began, and told them the information. "So," he said, finishing, "we are leaving today, and the queen and I would like you both to come."

Eyin's eyes widened. "What about Jor and Marc?"

"They will be staying. They have not progressed in their studies as you two have, and we do not have the ability to take all of you. A letter has been sent to the Academy to explain your absence, as well as Sodo's. Will you come?"

Meradyn nodded, and then looked at Eyin for conformation. The young king eyed him warily, and then nodded as well. "We will go."

"Good. You have thirty minutes to gather your gear. It will be cold," Losolin said, standing.

Within the hour, thirteen people, including the two bannermen to accompany them, milled about in the stables, mounting their horses and squinting up at the gray sky. Snow fell gently all around, but small drifts were already forming near the walls. They rode out of the gate and onto Obsidian Way, heading toward the castle walls and the city. The two bannermen rode in front, one with the Tree of Blackhaven, the other with the Sun and Star of House Ewôsdírn. Yayènia, Ghealan, and Aladorn rode just behind, Tlonna and Losolin next, with Eyin and Meradyn behind them. Suneelo and Sodo rode on the rear flanks, with Miazie and Erdwyf between them.

People stood on the side of the road and watched them pass, their eyes straying to the large gray flag with the white and black crescent moons that had suddenly appeared above the castle. The Mourning Flag. The people of Blackhaven wondered.

Once out of the city, the formation spread out slightly, but did not change. Takîreaes snorted, wanting to run faster, but Tlonna reined him in, keeping the stallion in pace with the other horses. Eyin clung to the large bay gelding loaned to him, a nervous rider at best. Meradyn fared slightly better, having been tutored by Yayènia. His leggy mare made him nervous, but he sat more relaxed in the saddle than his king.

The thirteen horses and their riders thundered along the forested road, the pennants snapping in the wind and snow. By nightfall, they had cleared Blackhaven Forest and were camped on the Elnya Highlands. Yayènia forced Eyin and Meradyn into sparring with her, and within seconds she had them on their backs in the snow. After a while, Suneelo joined in, working with the two young men, ganging up on his wife. The High Commander easily evaded them all, though it was obvious to the others that Suneelo was barely trying.

The rest of them huddled around the fire and spoke of the things that had happened recently, and of what might be ahead. The bannermen sat between Sodo and Ghealan, but their eyes were riveted on Yayènia, Suneelo, and the two Purheaens.

Morning came with a snowstorm, but the group struck camp and moved on in spite of it. Bundled in thick winter cloaks, Miazie, Losolin, and Tlonna also wore their slippery black cloaks from the Cyree. By late morning, they were at Lybera Bridge.

The thirteen crossed the white bridge carefully, mindful of ice patches. Eyin closed his eyes and kept them shut until they were on firm ground again, mistrustful of his horse's intentions. It took them a week and a half to make it to Kajgenia, arriving the day of the funeral.

Tristan and Aidyn met them at the castle steps, the former looking exhausted and lost, the latter worn and beaten. Tlonna, damning etiquette, rushed up the stairs and embraced her friend, and then hugged Tristan tightly.

"Tlonna...I am glad you made it," Aidyn breathed, attempting a smile as the others followed the queen.

Everyone greeted each other, and it was Tristan who eyed Eyin and Meradyn with suspicious eyes. Tlonna caught the look and laid a hand on the prince's shoulder. "Prince Tristan, may I introduce Eyin Thorn, First King of Purheae, and Meradyn Obren, Commander in Training. Eyin, Meradyn, I give you Prince Tristan of Kajgenia."

The three humans bowed, the prince the more elegant of the three, but he seemed not to notice the others' fumbles. "Tlonna...Losolin...everyone. Thank you for coming. Come in. The...ceremony...does not start for another hour, so you have time to wash and dress. I am sorry there is not time enough for you to rest."

"It is all right Tristan. We are here for you, and Demetri," Losolin replied, putting his arm around Tlonna's waist.

The young man nodded, and led them to their rooms. "I will have someone collect you when it is time," he said quietly.

Tlonna was adjusting her cloak when a knock sounded on the door. When she opened it, a young guard was standing there, gazing up at her with large eyes.

"Queen Tlonna...King Losolin, Prince Tristan is ready for you. I am to escort you to the ceremony."

"Very well," Tlonna replied, and she and Losolin followed the human out of their room. All down the hall people were being chaperoned from their rooms by stiff-backed guards.

The Blackhaven ensemble grouped together, Aidyn included, walking close to his brother. Aladorn made no mention of the black scars on his sibling's cheek, but he was curious and worried about them. The assassin was also rather worn looking, emerald eyes dull, his skin lighter than normal. The wiat eyed his brother through his peripheral, forcing himself to stay silent on the matter, for the others were still unaware of their relation. Aidyn said nothing as well, lost in some inner turmoil.

Together, the large group of people, Blackhavenites and Kajgenians, followed the guards garbed in full green and teal regalia. Swords gleamed, black boots shone in the torchlight, and those that carried bows had them polished to a high sheen, their arrows sharpened. Silver chain mail peeked out from between sleeves and vambraces, their green enameled helmets sporting short teal plumes.

They were taken out of the castle into the snow-blown courtyard where Tlonna and Losolin had once individually dueled members of the army. Once there, their escort took them through a small side door in the wall, and into a more sheltered yard. Large yew and ash trees stood sentinel along a pathway, shielding the passersby from the worst of the snow.

More than twenty strong, the group followed the guards to a large circular clearing. Aged stone benches, carved in an arc, faced an equally aged dais on which Tristan stood, listening with bowed head to an elderly man in plain green robes. Tlonna, Losolin, and their companions were guided to the front row of benches, and were bidden to sit. Along the row sat a few of the other rulers of Nymyños, but other than to nod silently at each other, none were in the mood to talk. Miazie shivered slightly and pressed against Sodo, pulling Aladorn close on her other side. The elves bore it with resigned grace, sharing their warmth with the human.

Eyin and Meradyn sat rigid in their borrowed clothes from Blackhaven, sandwiched between Aladorn and Aidyn, glancing up at the dark elves with nervous expressions, silently noting their similar appearance, but smart enough to keep silent. Quickly, the clearing filled with mourners, and Tristan moved off to the side of the dais, hugging himself to stay warm, pulling a black and teal cloak about his shoulders. On his auburn hair rested a thin gold circlet, emeralds embedded along the band. Two spears crossed above his brow, the points made of emeralds as well.

Finally, the green-robed man held up his hand and the smattering of conversation died away. The old priest folded his hands together before him and began the opening recitations. Once he had finished, he held up his hand and a murmur began from the back.

Tlonna twisted in her seat and her heart thudded slowly in her chest. Four soldiers in full armor carried a litter, Demetrius's body arrayed on top. The queen turned around again and locked her gaze on Tristan. The young man had his hands clenched tightly before him, gray eyes tight, jaw clenched, shoulders hunched forward. He was a study in grief and restraint.

Slowly, the king was borne up the long aisle and placed upon the altar on the dais. Demetrius's body had been preserved for death, dressed in ceremonial robes, his crown gleaming on his brow. He looked as though he were merely sleeping, though his skin was ashen and his eyes sunk too deep. Tlonna squeezed her eyes shut for a moment, trying to stop herself from crying. Behind her, the elf could hear the sobs and moans of people unable to contain themselves.

Tristan was staring at his father's body, unable to look away. Aidyn clenched his hands together, but they still shook. The priest began talking again, recounting Demetrius's life, his victories, and his passions. He talked of the fallen king's generosity, kindness, and firm handedness. He had brought much to Kajgenia, Derid, in particular. He had never failed to back up his friends and allies, marching across the continent to aid Blackhaven in their plight against Zaedic.

Tlonna felt her tears come, and let them. They fell silently, as did all the elves' tears, but they came fast and hard. Miazie had her head in Sodo's shoulder now, trying to muffle her crying. There were no dry eyes. Demetrius had been a beloved friend, father, and king. He had brought his people to wealth and health. He had saved them time and again from persecution, refusing to submit to Stoffnias Lostug, Aderiaen and Midian Rahlan. He had forged iron alliances and always kept them. He had left a legacy of benevolence and wisdom.

Finally, the priest stepped down from the dais, and bid those willing to come forward and say their private goodbyes. Tlonna and Losolin went first, as fit their stature. Together, they stood at Demetrius's head, gazing down upon their friend.

"We would never have made it without you, Demetri. You gave us so much, and never asked for anything in return. We will try to make you proud," Tlonna whispered, clutching Losolin's hand.

The elf king swallowed and looked down at the human who had meant so much to him. Memories and emotions flooded him, and he gripped Tlonna's hand back. "Goodbye, my friend," he murmured, and they walked away from the altar.

They found Tristan and stood nearby, watching the young prince, worried and saddened for him. He gave them a small smile, and then went back to staring at the ground. Once everyone had said their goodbyes and departed the clearing, but for Tlonna, Losolin, Aidyn, and Tristan, the priest returned. Much less formal, now, he walked up to the prince and conferred, glancing at the three elves.

Finally, Tristan turned to his companions. "We are going to place him in his tomb, now. You may follow, if you wish."

From the side of the courtyard, the four ceremonial guards reappeared and picked up the litter, after bowing to Tristan. Together, the small procession went through a narrow corridor of trees, one so low it forced the elves to hunch down. The passage turned sharply at one point, and then began to decline. Tlonna glanced at Aidyn, who shook his head. With the priest and Tristan leading, the guards and their precious burden in the middle, and the elves trailing, they descended underground. It was nearly a mile of tunnel before the priest brought them to a stop.

"You are about to enter the Tomb of the Kings. You may not speak, you may not touch anything. Tristan, step aside," the old man ordered, and pushed against a section of stone wall. It opened on heavy hinges, but swung silently, and they proceeded inward.

The funeral procession was now in a long cavern, carved from the bedrock. Lining the massive room were dark niches in which stood statues of kings in detail, though some were so old they seemed rudimentary. Tlonna gazed upon the faces and felt as though she were being judged. She wondered how Tristan felt, being stared at by all of his predecessors, his ancestors.

Faded frescoes adorned the ceiling and walls, carvings and gilt worn smooth and dull by the passage of time and underground air currents. The floor was made of block limestone, once stark white and gleaming, now warped and uneven, dull and chipped. Tlonna knew that this room was older than Blackhaven, older, yet, than the Tower of Magins. It was over two thousand years old, a long time indeed. Few elves even lived that long, growing weary after such a long time on earth. The weight of the earth pressed down upon the group, and they hastened forward.

Finally, after passing dozens of tombs, they came to a halt. They stood in front of an empty sarcophagus, but at the foot was a statue of Demetrius as he had been forty years ago, at the time of his coronation. Tristan gazed up at his father's effigy with forlorn eyes.

They looked much the same, with their wide cheekbones, hawk noses, and strong chins. Even their hair lay flat and straight, though Aidyn had once said Demetrius's hair had been red before it turned gray.

Tlonna moved over to the prince and put her hand on his shoulder. He looked up at her with a teary smile, and then went back to staring at his father. The priest and the guards were busy transferring Demetrius from the litter to the sarcophagus, lifting his body by the dark green cloak and laying him carefully within the stone bed. With a thud of grave finality, they slid the carved lid of the coffin shut. Tristan took a deep breath and shuddered, turning into Tlonna's arms, burying his head in her chest like a small child. The elf hugged him close until the priest gently coaxed him away, and the group began their slow ascent back to the world above.

Once above ground, the priest shuffled away, and the four guards dispersed, leaving the three elves alone with the prince. Tristan wiped his eyes with the back of his hand and looked up at the overcast sky.

"I miss him so much," he whispered. "I know it's ridiculous, but he taught me everything. He was the only family I had left. Now he's gone, and it's just me. Just me."

Tlonna took his hands in hers. "It will never be just you, Tristan. We are here for you. When my father died, I felt horribly alone, abandoned and lost. But I had friends, and loved ones who helped me get back on my feet and remember that I had a purpose, a duty. And you have a life of your own. Your father would not want you to regret his passing, but to value the memories, and embrace the future. Do not dwell on those who have passed and forget to live."

Tristan nodded, and together the four walked slowly back to the castle. Once there, they were met by the Blackhaven ensemble, and they secluded themselves in a large private dining hall. As dinner was served, the prince began to speak of the things yet to do.

"And...in a week's time, as is customary, I am crowned king," he concluded, expelling a deep breath. "I am not ready for it."

"Yet you must be," Losolin replied gently, patting his hand. "We will remain here, if it does not impose on you. We are here to aid you in any way, and to renew the alliance between Blackhaven and Kajgenia."

"Renew?"

"With your father's passing, the alliance was rendered invalid. Each treaty must be signed anew," Tlonna explained, looking to Erdwyf.

The High Advisor nodded. "I have all the papers, Prince Tristan. But they do need to be signed by you, Tlonna and Losolin, myself, Yayènia, your highest ranking advisor, and highest ranking military officer."

"Why wouldn't the alliance just pass from each generation? Would that not be easier, and assured?" the prince asked, brows knitted in a frown.

Aidyn shook his head. "It is something King Dietirin and your great-great-grandfather Baylien Plaukler decided upon. It ensured that with each passing of a king, the two ruling houses would be *forced* to meet and agree upon the alliance. Otherwise, treaties can go on and on for hundreds of years, and the rulers never meet. And if the next generation does not want the accord, then he can just ignore it. The alliance is pushed to the back of everyone's mind, and it seems nearly unnecessary to keep it."

Everyone at the table was staring at the assassin in amazement. With a shrug, he explained. "I was there."

Tristan shook his head in disbelief, but resumed picking at his food. Dinner passed swiftly, and the Blackhavenites, with their two Purheaen members, went back to their rooms. Eyin followed Tlonna and Losolin into their room.

"I'm sorry to intrude, but this is all rather new for me. Why is this such a big deal for everyone? Why is King Demetrius so important?"

Losolin turned to the human. "Demetrius, and now his son Tristan, held the strongest alliance with Blackhaven. Half of our army was once comprised of Kajgenians, recruited in this very spot, nearly four years ago. Demetri funded our campaign, and commissioned the armor you see on all of our soldiers. And...he was our greatest friend."

Eyin nodded. "I meant no disrespect."

"We know, Eyin. That is why we answer," Tlonna said, coming forward to stand before him, one hand on his shoulder. "Hopefully, in the years to come, you and I, and Losolin, will have the same strength of friendship and union that we had with Demetri. It is our hope that Purheae and Blackhaven will once more be ironclad allies."

The young king smiled. "I hope that, too."

"Good," Losolin said. "Now go get some rest. Tomorrow will be a busy day."

As soon as Eyin was gone, the king turned to his wife. "I am going to find Tyular and see if he can help me with something."

Tlonna frowned at him in confusion. "What?"

Losolin dug around in his belt pouch for a moment and then held something out to her. It was a ring, battered and old, but Tlonna recognized it immediately. "Oh, Losolin," she whispered, smiling sadly.

It was the ring of a man who had died in Losolin's arms years previous, asking with his last breath to return it to his son. The elf nodded slightly. "I never forgot, but things always seemed to get in the way. Now, I have no excuse."

Tlonna squeezed his arm in understanding and he left, searching for Tyular. He found the king in Tristan's study, along with the prince, staring out of the window, leaning against the sill. Aidyn was there as well, standing silently off to the side, dutifully cleaning one of his knives. The assassin looked up in surprise as one of the guards announced Losolin, and then looked away when the king stared at him.

Tristan turned and watched Losolin, confused as to why the elf was there. Tyular looked up as well, his gaze previously on the prince. Losolin pulled his gaze from Aidyn and turned to look at the older human.

"Tyular, I have need of your assistance. Three and half years ago, a man from Arseninis died before I could heal him. He gave me this, asking me to return it to his son. I do not know his name, or his son's name, I was hoping you might recognize the signet."

Tyular took the ring and studied it, a frown creasing his forehead. Aidyn came over as well, trying to ignore his king's wondering look. After a moment, the human king sucked in a breath.

"I do know it, though I'm surprised to. There are hundreds of family signs all over Arseninis. This belonged to Davide Giachino. It's one of the older families of Arseninis , and his father was my father's scribe several years ago. Died of old age about a dozen years ago. Davide was a bard," Tyular handed the ring back to the elf.

"Last I heard, his son had taken up his mantle, though he conveniently moved here, to Derid, after his father's death. You can probably find him at one of the inns in the city."

"I will have someone bring up a list of the names," Tristan offered, having come over to examine the ring.

"No need, I will find him. Thank you though," Losolin replied, once again pocketing the ring.

Tristan nodded and moved back to the window, his movements sluggish and pained. Aidyn hesitated, unsure of what to do. "I think I will go with you," he said finally, to Losolin.

The king looked at him blankly. Tristan gave Aidyn a sidelong glance and nodded, leaning his forehead against the glass.

As the two elves moved through the castle, Losolin refrained from asking Aidyn all the questions that ate at him. As soon as they were outside, however, the king could no longer help himself. "I noticed you were quite friendly with Tristan when he was in Blackhaven, but you seem more deeply attached than ever, almost like a father," he said blandly.

Aidyn shook his head at the statement. "I have known him for a long time. I taught him how to use a sword, how to shoot a bow...I was close to his father, I knew his mother, and I was there when his father died. I have a great deal of respect and love for the family, and now he is all that is left."

"I did not know you were so close with the Plauklers. How long have you...did you know Demetri?" Losolin asked, surprised.

The assassin shrugged. "Put it this way...I was in the castle the day Demetrius was born. I was also here when his father, Tristan's grandfather, was crowned. Dietirin and I had come for the coronation, leaving Constancias at home to deal with the kingdom while we fled her side. When Demetri was born, I was here to give King Michel Plaukler Dietirin's gift, a sword. Demetri wore it his entire life, and now Tristan does. The two families, Ewôsdírn and Plaukler, have been tied for centuries, simply through friendship."

"I can see why Tristan seeks your companionship," Losolin replied sincerely, eyeing his mysterious friend. "You have had a life of many turns, Aidyn."

"All in the form of an assassin," the dark elf said, shrugging again. "We are more than just killers, those of us from the College. We are oath-bound to be noble, to uphold our beliefs and we have the right to live as we choose, to be loyal to those we are bound to, and to be brave in the face of evil and injustice. We are the protectors within the shadows."

The king smiled faintly as they neared an inn, knowing that Aidyn held to his honor more tightly than anyone he knew, Yayènia included. To do otherwise was to lose everything he had worked for in his long life, and to end up a mindless killer like those within the Shitan-Kulata. The two males entered the inn, causing a great silence to fall as people recognized either or both of the elves. Losolin found the innkeep behind the bar and moved quickly to speak with him.

"What can I do ye for, my lords?" the man asked, eyeing them curiously.

"We are looking for the son of Davide Giachino, do you know where to find him?" Losolin inquired softly.

The innkeep frowned. "He don't work here, but ye'll probably find him at the Golden Carafe, down on Sonder Street. He in some sort o' trouble?"

"Not at all," the king said quickly, "I knew his father."

"Ah, well, I'd try the Carafe, like I said."

"My thanks," Losolin replied, sliding a gold piece across the table to the surprised man. Behind him, Aidyn subtly let his left scimitar fall back into its scabbard, glaring at the hulking man who had begun to step toward the elves, flexing his gigantic muscles. The man whitened and sat back down.

Once outside, the assassin shook his head. "You are an idiot sometimes," he chuckled good-naturedly.

Losolin frowned. "Aladorn once said much the same thing. Why?"

Aidyn tried to ignore the similarity between him and his wiat brother. "Flashing gold about in a place like that. You nearly got bowled over by a giant."

"Well," the Magin said, grinning, "good thing I have you with me then, eh?"

"Indeed. I know the Golden Carafe, it is down this way," Aidyn replied, and took the lead.

Minutes later, they were striding into the yellow-painted inn, once again causing all conversation and gambling to stop, allowing the more dishonest gamers to slip a few coins off the table. Losolin hailed the innkeep and when the man reached them, the king smiled disarmingly.

"Is Davide Giachino's son in residence?"

"Who? There's a Phillipe Giachino, I don't know if his papa's name was Davide, though," the round human said, looking beyond

Losolin's shoulder to stare at Aidyn. "We uh...do you have need of that many weapons, there, dark one?"

"What?" Aidyn snapped, confused and irritated.

"The people here, they're safe people, gentle people. So many weapons might make them nervous."

The assassin frowned. "I will not draw them unless provoked, you may be assured," he growled, folding his arms across his chest.

Losolin patted his shoulder. "He is my guard, good sir. I am Losolin, King of Blackhaven, and this is Aidyn Sestuns. You may know of him."

Once again the room went deadly silent, this time even the pipe player on the little stage stopped playing. "Aye, I know of him, and you, King Losolin. What can I do for you?" the innkeeper wheezed, suddenly very pale.

"I look for Davide Giachino's son, as I said," the elf reiterated.

A young man stood, looking shaken. "I am Phillipe Giachino, milord. Do you have need of a bard?"

Losolin looked to the squat man before him, his brow raised. "Do you have a room in which we may speak privately?"

"Of course, of course, this way. Phil, this way."

The four moved to the back of the inn and down a short hallway. The proprietor left them in a small room with a tiny hearth, two chairs, and a rickety table. Losolin sat in one of the chairs and gestured for the terrified bard to take the other one. Aidyn positioned himself against the wall, idly picking at the pommel of one of his scimitars.

"My name is Losolin Grisholm-en'Ewôsdírn, King of Blackhaven, and this is my good friend Aidyn Sestuns. You are indeed Davide Giachino's son?"

Phillipe nodded, swallowing. "Aye."

"Does this belong to you?" Losolin asked, pulling out the ring.

The bard took it with trembling fingers, his eyes wide. "It was my father's. It has been in my family for generations. I thought it lost with him."

The king sighed. "I was there when he died, in fact, he died in my arms. His last words were to ask me to return this to you. I am sorry it took so long for me to return it."

"No, it is enough that you did," Phillipe replied, astounded by the king's thoughtfulness. "I never expected to see it again. Thank you. I am afraid I have nothing to give you in return."

"I would never ask for anything," Losolin said. "Your father gave his life protecting several others, including myself." Struck by a sudden need, the elf untied his money pouch and tossed it to the young man.

Aidyn shook his head, but remained silent. Phillipe stared at the king in disbelief.

"Take it, please. I cannot offer you your father's life back, but perhaps I can make yours a little easier. There is something around eighty geld in there, maybe a little more. Not much, but it is all I have on me at the moment."

The bard's eyes nearly popped out of his head. "I could not make so much in a year! King Losolin, I could never take this!"

"What, you would refuse a king?" Aidyn said suddenly, staring at the human.

Phillipe swallowed and quickly took the purse. "No, never."

Losolin smiled. "Good. We must be going, but I am glad to have finally met you. I carried that ring around for nearly four years, and I am relieved it has finally come home. A good evening to you, Phillipe."

"And you, King Losolin, Lord Aidyn...thank you."

The two elves left the room, leaving the still disbelieving bard behind. As they strolled through the darkening streets of Kajgenia, they said little. Once they were nearing the castle grounds, Aidyn sighed deeply. Losolin looked at his friend with concern.

The assassin sighed again, and this time stopped, his ragged black cloak settling about his body. "Losolin...I have been working on the Eseirik who killed Demetrius. He has said some odd things, other than the usual evasion and desperate attempts to curry favor. I think something is going on within Seaduens that we are unaware of."

"How do you mean?" the king asked, unsure of what the dark elf meant.

"Well, he has said that the elves are in a far more desperate situation than we perceive. That our people are down to one kingdom. It does not make sense, but I can think of no other answer than that Seaduens is in trouble."

"If it is, there is little we can do about it," Losolin said, shaking his head. "Stoffnias would never agree to us going to see what is going on. If anything, he is probably involved in...whatever it is."

Aidyn nodded. "I know, but I figured you should know."

"I should. I will talk to Tlonna, but there really is nothing we can do until our own problems are solved."

The assassin nodded again, and the two continued on to the castle.

The next week was filled with treaty renewals, tailoring for the coronation, and helping the young prince get his life back on track. Finally, the day of the coronation arrived, and everyone convened in the corridor outside their rooms. The females, excepting Yayènia of course, were in long, floor-length dresses with full sleeves and skirts. Each was made in the same white and pale blue, with black embroidered trees on the bottom hem. Yayènia wore white pants and a pale blue over-dress, also embroidered with black trees.

The males all wore matching colors, but with black pants, white tunics, and pale blue cloaks. Eyin and Meradyn, however, had made a critical decision. They decided on the Purheaen standard, a red elk, which they said was populous in Purheae, and a symbol of both strength and purity for their people.

So Tlonna commissioned for them a set of clothing that went along with their choice. Pants of black and tunics of crimson with brown leather trim. Eyin was also given a royal cloak, black leather stitched with the Red Elk in the center. Meradyn, in accordance with Yayènia's wishes, was given a leather cuirass with the elk on the breast. The two men gaped in shock when Tlonna and Yayènia presented them with the items.

"Given to the King and his military commander, of Purheae," the queen said formally, handing the packages to them.

Eyin took his with trembling hands and opened it, the cloak slipping out of the paper to reveal its crimson elk. His light green eyes were riveted on the picture, as Meradyn tore open his package. Holding up the cuirass, he stared at Yayènia.

"You did this, didn't you?"

She smiled, and said nothing. The two young men donned their new items, fitting them carefully over their equally new clothing. Tlonna looked proudly upon them, standing before the boys as they grinned at each other.

"Eyin, the next step is a crown. It need not be a hulking thing of gold, or even silver, but it is a symbol of your stature, and it will be recognized for what it is by all the citizens of this world. It is not something I can give to you, or design for you. It is something you must commission yourself, for it will be your throne when you are not sitting, which will be often."

The young king smiled at her. "Thank you, Queen Tlonna. High Commander Yayènia. I... *we*, owe you both so much."

"And you will pay it back by being good leaders. Now come, we have a coronation to attend," the Magin replied, and the four stepped from the room.

All together once more, the Blackhavenites and Purheaens were escorted to the massive ballroom and given places of honor at the front. The hall was filled with people, nobles and commoners alike, all there to see their young prince crowned in his father's place. Tristan was well liked, but he had large shoes to fill.

As Tlonna turned to sit, she spotted another familiar face that made her furious. Tyular smiled at her from beside Athelias, rolling his eyes. His face lit up when Miazie, arm in arm with Sodo, strode up to him. They spoke shortly, and then the King of Arseninis stepped over to greet Tlonna.

"Tlonna, I am sorry I have not come to speak with you this whole time. Look at you and all your people! Losolin, did you find Davide's son? Aladorn!" Suddenly the king seemed overwhelmed and he grabbed them all into an ungraceful hug, having been too busy with Tristan to be able to greet his friends properly.

The three elves extricated themselves carefully and grinned back at the brash young king. The wiat shimmered for a moment and then snapped back into focus. "Tyular...what is *he* doing here. He is part of the reason Demetrius is dead."

Tyular turned and looked down the bench where Athelias sat, coldly ignoring everyone around him. He shook his head. "He is King of Talenias. He has to be here. At least he didn't bring Athelan."

Tlonna glared unabashedly at the murderous man. "He should be hanging from the rafters, Tyular, not sitting there gloating over his victory."

"I know, I know, but there is nothing we can do about it here and now. This moment is Tristan's, whether he wants it or not. Poor kid."

"He will be all right after a while. Oh, Tyular, come over here for a moment," Tlonna replied, and guided the king over to where Eyin and Meradyn were sitting between Yayènia and Ghealan.

"King Tyular, I give you First King of Purheae, Eyin Thorn, and Meradyn Obren, Commander-in-Training. Eyin, Meradyn, I give you King Tyular of Arseninis."

The two young men stood and bowed much more gracefully to Tyular than they had to Losolin and Tlonna back at Blackhaven. They had learned much. Tyular, on the other hand, nearly missed his from shock.

"Purheae? King?"

"Yes," Losolin butted in. "We will talk later. Tristan is coming."

Everyone turned around and caught a glimpse of the king-to-be standing outside the doors to the ballroom. As the various leaders of nations and their people found their seats, a herald pounded his staff on the floor.

"Enter, Prince Tristan Plaukler of Kajgenia!"

Tristan strode through the double doors, resplendent in an emerald cape lined in black fur, shining black knee-high boots, black cotton pants, and a teal silk tunic. On his head was the Heir Crown, the emerald-studded band with the crossed spears. He looked powerful, his broad shoulders thrown back as he advanced to the throne. The prince took his place, an uncomfortable expression crossing his face for an instant, immediately replaced by stoicism.

The same priest that had presided over Demetrius's funeral now stepped up to stand on the right hand of the throne.

"Prince Tristan, you have stepped up to fill the Crown of Kajgenia. With this honor comes the obligation to protect your people, your land, and your throne. You have come here today with the purpose of obtaining said throne?"

"I have," Tristan intoned.

"Do you swear to fulfill said obligations?"

"I so swear."

"Do you swear to uphold the laws of your fathers, justice for your people, and to protect them against those who would mean harm?"

"I so swear."

And it went on, oaths and promises yelled out by the priest, and answered in Tristan's monotone. At one point, Athelias yawned loudly, and Tyular smacked him hard on the back of his head, inciting murmurs and snickers. Tlonna shared a look with Losolin, but the proceedings did not halt. Finally, the priest stepped away from the throne and stood on the step below.

"Good people of Kajgenia, and her friends, rise for the Coronation!"

With a loud rustle, everyone in the hall stood, and those already standing stretched their necks. Tristan stood as well, and then knelt on the verdant pillow before the throne. The priest took off the Heir Crown, and with great ceremony, accepted the Crown of Kajgenia from another robed-man holding another green pillow.

The Crown of Kajgenia was a masterful creation of wrought gold and silver. It had no discernible object, as the Heir Crown had spears, but among a web of thin arms of gold rested an enormous emerald. It caught the light and shone outward, winking through the crowd. Demetrius had worn it, but it had seemed simply a part of him, nothing of great excitement. Now, Tlonna saw it for the first time in a different light. It was truly beautiful. She herself was wearing her crown, as was Losolin, Tyular, Athelias, and a powerful looking dwarf she took to be King Barukh of Florwen Hune.

So much power in this room, Tlonna thought, and yet they were at odds with each other. It was disheartening and disturbing, but the Magin had hopes to bring them all together, excepting Athelias. She merely wanted him dead.

Tristan had his head bowed, and the priest said something to him. The young man looked up, gray eyes hard with determination, and the Crown of Kajgenia was placed on his brow. Tlonna took a deep breath, staring at him with optimism and motherly affection. She wished Haydyn were beside her. It suddenly struck her how young they all were. Tristan, at twenty-five, Haydyn at nineteen, Eyin at twenty-three, Tyular at thirty-six, even Sithian at nearly twenty. She herself was extremely young for an elf at one hundred and forty-six. Athelias she knew was in his forties, now, and Barukh over two hundred, making him middle-aged.

Demetrius had been the eldest, the longest as king, and the patron of them all, after Dietirin. Tlonna felt a sudden and intense longing. Both her fatherly connections were dead, and she was the second eldest, though not the most experienced. That would be Barukh. He had come to power fifty years ago, when his father had died.

Putting her morose thoughts away, Tlonna returned to the present and watched Tristan rise, accept an ornamental spear with emerald and teal tassels tied just under the head, and stand tall before his people. The priest turned once more to the congregation.

"I give you King Tristan of Kajgenia! All Hail King Tristan!"

"ALL HAIL KING TRISTAN!" the crowd roared, and then everyone, rulers included, got down on one knee.

Tlonna glanced at her sister. Yayènia grimaced, but she followed the crowd to the floor. The warrior believed no one but an enemy should abase themselves by getting on their knees. Tristan hefted the spear in the air, and everyone returned to their feet, roaring and applauding. Losolin and Tlonna smiled at each other, remembering their own coronation at the top of the Steps of the Winds.

A guard came over to them, gesturing to all the kings and Tlonna, as the only queen present. Tyular, Losolin, Tlonna, Athelias, Barukh, and Eyin, yanked by Tlonna, stood before the guard, eying each other. Tlonna and Losolin bowed their heads to Barukh, who did the same.

"If it please you...my Kings and my Queen..." the guard was sweating with nerves. Tlonna pitied him. "You may go before King Tristan and have a private word. It is custom my Lords and Lady."

"Thank you, lad. We are not going to behead you just because we each own a kingdom," Barukh said gruffly, laughing slightly.

The guard wheezed, and gestured weakly to Tristan, who was watching them. Athelias turned and strode up to the throne, the others hastening after. Tlonna tuned her hearing so that she could eavesdrop.

"Enjoy it while you can, boy. Times are changing, and the weak will be swept away like leaves in a wind," Athelias muttered, and Tristan's chin rose marginally.

"I am a tree, and all *leaves* will blow around me, Athelias."

The traitorous king snorted and moved off, beckoning his entourage. Tlonna silently applauded Tristan, sharing a triumphant grin with Losolin, who had also heard. Tyular and Eyin were talking, oblivious to what had just transpired, and Barukh stepped up to talk to Tristan.

"As sorry as I was to see your father go, lad, I am glad to see you step up," the dwarf king said in his rough voice. "As I did with Demetrius, I will stand by you, and Florwen Hune will stand by Kajgenia."

"Thank you, Bar. I would like a meeting with you, and the other rulers later today if possible. In Council Hall," Tristan said, his voice hearty with appreciation.

"I will be there."

He moved off, and Tyular stepped up. Tlonna quit eavesdropping and turned to Eyin. "How are you holding up?"

The young man shrugged. "King Tyular said he would be interested in trade, once we get it going."

"Excellent. That will be very beneficial. Tyular is a good man."

"What do I say to him?"

"To Tyular? Yes! Of course!"

"No, to this fellow...Tristan?"

Tlonna smiled. "Whatever feels right, Eyin. You are a king, and he is a king. He is only two years older than you, remember that. Look, it is your turn. Go on."

Eyin hesitated, and Losolin pushed him forward, hiding a grin. Both elves turned to hear what he would say.

"Ah..." Eyin stammered, looking up at his colleague.

"King Eyin, wasn't it?" Tristan said, sticking out his hand. "Listen, we're both new to this arena, perhaps we can help each other? I'm holding a meeting tonight, will you come? Tlonna and Losolin will know where it is."

Eyin shook his hand. "Yes, of course I will come. I am...very glad for you. And very sad for you as well. I lost my father when I was seventeen, to a fever."

"Then we have much in common. I hope we become friends, Eyin," Tristan said, smiling sadly.

"Me too," the Purheaen hesitated again, and Tristan discreetly pointed over to where the Blackhavenites and Meradyn were standing.

Tlonna and Losolin smiled as they walked up to the new king. "We are proud of you, Tristan. And we will be at the meeting in Council Hall."

Tristan laughed, shaking his head. "I forget you people have such good hearing. Did you hear what Athelias said?"

"Yes, and you handled it well. We will take care of him and his son when the time comes," Losolin replied, gripping the man's hand.

"We love you Tristan," Tlonna said, and hugged him.

"I love you too, Tlonna," he replied, and hugged her back. "Thank you. Oh, will you ask Aidyn to come as well?"

The elves smiled, said they would, and walked back to where their friends were standing. After conveying the message to Aidyn, the troupe made their way through the crowded hall, most people parting when they saw the Blackhaven Tree, or recognized one of the elves. Some even bowed.

Chapter 29

A Council of Kings, a Queen, and an Assassin

Tlonna, Losolin, Aidyn, and Eyin were ushered into the Council Hall and were greeted by Tristan. Already seated was Barukh, and Tyular was pouring himself a glass of rum. The only queen present sat next to the dwarf, her two companions on her right side. This forced Eyin to take a seat next to Tristan, making the younger human look uncertain, while Aidyn sat on the other side of the king. They were sitting at a round table, small enough for there not to be any more room for someone else.

"Rather cozy, isn't it?" Tyular chuckled, nudging Barukh, who took the elbow in stride, obviously accustomed to the younger king. "So, Tristan, what are we here for?"

The newly crowned king sighed, twisting his glass of brandy. "We are in a state of unrest. It has been a thousand years since Nymyñosians have been at war with each other. Now, Seaduens and Talenias sit like hungry dogs, waiting for a weak spot. They almost had one, two, if what Aidyn says is true."

The assassin nodded. "They deeply underestimated Tlonna and her family's reaction. The attempt to kidnap, torture, and murder all the males was turned on its head."

"Who are 'they'?" Barukh asked, tugging at his brown beard.

"The Eseirik, hybrid killers from the Age of Kings, created in Arseninis," Aidyn replied, glancing at Tyular.

The Arseninisian King looked flabbergasted. "I've never heard of such creatures! There have always been rumors of odd experiments gone wrong, but no mention of these Eseirik."

"They were created two thousand years ago, Tyular, and they can breed only once, if that, we have discovered. They are mutants, creatures, Elf, Man, and Goblin, brought to insanity by their own twisted minds," Tlonna explained.

"Elf, Man, *and* Goblin?" Barukh gasped, horrified. "It is no wonder they cracked. The three races are as different as can be. We must find them all, and destroy them."

"Already done," Aidyn said quietly, touching his scars. "The seven from Blackhaven were destroyed by Tlonna, Yayènia, Erdwyf, and Miazie. Twenty-one of them, I tracked down to their den and slew them all. The last remaining septet was here. They assassinated Demetrius before my own eyes. I was just too slow to save him."

Tristan gripped the elf's shoulder in condolence. "There is one left alive, down in the dungeon. Aidyn has been...talking with him, which is why we know there are none left, and what their purpose was in both attacks. At Blackhaven, they aimed to cut off the right hand of power by kidnapping and murdering all the males. They planned to torture you," he said, looking directly at Losolin. "They were supposed to find out the weaknesses of Blackhaven, including Yayènia's and Tlonna's. They work for Sithian Rahlan, Athelias, and Stoffnias."

"We knew that," Tlonna said, looking at Aidyn, who extracted the medallion from his belt.

"We found this embedded in the flesh of one of our attackers. It has three rudimentary symbols of each kingdom. The same was found in the skin of the Eseirik who slew Demetri."

Barukh and Tyular looked beyond furious, and Eyin simply looked confused.

"What do you propose we do?" the dwarf asked, his voice a calm rumble, countering his apparent rage. Tlonna was impressed.

Tristan shook his head. "My father was attempting to work through an alliance that would bind us all together, tightly. Other than that, I do not know."

Losolin now spoke up, leaning onto the table. "Tlonna and I are in good relations with Furntil Eldrout, King of Flousen Dua. He is alive, and his son came to our aid at Alchemian, just like all of you."

"My captain spoke of him," Barukh nodded, narrowing his eyes in thought. "Anadin spurns most elves, but he spoke very highly of this...Erandur."

"Yes, Erandur elicits great admiration," Tlonna said. "He is a great elf. Two weeks back, I sent out an invitation to Furntil, and the figurehead in Schelum. I hope to form, as Demetrius did, the strongest alliance Nymyños has ever seen. A binding of our great kingdoms, and theirs. The Great Nymyñosian Alliance, an ironclad peace treaty between Blackhaven, Schelum, Flousen Dua, Florwen Hune, Arseninis, Purheae, and Kajgenia. We were hoping to hear back from Furntil before asking everyone else."

"What of Narnen and Zeynuwn?" Tyular asked, an excited fire in his eyes.

"Narnen has all but been obliterated, and Zeynuwn will be the hardest. I was planning on waiting until the final word from everyone before approaching Tahi-Tat with the idea. That way whoever agreed would be behind it, and he would be cornered. The Zeynuwnians saved us at Alchemian, all of us, but that does not mean they plan on allying themselves with us. Tahi-Tat does not like Losolin and I, for whatever reason, and he will be hard to convince."

"Aye, General Shin ran his soldiers through the Liberated Lands all last summer after the battle, but returned to Zeynuwn at the onset of autumn."

"Did they accomplish anything?" Tlonna asked, having wondered about that for a while.

The human shrugged casually. "They wiped out the garrison at Anutch, but it was eventually reclaimed anyway, at least there have been sightings of activity up there."

"All the more reason to bind ourselves together, then," the queen muttered, fiddling with the cuff of her sleeve.

"You have it all thought out, Tlonna, and I like the sounds of it. Draw up the papers and I will sign it," Tyular said.

"As will I," Barukh stated, slapping the table. "It is about time Florwen Hune and Blackhaven were allied. Elf and Dwarf and Man, we will be unbeatable!"

As everyone put their hands in the center of the table, all eyes turned to Eyin. "And what of you, Eyin Thorn, First King of Purheae?" Tlonna asked quietly.

The youngest person present went white, shaking as seven very strong rulers watched him. Aidyn sat back, his part done with.

"I would not want to be left alone and naked when Zaedic and these traitors come calling. Purheae is in," he avowed, and placed his hand on top of everyone else's.

"To the Great Nymyñosian Alliance!" Tyular shouted, and the eight kings and queen followed his example, tossing their hands in the air and grinning.

Once they had all settled down once more, Tristan assumed a grave countenance. "What of Athelias?"

"Kill him," Tlonna snarled, startling the males.

"We can't just slice his head off, Tlonna. He remains a part of the East Nymyños Alliance, whether or not we want him to be," Tyular reminded her. "As much as we all want him dead, it is much more complicated than that."

"He attacked me some few years ago, played a part in Demetrius's murder, hosted the Eseirik in his country, and threatened Tristan not five hours ago," the Magin spat. "We have more than enough reason to kill him."

"And he sat back while the rest of us fought at Alchemian," Losolin put in.

"True, he does deserve to die a most painful death, but it would tear Talenias apart, which we do not want, and we cannot forget Athelan. He is young, but he is cruel and ruthless. He makes his father look like a saint," Barukh countered.

"Then kill them both and put an end to it. There must be someone in that blasted place that is not blind to the rest of the world," Tlonna motioned, folding her arms.

The dwarf smiled, liking the elf queen. "We cannot be hasty in this. Otherwise, what makes us different from Rahlan, Stoffnias, and Athelias? I am sure they thought much the same about you."

Tlonna slumped her shoulders, defeated. "Then what do you propose?"

Silence filled the Council Hall as the leaders looked at one another, each filled with a loathing, but unable to voice their true desires lest it be accepted. Finally, it was Aidyn who sat forward.

"Look, Athelias is mad. He can hardly contain himself these days. Just look at him. Get him in a public place, where there are lots of witness, and goad him until he breaks. Guaranteed he will want to brag about his triumph, and most likely he will drag his son into it as well. And he will not do it quietly, either. Tlonna, remember what you said when he attacked you?"

Tlonna nodded. "He was screaming at the top of his lungs. He wanted everyone to hear what he had done. I almost think he wants to be caught and stopped."

"And how do you say we do this? We cannot just pull him into the middle of the street and start badgering him. That would be too obvious," Tristan asked, frowning.

"So host a feast, a ball, a bloody contest, just some sort of public affair where there will be tons of people," Aidyn said, spreading his hands on the table.

Everyone sat back in their chairs, smiles spreading on their diverse faces. Tristan folded his arms. "I hope everyone is up for some dancing," he said, and laughed.

Chapter 30

A Family Dethroned

The King's Coronation Ball was scheduled two days hence, with invitations to each ruler present. Though Tlonna was nervous about what might be happening at Blackhaven, she looked forward to finally calling out Athelias. The castle buzzed about the looming festivities, and the foreigners kept together, feeling more comfortable among each other than the denizens of Kajgenia.

Tlonna, Losolin, and Barukh holed up together quite often, finally getting to know each other. The dwarf king was rather jovial, but also iron-willed and blunt. Tlonna thoroughly enjoyed his company, and Losolin found himself smiling more than usual. Finally, when the day of the ball arrived, everyone convened in the corridor outside the ballroom. But, according to tradition, only the rulers and their partners were to enter in procession, so the entourage headed into the ballroom to wait like everyone else. Yayènia huffed, but Suneelo pulled her away from Tlonna, whispering something in her ear that made her laugh. Tlonna shook her head at her sister's devotion to her protection. The entire Blackhaven entourage was in their newly tailored dress once more, Meradyn and Eyin in theirs.

Barukh was clad in his country's colors, gray and brown, but surprisingly his pants and coat were of velvet. Tlonna met him with a curtsey, spreading her white and blue skirt and smiling. The king kissed her knuckles, and bowed his head to Losolin. Tristan arrived a minute later, resplendent in black and teal, a pretty young woman on his arm.

"This is Aleyjandra Bishop, Duchess of Aedrid," the prince introduced her, and the gathered rulers greeted her.

Tlonna eyed the woman, wondering if she was just a prize for the night, or if there was something deeper. She was certainly pretty enough with a soft face, kind hazel eyes, and curling black hair that tumbled to her mid back. Aleyjandra carried herself with the grace of one born into nobility, and though she was definitely of the lowest stature in the hall, she did not seem fazed.

"Queen Tlonna," she murmured once all had been introduced. "Tristan has told me of your kindness and your valor. You are a great leader."

The Magin turned and looked down at the girl. "I do only what I believe to be right, Duchess Aleyjandra. Have you known Tristan long?"

The human smiled faintly. "I have no designs on the throne, your Majesty, but if Tristan asked my hand in marriage, I could not decline."

"Because he is your king?"

"No, your Highness, because I love him," Aleyjandra whispered, leaning forward so that no one else could hear. "We have been lovers for three years, now."

Tlonna's eyebrows rose in surprise. "Have you really? Well, that is a surprise. I never knew. Demetrius never said anything."

"That is because King Demetrius did not know. Tristan knew his father did not want us to marry."

"And why is that, Duchess Aleyjandra?" the Magin asked, suddenly concerned.

"Aley, please. It is because I am King Athelias's cousin, on his mother's side. Though we have spoken only twice, King Demetrius worried that I was an agent for my cousin."

"And are you?" Tlonna asked coldly.

"My Lady, if I were, I certainly wouldn't have told you that I could be," Aley said with a coy smile.

The elf narrowed her eyes in suspicion, but before she could say anything else, Athelias himself appeared, also with a woman on his arm. She was a tiny thing, obviously young and vaguely familiar. The king looked haughty, as though, among all the kings there, he was the most powerful of them all.

Tristan ignored his presence, but he raised his arm and beckoned to everyone gathered. "As custom would dictate, I will go in first with Aley, followed by Tlonna and Losolin, then Tyular,"

"Wish I had a woman," the king muttered, eliciting chuckles.

Tristan smiled, but did not stop talking. "And Barukh, Eyin, and finally Athelias and his guest."

"Apparently it is not in order of power or prestige," Athelias snapped, glowering at Eyin as the young king took his place.

No one replied, but Tristan rolled his eyes and took his place, Aley standing beside him in her glittery red gown. The young king quietly rapped his knuckle on the door, and within the ballroom came the sound of the herald pounding his staff on the floor.

"All attend King Tristan, and Duchess Aleyjandra Bishop! Queen Tlonna Ewôsdírn er'Grisholm and King Losolin Grisholm-en'Ewôsdírn! King Tyular Ambrose! King Barukh Odrinsson! King Eyin Thorn! King Athelias Embina and Lady Jezebel Et!"

As they were named, the rulers marched through the doors into the ballroom to the clapping and gaping of the people. Eyin received the most stares, as no one knew who he was or where he was from. All the single kings moved to stand at the edge of the crowd, while the three couples took up a stance, and the orchestra began a mid-tempo waltz. Halfway through the song, people were allowed to join, and soon the ballroom was filled with dancers. As the night wore on, Tlonna danced with Eyin, pulling the protesting young man onto the floor and leading him through a simple routine. She caught Yayènia dancing with Meradyn as well, and Miazie with Tyular. However, most of the time they stayed with their respective partners, reveling in the frivolity. Only the members of the king's council two nights earlier knew of the plan, and they waited anxiously for the appointed hour and song to draw near.

Barukh, Tlonna saw, was dancing with a short human with a broad-featured face, and Tyular with an elegant woman who kept leaning in and making the king laugh. Even Meradyn had found a girl his age and they were absorbed in each other. Tlonna grinned at Losolin, who smiled back and held her close.

Finally, the first notes of the chosen song were played, and Tristan glanced at Tlonna, who looked to Tyular, who in turn nodded discretely at Eyin, who looked at Barukh. Slowly, deliberately, the five pairs moved in around Athelias, dancing in a rotating circle, surrounding the oblivious traitor. Tyular had the first cue, and he swung close to Athelias.

"Did you hear that Stoffnias was behind Demetrius's murder?" he whispered, and then moved away.

Athelias's head jerked up, envy and rage in his eyes. His partner, Jezebel, glared viciously at him.

Now Losolin stepped up. "The assassin caught by Aidyn is claiming that his faction acted alone on Demetri's death."

Now the Talenian looked violent, and Jezebel pale. Tlonna suddenly remembered where she had seen the girl. Leaning in to her husband, she whispered in his ear.

"Losolin, Jezebel was Midian's pet when I was captive there. She was one of his favorites. Sithian must have given her to Athelias as payment."

The king shook his head in disbelief, but his part was done in goading Athelias, so he was forced to stay in their spot.

Barukh was now leaning in to the king, keeping his partner out of hearing range. "Did you know your son put forth a proclamation saying he was in league with Stoffnias and the murder of Demetrius?"

Eyin was next, also keeping the girl he was dancing with away from the conversation. "I'm new to all this, but I heard Sithian Rahlan is taking all the credit for killing King Demetrius."

Finally, Tristan swung close to the now livid Athelias and his petrified date. "I know you did nothing to my father. You are too weak and scared to try and pull such strings."

Their ridiculously simple plan worked. Athelias's mind snapped like a taught string. He roared in fury, bringing the entire room to a standstill.

"I did it! I did it! That's right, boy!" he pointed a menacing finger at Tristan. "I hired the assassins that slaughtered your foolish daddy. Me and Athelan, alone! We killed your precious king, and we would have had you too," the lunatic gestured at Losolin, Suneelo, Aidyn, and Ghealan, who had moved close to their king and queen, along with the rest of the Blackhavenites. "Yeah...we would have had you, but your freaky little whore-queen got in the way."

Tlonna stiffened her back in an attempt to control her temper. Erdwyf laid a hand on her arm.

"And you..." Athelias took a step toward Eyin. "Who are you to dare speak to me in such a way? You little upstart simpleton!"

Losolin started to defend the young man, but Eyin raised his chin, and the king stopped, wondering what the youth intended. Meradyn had moved up behind his friend and stood tall, arms crossed, his striking face tense and defiant.

"I am Eyin Thorn of Purheae, and I stand as your equal, if not your better, for I have never been a traitor, nor a murderer," he said coolly, green eyes hard.

Tlonna and Losolin shared a stunned look, proud of their young protégé. Among the crowd were surprised murmurs, mostly consisting of the word Purheae. Tristan sauntered over to stand next to Eyin and looked at Athelias with steel gray eyes.

"Athelias Embina, as King of Kajgenia, I place you under contempt of the East Nymyños Alliance."

Barukh and Tyular followed him, so that the four males stood side by side, Eyin obviously uncomfortable. "As King of Florwen Hune, I too place you under contempt of the East Nymyños Alliance," Barukh thundered.

Tyular did the same, and Athelias shuddered when Tristan stepped up to him, putting his face inches away from the doomed king's. "You are the reason my father is dead, and I will see you rot in hell," he hissed, and then in an official tone, "Athelias Embina, you are hereby dethroned by the joint authority of the East Nymyños Alliance, and by that power, know that Athelan Embina is also disinherited on the same charge of sedition and treason."

"You can't do this! You will be hunted by men a thousand times your strength, and they will crush you like ants. They will crush all of you!" Athelias cried, spinning around and pointing at Tlonna and her companions. Then he suddenly rushed the Magin Queen, clawed hands outstretched toward her throat.

As her various protectors and family members leapt forward to stop him, Tlonna held out her own hand, palm perpendicular to the floor, and Athelias ran face first into a wall of air. He was knocked backward and landed hard on his back. People screamed and looked around in confusion before locking eyes on the elf. She stood calmly as her family regrouped, elfin faces unreadable. Even Miazie was blank-faced, standing in front of Sodo with her back rigid.

"Have you not yet learned that attacking me is a stupid idea, Athelias? You always end up on the ground," Tlonna said frostily.

The man groaned and staggered to his feet, blood fanning out from his nose. He shook his auburn hair back and glared at her. "This is not over, elf."

"It is for you, and your vile son," Tyular growled, coming forward and yanking the older man's arms behind his back.

Tristan beckoned to his guards and they marched forward and dragged the dethroned king from the ballroom. Tlonna stepped up to Jezebel, who was standing silently off to the side.

"I know who you are," the Magin said to the girl, looking down at her.

"I'm surprised you would remember such an unimportant face, Queen Tlonna," the Zaedican replied stiffly.

"What are you doing here?"

The woman smiled an eerie smile, dark eyes full of malice. "I am the payment, only a reward, as I have always been. Your son could not abide seeing me, knowing his father had enjoyed me so much. He's going insane, did you know? Your precious baby boy is losing his mind faster than Midian ever did. He sucks blood from the women he lays with, drinks it like wine. He ignores his wife and fucks every other woman in the city."

"No need to be vulgar," Erdwyf said, coming to stand next to Tlonna.

"Vulgar? When is the truth vulgar?" Jezebel asked innocently. "King Sithian is losing his mind, and when it is completely gone, that is when your world will turn to...ash." The last word she drew out with a hiss, giving the two elves a wicked grin.

As she sauntered away, Tlonna turned to Erdwyf, concern etched on her face. "Ash? Do you think Sithian will cause the Taint to return?"

The High Advisor shrugged, glaring after the woman. "I do not know, Tlonna, but he is your son. Perhaps he will."

"I hate this. I hate knowing I helped bring such a monster into this world. When the world finds out, everything will be thrown askew. How can I expect people to trust and follow me when they know that I birthed children to Midian Rahlan?"

"By knowing that you did it unwillingly," Erdwyf said forcefully, patting her friend's back. "It will be a hard blow, but you were a captive for months. You were raped and tortured. You did nothing wrong."

"I should have killed them when they were infants," the queen breathed.

"And what of Haydyn? Did you know that he would be good? Or do you wish you had killed him as well?"

Tlonna's shoulders slumped. "Hindsight. It is an evil thing."

Erdwyf smiled wryly. "True."

When they turned around to return to their group, they found Eyin and Meradyn being congratulated by the present kings. Losolin beamed at the young Purheaens, oceanic eyes sparkling with pride. When Tlonna approached, Tyular turned to her, grinning like a fool.

"You have trained him well, my friend. Young Eyin will be a force to be reckoned with. I've never seen such pluck!"

Tlonna smiled at a blushing Eyin. "He has a lot yet to learn, but he is a good student, attentive, inquisitive, intelligent. You showed true grit today, Eyin, you did well."

"I did not like him at all," the Purheaen stated quietly, glancing at Meradyn, who was being commended by Yayènia, Suneelo, and Ghealan. "Mer was behind me the whole time?"

"As a true protector should," Barukh replied, slapping the young man on the shoulder. Eyin lurched forward a step from the strength of the blow.

"You two make a good team," Losolin said, still smiling. "Tristan, your people are staring."

The new King of Kajgenia spun around and raised his hands, pointing at the orchestra. Immediately the conductor raised his baton and began a fast-paced tango that moved the party-goers back onto the dance floor.

Tristan turned back around and grabbed a glass of cordial off a passing servant's tray. "To a successful plan!"

The kings and queen toasted each other, and the ball wound into the late hours of the night. Finally, when even the most emphatic of dancers were tiring, Losolin pulled Tlonna out of the hall, tugging at her hand. Their friends watched them go with knowing grins.

Once alone in their room, Losolin pushed Tlonna against the door and kissed her, running his hand through her hair. Slowly, with the infinite patience of his race, he undid the stays on her dress and unclothed his wife. When they finally stood naked, Tlonna buried her face in his neck, holding him close, breathing in the comfortable and arousing scent of him.

Losolin trapped one of her hands against the door and moved within her, his heart thudding against his chest. His teeth scraped along Tlonna's lower lip and jaw as their bodies moved in tandem.

As dawn approached, Tlonna hissed Losolin's name in ecstasy, and they fell asleep entangled in the sheets of the bed and each other's limbs.

Aidyn slipped out from between the sheets of his bed and dressed quietly, so as not to disturb the woman still sleeping. He had watched everyone return to their rooms with someone, including his brother, Eyin, and Meradyn. At the last moment, the assassin had invited the woman he had been dancing with up to his bedchamber. She had agreed, gleefully. It had done nothing for him, but his partner had nearly screamed in pleasure, and claimed her entire body was numb from the waist down. The elf had lain awake for a long time afterward, thinking of the hallucinations brought on by the Eseirik poison.

It was the first time he had evaluated them fully, running through each one, dissecting them. The ones with Yayènia and Erdwyf he dismissed. They were like his sisters, beautiful yet he was not attracted to them. Miazie, Aidyn sighed, she bothered him. A human yes, but something had changed since the trip to Purheae. Though those who had gone did not speak of the things that had happened, Aidyn had gleaned that Losolin had pulled a frightening amount of magic into his body, and then released it with catastrophic consequences.

The assassin wondered if Miazie, as the only human present, had been altered somehow, for she seemed more radiant, renewed, even. Then there was Tlonna. Somewhere deep in his heart there was an ache that would never fade, a deeply buried love. Aidyn cursed himself, shaking his head, staring up at the canopy of the bed.

So now he crept from the bedchamber into the early morning hallway, barely glancing at the guard outside his door. He needed to release the pent up energy and emotion inside his body, and it was a two-fold process, if he could not couple with someone who could match his skill. Moving through the castle on silent feet, Aidyn slipped outside and looked up at the fading moons.

Acutely aware that today was beginning the exact same way the day had gone when Tlonna had been abducted by Midian from this very city, he walked to the training yard. A few soldiers, most likely officers, moved about the yard, sparring and preparing for the day. Ignoring the humans, the elf threw off his cloak and went through his warm-up formations. Slowly, meticulously, Aidyn sped up until he was just a blur to the soldiers watching.

Then he drew his sword in one fluid motion and went through the sequence he had followed nearly every day of his life since he was six years old. Next were his slim scimitars, flashing through the now bright morning air. Though no snow fell this morning, it laid in drifts all over the place. Aidyn moved through them easily, tracing a near perfect spiral, unconscious of the fact.

When he finished, an entire regiment was gathered at the training yard, sparring, running, or observing. Though they had watched him for over a week, the Kajgenian militiamen still were impressed by the awesome spectacle. Aidyn laid his arms down next to his cloak, still frustrated and tense.

Annoyed, he moved onto the dirt track and began running, passing a group of trotting soldiers twice before they completed a single lap. He moved easily, lightly, hands open for better circulation. By mid-morning he had stripped down to his waist, steam rising off his body as he kept his blood pumping.

Aidyn was about to give up and head to the second part of his day when Yayènia arrived, unusually alone and dressed in loose clothing that did nothing to hide her lethal grace.

"Rough night, my friend?" she asked, pacing with him along the track.

The assassin shook his head, not wanting to talk. Yayènia did not badger him as they ran side by side, thinking private thoughts. After a while, Aidyn veered off the track and the warrior followed him. Yayènia blinked at him, not even winded after the four and half miles they had run. Aidyn pulled in a breath and gazed at her.

He was still staring when she punched him. "What in the nine hells was that for?" he growled, wiping the blood from his lip.

"There is something seriously wrong with you, Aidyn. What are the tattoos about? What happened when you went after the Eseirik? Why are you acting like a spurned lover?" Yayènia demanded, raising her fist again.

Aidyn eyed her hand, wary. "They are not tattoos, they are scars. I killed all the Eseirik, and I am *not* acting like a spurned lover."

"I have known you for four hundred years, Aidyn. Do not lie to me!" the High Commander lashed out again, this time striking him in the gut.

Riled now, the assassin lashed back, but Yayènia caught his forearm with hers and shoved him back. For a long time, they simply fought hand-to-hand, drawing the astonished and disbelieving gazes of the soldiers. The two elves were the best in the land, Aidyn second only to Yayènia herself, and only just, or so it seemed. Together, they battled back and forth, rarely landing a blow, but when one hit, blood sprayed or skin bruised. Their bodies blurred to the eyes of the humans, long limbs moving faster than they could imagine.

Aidyn was furious and confused, and he kicked his friend hard in the hip. She went down and was up again in a flash, having grabbed two blunt wasters used for training in double-hand sword fighting. Nia swiped at him, battle fury creeping in on her mind in spite of her attempt to keep the fight solely for Aidyn's benefit. Her icy blue eyes flashed and the assassin caught the look. A tinge of nervousness stole into him as she came at him, the poles moving so fast even he could scarcely see them. Cursing, Aidyn backed away, looking for something to defend himself with. Someone tossed him another set of poles and he barely got them up in time to block Yayènia's onslaught. Together they battled across the training ground, their minds locked in instinctive rage. Aidyn had been trained always to be offensive, to turn every move into his advantage, and he found himself hard put to do so now. He and Yayènia had dueled together, but only rarely, and never with anger. She snarled at him now, her mind completely wrapped in the battle fury.

Aidyn swore again as one of her poles cracked into his shoulder and he returned it with a vengeance, whacking one across her ribs, and jabbing the other into her chest. Yayènia gasped and stumbled back a step, but her eyes were dark with anger now, and she doubled her attack. Their wasters cracked against each other, splintering slightly from the force of the blows. Aidyn saw a dangerous move coming when Yayènia swept one of her weapons up high and the other down low, advancing.

The assassin had seen her do this before, and it never turned out well for her opponent. Thinking fast, he slapped his right waster against the tip of the low one, trying to throw off the attack. Nia growled again, then lunged, spinning in mid-air, her blunt weapons hitting against Aidyn's, throwing his arms out wide, making him vulnerable. Desperate, the male kicked back, flipping over his own head, his left foot connecting with Yayènia's chin. When he landed in a crouching position, the warrior was on top of him, blood covering half her face.

Still crouched, he scooted back, swiping at her legs. Nia let out a cry and came at him, forcing him to stand or be run over. She stretched her poles out in front of her, and then arced one up at the last moment to strike him in the face. Aidyn retreated another step as she came, crossing his wasters and trapping the low offender between them. With a lightning fast move, he flipped all three weapons up and caught Yayènia's other pole just before it smashed into his face. The parry caught the female off guard as both her weapons were torn from her hands, and she looked up at him in stunned fury.

With a snarl, Aidyn leaned back, sweeping his wasters back to either side, and kicked Yayènia in the face. Blood exploded from her nose and she landed on her back, the very breath knocked from her lungs. She blinked to regain her vision, and then rolled onto her feet. Aidyn's chest was heaving, fists clenched in anger.

"What the *hell* was that for?" he shouted, wiping blood from his lip.

Yayènia shook her head, trying to dispel the voice in her head that screamed for her to kill him. After a moment she glared up at him. "Tell me what is wrong!"

"You want to know what happened in the defile of the Eseirik? I killed them all, but they poisoned me with their magic, slashed me across the face with some instrument of power, and stabbed me all over. I hallucinated for three days. I saw you, naked as the day you were born, riding me like a thrice-damned horse," he hissed in her ear. "You, and Erdwyf, and Miazie..."

"And Tlonna," Yayènia breathed, suddenly understanding. "Aidyn...you cannot..."

"I know damn well that I cannot, nor do I flaming want to. But gods forsake it, I am nearly eight hundred years old! I should have someone!"

Yayènia looked down at the narrow space between them, avoiding his gaze. "Is there something I can do?"

Aidyn stared at the top of her head. Slowly, he brought her chin up with a finger. Her cold blue eyes were full of concern. "There is nothing you can do, Yayènia, and you know it. This is something I must resolve myself."

The warrior hugged him then, wrapping her arms around his middle and pressing her cheek to his chest. He was so astonished that his mouth dropped open. Slowly, he folded his arms around Yayènia's shoulders and hugged her back.

"I love you Aidyn," she murmured, and pulled away. "I really do."

"I love you too, Nia," he replied quietly. "I just wish someone would love me enough to want to be with me, forever."

Yayènia dropped her gaze once more, suddenly uncomfortable. "You will find her, my friend. You are gorgeous, and kind. I am sure there are tons of ladies at home just wishing they could take you to oblivion, you just have to stop looking into the past, and accept the future."

Aidyn nodded. "I know. Do they really look like tattoos?"

The High Commander chuckled. “Very much so. It is kind of striking, actually. They might even look wicked if you did not have such a dainty little nose.”

The assassin scowled, thinking that Yayènia was the last person on earth to say who looked ferocious. She looked like a poppet. The warrior caught the look, knowing what he was thinking, and shoved him hard.

“I would kill you if you were not so bloody pretty,” she snarled, a smile tugging at her lips.

Aidyn spread his hands and assumed an innocent look. “You did your best.”

Yayènia shook her head, thinking that she had indeed, and together they gathered their things and headed back toward the castle proper, ignoring the awe-struck and confused humans still watching them. “What are you about today?”

The assassin sighed. “I am going back to the dungeon. I want one more crack at our assassin before we leave.”

“Mind if I come?”

Aidyn said he didn’t, and they descended the winding stairs from inside one of the castle towers. Above the stairs there was only air, a few lofty windows barely illuminating the stone obelisk. Yayènia glanced upward with a disgusted look.

“I can never understand humans. So much enclosed space, useless and dank. Why do they need a tower for a set of stairs that begins at the floor?”

The assassin shrugged and led the way down. Halfway down the elves came to a landing that opened up into a short hallway illuminated by one torch. Yayènia started to continue on, but Aidyn stopped her.

“That way lay the Deep Cells, reserved for dangerous criminals. Athelias is in residence right now.”

“The assassin who killed Demetrius is not considered dangerous?”

Aidyn gave Yayènia a meaningful look. “Not anymore.”

The High Commander’s eyebrows climbed her forehead, but she said nothing further. The assassin moved into the hallway, nearly bent double because of the height restriction. Yayènia sighed in resignation and followed. A minute later they were standing in a small guardroom occupied by three bored guards. They snapped to attention when the elves appeared, dropping their dice and stumbling over their chairs.

Aidyn waved his hand at them. "At ease. We are here to visit the Eseirik one more time."

"Yes Lord Aidyn. High Commander," one of them said, breathlessly staring at Yayènia. "He has not taken a meal in two days, so he may be dead. We cannot force him to eat."

"Why would you want to?" Yayènia muttered, receiving frightened looks.

Aidyn shook his head and, taking the key from the guard, moved into an even smaller tunnel before emerging into a tiny cul-de-sac. Five iron doors gleamed dully in the single light of a torch on the wall, and scraping sounds emitted from two. The male went directly to the center cell and rapped his knuckle once on the cold metal. The sound reverberated through the small area like a bell. Then he inserted the key and yanked on the portal. The door swung open and Aidyn stepped inside, jamming the torch from the room into a bracket within the cell.

Yayènia followed him, peering at the huddled form in the corner. The Eseirik was a brown lump, the glint of his eyes the only sign of life. The form pressed itself tighter against the wall when Aidyn moved aside to allow her room.

"A broken creature," the High Commander breathed, revolted.

"He chose his fate when he stabbed Demetrius," the assassin replied coldly, glaring down at the hybrid with loathing. "Did you not?"

The Eseirik shifted slightly, but did not respond. Yayènia crouched down for a better look at him, appalled and fascinated.

"Do you maintain that you have nothing left to tell me?" Aidyn demanded, watching the assassin for signs of deceit.

"I have told you everything, dark elf. Now let me die in peace," the Eseirik grumbled, sounding neither remorseful nor interested.

"Why are you not eating? You have the blood of elves running in your veins. You will not die of starvation. Your death is sealed. Would you rather walk to it, or be dragged?"

The hybrid exhaled loudly. Yayènia looked up at Aidyn in confusion. "He is annoyed with me," the assassin commented dryly.

"Only a coward is afraid to face his rightful death," the High Commander said, and the hybrid's eyes snapped onto her.

"I am not a coward, high elf. I fulfilled my purpose, killing your weak little Man-King, and now I prepare for death," he snapped, leaning toward her.

Yayènia's lip curled in loathing, but she kept her ground, squatting mere inches from him now. "Only a coward goes against an unarmed opponent with six more cowards. Together, you accomplished a deed, while my friend here slaughtered your entire group, by himself. How does that make you feel? Dishonored? Inferior? Weak?"

"How dare you!" the hybrid hissed, jabbing out at her.

Yayènia caught his arm and slammed her knee upward into his reversed elbow. The Eseirik screamed as his arm was shattered by the blow, writhing on the floor of his cell. The High Commander stood, looking at Aidyn, who watched passively.

"You just assaulted the High Commander Yayènia er'Tiena, Eseirik," he stated blandly. "That is always a stupid decision."

The creature looked up at them from his vulnerable position, insanity and rage flashing in his eyes. "You will be dead, soon. The Tri-Kings march on you as we speak, and your home will be razed to the ground once more. Your children will be slain. Your women will be raped and enslaved. Your men will be burned alive. You will run home, but it will be too late. They wait for you, knowing you cannot stand by. You will all die!"

Yayènia and Aidyn glanced at each other, fury and worry writ on their faces. The hybrid was cackling now, clutching his ruined arm, the light catching his face. The female caught a glimpse of a deep groove in his cheek, and saw what Aidyn had done to get his answers. It was known as Syping. Slow, agonizingly deep cuts were gouged into the flesh, and then left to scab. Once the wounds were partially healed, the rough skin was torn off, taking with it the tender tissues beneath. It was always a last resort, but an elf could execute it with perfection, and Aidyn was well versed in all types of torture, though he rarely descended to such standards. Yayènia had only done it twice.

"May you burn in the deepest Ninth Hell," Aidyn whispered as they left, accompanied by the howling laughter of the mad assassin.

They crawled back through the two short tunnels, ascended the winding staircase, and hurried to Tlonna and Losolin's quarters.

When the king opened the door to their frantic knocking, he looked worried.

"What is it?"

"Call all the kings, if they are still here," Aidyn said bluntly, pushing into the room.

Tlonna turned at looked at her friend and her sister. The two were unnaturally tense, moving with the fluid grace of warriors, pacing the room. "What is it?" she echoed her husband.

Yayènia glared. "We just came from the Eseirik that killed Demetrius. We have some news."

Losolin sighed, resigned, and stepped outside to converse with the guard. Twenty minutes later, Eyin, Tyular, Barukh, and Tristan were all standing in the room, obviously confused as to why they were there. Tlonna and Losolin joined them, and they looked to Aidyn and Yayènia, who had not spoken a word the entire time.

"What is it?" Losolin said again.

The two fighters relayed their conversation with the assassin in hard voices. By the time they had finished, Tlonna was white with rage, Losolin's eyes hard as stone. The other kings looked worried and stunned.

"Well," Barukh said finally, "we can be sure of one thing. Athelias's men will not be there. Athelan was arrested this morning by Tristan's men."

"I doubt Sithian and Stoffnias were depending on Athelias counting for much," Tlonna snapped, her mind racing. "They would use him as a decoy only, sacrificing his men to gain access to the walls and gates."

Losolin nodded. "Sithian and Stoffnias have both been within Blackhaven's walls, alas, within the castle itself. I am sure they would have had scouts searching for weak spots in both walls, and the harbor."

"If Blackhaven falls under siege, then Kajgenia will be there with her."

"Florwen Hune as well."

"Aye, Arseninis too," Tyular said.

Eyin nodded. "I cannot do much, but I will do what I can to aid you."

Tlonna smiled faintly at her young protégé. "You will not waste your population on a battle that is not of your kingdom. You have too few people, and only one warrior."

"Then that will be one more warrior to stand for Blackhaven," the king stated boldly.

"No," Losolin said, quiet but hard. "No, Eyin, we cannot use you, or Meradyn. You will go back to Purheae immediately."

"What of Marc and Jorunson?" the Purheaen demanded, feeling useless. "They are still there! And what of our studies? We have months left in our semester!"

"Your education comes secondary to your life, Eyin Thorn. Marc and Jorunson will be sent home as well if such a thing is safe. If not, they will be sequestered within the castle until this battle is over. If there is to be a battle. We do not know yet if there is even an assault!" Tlonna snapped, slicing her hand through the air. "Tristan, we will stay one more day, to see those worthless monsters die, but then we must leave."

"I understand Tlonna. If you need it, send word and we will be there," the young king declared.

Tyular and Barukh nodded their assent. Word was spread through the Blackhavenites and the rest of the day was filled with packing and heartfelt goodbyes. The next day was chilly and snow covered. Tlonna and her entourage had their bags taken to the stables as they progressed to the courtyard. A small crowd was already gathered, mostly the royal ensembles of each present ruler. A wooden dais had been erected against the wall, empty save for a set of chains linked to the floor. The Blackhavenites assembled next to Tyular's group, right at the front, Eyin and Meradyn standing between the two.

The yard quickly filled with the stronger-stomached nobles and the more righteous commoners. Fifteen minutes later, the executioner appeared on the dais, and then Tristan, followed by a score of guards pulling along a stiff-backed Athelias, and the hunched form of the Eseirik. Tlonna felt wrath bubble within her chest, but she found Losolin's hand and clutched it tight, standing ramrod still. His fingers were hard between hers, and his eyes were chips of blue stone.

Tristan read the accusations of each, and then departed the dais, coming to stand between Tyular and Losolin. His young face was devoid of expression, but his skin had a sickly cast to it. The Eseirik was the first to die. His hands were chained to the dais, forcing him to kneel. His black eyes found Tlonna's, and as the keen blade of the executioner's sword severed his neck, he grinned.

Athelias was much louder, protesting his innocence, screaming his ire and twisting in the hands of the guards. They finally succeeded in shackling the deposed king, and he tried to stand. The executioner kicked him in the back of his knees, forcing him to his knees.

"You will all die!" Athelias screamed, baring his teeth in a feral snarl. "You will all burn!"

Tristan nodded once to the executioner, and the courtyard fell silent as Athelias's head rolled to the ground. Someone retched as his body toppled over. Tlonna looked at Aidyn. The assassin had a slight twist to his lips, almost a smile, and his emerald eyes burned above the triangular scars. The Magin Queen shuddered.

Immediately after the executions, the elves, with their three human companions, headed back to Blackhaven. Knowing that Athelan had received the same punishment in Talenias did little to still their unease.

Chapter 31

Honor of Assassins

The hurried ride back to Blackhaven was frigid and harsh. Aidyn stayed silent nearly the entire time, only speaking with his brother and Yayènia on occasion. Tlonna instructed Eyin as best as she could, giving him hasty lessons on crises and setting up plans for a rendezvous in Blackhaven two months from now. Meradyn trained even harder with Yayènia and Suneelo, Ghealan, even Aladorn.

They even sparred while they rode, training for cavalry raids. Yayènia watched with growing pride as Meradyn's arms became rock hard and skilled. She had taken to calling him *Leatran*, lightning, for his quicksilver parries and thrusts. The young man grinned every time the warrior called him so, proving her true by his actions. Now, Meradyn worked with Eyin as well, dueling with his king at night when they camped.

While the two worked, the Blackhavenites huddled about the campfire, discussing plans, discarding ideas that they feared might fail. Miazie tried scrying Blackhaven, but only ever received a blurry vision off the city. Sodo consoled her, but the Belau was disappointed in herself, looking to Tlonna with pleading eyes.

"Since Purheae, I have not been able to do it as readily," she cried, glancing uneasily at Losolin.

The king shook his head. "I have no idea what I did. I cannot imagine that such a backlash of power, one that affected the elder races, would have any impact on you, a human."

Miazie's jaw tightened. "I am not *just* a human, Losolin. There is something I never told you."

Silence fell around the campfire, all the elves turning their attention to the human. Only Sodo leaned back, looking annoyed. Ghealan turned from supervising the two Purheaens, green eyes flashing in the firelight.

"What?" Tlonna snapped coldly, feeling betrayed.

Sodo shook his head and put his hand on Miazie's shoulder. "I told you to wait, love," he said softly.

The Belau swallowed and took a deep breath, regretting her outburst. "There is more than one elf's blood in my history."

"So," Yayènia blurted, shrugging. "That hardly makes you any less a human."

"It was much more recent, enough to cause dissimilarities in my genetics. I am not fully human, and I am certainly not an elf, but I have some...attributes that make a substantial difference."

"Get to the point, Miazie," Tlonna demanded, white pupils contracting to pinpricks.

Again Miazie swallowed, clutching Sodo's hand. "Midian came to Anutch the same year Blackhaven fell, and told my father of you. It was at Anutch that your memories were taken from you. Both of you. They, Midian and Darren, injected me with some of your memories. It is why I manifested as a Belau long after the usual time. I was already an adult. Most Belaus are children."

Again a silence fell around the campfire, but this time it was hostile and tense. Rage built in Tlonna until it physically made her shake. Losolin's breath was whistling between his teeth as he stared at Miazie. Then Yayènia moved, whipping out her longblade and hauling Miazie up by her throat, putting the blade to the human's belly. Sodo reacted out of instinct, grabbing the warrior's arm and trying to free his lover.

Aidyn bowled into him, taking him out at the middle and then jerking him to his feet. The assassin flicked a knife up into Sodo's face, holding it a hair's breadth from his black eye. The alchemist froze, staring at the stock-still blade. Slowly, Tlonna and Losolin stood, betrayed and hurt beyond belief.

"You liar," Tlonna breathed, coming to stand next to her sister. "All this time, you have pretended to be my friend. Our friend. I trusted you. I loved you."

Miazie gasped, turning red from lack of oxygen. "No, I did not know. It only came to me after Purheae. I swear," she choked.

"Spy," Yayènia snarled, pressing her blade harder into the human's stomach. Blood began to stain the front of her shirt.

"No! Please...I swear!" Miazie cried, tears running down her face. "Tlonna...I'm so sorry. Losolin, believe me!"

Losolin looked up at Miazie, his dark blue eyes shimmering as they locked onto her terrified and pleading face. Behind her suspended form was Aladorn, fading slowly in and out as he gaped up at the woman he had once bedded. Ghealan and Erdwyf stood side by side in total shock, Eyin and Meradyn also. Suneelo was the only one sitting, his long legs stretched out in front of him. As always, he was the calmest, the most collected.

"I have had enough of defectors and infiltrators," Tlonna said, silent tears running down her face. "Kill them."

Yayènia and Aidyn snarled in angry compliance as Miazie sobbed in panic. It was then Suneelo stood, putting a hand on his wife's arm. "I would not do that, Tlonna. There may be more to the story."

The High Commander looked at her husband in disbelief, but she stayed her arm. Aidyn trembled as he held Sodo, the knife still hovering. The alchemist blinked, and an eyelash was severed. Tlonna pivoted to Suneelo, her face a mask of wrath and agony. After a moment, she nodded once. Yayènia made a sound of disgust, but she dropped Miazie to the ground, sheathing her sword and grabbing the human's hair.

Aidyn shoved Sodo away, turning the knife to his kidney. Miazie sobbed as she was wrenched onto her knees by Yayènia's cruel hand, made crueler by her own feelings of betrayal. Her throat exposed, the human gulped in air, green eyes rolling to find Tlonna's. Losolin remained silent, regarding his brother with hard eyes.

Suneelo again touched Yayènia's arm, this time firmly removing his wife's hand from Miazie's hair. The Belau lurched forward, clutching her neck and stomach, unable to control her weeping. Tlonna stood impassive, her arms folded across her chest.

"Tlonna," Miazie panted finally, having caught her breath. "I swear, I did not know. Eleven years ago, when Midian came to Anutch, I was only sixteen. He terrified me, but I had already been the victim of my father's 'affections' for ten years. I viewed him as only another monster in a world full of them. Then they brought you and Losolin. I never saw you, I only heard rumors. Then the rumors stopped, and the news had already come that you had been slain by Midian, weeks before. It was late one night when my father came to my bedchamber. I believed him there for his usual wants, but for once I was wrong. He jabbed me with a needle, and injected me with a bluish substance that didn't quite look like liquid. It was neither viscous nor solid.

"I became very ill for about a week as visions assaulted me, memories I never experienced. I did not know them for what they were, at the time. Then they faded, and I forgot all about them, believing them to be hallucinations of a bad fever," Miazie explained, her voice faint. "Then, when you appeared in the slave compound, I had no recollection whatsoever of previous events. I never deceived you, I promise."

"Why would they inject you with our memories?" Losolin asked, caught up in spite of himself.

Miazie shook her head. "I do not know," she admitted quietly. "I can only surmise they needed somewhere to put them. See, memories caught in such a Weave would never dissipate. They are not tangible, hence the fact that you both regained most of them. Most of them...not all. Those memories remain within me."

Aidyn jerked, accidentally pricking Sodo, realizing what her statement meant for him. Miazie knew of him and Tlonna all those years ago. As if reading his thoughts, the Belau looked straight at him, her cheeks heating from more than the fire. The assassin released Sodo and patted him on the shoulder.

"Just a precaution, mate," he muttered.

The alchemist nodded, knowing that what the assassin said was true.

"But why you? And why, if they could transfer some of them, did they not do so with all of them?" Erdwyf asked, sitting down once more.

Miazie reclaimed her seat, glancing warily at Yayènia, who muttered under her breath and stalked off, standing just within hearing range. "As I said, memories are not tangible. You cannot hold them in your hands, you cannot bottle them up for more than a few minutes. And, if you release them into the air, they automatically go back into their original maker. Darren and Midian needed someone who had no knowledge of what they had done, someone who would probably die from having memories of another race injected into them."

Miazie shook her head. "I nearly ceded to their wishes, but I survived. As for why they did not take all of them, I would like to think that they just messed up, but I really cannot say. I have tried time and again to scry back and find out, but as I said, since Purheae my power has been challenged."

"Why?" Aladorn demanded, fully visible.

The Belau shrugged. "I believe it has something to do with the fact that I have both elf-blood in my veins, and Tlonna and Losolin's memories and knowledge in my mind. I was affected because I am no longer quite human."

Sodo rubbed her back. "We believe that the elfin elements within her became augmented in the backlash of Losolin's power. Her eyesight has grown keener, her hearing sharper, among other things."

"You are becoming an elf?" Ghealan asked Miazie, incredulous.

Again Miazie shrugged. "I do not think so, but as I said, I am no longer just a human."

Eyin and Meradyn had sat during the conversation, their faces hidden in shadows as they kept them averted. When no one said anything further, the young king looked up, pinning Losolin with a green-eyed gaze.

"So, that is what happened. That is what caused the barrier to break."

"The alternative was not acceptable," the elf replied in a hard voice, finding Tlonna's hand and holding it.

"What alternative?" Eyin demanded.

"That I let Tlonna die," Losolin snapped. "If I had not broken your damnable barrier, she would be dead, and all that we worked for null."

"The barrier in Narnen was broken as well," Erdwyf put in suddenly, remember a letter her parent's had sent her. "Magic is once again allowed."

Losolin shook his head. "As I said, the alternative was not acceptable."

No one disputed his statement, and yet again, silence fell.

They reached Purheae the next day, riding between the haunted forest and the dominating Kismath Mountains. Eyin took a deep breath, leaning back in the saddle and closing his eyes. Meradyn looked forlorn.

"Guard your people well, King Eyin," Tlonna said, pulling Takîreaes to a halt. "It has been an honor."

The human's jaw clenched as he rode up to the queen. "I owe you so much, my Lady. I promise you, Blackhaven has a friend in Purheae. My thanks to you all. Come, Mer."

Meradyn bowed his head to Yayènia and followed his king, looking over his shoulder at the group that watched them go. Once they were out of sight, Tlonna urged Takîreaes into a gallop, her companions quickly following. They made it to Blackhaven City three days later, having pushed their horses to the brink of exhaustion, and themselves.

Tlonna burst through the doors of the castle, followed by Suneelo in place as guard, Losolin at her side, and Erdwyf next to the captain. People turned and stared at their king and queen with wide eyes, clutching their chests or whispering to each other. Haydyn rushed down the staircase, Kelus and Feorien on his heels.

"Mother, Losolin, you look terrible. What has happened? Was there another murder? We heard about Athelias' and Athelan's execution," the prince said, eyeing his parent with worried eyes.

Tlonna stopped short, staring at her son. "There has been no battle? No challenge?"

Haydyn glanced at Suneelo, caught off guard. "Of course not. Why would you think there was a battle? Is that why you are back so soon?"

Losolin gripped his wife's arm, casting cautious looks about. "Tlonna, perhaps this is not the place."

Aidyn shoved forward from outside, having quickly returned from the courtyard where he had been talking with Yayènia. "It must be coming. The Eseirik was not lying when he told Yayènia and me."

"Are you positive?" Losolin demanded.

"Aidyn! What happened to your face?" Feorien gasped, staring at the black scars under the assassin's right eye.

The dark elf's head snapped up and pinned the Advising Assistant with a glare that brought forth a cold sweat. Aidyn said nothing, but Feorien shivered visibly, taking his eyes to the floor.

Kelus stepped up to the assassin, fearless of the older elf. "I have seen such marks before," the ex-demon breathed, touching the scars with one slender finger.

Aidyn's back went rigid, but he did not step away from the other's touch. His dark eyes sparkled as he watched Kelus.

"Oh yes," the elf hissed again, sounding for a moment like the Darkwight he had been. "I have seen these. You must be a stronger creature than you appear, my friend. Such poison is meant for elves, intended to ravage the mind and destroy the soul. It kills the flesh and turns it black and hard."

"How do you know this, Kelus?" Suneelo challenged, stepping forward to push the elf away from his friend.

Aidyn's eyes were riveted on Kelus's, unable to look away. He remembered the agony of the wound, and the vividness of the hallucinations. He had believed them to be the result of the Magin's stab wounds, but apparently not.

"I was once covered in such wounds, Captain," Kelus replied quietly, looking at Tlonna. "These are of a different instrument, but they are from the same source. Repulsive evil brought on by pure hatred of the Elven Race."

Aidyn touched the scars on his cheek, feeling the tough skin with newfound revulsion. Though they looked like tattoos, he knew them to be a sign of failure. They would forever remind him of his struggle with the Eseirik, and Demetrius's consequential death.

"Will they spread? Is Aidyn in danger?" Tlonna queried, worried for her friend.

Kelus shook his head. "I do not believe so. They were put there by an instrument, probably a weapon with triangular blades, to create such a design. Mine were done by Midian himself, by his eager hands, a few different knives, and fire. No, Queen Tlonna, your assassin should be fine."

Though Tlonna and the others looked relieved, Aidyn dropped his hand from his face and looked away, ashamed. Haydyn broke in then, nearly shivering with anxiety.

"What is going on? Where is everyone else? Why would you think there would be a battle?"

Losolin grabbed his stepson and dragged him up the stairs to one of the informal meeting halls, the others trailing behind. Once sequestered, the king turned and began pacing, gesturing at someone to explain. Haydyn watched him, plainly baffled. Erdwyf took pity on him.

"Everyone is fine. Yayènia, Ghealan, and Aladorn are off at the barracks, checking stores and the soldiers. Eyin and Meradyn have returned to Purheae to protect their people. Miazie and Sodo are the Academy, informing Jorunson and Marc of their king's whereabouts."

"But what is going on?" Haydyn pleaded, involuntarily glancing at Aidyn, who was standing at a window, watching the snow fall outside.

"We do not yet know, son," Suneelo said, smiling half-heartedly at his nephew. "We received a threat, saying that Sithian, Stoffnias, and Athelias were on the war path toward Blackhaven. Athelias, as you know, has been killed, and Tyular now rules as regent while the Council of Nymyños debates on whom to give the Sun Throne."

"Council of Nymyños?" asked Feorien, sitting beside Kelus, amber eyes nervous.

"A newly formed council of rulers consisting of Tlonna, Losolin, Barukh, Eyin, Tyular, and Tristan. There are hopes of adding Furntil of Flousen Dua, and Tahi-Tat of Zeynuwn," Erdwyf explained, watching Tlonna and Losolin, who remained silent. "Speaking of such, any news from our messengers?"

At that Tlonna turned from watching Aidyn, her eyes sparkling with hope. It dimmed when Haydyn shook his head.

"Not yet. But the winter has been harsh, and people are frightened. The air is thick with tension."

"But those sent to Schelum should be back by now!" Tlonna said, crossing her arms. "We have crossed the continent twice since they departed!"

"I know, but perhaps finding the mayor is proving difficult," the prince replied, shrugging helplessly. "Erdwyf said he did not reside in Barl for fear of assassination."

Erdwyf nodded, folding her hands on the table. "Still, they should have found him and returned by now. Perhaps they were killed."

"Who was sent?" Tlonna asked, frowning.

The High Advisor shook her head and looked at Feorien. The male squinted, remembering. "An emissary...Wayn Nadir, and a guard, some human swordsman."

"David Axel, Second Company swordsman," Suneelo snapped, feeling defensive of his men. "He is usually on the gate."

Tlonna nodded at her brother. Second Company meant he was good, as First Company of the guard was reserved for officers and second sons of nobility. There were four companies all together, presided over by Lieutenant Selick Madren, second to Suneelo. If David was in Second Company, an attacker would have to be very skilled to kill him and his ward.

"I will give it three more days. If no word has come, I am going to send someone after them, understood?" the queen stated, looking at everyone in the room. Only Aidyn ignored her, still staring out the window at the snow.

It was then that the door opened and Ghealan entered, holding Jaryikin. He handed his daughter to Erdwyf and turned to

Tlonna and Losolin. "There was no disturbance in the ranks, but I put them on watch. Yayènia is holding a meeting with *Zephyr Leifen*, Sargotarh, and Orthak to inform them of the situation."

"Excellent. Ghealan, I want the city on guard. Send word to Belgarath, Andik, Asheyl, Hastert, and Mardyn. Tell them to be ready to flee to the city on a moment's notice. Erdwyf, Feorien, I want areas set up in the city able to house any refugees that come to us. Suneelo, make sure all the defenses are as they should be."

The four stood and bowed, hastening to do as their queen bid them. Haydyn stood as well. "I am going to the wall to see what Edwin needs immediately. I am glad you're back."

"Me too, Haydyn," Tlonna said, hugging her son. When only Aidyn remained, Tlonna turned to Losolin and nodded toward the door. The king smiled faintly and left, leaving his wife alone with the assassin.

"Aidyn," Tlonna said quietly, moving to stand behind her friend, placing a hand on his lower back.

The dark elf glanced at her out of the corner of his eye. "I am lost, Tlonna. Because of me, Demetrius is dead. I failed in my mission, and I brought us here in a panic when there was no need."

"No, Aidyn, it is not your fault Demetri was killed. You completed your mission. My friend, you defeated twenty-seven of the Eseirik, officially wiping out their faction. You were wounded in the act. That does not make you a failure, that makes you a person. You are not invincible."

"The things I have done in my life, Tlonna, the people I have killed, I do not regret it. Each one of them deserved their deaths. I am an assassin because I am good at what I do, and because I believe in it. Some people just need to die. But...at what cost? I am scarred now, flawed, hideous."

Tlonna's mouth dropped open. "Aidyn, you are beautiful, as you always have been. Look at me."

The male turned his face to the queen, gazing upon her features. "I am more flawed than you, my friend. Look at my eyes. Do you think I miss the stares, the looks of revulsion when I pass? People watch you in awe, envy, desire. They are afraid of me."

Aidyn shook his head, disagreeing. "You are exquisite, Tlonna, and you are different because of it. So you have been altered by power, it does not change your physicality. Me, I am tainted and weak."

Tlonna studied his face, the titling emerald eyes, sable hair, the light brown skin. Pain and shame filled those eyes, the inky lashes hiding none of it. "Aidyn..."

The male sniffed, a rare sign of emotion, his breath ragged as he sucked in air, trying to hold back the ache of his life. "I want the oath back," he said softly.

The Magin blinked in surprise and frowned, dropping her hand that had slid to his waist when he turned. "Why?"

"Because it linked me to you. I always knew where you were, if you were in pain. It was severed when Midian blocked you, but it gave me a sense of comfort knowing I had such a connection. Please, Tlonna, I beg of you."

"Aidyn, I am not sure I know how. The first time was a total shock, and undoing it was simply a matter of needing to release you."

"You just have to believe it in your heart, the need and want to have me as your oath-sworn companion. Just take my hand," the assassin took her hand instead, linking his fingers with hers, examining the difference in their skin. "And say the words."

"What words?"

"Whatever you need to say, and it will happen," Aidyn whispered, leaning close to her, closing his eyes as her scent reached him.

"Aidyn..." Tlonna said in a small voice, her fingers tightening. "Stay with me, protect me, by the spirits, I need you."

Silent thunder shook the room, taking both elves to their knees as light danced up Aidyn's arm and sank into his chest. He grunted, a bit of his pain lessening when the small sensation of Tlonna's presence filled his heart. The female wrapped her arms around his shoulders and hugged him.

"Oh, Aidyn, your pain. How can you handle it?" she whispered into his neck.

The assassin clinched her back, and then helped her stand. "By knowing you will not let me fall," he said, stepping away.

Tlonna clutched at her chest. "It is fading. It was so strong before, almost as though I was inside your mind."

Aidyn nodded. "You did not notice it before because you were so caught up in your quest. It only brought me comfort."

Smiling, the queen kissed the assassin on the lips, a chaste kiss of friendship, but Aidyn's heart beat faster nonetheless, and then skipped when her hand moved up to his face, her thumb brushing the scars. "You truly are beautiful, Aidyn, in body and soul. A better friend I could never ask for, nor imagine." Her hand slid down his neck to cup the back of his head, sable hair running through her fingers. "You will never let me down."

"By the Honor of Assassins, I am bound to you," he replied, a little shaken.

Tlonna smiled again, faintly, now gripping his iron hard bicep. "I would have it no other way."

Chapter 32

To See the Truth of People

Nebet'thu straightened, wiping his brow with the back of his hand. Behind him stood Eesa, equally weary. They stood in the middle of a field of snow, hauling large planks of wood stacked high with stone blocks. The village of Asheyl was building a wall, tired of the upswing in attacks by goblins from Kismath. The hundred or so citizen of Asheyl were all gathered in the snowy field, each working with stone and mortar.

Neb turned to Eesa, meaning to ask if she had his hammer, but his wife's eyes were looking beyond him. Confused, the hunter followed her gaze and frowned. In the distance a rider had appeared, moving fast. Minutes later he had ridden into a cluster of Plains Elves. After a moment, they pointed toward Nebet'thu, and the rider followed.

He was a Blackhaven City soldier, adorned in the winter leather and soft wool, silver greaves and vambraces glinting in the dull winter sun.

"Captain Nebet'thu," the elf said on arrival, dark eyes landing on Neb without hesitation.

The hunter frowned again. "I am Nebet'thu. Captain was a temporary standing during the Battle of Alchemian. Who are you?"

The soldier ignored his denial and his question. "I am to report to you and your Chief Tèkar."

"Report to me for what? Who sent you?"

"Captain of the Guard Suneelo Tiena, sir. I bear a message that should not be spoken amongst regular citizens," the elf replied, sounding as if he were not used to deferring to anyone, ever.

Neb looked around to find all of Asheyl gathered around, gazing curiously at the much taller elf in unusual garb. Tèkar appeared out of their midst and shooed them away.

"I am Chief Tèkar, who are you?"

Yet again the soldier ignored the question. "King Demetrius of Kajgenia has been assassinated. King Athelias and Prince Athelan of Talenias have been overthrown and executed by the Kings of the East. Queen Tlonna and King Losolin have issued a warning for all Blackhaven citizens. War is coming, and they will not have their people wounded again. At the first sign of unrest, you are to depart immediately for the capital, where you will be protected until it is safe to return. This is not a request, but a Royal Order."

Tèkar, Nebet'thu, and Eesa stared at the elf, stunned. It was the hunter who regained his sense first.

"Who is our enemy?"

The elfin soldier's eyes narrowed, not for the question, but at the answer he must give. "The combined armies of Zaedic, Seaduens, and Talenias."

"No," Tèkar breathed, horrified.

"Yes. Sir," the city elf added the title too late, adding to Neb's suspicions. "Captain Nebet'thu, I was there at Alchemian. We both know the sheer size of the army we faced then. This one will be many times larger. Do you understand the implication?"

Neb nodded, numb. The Zaedican army, even defeated, had been immense. "Why me, though? What do you need from me?"

The solider eyed him from the shadows of his crested helmet. "You fought at Alchemian. You are a trusted member of High Commander Yayènia's war council. She expects you to follow orders. Sir."

Tèkar patted Nebet'thu on the shoulder. "You have risen high, Neb. You have brought honor to your people."

The hunter looked down at his chief, feeling overwhelmed. The Blackhaven solider started to say something more, but his tilted eyes hardened, and he turned to his horse. When the elf yanked his sword off the pommel, Neb shoved Tèkar behind him, swearing. But the city elf was glaring in another direction, his faced clouded.

"What is it?" Tèkar demanded, stepping away from his protective subject.

"Movement. It looks like a fast moving patrol. Captain, do you have your mount?" the elf replied, his entire body assuming an aura of readiness and power. The three plains elves took an unconscious step backward.

Then Neb sighed, realizing what the soldier wanted. "I will get Learia. Eesa, bring my sword and bow from the yurt, will you?"

The female nodded and ran back toward the village, red hair flying. Neb turned back to his chief. "Get everyone inside. It is probably just another raiding party, but I want no deaths this time."

"As you wish...Captain," Tèkar said, smiling slightly as he turned to go.

The hunter shook his head and they rushed back toward the village, followed by the now-mounted soldier. Minutes later, Neb was following on his deer Learia. The soldier's black cloak fanned out behind him as he bent low over his horse's neck, bow ready as he held onto the saddle with his thighs only.

Neb frowned, remembering that soldiers in the Blackhaven Militia had pale blue cloaks. His suspicion sharpened, but then his concentration was grabbed by the squad of men riding toward them.

"This is no goblin attack! Those are humans!" the suspicious soldier called back, firing an arrow.

Neb watched as one of the twelve men fell, an arrow protruding from his neck. The plains elf shot off an arrow as well, but his landed in a man's thigh. At the same time, the stranger took down another human. Then they were on them, putting aside bows for blades.

With a cry of Blackhaven, the two slammed into the ten remaining men, swords arcing through the gloomy winter afternoon. Within moments, the skirmish was over. The dozen men lay strewn about, those not dead, soon to be. The solder lifted one up and inspected his unadorned armor.

"Talenian," he said after a moment.

"How can you tell?" Neb asked, nudging one with his boot.

The elf plucked a pendant from the man's neck. "It is the sun, their deity and symbol."

Nebet'thu smiled grimly. "Can you tell me your name, now?"

The taller elf laughed, and took off his helmet to reveal a startlingly familiar face. Aladorn laughed again at the look on Neb's face.

"Lord Aladorn!"

"Nebet'thu," the wiat returned, smiling. "You have learned a lot since you first came to the capital."

"Lord, you outrank me tenfold. Why would you even pretend to be a regular soldier? Why did Suneelo send you?"

"To keep up appearances, Nebet'thu. Even these days wiats are not accepted with grace, but when people hear my name, they automatically attach 'the Wiat', to the end. A little caution never hurt anyone."

Neb nodded, sheathing his sword. "And why did the Captain send you?"

Aladorn sighed, running a tawny hand back through his sable hair. "I am to bring you back to Blackhaven City."

"Why?"

"The city may be under siege soon. We are going to need all hands to keep from being overrun. Tlonna is determined to preserve the city. Yayènia is calling all warriors home."

The tribal elf shook his head. "I am no warrior, Aladorn. I am just a hunter."

"A battle-seasoned hunter who has been trained nearly every day of his life in the art of warfare," Aladorn said blandly.

"Lord Aladorn! I cannot be of any use to people like you, or Yayènia, or Aidyn, or Suneelo, or-"

"Yeah, got it, Nebet'thu," Aladorn chuckled, nodding. "But we are few against many. We need all the help we can get. Besides, it is not a good idea to ignore a request from Yayènia."

The hunter narrowed his eyes and nodded once. "Probably not. When do you leave?"

Aladorn looked at the shorter elf with a suspicious eye. "*We* leave as soon as you are packed. And...Eesa will not be coming."

Nebet'thu mounted Learia before speaking, mulling over the events. "Why not?"

"Well," Aladorn replied, moving his horse into a trot next to the deer. "Last time, she had tricked you into marriage, you hit her, and then she fled as soon as you were out of the city. And she is no fighter."

"Ah ha," Neb mused. "Well, things have changed."

"I see that."

"You do not understand, Lord Aladorn. She and I spoke about our debaucheries, our failures and our deceptions. It brought us closer, and now, we are in love once more. Not for a hundred years have I felt this way about her."

"And your other interest?"

"Kepthari?"

"If that was her, yes," Aladorn muttered.

"Well, she wed Daegin last summer, Eesa's brother. They love each other, and in two years, Daegin will take over as Chief, when Tèkar steps down."

The wiat rubbed his face as the plains elf continued to talk, wishing for the silent types that his friends were. It took Nebet'thu about an hour to complete packing, taking care of his affairs about the small village, and consoling Eesa. She was furious at Aladorn.

"You think you can make me stay? I am a free elf, wiat, and I will go where I please, thank you very much!"

"We are all free elves, but when Queen Tlonna bids you stay home, you bloody well stay home. She is dictating these circumstances in order to keep you alive. You may come to the city if and only if Asheyl is threatened. Is that unclear in any way?" Aladorn said coldly, not in the mood to deal with the female.

When Eesa made to argue more, Nebet'thu stepped in. "Eesa, I am sure Queen Tlonna has her reasons. Please do not make this any more difficult than it already is. I will be home in a few weeks, I am sure. I am gone longer during the hunting season."

"I know, Neb, but when you are out hunting, there is no one hunting you. This is different. I do not like it at all," she mumbled, embracing him.

Aladorn rolled his eyes at the two shorter elves, folding his arms impatiently. He had ridden for two days straight in order to reach Asheyl in time, and to give a runner from the village time to get to Hastert. He was weary, and the scuffle with the Talenians was not only disturbing, but had wearied him further. It made him wonder how his brother had done what he had in Talenias and Kajgenia. Aidyn was phenomenal in Aladorn's mind, but something had changed within him since the assassination.

"All right, Lord Aladorn, I am ready," Nebet'thu said, cutting short his musings. He had slung his pack over his shoulder and Eesa was standing behind him, glowering.

"Good. We will be back in the city in two days. We ride hard, and we will not stop for night."

"Is it really that urgent?" Neb asked, suddenly worried.

"Maybe, I have been gone for three days, the city may have been attacked in that time. Perhaps we will not be able to make it inside the walls. Perhaps everyone is dead. I do not know."

"Then there will be no point in going," Eesa snapped.

"Hold your tongue, I grow weary of your constant bleating, Eesa," Aladorn snarled, his patience at an end.

"There is no reason for you to talk to her like that!" Nebet'thu scolded, glaring down at the wiat.

"She is interfering with my mission, Nebet'thu, and I will treat her as I would any annoyance. Now come, we do not have any more time to waste," the dark elf growled back, grabbing him by the arm and dragging him bodily from the yurt.

Eesa followed them out, and the rest of the village watched as the two males mounted. Tèkar came forward and bid them farewell, with wishes for a safe return while Aladorn brooded at the delay. As soon as the Chief had finished talking, the wiat was off, galloping from the village.

Aidyn watched his brother drag the reluctant Nebet'thu through the snowy courtyard four levels below. Unconsciously, he touched the scars on his cheek as Yayènia and Ghealan argued behind him. It had been nearly a week since their return and no one was sleeping well with the threat of attack looming in the air. Tlonna had been distant, hardly acknowledging anyone other than Losolin, Aidyn, and Yayènia. He could feel her fury simmering in the corner of his heart.

"What if there *is* no attack forthcoming?" Ghealan said, a very common statement in recent days.

"There is. You were not in the room with the Eseirik, Lan. You have no idea how real it was. The hybrid was not lying, was he, Aidyn?" Yayènia shot back, dragging the assassin back into the conflict.

"No, he was not. Aladorn is back with Nebet'thu of Asheyl," he replied dully, turning to eye his two friends.

Yayènia rushed to his side to look out the window, pressing her forehead to the cold glass. "I really wish it would stop snowing. I feel so stuffed up in this place with the glass in the windows."

"I know. I only remember a few other winters that had this much snowfall," Ghealan said, joining the two. "We do not usually get hit this hard."

"At least it is the right color," Aidyn muttered, then turned back into the room.

They were sequestered in the top room of the seldom used Sha Tower, the whole of which was reserved mostly for private parties of nobles and other residents of the castle. It was a large room with vaulted ceilings and ringed completely with windows, which were all filled with their glass casements. A wide table surrounded by cushioned chairs took up the center, and a massive chandelier made entirely of *kairhotuss* wood hung from the apex of the ceiling. All along the walls were white and silver draperies that brushed the obsidian floor, alternating with the windows.

When in use, it was typically filled with chattering ladies and lords of Blackhaven on their namedays or anniversaries. Today, however, it was only the three apprehensive warriors waiting for Tlonna, Aladorn, Neb, and the others to join them. They turned when the door opened and Losolin walked in, his brother at his side. Suneelo looked edgy, the king irritated.

"What is it?" Yayènia demanded, crossing to her husband.

"There are rumors of spies in the city," Losolin replied dully, sitting in the chair he normally occupied whenever they met in the room.

"Rumors? Such as?" Ghealan asked, sitting as well.

The king sighed, resting his head against the high back. "You know, people knowing things they should not. Arganor was really upset earlier when he went to speak to a section of the Market District. People are asking detailed questions about the Eseirik, details, mind you, they should not even be aware of."

"Is this so troubling?" Aidyn asked, wondering. "Dozens of people were at the execution in Kajgenia, word has been spread of Demetri's assassination, and our abduction was not well hidden."

"True, but they know things like the medallion," Losolin said, looking at his friend, "and your struggle."

Aidyn's face tightened. "How do they know about that?"

"There is the issue. How do they know these things? How do they know that a king has risen in Purheae? No, we did not exactly hide the fact, but again, there are details out in the open about Eyin, Meradyn, and their two friends that we did not put out there. Someone within our circle of confidentiality has been telling secrets," the king explained.

"No one in the family," Yayènia countered immediately, referring to their large but close group of friends.

"I would not think so," Losolin agreed, "but there is always the possibility. Look at Miazie."

Yayènia folded her arms and glared out at the snow-swept sky, her hip cocked against Suneelo's chair.

"You still cannot believe that she, or Sodo, meant any wrong, can you?" Suneelo scoffed, squinting at his brother. "Personally, if I had been injected with your memories, I would not really want to tell you either. How hard it must be on her to know such things."

Losolin expelled a breath. "I know, it just was such a shock, and the fact that she did not confide in us, after being through so much, hurt."

Ghealan opened his mouth to say something but the door opened again to admit Tlonna, Miazie, and Erdwyf. Seconds later, Aladorn walked in with Nebet'thu. Sodo was at the academy, and no one else had been invited. Once they were all seated around the table, Tlonna tossed an object on the table, and it landed with a loud thunk.

"People have been asking about this. How they know about it, I cannot even imagine. It has been a secret of my family for eight hundred years," she muttered as everyone leaned in to see what it was. "It is called the Death Pendant. Miazie, Losolin, and I recovered it from a Cleick's house in Kajgenia. Midian had left it there as bait for me. It was not something he needed, having mastered the craft of torture and murder, so he felt no fear of me getting my hands on it."

"What are they asking about?" Ghealan asked, picking the pendant up and immediately setting it down again. "It feels wrong."

"It supposedly contains the souls of everyone that was killed by it. I have never tested it, of course, but I do not doubt it," Tlonna replied. "They are asking how much power it contains, do I think I can overpower Sithian Rahlan with it, what of Stoffnias Lostug? Would he survive such an attack? What if, Queen Tlonna, you used this weapon to carve out an empire, overpowering all the leaders of the province kingdoms, and finally bringing the Liberated Lands under your control?"

"Someone actually said that?" Nebet'thu gasped, reminding everyone that he was there.

"Unfortunately, yes. So, my friends, I believe we have a spy, or spies, within our ranks. I have no idea who it is, but I swear I will find them, and make them sweat blood," Tlonna replied coldly, her eyes showing no emotion.

Silence ensued after the queen's bitter words with everyone glancing at everyone else, shifting uncomfortably and trying to ignore the evil pendant glinting dully in the winter sun. Finally, it was Aladorn who spoke, slapping Nebet'thu on the shoulder.

"Well, we have here our good friend fresh from Asheyl. Yayènia, do you want to tell him why I dragged him from his wife?" the wiat said, sounding by far more gusty than usual.

Yayènia squinted at him, a dangerous sign. "You did not tell him?"

Aladorn sat back, putting his elbow on Aidyn's shoulder. Though only Miazie and Sodo knew of their kinship, their comfort with each other was becoming more and more evident to everyone around them. The assassin, who normally rejected elongated physical contact with other males, seemed to ignore the wiat's touch. Erdwyf and Tlonna shared a look of utter confusion, surprised by Aidyn's nonchalance.

"I told him the basics, Yayènia," Aladorn said. "But when you demand someone leave their home undefended, then I suggest you tell them why yourself."

Yayènia's lips parted at the unexpected words. No one spoke so brashly to her, other than her immediate family. Suneelo was chuckling silently, glad that someone wasn't afraid to talk straight to Yayènia.

"Fine, Aladorn," the warrior said, flicking her husband's thigh. "Nebet'thu, I am sending you to Purheae to train two humans in the art of warfare."

"What? Why?" Neb demanded, shocked and angry.

The High Commander's lips tightened. "Do I need to explain myself to you, Captain Nebet'thu?"

"Yes, you bloody well do! I was in the middle of building a wall to protect my village, my home, from goblins. And now groups of Talenians are attacking, and you want me to go train some half-wit humans in a haunted forest? Give me a good flaming reason to do this!"

"I am your commander!" Yayènia shouted.

"No you are not! I am a hunter! A hunter for the Plains Elves! The Hidden Ones! I want nothing to do with your politics or your wars. Asheyl was not affected during the last wars, and it will not be affected during this one. Leave me be!"

Tlonna grabbed Yayènia's sleeve and yanked her back into her chair as the warrior shot upward, her hand reaching for a weapon. "Nebet'thu," the queen said, still holding her sister down. "I understand your reluctance to undertake what seems to be folly, but the training of Purheae's king and military leader is very important."

"Purheae does not have a king, or a military!"

"Yes it does. King Eyin Thorn, and Meradyn Obren will open a new door for Purheae, bringing the defunct kingdom back into the mainstream of Nymyños. The economy is non-existent, the populace less than a hundred, but already Eyin has relations with us, King

Tristan, King Barukh, and King Tyular. When you leave, you will escort Jorunson and Marc, two of their countrymen, back to Purheae, and they will then guide you to their village."

"Why me?" Neb asked, starting to become desperate.

"Because you are closest to their civilization, and you are a fighter of immense skill," Tlonna replied soothingly. "Nebet'thu, I will demand this of you, but I would prefer you go of your own free will. Eyin and Meradyn are good men, intelligent and quick to learn. Yayènia has already spent two months working solely with Meradyn, teaching him the basis of his career, and I have tutored Eyin in the forms of diplomacy and leadership. They have attended the Academy of Blackhaven, received high marks from their instructors, and have developed a base understanding of the goings on of Nymyños."

"How long will I be there?"

"Until either we send for you, or four months have passed. The four months are to allow us time for battle, if it ever comes."

"What battle? I see no threat!"

"We received a warning that Blackhaven would soon be under siege. We are preparing for such an occasion," Tlonna explained, finally letting go of Yayènia.

The warrior tensed, but she remained seated, still furious at Nebet'thu's breach of propriety. Aidyn scratched at his cheek, glaring at the pendant still sitting in the middle of the table. Suddenly he shot up out of his chair and strode from the room without saying a word. Aladorn moved to follow him, but Miazie shook her head once. Tlonna winced, a sudden revulsion and pain jabbing at her heart where Aidyn's oath was. Confused, she pulled the pendant over to her and placed it about her neck, where it always stayed.

"Well, Nebet'thu?" she said after a moment, turning her gaze back to the plains elf.

"It is not as though I have a choice. When do I leave?"

"In three days. You will be supplied with everything you need. Jorunson and Marc will finish out their week at the academy, and then you will go. The quarters you stayed in last time are available to you."

"Why the rush to get here, then?" Neb asked, still miffed.

Losolin replied in Tlonna's stead, as she was now fiddling with the pendant. "A severe storm is coming. We received word of it from a merchant coming in to port."

The tribal elf sighed, and then bowed his head. "Well then."

"Indeed," Aladorn said, standing. "My part is done. I am going to wash up and retire for the evening. Good day to you all,"

He strode from the room and headed straight for Aidyn's room. He found his brother on his balcony, sitting on the railing with one leg dangling over a small lawn bordered by cypress trees, four stories below. The assassin had his eyes closed and his head leaning back against the wall.

"Are you all right?" Aladorn asked, leaning against the railing.

Aidyn nodded, his eyes still closed. His stomach heaved again, and he forced down the feeling.

"What happened?"

The assassin peeked at his older brother, still slightly amazed that he had found him so coincidentally. "I am changed, Aladorn. It creeps within me, twisting my stomach and making me ill. I am weakened and tainted."

"No," the wiat said, shaking his head. "A scar cannot change you."

"It can when it is made by Maginic evil. You did not hear Kelus's words, you cannot imagine the pain it causes me still. I have never felt so defeated."

"But you killed them all, Aidyn. You were not defeated. Why do you not talk to Losolin? I am sure he can heal you."

Aidyn shook his head once. "I could never reveal this to him. I could feel that pendant, Aladorn. I could feel its presence, its purpose. I could hardly stand it."

"But Tlonna wears it all the time, and you are always around her. Why does it not affect you then?" Aladorn asked, seating himself on the railing as well, watching his brother.

"Because her presence overwhelms it. She is so strong that the pendant has no power over her, and therefore, when it is within her aura it has no power unless she invokes it. As soon as it departed her aura, I could feel it, and I nearly lost my stomach."

"Why do you think it affects you so?"

"Because the scars are evil, and they are within me, therefore creating a link between me, and objects of intense evil. Just because I am not bad does not mean that I am immune to the scars' power. They are not ordinary wounds. They are semi-sentient, conscious to other evils around them. My right eye sees dark auras now because of them. If I close my left eye, I can see the truth of people."

"What do you see when you look at me?"

Aidyn opened his eyes all the way and gazed at his brother. "I see an elf afflicted by pains so deep he cannot rid himself of them. I see my brother's worries, and his secret fears. I also see an attraction to seeing his enemies die slowly."

Aladorn snorted, a little wary of his younger sibling. "You were not kidding."

"I rarely do."

"So, you can see inside of people's hearts and minds?"

"Not quite..." Aidyn sighed and looked out at the yard far below him. "I can see their weaknesses and evils, whether self-proclaimed or not."

"It must be wearing on you, Aidyn. Is there nothing I can do?" Aladorn asked, concerned. "You have changed so much since your mission. You are much more reclusive and you no longer trust me as you did."

The assassin closed his eyes again. "I have lost a part of me, the part that trusted people, the part that held hope and a dream of finding love. I am nearly eight hundred years old, and I am still alone. I do not know why it bothers me so, many elves live life without a spouse."

Aladorn's heart ached for his little brother, and he squeezed Aidyn's boot toe in an attempt to convey his feelings. "You will find someone, *bruun*. I know it. You are just too closed right now. You are an assassin, and despite the Honor of Assassins, that still makes people anxious around you. Loosen up and stop glaring about so much."

"Oh yeah," Aidyn snorted, chuckling, "because you are so carefree. Unlike you, I cannot just disappear whenever I look a fool."

"Well, that does help," Aladorn laughed, getting up from the railing. "So, is there anyone you are interested in?"

The assassin's face went blank and his fist tightened where it rested on his thigh. "It does not matter."

All humor evaporated from Aladorn and he studied his brother. "Who?" he asked simply, fearing he already knew.

Aidyn sighed. "Tlonna."

"Ah, no, Aidyn," Aladorn groaned, rubbing his face.

"I know! I know. But you do not understand. We were together, once. A long time ago," the assassin said quietly, looking away.

"What? When? How? Does Losolin know?" the wiat gasped, astonished.

"No, nor does she remember. It was on her forty-fifth birthday, and Dietirin asked me to. How could I say no?"

"By saying no!"

Aidyn sighed again. "I love her, Aladorn, I always have and probably always will. I took her virginity."

"Aidyn!" Aladorn wheezed.

"As I said, it was a long time ago, and she does not remember. It is one of the memories Miazie retains."

"Miazie knows?"

The younger elf nodded, sliding off the railing. "She has not said anything, but I know she does."

Aladorn studied his brother for a long moment, gauging his emotions and actions of the last few weeks. "We need to find you a girl," he said finally, smiling.

Aidyn smiled back, and then turned his face away, looking out at the moons, particularly at the large red one that had once been a very close friend. When he said nothing more, Aladorn quietly left the balcony.

Chapter 33

Deception

Yayènia smiled at Suneelo as he brushed by her on his way to the wash room, his hand trailing across her shoulders. When he was gone from the room, the warrior sighed and began folding her cloak. A quiet thump made her turn, thinking her husband had returned for some reason, but the strangest sight greeted her. Herself.

Suneelo rolled his shoulders as he walked back into his bedroom, a towel tied about his slender hips. Yayènia sat on the bed, her hair loose and in snarly tangles. Carefully, she ran a comb through the golden lengths, smoothing out the gnarls and bringing a lustrous sheen to the strands. When he crawled onto the bed behind her and gently took the comb from her hands, she barely acknowledged him, her face turning slightly and then faced the window across the room once more.

He frowned, but figured her mind elsewhere. Slowly, with the ease of many years of practice, he ran the comb through his wife's hair until it was silky all the way to her knees. The hour had passed in silence, which was unusual, but he kept silent on his confusion and started redoing the braid. Yayènia stopped him, finally turning to face.

"I do not want the braid anymore," she said dully, her eyes shaded.

"Why not? Are you going to cut it off?" Suneelo asked, wondering how else she could possible deal with the long hair.

"No. There are more attractive ways to wear it. I tire of looking the same."

"I think you are beautiful no matter how you wear your hair," he said, smiling mischievously. "In fact, I like it when you wear only your hair." He swiftly untied the laces that kept her blouse together and pushed it from her shoulders.

Yayènia responded with a fervor that surprised the normally unshakable Suneelo. His clothes soon lay in shreds on the floor, removed by a knife that had somehow been invisible to him as he undressed her. When she shoved him backward and straddled him, he scowled.

"Our marriage has gone into a rut, Suneelo. I am taking Aidyn as a lover. What do you say?"

"What?" the captain yelped, horrified by the thought. "What are you talking about? Yayènia?"

But she was not listening any more as her hips rocked furiously back and forth on him despite his struggles to free himself. When she finished, Yayènia did not cuddle against him as usual, but rolled away and covered herself in blankets, immediately falling asleep. Dumbfounded, Suneelo slid from the bed and, with shaking fingers, dressed in the closest things he could find. Minutes later he was riding full tilt to the castle, ignoring the fact that his hair, which had been wet from his bath, was now so tangled it would take another hour to reorder.

When he arrived in the stable yard, he tossed the reins to a surprised boy and ran into the castle, sprinting up to the fourth floor. When he shot by Losolin, his brother yelled at him but Suneelo was beyond control now. Aidyn nearly fell off the balcony railing when the captain burst into the room, hollering in a rage that was quite unusual for the composed elf.

When Suneelo's hands yanked the assassin from his perch, Aidyn yelped in surprise and astonishment.

"Did you sleep with my wife?" he bellowed, shaking the stunned dark elf.

"What? Suneelo, have you gone mad?" Aidyn gasped, unable to comprehend the pale elf's words.

"Have you taken Yayènia as a lover?"

"No! What in the nine hells would make you think that?" the assassin shouted back, irritated at being manhandled.

When Suneelo did not release him, he quickly sent his hands into a series of complicated slaps, disorienting the captain enough that he dropped his prey and stepped back, stunned.

"Yayènia said she was taking you as a lover," he snarled when he finally regained his senses. "That our marriage was in a rut and she was having you."

"News to me, Suneelo," Aidyn shot back, befuddled as to why Yayènia would say such a thing. "I would never do that, ever. Spirits, mate, you just about knocked me off my balcony."

Suneelo hesitated, his mind reeling. "So...she was lying?"

"Apparently. What is going on? Did you two get into it?"

"Not that I know of, I went to clean up tonight, came back and she says that, then rides me like a damn horse. I think she bruised me."

Aidyn curled his lip in an expression of confused sympathy. "I do not know what to say, other than no, I have never been with Yayènia. That is very strange. Perhaps she is just having a bad day."

"She seemed fine earlier," Suneelo countered, shaking his head. "When we were all gathered in the garret room, she was angry but no more so than usual."

The assassin shrugged, at a loss. "Stay in the castle tonight, let her cool off and talk to her tomorrow. I am sure she will have an explanation tomorrow."

Suneelo nodded, turning. "Yes, you are right. Ah...Aidyn. Sorry."

Aidyn snorted, "It is not the first time, I promise you. Apparently I am the scapegoat for every female having marital discord."

"How annoying," Suneelo muttered sarcastically, knowing full well the assassin had more than earned the reputation. With that he walked to his and Nia's castle apartment, his mind clouded.

The next morning everyone was gathered in the private dining hall for breakfast when Yayènia strode in, wearing the tightest possible leather pants and a red tunic that was low cut, exposing much of her breasts. Her boots clunked loudly on the stone floor as she passed Suneelo, ignoring the stunned and appalled stares she was getting from her friends. When she sat down in the empty chair next to Aidyn, the assassin's emerald eyes shot up in horror to stare at Suneelo, who was staring back just as widely.

"Morning," Yayènia murmured, pressing her hand against the dark elf's thigh.

"Good morning, Yayènia," he said sharply, pushing her hand away. "An unusual wardrobe today."

"Mm...yes. I have decided that I am bored with my marriage, and bored with my constant armor. So I dress the way I should. Do you not find it attractive?"

Aidyn's eyes widened even further as her hand slipped through his defenses and slid between his legs. "I am done. I have to go," he said, jumping up in his chair.

He grunted as Yayènia's hand slammed hard on his shoulder, shoving him down. Then she stood, smiling at the horrified expressions of her stupefied friends. "No, I shall go. Enjoy your breakfast. I will be at the barracks."

Her nails dug into Aidyn's temple and dragged through his sable hair as the changed warrior swaggered by, pulling his head to the side. When she was gone, the stares turned to him and Suneelo. The two males gaped at each other, disbelieving.

"What in the *nine hells* was *that*?" Tlonna demanded when the silence stretched on, her voice higher pitched than normal.

Suneelo shook his head, his indigo eyes filled with pain. "Something has happened to her. Last night she said she was tired of our marriage, and said she was taking Aidyn as a lover. That is why I stayed here last night. I do not know what to do."

"I have never seen her act like this," Ghealan added, studying the deeply shaken dark elf to his left.

"Yayènia is lost," Miazie said suddenly, her voice hollow and her eyes blank. "Lost amid a whirlwind of white and red. She does not know herself."

"What do you mean?" Suneelo demanded, not liking the sound of the Belau's words.

The woman shook her head, her eyes widening as she lost the vision. "What?"

"What do you mean Nia is lost amid a whirlwind of white and red? How does she not know herself?"

Miazie leaned back in her chair, shaking her head again. "I do not know. I am sorry."

Suneelo slumped, dejected. "I cannot lose her. There has to be a reason she is doing this. There must be."

The table went silent once more.

Yayènia floundered, her eyes blind, her mind in so much agony all she felt was the pain and small amount of pleasure that accompanied the pain in one such as herself. Confused and lost, her soul began to weep.

Tlonna stormed off after breakfast, heading straight for the military compound. She found her sister in the overflow armory, going over sets of armor with an air of deep interest.

"Care to explain yourself?" the queen nearly shouted, which, surprisingly, caused the warrior to jump. Tlonna's gaze narrowed suspiciously.

"Explain what?" Yayènia asked, running a hand through her hair, which was lifted and coiled about her head and shoulders.

"You claim to be sleeping with Aidyn! You tell Suneelo your marriage is in a rut! You come in wearing clothing fit for a Zaedican whore! I demand an explanation immediately!" Tlonna screamed.

Yayènia's eyes widened in fury and her face contorted with rage and disgust. "I could kill you, you know. I could drive my sword through that pretty little skull of yours, wipe out those creepy eyes, shut them forever so that we no longer have to look at them. Then I would become the rightful queen, perhaps I would take Losolin as my husband, keep Aidyn on as my consort. What do you think?"

Immediately Tlonna's suspicions were heightened and she started to turn away. "I do not know what illness has gotten into your mind, but know this," she said, stopping. "We will all be watching you, and do not believe for a minute that we will not defend ourselves if you come at us." With that she departed the military compound, sick to her stomach and beyond confused.

Later that night, Aidyn woke with a start at a soft sound outside his bedroom door. He allowed himself a second to let his eyes adjust to the complete blackness of his room, and then slipped out of bed, grabbing the knife he always kept beneath his pillow. Crouching, he padded across his room and pressed his ear to the door, listening.

He heard the barely audible footfalls of his kin, and his brow knitted, wondering who would attempt to surprise him, of all people. Whoever it was moved expertly and with purpose, crossing the anteroom quickly and stopping just outside the door to his bedroom. Aidyn moved away, bent down in the shadows, and located his scimitars in seconds. Discarding the knife, he carefully drew the slim blades and crouched, ready.

The door opened on silent hinges and a slim figure slipped through, apparently armed to the teeth and lethal as it moved toward his bed, still making only the faintest of noise. Aidyn was confused. The elf seemed very familiar, and it set his nerves on edge as slender fingers reached up and silently drew a wicked blade from a sheath on its back. With a quicksilver movement, the blade slammed downward, right where the blankets were bundled up from where Aidyn had pushed them.

When the attack produced nothing, the unknown assassin yanked the bedding away, spinning into a crouch as soon as they revealed Aidyn's absence. When the elf spun, a stray bar of moonlight slipping between Aidyn's bedroom curtains revealed a slim portion of a face he knew very well. His stomach dropped and his heart stopped beating altogether as betrayal, anguish, and bewilderment caused him to whimper slightly.

Yayènia's ice-cold gaze pinned him where he crouched, her hand pulling her embedded katan free. The warrior stalked toward him, her beautiful face emotionless.

"Nia? What are you doing?" Aidyn cried, backing away, holding his swords tip-down at his side.

"You deny me? You, who would have my sister but not me? You, who leaves for a mission and returns changed, altered and touched by evil so much so that we can no longer trust you?" came her frozen reply, no hint of sadness or remorse in her voice.

"What? I remain faithful, as always, you must know this! What of Tlonna? She knows! I promise you! And why would you want to be with me, Nia? I am not your husband, I do not love you as he does. What has happened to you?" Aidyn replied, stricken even as he knew it was useless.

The coldness of his old friend's gaze told him his life was forfeit unless he somehow managed to defeat her, and thinking about the oddness of her behavior, he was sorely baffled.

"I have decided to see the world for what it truly is, a blackened pit of despair and deception, filled with murderous kin and ruthless leaders. I shall no longer stand idly by and let rogues like you run free. I would have spared you were you willing to be my lover, but no, not the great Aidyn. He would never do such a thing. Heartless bastard that you are. I shall kill you tonight, and end all of our worries and our put an end to our questions of where your loyalties lie."

"No!" Aidyn said, tears sliding down his face. "I cannot fight you!"

"Then you will die without honor, and I will be forced to live with that knowledge. Fight me, Aidyn, and give me a reason to mourn you," Yayènia replied, sincerity in her words but not her voice.

Suddenly she was upon him, katan slashing in the dark. Aidyn leapt back, but felt the sting of her blade nonetheless, the warmth of blood on his belly. Swearing, he brought his scimitars up, resigned, but unwilling to die for no reason. With a ringing clash, their weapons came together, and then Yayènia drew her shortsword, grimacing. Aidyn's tears burned up as fury replaced his sadness, and he began to fight back. His heart was still grinding itself into dust, but he was angered by the fact that he had been given no choice in his fate.

The two elves fought cautiously for a time, probing for weaknesses, giving the other a chance to forfeit without loss of life, and then Yayènia whacked Aidyn across the face with the hilt of her katan, nearly knocking him senseless. The assassin dropped to the ground, but he recovered instantly and dove for her legs just as both blades came whistling down. He felt one sword graze his side, but he did not slow.

Yayènia lost her balance as Aidyn took out her legs, and they rolled around on the floor, each struggling to gain an advantage. Finally, Yayènia freed one of her arms and she slammed her palm into Aidyn's nose. With a cry, the dark elf reared upward, clutching his face, blood dripping between his fingers. The High Commander kicked him in the stomach and he fell backward, landing hard on his shoulders. He scooted away, searching for his scimitars. Already Yayènia was up, advancing toward him, determined to end the struggle.

At the last second, Aidyn found his weapons and swept them up in time to block a downward thrust that would have split him in two. With a jerk, he shoved Yayènia's katan out of his face and rolled onto his feet, trying to blink the blood out of his eyes. Then the female tossed aside both the katan and the shortsword and drew her longblade. Aidyn let out a desperate and incredulous breath, and readied himself for the attack, refusing to make any offensive moves. She came at him in a blur, longblade sweeping toward him.

The assassin ducked away and heard the sword bury itself in his bedpost. With an oath, Yayènia yanked her blade free, taking a large chunk of wood with it. She tossed the portion at Aidyn and he evaded it easily.

"Is this really what you want?" he asked, trying to stop the insane attack.

"It is what everyone wants," Yayènia replied, slicing at him again.

Aidyn wove his scimitars in an intricate dance to deflect her vicious sword, barely keeping a step ahead of the warrior, wondering if this was the reason she had changed so drastically. For a long while, they stood in the same spot, jabbing and parrying at each other, their blades only occasionally sliding across flesh. Blood ran down all of their limbs, and both elves were cognizant of the fact that they were at last of similar skill. Finally Aidyn stepped forward, within Yayènia's guard, and slammed his fist into her face. The warrior reeled back, surprised.

"Why?" he shouted, spreading his arms as he stood before her.

Yayènia did not answer, but darted forward, spinning deftly. Aidyn jumped back, ramming into his bed. He flipped over and landed on all fours on his mattress, glaring at his opponent. The look stopped the High Commander in her tracks. It was vile and cold, raging enough to send shivers down her spine. Aidyn could not remember ever being so livid. With a savage howl, he jumped off the bed, slamming into Yayènia hard enough to carry them both against the wall.

The female grunted as the solid obsidian wall smashed into her back, her head whacking it hard enough to cause sparks to appear in her vision. Aidyn's hands were all over her, punching and cuffing until finally he grabbed her chin and dug his fingers into her jaw, his entire body vibrating with the intensity of his wrath. Suddenly she realized his scimitar was pressing hard against her belly.

"Aidyn..." she wheezed, desperate.

"You are wrong," he sobbed, tears once again welling in his eyes. "I will always be loyal, noble, and brave. I would never betray any of you. Why would you do this to me?"

"Because you failed," Yayènia breathed, giving him a twisted grin. Her hand jerked up suddenly and he felt a sharp pain in his side where her dagger had pierced him.

Aidyn closed his eyes, and shoved the scimitar forward until he felt the tip bury itself in the obsidian behind Yayènia. After a moment, he stepped away, letting go of the hilt. Yayènia slumped forward, held up by the sword embedded in the wall. Aidyn fell to his knees and yanked the dagger out of his side, trying to staunch the blood with his fingers. When it did not stop, he buried his face in the rug that covered half of his room, weeping.

Moments later, his door burst open and light spilled into the bedroom.

"Aidyn!" Tlonna screamed, horrified by the scene before her.

Behind the queen crowded Losolin, Aladorn, Miazie, Sodo, and worst of all, Suneelo. The Captain of the Guard's dark eyes flashed between the assassin and his dead wife, his face unreadable. Aidyn did not move, unable to summon the willpower or strength to stand. His sobs wracked his entire body and he did not care that dozens of wounds were soaking through the rug. He did not care that some of them were serious and could prove debilitating, perhaps even fatal, if not tended to soon. He did not care that his back and neck were completely vulnerable, for his heart was shattered.

No one moved, stunned and dismayed. Slowly, Tlonna moved toward her dear friend, still huddled in the middle of the floor, his fingers digging into the side of his head.

"Aidyn what happened?" she cried, not daring to look at her sister. "Miazie and Sodo heard screaming."

"She came for me," Aidyn sobbed, "she drove her sword through my bed, and said you all wanted me dead. Why?"

"Aidyn...we would never want you dead. How could you believe such things?" Tlonna breathed, kneeling beside the shattered assassin.

He finally looked up at her, verdant gaze stricken. "What?"

"You are my closest friend, why would I want you dead?"

"Yayènia said...she said I had failed, that..."

At that moment Suneelo lost control, bursting into the room and grabbing Aidyn by the arms. He hoisted the surprised dark elf up and tossed him onto the bed, snarling viciously. He drew a dagger from his boot and prepared to leap on the wilted assassin, but Losolin and Sodo stopped him, yanking him back with every ounce of strength they had.

Aidyn slowly rolled onto the foot of the bed and dropped his head into a position that told everyone in the room that he had just lost the will to carry on.

Aladorn rushed to his brother's side, not caring that only two of the people in the room knew of their relation. He knelt before the younger elf and grabbed his face, peering deep into the assassin's suffering gaze. Tlonna moved to stand next to her dead sister, a look of confusion, rather than horror, now on her face. Miazie came over to stand next to her, ignoring the now sobbing Suneelo being supported by Losolin and Sodo.

"This is very odd," the Belau said flatly.

Tlonna nodded, and without a word yanked Aidyn's scimitar from Yayènia's belly. The corpse drooped forward, and the Magin felt the slightest residue of a Weave. Still silent, she grabbed a fistful of golden hair and held the body up at an awkward angle, its mouth gaping open. Miazie lurched away at the gruesome sight as Tlonna began muttering under her breath.

A dark aura appeared around the body and suddenly the female began to contort. There was a collective gasp as the dead Yayènia shrank and darkened, her face becoming fuller and her hair curling. Finally, Tlonna dropped the hair in dismay and surprise and stepped away, staring at the real corpse. Even Aidyn took note of the true identity, and his guilt lessened slightly.

Rhiannan lay flaccid on the floor, blood spilling from her mouth. The dead half-breed shuddered suddenly, and a black cloud puffed from her chest, and she again lay still. Tlonna stared down at her daughter, devastated. Numbly, she looked up and found Losolin's concerned face coming toward her.

"Anna..." she said blankly, letting her husband support her.

"Yayènia," Aidyn uttered, motioning Aladorn to the side and getting to his feet. "I did not kill her, I...Yayènia is alive somewhere! Suneelo, it was not her!"

The stunned captain fell to his knees before the dark elf and leaned forward, hugging his legs. Aidyn stumbled in surprise but then felt his brother's hand on his shoulder. He shared a look with Aladorn, a look that quickly turned to surprise as he tensed suddenly.

"Aidyn!" the wiat cried out as the dark elf sagged to the side as Suneelo let go of his legs in shock.

Clutching his side where Rhiannan had stabbed him, the assassin fell to his knees and cried out in pain as all his many injuries came roaring to the fore. Distantly, he heard someone calling for Losolin, and then all went blank.

Suddenly Tlonna pivoted, her eyes wide with fear as Losolin left her to tend to Aidyn, who was convulsing slightly on the floor.

"Suneelo, Miazie...find Haydyn!"

The two looked at each other and then sprinted off, driven mostly by the urgency in their queen's voice. Once they were gone, Tlonna went to her knees beside Aidyn's head and brushed the sable hair from his face. Losolin's hands roamed his entire body, locating and healing the several wounds the weapons master had received.

Slowly, the jerking dark elf's body calmed and his rasping breath became more regular as he succumbed to sleep. The king sat back, exhausted as Aladorn and Sodo hoisted the assassin back onto his bed, trying to ignore the hole driven through the blankets and mattress by a sword.

Then he stood and picked up the weapons that had belonged to Rhiannan in the guise of Yayènia. She had somehow stolen the weapons from the real warrior, probably when she had done whatever to disable the High Commander in the first place. His worry for his sister increased tenfold when Miazie and Suneelo returned.

The Belau stepped forward, her hand reaching for Tlonna. The queen knocked the appendage away, her eyes wide with denial.

"No, no."

"Tlonna, I'm so sorry," Miazie said, tears on her face.

The queen's face crumpled with grief and she buried her head in Losolin's shoulder, weeping. The king looked at his brother and saw the terrible truth in the indigo gaze.

"How?"

"His throat was slit. He was still in bed," the captain supplied quietly, watching the trembling shoulders of his sister-in-law.

Tlonna's knees buckled and she was supported only by Losolin's strong arms. Her wails of anguish filled the entire room at the news of her son's murder, and everyone bowed their heads and cried.

Only minutes later though, Aidyn resurfaced enough to warrant attention. He grasped his brother's hand and pulled himself up. "Yayènia is still out there, somewhere in the city. She may yet be alive."

Those few words had everyone sprinting for the door, but when the assassin moved to get up, Aladorn pushed him back down. "Stay, and rest."

"But I—" Aidyn began desperately, but his brother cut him off.

"Stay."

When the wiat joined the others, they were standing in Aidyn's front room, surrounding Miazie who was clutching Sodo for support. Her eyes were open and staring, the pupils dilated enough to take up her entire iris, her face tense. For a long while she remained so, hardly breathing. When she came out of her trance, she sucked in a great breath and uttered a single word.

"Harbor."

Tlonna and Losolin had volunteers from the castle spread out and search the buildings all over the docks. It was almost dawn when they found her. Suneelo and Aladorn came running, shouting and waving their arms in the air. They guided the king and queen to where a young nobleman was standing outside a small storage hut, nervously wringing his fingers together. Without hesitation, the four elves went into the dark building and there they stood in stock horror.

The High Commander was curled into a ball, loosely wrapped in a white sheet, the floor beneath stained crimson while fresh blood seeped from her naked body.

"Dear gods," Tlonna choked and went to her knees by her sister.

Losolin positioned himself by Yayènia's head and lifted it. Both her eyes were blackened and swollen. Her lips were cracked and bleeding, her teeth stained red. Suneelo's breath came and went in a desperate wheeze and he slammed to the floor, shaking so hard he could hardly stay in one spot. Aladorn gripped his shoulders in support, unable to look away from the horrible sight.

"Rhiannan broke almost every bone in her body. Losolin...help her. Save her! Please!" Tlonna sobbed, gingerly picking up Yayènia's mangled hand.

Losolin swallowed, blinking back his tears. As green light expanded from his hands, Yayènia moaned. Tlonna watched as her sister writhed on the floor. Her fingers straightened and the hand Tlonna held slowly began to grip harder and harder.

"She is helping me. She is giving me her power," Losolin said, breathing hard.

After a few moments he frowned and stopped, a look of dismay crossing his face. "She has the same injuries Rhiannan had, the same ones Aidyn gave her. Every blow that Aidyn landed on Anna, landed on Yayènia as well. She is only alive because of her being a Maig. She has several other injuries as well, most likely from when Rhiannan attacked her in the first place, but that was the plan. Every strike Anna got, Nia got too. Dear gods, Aidyn..."

Everyone was staring at the king in desperation, unable to summon words. Losolin shook his head, blinking away the tears that welled in his dark eyes, and began to run his healing power over Yayènia once more.

The shaft of light coming through the partially open door widened suddenly and Aladorn turned in rage to the nobleman who had found the building. He held up his hands in a desperate sign of innocence and stepped aside as an undulating ball of dark blue light drifted by him. Tlonna heard the wiat's intake of breath and turned to see what had caused it. She immediately recognized the color, and knew it to be Sithian's.

The ball floated to the queen's side and there it sat for a moment, as though taking in the scene. Finally, when the female was getting ready to blast it with her own power, it spoke.

"I see my sister has failed me yet again," Sithian's voice said casually. "She was not supposed to survive, but neither was Yayènia. If she'd killed the dark elf, then even better, but it was not part of the plan. Fortunately, I have done the deed of destroying the assassin's heart enough that he will probably be of little use from now on. Anyway, I needed Anna's power for my own, and this just seemed the perfect opportunity to use her body. What do you think? Oh never mind, I know what you think. So, both the assassin and the bitch will survive, but at what cost? Will they ever be able to look at one another again? Will Aidyn be able to lift his scimitar again if he knows there is a possibility it might be one of his friends he is about to kill? And by the way, Mother, I am so sorry about Haydyn, but he was such a thorn in my side. And Kelus," Sithian's voice grew mocking, "such a loss. He was a great demon, but a sad little elf. All in all, I feel rather good about all this, though I'm sorry Anna wasn't able to finish off her other targets. Also, I expect you really won't have time to mourn the way you elves do. You're soon to be very, *very* busy."

The ball winked out and Tlonna stared at the empty space for a long, long time. Slowly, she turned back to Yayènia, and used the cuff of her sleeve to wipe the blood and sweat from Yayènia's forehead. Aladorn, Sodo, the nobleman, and even Suneelo were in complete shock from the message, knowing full well the damage that had been done this night.

Slowly, Losolin resumed his healing and the warrior's limbs became normally shaped, though she still was not conscious. It took another half hour for Losolin to heal her enough to waken. Yayènia's eyes, though no longer blackened and swollen, were glazed with pain. Her lips twitched into a small smile.

"She did her damnedest, did she not?" she said quietly.

Tlonna let out a relieved sob. "Oh spirits. I thought we might have actually lost you this time."

Yayènia winced as she sat up. "I am harder to kill than death itself. Losolin, my brother, my thanks. I was so caught up by the image of myself striding toward me I did not think to react until Rhiannan had driven her knife into me. If I did not have the healing power I do, I would surely have died within the hour. What happened? You all look so...grave."

"Rhiannan murdered Haydyn, and apparently Kelus. Yayènia, in your body she fought Aidyn, and he believed he had killed you. He...did it to save his own life, and only barely. He was hit several times, nearly as grievously as you. You must not blame him," Suneelo said quietly, stroking his wife's face with his knuckle.

While Yayènia began demanding answers, and Suneelo and Losolin tried to answer her, Tlonna pulled Aladorn aside. "Find Kelus. If he is indeed gone from us, have him brought to the castle."

The wiat nodded and ran off along the harbor that was already filled with milling sailors and merchants. Suneelo and the nobleman helped Yayènia to her feet as Tlonna instructed the group of guards that had arrived to help them back to the castle. Once there, the queen set off immediately for her son's room.

Haydyn still lay in bed, his eyes closed in peaceful slumber, and it would have been just that if not for the crimson smile carved in his throat. Tlonna gently shut the door and went to his side, tears of anguish rolling down her face as she gazed down at her murdered child. Slowly, she sat on the edge of the bed and began wiping the blood away. He had bled out already, so when she cleaned off the final smudges, no more fluid came forth, and the wound did not look so ghastly. Still sobbing, Tlonna tore a clean strip from her shirt and gently tied it around her son's throat, covering the gash.

Then all strength seemed to leave her and she doubled over, gasping for breath and weeping inconsolably, clutching her stomach.

Aidyn was moving slowly down the corridor when Suneelo and Losolin brought Yayènia up. The three elves stopped before the single and a sudden tension filled the hall. The dark elf's eyes went wide at the sight of Yayènia, wrapped in the blood-stained sheet. He stumbled, still weak from his ordeal, and would have gone to his knees had Sodo not grabbed him. He and Miazie had returned to the castle in the wake of the guards surrounding Yayènia, Losolin, and Suneelo, and now they stood on either side of the assassin.

"They say you held the sword that killed Rhiannan," Yayènia murmured quietly, "while she was impersonating me."

"I did not know," Aidyn rasped. "She came in trying to kill me, stabbed your sword through my bed. When I saw it was Rhiannan, my relief was profound. Nia, can you ever forgive my mistake?"

The stunned commander backed away from the assassin as he reached out. "You still drove the sword through my body."

The dark elf's entire body wilted at the words and he went limp in Sodo's arms. "Yayènia...please, you...she...I had no choice! It was not you in the end!"

"Yes it was. Every wound you inflicted on Rhiannan you inflicted on me at the same time. Your scimitar went right through my stomach, and I felt it as keenly as though I were the one physically standing at the end of your sword. I have long defended that assassins have honor, and that their oaths held true, yours most of all. Now I am not so sure. Were it me, I would not be so able to drive my sword through your belly," Yayènia returned frostily, though her voice trailed off at the end.

Suneelo tried to grab his wife as she stormed by him, but she shook him off, lurching to the side, but continuing onward to their castle apartment.

The captain turned to his devastated friend and held out his hand imploringly. "Aidyn...she did not mean it. We all know that you have honor, and that you were only defending your life. I am so sorry," he said, his voice breaking.

When Aidyn barely responded, the other elf sent a look of hopelessness at Losolin, and then turned and ran after his wife. Aladorn returned later that night with the grave news that he could not find Kelus anywhere, and he had asked several people about the elf's whereabouts. No one had seen him for days.

Three days later, Haydyn's funeral took place. Tlonna, swathed completely in black and silver, stood rigidly, her face concealed. Losolin too was clothed in mourning garments, and his eyes were red-rimmed with sorrow. All around them stood the family, each one of them silent in their grieving. Yayènia stood next to Tlonna, which forced her to be near to Aidyn, and they could all feel the tension emanating from the two elves. The assassin's face was blank, his usually vibrant eyes dull and discouraged, whereas the High Commander's were full of rage and distrust. Tlonna felt Aidyn's pain and sadness within her heart, but it was a distant feeling. She could not think of anything but her son and her daughter, dead.

Though Rhiannan had been evil and vicious, the queen still felt in her heart the love of a mother, the desperate attempt to see past the ugliness and the cruelty. The knowledge that her only surviving child was responsible for taking both their lives ate at her insides, sent breathtaking pangs through her limbs.

The princess had been quietly buried within the family graveyard with a headstone reading her true name. Rhiannan Rahlan-Ewôsdírn, Princess of Zaedic and of Blackhaven. Haydyn, however, was entombed in a raised coffin with a carved likeness on the lid, a few feet away from Dietirin's mausoleum. His name and title had been emblazoned by magic on a small obelisk at his head.

Here lies Haydyn Rahlan-Ewôsdírn
Prince of Blackhaven
Beloved Son and Friend
Light of Zaedic

As soon as the priest finished his oratory, Tlonna fell to her knees before the tomb, her fingers clutching at the harsh stone. Tears rushed from her eyes as loss overwhelmed her, and she cried out meaningless syllables as grief stole her words. Swiftly, the family moved the onlookers away from the cemetery and then ringed their friend and queen in a protective half-circle, standing like black statues in the frosty winter evening.

Feeling utterly alone, Tlonna rested her forehead against the foot of the coffin and cried out to her son. The loss she felt was unbearable, the pain nearly debilitating. Even the death of her father had not been this terribly heartrending. Within her mind flashed memories of Haydyn's mischievous grin, his summer-blue eyes dancing with glee, and the look of determination on his face whenever he trained with Yayènia. Tlonna remotely felt the icy wind ripping through her garments, but she did not care.

Clutching her son's final resting place, the queen screamed at the cruel gods that had taken so much from her and demanded more. When the spirits began whispering to her, the Magin tried to block them out, tried to ignore their nonsensical babble. But they refused to quiet, instead raising their voices until they were nearly screeching within her head. The part of her that was Jair rose up, angry and violent. Together they lashed out at the spirits, not caring if they destroyed or simply silenced them.

Losolin watched as Tlonna huddled before Haydyn's tomb, his heart grinding itself into dust. Beside him stood Miazie, and on his other side, Suneelo. They were both crying, saddened by the loss of the vibrant young half-blood. Losolin felt guilty and remorseful, wishing he had told Haydyn that he loved him. He wished he could have hugged his stepson at least once, given him the father he had so desperately wanted.

The king brushed the tears from his face and took a shaky breath, trying to be strong for his wife. He started to turn to Miazie when a blast of burning hot air knocked him, and everyone else, to the ground. Stunned, Losolin stayed on his back for a few seconds, trying to gather his wits. Another blast rolled over him, and he heard Yayènia swear as she was flattened again.

Turning onto his side, Losolin searched for Tlonna and found her still kneeling at the coffin, her back bent and her forehead pressed to the stone. Heat so strong it made the air shimmer radiated from her body, colored lights flickering sporadically all around her. On his hands and knees, the male forced his way to her side.

"Tlonna?" he whispered, wrapping one arm around her shoulders.

She turned her face away and sobbed, for once not caring about him. Within her, anger and sorrow warred, battling back and forth in her mind. Jair was aroused as well, muttering darkly from the depths of her soul.

"Loni?" Losolin said, afraid he was losing her. "My heart, come back to me."

Tlonna forced Jair's morbid utterances away and slowly turned to confront her husband. When her eyes landed on his face, she collapsed into him, needing his strength. Digging her fingers into his arms, the elf pressed her face into his neck and felt his arms encircle her.

"I cannot do this, Losolin. I cannot continue to lose everyone I love," she wailed softly.

"I know, my heart, I know. Come, let us away from here. Can you stand?" Losolin asked, pressing his cheek to her hair.

Tlonna tried to get up, but her willpower failed her, and she slumped into him. Without another word, Losolin lifted her in his arms and stood. Everyone was back on their feet now, and they met the king's gaze with despair. Aidyn was rubbing his hand over his heart, his mouth open as he sucked in breath after breath, trying to put up a block against Tlonna's emotions. Though Losolin knew about their connection, no one else did, and they stared at the assassin in confusion. Yayènia strode by him without a glance, taking up point position, though it was Ghealan's place to do so.

The Second Commander moved toward his friend, but Suneelo stopped him, shaking his head. Together, the two males flanked Aidyn, with Aladorn trailing, giving the dark elf moral support. Erdwyf, Miazie, and Sodo moved behind Losolin, guarding the rear. Together, the entourage walked back to the castle, where they went their separate ways.

Losolin, still carrying Tlonna, gently put her down on their bed where she immediately curled into a ball. He removed her veil and lay down beside her, drawing the female close and lending whatever comfort he could. They stayed there for the rest of the day, neither sleeping nor awake, but somewhere in limbo where the pain and sorrow became a dull ache, unable to create nightmares or encompass their thoughts as it waited like a sentience in the air.

Chapter 34

To Lose Everything

Erdwyf took up the king and queen's mantle for the duration of their seclusion, with the aid of Miazie, Feorien, and Narda, the seneschal. The High Advisor was standing on a turret, trying to escape the constant needs of the people, when there came a quiet knock on the door behind her. Turning, the elf eyed the nervous messenger with wary eyes, fearing more bad news.

"What is it?" the female demanded when the boy just stared at her.

"Uhm...High Advisor, I was told to give you this, and to tell you that only the king and queen may see it," he said, handing her a folded bit of vellum.

"Who from?"

The messenger shrugged nervously. "Lord Arganor."

Erdwyf frowned, thinking that few things would come into Arganor's knowledge that needed her ignorance. "Then I will do as he asks."

When the boy remained, shuffling from foot to foot and staring at her midriff, Erdwyf's patience ran out. "What?"

"I am to report back to Lord Arganor that you have handed the unread message to the king and queen," he said in a small voice.

Suddenly Erdwyf remembered that it was this same boy that had announced Sithian's arrival, and then later been attacked. She felt little remorse for him at the moment. "I am High Advisor, acting as regent. You may tell Lord Arganor that in the future, if he has discretional material, he can either hand it to Tlonna and Losolin himself, or deal with the fact that I, and several others, have the right and privilege to be privy to any and all information. Do I need to repeat myself?" she snapped, her temper frayed.

"No, High Advisor."

"Good. You are dismissed," Erdwyf snarled, and then turned her back on the boy, ripping open the message as she did.

By the time she read the last line, the female was shivering with anger and sadness. "How many more are we to lose?" she murmured to herself, turning into the castle.

Finding Tlonna and Losolin was easy, as they had been in their quarters since Haydyn's funeral. Erdwyf knocked on the door and strode into the foyer without waiting. The room was deserted, so she headed straight for the bedroom. She was halfway there when it opened and Losolin stepped out, half-naked and weary.

Erdwyf halted, staring at the king's supple muscles as he walked over to her. He looked exhausted, but otherwise as beautiful as usual, his oceanic eyes taking in her distressed visage.

"What has happened now?" he asked, his voice a little shaky.

The High Advisor handed him the message. "Kelus was found dead in an alley earlier today. By the looks of it, he had been dead for days."

Losolin read the message, his broad shoulders slumping. "I had hoped Rhiannan had failed, that he had somehow escaped," he said finally.

Erdwyf nodded. "Myself as well. As much as I hate to say it, I am glad Aidyn had the courage to drive his scimitar through her belly. I just wish Nia would see the folly of her hurt and anger."

"She is still not speaking to him?" the king asked, finding a shirt and pulling it on.

"No. She is not even talking to me, and barely standing Suneelo's presence at the moment. I am sure there is something more to her actions than just Aidyn beating her doppelganger."

Losolin shrugged. "Maybe that is it. He beat her. No one has beaten Yayènia since her rise to High Commander, and now two people have. Remember what she did as soon as she was able to walk after Midian slit her throat?"

Nodding, Erdwyf sat down in one of the elegantly carved lounge chairs. "Her mind is not stable, never has been. Did you hear about their duel in Kajgenia?"

"What duel?"

"Aidyn and Yayènia fought in Kajgenia, the day they went to the Eseirik's cell. Aidyn defeated her then, too. Knocked her to the ground so hard she could not get a good breath in for a long time. Nearly broke her nose."

"Why? What caused such violence between them? They were such good friends, as we all are," Losolin replied, thoroughly confused.

Erdwyf shook her head. "Yayènia was trying to get him to talk, to let out some of his anger and desperation. He feels responsible for

Demetrius's death even still. It is the only way she knows how to deal with such situations, and the only way he knows. They are warriors to very end."

"So, Aidyn bested her twice. That would certainly rub her the wrong way, would it not?" Losolin said, more of a comment than a question. "Nia even beat Tlonna, which is no easy feat. But still, Aidyn is an assassin, the best in the world. How could she take offense?"

"Yayènia does not like being second to anyone. Ghealan says she goes into a battle rage every time a fight has any sort of anger behind it or if blood is drawn. She broke his legs in their competition to become High Commander. She cannot shake the feeling that even though it was really Rhiannan that Aidyn killed, he is the better fighter. It bothers her."

"Well she can get over it," Tlonna snapped from the bedroom door. The queen was wrapped in a thin robe and her hair was puffed up to nearly twice its size from being constantly run through with her fingers. "Aidyn did what he had to do in order to survive. Anna killed Haydyn, there can be no forgiving that."

"She also killed Kelus, he was found in an alley," Losolin said quietly, walking over to his wife.

Tlonna looked up at him in disbelief, her white pupils dilating. She sucked in a very shaky breath and dropped her forehead against his chest, suddenly numb. "Why must I continue to lose everyone I love?" she whimpered.

Losolin wrapped his arms around her and drew her to the chairs where Erdwyf waited with averted eyes.

"He had only just reclaimed his old life, to have it ripped away in such a fashion, by someone whose life they owed to him. He was the reason all three children survived. He would not let me kill them, knowing that they had a chance to be good. He would never suffer a child to die at the hands of anger or vengeance," Tlonna said softly, sniffling. "He was a good, kind person, trapped in a world of evil and violence. He kept me alive those months I was a captive. He healed my wounds and gave me company, making sure I was fed enough to survive, given clean water as often as possible. I trusted him implicitly. I loved him as a brother."

Losolin rubbed her back while Erdwyf knelt before her friend. "We will find a way to stop this all, Tlonna. I swear to you, we will find a way, or we will make one, either one. Please do not give up. We are all here for you, as we have been, and always will be."

"Not so much, Erdwyf," someone said savagely from the foyer doorway.

When all three elves looked up, Yayènia strode into the room, a furious and somehow helpless look on her face.

"What do you mean?" Losolin demanded, realizing that she too held a message.

"I mean this," the warrior snarled, tossing the letter at Tlonna. "It just arrived, from Narnen."

Erdwyf scowled. "From my parents?"

"No, from Emar and Atlan," Tlonna said faintly, her heart breaking into even smaller pieces. "Or more correctly, from their councilors. The king and queen have passed on, found dead in their bed. Suicide."

Erdwyf and Losolin gaped at the Magin, at a loss for words. "What does it say?" the king asked, worried by his wife's ashen face.

"They have named Erdwyf and Ghealan their heirs."

"What!" Erdwyf shrieked, disbelieving and horrified. "You cannot be serious!"

"Indeed she is," Yayènia interjected angrily. "It also says that, though they realize this to be a surprise, that you must be prepared to take the throne within two weeks."

"What of Volker?"

"Dead," Tlonna supplied coldly. "Like everyone else."

"They cannot be serious!" Erdwyf said again, more frantically, her eyes huge. "I am not fit to rule! I have no blood ties to them! Why me? Why Ghealan! We cannot leave here! This is our home, our friends are here! Our jobs, our family! What of Jaryikin?"

"She will be the heir-apparent," Yayènia snapped.

"Yayènia, this is not my fault!" Erdwyf screamed at her irritable friend. "Stop striking at your friends because of your own insecurities! I have had enough of your constant anger! Give it up already! I swear to the gods you are going to lose everyone if you do not rein in your bloody temper!"

Yayènia stood ramrod straight, fury and hurt warring in her eyes. She said nothing, however, but continued to stand right where she was.

Tlonna placed a hand on Erdwyf's shoulder. "I do not believe you are being given a choice, Erd. As far as everything here, we can figure that out in due time. Tell Ghealan, and we will speak of this tomorrow."

"Oh, spirits, Ghealan. He has no desire to rule. He will not go. He will stay here," Erdwyf said, her anxiety rising.

"I think Ghealan would give up anything to be with you," Yayènia said cruelly, as she turned around, flopped down into a chair, and dropped her face into her hands.

Erdwyf stared at the warrior, but did not lash out her again. "I do not want this, Tlonna. Please, can you do anything?"

"I am afraid not. You are a native Narnenian, and Emar's will is not negotiable. My rule over you lasts only to a point. Because Blackhaven has no civilian contract, I cannot argue your citizenship. I can only argue Ghealan's because he was born here," Tlonna replied sadly.

Erdwyf was crying now, her entire demeanor one of defeat. "I am not qualified to be a queen!"

"Better than most, Erd. Think of it this way, you have often run this kingdom by yourself when I was gone or otherwise incapacitated, such as this week. Narnen is much smaller than Blackhaven, with far fewer citizens. Your parents are there, and they have been leaders of their community for years, I am sure they will help you."

"Why are you not fighting this?" Erdwyf asked Tlonna, breathless.

"Because it is out of my hands. It is not my place to gainsay other rulers," the queen said gently. "I have no power over anyone out of my kingdom."

"That includes me! Please, Tlonna, tell them you need me! You do need me, right?"

"Of course I do, but Erdwyf...I am powerless here. I will write back, but I do not feel that they will allow me to hold you here."

Erdwyf nodded in a defeated way and taking the letter, left the room to find her husband. Yayènia still sat in the chair with her face covered. Losolin had been watching her the entire time and he was gravely concerned for her. He felt a deep pity for her, and wanted only to find out what was wrong by being gentle with the troubled warrior. Tlonna did not have any such reservations.

"What in the nine hells is the matter with you?" the queen shouted at her sister.

Yayènia's head snapped up and tear-rimmed eyes tried to burn a hole through the Magin. "I am about to lose my oldest friend, and my trusted second! I am already losing one friend, and now I must lose two more! I lost Haydyn, who was my greatest protégé and my nephew! I have lost my respect for myself, and the one thing I always have counted on, my infallibility, has been thrown to the winds! What am I now? A friendless, fallible she-elf with no spectacular talent!"

"Just because Aidyn killed Rhiannan in the guise of you does not mean you have no talent, or that you are even with fault," Losolin countered, butting in before Tlonna could lose her temper again. "He has been training nearly every day of his life to be the best, to be perfect, you have done so as well. You are both of equal skill, and you know that to be true. Do not beat yourself up over something that is false. And as far as friends, you still have all of them. Just because Erdwyf and Ghealan must leave does not mean that they will forget us as soon as they step within Narnen. And you will not lose Aidyn if you do not want to. You are pushing him away, not the other way around."

Yayènia dropped her gaze and leaned back in the chair, her legs stretched out in front of her. "Still. How can I salvage our relationship after what happened? He drove a scimitar through my stomach!"

"Not your stomach, Nia. Rhiannan's, though she was disguised as you. What else was he to do? Let himself be murdered?" Tlonna argued, a little calmer.

The warrior sighed. "I suppose not, but it was just really hard to see when the same wounds he inflicted on her happened to me."

"You would be more inclined to forgive him if you had seen him as we did. He was shattered, Yayènia. Absolutely devastated."

When the warrior did not reply, Tlonna inhaled deeply and sat down. "Look, you need to speak with him. For once, let your true feelings guide you, release your bitterness and your anger and fill yourself with the pain and fear that you really feel. Aidyn will understand that. Trust me."

"What is between you two? Why are you so close? You were never this close before," Yayènia demanded, uncomfortable with the topic of her emotions.

Tlonna smiled faintly. "He is bound to me by oath."

"What oath?"

The Magin looked at Losolin, unsure how to explain the strong bond between her and the assassin. "Well…it is an oath between an assassin and a Magin. There is an emotional connection between us, a small part of my heart is bonded with his, and we can feel each other's stronger emotions. Right now, I can feel only sadness and loneliness."

Yayènia nodded slowly, ashamed of her attitude toward one of her oldest friends. "I have betrayed him."

"No, but you certainly hurt him," Tlonna countered gently.

"I attacked his honor, which is all he has as an assassin. It is his precept of life. Nobility, Loyalty, and Bravery. It is their creed."

"And something he would never abandon," Tlonna agreed. "Go to him, Yayènia, be the warrior you claim to be and face your demons."

"What of Erdwyf and Ghealan? Who will take their place?"

Tlonna had known this question was coming, and she again looked at Losolin. "Miazie will take on the mantle of High Advisor. As High Commander, it is ultimately your decision who gets the Second Commander position. But I would suggest Suneelo, or Aladorn."

Yayènia nodded, standing. "Then I will do as you say, and speak with Aidyn. I am sorry to have made this week worse for you. I know you have been in pain. And I am sorry about Kelus. I do not believe he ever forgave me for the arrow I put through his hand, but he seemed a good fellow once he turned."

The queen did not reply other than to nod, but Yayènia knew she had been forgiven. When she had gone, Tlonna turned to Losolin and smiled. "You have been my savior, love. Thank you for staying by my side."

"There is no other place for me, Tlonna," he replied, embracing her.

Aidyn shot to his feet when Yayènia walked into his anteroom. Though his hands went instinctively to his scimitars, the dark elf forced himself to stay unarmed. Yayènia saw the motion, and her pale eyes narrowed. For a moment the two warriors watched each other, both wary of the other's intentions. It was the female who looked away first, folding her arms across her chest.

"I have come to mend things," she said bluntly, not looking at him.

The words caught the assassin by surprise, but he did not reveal his inner turmoil. Instead, he dropped his hovering hands onto the hilts of his blades and held them there, resting. "Is there anything left to mend?" he asked, sharper than he had intended.

Yayènia's lips thinned and she nearly left, but remembering her sister's words, she remained. "I have wronged you, and betrayed your honor. I was misled in my anger and doubt, and I realize that I need my friend more than I need another enemy."

Aidyn's shoulders loosened visibly with relief and he reclaimed his seat, shoving the book he had been reading off the chair. "I am glad you came to that realization. It has been a trying week."

The female also sat. "I know, and it is about to become more so."

At Aidyn's worried expression, she explained Kelus's death, and Erdwyf's and Ghealan's sudden situation. When she finished, the assassin slumped in the chair, at a loss for words. "What are we to do?" he asked finally.

"Tlonna says we will be fine, that Miazie will take Erd's place, and that either Suneelo or Aladorn will take Ghealan's. But I do not know. Lan and I have been a team for two and half centuries. Erdwyf has been High Advisor for well over a hundred years as well. This will be such a drastic change."

Aidyn nodded, still shocked. "It is too much at one time. All my long years I have lived, and now everything is happening too fast."

"Mm..." Yayènia grunted, her mind elsewhere. "It will be so hard to see them go, knowing they will never return."

The assassin shook his head, remembering the other part of her news. "Kelus was a good person. Did you know he gave me a salve for my scars?"

"I did not," Yayènia replied honestly. "My opinion of him was tainted by his association with Midian. I fought him twice on the battlefield, but he slipped away before I could finish him off both times. He was a cunning fighter. And I shot him once, let him run off like a dog to his master."

"And loyal to Tlonna," Aidyn added, hearing her voice lower with dislike.

The female smiled at his words, knowing them as truth. Her smile faded when she looked up and saw the assassin watching her, his almond shaped eyes still shadowed by an emotion deeper than she had ever seen.

"Something still weighs heavily upon you," Yayènia stated quietly, meeting his gaze.

Aidyn looked away, the muscles in his jaw tightening. "It is something I must solve myself. A battle of two wills within one being."

"I understand, but for what it is worth, I am truly sorry."

"I know," the male said, not willing to insult her by denying her hurtful actions, and discarding her honest apology.

Yayènia stood, rolling her shoulders. "I received a notice today from Master Smith Ulrow that my katan was finished. Would you like to come with me?"

"I would," Aidyn replied, following her out of his apartment.

Together, they descended the four floors of the castle and, forsaking their horses, walked into the city. The citizens moved respectfully out of their way, but did not look upon them with fear or awe. They were heroes of Blackhaven, but they were also respectful of their fellow people, and did not demand obeisance. Soon they were standing in the warm front chamber of the Master Smith's forge as one of the dwarf's assistants went to fetch him.

"His great grandfather made my longblade and my scimitars," Aidyn said suddenly, remembering. "It has been six hundred years, and still they are as keen as the day they left this shop."

"That is the truth of Hylen steel," said a gruff voice as the dwarf came into the room carrying a long wooden box. "The strongest material in the world, and forged by the greatest smith in history."

"Master Ulrow," Aidyn and Yayènia said in unison, bowing respectfully to the blacksmith.

"Your blades are right next to the High Commander's as legends in this forge, Lord Aidyn. Their design remains a secret, shown only to the descendants of my family."

"Glad I am to know that they mean so much," the assassin replied, smiling.

"Yayènia, your katan," Ulrow said, turning to the female and handing her the box.

She took it with trembling fingers and removed the lid. Her breath was stolen by the blade within. It was a few inches shorter than it had originally been, and slightly more curved. The hilt was wrapped the same way it had been, with black and blue alternating leather crossing the *kairhotuss* wood. The pommel was small, as she liked, and shaped like the top of an onion. Yayènia gazed at it in awe. The blade was so flawless it shone nearly white. Twining away from the hilt was flowing script in Parlêthian.

"*Zuskadi naht xellt,*" she breathed, immensely touched by the dwarf's addition.

"Duty above all," Ulrow repeated, "your house motto. I also crafted a new scabbard for it, as the old one will be too long and not the correct shape." He handed her the sheath. "It will fit in place with your other katan."

Yayènia pulled her baldric off and disengaged the two scabbards from each other. Sliding the new sheath into place, the elf put it back on, adjusting it to fit. Handing the old scabbard with the shortsword Ghealan had given her to Aidyn, the High Commander lifted the finely crafted new blade and sheathed it.

Ulrow grinned. "How does it feel?"

"Perfect. You are indeed a master of your craft," Yayènia replied, comforted by the even weight of her two katans once more.

"Then I am glad," the dwarf stated. "Once you have felt the slice of the blade, you must tell me how it works for you."

"I shall. My deepest thanks, Master Ulrow."

The two elves left the forge moments later, once Yayènia had paid the final balance. They strolled through the town slowly, taking in the winter sights. The forested city was blanketed in white, though there was no glare except for in the few open squares, by nature of the thick canopy above them. Elves and faery creatures glided by them, dressed in flowing capes and coats that were insufficient for the other races. Humans plodded by, doggedly braving the snow and wind chill, bundled up until they seemed much larger than they were, and dwarves as well, though they wore their customary leather and fur, their tough skin helping to keep them warm.

Aidyn and Yayènia talked casually, greeting their neighbors with smiles and nods, never breaking stride. They talked of Ulrow and his ancestors, of the city's defenses, and the small trickle of folk that had come in with Tlonna's decree of protection. Then Aidyn saw his friend's hand press against her belly and he winced.

"I did not know," he whispered suddenly, staring at her hand.

Yayènia pressed her lips together and shook her head. "I have never felt so weak or vulnerable. Even when Midian cut my throat I was still able to fight back, if feebly. As I lay there, wrapped in the cursed sheet, unable to move because of my broken bones, I felt every stab, every slice and could not counter them with anything. I could not dredge up any battle fury to mask the pain, I could not defend myself, I could only think of the pain, and then I felt the steel slide inside me, and I lost it. I was able to keep myself alive, but gods above, I have never been so defeated. And to know it was you who delivered those blows..."

Aidyn's tawny skin had a gray cast to it as he stared at her in self-loathing. "I was shattered, Yayènia. I wanted to die. Rhiannan stabbed me, pierced my lung according to Losolin, and I was ready to die. I could not live in a world where I had killed one of my oldest friends."

Yayènia grabbed him suddenly and pulled the taller elf into a fierce embrace. Her face pressed against his neck and she sniffed, inhaling the surprisingly arousing scent of him. Aidyn slowly lifted his arms and wrapped them about the female's shoulders, uncertain.

The warrior pulled away after another moment and then blinked up at him. "I do not want to lose you, Aidyn."

"Nor I you, Nia."

They were headed back to the castle when a rider galloped by them, nearly running the two over. Stunned, the High Commander and the assassin watched the rider disappear around a bend, and then raced after it.

Their swift strides carried them to the castle gates in minutes, where they were informed that the rider had been allowed within, and was currently on its way to the castle. The two elves hastened to the obsidian palace and were told by a messenger that they were expected in the map room. Curious, they hurried up the four flights of curving stairs and strode into the large room.

Everyone looked up in surprise to see Aidyn and Yayènia together, plainly on friendly terms once more. The mystery rider was also there, turning out to be the messenger sent to Schelum.

"You nearly ran us over," Yayènia accused, though her heart was not in it, for she had spotted Erdwyf and Ghealan sitting near to Tlonna.

"I am sorry, but I knew Queen Tlonna would be anxious to hear from me," the man said, his eyes darting from the unpredictable warrior to the Magin.

"And I indeed am. What news do you have?" Tlonna said, relieved at Yayènia's relaxed bearing.

"It was very difficult to locate Mayor Ardyce. He moves about Schelum constantly, keeping his whereabouts known only to a select few leaders of the villages. He is a squirrelly little man," the messenger said, obvious dislike in his voice.

"What did he say of the alliance?" Losolin pressed.

"Once I found him and told him of your proposal, he nearly spat in my face. He said that the only way he would even consider such an 'irrational and ridiculous idea', he would have to be shown the merit of the others involved. And also that with the sudden drop in leaders all around Nymyños, he doubted the fortitude of one she-elf sitting at the head of a bastardized city of mongrels and bigot elves."

Silence filled the room at the messenger's words. Tlonna stared open-mouthed at him, taken totally by surprise. Finally, she found her voice. "What?"

The messenger nodded, his lips thinned. "Aye. Nedd Ardyce is an ignorant and racist little prick. He is not worth your time, my lady. Neither is Schelum as a group. The whole lot of them are racist and mean-spirited."

Tlonna was dumbfounded, meeting the stunned and angry gazes of her council. After a moment, she spoke the condemning words. "Then Schelum stands alone."

"Have the others returned from Kismath and Flousen Dua?" the messenger asked, agreeing whole-heartedly with his queen's declaration.

"Not yet, though we expect them within the next few weeks. Thank you for your service," Tlonna said, dismissing the man.

When he was gone, Yayènia turned to her sister. "Any ideas?"

"Not yet, but we have more pressing matters. Kelus's funeral has been set for tomorrow, and Erdwyf and Ghealan have made their decision."

The warrior's heart dropped as she looked at her oldest friend and his wife. Aidyn sat by Tlonna, and too felt sickened. Ghealan looked depressed, plainly not happy with the sudden twist of fate. Erdwyf took a deep breath and looked down at her folded hands, unable to meet any of her friends' gazes.

"I will leave for Narnen in seventeen days. Ghealan will remain here until the forthcoming battle is finished. Because neither of us was given a choice in this matter, I do not have the option of staying here as well. Narnen is leaderless right now, and despite my inadequacies as a ruler, I must take up that mantle."

Everyone burst into protestations as soon as Erdwyf finished speaking, but the High Advisor simply waited it out. "I am not doing this willingly, as you all know. Though I will be in another kingdom, it does not mean our friendship will diminish, or mean less."

"Why seventeen days?" Sodo asked, bringing the odd number of days into the thoughts of the others.

Erdwyf looked at Yayènia. "Because Yayènia and Suneelo's anniversary is in sixteen."

Everyone looked at the High Commander and the Captain of the Guard, who were staring at their friend in utter shock. Suddenly Suneelo grinned, wrapping an arm around his wife's waist and tugging her close, indigo eyes sparkling.

Tlonna smiled as well, for the first time in many days looking forward to something. The expression on her sister's face was priceless. Yayènia, so stoic and guarded, was still gaping at the absurdity of the notion of their anniversary. She rarely even mentioned it, though Suneelo always tried to do something for her. Suddenly, she realized that she was not so alone in her world as she had always believed, and a smile fought its way onto her face.

Chapter 35

Rat

The next day dawned reluctantly, mist clinging to the trees and the snow stubbornly refusing to give way to the spring melt. Tlonna walked to the military compound to watch Locton, Aladorn's son, spar with Yayènia. When they took a break, the queen summoned the warrior over to her.

"Will you walk with me?"

Yayènia snorted, "Do I have a choice?"

"Not at all," Tlonna replied, smirking.

"All right," Yayènia replied, "what do you want?"

The queen sighed. "How are things down here?"

"The training is going well, actually. More recruits show up every day, boys, girls, women, men, even grandfathers," Yayènia said. "Those who went to war want to learn the fighting styles of the Zeynuwnians, and many and more are trying for the silver cloak. The barracks are full to bursting, even with most of them staying at home. We are going to have to build onto the compound."

Tlonna sighed. "I will send Daphne over to your office tomorrow to see about finances. The war ate up a lot of geld, along with the demand for the issued armor. She is having some trouble finding money in places other than taxes. The kingdoms are losing geld steadier than Furntil's aim trying to pay for the wars and reconstruction."

"There are always ways to make money, Tlonna. Private financing not being the least of them. Suneelo and I have a rather substantial and mostly unused treasury, so does Aidyn. We get paid more than anyone else in Blackhaven, and we live mostly off the castle. Tomorrow, I will give Daphne a tender for..." the female did some quick calculations in her head. "Sixty thousand geld."

"Yayènia!" Tlonna gasped, amazed at her sister's wealth.

The warrior shrugged. "Almost three hundred years of service, and we have barely spent any of it. Most of our expenditure went toward rebuilding our home, and that hardly broke the coffers. Suneelo and I are more than capable of giving the throne so much. Trust me, it will be replenished soon enough."

"How?"

"You pay me a lot of money to stand at the head of your army," Yayènia explained blandly, giving the younger elf a wicked smile.

"Ah..." Tlonna said, shaking her head. "Speaking of that...do you think we will be ready if Sithian attacks?"

Yayènia bit her lip. "The seasoned soldiers are good for it, but unless we are given at least a week's notice, we would be hard pressed to keep up. With so many recruits, we are just not getting the quality we want. Ghealan has taken to splitting his command with the officers, and I have set the Silvers to training the different companies. Which makes it so neither the officers nor the Silvers are getting the attention they need."

"How are you with weapons?"

"A bit short, but many of them are getting their own made, or already own a sword or bow."

"All right," the queen breathed. "I will get the forges to up their output as much as possible."

Yayènia stopped and put a hand on her sister's arm. "Tlonna, it will be okay. The army is doing fine, the kingdom is prospering as much as can be hoped after such devastation, and the winter is soon to fade."

"I know, but this last week, this last month really, has been so hard. It seems as though we have lost the backbone of our work. With the loss of Demetri we were robbed of our greatest ally. Now Hayd is gone," Tlonna choked on the words, but forced herself to continue, "I have lost the security of an heir. And now...losing Erdwyf and Ghealan...I just do not know what to do."

Yayènia nodded. "I cannot even think of Lan leaving. But...I have made my decision on his replacement."

Tlonna simply waited for her sister to reveal her choice.

"Suneelo and I talked it over last night. He never wanted to be a commander. Though he is officially Third Commander, he enjoys being Captain of the Guard. I have chosen Aladorn to be my Second."

"A good decision. Aladorn is a great warrior and he has a cool head on his shoulders. He also led Tyular's men for a while. Have you told him yet?"

"No, I figured we should probably do it together. He will be down here in about an hour, if you are able to stay," Yayènia replied.

"Why?"

"Locton. When they are together, it is quite obvious that they are father and son, you will see."

Tlonna nodded, and the sisters turned around on the pathway and headed back toward the training compound, speaking of things both mundane and not. For a while, the queen simply observed the warrior training the young elf, feeling hollow inside as she thought of her son. If it had been any other time, Haydyn would be there as well, sparring with Locton.

Her bleak thoughts, however, were interrupted by the arrival of Aladorn. The wiat appeared in the training yard and stepped over to lean against a post near the queen.

"I did not expect to see you here," he said, continuing to watch his son.

Tlonna stared at his back. "I needed to speak with Yayènia, and she and I need to speak with you."

Aladorn grunted in response and then kicked a stick into the path of his retreating son. Yayènia saw the move and guided the poor boy directly onto the obstacle. Locton stumbled and went down, coming back up only to find Yayènia's wasters at his neck.

"Be aware of all of your surroundings," she instructed with the bite of a common phrase. "You should have seen your father kick it into your route, and adjusted accordingly. Even defending, you need to be aware of everyone around you. Remember, in war, it is not one on one fighting. There are enemies all around, and they do not care if you are already engaged."

Locton took the reprimand stoically, but turned a glare on his parent. "You are unkind," he accused.

Aladorn straightened and spread his arms wide. "Ah, son, it is my obligation to be so. And my privilege."

The young wiat crossed his arms defiantly, though he wisely kept his mouth closed. Yayènia patted him on the shoulder and gave him a new set of instructions. As the male moved farther off into the compound, the warrior shook her head at Aladorn.

"He does not ever seem to learn!" she cried. "He has the potential to be a great fighter, but he becomes too engaged in the fight before him."

"What would you propose we do to rectify it?" the wiat asked, turning back to face Tlonna as Yayènia stepped inside the observation porch, standing next to her sister.

"I think you should fight him while invisible," the female replied immediately. "It will take away the advantage of sight, force him to rely solely on his other senses."

"If you think it will help, then I will do so," Aladorn conceded somewhat reluctantly. He did not like sparring with his son, for it reminded him of his long-absent father. "What did you want to talk to me about?"

Yayènia shifted to look at Tlonna, who simply looked back, apparently wanting the High Commander to make the appointment. With a gusty sigh, the shorter elf turned back to face Aladorn.

"I would like you to take Ghealan's place as Second Commander when he leaves for Narnen. I will not demand it of you, but I think you would make a fine second."

Aladorn blinked. He was completely taken by surprise, but like normal, he did not show it. For a long while he simply looked at the ground between him and the two females, running the idea over in his mind. He went through several denials, but slowly he warmed to the thought. It would be a vast and long-term undertaking, a full time job and constant effort. His dark eyes found his son a few yards away, moving through intricate sword patterns.

Locton was seventy-seven now, fully-grown and living on his own. Though still young for an elf, he had matured quickly, having watched his own mother die. He had also struggled with the hardship of being a wiat. The Sestuns line was cursed, for the children had all been given some sort of mutation, whether the dark elf strand or the wiat gene, or both. Aladorn shook his head and turned back to Yayènia.

She watched him patiently, her light blue eyes steady on his face.

Finally, Aladorn sucked in a deep breath. "I will do it."

Tlonna smiled and Yayènia looked relieved. The male felt a ball of tension appear in his abdomen, but he pushed it away. Shaking his head, Aladorn moved out onto the training yard and began working with his son, fading out every now and then as control over his emotions got away from him. Tlonna stood and stretched, rolling her shoulders for good measure.

"I should be getting back. The gods only know what has been going on there while I have been strolling along. Will you be at the meeting tonight?"

Yayènia hefted a giant iron ring over her shoulder and turned to face her sister. "Yeah, I might be a bit late though. I am going to the harbor to find a few out-of-work sailors."

"Sailors?"

"The Black Armada has all but dissipated these past few years, and I think it would be a good idea to start it up again."

"Ah, what would that entail, exactly?" Tlonna asked, squinting.

Yayènia smiled. "Oh, just a few hundred workless sailors, a dozen or so ships, a few signed papers, and a lot of scary commander."

Tlonna nodded sagely. "I am sure that will be just the thing. I will see you tonight."

The sisters waved farewell and the queen took the path back to the castle. Once there, she found things in total hysteria.

"What in the nine hells is going on here?" she demanded of Narda.

"A message came of heavy news, my queen. The King and Princes of Seaduens are approaching the kingdom. They will be at Lybera Bridge by dusk. A small court is following them, along with over five thousand armed soldiers."

"So it has come at last," Tlonna said to herself. "Have they come to attack for certain?" she asked Narda.

The dryad quailed. "No one knows, your highness. It was a merchant that saw them and sent his boy with the news. They have not sent forth any riders or even scouts since they were sighted."

Tlonna was not surprised, but she was unnerved by Stoffnias's subtlety. How had they marched the entire breadth of Nymyños undetected?

"King Losolin is in the War Chamber with the High Advisor and Advisor Miazie, along with most of the Council. They dared not wait for your return, had it not been so soon," Narda was saying, panicking.

"All right. Go to the barracks and bring High Commander Yayènia and Aladorn up. I am going to the Chamber."

"Of course your majesty. I shall return as fast as possible."

The nymph fled in the direction of the stables and Tlonna hastened to the War Chamber. When she opened the thick door, she found her councilors and her husband in heated argument. They did not quiet until Tlonna slammed the door shut behind her.

"What. Is. Going. On. Here?" She bit the words off as she said them.

Losolin stood with the rest as they bowed to her. Erdwyf was tugging her dagger out of the large map spread out on the table.

"Tlonna, Stoffnias has begun the attack. He marches with five thousand armed soldiers behind him. They will reach Lybera Bridge by nightfall and be here within the week."

"I know. What I mean is why is my council bellowing like a bunch of witless old men when they should be working together to come to an agreeable solution?"

The councilors mumbled their apologies and sat down as Tlonna crossed to her high-backed chair carved from a single trunk of a *kairhotuss* tree. Losolin handed her a couple sheets of parchment and her utensils.

"All right council, what the bleeding blazes is going on? What did the merchant's son say exactly, what path are they taking, tell me what I need to know to defend my country and my people. Have they attacked anyone?"

Erdwyf carefully laid her dagger back on the table. "Not as yet. The boy said that about five thousand arms are marching behind King Stoffnias, Prince Isadorr, and Prince Gothier. They carry the Seaduens banner, and their house banner, but no white flag of peace. They were sighted just outside Purheae, so we must assume that they came by sea and landed at Purheae Harbor. They certainly were not concerned about being seen."

"So why did we not hear of them until now?" Tlonna mused, studying the quill in her hand.

Erdwyf shook her head, dismayed. "I do not know, Tlonna. I know they are not here for trade talk and company."

"You tell me things I already know, High Advisor," Tlonna broke in sharply. "We have been waiting for this attack to come."

"With five thousand men?" the aging Steward of the Walls croaked. Edwin was one hundred and fifteen years old, but still went out every morning to walk the length of the two walls of the city.

"Yes, Stoffnias is not known for his tact. He is a brute, and linked himself with the one other country that hates Blackhaven enough to declare war. The Zaedicans hate elves, but they would be willing to ally themselves with the only army that has a chance to best ours," grumbled the Captain of Cavalry, Sargotarh.

"Ah," Tlonna raised a finger. "*Midian* hated elves. Sithian is half-elf. He is a selfish child wanting to be in control of everything. He will do as he pleases to get what he wants."

Just then the door opened to admit Ghealan and Suneelo. The males looked fit to kill as they took their respective places. Ghealan in the second chair to the right of Tlonna, and Suneelo, as Captain of the Guard, took his on the immediate left of Losolin. Before anyone could so much as speak, the Second Commander drew his dagger and shoved it into the table. The blade, made of the Maginic metal Hylen, did not break but rather sank halfway through the wood before sticking. The elf was raging.

"Someone has betrayed us. Someone on *this* council."

Silence ensued for almost an entire minute before the door opened again and Yayènia and Aladorn strode in. They were both bloody.

Tlonna and Losolin stood in unison, staring at the blood-soaked newcomers. It was Yayènia who broke the long hush.

"Four people are dead, and there were only two of the enemy. Someone with a key to the city let a murderer into my home and has henceforth caused the death of two of my soldiers and my horse Verity. I vow to each and every one of you, I will find the traitor, and by the time they even *begin* to pay their debt to me, the walls will run red with their blood, and I will make you scream for every drop I take. Know this, you cannot hide from me, or those righteous and true. You will pay for your sins many times over before your death, and that will be only the beginning."

The High Commander pivoted on her heel and left the room full of tense silence. Aladorn remained, a long slice running from his jaw to his ear. Tlonna walked over to him.

"Are you all right?"

The wiat nodded and moved around her to take his usual seat next to Sargotarh.

"I am fine," he said, ignoring the wound on his face. "Yayènia will need healing, though. The bolt that slew her horse first went through her foot at point-blank, from a crossbow. The Black Gate had been unlocked and left open from the inside, no force was necessary to enter. We had been at the compound only a moment after you had left," Aladorn gestured to Tlonna, "when a squire came to tell us that the door was open. When we arrived, we found two men sneaking inside the walls. Yayènia questioned the second man until he confessed that there was only the two of them, but more were to come later in the night. She put a dozen city guards on watch, asking for Suneelo's forgiveness."

The council frowned together. The High Commander ruled over all the militant branches, city guard included and did not need to tell any of her officers a thing about it, much less ask for forgiveness for issuing an order. Suneelo nodded in acknowledgment, meeting Tlonna and Losolin's knowing gaze. Yayènia was apologizing for what she was doing to herself at the moment, a brutal self-abuse that she induced every time she felt she had failed at something, if allowed to do so.

Suneelo followed his wife's path out of the room.

Aladorn continued his unsettling narration. "We were not able to discern the exact objective for Seaduens' offensive, but they are here for war, as we have expected all along. I do not know what they hope to do with five thousand men against the entire militia, but I believe it a diversion. Perhaps a siege by sea while the troops are at the wall keeping off the land invaders. However, we were told that they are moving slowly, and plan to move even slower once they get close to Blackhaven. They will not be attacking alone, and will probably wait for whoever else is coming."

When he finished, Tlonna sat down heavily in her chair, overwhelmed by all the bad news she had received in the last week. However much her desperation, her anger completely overrode it.

"Well now, what do we think? Is there a traitor among us? A key holder to the city means it has to be someone in this room, High Commander Yayènia, Captain Suneelo, or Lord Aidyn. Now, if any one of you thinks to blame one of them, I will know who the true turncoat is. Advisor Miazie, will you go to the docks and inform Harbor Master Jamìn of this little problem?"

The advisor bowed and left the room quickly. Tlonna scanned the faces still at the table. Steward Edwin looked so shocked and angry that Tlonna nodded to him. "Steward Edwin, you may go. Prepare the wall for battle. Captain Sargotarh, I want half of your cavalry at the wall, and the other half ready to defend the harbor. Feor, find every access point to the city and lock it down. Once you are finished, send out a missive to Flousen Dua. Our messengers have not returned, and I do not want them riding in to be trapped by the Seadueni."

The human and elves bowed, and with an uneasy sweep over the room, left. The next to leave was Daphne with instructions to see to the depleted treasury. Those left stared at her, some in fear, and others in worry. The queen regarded them coolly.

"Now, if you want to save us all a long, arduous task, why does the betrayer not come clean?"

The Grand Duke of Merchants cleared his throat and raised a knobby hand. "Your Highness, I don't mean to impugn myself, but I wonder if perhaps you let the culprit go?"

"And what would make you say that, Lord Marco?"

The old man cleared his throat again. "That...that Feorien. He was the late queen's personal advisor and was oft known to seek the throne. Mayhap this be his way to gain it?"

Losolin touched Tlonna's hand before she could reply. "Lord Marco, Lord Feorien has proven his worth to us, and we have no doubt of his innocence in this matter. He was indeed Constancias's lapdog, but has since then shown his loyalty to both the queen and I. Your fears are not misplaced, but your judgment is."

"Yes, of course, my apologies your highnesses," the human said in his gravelly voice.

Losolin inclined his head to acknowledge the apology. Tlonna did the same. "Now, councilors, if we may proceed. I do not know who the traitor is, but I hope that you believe the High Commander. I will give her no limitations on her punishments. No matter what, we will find the person responsible and they will get their payments. The High Commander will make sure the death is extremely drawn out, and she will squeeze every ounce of information from said person." Tlonna stopped, scanning the faces watching her. After a moment, she said, "It burns me to know someone here has betrayed us all."

Everyone remaining at the table looked down in shame, but for all her study, Tlonna could not see any sign of fear or slyness in any of them. Whoever had betrayed her people had done it well. The meeting was adjourned and all the staff and council members fled the room. Tlonna dropped her head into her hands. Ghealan patted his wife's arm and stood, pushing a curly strand of hair behind one pointed ear.

"I am going to the barracks to start preparing. Is there anything you require of me before I go?" he asked Tlonna.

The queen sighed. "No. You know what needs to be done, Lan, and for the last time, too."

"A grand finale it will be, then," he replied, kissed the top of Erdwyf's head, and left.

Now only the two females and Losolin remained. The High Advisor watched the couple, pale blue eyes unreadable. Tlonna squeezed Losolin's hand before speaking. "Erdwyf..."

The older female raised her chin slightly, waiting.

"You know the most about everyone on this council. Who would do this?"

Erdwyf slumped in her chair, frustrated. "I do not know. I would have never suspected any of them. A few are newly appointed, but they have never shown any sort of malcontent or two-facedness. I just...I do not know."

"What can you do?" Losolin asked, fiddling with Tlonna's seal. "Or more rightly, what will you do? It is no longer your issue if you do not want it to be."

The High Advisor thought for a moment, ignoring the last statement. "I will check with their families, find out of any of them have been keeping strange hours or exhibiting odd behavior. I will also look into their records, see if any of them have ties with Seaduens."

"Good," the king murmured. "Start with that and tell us what you find. How long?"

Erdwyf shook her head. "At least a day, perhaps longer. I will go as fast as I can, but there are seven possible people to research. We cannot afford mistakes Losolin, and thorough research takes time."

The male wiped the impatient look from his face. "I know, I know but...we do not have long."

The advisor nodded and stood. "I will find the traitor, and justice will be dealt. I will let you know when I have something."

"Be careful, Erdwyf," Tlonna said as her friend walked to the door.

She smiled, a wicked grin reminiscent of Yayènia. "I will welcome any threat. It will make my search much easier."

Erdwyf went first to the Archive Tower. Finding the book of records for City Council members, she walked to her office. Narda and Daphne she dismissed easily. Both were Blackhaven natives, outspoken in their support of Tlonna and Losolin, and they had both looked downright furious when Aladorn had related his news. Steward of the Wall Edwin was much the same.

Most of the files were similar. Native Blackhaven, no contact with Seaduens on file, no notes in the margins. But the fifth file she read was different. Arganor, the Public Liaison, had a vague background. Born in Belgarath, he had appeared in Blackhaven eleven years ago. It had taken him two years to be elected as the Public Liaison, and mere months later, Blackhaven fell. The Liaison was the person responsible for dealing with boundary feuds, petty judgments, and any sort of citizen issue that was not brought before a local praetorian or the throne on petition days.

Erdwyf found the coincidence disturbing, but she moved on. It was the seventh and last file that she found another anomaly. Jayce's file was clean. Born in the city, a son of wealthy merchants, he had risen fast to the position of Royal Diplomat. He was also very popular, handsome, and well-liked. It was impeccable until the very last page.

Scribbled in the margin as though whoever had written it had wanted it to escape notice was a footnote.

Resident of Seaduens 9530-9541

"Flaming...bloody nine hells," Erdwyf cursed in a whisper. The male had lived away from Blackhaven the entire time Midian had occupied it.

Grabbing the two suspicious files, the advisor ran down the hall to Miazie's office. She knew the Belau was back from the harbor from the way her door was cracked. The human always left it slightly open when she was working, but locked it when she was out. Miazie was reading a long parchment, her green eyes dull. Erdwyf knew the feeling.

"Miazie, I have something much more interesting than reports on over-budget lumber," she said, startling the human.

"Reframing the portrait hall, actually," Miazie intoned as Erdwyf sat on the corner of her desk.

"Fascinating. Check this out."

The woman read Arganor's file with a frown, and went pale when she saw the note on Jayce's. "Have you shown Tlonna and Losolin yet?"

Erdwyf shook her head. "I wanted your opinion first, figured you might as well get used to dealing with this if you are to take my place."

Miazie leaned back in her chair and studied the elf, very unhappy about the sudden rise in station. "I don't like making hasty conclusions," she said after a moment, "but...I suspect Jayce most, obviously. However, both of them were gone during the siege. Mayhap they were working together?"

Erdwyf nodded. "That is what I thought as well. Stab me thrice, I never would have suspected either of them. Well-liked, wealthy, outwardly happy. It makes me paranoid about everyone else."

The Belau twisted her lips a little. "Don't be hasty, Erd. You were made High Advisor for a reason, and now a queen," she reached out and tapped the curled silver band on Erdwyf's left bicep, that which would soon be hers. "Use your brain."

When Erdwyf left her office, Miazie stood and stretched. Feeling uncommonly bored with her job, she stared out of her window into the courtyard. A group of students was gathered around a patch of shrubs, Professor Alisimon pointing at the center. From this height, Miazie could hardly see the bush, much less identify it.

She had toyed with the idea of teaching an ancient history class. The three lecture halls in the castle were only used two or three times a week, and were on the same level as the library. Tlonna had given her leave to do so, but Miazie was still hesitant about it. She had always taught herself, and Tlonna and Losolin and later Haydyn, Eyin, and his three companion, but never an entire class.

Sodo had offered to help, having taken to teaching with an unexpected finesse. Thinking of him made Miazie smile. He had long since adapted to his mismatched appearance, along with everyone else. They had not spoken of marriage yet, but Miazie could tell it was in the offing.

A sudden gloom took her, there was no way around it. She was twenty-seven, young even for a human, but she would age and die with certainty. Sodo would live on for ages before performing *Haithen.* Would he still love her when she was wrinkled and bent with age? Even though she had been changed by Losolin's aftermath in Purheae, her body altered and her mind opened, Miazie feared she would be but a tick mark in the length of Sodo's life. She had gone to a healer when they returned from Kajgenia, and been told that her heartbeat had slowed considerably, though it was not as slow as an elf's.

Their hearts beat at less than half the speed of a human's, and a rapid beat for them was just under a human's regular pulse. Miazie had not noticed the change, but she had noticed the physical alterations. Her skin was smoother than it had ever been, and blemish-free. She also had more stamina and more strength than ever before.

The healer had told Miazie that she would have the lifespan of a half-breed, perhaps even seeing a couple centuries. Sodo had been thrilled, but the Belau was more apprehensive. She feared living so long. Would her body still age as a human? Would her mind go as well? The healer had not been able to answer the inquiries, but had assured her she had a long time before such things were a worry.

However, the constant plague of Tlonna's and Losolin's memories gave her headaches and had caused a rift between them. It had even driven a wedge between her and Aidyn, as though the assassin mistrusted her with the knowledge she had. She had seen him, through Tlonna's eyes, uncertain and desperately in love. She had also experienced his skill in bed, and it had brought her a very tense and uncomfortable night. Miazie had locked herself in the washroom of her and Sodo's apartment and wrapped a large towel about her body. For hours she had sweated through the memory, gasping for breath and clenching her hands against the sensations.

Fortunately, Sodo had taken it as some sort of human illness, and left her alone. The next day, Miazie had not even been able to look at either Tlonna or Aidyn, or really even been able to walk without discomfort.

Thinking of the dark elf, Miazie frowned at her reflection in the glass. He had become a recluse, his honor suspect and his sanity questioned. Though she knew Aidyn to be incorrupt, the Belau feared the thoughts of the others.

"No use worrying about things I can't control," the Belau muttered, moving away from the open window. "There's a war to plan for and a traitor to catch."

"Talking to yourself, Miazie?" an amused voice said from the doorway.

The human spun to find Suneelo leaning against the doorjamb.

"Gods, Suneelo you scared me!" Miazie laughed, slightly confused as to why the elf was there.

The Captain of the Guard and she got along fine, but really had nothing in common. He moved into the office with the fluid grace of a warrior, dark eyes crinkling as he smiled.

"Wondering why I am here?" he asked.

"Yes...a little," Miazie replied, watching him. "Last I heard, you were with Yayènia."

Suneelo's face took on a look that defied emotion. Miazie had never seen a look so pain-filled, lost, and yet somehow resolved. The expression passed, and the male took a deep breath. "Yayènia will do as she always has, and I will be there for her when she is ready. What I need from you is something less onerous. I need your advice."

"On what?"

"Our anniversary is coming up. Her birthday as you know was months ago, but we were not able to celebrate it because she was in the infirmary. I want the gift I get to be special, not what I normally get her."

"Which is?"

Suneelo shrugged. "Weapons."

"Of course. And why are you asking me this?" Miazie inquired, baffled.

"Because you are more feminine than Erdwyf or Tlonna."

"Ah," Miazie grunted. "What anniversary?"

"Two hundred and seventieth."

Miazie flopped into her chair. "That's quite a run, Suneelo."

The male grinned. "Maybe. But what do you suggest?" he replied, sitting across from her, stretching his long legs.

The Belau stared at him. "What does she like? Other than the obvious."

"Books. Art. Music."

Miazie blinked. She would never have thought the lethal and domineering Yayènia would enjoy such tame avocations. "Surprising."

Suneelo snorted. "She is a female, Miazie."

"I know, it's just a little unexpected is all. Now...do you have room for artwork in your house?"

"Not really. All the space is already taken up. The library as well."

"You have a library?" Miazie gasped, jealous.

"Yes. Do you want to see our home, Miazie? Will that make it easier on you?" Suneelo asked, laughing.

The woman nodded. Tiena Manor was rumored to be the most beautiful house ever built, and few were allowed to see it. It took them twenty minutes to reach the tree-lined pathway, and soon Miazie was gaping at the house that rose from the ground. It was bathed in evening sunlight, the rosy sandstone glowing softly in the hazy light.

Gauzy curtains swayed gently in the light breeze, obscuring the interior view, but Miazie caught a glimpse of dark red tile on the floor.

"Jordan, this is Belau Miazie, Advisor to the Queen," Suneelo was saying to a youth who had wandered out of the small stable to take their horses.

"My Lady," Jordan said, helping Miazie from the saddle.

"Nice to meet you Jordan," Miazie replied, still staring at the house.

Suneelo took her to the backyard where a small pond glittered amidst the masterfully crafted garden. There were orbs of light sitting in the trees, flickering alight as the sun lowered. Then he guided her into the house. It was spacious and calming, as most Elfin dwellings were. A cook was humming in the kitchen, another servant lounging at the round dining table, reading.

The cook looked up as they entered, a human in her middle years. "Suneelo, will Yayènia be home tonight?"

The elf shrugged. "She is atoning, Heidy."

The cook looked sad. "Very well. Will the lady be joining us, then?"

Suneelo looked at Miazie. "Oh, no. Sodo and I are dining with Aidyn and Aladorn tonight, but thank you," the Belau replied, stunned she had been invited.

Hiedy sighed, but she fixed her employer with a hard look. "You will be eating here, I presume?"

"Yes, Hiedy. I would not miss it."

The woman snorted, and Suneelo hastened Miazie out of the kitchen. "You have a very odd relationship with your servants, Suneelo," she remarked as they climbed to the second floor.

"So we have been told," the elf replied. He led her into a large room and Miazie's breath caught.

The library was massive, easily holding over a thousand books. A worktable sat in the center and a fireplace dominated one corner. Above the eight foot shelves were paintings of landscapes and one Zeynuwnian watercolor of a young woman holding a sword.

"You are welcome to it anytime, Miazie," Suneelo said behind her.

"Oh, thank you Suneelo. It's magnificent."

"Indeed. Now come on."

Miazie followed him reluctantly out of the library, across the hall, and into the bedroom. The bed was ridiculously large, canopied with sheer creamy curtains. It was unmade.

"Do the maids not come in here?" she asked.

"Only twice a week. Nia and I like our privacy, and a bed that is always made never seems as inviting as one that is not. So, what do you think?"

Miazie gazed about the unexpectedly casual room. The rest of the house was decorated with battle tapestries, weapons, and armor. This room, like the library, had landscapes and personal items scattered about the mantle and furniture. Her eyes widened when she saw a little carved figure of a creature only heard of in stories, and one she had seen on Yayènia's old sword. Elephunts were fantastical beasts, taller than a horse and skinned in rough hide. They were supposed to be extremely intelligent, and protective. Their long noses and sharp eyeteeth gave them an odd appearance, but they were also very beautiful.

There was a large wedding portrait above the fireplace, and Miazie saw just how beautiful Yayènia really was. Usually, her face was hard and unsmiling, and nervousness tainted the human's perspective. The artist, however, had caught the couple with their eyes alight with love, faces softened in contentment. The Belau sneaked a look at Suneelo, who was also staring at the portrait, a small smile on his lips.

"I think you're right. No books, no pictures," she said finally.

The elf looked at her. "Then what? I cannot buy an orchestra to sit in the backyard!" Suneelo exclaimed desperately.

Miazie smiled. "No, but you can get her a music sphere, hire various musical groups, and fill it with her favorites."

Suneelo frowned. "I have never heard of a music sphere."

"You wouldn't have. It's something the Council of Magins created, no one has figured out how to make one since. However," she said loudly when Suneelo opened his mouth, "I would bet Losolin could do it."

"Really? Why him?"

"He's a Healer Magin, not a 'Destroyer' Magin, and he has the elemental talent to Weave the right flows of power."

"I hope so. I will ask him tomorrow."

Miazie nodded. "I'll get him the book tonight."

"My thanks," Suneelo said heartily.

"Thank you for showing me your home. It really is the most beautiful I have ever seen."

The male smiled. Miazie rode back to the castle alone, smiling and content. She found the book on the first Magin's obscure creations, handed it to a confused Losolin, and went to dinner with her lover, Aladorn, and Aidyn.

The next morning Losolin was having an impromptu meeting with Edwin to discuss areas on the wall that needed immediate attention when Suneelo strolled in. The king concluded his business with the aged human and then turned to his brother.

"I am guessing you are responsible for this?" he asked, picking up a book and shaking it at him.

Suneelo grabbed it so he could read the title, *Creative Creations of the Council.* "Miazie gave you this?"

Losolin nodded. "Most of it is very dull magic tricks. Seduction Weaves, different colored flames and the like. Why am I reading it?"

"I want you to make me a...a music sphere, for Nia," Suneelo replied.

"Ah. I can do that. Let me see the book."

Suneelo handed the book to his brother and waited while he searched for the right page. "Here we are. I need a glass ball, hollow, and whatever you want it to sit on," Losolin said after a minute.

"All right. How long does it take?"

Losolin shrugged. "A couple of minutes. I have a feeling I will be here all day so you will know where to find me."

Suneelo stood, but hesitated, looking down at his young sibling. "You are a good king, Losolin. We have hard times ahead of us, but we will persevere. Do not doubt that."

The Magin looked up and smiled, his oceanic eyes grateful. "Thank you, Suneelo, I know."

The captain left and returned a few hours later with a pale pink glass ball and a silver pedestal. "I had to get it blown, and this is what I got. Is it okay?" he asked, handing the items to a weary Losolin.

"Perfect. All right...where is that flaming book?" the king muttered, pushing numerous bits of vellum around to reveal the book. Green light surrounded his hands and he placed them on the orb.

Suneelo felt a pulling in the air around him and stepped back. After a minute, a slight humming noise began to emanate from the sphere. It grew louder until Suneelo had a nagging urge to cover his pointy ears. Then there was a loud twang, as if a low harp string had been plucked hard. Losolin stepped away and revealed the glass ball. It was fused to the silver stand and glowed faintly.

"Now what?" Suneelo asked.

"Sit it next to a musician and let them play until the sphere turns opaque. That indicates it is full. When it reaches that point, just press your hand on the top and it will play. To empty it and start over, shake it till it reverts to its original translucency."

Suneelo picked up the sphere and exhaled. "It is perfect. Thank you, *bruun*."

Losolin smiled at his older brother. "Well, what better time to celebrate love and life than just before a war? Will there be a celebration?"

Suneelo shook his head. "I do not know. I think Erdwyf is planning something from the way she was talking earlier. I expect it will probably just be the family if anything, though."

The king nodded. "Understandable. Let me know the plans, then."

"I will, thanks again."

Just as the elf turned to leave, Erdwyf burst into the office, her eyes shadowed with lack of sleep. "I have the only two possible traitors. Their records both have suspicious notes in them, and both were about the city two nights ago," she rambled, catching Suneelo's arm to stop him.

Losolin's face went stony, his eye twitched once. "Who?"

"Jayce and Arganor."

"No," the king breathed. "Not Jayce. I cannot believe it. And Arganor? Maybe someone stole one of their keys?"

Erdwyf looked at him with pity. "I doubt it. Losolin, it had to be one or both of them. Everyone else checks out."

Suneelo plucked the folder out of her fingers and laid it open on the king's desk. Together, the brothers read the two files and

Erdwyf's notes. When they finished, an angry tension filled the office. Losolin looked at his two friends.

"Find them," he commanded coldly.

Tlonna smiled as Losolin strode into her office. Even though his face was darkened with anger and hurt, it was still the face that filled her heart with love and joy. She stood, walked around the desk, and wrapped her arms around him.

"Ah, love..." she murmured into his shoulder. "Will life ever be simple?"

Losolin chuckled faintly. "Would you want it to be? Would you rather be bored?" he joked.

Tlonna shook her head, "I love you."

"And I you, Loni." He paused. "We found two of them. Arganor and Jayce."

The queen sucked in a breath and let it out slowly. "Have they been found?"

"Suneelo and Erdwyf just went out to do that. Tlonna, what will we do when they are found?"

The female pulled away from her husband, looking down to hide the pain in her eyes. "We give them over to Yayènia to get the answers we need. Losolin, one or both of them betrayed our people. Had Yayènia and Aladorn not gone to the door, we would have already lost."

Losolin sighed. "I know. It is just hard to think that it might have been one of them...or both."

"When they are brought in, we will see."

"I suppose."

Tlonna ran her hands over Losolin's shoulders and drew him down so she could kiss him. The male kicked the door closed and pressed Tlonna against her desk, his blood pounding. Losolin moaned as Tlonna wrapped her legs around his waist, digging her fingers into his hair. Their nights had been short and filled with loss, and Tlonna had been unable to drag herself out of mourning for a long while.

"Losolin..." Tlonna breathed as his lips danced down her throat.

"Shh," he groaned, pulling at her laces.

Tlonna felt his hands touch her, and her mind went blank.

An hour later, the rulers of Blackhaven lay sprawled on the large desk, their limbs limp and glistening with perspiration.

"I think we need to spend more time in bed, Losolin," Tlonna remarked as she rolled off him.

The king laughed, but nodded as he slid from the desk. "We are lucky no one walked in."

Tlonna grinned. "Would you have stopped?"

"Not bloody likely," Losolin chuckled. "I have not touched you in nigh three weeks."

"Mmm...the joys of being in charge, yes?"

Losolin knotted the laces on his pants and was bending over to grab his shirt when the door opened. Tlonna let out a shriek and ducked behind the door, yanking on her shift as Ghealan strode in. The warrior eyed the shirtless king with amusement before peering around the door at the lightly clad queen.

"Well," he grunted, grinning widely and planting his hands on his hips. "Should I come back later?"

"No, no...what is it? Tlonna breathed, shutting the door behind the male.

"A private audience with the king and queen of Blackhaven in their small clothes?

Losolin snorted and yanked on his shirt, eyeing his wife as she calmly sat behind her empty desk in only her thin shift. All of her papers and items were scattered about the floor, knocked off in their haste.

Ghealan eyed his friends, sympathizing for them. "Perhaps you should take a retreat after the battle with Seaduens."

Tlonna sighed wistfully. "I wish. How are you doing...King Ghealan?"

He glowered at her, still furious at his new position. "Well enough, considering. I wanted to tell you Yayènia showed up at the barracks this morning and she seemed decent, her foot pains her, but nothing she cannot handle. Our main concern is the lack of news of Stoffnias's army. Why did we not hear anything before they entered the forest? What happened to everyone along the way? Even if they used Purheae Harbor, Eyin Thorn promised to destroy any Seadueni that crossed his borders."

Tlonna sat back. "Perhaps they tried, and were annihilated."

Ghealan shook his head. "We would have heard of it."

"I will send a rider out to check it out," Losolin said quietly. "There is definitely something wrong."

"Nebet'thu leaves tomorrow, with Jorunson and Marc," Tlonna added.

The older male nodded. "I need to get back to the barracks. I just wanted to let you know Nia is all right," he started to leave but turned back with a grin. "Next time, lock the door."

Erdwyf and Suneelo returned to the castle late in the evening with their two suspects. Arganor and Jayce were fidgety, their eyes flashing in the lamplight. Tlonna met them on their first floor.

Jayce stood tall and proud, though his face was white with fear and his eyes wide. "Please my lady, why am I being brought in? They would not tell me!"

Tlonna glared at him. "You will find out soon enough. Take them to the guard tower for holding. Yayènia will be down to see them later."

The two men began convulsing in terror. Jayce's youthful face went even whiter and the queen feared he would swoon. Arganor began weeping hopelessly, his usually proud demeanor ripped from him. Tlonna swallowed and deliberately turned her back on them. The weeping faded as Suneelo and Erdwyf hauled the two away.

"You are much stronger than you look, Majesty," a male voice said behind her.

Tlonna turned to find a dark-eyed elf watching her from an intersecting corridor. He was astoundingly pretty, even for an elf. His face was angled and framed by fine white-blond hair, and his eyes were a rare dark hazel.

"Is that a compliment, or a doubt, my lord?" the Magin asked, trying to recognize the elf.

"Merely an observation, my queen, and I am no lord. I am Lorne Jesman, only."

"Ah," the queen replied softly, an alarm going off as the male continued to move closer, circling slightly. "And what can I do for you?"

Lorne smiled faintly, a mere tightening of the lips. "I live in the south of Blackhaven, right on the Strait of Arwênlhias, near where it opens to the sea."

"Mardyn," Tlonna said automatically, thinking of the little village situated on the coast.

Lorne nodded. "Yes."

"You have come quite a distance, Master Lorne. Surely you have a reason?" Tlonna said, her heart starting to beat a little faster as the male circled slightly to her right.

"Oh...I do," he whispered and moved suddenly, white hair flying.

Tlonna cursed as something sliced across her cheek as she jerked to the side. Twisting, she caught the assassin's wrist as it flicked upward, causing the throwing knife to thunk into a table. Lorne's dark eyes widened as she yanked him around. Bending his captured hand, he released his wrist blade.

The Magin saw the flash the silver out of her peripheral. Lorne bared his teeth as he slowly forced the knife close to the queen's neck. Tlonna released him suddenly, stepping back, causing him to stumble. With a speed that shocked him, the female pinned him against the wall. A massive pressure built up around his calves, wrists, and thighs. The Magin Queen stepped back, leaving the would-be assassin stuck to the wall by her Weave.

"Now," she said calmly. "Who do you work for?"

Lorne stayed silent, the left side of his face smashed against the cool obsidian wall. Tlonna sighed resignedly.

"Did you really think you could kill me? Do you think you are the first? You certainly will not be the last." Her voice took on a tone of great defeat. "My fate has already been decided, Lorne, and no one can change that. Trust me, if killing me would put an end to this war right now, I would gladly hand you the blade, but it would not. Things have already been decided for me."

Lorne found himself listening to the queen with a heavy heart. He was about to confess all when another female entered the corridor. His throat clogged and his heart began to race with panic. Tlonna watched Lorne's face lose all color and turned to find Yayènia striding toward them.

"What is this?" the warrior asked when she drew up to her sister.

"An assassin. I was just about to find out who sent him."

Yayènia turned to the trapped male with a frown. "He is a pretty one, that is for sure. You let him inside your guard."

Tlonna touched her cheek to find blood crusting on her skin. "Indeed. He caught me by surprise. Throwing knives."

"I think we need to start up another training regime. You cannot afford to let your skill leave you," she stated, brushing the flakes from the Magin's cheek.

"If I have time," Tlonna hedged.

Yayènia was about to reply when Lorne let out a strangled sound

"King Stoffnias!"

Both females turned to Lorne in surprise. "He promised me land, and a title once the city was won."

Tlonna sighed again. "Lorne, did you honestly believe he would keep his word? Now you must pay for his lie. Yayènia?"

"No!" Lorne screamed against his will.

Yayènia looked grim as Tlonna released the Weave and he dropped to the ground. The male scrabbled to his feet and backed up to the wall. "Stoffnias promised me ten thousand geld! How was I supposed to turn that down? I have a family! That amount of money could renovate all of Mardyn."

"I am your queen, Lorne, and I have made a promise to all of my people to help every person I could within these borders. If Mardyn needed anything, I would give it to you, all you had to do was ask. Do you know what the Seadueni do to their own people when they are untitled? Stoffnias would never grant you a thing. He would have killed you rather than risk exposure," Tlonna seethed.

"You are a Blackhavenite! How could you do this?" Yayènia growled, forcing her hands away from her swords.

"I know!" Lorne cried. "But there are so many more of them! Blackhaven is becoming a human city like all the rest! Seaduens is now the largest kingdom of Elf-kind. They only allow humans in as slaves, or low worker class. Here, they run rampant like ants, tainting our places of beauty with their heedless disregard of natural perfection. They must not be allowed to continue their destructive lives!"

Both females stared at the traitor in disgust, frozen solid by his racist attitude. Finally, the Magin Queen summoned up the words lodged in her throat. "What right do you have to make that decision? They live and breathe the same as we do, Lorne, and deserve a chance to discover their faults on their own. They are a young race, untried yes, but valiant and honorable. Were it not for Man, Blackhaven and I along with it, would be dead. Our race would be wiped out, even the Seadueni, who have interbred so long their population is decreasing rapidly as the availability of new blood becomes slimmer, would have soon died out. Now we flourish once again, strong in our alliances with the humans. It was the humans that came to our aid in droves during the last battle, and it is because of them we won."

Lorne swallowed, looking defeated. "Still, they are overrunning our home."

Yayènia rolled her eyes, studying her fingernails. Tlonna rubbed her forehead. "It is their home too, Lorne. Now, you can either go with the High Commander quietly, and stay in one of the upper cells where you will be treated fairly and be served three meals a day, or you can go unwillingly to the deep cells, and be forgotten."

The village assassin looked at the passive Yayènia and took a deep breath. "I will go willingly. But...what happens to my family?"

Tlonna cocked her head. "You should have thought of them before you decided to try and kill me. They are no longer your concern."

"What? No, please! They know nothing of this, I swear!" Lorne cried as Yayènia straightened.

"We will see," the queen said coldly, nodding to her sister.

"Come on," the High Commander growled and Lorne turned obediently to follow her, glancing back at Tlonna, regret etched on his face.

Tlonna wearily climbed the stairs to her quarters and found Losolin sitting on the balcony facing the harbor. He was sprawled in his chair, long legs placed on either side of the small table, and his head resting on the back of the chair. She stared at him, transfixed by the glow of moonlights casting different colored shadows on his shoulder-length hair, unbound and tumbling over the back of the chair. Beyond the open doors, Tlonna heard the sounds of the ocean lapping at the harbor a mile away, night creatures coming to life as the city quieted. Somewhere distant, a slow song wound through the air from one of the numerous music halls.

It seemed to her that Blackhaven City never really slept. There was always some group doing something, and music was always playing; a soft soundtrack to the normally restful life of Blackhaven. For a moment, Tlonna forgot that she was the ruling monarch of a besieged kingdom, harried with traitors and assassins, that two of her children were dead, and that she was about to lose two of her closest friends and important council members. Losolin pulled one of his legs up and scratched at his knee absently, turning his head to look at her.

"Hello," he said quietly.

"Hello," she replied, moving to join him. "It is a beautiful night, is it not?"

"Mm...now it is," the king returned, smiling gently as she sat down across from him. "What happened to your cheek?"

Tlonna touched the cut. "An assassin. Yayènia has him now. I do not want to think of that right now. I just want to enjoy this."

Losolin rolled his head back and stared at the inky sky illuminated by the moons. His eyes found the red moon that was new to the celestial painting and felt a sudden peace. Dietirin was watching them, guarding over them.

"I miss him so much."

Losolin looked over at his wife to find her staring at the moon that had once been her father as well. "He is still with you, Loni."

Tlonna smiled faintly. "I wish he were here now, beside me. I do not understand why he had to die when so many others live when they do not deserve to."

Losolin breathed in slowly and let it out. "It was time for you to rule, my heart. The gods knew that, the spirits that rule our existence knew it as well."

"Why can they not share their knowledge with us? Why must they make everything so difficult and hard to understand when they have all the answers? What gives them the right to rule our lives so completely?" the queen ranted quietly, still staring up at her celestial father.

"We would never truly learn anything that way. You know that as well as I, love."

"Why do you have to be so bloody insightful all the time?" Tlonna laughed, finally looking back at him.

The king smiled, but stayed silent, content just to gaze at her. They remained so for a long while, soaking in each other's presence, letting the apprehension of their turbulent duty drain from them momentarily. Finally, the queen brought up Lorne. As she told him, Losolin shook his head in bewilderment and exasperation. When she finished, he sighed, standing. It was nearing midnight and they were usually up just before dawn.

"Well, now all we can do is wait," he said as he yawned. "I have asked Aladorn to seek out any other spies and turncoats in the city. There must be a contingent within the walls for it to have penetrated this deeply. Because of the circumstances, I think we should try and keep this as under the table as possible. We do not want to cause any more panic."

Tlonna nodded her agreement and readied for bed.

The next few days were filled with anxiety. The castle nearly vibrated with the rushing of people as servants ran from one errand to the next, nobles rushed about in clusters, as though expecting attack at any moment. Guards stood stiffly, watching the nervous crowds with glittering, war-hardened eyes. Yayènia was seen every now and again, striding along the corridors as the inhabitants whirled out of her way, creating a ripple effect everywhere she went. The High Commander was always clutching a folder, or dragging along a nervous-looking soldier. Tlonna tried to catch up to her several times, but the warrior was too absorbed in preparing for battle that she did not see the queen.

Suneelo also was seen roaming the castle more often than usual. Sometimes Ghealan was with him, the two talking with heads close together, seemingly unaware of the skittish people around them. Even Erdwyf, with the young Jaryikin in her arms, moved about more frequently, keeping a firm hand with the goings on of the politicking nobles.

Losolin sighed inwardly as yet another maid put her head to the floor in a deep curtsey. Conscious of the circlet on his brow, the king smiled as graciously as he could to the girl, and continued on.

"Is it so bad, Losolin?" an amused voice said next to him.

Smiling, Losolin shook his head. "You cannot startle me anymore, Aladorn. I have known you long enough for that."

The dark elf appeared suddenly, causing people to jump a few feet in terror, and then, realizing who it was, visibly calm down. Aladorn laughed heartily, sticking his hands in his pockets and slouching comfortably, as much as an elf could slouch. Losolin smiled crookedly, slightly envious of the older elf's nonchalance in all things.

"So...have you found anything?" he finally asked, dreading the answer, yet at the same time hoping there was one.

The wiat seemed to stiffen a little, and then resumed his slump. "Only one thing. No names yet, but perhaps a meeting place.

There is an inn down off Mafien Street that has ill repute, and a few people have seen a more elegant crowd frequenting it lately. Brashnard's Tavern. I have not yet been to visit it, but I planned on going tonight. What would you like me to do if I find something?" This was all stated in a hushed voice, barely audible even to Losolin, but he nodded slightly to acknowledge that he'd heard.

"We will go in force and collect the bloodless cowards," Losolin hissed back.

Aladorn nodded, and they walked on in silence. After a while, he started to fade in and out of focus. Losolin glanced at him out of the corner of his eye, wondering what was taking the wiat's focus. After a while, he asked.

The dark elf sighed, and then came back into focus so fast Losolin blinked. "I have been keeping a secret from you, and Tlonna. Well, from everyone. Aidyn and I have spoken about telling you for a long time, since Miazie realized it back when she was in the hospital, when Stoffnias delayed the army from reaching Blackhaven."

Losolin frowned. What could the three of them have in common? As far as he knew, the two dark elves were good friends, having found a connection through their dark elf heritage. And Miazie...well, she was a puzzle all on her own. Rather than voice his confusion, he waited. Aladorn stepped into an empty room, which Losolin realized was one of the common rooms for nobles to gather. It was a sign of the tension of both the elf and the nobles in the castle; Aladorn for the apparent need for privacy, and the nobles for the fact that it was empty.

"Aidyn and I are...we are brothers. I was raised by our mother, Aidyn by our father."

Losolin stared at his friend a long moment before the words truly sank in. Before he could stop it, he laughed. The wiat started, another sign of how unsettled he was. His dark green eyes widened as well, before narrowing dangerously. "What is so funny?"

"How could we have missed it? Spirits! It is so obvious now!" the king chuckled, unable to contain himself. "Why in the world did you not tell us sooner?"

Aladorn shifted. "Aidyn nor I realized it until after Blackhaven was reclaimed. He mentioned in passing his father's name was Bailan, which was my father's name. He was only a few weeks old when our family was separated, and after a while, I simply forgot about him. I knew that I felt a sort of kinship with him when we met in Kajgenia, but I really did not remember. It had been seven hundred and eighty years, after all. When I asked him about his mother, he told me she had died when he was young, too young to remember the two brothers who had died with her in a freak fire accident."

"Two brothers?" Losolin asked sharply, wonderingly. Few elves had more than one child, but it seemed his life was full of siblings. Tlonna and Yayènia, he and Suneelo, now Aidyn, and Aladorn, and this unknown third brother.

"Yes, I had a younger brother, named Aolan, who was ripped apart by a mob a few hundred years ago. He was an ash-toned dark elf, not like Aidyn and me, who are merely darker hued than the rest of you. Aidyn believed us all dead, and our father was killed in a battle with Aderiaen."

"And your mother?" Losolin asked quietly, all mirth forgotten.

Aladorn looked away from his friend. "She fled with me and Aolan because we were different. Me a wiat, he an ash-elf. She feared for us, and rightfully so. Aidyn stayed with Bailan because he was neither of those things, merely a normal dark elf, more accepted by the general public. My mother, Alena, was killed by Aderiaen Rahlan some hundred and seventy years ago. Not by him personally but by his minions who were searching out elves and slaughtering them. I believed I was the last surviving member of my family. When we were separated, my father, Bailan, with little Aidyn, promised to meet us at a monolithic stone in Cleshnoe Forest. My mother, Aolan, and I were accidentally taken aboard a ship, and when we got ashore once more, there was no sign of them."

Aladorn's voice was quiet, his eyes pinned to the floor. "It was my idea that we separate, and it destroyed my family. Father and Aidyn had simply...disappeared. Aolan and I tried to find them, but we never succeeded. Now I know that Aidyn was taken up by the College of Assassins, and our father was basically a nobody living off his son's wealth, once Aidyn was appointed Dietirin's personal guard and assassin." Aladorn sighed. "When he mentioned his parentage, I finally saw in him the brother I had lost. The same active senses, the same intense eyes. So, we found the birth records for Bailan and Alena Sestuns, and there we were, all three of us, forgotten in nearly eight hundred years of new births. Aolan was the middle brother, he would have been eight hundred and seven this year."

Losolin was speechless. He had subconsciously noted the visible similarities between his two friends, but never really thought about it. Aladorn noticed his silence and smiled crookedly, dark eyes shining slightly with moisture, a rare sign.

"Aidyn wanted to be here, but with everything going on, he could not get away. And he feels not himself since the attack on Demetrius. So," the wiat said shortly, "you and Miazie know. I would ask you to tell Tlonna. There is one other thing we would ask of you."

The king waited silently.

"Aidyn is the holder of both title and land, though I am older by a large margin. We do not want this to change. We are happy in our positions. I know it is against custom for the younger sibling to be lorded while the older is not, but this is how we like it."

Losolin scowled at his friend. "You do not have to even ask that, Aladorn. Now, if you wanted a title and land as well, it is yours, but I would never strip Aidyn of his honors just because you happen to have been born first."

The dark elf laughed in relief. "No, I would hope not. Besides, Aidyn would kill me, and I think him quite capable of doing so."

Finally Losolin smiled. "He is capable of doing anyone in, I think. Now, go spy on some traitors please."

Aladorn bowed sarcastically, and left the room, followed by the king.

The wiat found his brother a while later striding up the fourth floor corridor where the Head Staff offices were held, along with apartments for a select few members of the Royal Council. He and Aidyn both had suites, along with Miazie and Sodo. Both the Tienas and the Tomyvons had apartments as well, though they were seldom used. The assassin was about to enter the private library when Aladorn called to him.

"Aidyn! I have found where the infiltrators have their main headquarters. I am going down tonight."

The younger male opened the door to the library and led his brother in. "What is your plan? You are well known throughout the city, now. They will recognize you immediately and either run or attack you."

Aladorn grinned. "That is why I want you to come with me. I have asked Sodo to come as well."

Aidyn eyed his brother warily. "I am surprised he acquiesced."

"He has come a long way since Purheae. So, what I plan is that we go in the back, nab the cook and the innkeeper, and find out if they are in on the coup. If not, we go around to the front, and act like regulars with the aid of the innkeep. If they are, we knock them senseless, bar the doors from the outside, and bring down one of Suneelo's squads."

"And if they have Magins? What then?" Aidyn asked dubiously.

Aladorn shook his head. "They will not have Magins. My intelligence says they have Cleicks with them. No Magin would be in the same room as a Cleick, and vice versa. But before all of this, I will slip inside and make sure our targets are there."

The assassin finally nodded. "Then I will go. When do we leave?"

"One hour."

The brothers bid a short farewell and Aidyn left the library behind his elder sibling, regretfully giving up the hour of respite he'd planned.

An hour later, he was standing in the stables dressed in his inky black assassin's clothes when Aladorn and Sodo strode into the building. His brother wore a black tunic and dark gray trousers that fit snugly, making it easier for him to disappear. The alchemist wore a white belted tunic over a pair of brown breeches, his black-streaked hair tied in a long cable braid. Aidyn acknowledged them both with a wave and resumed saddling Whäd. Minutes later, they were riding over the wide bridge that spanned the clear stream just before the castle gates. They wound through the city streets, veering off Obsidian Way a third of the way down.

Aidyn's memory was triggered as they turned onto Mafien Street, vividly remembering his first encounter with the place. Automatically, his eyes sought out the face of the inn that housed the College of Assassins, though it had long been torn down. The Blackhaven College was now housed entirely in Aidyn's manor house deep in Blackhaven Forest, south of the city.

Though all of Blackhaven was well-maintained, and every spare inch was taken up by trees and plant life, this part of the Market District was known for its crudeness. The three elves rode down the quiet side street to the stable of Brashnard's Tavern, and relinquished their horses. They rounded the back corner of the building and Aladorn faded from sight. Aidyn and Sodo waited calmly as the older elf slipped inside the rowdy tavern, lounging against the siding. After a few silent minutes, the wiat reappeared before them, his face shadowed.

"They are here. About twenty of them, and some are definitely Cleicks. Drinking and carousing as if they have not betrayed an entire city. The innkeeper is not reachable, yet, but the cook is just inside this door," the wiat relayed quietly.

His two companions nodded and adjusted their various weapons. Sodo scanned the dark façade of the building, pausing at each lit window. Aidyn watched him passively, wondering what the tainted alchemist saw. Then the trio slipped inside the back door, shutting it quietly behind them. The cook stared at them uncertainly, her scarred face slack with age.

Aidyn moved, as he was the fastest of the group. A second later, he had her wrists behind her back, one hand clamped on her mouth. "If you are true to Blackhaven, and Queen Tlonna, you are in no danger. Now, where do your loyalties lie?"

The woman froze, her eyes riveted on Sodo as she caught sight of him. The elf stared back at her daringly, his jaw clenching. Aidyn lifted his hand from her mouth. She sucked in a breath and let it out, suddenly trembling violently.

"I am a true Blackhavenite, and I wept at King Dietirin's funeral, and Prince Haydyn's. His daughter is my queen as much as he was my king," she whispered in a tremulous voice.

"Good, then you are safe. Tell me," Aladorn said gently. "Do you know of the conspiracy taking place in your common room?"

"You mean the twenty-three traitorous bastards who dug a rusty knife into my face in order to ensure my silence?" the woman spat.

The three elves unconsciously drew themselves up to their full height. Sodo, the shortest of them, stood at a solid seven foot one. The woman drew back in sudden fear as she gazed at the three towering strangers in her kitchen.

Aidyn noticed her unease, and smiled slightly. "As we said, you are in no danger from us. Tell me, is the innkeeper part of this?"

The cook swallowed, "I don't know. Sometimes, I believe he is, at others, no. He caters to them, more than other customers, but then snarls about their presence when they're not around. He is in his office at the moment, hiding. Should I fetch him?"

"No," Aladorn said. "I will."

The woman let out a gasp as the elf faded from sight. Aidyn grinned at her reaction. "He is a wiat, madam. My name is Aidyn Sestuns, this is Sodo of the White, and that was Aladorn. What may we call you?"

The cook looked apoplectic. "Lianin," she managed in a rough voice. "Are you really Aidyn Sestuns? That was really Aladorn the Wiat?"

"Yes."

Lianin's eyes rolled up in her head and she fainted. Aidyn just managed to catch her before she hit the hard stone floor. Sodo cleared off a preparing table and the assassin laid the human down.

"Is that reaction normal?" Sodo asked quietly.

Aidyn shrugged. "Depends. Normally I am with Yayènia or Ghealan, or someone like that, and just their appearance will send people into fits. We can never be sure if it is fear or awe that does it. Gets a little tiresome after a while."

The alchemist chuckled quietly, studying the aged woman's face. "That is a nasty scar," he said after a moment.

Aidyn followed his gaze and scowled. The scar was nearly a half-inch wide, puckered and red. It ran from her temple to her earlobe. "It was definitely done purposefully, and viciously. I wonder why she did not flee."

"Because she could not," Sodo said furiously, pointing to the floor. An iron chain attached to the middle of the floor was cuffed to her skinny ankle. It had just enough slack to allow the woman full access to the kitchen, but no further.

"What did you do?" Aladorn said, appearing suddenly, a large man cowering before him.

The two younger elves frowned at the accusation. "Introduced ourselves. Is this the innkeeper?"

"Unfortunately. Master Haerford, meet Lord Aidyn Sestuns, and Sodo White of the Guild of Alchemists."

The man went pale as all the blood rushed from his head. He sagged in Aladorn's grip, and though he was a big man, he looked like a doll hanging from the elf's hand. He shook the innkeeper roughly. "Tell us everything, human, or suffer the wrath of the Magin Queen and her Council."

The threat was all it took for the man to accept his fate. "I didn't know they was coming until a few months ago. I got a letter from the king of Seaduens demanding that I house his friends. You must understand Good Masters, me tavern does little business these days. I didn't know who they was, or what they was up to until they got here. I swear."

"Why did you not report them as soon as they arrived?" Aidyn asked calmly.

Haerford began dry-washing his hands. "I was scared, me lord. I saw what they did to Lianin, and I was afeared they'd do it to me if I didn't obey 'em. They're rough men, Good Masters, tough and dangerous. They threw out me guard as soon as they got here, didn't want no trouble."

"So you let them abuse a woman rather than yourself? You are truly chivalrous, Haerford," Sodo growled.

"Please! I couldn't stop 'em! They're near two dozen of 'em, all told. I'm just one man, and Lianin tried to make 'em stop destroying me inn, so they did that to her face when she said she'd report 'em."

Aidyn looked at his brother. The wiat nodded once, and the assassin slipped out of the kitchen back into the night. Haerford began whining in terror. "Where's he goin'? What are ya gonna do?" he cried, his words becoming more and more jumbled as his anxiety grew.

"He is going to the castle to gather Captain Suneelo Tiena and his guards to arrest these turncoats. Do you have a problem with that, Master Haerford?" Aladorn hissed.

"No! No, I swear I don't have nothin' to do with 'em."

"Then why did you not let Lianin run? Why did you keep her here?" Sodo queried angrily.

"She'd have run and told someone. She'd have got me killed!"

"You nearly got her killed, man. Did you put the chain on her, or did your friends?"

The innkeep quailed before Aladorn, writhing in his strong grip. "I didn't *want* to!"

"But still you did it. You are worse than a traitor, Haerford, and you will pay for your cruelty," the wiat snarled, and slammed his elbow into the man's neck.

He went down in a heap. Immediately, the two elves trussed him and threw him in the cellar. "He does not have the key on him," Sodo said after a minute of searching.

Aladorn shrugged and gripped the cuff around Lianin's ankle. Straining, he slowly pulled the iron ring apart until the lock snapped and the unconscious woman was freed. Then they went out the back door once more after securing the kitchen door. They had to attack three men before reaching the front door, dragging the unconscious bodies to the back door. They found a few heavy timbers from the stockpile on the other side of the tavern and quietly barred the door from outside. The enemies on the inside were oblivious to their entrapment, and went on with their debaucheries.

It was over an hour before Aidyn arrived with Suneelo and fifty armed guards. The assassin, the wiat, the alchemist, and the captain slipped inside the back door one more time. Suneelo frowned curiously at the still listless Lianin, glancing at Aidyn for an explanation.

"Prisoner," the assassin said shortly, drawing two throwing knives from his belt. "So, did Losolin say to kill them or take them alive?"

The king's brother shook his head. "He just said to do what was necessary. We will need captives though, so try not to kill them all."

"Take the fun out of everything, then," Aidyn joked, and kicked open the door.

The four elves rushed into the common room, which exploded in a maelstrom of surprised renegades and infiltrators. Immediately, the barricaded door burst open and Suneelo's guards poured in, armed to the teeth and ferocious in their anger. Within minutes, the entire common room was filled with the howls of desperate people. Men and elves sat tied back to back, faces slack with the shock of being caught. The four leaders sprinted up the stairs as movement was heard above.

Three males were wresting open a window as they burst into a room, a few of the guards checking the other rooms. The four elves pulled up short as the three fugitives succeeded in opening the second floor window. Suneelo and Aladorn rushed two of them, but the third leapt from the sill into the night. Cursing, Aidyn followed.

His lithe body flew through the air seconds after his target. He landed in a roll and was up and running immediately. His prey was obviously an elf, or a highly trained human, for he was already halfway down the street. Aidyn sprinted after him, nocking his bow on the run. It was a dark night, the moons obscured by heavy clouds, and the elf prayed for it not to rain.

The male ahead of him ducked into an alleyway and Aidyn followed, cursing again as he saw the bottom of the other's cloak disappear over a low-hanging roof. Leaping onto the building, the assassin caught sight of his target hurdling onto another roof. Irritated now, Aidyn watched him for a second before sprinting off in another direction.

It took only moments for him to overtake the other male. Aidyn judged his placement, and dropped from his higher roof to land in front of his victim. The elf, as it turned out, reeled back in surprise and fear, and turned to run off in another direction.

"Oh no, you will not!" Aidyn growled, loosing his still-nocked arrow.

The arrowhead buried itself behind the elf's knee, knocking him over. He rolled desperately, bellowing as the arrow shaft broke off, leaving the iron head imbedded deep in his leg.

Aidyn strolled over to him, spreading his arms wide, his cloak billowing out behind him. "Did you think you would win? Where were you going to go? You betrayed this nation! No one would give you shelter!"

"You are wrong," the other elf hissed, still trying to crawl away.

Aidyn laughed viciously, coming to stand before the wounded male. "Do you know who I am?"

"Does it matter?"

The assassin grinned maliciously, squatting before his captive on the dark rooftop. "Oh, I think it does. My name is Aidyn Sestuns."

The other elf's breathing became harsh and rapid. "Then kill me and finish it."

"Oh no, I am not going to kill you. I am going to hand you over to Queen Tlonna Ewôsdírn and High Commander Yayènia er'Tiena. They will get all the answers from you, trust me."

"I have no answers!" the elf wheezed frantically. "I am just a runner!"

"No you are not. You are an operative, a weapon. No one else could get away from me as long as you did, especially not a flaming runner. You are no errand boy. Now, get down," Aidyn snapped, and kicked the wounded elf over the edge of the roof.

He jumped down lightly after him, grabbed the other by his cloak and dragged him through the streets back to the tavern. It started to rain halfway, and Aidyn pulled his hood up to shield his face from the torrent. "What is your name?" he asked after a while.

"Nydis," his prisoner mumbled sullenly as he was dragged through the wet.

"Well, Nydis, was it worth it?"

When the male stayed silent, Aidyn laughed quietly. Soon, they were back at the inn and Nydis was tied up with the rest of his comrades. They looked at him with sullen eyes, hoping that at least one of their number had escaped. Haerford was brought from the cellar and added to the group. Suneelo directed his men, and within the hour they were marching the twenty-four captives to the castle. Sodo carried Lianin, who had regained consciousness, but was so weak from her ordeal she had collapsed after a quarter mile.

Tlonna, Yayènia, and Miazie met them at the stable yard, grimly watching the captives as they were brought shuffling into the yard. Servants rushed forward to take horses, and two took care of Lianin, carrying her off to the hospital wing. Miazie and Yayènia briefly met with their lovers while Aidyn and Aladorn filled Tlonna in. The assassin abruptly hauled the panting Nydis forward, dumping him unceremoniously at the queen's feet.

The injured elf peered up at the Magin, his angled face slick with rain and frozen in dread. Tlonna glanced at him once and then ignored him, turning her attention to the twenty-three other men being individually carried off to the guard towers where they would await their fate in tiny cells in the middle of the two towers. "Did you get them all?" she asked finally.

"All those were at the tavern. If there is another contingent in the city, we have not found them yet," Aidyn replied.

"Let us hope this is all of them. I believe Yayènia has made a judgment on Arganor and Jayce. She was about to tell me something when were called to the stable," Tlonna said quietly. "Losolin is at the north wall with Edwin. They found a small fissure near the base of the wall and are trying to get masons to replace the blocks before Seaduens gets here."

Aladorn shook his head. "Why do things go wrong all at the same time? Where there is one fissure, there will be another."

Tlonna smiled. "Are you worried Aladorn? We will be fine, I promise. Now, who is this?"

Aidyn yanked the pitiful Nydis to his feet and held him firm. "This is Nydis, a weapon for the traitors. I have not questioned him. I thought you and Nia would prefer to do it."

The Magin eyed the shaking Nydis through the dark and rain. "Yes. Thank you, Aidyn. I will take him to Yayènia's office. Send her there when she is done with them," she said, gesturing to the remaining captives.

"As you wish," Aidyn said, and handed Nydis to his ruler.

Tlonna shoved the male ahead of her and watched him stumble toward the castle. Once they were inside, she took him roughly by elbow and steered him all the way to the fourth floor. By the time they reached Yayènia's office, Nydis was near to crawling, being dragged by Tlonna.

She shoved him inside the large room and shut the door behind her. "So, Nydis, is it? Where are you from?"

The male struggled to his feet and dropped into a chair. "Amaden."

"The capital of Seaduens? So, you are a direct link to Stoffnias, then?"

Accepting his defeat, Nydis nodded, slumping in the chair and avoiding Tlonna's eye. "I am his personal assassin."

Tlonna's chin rose slightly and she sat on Yayènia's desk, thinking. "So, Stoffnias's assassin against mine..." she mused, "How true the outcome was. Tell me, were you sent here to kill me or someone else?"

"King Stoffnias sent me here to assassinate Aidyn and Aladorn Sestuns, and to capture Miazie Paron of Anutch. My Lord wishes to have her for his family, to have her in his harem."

Tlonna jerked slightly, fury and surprise shocking through her body. "Aidyn and Aladorn *Sestuns*? His *harem*? What the flaming nine hells is wrong with that elf?"

Nydis winced in his chair. "They insulted him, three years ago! He could not let such an affront go by unpunished!"

Tlonna forcefully calmed herself down. "You believe that Miazie belongs in the Lostug Harem? Did you know that the three elves who caught you tonight were Aidyn, Aladorn, and Sodo, Miazie's consort?"

Nydis shook his head. "I believe that she is a human, worth less than elves, and if the royal family desires her, then she should oblige, happy she is attractive enough to warrant the attention of such great males. If she is with an elf already, then she will better serve my lords."

Tlonna's slap lifted him over the arm of the chair and he collapsed against Yayènia's desk just as the High Commander strode in. "What happened?"

Tlonna related the preceding conversation, and Yayènia listened as she shut her office door and walked to the other side. Nydis tried to curl into an insignificant ball, but the warrior ignored him as she slid open a door and stepped inside. The queen watched her curiously, never having seen the small dark room, but she could only make out vague shapes in the shadows, and then a flame flickered to life in the darkness. Finally, the silent warrior stepped out and looked upon the trembling male with ice-cold eyes.

"I do not take care with assassins bent on killing my friends because their king believes they have been slighted when they have not. My name is Yayènia er'Tiena, and you will tell me everything."

Tlonna took a deep breath and put a hand on her sister's shoulder. "Do not lose yourself, Nia," she said quietly.

"I locked myself away long ago. I will take it from here," Yayènia replied in the same manner.

The queen opened the door and let herself out as Nydis began to scream.

Losolin found Yayènia several hours later, standing in the rear courtyard, leaning against The Archer that stood above the underground entrance.

"Nia?" he asked quietly, coming up behind her.

The warrior had her arms wrapped around herself, and she stood perfectly still in the early morning light. She did not respond to his call.

"Nia, are you all right?"

"Well over two hundred years I have been known as the hardest warrior in Nymyños, and I have never lost control. Losolin...the things Nydis was saying, he truly believed them. The things he said about Miazie, and Aidyn and Aladorn...all of us. I... lost control. I finally snapped. I nearly tore him to pieces. I was not even aware of it until I was washing the blood from my skin. I have never been so far gone."

"Yayènia..." Losolin said, unable to comprehend her pain.

"Losolin!" she cried, turning.

The king blinked in surprise as his sister-in-law buried her head in his shoulder and wept. Slowly, he wrapped his arms around her small body and held her close. He had never seen Yayènia cry more than a few silent tears, and now she was bawling unrestrained into his shoulder.

"You are the strongest person I know, Yayènia, and no one can handle what you have handled. But you must know that even you are not invincible. You must not expect yourself to deal with things that are beyond normal emotional capacity."

"What?" the High Commander breathed, pulling away, large blue eyes wide.

Losolin grinned. "I love you, and so does Tlonna, and Suneelo, Erdwyf...everyone. You are not alone."

"I love you too, little brother," Yayènia sniffed and stepped completely away from the king. "Thank you for dealing with that."

"I am quite used to it. Tlonna cries at least once a week."

"Really? She is always so stoic," Yayènia said, laughing.

Losolin stared at her, open-mouthed. "*Tlonna* is stoic? Yayènia! I have never even seen you sniff!"

The warrior laughed louder and gently punched her brother-in-law. "Now you know my dirty little secret. I cry alone."

Losolin sobered at the sad words. "You do not have to. I am always here, and I know for a fact that Suneelo is as well."

"I know. It is not that I doubt it, but merely the fact that I cannot do my job if people knew that I succumbed to emotion. I am not a person who is allowed to feel, at least in the presence of others," Yayènia explained quietly. "Have you spoken to Tlonna?"

Losolin nodded. "She is not happy. She did not want to leave you alone."

"It is my job, Losolin, as she has hers. So...did you know about Aidyn and Aladorn?"

The king grunted. "Aladorn told me earlier today. Tlonna did not take it well. What about you? What do you think of it?"

The warrior shrugged. "It is odd there are so many of us who have siblings. Rarely does an elfin couple have more than one child. But I understand their want for secrecy. If it were any other monarchy, Aidyn would be forced to abdicate his position to Aladorn, and neither would be happy with that. I wonder how they will take it when they find out Stoffnias knows. As a matter of fact, I want to know how Stoffnias knows. None of us did, and they are our friends!"

Losolin stared at the rear wall of the courtyard that separated the castle grounds from the harbor district. "Stoffnias knows too much about everything. Speaking of which, have you come to a conclusion about our traitor?"

Yayènia nodded silently. After a while she said, "Let us find Tlonna, and I will tell you both, all right?"

The two walked back to the castle and found the queen standing in a third floor corridor, conversing quietly with a disturbed looking group of resident nobles. When he and Yayènia approached them, the group broke away with quiet murmurs and genuflections. Tlonna turned to face her sister and husband, eyes darkened with the pain of knowledge.

"You know who the traitor is," she stated softly.

Yayènia nodded and took a deep breath, and related her news.

The City Council convened immediately in one of the large meeting rooms on the fourth floor of the castle. Yayènia stood and waited for the excited and apprehensive council to quiet. "I have determined who the traitor is, and you may be relieved that it was only one of those taken into custody. The innocent man has been apologized to, and has been released, though he is being watched very carefully in case he does decide to turn. You may also be relieved that he showed little ill will toward us, though he was, understandably, deeply insulted. However, what he showed most was relief, and concern for the city. He has been examined multiple times by myself and others to make sure of his honesty."

There was a collective sigh of relief, though the council still stared at the warrior with tight eyes, wondering which of their comrades had betrayed them.

"Arganor is the traitor," Yayènia stated bluntly, and sat down as the room erupted.

Though there was much relief that it had not been young Jayce, Arganor had been well-liked, and it came as a hard blow that he had deceived them so. Now Tlonna stood, her head held proudly as she waited for her council to quiet once more. "Arganor will be brought to the throne room in a short while, and we, as a group, will decide his fate. Jayce has been invited to take part as well, being as he is still a part of this council, but he was given full leave not to come. Now, the charges against Arganor stand thus: Sedition, Murder, Espionage, and High Treason. Each of these charges by themselves is viable for death, but I will leave that to discussion."

The door opened and everyone turned, expecting to see the guards with Arganor, but Jayce walked in, still shaken by his ordeal. He met everyone's stare, however, and bowed to Tlonna and Losolin. "I believe I have the need to be here. I have been personally affected by Arganor's treachery, and I want to see some justice."

Losolin smiled grimly at the human. "So you shall, Jayce. You have my deepest and most sincere apology for your detainment."

"I accept it, my lord. Know that I realize the necessity for taking me in, as my record must look suspicious, but I am and always will be a loyal Blackhavenite."

"And we are glad of it," Tlonna said, and gestured for everyone to rise. "Let us go now to the throne room, and await our traitor."

The council descended the three flights of stairs to the ground floor and reconvened in the throne room, which had been sealed off to the public for the occasion. Already two royal scribes were setting up, along with guards at every open interval along the wall. The council took their respective seats in a semicircle that was absent during petitions, while Tlonna and Losolin seated themselves on the dais. Yayènia stifled a yawn behind her elbow, and Losolin realized she had not yet been to bed.

It was early in the morning, and they had several verdicts to make today. Ghealan arrived a few minutes later in full armor, having just come from his duties at the gate, preparing for the imminent battle. Everyone was present for the hearings, and all other duties had been handed off to seconds and thirds. Aidyn nodded to Tlonna, who stared back, still unsure about the revelation. Suneelo smiled at Miazie, who blushed and turned to speak with Sodo. They all stood in their respective places behind the thrones, also in a semicircle.

At the entrance to the throne room, the herald pounded his staff on the floor and the anxious council went silent, expectant. The door opened and a contingent of guards marched in, forming a tight box around the twenty-six defendants. Lorne, Nydis, and Arganor were foremost, stiff-backed and pale as they were led to the side of the room where rows of chairs had been arranged. As they were seated, Suneelo looked proudly on as his guards moved into precise lines about the prisoners, their faces impassive as they once again boxed in their charges.

Once everything had stilled, Tlonna stood, her crown catching the light as she did so. She had dressed carefully for this event, choosing a gown of black silk embroidered with white and silver crescents, the long, dagged sleeves were lined with white voile and gathered at her elbows. Her hair she had left unbraided so that it hung in a golden sheet to her back, her coronet catching only a small amount to fall in ringlets at her temples. Everyone present stared at her in awe, even the prisoners.

Her crown was elegant in its simplicity. Made of pure silver, it was embellished with moonstones, white diamonds, and one thumb-nail sized black diamond that sat between her brows, suspended by two crescent moons. The silver vines curled about a quarter-inch base, moonstones and diamonds dotting the center of each delicate leaf.

As she stood, Tlonna mentally prepared herself for the decisions she must soon make. “Lords and Ladies of the Blackhaven Council and Royal Court, I, Tlonna Arune Ewôsdírn, the Everwood Magin Queen of Blackhaven in this five hundred and forty-fifth year of the Eighth Age, do convene this court against these twenty-six charged people. I call upon all present to make fair and honorable rulings, and to commit no perjury. Do you swear so to do?”

The council all rose and in unison spoke the formal words. “We swear so do to, in witness to the gods above, may our souls be condemned if foresworn.”

“Then let this ruling commence,” Tlonna replied, and sat.

Losolin shifted and studied the gathered defendants for a moment. “I call upon Lorne Jesman to make his stand.”

The Mardyn assassin stood and slowly walked to the front of the dais, where he looked up at Tlonna with large eyes, obviously terrified.

“Lorne Jesman, did you or did you not come to Blackhaven with the intent to kill the queen?” Erdwyf asked stiffly.

“I did.”

“Did you or did you not accept payment from King Stoffnias of Seaduens to commit this act?”

“I did.”

“Your reasons for these acts?”

The elf took a deep breath to steady himself. “King Stoffnias promised me ten thousand geld, along with land and a title if I killed Queen Tlonna. I am from Mardyn, a small village on the Strait of Arwênlhias that does not receive benefit from the royal city. We have very little, and ten thousand geld would not only improve conditions beyond imagination, but would provide my community with future insurance. It was not an offer that I could refuse."

Erdwyf sighed. "Mardyn is a Blackhaven community, which means it is under the full protection of the crown. If conditions were so bad, could you not have come to petitions? Your request would surely have been granted."

Lorne shook his head. "We have petitioned before, Lady High Advisor, and were given minimal aid. Five hundred geld, or supplies for new fishing boats, nothing that would permanently fix the problems."

"Were you aware that a ruling had already been signed to send a representative to Mardyn so that the problems be assessed, and therefore rectified?"

Lorne looked dumbstruck. "No, I was not."

"Perhaps next time you should speak with your village council before making irrational decisions that could send the entire kingdom into a downward spiral. I call upon this honored body to make a judgment on Lorne Jesman," Erdwyf declared.

The council and its rulers leaned inward, and after minutes of debate, Tlonna stood once more. Lorne stared at her fearfully. "Lorne Jesman, you are to return to Mardyn a free elf."

The male went white with relief.

"However, if you ever step foot within this city again, you will be executed immediately. Is that clear?"

"Yes, my Queen," Lorne replied shakily.

"You have one hour to depart. I suggest you use it wisely. Dismissed."

Lorne fled the throne room, followed by three guards.

Losolin spoke as Tlonna sat. "I call upon Nydis Karnahan to make his stand."

The Seadueni assassin stepped forward, limping heavily from the arrow Aidyn had embedded in his knee, and the severe beating from Yayènia. The High Commander watched him coldly. He bowed low, stumbled, and needed the aid of a guard to regain his feet.

Erdwyf sighed quietly. "Nydis Karnahan, did you or did you not come to Blackhaven with the intent of kidnapping Miazie Paron, and assassinating Aidyn Sestuns, and Aladorn the... Sestuns?"

The assassin found his three targets among the seated council and swallowed. "I did."

"You are from Seaduens?"

"I am."

"Your reasons for coming all the way from your home kingdom to murder three innocent people?"

"They are not innocent!" Nydis cried, his bugging eyes riveted on Yayènia. "They insulted my king! They must be punished!"

"You do not protest your innocence, then?" Erdwyf asked loudly.

"I *am* innocent! It is you who are guilty! Spending the lives of elves to protect that of a human! You must see the heresy in that!" the raving elf screamed.

"Silence!" Erdwyf yelled as the council burst into furious reprimands. "I call upon this honored body to make its judgment."

Barely a moment had passed before Tlonna stood. "Nydis Karnahan...I sentence you to death by beheading. Tomorrow at dusk, you will be executed. Go now, and contemplate your life."

The zealous elf was dragged screaming from the hall and Losolin spoke once more. "Lord Arganor, you stand accused of High Treason, Murder, Sedition, and Espionage. You have been questioned and examined, and you have admitted to these crimes. What say you now?"

The human stood before the dais and glared at his rulers. "You promise only good feelings and peaceful times. King Stoffnias promises honor, and glory. Your gifts are weak compared to his. He knows the value of heroism. You are weak, as are your followers," the man wheezed, glaring up at the elf.

"That may be, but we will win this battle, as we have won all the others. King Stoffnias and his spoiled sons are fools to believe they can attack Blackhaven, and win," Tlonna replied. "But not only that, you are human, Arganor, and Stoffnias would never allow a human to keep his life as long as he were no longer useful. Did you honestly believe he would forsake his own law for you? You are but a tool to him, and now you are traitor to your own people."

"No more than you, my *Queen*," the human sneered, and lunged forward.

Yayènia leapt forward, but too late. Tlonna yanked her arm up to deflect the knife the human had somehow kept away from the guards, earning a deep gash across her forearm. Shouts erupted throughout the hall, but Yayènia calmly drew her longsword and buried it to the hilt in Arganor's chest. With a grimace, she yanked it out and the man crumpled to the floor. Already, Losolin had his hands on Tlonna, but she shook him away, ignoring the wound as it splashed blood on her dress, throne, and the floor.

The others in the room stared in shock, unable to comprehend what had just happened. Arganor was still moving slightly, writhing on the floor in a pool of his own blood. The queen shared a long look with her sister and personal guard. After a while, Yayènia nodded faintly, so small a movement Tlonna thought she might have imagined it, but then the High Commander turned to Losolin.

"My king, will you heal this man so that he may live long enough to be brought to true justice before the people of Blackhaven?"

"I will," Losolin replied hollowly, bending over the human.

After a moment, Arganor was hauled to his feet by the guards and dragged bodily from the throne room. Tlonna smoothed her skirt unnecessarily, smearing more blood on it, and sat back down on her throne. Taking a deep breath, she called softly to Erdwyf. The High Advisor turned and lowered her head so that the queen could speak directly to her.

"Would you suggest continuing on, or delaying until tomorrow?"

The fey-faced elf shook her head. "Delaying would only give the rest of them more courage. Let us finish this now."

"Fair enough," Tlonna breathed, and stood once more. "High Advisor Erdwyf, will you please continue the trial?" she said loudly.

Erdwyf adjusted her armband as the council and the prisoners quieted. Finally, when silence ensued once more, the High Advisor looked up. "As High Advisor to the Queen of Blackhaven, I do re-commence this trial, and ask that all remaining defendants be brought before the dais of the Rulers of Blackhaven."

As one, the twenty-four accused rose and were herded to the front of the thrones. Tlonna looked them each over, studying every face, every nervous twitch. Finally, her gaze landed on Brashnard Haerford and she could not stop a glower. The innkeeper saw her scowl and his face and neck went white.

"Master Haerford, you are the gravest of traitors in this room. You allowed these twenty-three men to take refuge in your inn, and to abuse the woman Lianin. You had her detained against her will, and from what she has said, you allowed these men and elves to rape her,"

Erdwyf spat, unable to contain her disgust. "You stand charged with High Treason, Rape, and Domestic Abuse. Your reasons?"

The man fell to his knees, clasping his hands together in abeyance. "I did it to preserve meself. I meant no harm to her, she just was too flighty for me to allow her freedom. Please, Good Mistress, grant mercy on me. I was only doin' what I had to do to survive. These men...they's the ones as did it. I never touched her, Good Mistress, I never did."

"Be that as it may, Master Haerford, you allowed it, you even encouraged it in order to keep yourself in good graces. Now, what made you allow these people into your inn in the first place?"

"King Stoffnias, he sent me a letter saying he needed a favor. Who am I to refuse a king? An' as I told the good masters as found me, business is slow, and I need the pickup, see. I ain't done no real treason. It were an innocent mistake, I promise!"

"Somehow, I find you hard to believe. So, Council, what is the fate for Master Brashnard Haerford?" Erdwyf asked coldly, turning away from the man.

There was a stiff silence as the members of the council remained staring at the human. One by one, they turned to Tlonna and Losolin. Losolin took his wife's hand and gave it a gentle squeeze, and shook his head minimally. Tlonna raised her chin slightly.

"Master Haerford, your crimes outweigh your pleas. Tomorrow, you will hang by the neck until dead. Go now and think on your life, and hope the gods find some pity on you."

The human began wailing as he was taken from the throne room and the queen rested her head against the back of her throne. Erdwyf was reading the long list of names of the twenty-three Seadueni infiltrators and their crimes. Tlonna already knew the outcome of their judgment. Though each one would have the opportunity to lay their case before her and the council, their lives were forfeit. No one in Blackhaven would give an ounce of mercy to Seadueni murderers, especially now. Already her peers were angry and deceived, bitter toward the treacherous acts of their comrade and sickened with the racist remarks of the previous defendants.

The day wore on as the trials continued. At midday, servants brought lunch to the court and the prisoners were given slices of bread and water. As Tlonna picked at her buttered red potatoes, her appetite waning, she heard Aladorn and Aidyn's low voice conversing behind her. Their secrecy hurt her. She had found out about their relationship through a Seadueni assassin, then Losolin had told her the whole story hours later. Despite the fact that it was now glaringly obvious, Tlonna had never even considered the idea. Against her will, the queen began to listen to their whispered conversation.

"...told her ourselves."

"And her reaction? Aidyn, she has not said a word to us since."

"Maybe she is too angry with us to speak. I would not blame her. We told Miazie and Losolin. We should have told her."

"Miazie figured it out by herself, and I told Losolin," Aladorn's angry voice spat back.

Tlonna frowned at her potatoes. Finally, she twisted in her chair and pinned the brothers with a solemn stare. They both went stiff-backed, dark green eyes tightening as they tensed.

"I am your friend, not just your queen," Tlonna said quietly, though her words were clipped. "You should have trusted Losolin and me to keep your secret. I am hurt you did not believe me capable of taking such news. However, as I am your friend, I will try my best to accept your deception and move on. I wish you to do the same."

"Tlonna...I am sorry," Aidyn replied, leaning forward to touch her hand. "Honestly, it is still new for us, so sharing it with others was a daunting prospect."

"Be that as it may, I learned it first from Nydis...which I do *not* appreciate."

The dark elves stared at her in shock. "What?"

"That is right. Stoffnias must know, for that is what Nydis said. Our enemies have the unfortunate habit of knowing more about us than we do. I believe it was Midian who told Stoffnias, for it was Midian who knew of Yayènia and me."

Aladorn frowned. "But how?"

Tlonna shrugged. "He had ways."

The brothers snorted, then glanced at each other in surprise. Tlonna shook her head in exasperation and turned back around to her cooling meal. Losolin pushed his half-empty plate away and leaned back as servants came to take away their dishes. Tlonna's cupbearer, a young wood nymph, gave the queen a knowing stare as she picked up the full plate. The Magin tried to ignore the reprimand, but she nodded silently to her cupbearer, knowing that when she returned to her rooms tonight, there would be a hearty meal waiting for her.

The day wore on.

Chapter 36

Celebrate Life with Death

The next morning dawned gray and drizzling. Losolin watched with uninterested eyes as the servants swiftly placed the glass panes in the window casements, shutting out the weather. He donned his robe and stepped onto the courtyard balcony, letting the rain run down his face and soak his hair. It was a fitting start to a day full of executions. Indeed, all but one of the trials yesterday had ended with the death sentence. It had taken a toll on everyone involved. Even the guards had looked ill-at-ease by the end of the day. Tlonna had barely spoken a word since, and had eaten very little of the large dinner awaiting her.

The king sighed, already weary. A soft noise behind him made him turn.

"Oh, please forgive me my lord," a maid said quietly, curtsying. "I did not mean to disturb you. I was only bringing up the royal breakfast."

Losolin smiled. "It is all right, girl. What is your name?"

"Sera, my king."

"A lovely name. How long have you worked at the castle?"

The girl blinked. "Seven years, King Losolin. The Late King Dietirin hired me in the underground when my predecessor died."

"Ah. Tell me, what do you think of today?"

Sera looked down at her feet. "I think it sad when any life must be taken, my lord, but those men...they betrayed us all, didn't they. How many would have died had they not been caught?"

"That is a hard statement to make," Tlonna said unexpectedly, waking.

The two turned to look at the queen as she slid out of bed.

"My Queen," Sera said, curtsying low, lower than she had for Losolin.

"Stop that. I will not stand on ceremony with people I see every day. You may call me Tlonna."

"Thank you my-Tlonna," Sera replied, blushing. "You are much like your honored father."

"I hope so," the Magin murmured, coming to stand next to her husband. "So, you believe the trial judgments to be correct?"

"Yes, though it is not my place to say. They are hurtful people, and we have done them no true wrong."

Tlonna and Losolin smiled at the human. "You are much wiser than many people in positions of power, Sera," the queen stated. "Come, eat with us."

"Oh! Your majesty! I could never break protocol so!"

Losolin frowned. "We are the makers of protocol. We can break it when we want to."

"But my duties-"

"Are to obey the king and queen, yes?" Tlonna cut in.

The human dipped her head. "Yes."

"Then eat with us, and tell us of yourself. Were you born here, in the city?" Losolin said, sitting at the small round table with the two females.

"Hastert, actually. I came here with my parents fourteen years ago when news of trouble throughout Nymyños reached us. We thought we'd be safer in the city. It was our misfortune that we were not. My father died during the siege. He was a volunteer archer in Captain Suneelo's wall guard. My mother and I fled with the rest of the population underground, but she died four years later from illness."

"I am so sorry, Sera," Tlonna said, touching the human's hand.

The maid gave her queen a small smile. "It was a long time ago, now. I was in the room when you came back, did you know? I was waiting on King Dietirin when everyone arrived. It was a moment I shall never forget. Your presence seemed to be hope incarnate."

Tlonna smiled, swirling her spoon in the cream of wheat that was her breakfast. Losolin was half finished with his, and crumbs were all that was left of his bread. The king drained his steaming mint tea and leaned back contentedly, picking up his bowl and finishing off the porridge. Sera took a bite, and then stared at the queen.

"My...Tlonna, is it not to your satisfaction?"

The Magin frowned, and then let out a small laugh. "No, it is delicious. I just have little appetite recently, Sera. Something I, unfortunately, picked up in Zaedic. The worse the situation gets, the less I eat."

"Oh, your majesty, that is awful. You should eat."

"Yes, you should," Losolin said in a hard voice, still leaning back in his chair, when Tlonna opened her mouth to reply.

"Thank you, Losolin," she snapped, and deliberately drank her tea.

Standing, the queen smiled down at the worried human. "Do not worry about me, Sera, I have plenty enough people doing that already. Instead, I want you to take the day off, go do something for yourself. It will not be long before this city is besieged, and such activities will no longer be available. I will give you a leave note to give to the Head Maid. Understood?"

Sera gaped at the elf. "Yes...thank you."

"No worries, now," Tlonna replied, hastily writing out a leave of absence and sealing it with her signet. She handed the letter to Sera and bid her goodbye.

As the young woman scurried out of the royal apartments, Losolin walked over to Tlonna and wrapped his arms around her from behind. "You should eat, you know."

"I do, but I cannot get it down. Losolin, I know it is foolish, but it is how my mind works. Even now, four years later, I cannot get my mind out of that cell in Zaedic. It twisted me, *he* twisted me, made me something less than I was."

"No." Losolin said sharply, but kindly. "No, love, you are more than you were. You are stronger for it, and though it was terrible and cruel, you are a better leader for it. And I love you."

"I love you, too," Tlonna whispered, leaning against him.

Minutes later, there was a knock at the door and Carlotta and Coran, the royal dressers, walked in. Tlonna and Losolin washed and readied for the day. Tlonna was laced into a gown of silver crepe with a black chiffon overlay. As was custom for such days, a white veil was placed over her face, attached to her crown. Every single gown she owned had been custom tailored by Mattie, the royal seamstress, and Carlotta, so each one was made to enhance her appearance. Though the neck was higher than usual, squaring out at her collarbone, it clung tightly, the overlay flowing about on its own. The sleeves were loose, as usual. Tlonna had made the point that she didn't like tight sleeves, and the two women had obliged her.

When she was ready, the queen turned to find Losolin and grinned. He was tugging on his left boot, looking glum. Coran was fastening a white leather cloak to his shoulders. The leather had been treated to withstand the rain, but it was heavy and irritated the king. Gray pants and a black cotton tunic completed the ensemble. When he stood, Losolin shook his shoulders in an attempt to get the cloak to lay right. Tlonna swallowed a lump in her throat. Her husband looked every inch a powerful king.

Coran stood on a stool in order to place the crown on the king's head, catching Tlonna's knowing eye with a grin. Losolin's crown was a silver band with black enameled *kairhotuss* trees marching along the center. A black diamond, the same shape as the one on Tlonna's, rose from the hilt of a silver sword. The sword point reached to the middle of his forehead. Losolin often commented that it pricked him when he scowled. It was not a crown he could wear easily.

"Are you ready?" Tlonna asked him as he came to stand next to her.

"As ready as I can be," the male replied, kissing her lightly on the cheek and dismissing the dressers.

The couple descended the widening spiral staircase through the center of their tower until they reached the ground floor. Already the council was waiting, all dressed in their ceremonial garments and fidgeting restlessly. Yayènia, Ghealan, and Suneelo were all in full armor, long cloaks of office billowing in the wind. Rather than their plumed helmets, however, Yayènia wore a veil similar to Tlonna's, as sister to the queen, and the two males wore circlets befitting their ranks. Erdwyf was draped in the flowing white, black, and silver robes of High Advisor, her left arm and shoulder bare to reveal the band of office on her bicep. Miazie was there in silver and white robes, Aidyn and Aladorn in their dark profession garments, and Sodo in his white caste robes. They made a stunning and powerful group, daunting even the Royal Council, who knew them all personally as well as professionally.

Erdwyf curtsied low, as was custom, and the rest followed. Servants appeared at the tower door with large oiled parasols, waiting to escort the company to the small north courtyard where such proceedings took place. Despite the parasols, the company was battered by winds and spraying rain, and soon Tlonna's and Yayènia's veils were soaked. The sisters exchanged long-suffering glances and resolutely kept their hands from yanking the things off.

They soon reached the secluded courtyard and settled into place on a large wooden dais. The sentenced prisoners were marched up and secured in place. Erdwyf stood, shielded partly by a servant holding a parasol to the side to block the sweeping rain, hiding himself behind it as well.

"Today we gather here to acknowledge that these sentenced men and elves are to be executed for their crimes of treason, rape, and murder. Individually, they will be allowed to speak their last words, and be hanged by the neck until dead. May the gods find compassion for your souls."

The hangman stood and called the first name. "Ressing Mathers of Purheae."

A tall elf walked hesitantly up the gallows and stood trembling as the noose was tightened about the neck. "I die an honorable elf of Seaduens, and I regret nothing."

Tlonna jerked involuntarily, squeezing her eyes shut as the trap door swung open and the elf dropped. Against her will, she reached out and grabbed Yayènia's hand, needing the connection. When the strong hand squeezed back momentarily, the queen looked at her sister and was a little disturbed, but not surprised. The warrior was sitting comfortably in her chair, steadfastly ignoring the hated water soaking her. The expression on her face was one of pure disregard. Yayènia watched the dying elf with the calm gaze of someone who had seen hundreds die at her own hands. Ressing was loosened and taken away, and the executions resumed.

Brashnard Haerford was the last to mount the gallows, and Tlonna swallowed. The human was shaking so bad he could hardly stand. His pleading eyes found the queen's and locked. She stared resolutely back, gripping both Losolin's and Yayènia's hands, their own fingers clasped tightly on hers.

"I have done nothing wrong! Please! Please! Spare me!" the human wheezed as the noose tightened around his neck. "I beg of you!"

The door swung open and the human dropped to his death, twitching and jerking on the line until he died. Tlonna released her husband's and sister's hands and stood. It was well into the afternoon now, and everyone was sick to the stomach. Suneelo discreetly moved to his wife's side as they proceeded back to the castle, rubbing her neck above her cuirass. The High Commander wrapped her left arm around her husband's waist and, to the shocked eyes of everyone gathered, hugged him close.

Suneelo closed his eyes as his wife gripped his waist, love washing through him. Over Yayènia's head he caught Ghealan's gaze, and found his friend grinning from pointed ear to pointed ear. Even Losolin was smiling, his long arm draped about Tlonna's shoulders as they moved into the High Hall. Fires were roaring in the massive hearths at both ends of the hall and a steaming meal was waiting for the entire council.

Yayènia let out a breath as she took her seat next to Tlonna and, oblivious to the stares she was receiving from the shocked council, tucked into her food. Suneelo gave the queen a wicked grin and kissed his wife on the cheek. Erdwyf stared open mouthed at her friends, disbelieving Yayènia's sudden show of affection.

After lunch, the council departed so that they could gather themselves for Nydis' and Arganor's beheadings that evening. Tlonna grabbed her sister's arm on the way out and pulled her to one side.

"Are you taking a new position in life?"

"What?" Yayènia murmured, frowning.

"I have never seen you show so much affection toward Suneelo in public. You have everyone wondering," Tlonna said, watching her sister's face.

"Well, pardon me for loving my husband too much. And despite my profession, even I have a problem watching twenty-five people get strangled to death," the warrior snapped defensively.

"I am not saying it is a bad thing, Nia!" Tlonna laughed. "It is wonderful to see, it is just unusual. I only wondered if something was going on."

Yayènia shrugged. "Suneelo and I will have been for married two-hundred and seventy years in three days. And after what happened with Rhiannan, how she abused him, it seems as though our need for each other has grown. I do love him."

"I know you do," Tlonna said softly. "And he is also very impatient. Are you going home or staying here until the beheading?"

Yayènia twisted to look at her husband who was waiting with Losolin, both males had their arms crossed and an identical look of eagerness on their faces. "Staying here. It is too wet to ride back and forth all day."

"True. So...I will see you later, then?"

"Indeed," the High Commander affirmed and went to join her husband, who nearly yanked her off her feet in his haste to get to the fourth floor where their suite was.

Tlonna chuckled as she and Losolin headed back to their tower. The king was already shrugging off the cumbersome cloak as they began to mount the stairs.

"What are you expecting?" Tlonna asked coyly as she followed him upward.

"We just watched twenty-some odd people die. Now...I need to celebrate life, which is also what Ghealan, Erdwyf, Nia, Suneelo, Miazie, and Sodo are doing right now as well, I am sure," the king said breathlessly as he opened the door to their apartment and rushed inside.

Tlonna laughed again as she entered behind him. His crown was already on the desk, his cloak in a pile on the floor, and he had one of his boots off. The queen locked the door behind her and moved slowly to stand in front of her husband.

"You are in such a rush, love," she commented dryly.

"Yes, well, we do not have much time, now do we?" Losolin panted, untying his breeches.

Tlonna made a noise in her throat. "We have...seven hours!"

"Not long enough."

The queen shrieked in surprise as her husband yanked her onto the bed. She floundered in pillows and her own clothing, laughing uncontrollably as Losolin wrestled with her shoes. Finally, he succeeded in freeing her feet and his hands slipped up her ankles to roll down her thin stockings. Tlonna gasped in air, trying to stop laughing, but could not. Even the amorous male started to chuckle as they wallowed ineffectively on the bed.

"Why do you have to wear so much clothes?" he growled, tugging on her dress laces.

"So...you...can...struggle..." Tlonna gasped.

"Torture is what it is," Losolin grumbled, victoriously undoing the last lace and pushing her dress over her head. He gaped in disbelief at the chemise and undergarments, flopping onto his back in defeat.

"Giving up?" Tlonna asked, giggling now.

"Not a chance," he returned, simply ripping off the rest of her clothing. His lips found her collarbone and traveled downward, covering every inch.

Tlonna arched, digging her fingers into his tunic. She tugged it off and tossed it on the floor where it joined her dress. The king twined his fingers in her hair, capturing her mouth with his. The Magin's hands gripped his strong shoulders, bracing herself. Already sweat slicked their skin, the blood leaping through their veins as physical excitement grew.

"I love you," Tlonna breathed in his ear.

Losolin moaned in answer.

Unacknowledged by the ardent elves, the flames illuminating their bedroom leapt higher, burned brighter.

On the other side of the fourth floor, Miazie stepped out of the tub to find Sodo waiting for her in all his natural glory. Her heart skipped a beat as the blood rushed to her head. The elf grinned and swept her off her feet, carrying her to their bed. The alchemist trailed his fingers down her breasts, over her belly, and all the way to her toes and back again. Miazie whimpered as her lover followed his fingers with his lips, leaving burning traces of desire on her skin.

Slowly, he unbound her long raven hair and wrapped it in his fists. Pulling her chin up, he kissed her slowly, deeply. When the Belau was trembling with yearning, he succumbed to her wishes and sheathed himself. After a few agonizingly controlled strokes, he stopped, gazing down at her face.

"Miazie..." he breathed, kissing her throbbing pulse just below her ear.

"Sodo." Miazie exhaled, drawing out his name.

"Will you marry me?"

"Sodo?" she gasped, fully lucid now.

The elf rose up onto his elbows, still linked with her. "I love you. I want to be your husband. Will you be my wife?"

Tears burst unbidden into Miazie's eyes as she gazed up at him. "But I am human."

"Not wholly, and even if you were, I would not care. We will find ways to get beyond such trivial matters, if you want to."

"Yes. Yes I do, and I will. I will marry you Sodo," Miazie cried. "But if you don't finish this, I am going to kill you, and the point will be moot."

Sodo laughed joyously and made love to his fiancée.

Hours later, they were all once more assembled at the wooden dais, the rain having slackened only a little. Everyone looked oddly sated, their faces radiating with some inner satisfaction, but Miazie merely looked about to explode. Tlonna noted the extreme happiness on her friend's face and wondered. Even Sodo seemed unable to keep a smile off his face, despite the rain streaking down his face and the rather unhappy proceedings about to take place.

Shaking her head, Tlonna took her seat between Losolin and Yayènia and steadied herself for the beheading. As the council arranged itself for the final execution, there was movement off to the side of the courtyard and six guards appeared, marching Nydis and Arganor to the dais. The elf and the human walked as far away from each other as possible within their box. Tlonna tensed as Arganor looked straight at her through the haze, his shadowed eyes blaming her for his predicament. Yayènia also saw the look and growled, shifting in her chair, resisting the urge to slice the man's head off herself.

Tlonna patted her sister's hand and gave her a knowing smile. "Let him die at the hands of another, rather than sully your own with such a traitor's blood."

Yayènia's upper lip curled. "I already have his blood on my hands, I just wish I had a little more."

"Do not let justice deter you from enlarging your ego," Miazie said, leaning forward to stick her head between the sisters' chairs.

The warrior snorted and swatted at the human in a good natured way. Tlonna grinned, watching the Belau with a suspicious eye. Miazie gave her a wicked grin and settled back in her chair, raven hair plastered to her face. Next to her, Aidyn also studied her with suspicion, his verdant eyes narrowed. Instead of speaking, the assassin planted one foot on either side of Yayènia's chair, resting his boots on her armrests. The warrior hooked her elbows around the toe of each and leaned back, perfectly at ease.

Tlonna was amazed at how the comfort level of her friends had risen so substantially, but she did not question it.

"Arganor Jamson!" Erdwyf called loudly, standing tall against the rain. "You stand before us today to pay for your crimes against the Throne of Blackhaven, and its citizens. You are a traitor to this nation and your name shall forever be burned with the knowledge. What final words do you have to say?"

The human set his jaw and remained silent, eyes steady and cold. The executioner waited only a moment before kicking him in the back of the knees. Arganor went down hard, but his eyes stayed hard on Tlonna. With a thud, his head landed off to the side and he slumped over. Tlonna took a steadying breath and shook her head, looking at Yayènia. The warrior's face was iron hard and her jaw tense. When she looked at her sister, the High Commander smiled a feral smile, one of paid justice. Then Nydis was dragged onto the dais and Erdwyf rose once more, her white and black dress billowing in the wind.

"Nydis Karnahan! Today, you pay for your crimes against the Throne of Blackhaven with your life. What final words do you have to say?"

The Seadueni elf glared at the gathered council, his proud chin in the air. "You will find your victory short lived, and soon you will face the full wrath of your enemies. I die without regret, and I die with my dignity!"

Erdwyf nodded once. The executioner forced Nydis to his knees and the proud elf kept his eyes on Tlonna, only the way his fingers were clasped before him betraying his true emotions. Without another word, the executioner lifted his broadsword and swept down, cleanly taking the elf's head off. The body of Nydis slumped to the side and then fell over while its head landed with a thud off to the right. For a moment, no one moved or said anything. Yayènia shook her head and sighed, glad to be done with the whole thing. Shaking Aidyn's toes, the warrior turned to face Tlonna.

"Now what?"

The queen did not reply for a moment, watching the priests gather the remains and take them away. Finally she looked at her gathered friends and council and attempted to wipe the rain from her face.

"Now, we prepare for war."

Chapter 37

Goodbye

The next day, everyone gathered at Tomyvon Manor for a final time in order to celebrate the two hundred and seventieth wedding anniversary of Yayènia and Suneelo. Erdwyf had insisted that the party take place at her home, for it was the last time it would ever happen. The High Advisor greeted her guests at the front door in a flowing gown of red and silver, her golden hair piled atop her head in elegant spirals. Miazie and Sodo were the first to arrive, then Aladorn and Aidyn. The brothers were, for once, dressed in finery rather than their usual black silks and leathers. The assassin still wore black, but slashes of white and red were visible in the folds of his sleeves, and though he still wore his scimitars, the rest of his weapons were gone, and his boots were tooled in silver. The wiat, however, had decided to be daring, and he wore a white tunic with light gray pants, creating an alluring yet noble vision with his dark features.

After the brothers came Tlonna and Losolin. The monarchs were stunning as usual, the queen in a simple gown of blue velvet and white hem, the king in his normal black and gray. Sargotarh arrived moments later with Orthak on his heels. Finally, once everyone was gathered in the main hall of the manor, Ghealan strode in, resplendent in green silk and black leather, his auburn hair tied back by a leather thong.

"They should be here any moment," the warrior said, grinning. "Erdwyf told them a later time so that they would be last to arrive."

Knowing smiles were passed around the room, as everyone knew of the Tienas' habit of always being the first to turn up. Tlonna moved to stand by her friend.

"Thank you for doing this, Lan. I know it must be hard at this time."

Ghealan sucked in a deep breath. "Well, we could not leave without having one last fête, now could we? Besides, they are our closest and oldest friends. We could not let their anniversary go by unnoticed. Two hundred and seventy years is quite a run, even for elves. Usually couples tire of each other by then, though they cling to each other in order to preserve their lives. Rarely do couples hang on to the love and friendship that Nia and Suneelo have. Even more rarely do they survive the trials those two have gone through."

Tlonna nodded in agreement, though it was a sad truth. "You and Erdwyf have not lost it, though," she said after a moment.

"No, we have not, but our love is made stronger by theirs, and yours and Losolin's. Erdwyf and I will persevere through anything, including this new post, and now we have Jaryikin. As long as we are together, we will make it through."

The Magin started to say something more, but just then Erdwyf entered carrying the child and beaming from pointed ear to pointed ear. "They are in the yard," she announced, causing excited murmurs to rise from the small but close group.

Tlonna moved away from Ghealan to stand next to her husband, linking hands with him. Losolin smiled down at her and tugged her close, happy to be there. After a moment of silence, the door opened and in strode Yayènia and Suneelo, who stopped dead at the gathered people. Equally stunned was the group, who gawked at the High Commander in absolute disbelief and awe.

Yayènia was wearing a dress. It was elegantly cut, with flared hems and thick silver straps crisscrossing the bodice in the style of a corset. The whole thing was dark blue with touches of silver and black inside the jagged hems. Her hair was not in its customary braid either, but lifted by combs and sticks, framing her beautiful face in gold, rippling all the way to the small of her back. She was breathtaking, and no one could stop staring.

The High Commander blushed crimson and tried to turn away, but Suneelo stopped her with a soft smile. He too was in dark blue, though his trousers were black cotton and his boots and belt tooled in silver. Yayènia turned around to face her friends, once more composed, though her lips were thinned in resignation.

"To Suneelo and Yayènia," Erdwyf said suddenly, raising her glass of mulled wine. "May you find love and companionship with each other for another thousand years."

As everyone raised their glasses to the couple, Tlonna could not help but notice the extra gleam to Yayènia's eyes, the telltale sign of wetness. Though the warrior did not allow it to show, her sister knew that she was deeply touched. As everyone moved in to start up conversations, Tlonna stayed back, observing. She had learned things about her friends in the recent weeks and wanted to see if things had changed. Her eyes shifted to Aidyn and Aladorn, who smiled easier and laughed more often, though the assassin still wore about him a cloak of foreboding, as though he was simply waiting for the happiness to fade away. The elf could feel it within the part of her heart that was him. She could push aside the seeming relaxed emotions and reveal the tense, quivering ball of desperate pain. Looking at the dark elf, Tlonna could see it in the way he moved, the straightness of his shoulders, the way his hands clenched and unclenched unconsciously, even the constant shifting of his emerald eyes spoke of readiness.

Next to him stood Sargotarh who also moved with an air of impending action. He was a tall elf, even for his kind, for he stood only an inch shorter the Ghealan, the tallest of them all. Sargotarh had his head bent and was smiling as Yayènia told some tale from her long life. Suddenly the group erupted with laughter, and Tlonna found herself smiling.

"It almost seems as though it will never change," someone said from behind the queen, and she turned to find Erdwyf.

"I wish it did not have to," Tlonna replied sadly, holding her arms out for Jaryikin. Though the child was nearly two years old, she could only walk a few steps and speak a few words, for she was elf-kind, and they matured much slower than humans. It would be another year before she could walk by herself, and yet another before she was fully cognizant.

Erdwyf nodded, her eyes sparkling with tears. "Oh, how I do not want to go, Tlonna. Why did they do this to us?"

"I have no answer, my friend. But know this, you will make a great queen, and Ghealan a great king. You will bring Narnen out of its terrible state and back into prominence. I can feel it."

"Narnen was never prominent," Erdwyf snorted. "It is a small little kingdom known mainly for its ports and fish trade."

"Then turn it into something grand, Erd. You were born to be a ruler of Narnen, and now you have your chance to make it really happen. You left your birthright to come here and be the wife of Ghealan, and now you must go back, and show all of Nymyños that Queen Erdwyf er'Tomyvon will not make her predecessor's mistakes. You have me, Tristan, Barukh, Tyular, and Eyin to stand with, and together we shall reforge the face of this world into something beautiful once more," Tlonna said, her words thick with belief and strength.

"And of the halls I must live in? What of the things we have heard, of the floor turning crimson with the blood of all who lived there? The doors painted red with that same blood? How can I turn such a horrible place into something beautiful?" Erdwyf asked, overwhelmed by the upcoming tasks.

"Did we not do the same here?" Tlonna countered, sweeping her arms out to encompass all of Blackhaven City. "Was not the castle a tomb? Was not your home torn to pieces and left to the elements? Have we not rebuilt this city into twice what it was?"

"Aye, but we were all together, and I must do this alone."

"Not alone, never alone. You will have Ghealan, and I am sending Feorien and his wife, Sharntun with you, as well as three dozen of the castle staff. Daphne is finding someone within the treasury to accompany you, and Narda a seneschal. You will not be alone in this."

"Tlonna, I cannot take them! They have homes here, families and lives!" Erdwyf replied, deeply touched but nervous about such a thing.

The Magin Queen shook her head. "They have all volunteered to stand by your side. Erdwyf, you have been a figurehead in Blackhaven for nearly three centuries. You kept the city alive even during the darkest of hours, and no one looks upon you with disrespect or malice. You are loved, and they are all more than willing to go with you into your new life. I actually had to turn several others down, else there would be none left here," she laughed, bouncing Jaryikin in her arms. "And this one needs to know where she came from."

Erdwyf stammered for words, but suddenly her throat had constricted and she could not find the words to speak. Instead, she pulled Tlonna into a hug, careful not to squash her daughter. Wiping moisture from her eyes, the new Queen of Narnen took a deep, shaky breath. "Ghealan does not want to go."

"Nor do you," Tlonna replied.

The fey-faced elf smiled. "True, but he was born here, grew up here, loves everything here…Yayènia is here."

"And you will be there," Tlonna said, "which is where he would rather be. By your side in a foreign kingdom. Trust me, the elf loves you more than life itself, and Yayènia loves Suneelo. It is high time for the four of you to get over something that happened three hundred years ago."

Erdwyf blushed at the ridiculousness of the issue, and finally nodded. "We have been foolish."

"Yes you have, though I understand."

"Then, it is time to celebrate a love stronger than our foolishness," Erdwyf stated, and, taking her daughter, moved to mingle.

Again Tlonna stood alone, but she caught eyes with Suneelo, who gave her a knowing smile and lifted his glass to salute her. The queen mimicked him, and she downed the rest of her wine. The party lasted well into the night with much laughter, dancing, toasts, and drinking. Even the elves felt slightly askew as they left Tomyvon Manor, though they soon sobered as they said goodbyes to Erdwyf and Ghealan, realizing what it meant.

When they arrived home, Yayènia and Suneelo rushed up the stairs and into their bedroom, trying to forget their sadness and revel in their years together. The captain, however, gently pushed his half-clad wife away and smiled wickedly, turning to open the chest at the foot of their bed.

"I have something for you," he said gently, lifting the music sphere and holding it out to her.

Yayènia's breath caught in her throat as she stared at the gently swirling rose orb, taking it from Suneelo with trembling hands. "What is it?"

"It is called a music sphere, here," he replied, and placed his hand on the top, pressing slightly.

Music filled the room, a large orchestra piece called *Love of the Warrior*. Piano and violin cascaded over each other in soft waves, backed by flutes and horns and a single deep drum. It was one of Yayènia's favorites, and tears spilled down her face as she stared at her husband.

"Suneelo…" she breathed, unaware of the unusual display of emotion.

The male found himself on his back, his wife's fingers hastily removing his belt and yanking down his pants. Yayènia kissed him deeply, pressing against him as though trying to actually merge. She felt his thumbs wipe away her tears and more came as she realized just how much she loved him, how much she needed him.

"I love you," Suneelo breathed, as though reading her mind.

Yayènia pulled away from him in order to look him in the eyes, her arms braced on either side of his neck. The violet hue of his eyes seemed brighter to her than ever before, and she noticed the thin white scar running from his temple to his eyebrow. Running one finger along the mark, Yayènia smiled sadly down at him.

"You have been hurt so many times, often because of me. I remember when you got this," she whispered, taking a breath. "You pushed me out of the way of an arrow, and it caught you here. I would have died if not for that."

"You would have come back to me, as you always have," Suneelo murmured, taking her hand away from his scar and kissing it. "And if you do not, I will follow you. To the ends of anywhere, I will follow you."

Yayènia pressed against him again, running her lips along his collarbone. "I will always come back," she sighed.

Suneelo wrapped his arms around her and they made love as the music sphere serenaded them in the background.

The next day dawned foggy and gray, the vegetation gleaming with dew. A clipper ship waded in the harbor, the black and silver pennants of Blackhaven hanging limply in the still air. Erdwyf stood before the gangplank wrapped in a thick cloak. Behind her stood everyone, their faces somber and drawn with grief. Only Ghealan stood apart, his green eyes red-rimmed from crying. He planted a kiss on his daughter's head and handed her to Erdwyf with obvious reluctance. The female then handed Jaryikin to a maid and threw herself into Ghealan's arms, sobbing into his broad chest.

Everyone watching averted their eyes and sought each other's hands, needing the reassurance of their company. Finally, Erdwyf tore herself away from Ghealan and walked over to her beloved friends. She went first to Aladorn, and then moved to Aidyn, Miazie, Sodo, Suneelo, Yayènia, whom she embraced the longest, then to Tlonna and Losolin. With each person she cried harder, clinging to their familiar faces and presences with everything she had. Then suddenly, the horn of the ship was blown and there was no time left.

Erdwyf once more took Jaryikin into her arms and slowly walked up the plank and stood upon the deck. As the sails caught wind, she raised her hand in a final farewell, and her friends and family left upon the dock waved back, tears staining their faces as they said goodbye.

Chapter 38

At Long Last

The following morning was as overcast as the previous, and the occupants of the city awakened feeling miserable. There was no breeze, and the forest lay heavy with frost as the early stirrings of life began to fill the great city. Tlonna leaned out over the city-facing balcony of her apartment and closed her eyes, trying to will away all the terrible things that had happened recently. Behind her, Losolin was combing out the snarls in his wet hair, the moisture falling down to land on his bare chest and race to his belt. He sighed with resignation and nodded to Coran, who was holding up a dark red shirt of suede and black leather laces that fell to his navel.

"Choose your battles, my lord," the man said lightly, trying not to reveal his triumphant grin.

"I try, Coran, I try," Losolin sighed, allowing himself to be dressed.

When the man tried to undo the elf's belt in order to tuck in the shirt, Losolin batted his hands away and pointed toward the door. Coran chuckled, but he followed orders and left the king in peace. Shaking his head, the elf readjusted his belt, leaving the shirt untucked, and went to stand behind Tlonna.

"The man is going to drive me mad one day," he muttered, wrapping his arms around her shoulders.

"And you him," Tlonna replied, twisting in his arms so that she faced him. "He does know what he is doing."

Losolin frowned at her. "I do not care. I like my clothes how I like them, not how he does. I am the flaming king!"

"Yet you are a peasant at heart," Tlonna laughed, noting his language. "I do think you look good with your shirt tucked in, but this works as well, I suppose."

Losolin grunted, but he silenced her next words with a kiss. Their embrace was suddenly interrupted by a blasting horn, the clarion ring breaking the heavy silence of the morning. The king and queen spun apart and stared outward, their eyes going immediately to the far eastern gate. Another three blasts ran out, and Tlonna turned to look at her husband with cold eyes.

"They are here," she said simply.

"At long last," Losolin replied, and they moved back inside, calling in their dressers to help them don their armor.

Twenty minutes later, they stepped out of their room and descended the spiraling stairs that coiled to the very bottom of the tower. Once they reached the bottom, the couple strode through the doorway leading to the foyer of the castle and found Yayènia waiting for them, armed and armored, her shoulders back and her feet spread.

"The Seadueni have finally reached the gate, and are making camp about three miles east and north. No word yet of their reinforcements, but from what Arganor told me, they are expecting thousands more from Zaedic and Talenias," the warrior said immediately. "And Aladorn was right in his assumption of both an attack by land and sea. We will be pressed on all fronts."

Tlonna nodded. "They must have regained a lot of forces from wherever their reinforcements came from, though. And an attack by both land and sea, that will be hard to defend against. Nia, how is the Black Armada coming along?"

"Slow. Sailors are flocking in, but we only have two available ships, besides the ones already in use as temporaries, and nowhere near enough time to build more. I only thought of it a few days ago, remember?" the High Commander replied.

Tlonna sighed. "Yes, I know. I guess I was just hoping something might go right for once. How is your foot?"

Yayènia frowned and then realization dawned on her face. "It was nothing I could not handle."

Losolin swore. "You took a bloody crossbow quarrel through your foot. You are not invincible, Nia."

"I had my throat slit, and I can still talk and walk, can I not?

When neither of her friends responded, the warrior rolled her eyes. "I am fine. Trust me."

Tlonna nodded and said, "What of Erdwyf? Do you think her ship will be attacked?"

Yayènia's head snapped up, her eyes going wide at the possibility. After a moment, she shook her head. "No. If they are coming from anywhere other than Narnen, or Purheae, the ships will not cross paths. And our clipper is much faster than those wallowing white ships of Zaedic, or the thin triremes of Seaduens. If nothing else, she can always simply run over the trireme."

The queen nodded, pushing the horrid thought from her mind. "What now?" she asked after a moment.

The warrior gave her an odd look. "We kill them."

Tlonna folded her arms. "I am aware of the basic point of war, Yayènia."

Losolin put his hand on her shoulder and massaged it gently, but the High Commander's face turned so furious for a second they both stepped back.

When she spoke, her voice was callous and dripping with hatred. "Stoffnias wants an immediate audience with you, but I will not let him through the gate. Isadorr shot one of Suneelo's guards through the head. What do you want me to do?"

Tlonna closed her eyes for a brief respite. "What damage would it do to let him and his sons through?"

"Not too much, I think. Even if the traitor demands to bring an armed escort, my Silvers would accompany them at all times. I just do not want him in my city. The last time he and his sons were here, it caused death, and it marked the beginning of your departure. I do not like the idea of them being anywhere near you...or me."

"Nia, Losolin and I are not going anywhere. We are more powerful and have more knowledge now than we did ten years ago. I do not fear him, or his army, and I know you do not," Tlonna tapped her fingers against her lips. "It would have to be formal, with your *Zephyr Leifen* watching them at all times. I want you, Suneelo, and Ghealan there."

"Which room?"

"Throne room?"

"No, too big. Too much chance of an attack," Yayènia muttered.

"Then, the formal reception room. It is big, but not nearly as big as the throne room. It will give no cause for insult, but small enough to make the presence of your warriors a deadly threat. What do you think?"

Yayènia unconsciously rubbed at her scar, running possible scenarios through her mind. "It would be the safest, I think, other than standing above the wall and shouting down at the bleeding cowards."

Tlonna smiled slightly. "Then I will expect them in...an hour?"

"I will get to the gate, then."

The elves bid each other goodbye and went in separate directions. Tlonna and Losolin to find Miazie, and Yayènia to the stables to get her remaining horse, Udu, the massive dun stallion she'd ridden at Alchemian.

Minutes later, the king and queen were striding down the fourth floor corridor, when Aidyn stepped out of his room, looking deadly in his assassin's garb, his scimitars and longsword settled in place like extra limbs. "What is it?" he asked, rubbing his hand over his heart and looking pointedly at Tlonna.

"The Lostugs want an audience," she replied coolly, ignoring Losolin's grunt.

"And you granted it?" the assassin gaped, astonished.

The Magin shrugged. "Why not? What true harm can they do to us? And what sort of precedent would I set if I refused? Surely not a good one."

Aidyn looked to Losolin, but the king merely shook his head. Tlonna let out a breath. "Will you come?"

The assassin eyed her for a moment, remembering his last encounter with the Seadueni king. "It is my duty," he said finally. "I will get Aladorn."

"Very well. We were going to find Miazie."

Aidyn stopped in his tracks. "Are you sure that is a good idea? After what the bastards put her through, one would think she would want to stay as far away as possible."

Tlonna nodded. "Aye, but she is my High Advisor now, and I believe she would like to at least be given a choice. I will not force her to come."

Satisfied, the assassin moved toward his brother's room as the couple continued on toward the Belau's apartment. She answered their knock immediately, already dressed in formal attire, with Sodo tightening his belt behind her.

"First day on the job and it's a bloody war," the human said, holding the door open for them.

Tlonna and Losolin did not move, but they both stared at her, unsure of what to say. Finally, the queen blurted out the message. "Stoffnias and his sons have been granted an audience. If you so choose, you may sit it out, but you are also welcome to come."

Sodo's head snapped up and he glared at Tlonna, though he said nothing. Miazie's face was frozen into a dumbfounded expression, her eyes wide. After a moment, she took a shuddering breath. "I will come."

"Miazie!" Sodo exclaimed, coming to stand behind her. "Are you sure that is wise?"

The human shrugged halfheartedly. "It is my job, correct?"

"But no job is worth this! Please reconsider," the alchemist pleaded, placing his hands on her waist.

Miazie shook her head. "If I cannot face them now, how will I be able to face them in the future? No one should be able to hold such power over me."

Tlonna smiled faintly and moved aside as the couple departed their room. "Aidyn and Aladorn will be there as well," she said.

The Belau nodded in acknowledgment, though her insides were churning at the thought of meeting the elves who had so misused her. She self-consciously adjusted the armband that for so long had been Erdwyf's, and straightened her spine in defiance. Just as they reached the stairs, Aidyn and Aladorn caught up to them, and the six made their way to the second floor.

They entered the formal reception room and took their places on the dais. The chairs were not thrones, but were high-backed enough to be imposing. Suneelo, Ghealan, and Yayènia were waiting for them, armed to the teeth. Tlonna gave them an uncertain laugh.

"Do you think they are that much of a threat?"

None of them even cracked a smile. Suneelo bowed his head slightly. "We are taking no chances with these turncoats."

Ghealan nodded in agreement.

"The Silvers are bringing the contingent up the Way now," Yayènia added, playing with her left katan hilt.

"Good," Tlonna replied as she leaned her head against the chair back and closed her eyes. "I am a little worried. I fear that this may be a large mistake. I do not remember the last time, but the dreams I have had are not pleasant."

"That is because these people are not pleasant, Tlonna," Miazie snapped before she could stop herself.

Yayènia sent the human a ferocious grin, and the friends settled in to wait, hiding their individual nervousness. Aidyn and Aladorn stood to the right of Tlonna's chair, Yayènia slightly off to one side. Ghealan and Suneelo were to the left of Losolin's, and Sodo stood behind Miazie's, his tainted eyes hard. Few words were spoken during the seemingly interminable wait, but less than ten minutes later a thump outside the door announced the arrival of the Seadueni contingent. The herald's voice was heard through the thick doors.

"Announcing King Stoffnias, Crown Prince Isadorr, and Prince Gothier of Seaduens, and their royal company."

The double doors opened and three richly clad elves strode in looking about in a superior manner. Behind them crowded fifty retainers and the *Zephyr Leifen*, the guards glancing uneasily at the warriors standing stolidly beside them.

King Stoffnias, a regal elf of massive build and auburn locks bowed ever so slightly to Tlonna and Losolin. He then glared openly at the couple. Behind him, his sons sneered at the gathered council, the elder leering at Miazie in an open insult.

"Expecting an attack, Queen Tlonna?"

"Is this not one? Perhaps I have misread your army camped outside my walls?" Tlonna replied coolly, reclining in her chair.

Stoffnias chuckled. "There will not be a war if you cede to my conditions."

"And what conditions would that be?" Losolin asked, sitting forward to lace his fingers loosely between his knees.

Stoffnias looked furious at Losolin, as if unable to believe he would speak to him. "The conditions are thus: you will open your gates to my men. You will accept me as your liege, and name Gothier your heir. You will rule as regent until I decide he is ready to assume the crown. Do not accept these terms, and your city will be destroyed, far worse than before."

There was a tense silence before Tlonna burst out laughing. "You expect me to accept these heinous conditions? Are you mental? What sort of ruler would just hand over her kingdom to blood traitors and murderers? No."

Stoffnias had the decency to look taken aback. His sons looked murderous. "Then, you will all die."

This time it was Yayènia who snorted with laughter. "Stoffnias, we have many times your men, many times your skill, and many times your intelligence, not to mention supplies. Do not pretend that you can win, even if you do have Zaedic backing you. We have defeated them twice, we will defeat them again. Now, I think it in your best interest if you leave this land and never come back."

The king shook with rage. "How dare you, how dare you? You speak to me as if you are equal to me? You are nothing but a maniacal soldier with big swords. I do not fear you."

Yayènia sneered and moved so fast everyone gasped when she appeared at Stoffnias's back, holding a dagger to his throat. "Too bad."

Gothier and Isadorr pulled their swords and put them to Yayènia's back, and the guards found themselves staring down the swords of the Silvers. Tlonna rose slowly from her seat.

She advanced down the steps until she stood eye to eye with the fuming king. "Your presence here, in my home, is an insult. We will meet you on the field of battle...and you will die."

Tlonna pivoted and strode out of the room, Suneelo on her heels as guard. Losolin remained seated, chin on fist. "Ghealan, will you disarm the princes?"

"Of course," the Second Commander deftly twisted the swords out of the younger elves' grasps and knocked them to the ground for good measure.

The brothers attempted to rise but Ghealan planted a boot in the back of Isadorr and a sword to Gothier's. Stoffnias's face turned crimson.

"You make a mistake, peasant boy. I have often dreamed of taking your life as you did my son's. You will pay, boy, and your life will be the price."

Losolin lifted the corner of his mouth in a mocking smile. "Is that so? You do not seem to be doing too well, right now." The smile disappeared. "King Stoffnias, you are my enemy, and will die as such. You insult my High Commander, allow your sons to draw weapons in my castle, and threaten my people. You have already lost one son, do you wish to lose the other two in battle? We will give no quarter, no mercy, if you march against us, you will die. You have one day to remove your troops from my land, or pay with blood."

The older king's face went from crimson to sheet white and then back again before he spoke. "My men will take your city tomorrow."

Yayènia made a disgusted noise, withdrew her blade from his neck, and shoved him forward. "Get the bloody nine hells out of my sight."

Ghealan allowed Isadorr and Gothier to stand and then yanked them around so that they faced the door. "Get them out of here."

The *Zephyr Leifen* bowed as one and escorted the entourage out of the reception room. Gothier started to follow them out but his older brother grabbed his sleeve and held him back. Stoffnias gifted a furious glower on all of the Blackhavenites assembled.

"You will all pay for your impertinence. When you are under my rule, you will be stripped of title, rank, pay, and lands. You will serve me as slaves. King Sithian has also demanded that you," he jabbed a finger at Yayènia, "are to be his personal slave."

"Is that so?" Yayènia replied running a finger along her dagger's blade. "Perhaps when he is done with me, he will turn his attentions on your wife. I hear he has a thing for whores."

Stoffnias lunged forward but came up short when the warrior slammed a naked fist into his mouth. The king reeled backward a step and then wiped the back of his hand across his bloody lips. "Tomorrow, you will pay dearly, bitch."

The three strode out of the room as Yayènia shook the blood off her knuckles. "Turncoat bastard."

"Aye," Miazie said as she grabbed her friend's hand and examined it. "You got blood on your shirt."

Yayènia looked down at the splotch of crimson staining the hem of her blue tunic. "Damnation. Sayoir is going to yell at me."

"Sayoir?" Losolin asked, grinning.

"My maid, from Zeynuwn, remember?"

"I am sure you will be fine, Nia," Miazie said, releasing the warrior's hand.

Yayènia snorted and then turned to Ghealan. "Can you get the troops into the barracks? I am going to run to the harbor and see what I can do there."

The Second Commander nodded. "Yeah, sure. When can we expect you?"

Yayènia shrugged. "Two or three hours should get me there. Stoffnias knows we know he wants to attack at dawn, therefore, he might attack as soon as he gets back to his camp. Try to catch us off guard, so we need to be ready if that happens. I think Suneelo has a lot of men up at the wall, so we will not be totally caught off guard."

Ghealan rubbed his chin, eyeing his oldest friend. "As you wish."

Yayènia watched her friend and partner for a few silent seconds before grabbing his elbow. "Lan...Lan you can stay here, if you want. You have a lot to lose, if you die. You have a family and Jaryikin is old enough now to be able to remember you. I would not want Erdwyf to worry."

Ghealan placed one big hand on Yayènia's cheek and then cupped her chin. "You too, have a family, Nia. And I know you will not stand aside, so why should I? Am I not your second? Am I not the person you are supposed to depend upon? What good would I do cooped up here? No. I fight by your side, as always. Besides, this is the last time we fight together as partners. How could I miss it?"

With a sniff, Yayènia embraced Ghealan, their weapons clanking against each other.

The harbor was unusually quiet. The sailors were all on deck waiting for orders, the shops closed, and their owners home within the city proper. Yayènia walked alone, her boots ringing off the cobblestone street, the only one in the city, as the grass weave was prone to mold in close proximity to the ocean. The High Commander allowed herself the luxury of limping. The stars shone brightly in the sky, the moons casting colored shadows on the silent harbor. Only one building was alight, and Yayènia knocked on the door before striding in. Harbor Master Jamìn looked up and smiled.

"High Commander Yayènia, what a surprise!"

"Indeed, Jamìn. I have some dire news."

The miniscule man tilted his head to the side as he waited. "Of the Seadueni?"

"Aye, and more. Zaedic is coming, Harbor Master. Land and sea. I had hoped to have the Black Armada up and running before the next battle, but time is up. Can you pull the chains?"

Jamìn's face went from worried to terrified. "The chains, High Commander? They have not been used in-in many years. Before even you were born, my lady."

Yayènia lounged against a pole in the center of the room. "Have they not been maintained?"

"Oh, they have been maintained, but Lady, what of those still coming? Of *The Silver Crest* and *Zaedic's Bane*? They have not reached port yet, and they would be destroyed."

"Raise them Harbor Master. Send a bird to Alexander and Troaz and hope to the gods they reach them in time. The corsairs know war, they will deal with it," Yayènia said coldly, staring down at the human.

Jamìn bowed low. "As you say, High Commander."

"Good," Yayènia pivoted and strode out of the building and immediately resumed her limping. She hadn't yet taken the time to fully heal her foot from the crossbow bolt.

Above, a lantern was lit in the bell tower of the harbor offices. The elf climbed onto one of the main dock lantern posts and watched as harbor workers rushed toward the two sandbars that curled into the ocean like arms about to embrace a lover. The massive obsidian walls that sat atop them gleamed in torchlight as men rushed to the ends. A few minutes later, they reached the end of the sandbars and a low vibrating rumble echoed across the dark water.

Yayènia watched solemnly as three massive chains slowly rose from the depths of the ocean, each sporting several enormous balls of iron studded with spikes. Sailors rushed to the decks to stare out across the deep to see what was making the noise and the vibrations. Yayènia heard the deep clunk that meant the chains had been locked in place and were now strung across the mouth of the harbor, just above the surface of the water, invisible until it was too late for oncoming ships.

She was a small jump down from reaching the dock street when an arrow thudded into her shoulder. Crying out, Yayènia fell the rest of the way and then clamped a hand to the wound. Gasping, she broke the shaft off and got to her feet. Spinning around, she yanked a dagger out and held it before her. Figures appeared in the dark like wraiths, each holding weapons in both hands. Yayènia searched in the dark for a face she knew, but saw only foreign faces and grim expressions.

"Who are you? What do you want?"

Someone chuckled. "Our master is very upset with you. Very upset."

Yayènia rolled her eyes. "And who is your master?"

"Someone much greater than you."

"Wonderful. What is your master's name?"

"His name is too perfect to be heard by peasants like you."

A snort escaped the warrior. "So you do not know the name of your master. I wonder if it is Stoffnias or Sithian. Either one have reason to kill me. It just saddens me that they are too afraid of me to come after me by themselves."

"Shut up bitch!" One of her attackers lunged forward.

Yayènia stepped forward, brought the heel of her hand up into his nose, kicked his knee backward with such force it snapped, and then slammed her other elbow into the soft spot where neck joins shoulder. The man gurgled as he died. The others attacked her, two of them swinging low, the others high. Yayènia leaned back to avoid the crushing blows coming toward her face, accepting the hits to her legs. She went down on one knee, feigning injury, one hand clutching the side of her boot.

Someone stepped in close to finish her off, but she lunged suddenly, driving her boot dagger into his groin and twisting between his legs, coming up behind the attackers. Yayènia leapt in the air, spinning her leg out and whipped her foot into the two closest faces. Their heads snapped to one side as she landed, drawing forth her katans. One blade went low, the other high and she twisted, remembering for a moment as she did how Aidyn had countered this very move in Kajgenia. Luckily, none of her assailants were anywhere near the assassin's skill, and her blades carved deep arcing lines into two more of the thugs.

With four down and two severely injured, only three remained. Yayènia skittered back, grimacing as she stepped hard on her wounded foot. She brought her right blade up to parry a cutlass coming for her exposed midriff and danced the left around to fend off the scimitar coming for her neck. With her feet, she kept the third man at bay, leaping and spinning about, kicking her legs out, connecting solidly several times. He reeled backward, clutching at his shattered breastbone, finding it hard to draw breath. With one more powerful blow, Yayènia slammed the heel of her boot into his chest, shoving the process into the diaphragm. With him out of the fight, she focused on the two swordsmen circling around her.

With a lightning quick set of jabs, the elf knocked the left blade out and up high so that she could step inside his guard. Yayènia spun and slammed her right katan into his chest with a hard backhand thrust, keeping her left sword out in front of her to fend off the remaining attacker. He dived to the side and came up with a dagger in his other hand.

"Who sent you? You must have known this to be a suicide mission," the High Commander said casually, circling with him.

"Think you and your assassin friend can torture the answer out of me?" came the snide reply, though his voice did quaver a bit.

Yayènia shrugged nonchalantly. "I do not see why I would need to do that. You are not the first group to be sent against me, and certainly will not be the last. I am not really all that concerned by your puppeteer. I will just search your body for clues once you are dead."

The man came forward in an angry rush, swinging his sword in and low while sweeping his dagger out to block. Yayènia danced back, not really pushed but interested by the fight. He jerked his sword up and came at her again, bringing it down at an angle. The elf knocked his parrying dagger away with her katan, keeping it out wide. The man rushed her again, trying to keep her off balance, but the warrior sidestepped and let him pass, not even bothering to hit him as he went by. He staggered slightly, surprised to find himself facing empty air, but turned immediately, his eyes wide. He instinctively brought his sword up to block a thrust that was not coming.

Yayènia stood in the same spot, watching him with narrowed eyes. "Whoever sent you did not intend for you to survive. You nor any of your partners have the skill necessary to take me down. So either you are a distraction, or sad waste of time."

"Or simply something to snag the wheel," was the unexpected reply and the man rushed her once more, but he veered off at the last moment and slammed his side into her, knocking her off the dock.

As she fell toward the water, Yayènia drew forth a throwing knife and saw the man clutch at his throat. Then she hit, and had other things to think about.

"Where in the nine hells is Yayènia?" Ghealan demanded of Tlonna as he stormed into her bedroom.

Losolin poked his head around a folding screen and scowled. "Do you bloody well mind, Ghealan?"

"No, I do not! Where is Yayènia? No one has seen her since early last night. Master Jamìn said she left about an hour after midnight, said she had the chains ordered up and then left. It is daybreak, and she has not returned. Suneelo said she did not come home last night, nor did she return here. She is not at the barracks either, or the gate. Something is wrong."

Tlonna finished putting on her gauntlets and reached for her helmet. "What do you think happened?"

The Second Commander sighed. "I do not know. I do not like this, Tlonna. Something is wrong."

The queen echoed his sigh. "All right Ghealan. You head to the gate, command the troops. I will go to the docks and look about. We will find her, Lan, do not worry."

He gave a short nod of his head and strode out of the room. Tlonna looked at Losolin who shrugged and yanked his cloak out from underneath a spare cuirass.

The sounds of battle rang out over the city to reach the harbor as the couple headed for the docks once more to find Yayènia. Few people roamed the cobblestone street, but several people were standing around a lamppost, muttering darkly. When Tlonna, Losolin, and their guards moved toward them, they parted without a word of command. Within the ring of people lay nine men, all of them dead.

"Yayènia's cuts," Losolin said, bending over two who seemed to have fallen at the same time, arcing slices curving across their chests and thighs. "They died from bleeding out, both the femoral artery and the aortic arch have been severed. Only she knows how to do that."

Only one of the corpses was facing toward the water, a dagger, carved with the head of a badger, stuck in his throat.

"Yayènia's," Tlonna said, pulling the throwing knife free. "From the direction the blade landed, it was thrown..." she walked a straight line from the man until she stood at the very edge of the stone dock.

Losolin came to stand next to her and they gazed out over the calm harbor waters. "Does Yayènia know how to swim?" he asked quietly.

Tlonna shrugged and began removing her armor. When the guards came over in a rush, she held out her hand. "I will go in, and you will stay right here. Understood?"

"But, my Queen, we cannot allow you to place yourself in such danger," one of them countered, looking frightened.

"Do you want to be the one to find the High Commander in what is probably going to be a *very* bad mood?" Tlonna asked calmly, though she was secretly terrified she would find her sister's body, trapped beneath the water by the weight of her armor.

The guards backed away and Tlonna nodded once, kicking off her boots. Then she dived gracefully into the cold waters of the Fãrthyn Ocean. It did not take her long to find Yayènia, for the warrior was clinging to dock post some ways away, unconscious. The warrior had taken her sword belt and tied it around the post and one shoulder to keep her head above the lapping water, but had not been able to pull herself up with the added weight of her weapons and armor, along with the arrow wound in her other shoulder.

Carefully, Tlonna removed Yayènia's weapons and tossed them upon the deck several feet above them. Then she untied her sister and grunted as the surprising weight began to pull her down. Cursing under her breath, the queen strapped Yayènia back to the post and began removing her armor, also tossing it above her head. She was tugging on the warrior's left greave when she heard the horns blaring in the distance. Tlonna poked her head further above the water and gasped in a frustrated and dismayed breath. The white ships of Zaedic had appeared on the horizon not too far away, and as they were out away from the main docks, Tlonna and Yayènia were in a sore spot indeed.

Giving up on the greave, the queen untied her sister once more and, groaning with the effort, lifted her above her shoulder. Yayènia lay limp against her, breathing steady but shallowly. Tlonna gritted her teeth and dug her fingers into the wood of the post, Weaving strands of Air to help boost them. She would have Woven a ladder, but she did not have the ability to move her hands in the precise way, being rather encumbered in the water, so she settled for the boost. Several difficult minutes later, she had Yayènia on her back gasping in air.

"You look like death itself," Tlonna mumbled, helping her stand.

"Thank you," the High Commander said, swiftly donning her armor and weapons. "And thank you."

Tlonna smiled. "You are welcome. Who was it?" she asked.

"I do not know. Said they were doing their master's bidding. I would say Sithian or Stoffnias. Either one has sufficient reasons to want me dead. I have had a nasty habit of killing their family members."

"Losolin killed Stoffnias's son."

"He had five sons. Now he has two," Yayènia replied, took a step, and stumbled. Cursing, she focused her mind. Her head snapped up as the horns sounded again.

"How long has the attack been going on?"

"Since about four this morning. Zaedic's ships are almost to the harbor," Tlonna replied.

"What? We need to go. If any of the ships make it through, the harbor will be the first to fall," Yayènia said, looking about for a way to get off the floating dock.

Tlonna pointed as a small boat rowed out to them, Losolin sitting in the prow. Once aboard, they turned swiftly back toward the docks, and the anxiously waiting guards. There they sprinted back to city proper, leaving behind a large contingent of archers.

Arrows flew everywhere. Sailors on the Blackhaven ships were shouting back and forth to each other as the whitewashed ships of Zaedic approached the invisible chains. With a horrible crack, the first ship rammed into the chain, directly on top of one of the studded balls. The ship groaned and then splintered down the center.

"Move!" Yayènia commanded, and they moved.

They made it back to the castle and barred the Harbor Gate tight behind them after making sure one of the guards keeping watch had a way to open it for a retreat, if necessary.

"I need to go to my house. Get my armor dried and clean off a bit," the warrior said as the three reached the stables.

"We will go with you. Do not argue with me!" Tlonna snapped when Yayènia started to shake her head.

They made it to Tiena Manor and Yayènia let them in. The servants rushed their mistress, but she gathered them all into a room and addressed them.

"I want you all to leave for the castle, now. When you get there, go to my apartment and lock yourself in. Sayoir, you know where it is?"

"Yes my lady," the Zeynuwnian girl said morosely.

"Do not despair my friends. This is not my first battle, and we are more prepared now than we ever were. It will be fine. Go, now."

The twenty odd people bowed to their employer and left. Yayènia nodded to Tlonna and the queen followed her into her and Suneelo's bedchamber.

"I have never been in here before," Tlonna said in wonder as she looked around.

"Is it so surprising?" Yayènia asked, pumping water into a large basin.

"Well...a little," Tlonna admitted.

The walls were the same sandstone of the rest of building, and in the middle, a massive canopy bed that rivaled even Tlonna and Losolin's. What surprised her, though, was the almost complete absence of weapons. Tlonna chuckled when she saw the painting of Yayènia pulling back a bow, her eyes aimed on a target out of the picture. What made her chuckle was the picture next to it was one of Suneelo crouching with a shield before him, roaring as something blasted by him. It appeared that Yayènia had just fired at her husband and was preparing to do so again. Obviously the artist had not intended for the pictures to be hung together, but the couple had found a great bit of humor in them. Above a large fireplace was a portrait of Yayènia and Suneelo. Yayènia wore a floor length wedding gown that spread out behind her while Suneelo wore black pants and coat embroidered with dark blue.

The only weapon in the room was a large recurve bow hung on the wall next to the fireplace.

"That was Suneelo's grandfather's," Yayènia said, pointing to the bow.

"He must have been a powerful fellow," Tlonna replied.

"Yes, he was. Why is my room surprising?" Yayènia asked, turning back to her basin of water.

Tlonna shrugged. "You and Suneelo are warriors, and the rest of your house is decorated with weapons, flags, armor, and artwork from battles. It is odd to see the most personal of your rooms as very delicate and comfortable. It is a room I could live in."

Yayènia's laugh was gurgled due to the fact she had her face in water. "Are you saying Suneelo and I are bad decorators?" she said when she surfaced.

"Of course not! I like your bedroom, it is just hard to see you and Suneelo sleeping in it."

"Among other things, we do indeed sleep in it."

Tlonna grinned. "Well...with such a big bed I do not wonder."

Yayènia finished washing and Tlonna helped her don her armor. Looking thoroughly exhausted and sore, but much better, the High Commander started placing her weapons back on her person.

"Come on, then," Yayènia said and then put her hands on her hips.

Tlonna was staring at the wedding portrait in wonder. The warrior came to stand next to her queen, gazing up at her own face.

"You both look so beautiful," the Magin said after a while.

Yayènia nodded. "Aye, but it was a long time ago."

"Do you remember it?"

"Of course. Like it happened yesterday. We both do," Yayènia replied, moving her gaze to Suneelo's beaming face. "I even remember how he proposed to me. He was so nervous," she laughed.

Tlonna looked at her sister in a new light. A female in love, even after two hundred years and more. "How did he do it?"

Yayènia turned and guided Tlonna out of her room by the elbow. "I will tell you on the way to the wall."

When they reached Losolin in the foyer of the manor and had remounted their horses, Tlonna looked at Yayènia expectantly, the High Commander sighed.

"It was Erdwyf's birthday and we threw a celebration. There was a ball, and contests, all manner of things. Suneelo and I...escaped...into the garden and got to it."

Losolin grinned at Neñyos's head. "I take it this is how you got engaged?"

Yayènia nodded.

The king grinned even wider. "It must run in the family."

Tlonna snorted. "Just because you shouted it at me in the middle of your peak does not mean your brother did. Perhaps he had a little more finesse?" she directed the question at her sister.

Yayènia was laughing so hard she nearly fell out of her saddle. Udu snorted. "That is how you proposed?" she guffawed at Losolin.

The male colored. "The first time."

"You said no?" Yayènia asked incredulously.

Tlonna nodded. "I was not going to say yes until he did it correctly. Imagine it, Nia. Really."

The High Commander collapsed into peals of laughter. It took her almost an entire minute to compose herself. "Well, yes, I suppose. Anyway, *afterward*," she said with a pointed look at Losolin, "when we were *finished*, he got all nervous and fidgety. Put his pants on backward, I think. When I had put them back on myself, I asked him what was wrong. If I remember correctly he said some very embarrassingly squishy things and then whispered 'will you marry me' in my ear, and ran off."

Losolin glared at Tlonna. "At least I did not run away."

"No, but you were all sweaty and laying on top of me," Tlonna replied primly.

Yayènia snorted. The queen motioned for her to go on.

"Well, once I found him shaking like a leaf and telling it all to Ghealan, I said yes. Then we went to my apartment in the castle, where I lived, and Erdwyf claims she could hear us in her apartment, but I think she is lying."

Tlonna chuckled, but she could see Yayènia at the corner of her eye. Her face was soft, and her eyes were looking toward the wall where Suneelo would be commanding his guard.

"Losolin finally got dressed and actually went to one knee. He too was shaking rather hard, as if there was any doubt," Tlonna said softly, meeting her husband's smiling gaze over Yayènia's head.

The High Commander was silent for a moment, then sighed. "I figured it was something romantic like that. I rather like the first one."

"Me too," Losolin said heartily.

Then they reached the wall.

Chapter 39

The Machine

Booms echoed in the air along with the screams and shouts of soldiers as the trio dismounted before the gates. Yayènia casually walked Udu over to the hitching post by the gatehouse and loosely wrapped the warhorse's reins around the wood. Tlonna and Losolin followed her, donning their helmets. The High Commander rolled her shoulders a bit and winced, reminding Tlonna that the female was recovering from a very long, difficult night.

"Are you sure you are up to this?" she quietly asked her sister.

Yayènia nodded, perhaps a little more hesitant than usual, but still quickly. "I ache, and feel as though I have been running nonstop for days, but adrenaline should take care of that, soon," she said, tugging her gauntlets tighter. "And I can feel the ache diminishing quick enough. Being a Maig comes in handy, sometimes."

Losolin lifted an eyebrow at his sister-in-law, but said nothing as they climbed the stairs to the wall. Soldiers bowed their heads respectfully as they passed, but did not stop whatever they were doing. Silver cloaks flashing in the sunlight announced the presence of *Zephyr Leifen* at the crenellations as well. Yayènia stopped for a moment as she reached the wall, looking around, ignoring the multitude of attacking elves and men on the ground. She spotted her husband and made for him.

Tlonna and Losolin followed her, watching the lines of Seadueni soldiers. When they reached Suneelo, the Captain of the Guard looked around for whoever had tugged on his sleeve and then saw his wife. With a relieved cry, the male grabbed Yayènia's face and kissed her quite vigorously. The militiamen who saw hooted and laughed as their leaders embraced. Tlonna and Losolin grinned, but their eyes strayed to the ground. Wave upon wave of Seadueni crashed against the wall and gate, shooting arrows up at the great wall, though most fell short. The booms they had heard were coming from cloaked figures deep in the tree line. Magins. Tlonna snarled and lifted her hands, but Losolin grabbed her wrist and shook his head.

"No. We do not want them to know you are here, yet," he shouted.

Grudgingly, Tlonna let her hands fall and pulled off her bow. "One more bow will not alert them to me, though."

Losolin nodded and let his wife go, looking around for Ghealan. The Second Commander was standing a hundred yards away from them and had not noticed their or Yayènia's presence. Losolin moved toward him, weaving through the anxious soldiers moving back and forth on the wall in order to keep a constant volley of arrows raining down on their antagonists. The older elf looked down from his spot on a rear crenellation that allowed him a better view of the forces and saw the king. He jumped down and stalked close.

"Did you find her? Is she alive? Where is she?" he demanded, shaking Losolin a bit.

The male brushed his hands off and nodded to where Yayènia and Suneelo were now talking. Ghealan visibly relaxed.

"Where was she?"

Losolin told him and watched Ghealan's face go from red to bloodless and back again.

"What?" he finally roared, startling the archers around him. "Why did you let her out here? Yayènia!" the warrior bellowed, and stalked off.

Yayènia turned and glowered at Ghealan as he stomped up to her. "What are you doing here? You should be resting!"

Suneelo placed a hand on his wife's shoulder and stared at Ghealan. The female went rigid with fury and humiliation. Tlonna turned from her spot on the wall and joined the little group. Losolin fingered the hilt of his sword, leaning back from the tense situation and gesturing at the curious fighters around him to get back to their posts.

"I am fine, Second Commander Ghealan," Yayènia snapped, glancing pointedly at the soldiers milling about them.

Ghealan glowered at her. "I do not care whether you think you are in fine form or not, you should not be here, *High Commander*," the male snapped.

Yayènia's back stiffened even more, which Tlonna thought must be impossible. Somehow she looked taller, managing to loom over Ghealan, who stood head and a few inches taller than her.

"Second Commander Ghealan, I command you to get back to your post immediately, and leave my personal affairs alone. We are under siege, and only constant vigilance will keep very recent history from repeating itself. Am I understood?" Yayènia said coldly.

Ghealan's mouth tightened, and even Suneelo's eyes widened a bit, though he too agreed with Lan's opinion. The older male bowed formally, right hand on his belt sword, and left hand on the hilt sticking above his shoulder.

"Your orders are understood, High Commander Yayènia," he said, and stalked back down the wall.

"Was that necessary?" Tlonna asked Yayènia quietly so that Losolin had to strain to hear.

"For the sake of my command, and the soldiers' peace of mind, yes, my Queen, it was," Yayènia replied stiffly, performing the same bow as Ghealan.

Losolin did not think he had seen his friends in such a fit ever before. Tlonna's next words startled him from his idle thought.

"As you will, High Commander. I do not want this battle to last long. I expect you to move quickly, and you as well, Captain Suneelo. You have my permission to use whatever means you have to defend this city. Is that clear?"

Both Yayènia and Suneelo bowed again, almost identically. "Yes, Queen Tlonna, it shall be as you say. King Losolin," they said, and strode away, cloaks of office swaying in the wind.

Tlonna turned to look at Losolin and her heart soared at the sight of him. He *looked* like a king in his armor, tall plumed helmet standing proud a few inches above hers.

"My heart," she said and waited until Losolin bent down so that she wouldn't have to shout. "I *will* see you tonight."

Losolin straightened and nodded, brushing a finger along her jaw. "I love you," he said quietly and she smiled.

"You as well, Losolin," Tlonna murmured, and strode away after Yayènia and Suneelo.

Taking a deep breath, Losolin moved a little further down from Ghealan, who was roaring at the top of his lungs for no apparent reason other than to vent his frustration. The militiamen around him nearly leapt out of their skin every time he issued a command.

Tlonna swiped her forearm across of her cheek, pushing her helmet up awkwardly. Dust seemed to coat her skin like a second layer. Grimacing, the Magin pulled her bowstring to her cheek, chose a target, and loosed. The elf screamed as the arrow slammed into his eye socket.

A man standing next to her whistled and smiled at her, then went pale when he saw who she was. Tlonna smiled back until he laughed, a joyous sound among the screaming and shouting. Loud curses from below drew the elf's attention and she leaned over the wall at the gate below, on the city side. Blackhaven pikemen were crammed against the heavy gate, bouncing back every few seconds as something heavy slammed into it on the other side. Cursing Tlonna sought out a plumed helmet among the many people atop the wall. Shoving through the archers, the Magin grabbed Sargotarh and yanked him down so that he could hear her.

"They are trying to ram down the door. Get some archers over to cover the area while I go down," she said, and then released the male.

"Go down where?" the elf demanded, not at all cowed by his risky queen.

Tlonna, who had started to turn away, spun back to the male, her face incredulous. "To stop them," she said as though the answer were obvious.

Sargotarh shook his head but he sprinted off, shouting. A few seconds later, archers were packing tight at the curving portion of the wall that sat above the gate. Tlonna jogged down to the ground where she could check the gate itself, drawing her sword as she did so. The pikemen were chanting as they pushed against the door, despite the fact that they kept bouncing back. Soon she was joined by Ghealan.

"They have two rams and a few Magins hitting against it, Tlonna," the warrior said as he watched the soldiers.

"Aye," Tlonna replied absently.

She was slowly filling herself with power, her body trembling as the immense magic rose from her belly to suffuse her entire body, even crackling down the blade of the sword. When she felt full to bursting, the queen spoke again. "Tell them to open the gate as fast as they can, Ghealan."

"What?" the male snapped incredulously, noticing the colored lights sparking along the blade of his friend.

"I want you to tell the pikemen to open the gate and get out of the way as fast as they can."

"No. No, I do not think so," he replied.

"Do not make me command you, Lan. As soon as I clear the gateway, get them to close it again," Tlonna said calmly.

Swearing loudly, Ghealan gave the command. He had to repeat it twice more before the pikemen complied. With a bang, they shot back as the gate was hit yet again. As soon as the last man cleared the space with a flying leap, Tlonna shoved her sword forward, clutched in both hands and moved it back and forth, releasing all the power she held. The milling mass of startled elves that had shot through the enormous gate made a fine mist as they simply dissolved. Those farther behind screamed as they were blasted into pieces. A clear space of nearly twenty yards now stood between Ghealan and the forest. Tlonna was on her back several yards away, dazed by the concussion. The Seadueni soldiers on either side stared in horror at the floating red mist, completely ignoring the screams of their fellows and the dismembered arms and legs that now littered the ground. Eyes turned up to stare at Tlonna and Ghealan, finely coated in blood.

Before the attackers could recover from their shock, the pikemen rushed to close the gate again, bringing extra bars of wood to reinforce it. Most of them left a wide area around the two elves, though several could hardly lift themselves up from the ground where they had fallen to retch. The mist finally dropped, leaving the ground a fine sludge.

Tlonna exhaled and wiped the unprotected portion of her face. Her helmet had provided some shield, but she grimaced when the taste of blood lingered on her lips. Ghealan, who had not moved since the gate opened, promptly leaned over and vomited. When he recovered, the warrior turned his gaze to Tlonna, who was slowly getting back to her feet.

"I did not know you could do that," he whispered hoarsely.

Tlonna shivered. "Nor did I. I was expecting to take down the first few lines, not clear an entire space, and those in front..." Her stomach heaved.

When Tlonna had completely emptied her belly, she looked up and saw that Yayènia, Suneelo, Aidyn, and Losolin had joined Ghealan. They all were staring at her.

Losolin was the first to speak. "I was standing above the gate when...when..." He made a slashing gesture with his hands. "They all just...*psst.*"

Yayènia nodded, her eyes huge. Suneelo looked like he too wanted to sick up. Aidyn's jaw was clenched hard enough for Tlonna to see that it was so for him as well. She swallowed dryly, trying to work moisture back into her mouth. Ghealan was behind her, trying to wipe off the sheen of blood by the sounds he was making.

"I did not know...I was not expecting that to happen. Did I hurt anyone on our side?" Tlonna finally said. She was surprised her voice was so steady.

Yayènia shook her head. "No, though a good many just about lost it when they saw an entire company explode. I believe seven fainted. Most of Stoffnias's ranks fled. I think, barring those few who were too stunned to run, we are finished for the day."

Tlonna nodded, and looked at Losolin, fearing to see what she expected. Her heart suddenly seemed to beat again when she saw only concern and love in his face, no fear.

"Are you all right, Loni? You look really pale," he said, moving to take her arm.

Tlonna nodded again, leaning into him. "Yes. Shocked, and more than a little appalled, but I am all right. I do not think I will sleep well, though."

"Nor will anyone else, Tlonna," Aidyn said, snorting. "That is just not something you see, ever."

Murmurs of consent passed around the small group, though none looked at her any different from ever before. There was no fear or anger in their eyes.

The next morning brought a whirlwind of messengers, running back and forth between the wall and the castle. So far, only one ship had breached the harbor, though dozens of sailors had swum the distance and gained the docks, only to be cut down by the defenders of the city. Guards from the south-westernmost tower on the wall had reported seeing a few squadrons of Talenian soldiers trying to sneak about in the forest, apparently to see if the southern wall had any weakness. Those soldiers were no longer breathing.

The main attack seemed to be focused mainly along the eastern wall, centered on the gate and its two flanking towers. Laddermen had been brought in, but had failed utterly as the defenders simply leaned out and chopped at the topmost rungs, rendering the ladders useless. However, one obviously terrified messenger had sprinted into the castle just as Tlonna, Losolin, and Aidyn were heading out.

"Your highnesses! There's something headed toward the wall, and nobody knows what it is."

"A beast?" Losolin asked the trembling boy, frowning.

"A wooden beast, my lord. It stands as tall as the wall and rolls on heavy logs. It has not reached the wall, but High Commander Yayènia said to get you there at once."

The three elves rushed to the wall, flying through the abandoned streets on their horses. They nearly flung themselves out of the saddle when they reached the gate and charged up the stairs. The queen, flanked by her worried officers, and stared outward in confusion. A massive wooden contraption crawled toward the wall as dozens of soldiers marched beside it along with a few unarmed men who were constantly touching the machine. The soldiers in front had thick ropes over their shoulders and they were heaving forward, moving the thing in lurches.

"What is that?" Losolin asked, clutching the edge of the wall. "What is it?"

Yayènia shook her head and looked to Aidyn, utterly baffled. Even the assassin had a scrambled look, as though he were vastly unnerved.

"Shoot it down, take it out!" Tlonna shouted, pointing frantically to the archers.

They obeyed immediately, pulling back their strings and sighting on the monstrosity. Five hundred arrows thudded into the wood, but did nothing. Yayènia spun toward the gate, shouting down at the soldiers below.

"I want torches and whatever oil you can find up here now!" she barked, freeing her own bow and setting her quiver against the wall.

Aidyn and Aladorn moved to flank her, the dark elves waiting patiently as the engine moved closer. Arrows whipped through the air, taking out the surrounding guards and mechanics with alacrity, but the machine continued lurching onward.

Tlonna and Losolin watched as it suddenly stopped and the surrounding soldiers scattered, leaving the civilians behind. "What is it?" Tlonna demanded, gripping Losolin's hand.

Everyone on the wall stared down at the foreign thing, including the archers who had, for the moment, given up on their futile barrage in order to spare their arrows. Someone stepped forward, arms spread wide, a pulsing aural shield protecting him from the arrows that suddenly sped toward him.

"Well, Elf Queen? What do you think of my mangonel?" he cried, spinning around and gesturing to the machine.

"Who are you?"

"My name is Orlando, General of the Zaedican Force!"

"I have heard of him," Yayènia muttered, her eyes narrowing. "Cruel bastard if even half the rumors are true. I want to kill him."

"Then you shall," Tlonna growled, eyeing the man.

He was young, probably just under thirty, but he had a rough face, scarred and pocked. His arms bulged and his legs were bowed out with muscles to the point of extreme.

"Ugly bugger," Aladorn snorted, leaning on his bow.

"High Commander!" a soldier yelled from the stairs, leading a long line of torch bearers and people with buckets of viscous liquids. "We've got lamp oil, cooking oil, and fat grease."

"Excellent, I want a torch bearer for every two archers, and the same with the oil," Yayènia instructed quietly, giving the order to the interested archers.

"This is not honorable warfare," Aladorn muttered, glaring at the burning torch by his shoulder.

"They took out honor when they made that monstrosity, Al," Yayènia replied, touching her oiled arrow to the torch.

Fire erupted along the haft and she quickly loosed it, fearing for her string. The arrow thudded into the mangonel and nothing seemed to happen until a hundred more smacked into the wood. Orlando spun around, his eyes wide with rage and thick arms waving. With a sudden crack, the large arm of the thing swung forward and down, whipped up a giant bucket, and launched massive boulders at the wall.

People screamed and scrambled for cover as the wall shuddered and groaned, but held. Yayènia swore, gesturing to Aladorn who loosed another fire arrow. The mangonel was able to get out two more rounds before, with a resounding splinter, one of the supporting arms of the machine crumbled downward, effectively destroying the thing.

"Kill the engineers!" Yayènia screamed as they began to run away.

Her militia responded with amazing speed, launching volley after volley into the fleeing people, taking out every one. Orlando called the retreat then, and he sent the elves atop the wall a malevolent glare.

"You will all burn!" he screamed, running after his troops.

Aladorn leaned over the edge of the wall, watching the clearing ground. "Two of them are alive, get them inside the walls!" he called, shoving the closest soldiers down the wall.

Ghealan and Suneelo arrived then, looking disturbed. "What happened? We were at the north tower and felt the wall shake. What is that?" the latter asked, gesturing to the burning siege machine.

"Some sort of weaponry, I believe they called it a mangonel?" Tlonna said, looking around to see if anyone would correct her use of the strange word.

"Ingenious," Ghealan muttered darkly, though there was indeed a glimmer of appreciation in his light green eyes.

"We've got them!" someone called from down below and the elves leaned out to see that the soldiers sent to retrieve the engineers had returned with their injured charges. Tlonna led the way down the stairs and came to a stop before the men.

"How many more of your war machines do you have?" she demanded of the more cognizant human.

"None," he replied angrily. "Spent years creating it, and in a few minutes it's gone. All my work, all my research."

Yayènia scowled and shoved him hard. "Your machine nearly took down our wall. Who else knows how to build them? How many?"

The engineer glowered up at her. "Besides myself, none now. You killed them all. Brilliant minds all, wasted on this stupid battle. Why can't you just leave well enough alone, eh?"

"We would like to, but you might take care to notice that we are the ones under siege, not the other way around. We did not want this," Tlonna replied softly. "Are you sure there is no one else, and no more mangonels?"

"Positive," the man responded immediately. "Do you think you have a chance to defeat the three combined armies?"

The way he asked it had everyone back on their heels a little, for he did not say them with malice or sarcasm, but with true curiosity, and perhaps a little hope.

"You want us to defeat them," Losolin stated, folding his arms.

The engineer shrugged. "All my life I've toiled for the Rahlans, and never been given more than a sad pittance. I was told I would be sailing with several others from my guild to the mainland, and there I would build my design to help win the war, or else my family would be murdered, my belongings seized, and my family named burned with dishonor forever. What would you have me do?"

Tlonna studied the man for a minute before stepping away. "Release him," she said suddenly. "So, if I offered you the chance to work on this side of the wall, what would you do?"

The man stood gingerly, nursing his injured leg and stared up at the elf. "Fight for you? You ask me to change allegiance very quickly, Queen Tlonna."

"Your words indicate little allegiance to Zaedic, good sir," the elf countered.

He shrugged one shoulder. "True enough. What would you have me do? I can build you machines to take down enemies from afar, to smash great numbers, anything, really."

Tlonna smiled slightly, glancing at the warriors around her. "We fight with honor and dignity. I would never have such machines inside my walls. What I would have you do is work on something to better our chances of winning, without sacrificing our moral integrity. Can you do such a thing?"

The engineer continued to stare at her. "I do not know what you want from me," he sighed with honesty. "I can build rams and trebuchets, catapults and ballistae, but they are all devices similar to the one you find dishonorable."

"Who says I want something to destroy? Can you not put your mind to the task of finding a way to help the injured, protect those fighting, or improve our weapons in a way that still makes use of true skill and personal adherence to codes of morality?"

The engineer frowned, but his mind was racing with possibilities. "Perhaps. If I have access to the readings I will need, and space in which to work, I will do as you ask."

"You will have such access, but you will be guarded for signs of treachery."

"Then these things you shall have. I present myself, Matthias Goss, and my friend here is Lukan Morholn. We shall serve you proudly and to the best of our abilities, and most importantly, willingly."

"Then I am glad.

Another two days passed as soldiers were rammed against the wall, carelessly spent by their leaders. The reconnaissance from the deep forest informed Tlonna and her companions that the rest of the mainland Zaedican force had arrived, led by none other than Sithian Rahlan.

"I fear that Eyin and his people are done," the queen confided to Miazie as she read the latest report. "He and Meradyn were too eager to be of worth in this war, and I do not see them sitting idly by when they spoke an oath to do otherwise, no matter what we said to them."

"Perhaps, but those boys have good heads on their shoulders. Maybe they let them pass, and are hiding within their forest," the Belau replied, placing a hand on her friend's shoulder. "Tlonna, may I speak to you of something besides the war?"

Tlonna looked up and scowled. "Of course. Since when do you have to ask?"

Miazie shrugged, plainly uncomfortable, and then bit her lip. "Sodo asked me to marry him."

The queen's look of sheer delight took the human by surprise, and she felt a great weight lift from her chest. "I hope you said yes."

"Of course I did, but I have worries. Since Purheae I have been changed," Miazie noted with sadness the shade of hurt and reservation on the elf's face, but continued anyway, "but still I won't live to see the centuries all of you will. Sodo and I have spoken of this, of course, but he maintains that it does not matter to him. Whether I live another ten years or another thousand, he says as long as we're together he'll be happy, but..."

"It is a big step," Tlonna agreed. "But what is life worth if you do not take chances on love? If your only worry is the race card, then worry no longer. All of us will support you in whatever way you can, you know that."

"I do, and it is indeed the largest fret I have. The others are, I'm sure, just engagement jitters," Miazie conceded.

Tlonna leaned back in her chair. "When are you to hold the ceremony?"

The human shrugged one shoulder, unsure. "After the siege, of course, no point in stressing everyone out further. I just...would you be my Matron of Honor?"

Tlonna grinned from pointed ear to pointed and hugged her friend. "Gladly. And we can have the wedding at anytime. No reason for this stupid battle to keep you two single longer than you desire. Just say the word and we shall have it done."

Miazie wiped happy tears from her eyes with the back of her hand and hugged Tlonna again. "Thank you, this means so much to me."

"And to me. You deserve to finally be married to the elf you love, after all you have gone through. Now off with you, go to your fiancé and the both of you abstain from the battle for today, unless desperately needed."

The woman smiled and bounced from Tlonna's office. Once she was gone, the queen stood and, after donning her armor and weapons, hastened to the wall.

Chapter 40

Saddest Day since Yesterday

The battle was in a fine frenzy when she arrived, the gates open wide in order to allow the defenders to get down and dirty with their enemies. The melee was brutal, mingled amongst the giant *kairhotuss* trees, giving and taking advantage with ambivalence. Seadueni elf struggled against Blackhavenite elf, Zaedican human against the same, with ferocious dwarves standing shoulder to shoulder with their elven comrades, and humans on the other side. Only the defenders had any sort of cohesion, for the Seadueni were just as prone to cutting off the head of their human allies as their enemies. The few remaining Talenians had little fight left in them, but had no choice, for they were now nothing more than slaves to the more powerful armies.

Tlonna dove into the fight after looking around for her companions, and not spotting a single one. She was loath to use her magic in such a constrained space, where she might lose control and hurt her own people, so she settled for her forged weapons. The elf queen danced through the masses, her blades flickering, coated with a fine sheen of blood. She had no idea she was heading straight into a trap, straight into the worst day of them all.

Aidyn heard screaming behind him, and a terrible pang nearly ripped his heart in two. Spinning, the assassin sprinted back the way he had come, sheathing his scimitars and drawing his longsword as he leapt over the bodies littering the ground. Through the milling fighters, the dark elf caught glimpses of Tlonna struggling with several Cleicks, their antimagics rendering her immense power useless. She downed two of them with a single swipe of her sword, and then ducked, slashing out at their bellies. Three burly men grabbed a hold of her writhing body, trying to overpower the elf.

Aidyn tore through a group of Seadueni like a tornado, leaving only destruction in his wake. Seconds later, he was at his queen's side, whirling sword spraying blood and tearing flesh. He teeth were bared in a furious snarl and he opened a gnarly smile in a

Cleick's throat, taking out the last one. Tlonna stood behind him, shamefaced.

"I should have been able to take them all out," she said, gazing at Aidyn.

The assassin wiped blood from his face and looked away, burying the old desires. "Then I would have no job."

Tlonna smiled at the attempt to validate her weakness. She picked up the sword that had been wrested from her hands and sheathed it, watching the battle around her. The queen glimpsed Yayènia off to the right, both katans flickering through the air in a mesmerizing dance of death, creating a ring of dead around her. It was the first time she had seen anyone she knew, and having Aidyn beside her and Yayènia several yards away comforted her.

Together, the queen and the assassin started off to rejoin the fight, but a sudden explosion knocked them both off their feet. Before they could regain their senses, both elves heard the stamping of boots coming near to them. Tlonna twisted, hoping the antimagic had worn off, and pushed herself to her feet. Aidyn was standing already, but a wicked piece of shrapnel was buried in the side of his thigh, and he could hardly plant his feet. Shaking off the agony, the assassin housed his sword and once again drew his scimitars, knowing he could not go through the longsword positions with the injury.

Tlonna saw the movement, and worry filled her, and she tapped into the bond in order to share his pain. Aidyn felt the hurt lessen slightly and sent a sidelong glare at his friend, knowing what she had done. Before he could say anything, however, they were attacked.

Several Seadueni and a handful of Zaedicans rammed into the two elves, trying simply to overrun them. Aidyn sliced the first few to reach them into ribbons as Tlonna lopped off the heads of those nearest her. But then the enemy elves and humans kept on running, not stopping to fight the pair. Staring at each other in confusion, Aidyn and Tlonna did not see the reason why until it was too late. A cloud of blackness engulfed them, taking away their sight. It did not bother the assassin, who did not need to see to know where his enemies where, but it disoriented Tlonna.

Aidyn stepped close to the queen, pressing his back against her to let her know it was he. Her breath was hot on his neck as she muttered something. A tiny flame appeared, but the darkness immediately ate it up.

"That should have illuminated this like a bloody sun," she whispered.

Aidyn felt her move away from him, and suddenly she appeared next to him, shining as though a light were coming from within. Her beautiful face seemed carved from marble as she stared outward.

"We should move," the male said quietly, knowing that their enemy was approaching.

Tlonna shook her head. "It will only move with us, and we might step into another fight. At least here we know the landscape a little."

Aidyn nodded in assent, unsure if she could see him. When her eyes locked onto his, he knew she could, and was relieved by the thought. Side by side, they waited.

They did not have long, for moments later a flickering blue form materialized within the dark. At Tlonna's sudden intake of breath, Aidyn knew they were in trouble. His mind automatically went back to the time they had watched Midian approach in much the same way. He shoved the memory away and focused on the enemy.

"You should not have come here," Tlonna said loudly, apparently knowing who the person was.

"Why not? I like it here," came the reply in a voice that sent disgusted chills down Aidyn's spine.

"Even if you kill me, you will not win in the end, Sithian," Tlonna spat, sheathing her sword and glaring at her son. "You do realize that, do you not?"

The boy shrugged, the action limned in blue flames. "We shall see."

"You murdered both of your siblings because they were irritating to you, your father is dead, and now you are here to finish off your mother. You must really want to be alone in this world, my son," Tlonna replied coolly, outwardly unperturbed by the Magin's words.

Sithian's lips curled into a parody of a smile. "I am never alone."

"Neither am I."

Aidyn stood perfectly still next to Tlonna, wondering what was going on. He wondered if Sithian knew he was there. As if in answer, the half-breed shifted his dark gaze to the assassin.

"So..." he said quietly, licking his lips in a very disturbing way.

The male elf tensed, checking his grip on his scimitars.

"I do not like you, Dark Elf. You caused me to have a limp and a scar, but were too afraid to go against *her*, so you stopped when you could have finished me. And here we are again, all alone. Do you think you can best me when you could not even best my father? I am tenfold his strength," Sithian crooned, eyeing the older male. "Do you know that I know what memories lurk behind those shifty eyes of yours? I could undo you right now...but why spoil the fun? See...my forefathers were skilled in the art of scrying, and you were of great interest to them. I know what you have done."

"What is he talking about Aidyn?" Tlonna said, unsure of the suddenly desperate look on her closest friend's face.

Aidyn said nothing, unwilling to play the boy's game. He made sure his gaze and stance did not alter, forced his heart to slow and his mind to clear of all thoughts. The Magin moved slowly closer and lifted his hand to the scars on Aidyn's cheek. His cool fingers brushed against the flesh, lightly caressing them, sapphire eyes half closed in what could only be described as ecstasy. Suddenly he moved again, sweeping his flame-covered arm upward and across. The assassin stepped back as something swept by him, brushing by his cheek.

Pain exploded from the triangular scars, dropping the elf to his knees. He roared in defiance, forcing himself to keep his hands on his scimitars, and launched his body forward, catching the overconfident Magin by surprise.

Sithian was knocked backward, landing hard on his shoulder as Aidyn slammed the hilt of his left blade into the boy's face. Tlonna watched the struggle in amazement, knowing that Aidyn was in such agony that even she was nearly doubled over. Sithian's blue-limned hands locked together and slammed into the side of the assassin's head, Maginic flames whooshing around his head and shoulders.

The dark elf bellowed again, squinting through the fire and sliding his scimitars across Sithian's vulnerable flesh. The boy cried out as his skin was shredded, but he called up another Weave and launched Aidyn skyward. The assassin landed heavily on his stomach and groaned, feebly trying to stay conscious. Tlonna gasped as her son rounded on her, anger and insanity flaring in his dark eyes.

"Will you let him die for you?" he asked, walking over to the barely stirring elf.

Tlonna rushed forward and knocked her son aside with a powerful blow to the head. Sithian shook his head and stared up at his mother in shock. She kicked him in the ribs, snarling.

"I will let no one die for me, Sithian. Do not ever believe that a weakness," she hissed, grabbing him by the collar of his shirt and hauling him to his feet.

Knowing he could not win in a fight against his mother, Sithian once again clasped his hands together and put all his strength behind the Weave. It hit Tlonna in the middle and sent her flying. Before she had time to retaliate, the young king picked up the unconscious Aidyn and fled the globe of darkness.

Aidyn came to groggily, squinting his eyes against the flaring light that undulated before his eyes, shaking his head to dispel the last fingers of drowsiness. The dark elf grunted softly as he tried to roll his shoulders, discovering as he did so that his wrists were bound behind him, tethered to the opposite side of the back of his chair, and that one shoulder was dislocated. His slender fingers began playing with the strings, but whoever had tied him had not been gentle, and the rough line dug into his skin, making his work decidedly uncomfortable. More annoyed than worried that he was captive, Aidyn glared at the entrance to the small tent he occupied.

His legs were also tied to the chair, straining his thighs as they bent at an awkward angle. He took a deep experimental breath and found that several of his ribs were broken. Shaking his head again, Aidyn gave up trying to free himself and began studying his surroundings. He was directly behind the opening of the tent so that every time a gust of wind came through bright sunlight glared into his face. The tent was small, with enough room for him and perhaps someone else. Aidyn craned his neck forward, trying to see through the shivering flaps and saw several forms standing to either side.

Satisfied with the information, the assassin began pulling at the stays on his wrists once more, not straining, simply tugging, stressing the ropes a little further each time.

He was nowhere near free when Sithian strode into the tent. Cursing, Aidyn strained one of his legs so much that it snapped the back leg off the chair, and sent it swinging toward Sithian. His booted foot caught the unsuspecting Magin in the groin, and the leg ricocheted off his hip. The young king flicked his hand outward as he stumbled backward, sending a dark blue jet at Aidyn, which hit the elf square in the face.

The dark elf bit his lip to stop from screaming, balanced precariously on the remaining three legs of his chair. "What do you hope to achieve by having me as a captive?" he demanded as Sithian righted himself.

"I'm not sure yet," the boy answered honestly, wincing as he took a step forward. "I saw you and my mother and decided I could get either of you and give myself quite an advantage. If I got her, I would steal her power and then kill her. With you…you're the best, I hear. You even defeated the bitch Yayènia, twice, if I heard correctly. I want your skills. I will take your mind if I have to, but I would rather you just convert to my side and save me the trouble."

The elf let out a short laugh, absolutely dumbfounded by the half-breed's gall. "You will never be able to hurt me enough to make me join you, trust me. You can do what you want, boy, and you will still fail."

Sithian lifted an eyebrow at his captive. "Very confidant."

Aidyn glared at him, his breathing coming hard and fast with rage. "This will be the end of you."

"So everyone keeps telling me. Personally, I'm not too worried. But as for you," Sithian smiled cruelly and bent over the elf, holding the chair leg. A flash of blue light and the chair was stable once more. "Can't have you toppling over on me every few minutes."

Then, with a malicious snarl, he clamped his hand over Aidyn's mouth and jaw and roughly jerked his head up. The assassin's emerald eyes rolled downward in time to see pulsating blue Weaves writhe out of his captor's fingers and sink into his face. Then his eyes rolled upward as agony such as he had never experienced before splintered through him. Mere seconds later,

Sithian dropped his hand and stepped away, nonchalantly wiping clean the thick coating of blood that had burst forth from Aidyn's mouth onto his hand.

"I will return tomorrow."

Aidyn's head fell limply onto his chest, strings of blood hanging from his mouth and nose. He did not hear Sithian's promise.

Tlonna got to her feet seconds after the darkness disappeared, and then shot forward in horror when she realized Aidyn was gone. "Aidyn!" she screamed, casting about for him.

"What happened?" Yayènia said from behind, having seen Tlonna fly through the air moments earlier.

"Sithian has Aidyn!" Tlonna cried, grabbing her sister and pulling the warrior into a run beside her.

Yayènia stopped running and crossed her arms. "The assassin can hold his own just fine, even against that twisted offspring of yours. We have a battle here, and we cannot afford to go running about after some dark elf who can land even me."

Tlonna spat in disgust, glaring at her sister in disbelief. "So you are willing to let him die?"

"Aidyn will be fine, Tlonna. Trust me."

The queen shook her head and turned away, resisting the urge to slap the warrior. "Then I will go after him myself."

"What is with you? You know bloody well that Aidyn will be just fine. Flaming nine hells, you are being ridiculous!" Yayènia cried, about to knock her sister out.

"He would do the same for you or me!" Tlonna retorted angrily.

"Because you or I would be hard put to stay alive!" the High Commander yelled, turning in time to open the belly of a Seadueni elf who had noticed them standing idle.

"We have to go after him!" Tlonna shrieked, but Yayènia shook her head.

"As I said, Aidyn can take care of himself, we need to protect those who cannot. Remember where your duty lies. He would not be happy to find out you left the defense of the city to follow him. He is your protector, not the other way around."

"Sithian has him, Yayènia! He cannot fight him and hope to win, not if Sithian gets the slightest chance to Weave," the queen countered frantically, despair welling inside her.

Yayènia shoved her sister back, nearly pushing her over. "He knows that, and he will not allow Sithian that chance. Trust in Aidyn, trust in his blades if nothing else."

"I will not lose him," Tlonna swore, tears streaming down her face.

"No," the warrior shook her head in agreement.

"I cannot," the queen whispered, terror making her voice shake.

"I know," Yayènia responded quietly, patting her sister's shoulder. "I know."

Tlonna sank down on the steps and buried her face in her hands. There was a moment of utter silence as Tlonna sat there, the warrior standing over her, and then a cry that was repeated several times along the wall rent the air.

"Fire!"

Yayènia and Tlonna sprinted up to the top and stared outward in fury and disbelief. There, on the edge of the forest billowed great black plumes of smoke. As they watched, many and more fires erupted throughout the great forest, turning the darkening sky orange.

"They are burning the forest to keep us from retaliating," Ghealan said as he joined them.

"Where are they?" the queen asked, trying to find the invaders in the smoke.

"Gone. They burned as they retreated and we cannot get it under control. They used some sort of fire aid that water does not affect. We are pulling our forces back, but a few are hanging in to try and get a sample of whatever it is. Then we can have Sodo look at it."

"They will burn along with it," Losolin said savagely. "No magic can keep a fire like this at bay for long, not without severe risk to the Magins, and Sithian will never put himself in such danger."

"Are you sure it would be him who is doing it?" Ghealan asked.

The king nodded. "No one else in his camp has the strength."

As everyone from the Companions slowly arrived, they turned back to the burning forest. “They certainly know how to push our buttons, do they not?” Yayènia said after a minute, her knuckles white with rage.

“We must not let them get to us. Where is Aidyn?” Aladorn asked, turning to Tlonna.

The female turned away and could not answer. Yayènia did it for her. “Sithian has him.”

The look of sheer horror that crossed Aladorn’s face was matched by everyone else, though the wiat’s pain seemed much deeper, matched only by Tlonna’s quiet sobbing.

Chapter 41

Firefight

Losolin took a deep breath and closed his eyes. "Aidyn has gotten himself out of worse places than this," he said halfheartedly. "For now, we need to focus on the fires."

Suddenly Tlonna took off, sprinting south toward the nearest tower. She disappeared within and everyone stared after her, confused and worried. Losolin handed the reins of battle over to Yayènia, Ghealan, and Aladorn, and followed his wife, twisting through the angry soldiers gathered on the increasingly hot wall. Finally he reached the southern defense tower, a spiraling affair that looked too insubstantial to do anything, but was in fact nearly indestructible. Even now, with Maginic blasts shaking the wall, Woven by Sithian's suicidal minions, the tower stood unmoving, small bits of stone flaking off where on any other wall it would have been massive chunks. Losolin ducked inside the low door and was heralded by the four guards standing there, their bows strung and ready, but useless with no enemy visible.

"Where is the Queen?" he demanded, a little breathless in the dry heat from the fire.

"Upstairs King Losolin. Are you going to stop this inferno? The trees…they are crying," one of the guards said, making the Magin take a closer look.

The male was a dryad, his skin rough like bark, eyes the color of a night forest. Losolin bit his lip, frowning. "We are going to try. Get as far away from this side of the tower as you can."

As the four soldiers moved away, Losolin sprinted up the spiral steps to the second floor, which was high up indeed, stepping through the small opening in the floor. In the little circular room stood Tlonna and Suneelo, their backs to him, the former staring out the small window.

"What are you thinking?" Losolin asked, emerging completely into the room.

Both elves turned to regard him with sad expressions. "I cannot stop it," Tlonna replied sadly. "I can only destroy."

"I know, but perhaps you can channel your power into me, and I can heal it. Probably not all of it, but enough," he replied, gripping his brother's shoulder.

"We have tried that before, and it wiped us both out, remember?"

"I do," Losolin said quietly, remembering the time Tlonna had used his magic to heal her own side in Kajgenia. "But it is worth the risk."

Tlonna nodded after a moment and pushed Suneelo out of the way. "Stand before me, then," she said, wrapping her arms about her husband's chest.

Losolin took a deep breath, feeling Tlonna's racing heart against his back. "Whenever you are ready," he whispered, and then grunted as a wave of colossal power rushed through him.

Along with the strength came the voices. He heard the mad mutterings of Jair and the soulful wailing of the spirits. Losolin squinted, trying to focus against the indecipherable voices, and stretched his arms out, fingers splayed against each other. Green light immersed in all the colors of Maginic Weavings shot out from his fingertips, spraying like water over the raging forest.

Below he heard the frightened screams of his people, and then slowly they turned into cries of wonder and relief as the fire hissed and steamed as it was covered by Losolin's Weave. Moving gently, he waved his arms back and forth in the window, trying to cover as much of the forest as he could, but still the fire seethed. However, where his magic touched, the trees bloomed healthy, sap springing from the bark as soon as the Weave passed on.

Losolin began to smile as he saw the fire abating, but then he shuddered as the toll on his body began to show. He was quickly losing his strength, and Tlonna clung to him in a desperate attempt to keep him upright. With an oath, she stepped away and caught his hand, sticking her free hand out of the window, pointing toward the sky with a rigid claw. She threw her head back in a savage howl of agony as she reversed the flow of power, turning it quickly back into her body.

Suneelo swore as his two family members convulsed violently, but when he tried to disconnect them, Losolin weakly lifted his head and shook it. Tlonna roared again and hopped a little in frustration, and then it happened.

A concussion shook the tower so hard that it threw all three elves to the ground, and everyone else within a five mile radius. The clouds directly above the tower roiled and rumbled, turning black and yellow as they did. Somehow, Tlonna still had her hand outside the window and from her palm shot wicked bars of lightning, dancing and crackling upward. People were screaming in fear again, covering their heads and crouching low in terror. Yayènia, Ghealan, and Aladorn sat against a crenellation, staring upward at the little hand barely visible in the tower window wreaking such devastation. Then suddenly the lightning disappeared and for a moment there was a deep quiet, punctured only by the frightened sobbing of civilians.

And then it began to rain.

Chapter 42

Repercussions

Yayènia led the charge into the tower, followed by Ghealan and Aladorn. The guards in the bottom floor were severely shaken, one completely cataleptic but otherwise unharmed. When the three barreled into the upper floor, Suneelo met them with a grimace.

"I have never seen anything like it," he muttered, gesturing to Tlonna and Losolin who were slumped against the wall, unconscious. "One minute he was doing just fine, spraying that mist, and then suddenly he shivered and Tlonna turned into this raving lunatic. I tried to pull them apart but Losolin stopped me."

"Have you looked outside?" Ghealan asked, bending over the queen.

Suneelo stepped to the window and gazed outward in amazement at the soft rain. What fire hadn't been put out by Losolin was now being efficiently doused by the magical shower. He shook his head in disbelief.

"Every day they get stronger and more out of control," he said, crossing to his wife. "I fear the day we dread is coming fast."

"We will be ready," Yayènia countered fiercely, staring at her sister. "We will be ready."

"Should we carry them out, or let them rest so they can walk out?" Aladorn asked, swallowing against the fear for his friends, and his lost little brother.

"Let them rest. The men do not need to see this," Ghealan replied, pulling off his cloak and spreading it over the comatose couple.

Tlonna came to her senses a few hours later, cracking her eyes open and glancing about. The scene before her made her blink several times. Aladorn was sitting against the stone wall across from her and Losolin, who remained unconscious, his arms wrapped around his knees and his forehead pressed against them, his shoulders shaking as he silently cried.

Suneelo and Yayènia sat side by side next to him, the latter's head on her husband's shoulder, sound asleep. The captain's dark eyes were red rimmed and bruised looking, his fingers loosely laced together between his knees, his head resting on Yayènia's. Ghealan sat apart from them all, staring blankly at the wall opposite, his body as slouched as possible while still remaining upright. His eyes too were swollen from tears.

"What happened?" Tlonna asked quietly so as not to disturb Yayènia or Losolin.

Suneelo lifted his head and stared at her, expressionless. "The fire is out."

"Then it worked?"

The male nodded silently. Ghealan stirred enough to take a deep breath. "Sithian's forces have fled. What remains only needs to be cleared from the walls and the surrounding forest. My boys found a large circular clearing that appears to have been surrounded by fire, but not broached by it. We figure this to be where your son made his camp. However, he was not seen by any of our reconnaissance teams, not even during the retreat. We believe him to have fled as soon as you began dousing the fires."

"Then it is over? We won?" Tlonna asked in a dully surprised voice.

Suneelo and Ghealan looked at each other and then back at her. The captain shook his head once, barely a twitch. "It is true we pushed them, hard, but they will bounce back with ferocity. I have seen it a hundred times. Never on this scale, but the theory is the same. Tlonna, this war is far from over. Not until Sithian Rahlan lies underground with his father and sister will this battle be won."

"You make it sound so easy," the queen said, sarcasm thickly lacing her words. She began to add more when a terrible pang nearly ripped her heart in two.

"Tlonna!" Ghealan shouted, springing to his feet, startling Yayènia and Losolin awake.

Tlonna was on her side, convulsing with agony as her heart pounded at nearly the speed of a human's; bloody foam dribbling from between her clenched teeth. Yayènia was at her side at once, kneeling over her sister, a terrified look on her face. Losolin was shouting, demanding answers, pleading to her, but Tlonna could only see their faces through a sparking haze of black as her vision tunneled inward, excruciating torment ripping through her body, stemming from her heart.

Then it was Aladorn's hands on her, his tortured visage coming through the blinking haze. "Tlonna, listen to me. It is my brother you are connected to, my flesh and blood. Take my strength, give it to yourself, and to him. Take it."

The Magin Queen clutched at the hand within hers and she let out a terrible scream as her vision blacked and suddenly she was looking somewhere else. A thin hand was clamped over her mouth, blue strands of magic waving before her eyes and then latching on. She felt warm blood rise up from inside and come gushing forth to fill her mouth and burst over the hand. A few seconds later the hand removed itself from her face only to backhand her so violently she felt her neck crick and half her tongue go numb.

"TELL ME!" a deep voice screamed, accompanied by another vicious slap.

"Never," croaked Tlonna, through Aidyn.

For a moment Sithian's eyes widened as he heard something else in the assassin's voice. He hid his surprise and fear quickly though, and did further to mask it by slapping his hand to Aidyn's face once more and Weaving the brutal magic into it.

Aladorn heaved, crumpling over Tlonna's inert body, his hand still clutched in hers. The two of them were linked, the queen's strange power writhing over their hands like a coiling snake. Suneelo braced the wiat, Ghealan and Losolin Tlonna, while Yayènia stood back, petrified. Then she snarled and went to her knees, lacing her fingers with Aladorn's. She cried out in pain as magic shot through the dark elf's body and began pulsating about their joined hands as well.

Tlonna felt the torment ease a little, and then a little more as Yayènia joined, though she did not know that was the cause. She grunted, gasping for breath as her elfin heart galloped, beating so fast her shirt moved beneath her armor. Then the pain lessened dramatically, not because Aidyn's torture had stopped, but because Ghealan, Losolin, and Suneelo had all grasped hands, forming a great circle, the latter clasping Yayènia's, and Losolin holding Tlonna's free hand. As though a jolt of electricity, her magic shot through them all, pausing only to wrap about the joined hands before moving on. When it reached Tlonna once more, it exploded, throwing all six elves outward so that they were stretched at arm's length, on their knees.

A pillar of pure white power stood in the center of their circle, flashes of other colors twining up it like a moving vine, and streaks of green lancing up the sides as Losolin's magic was joined in. Tlonna threw her head back and roared in primal fury, closing her eyes and opening them elsewhere.

Aidyn threw his head back and roared in primal fury, closing his eyes, trying to escape the pain. Sithian leapt backward in surprise, yanking his blood-covered hand away in the same movement. The assassin's emerald eyes opened and the young king swallowed in revulsion as he saw the white pupils, pupils that had seconds ago been black and dilated with agony. From within the dark elf came a light so blinding Sithian was forced to throw his arm up to protect his eyes.

The echoing sound of someone's voice reverberated through the small tent, making it seem somehow much larger. It was male and female, furious and filled with pain, both emotional and physical, it was righteous and vindictive, deepened with violence and heightened with purpose.

"VALÕN YERCHT UDUAN MUNNASAEQUEN. GÜNNA FEAEN YESTE."

The light faded and Sithian put his arm down, shaken to the core. He looked at Aidyn to see the assassin staring back at him, his emerald eyes normal once more, all signs of injury gone. He was laughing so hard tears were streaming down his face.

"What did they say? What did they say!" Sithian screamed, unable to take a step closer to the dark elf.

"You have doomed yourself. We are coming. *We are coming*," Aidyn laughed maniacally, gasping for breath.

Sithian's lip curled and he moved right up to the assassin, his rage outweighing his fear. His hand clamped, not on Aidyn's mouth this time, but directly on his throat. The dark elf went rigid, his veins and muscles straining against his tawny flesh…

Tlonna gasped as the pillar of light faded from the tower room, her five friends collapsing against the wall, clutching at their chests. Then suddenly pain greater than ever erupted inside the queen and she went taut, her eyes bulging, and then she stumbled, banging her hip against the window sill.

"It is gone," she wheezed, her hand flying to her heart. "I can no longer feel him."

"What?" everyone asked in unison, hardly able to stand for the power she had channeled through them.

"The connection, it has broken," Tlonna sobbed, going to her knees. "Aidyn."

Aladorn's legs went out from under him, dropping the elf like a stone to the floor. "He cannot be dead. Sithian would not dare. He cannot be dead."

Yayènia went down right beside him, tears rolling unabashedly down her face. "'Lonna," she whispered, gazing at her sister with desperate eyes. "Aidyn told me death or your choice alone could break the oath. Could he have done it, to stop us from doing what we did again?"

Tlonna squeezed her eyes shut, unable to look any of them in the face. "I do not know. He could have, only he would be able to stand the whiplash of power, I think. Only him."

"Then that is what we will believe," Suneelo said resolutely, dragging his wife and his brother to their feet as he stood. "I will not believe Aidyn is dead until I see him. He will come waltzing through the gate with that cocky grin on his face and a great story to tell. Aladorn, he will come."

The wiat looked up at his friend, a look of utter grief on his face. "He is my baby brother," he said dully. "I just found him."

"And now it is up to him to find us," Suneelo replied, giving Ghealan a pointed look, and the commander grabbed Aladorn and Tlonna.

The six elves left the tower, barely glancing at the forest to their right. Steam rose in wafting clouds, a heavy mist forming at the base of the trunks. Soldiers moved quietly about, dragging bodies of fallen comrades inside the walls to be buried, piling the enemy dead in large heaps and lighting them on fire, careful to keep them away from the trees.

The wounded were being tended to all along the wall, on the ramparts and down below, healers and apothecaries moving about like wraiths in the fog. Few looked up from their duties as the six went by, but those that did gave great cries and fell to their knees in awe-stricken homage. They were ignored.

The sextet met up with a harassed looking Miazie and a pensive Sodo about halfway up Obsidian Way. The alchemist had a large vial filled with a clear liquid striated with swirls of red. He held it up to the six.

"This is what they used to ignite the fires. I have not yet extracted all the components, but our Nytrynhimmel is the base. They must have gotten their hands on it somehow."

"What about the red?" Losolin inquired, frowning at the small bottle.

Sodo shrugged. "I do not yet know. I have a bit of it in my laboratory at the Academy separating as we speak. I thought to bring this to you and show you what it looks like in case we discover more."

"Let me know when you have the rest figured out," Tlonna said wearily, struggling to stay upright.

"I will. What happened to you lot?"

"Sithian has Aidyn," was all Ghealan said, and the couple immediately understood the gravity of the situation.

Miazie chanced a look at Tlonna and saw exactly what she feared. Her friend's face was a mask of torment and rage, an unbridled look of longing burning within her eyes. "What do we do?"

Tlonna turned her back on all her friends, facing toward the wall. "We find them, chase them to the sea and beyond. Anyone who stands before us will be cut down. We will break them, fast and hard, so much so they will not have the strength to pray to the gods for forgiveness. We will send them to the depths of the deepest hell, where their screams will be heard only by Maln, and he will smile, but I will come down upon them and take even that refuge from their vile hearts. I make now a promise that until I draw my last breath I will stand against them. In the end they will beg for the exquisite release of death, and, if I am feeling merciful, I may grant it."

To be continued in Prophecy's Final Price: Book 3 of The Graves of Good and Evil

Discover other titles by A.B.B.Olson

<u>Graves of Good and Evil Trilogy</u>
Elven Race Reborn
Honor of Assassins
Prophecy's Final Price *

Nkayt'hei

*forthcoming

www.ingramcontent.com/pod-product-compliance
Lightning Source LLC
Chambersburg PA
CBHW030838030726
47495CB00005B/1281
9780997257212